Heath
English

LEVEL
9

J. A. Senn
Carol Ann Skinner

HEATH D. C. Heath and Company
Lexington, Massachusetts/Toronto, Ontario

*A*bout the cover and the artist

The cover of *Heath English,* Level 9, is a collage of images that reflect American writer Maya Angelou's poignant memories of a childhood spent in a small rural town. On pages 3–6 of *Heath English,* Level 9, one of the most vivid and touching of those memories is excerpted from Ms. Angelou's autobiographical book *I Know Why the Caged Bird Sings.*

The cover, an artistic response to Maya Angelou's writing and recollections, is by Mahler B. Ryder, a visual artist and teacher at the Rhode Island School of Design. Among his many achievements, Mr. Ryder is one of the founders of the Studio Museum in Harlem and was the project director and teacher for *The Fantasy World of Children.* Mr. Ryder has been recognized in *Who's Who in American Art* and *Who's Who Among Black Americans.*

Editorial	Christopher Johnson: Managing Editor, Barbara Brennan, Barbara Brien, Kathleen Kennedy Kelley, Peg McNary, Nadia Yassa
Editorial Services	Marianna Frew Palmer: Manager, K. Kirschbaum Harvie
Series Design	Robin Herr
Book Design	Bonnie Chayes Yousefian, Caroline Bowden
Production	Bryan Quible
Permissions Editor	Dorothy Burns McLeod

Acknowledgments start on page 905.

Published simultaneously in Canada

Printed in the United States of America

International Standard Book Number: 0-669-22092-2

9 0

Consultants and Reviewers

Program Consultant

Henry I. Christ
Former Chairman of the English
Department
Andrew Jackson High School
St. Albans, New York

Program Reviewers

Arizona
Patricia Nash
North High School
Chandler Unified School District
Chandler, Arizona

Florida
Carol Alves
Apopka High School
Apopka, Florida

New York
William E. Ottaviani
Binghamton High School
Binghamton, New York

Ohio
Linda Fulton
Lincoln High School
Gahanna, Ohio

Oklahoma
Sandra L. Benson
Edison High School
Tulsa, Oklahoma

Pennsylvania
Bernadette Fenning
Archbishop Carroll High School
Radnor, Pennsylvania

Tennessee
Alan F. Kaplan
Hume-Fogg Academic High School
Nashville, Tennessee

Texas
Victor Valenzuela
South Grand Prairie High School
Grand Prairie, Texas

Jan W. Blount
Berkner High School
Richardson, Texas

Contents

Unit 1
Exploring the Writer's Craft

vii

Unit 2
Achieving the Writer's Purpose

Chapter **8** **Writing Personal Essays** **284**

Chapter **9** **Writing Essays about Literature**   318

xiii

Chapter **10** **Writing Reports**   358

Chapter **11** **Creative Writing** **400**

Unit 3
Applying Communication and Study Skills

Chapter 13   Speaking and Listening   450

Chapter 14   Vocabulary   466

Chapter **15** Spelling 484

Chapter **16** Reference Skills 494

Chapter **17** Study and Test-Taking Skills 514

Unit 4
Language Skills Resource

Grammar

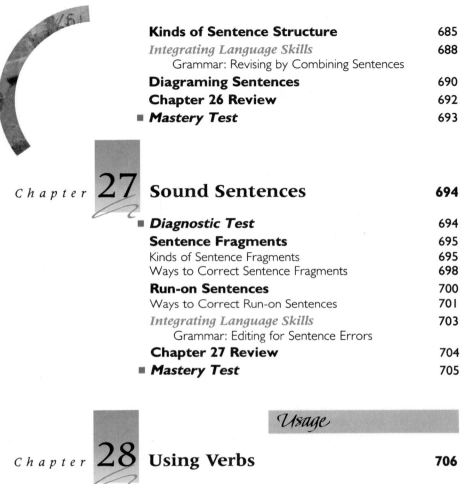

Chapter **27** **Sound Sentences**   **694**

Usage

Chapter **28** **Using Verbs**   **706**

Unit 1
Exploring the Writer's Craft

Chapter

1

The Writing Process

Part 1 — *Reading to Write*

THEME: *Self-Confidence*

In your high school career, you will have a wide variety of new experiences. Some of these experiences may challenge your old ideas about who you are and who your friends are. Other experiences may confuse or enlighten you about what you think and believe. As you sort out your thoughts and feelings, you gain confidence in yourself and your ability to win control of your life. Then, as you gain more experience and build friendships with people who like and accept you for who you are, your self-confidence grows.

One of the best ways to start building self-confidence is through writing because writing lets you express your thoughts and feelings in a concrete form. Then you can really examine those thoughts and feelings. As you learn about the writing process in this chapter, you will be exploring the theme of self-confidence. To start thinking about the theme, read the following autobiographical selection, in which the author tells about a time in her life when she could not bring herself to speak. As you read, think about what enabled her to overcome this crisis in self-confidence.

Maya Angelou was born Marguerite Johnson in 1928. She and her brother Bailey were raised by their grandmother, called Momma, who owned a general store in the black community in Stamps, Arkansas.

from

I Know Why the Caged Bird Sings

M a y a   A n g e l o u

For nearly a year, I sopped around the house, the Store, the school and the church, like an old biscuit, dirty and inedible. Then I met, or rather got to know, the lady who threw me my first life line.

Mrs. Bertha Flowers was the aristocrat of Black Stamps. She had the grace of control to appear warm in the coldest weather, and on the Arkansas summer days it seemed she had a private breeze which swirled around, cooling her. She was thin without the taut look of wiry people, and her printed voile[1] dresses and flowered hats were as right for her as denim overalls for a farmer. She was our side's answer to the richest white woman in town.

Her skin was a rich black that would have peeled like a plum if snagged, but then no one would have thought of getting close enough to Mrs. Flowers to ruffle her dress, let alone snag her skin. She didn't encourage familiarity. She wore gloves too.

I don't think I ever saw Mrs. Flowers laugh, but she smiled often. A slow widening of her thin black lips to show even, small white teeth, then the slow effortless closing. When she chose to smile on me, I always wanted to thank her. The action was so graceful and inclusively benign.

She was one of the few gentlewomen I have ever known, and has remained throughout my life the measure of what a human being can be . . .

---

1. **voile** [vwäl]: Light, thin fabric (French).

One summer afternoon, sweet-milk fresh in my memory, she stopped at the Store to buy provisions. Another Negro woman of her health and age would have been expected to carry the paper sacks home in one hand, but Momma said, "Sister Flowers, I'll send Bailey up to your house with these things."

She smiled that slow dragging smile, "Thank you, Mrs. Henderson. I'd prefer Marguerite, though." My name was beautiful when she said it. "I've been meaning to talk to her, anyway.". . .

She said, without turning her head, to me, "I hear you're doing very good school work, Marguerite, but that it's all written. The teachers report that they have trouble getting you to talk in class." We passed the triangular farm on our left and the path widened to allow us to walk together. I hung back in the separate unasked and unanswerable questions.

"Come and walk along with me, Marguerite." I couldn't have refused even if I wanted to. She pronounced my name so nicely. Or more correctly, she spoke each word with such clarity that I was certain a foreigner who didn't understand English could have understood her.

"Now no one is going to make you talk—possibly no one can. But bear in mind, language is man's way of communicating with his fellow man and it is language alone which separates him from the lower animals." That was a totally new idea to me, and I would need time to think about it.

"Your grandmother says you read a lot. Every chance you get. That's good, but not good enough. Words mean more than what is set down on paper. It takes the human voice to infuse them with the shades of deeper meaning."

I memorized the part about the human voice infusing words. It seemed so valid and poetic. She said she was going to give me some books and that I not only must read them, I must read them aloud. She suggested that I try to make a sentence sound in as many different ways as possible . . .

The sweet scent of vanilla had met us as she opened the door.

"I made tea cookies this morning. You see, I had planned to invite you for cookies and lemonade so we could have this little chat. The lemonade is in the icebox." . . .

They were flat round wafers, slightly browned on the edges and butter-yellow in the center. With the cold lemonade they were sufficient for childhood's lifelong diet. Remembering my manners, I took nice little lady-like bites off the edges. She said she had made them expressly for me and that she had a few in the kitchen that I could take home to my brother. So I jammed one whole cake in my mouth and the rough crumbs scratched the insides of my jaws, and if I hadn't had to swallow, it would have been a dream come true.

As I ate she began the first of what we later called "my lessons in living." She said that I must always be intolerant of ignorance but understanding of illiteracy. That some people, unable to go to school, were more educated and even more intelligent than college professors. She encouraged me to listen carefully to what country people called mother wit. That in those homely sayings was couched the collective wisdom of generations.

When I finished the cookies she brushed off the table and brought a thick, small book from the bookcase. I had read *A Tale of Two Cities*[2] and found it up to my standards as a romantic novel. She opened the first page and I heard poetry for the first time in my life.

"It was the best of times and the worst of times . . . "[3] Her voice slid in and curved down through and over the words. She was nearly singing. I wanted to look at the pages. Were they the same that I had read? Or were there notes, music, lined on the pages, as in a hymn book? Her sounds began cascading gently. I knew from listening to a thousand preachers that she was nearing the end of her reading, and I hadn't really heard, heard to understand, a single word.

2. *A Tale of Two Cities:* Novel by Charles Dickens.
3. **"It was . . . times"**: First sentence of *A Tale of Two Cities.*

"How do you like that?"

It occurred to me that she expected a response. The sweet vanilla flavor was still on my tongue and her reading was a wonder in my ears. I had to speak.

I said, "Yes, ma'am." It was the least I could do, but it was the most also.

"There's one more thing. Take this book of poems and memorize one for me. Next time you pay me a visit, I want you to recite."

I have tried often to search behind the sophistication of years for the enchantment I so easily found in those gifts. The essence escapes but its aura remains. To be allowed, no, invited, into the private lives of strangers, and to share their joys and fears, was a chance to exchange the Southern bitter wormwood[4] for a cup of mead[5] with Beowulf[6] or a hot cup of tea and milk with Oliver Twist.[7] When I said aloud, "It is a far, far better thing that I do, than I have ever done . . ."[8] tears of love filled my eyes at my selflessness.

On that first day, I ran down the hill and into the road (few cars ever came along it) and had the good sense to stop running before I reached the Store.

I was liked, and what a difference it made. I was respected not as Mrs. Henderson's grandchild or Bailey's sister but for just being Marguerite Johnson.

Childhood's logic never asks to be proved (all conclusions are absolute). I didn't question why Mrs. Flowers had singled me out for attention, nor did it occur to me that Momma might have asked her to give me a little talking to. All I cared about was that she had made tea cookies for *me* and read to *me* from her favorite book. It was enough to prove that she liked me. ◆

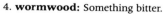

4. **wormwood:** Something bitter.
5. **mead:** Drink of the Middle Ages made from honey.
6. **Beowulf:** Hero of an Old English epic poem.
7. **Oliver Twist:** Hero of a novel by Charles Dickens.
8. **"It is . . . done":** Line in *A Tale of Two Cities,* spoken by a character who dies so that another may live.

Responding to the Theme

Self-Confidence

Responding in Your Journal   In this story the author describes the feeling of being liked just for herself—not for her family, appearance, or achievements. In your journal write about an experience you had that gave you the same kind of feeling. Continue to explore this subject. For example, write about experiences, relationships, and decisions that have raised or lowered your self-confidence. You may wish to use a loose-leaf notebook for your journal. Then, if some of your entries are too personal to share with your teacher, you can remove them before turning in your journal for review.

Speaking and Listening   According to Mrs. Flowers, reading aloud gives written words deeper meaning. With your teacher's permission, test Mrs. Flowers's theory by reading aloud from the selection. Work with two other students and choose a passage or piece of dialogue to read aloud. Then read the piece in as many different ways as possible, experimenting with the way it sounds. How do different readings change the meaning or the message? Take turns by having each member read the passage aloud in a different way.

Critical Thinking: Analyzing   In her autobiography the author remarks that "childhood's logic never asks to be proved." Find and explain the context of this remark in the story and give a similar example from your own experience.

Extending Your Vocabulary   Several words in this story, included in the list below, begin with the prefix *in-*. This prefix has two different meanings. Its first meaning is synonymous with *un-* or *non-*, meaning "not." *Insincere*, for example, means "not sincere." The second meaning of the prefix *in-* is "into" or "within." *Inflate*, for example, means "blow [air] into [something]." Use a dictionary to find the meaning of each word below. For each word write *first* or *second* to show which meaning of *in-* is being used. Then list the words in your notebook for possible use in your writing.

inedible	ingrained	infuse	intolerant
inalienable	inclusive	invalid	indelible

7

Part 2   *Writing*

Why write? As Mrs. Flowers said, language is people's way of communicating. To communicate well, you must be able to write well for a variety of purposes. Also, the stronger your writing skills, the better you will be able to complete writing assignments in school or in a future job. Another reason for writing, as you have already seen, is to discover and sort out your thoughts and feelings.

In this chapter you will learn to use the writing process. This process involves prewriting, drafting, revising, editing, and publishing a composition. The diagram on the next page describes these stages and shows the relationship between them. As you review the diagram, think about the process you use when you write a composition. Most writers do not simply complete one stage of the writing process and then move on to the next. Instead they move freely back and forth between stages. This is because writing is a creative process. As a writer you can shift from one stage to another or change the order of the stages you follow. For example, you may choose to revise your writing as you draft it, or edit your writing as you revise it.

The Writing Process

The following diagram illustrates the different stages of the writing process. Notice that the diagram loops back and forth. This looping shows how writers often move back and forth between various stages instead of going step-by-step from beginning to end. They can go back to any stage until they are satisfied with the quality of their writing.

Prewriting includes all the planning steps that you can take before you write the first draft. During pre-writing you find a subject, develop it, and organize the details.

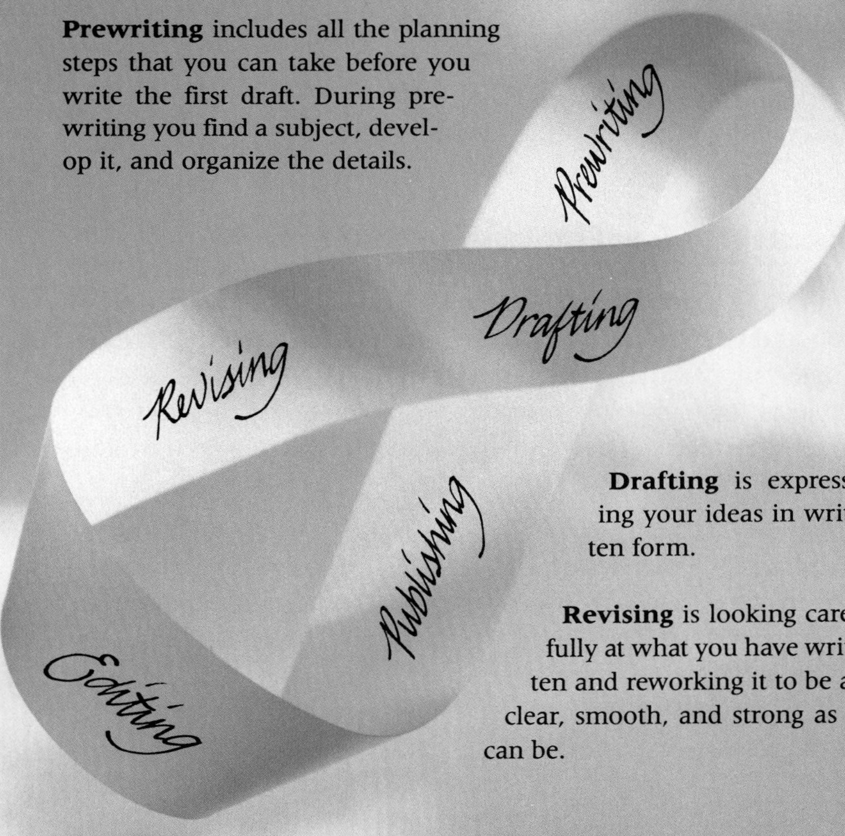

Prewriting

Drafting

Revising

Publishing

Editing

Drafting is expressing your ideas in written form.

Revising is looking carefully at what you have written and reworking it to be as clear, smooth, and strong as it can be.

Editing means checking your final draft for mistakes in grammar, usage, spelling, and mechanics and correcting any errors you may find.

Publishing means presenting your finished work to others in an appropriate way.

Prewriting

Writing Process

Something usually happens to trigger the act of writing. That something may range from a school assignment to the need to lodge a protest. All the planning that happens from the time an idea is triggered to the time you are ready to write the first draft is called *prewriting*.

Prewriting strategies that you can apply to your own writing appear on the following pages. The purpose of these strategies is to help you produce ideas for writing a composition. As you work through these pages, keep a writing folder in which you can put all your prewriting ideas.

Strategies for Thinking of Subjects

Finding a good subject—one that holds genuine interest for you and your readers—is an important first step in prewriting. Subjects have many sources. You may discover good ideas for subjects through your reading, for example, or through your own experiences. The following strategies will help you explore possible subjects.

Exploring Your Interests and Knowledge Much of the writing you do will grow out of your own interests, experiences, and knowledge. For this reason a good way to start thinking about subjects is to explore your own storehouse of knowledge and experience. You can do this by asking yourself questions like the following ones.

Questions for Exploring Interests and Knowledge

1. Whom do I admire and why?
2. What are my hobbies?
3. What at home or at school would I like to change?
4. What do I like to talk to my friends about?
5. What do I do best or know the most about?

WRITING ACTIVITY *Exploring Your Interests*

Complete each item as fully as you can and save your notes in your writing folder.

1. Movie and book characters I have admired include . . .
2. Aspects of my life that I would like to change are . . .
3. My favorite recreations, sports, and pastimes are . . .
4. My greatest accomplishments include . . .
5. Issues in the news that concern me the most are . . .

Freewriting   You can also use the strategy of freewriting to help you bring your thoughts to the surface. *Freewriting* means writing freely without stopping. Because the work you produce by freewriting is for your eyes only, you need not worry about making mistakes. Just write—and keep writing—whatever is on your mind. If you can't think of anything, choose an object you can see, such as a fire-exit sign in the classroom. Then write freely about the object, wherever your thoughts lead you. Following is an example of how you can discover ideas through freewriting.

Student Model: *Freewriting*

> I'm sitting here in my English class wondering what to write about. I'm supposed to keep an open mind, but it's not happening that way. I feel like I have to come up with a good idea. OK, so here I am in high school, working hard. And it is hard, or at least it's harder than junior high. Junior high was easier and I felt more comfortable there. I felt like I was somebody — somebody special I mean — but here I'm not too sure. I guess I felt sort of important before but now I'm kind of lost in the crowd.

As the writer wrote whatever came to mind, one idea—high school—began to emerge out of the muddle. Freewriting brought to mind a subject to write about.

WRITING ACTIVITY *Freewriting*

For five minutes, freewrite by jotting down everything that passes through your mind. Without stopping to think, keep your pen or pencil moving. After five minutes stop and place your work in your writing folder.

Exploring Literature for Writing Ideas   While your personal experience is a rich source of writing ideas, you may also find excellent writing subjects in your reading. For example, you may read a short story about the Alps, a poem about solitude, or a play set in a medieval castle—all subjects that you might like to explore on your own. If others have read the same selection, discussing it with them may help you discover additional ideas for compositions. Following are some strategies for finding writing ideas in your reading.

Exploring Literature for Writing Ideas

FICTION, POETRY, AND DRAMA

1. Write about the piece of literature itself, exploring plot, character, setting, or some other aspect of the literature. *(See "Writing Essays about Literature" on pages 318–357.)*

2. Write about the theme, or central message, of a story, poem, or play. For example, a story about a quest for the truth may give you ideas for writing about this theme.

3. Write about some trait of a character in a story or play. For instance, a character who envies others may give you ideas for writing about the problems envy can cause.

NONFICTION

1. Decide whether you agree or disagree with an editorial in a newspaper.

2. Look through newspapers and magazines to find issues or subjects that you could explore. For example, you may write about a particular event or an athlete or entertainer.

3. Think about biographies and autobiographies that you have read. Write about the subject of any of them.

Keeping a Journal Another good way to discover your thoughts through writing is to keep a journal. A *journal* is a daily notebook in which you record your thoughts, feelings, hopes, observations—anything you want. Since you most often write about subjects that are important to you, your journal entries will become a good source of ideas for compositions. Be sure to write in your journal every day and to date each entry. In this textbook you will also use your journal for the following additional purposes.

Additional Uses of the Journal

RESPONDING TO LITERATURE—A journal is a good place to write your responses and reactions to books, stories, poems, and other literature. After reading each literature selection in this textbook, you will have the opportunity to use your journal for this purpose, as you did on page 7. When you use your journal to respond to literature, be sure to start each entry with the author's name and the title of the selection.

LEARNING LOG—The Learning Log is a special section of your journal where you can write down ideas and information about math, science, history, health, or any other subject that you find particularly interesting. Facts from subject areas such as these may be useful when you are writing a composition.

PERSONALIZED EDITING CHECKLIST—The Personalized Editing Checklist is a section of your journal where you can keep a list of errors that recur in your writing. You might include words you frequently misspell, usage mistakes, mechanical errors, and so forth. Also list the page number in this book that will help you correct the error. Each time you edit a composition, you should refer to this checklist.

WRITING ACTIVITY *Writing in Your Journal*

Look carefully at the picture on the next page and freewrite in your journal everything that comes to your mind. Then, each day for the next several days, use a striking image from TV, magazines, or real life as a starting point for a journal entry.

Choosing and Limiting a Subject

How can you use the prewriting work you have done so far—exploring your interests, freewriting, exploring literature, and journal writing—to find a good subject? One good way is to review everything you have written to see if any ideas or subjects appear more than once. Ideas that come up often in your writing probably mean the most to you, which is an important characteristic of a good writing subject. Following are guidelines for choosing a good subject. Remember, though, that the most important guideline is your genuine interest in exploring a subject more fully in writing.

Guidelines for Choosing a Subject

1. Choose a subject that genuinely interests you.
2. Choose a subject that will most likely interest your readers.
3. Choose a subject you can cover thoroughly through your own knowledge or a reasonable amount of research.

WRITING ACTIVITY ◆ 4 *Writing on Your Own*

WRITING
ABOUT THE
THEME

Reread the selection from *I Know Why the Caged Bird Sings* on pages 3–6 and review all the prewriting work in your writing folder and journal. Search for potential subjects that have to do with gaining or losing self-confidence and jot down between five and ten subjects related to that theme. For example, you might write about a time when a burst of self-confidence enabled you to achieve the impossible. Use numbers to rank your subjects according to how well they fit the Guidelines for Choosing a Subject. After eliminating the weaker ideas, choose the one strong subject that you would like to write about the most. Then circle this subject and save all of your ideas in your writing folder.

Limiting a Subject When you choose a subject, you will often start with a general one, such as "sports" or "current events." Your next step, therefore, is to narrow, or limit, your subject. By limiting your subject, you are making it specific enough to cover completely in the amount of space you have for writing.

Strategies for Limiting a Subject

1. Limit your subject to one person or one example that represents the subject.
2. Limit your subject to a specific time or place.
3. Limit your subject to a specific event.
4. Limit your subject to a specific condition, purpose, or procedure.

Consider, for example, the subject of high school that was discovered through freewriting on page 11. To limit this general subject, you could write about only those aspects of high school that seem different from your experience in junior high school. Later, when you develop your subject, you could limit it even more by deciding to write about only two or three aspects of high school that are different from junior high.

WRITING ACTIVITY *Limiting a Subject*

For each broad subject, write two limited subjects. Then, for each limited subject, write one subject that is even more limited.

EXAMPLE: cats
POSSIBLE ANSWERS: cats I have known, my cat Frodo
cats in history, cats in ancient Egypt

1. games
2. movie stars
3. aircraft
4. novels
5. oceans

6. talk shows
7. football
8. emotions
9. money
10. reptiles

Considering Your Purpose and Audience

When you have decided on your subject, you should then consider your purpose for writing and your audience. Your *purpose* is your reason for writing. The box below summarizes the main purposes for writing and provides an example of each one.

Writing Purposes

- to **explain or inform** (a science book that explains how to conduct experiments)
- to **describe** (an essay that describes the features of Yosemite National Park)
- to **create** (a suspenseful short story about a detective on the trail of a bank robber)
- to **persuade** (an editorial that calls for greater public participation in local government)
- to **express your thoughts and feelings** (a poem or a personal essay on the value of friendship)

Keep in mind that writing purposes overlap and can be easily combined. For example, you might write a short story about bald eagles in which you want to describe but also to persuade others to conserve this species of wildlife.

WRITING ACTIVITY *Deciding Writing Purpose*

Decide which writing purpose or combination of purposes you would use for each of the following situations.

1. You won an art award for your T-shirt design and feel the urge to write about this for your own satisfaction.
2. A friend has composed a stirring melody for guitar, and you want to write lyrics for it.
3. You read about a proposed law to restrict skateboarding, and you want your community to vote a certain way.
4. You witnessed a hilarious case of mistaken identity that you want to share with others.
5. You did some research on tree farming, and you want others to understand what you have learned.

Considering Your Audience   Equally important in shaping your composition is knowing your *audience*, the people who will be reading your finished work. How you approach and develop your subject will depend in part on what your audience already knows about it. To understand your audience, ask yourself the following questions.

Audience Profile Questions

1. Who will be reading my work?
2. How old are they? Are they adults, teens, or children?
3. What background do they have in the subject I wish to write about?
4. What interests and opinions are they likely to have?
5. Are there any words or terms I should define for them?

WRITING ACTIVITY *Profiling an Audience*

Review the writing purposes that you wrote for the subjects in Writing Activity 6 above. Think of an audience that would be appropriate for each subject and purpose. Then write a brief description of each audience by answering the above Audience Profile Questions.

WRITING ACTIVITY *Writing for Different Audiences*

Imagine that you are writing about game hunting, a subject that you and others have different, strong feelings about. You know that to be effective, your writing must be appropriate for your audience. Explain, therefore, how you might modify your composition for each of the following audiences: very young children, game hunters, animal rights activists.

WRITING ACTIVITY 9 *Writing on Your Own*

WRITING
ABOUT THE
THEME

 Read the subject related to self-confidence that you chose in Writing Activity 4 on page 15. Limit that subject by following the Strategies for Limiting a Subject on page 15. Then decide on a purpose for writing about this subject and an appropriate audience. After you write your purpose and a brief profile of your audience, place your work in your writing folder for later use.

Strategies for Developing Your Subject

After you have chosen and limited a subject, you can flesh out your ideas with supporting details. *Supporting details* are the facts, examples, incidents, reasons, or other specific points that back up your ideas. Following are some prewriting strategies for developing supporting details.

Observing Observing is essential for developing supporting details—especially if you are describing a person, a place, or an object. *Observing* involves taking in sensory details—sights, sounds, tastes, feelings, and smells. Although your brain automatically records and interprets sensory input, observing as a skill requires both awareness and practice. Without paying particular attention, you may not notice all the small details that describe a scene. For example, suppose you were writing a description of a city street in the rain. Your senses automatically determine that it is raining because of the sound and feel of rain and the sight of pedestrians with open umbrellas. Observing more closely, however, you may notice less obvious descriptive details, such as the small rapids formed by water rushing along the gutters, the hollow sound of water dropping into a storm drain, and the rainbow-colored reflections of streetlights on the wet pavement.

WRITING ACTIVITY *Observing*

Look carefully at the picture on this page. Write freely for several minutes, giving a general description of the scene and an interpretation of what is happening in that scene. Then write for several more minutes, adding details about the scene and the event based on your closer observation.

Brainstorming for Details   Brainstorming is another good technique for thinking of supporting details to develop your subject. *Brainstorming* is like freewriting. When you brainstorm, however, you focus your thoughts on a specific subject. Also, you may pause to review an idea or to think of your next one, and you record your ideas in words and phrases rather than whole sentences. In the following brainstorming notes, the student wrote the subject at the top of a sheet of paper and then jotted down whatever came to mind about that subject.

Student Model: *Brainstorming List*

SUBJECT: high school versus junior high

— lots of homework (some of it interesting)

— big building (actually 3 buildings)

— nice pool and gym (brand new basketball court)

— crowded parking lot (looking forward to getting my learner's permit)

— lots of rules (hard to remember them all)

— crowded halls (I'm still getting lost!)

— real different from junior high

— lots of strange new people (miss my friends who went to different schools)

— all new teachers

— separate study halls (didn't have those in my junior high)

Group Brainstorming   Brainstorming can also be done in groups of two or more people. This strategy, known as *group brainstorming,* is an effective way to generate supporting ideas and details when everyone in the class is writing about the same subject. After forming a small group with three to five classmates, use the following guidelines. *(See pages 463 – 464 for more information about cooperative learning.)*

Guidelines for Group Brainstorming

1. Set a time limit on the brainstorming session.
2. Write the subject on a piece of paper and assign one group member to be the recorder. If your group meets frequently, take turns recording ideas.
3. Start brainstorming for supporting details, such as facts, reasons, and examples. Since you can eliminate irrelevant ideas later, contribute any and all ideas.
4. Build on the ideas of other group members. Add to those ideas or modify them to improve them.
5. Avoid criticizing the ideas of other group members.

When you have finished brainstorming, get a copy of all the ideas from the group recorder. Then you can choose the particular ideas and facts you want to include in your composition.

WRITING ACTIVITY *Brainstorming for Details*

On your own or with a group, brainstorm for ideas on the subject of status symbols, such as brand-name sneakers, jeans, or makes of cars. If you are working with others, follow the Guidelines for Group Brainstorming. When you are finished, save your notes in your writing folder for later use.

Clustering   Another strategy for developing supporting details is clustering. *Clustering* is a brainstorming technique that lets you not only record your ideas but also place them in groups. A cluster looks something like a wheel. At the hub, or center, you write your limited subject. Each idea or detail you think of to develop your subject is connected to the hub like a spoke in a wheel. Sometimes supporting ideas become new hubs with spokes of their own. The student who was writing about the differences between junior high and high school created the following cluster.

Student Model: *Clustering*

After clustering, the student further limited the subject to three aspects of high school that are different from junior high. This subject was suitable for the student's purpose (to inform) and audience (students).

WRITING ACTIVITY *Clustering*

Using the brainstorming notes you developed in Writing Activity 11 on status symbols, create a cluster like the one on page 22. If you prefer, you may create a cluster on one of the following subjects or on a subject of your own instead.

1. music of the 1990's   **4.** fishing
2. prehistoric people   **5.** movie ratings
3. environmental protection   **6.** team sports

Inquiring   Another good way to generate the supporting details you need to develop your subject is to ask yourself questions. Questions that begin *who, what, where, when, how,* and *why* can produce answers that are helpful in developing a subject. The following model shows how one writer used *inquiring* to develop details on the subject "an unforgettable cast party."

Student Model: *Inquiring*

> SUBJECT: an unforgettable cast party
>
> **Who?** All the cast members from the play *West Side Story* and the director, the stage manager, and the wardrobe manager
>
> **What?** Celebration of a successful play and a chance to wind down after closing night
>
> **Where?** Director's home — Mr. Timberlake's apartment
>
> **When?** After we had struck the set after our final performance last Saturday night
>
> **How?** We brought music tapes, snacks, and soft drinks — also gifts of appreciation for Mr. Timberlake and the stage manager
>
> **Why?** It is traditional to have a cast party after a school play. This particular party was "unforgettable" because we all felt especially close, like a family

WRITING ACTIVITY *Inquiring*

Practice the strategy of inquiring by using it to develop details on two of the following subjects. To write answers, follow the form of the student model on page 23.

1. a memorable trip   **4.** a wise decision
2. a lucky break   **5.** a dangerous encounter
3. a foolish mistake   **6.** a welcome surprise

WRITING ACTIVITY

WRITING
ABOUT THE
THEME

Review your limited subject for a composition on the theme of self-confidence, which you chose in Writing Activity 9 on page 18. Also look over your notes from that activity on purpose and audience. Then use observing, brainstorming, clustering, or inquiring to develop supporting details for a composition about your subject. Use more than one strategy to see which works best for you. Then save all your prewriting notes in your writing folder for later use.

Strategies for Organizing Your Ideas

When you brainstorm or cluster, you record your ideas in the order they occur to you. Before you share your ideas with a reader, however, you must organize those ideas clearly and logically. To do that you first focus your subject.

Focusing Your Subject   Before you arrange your ideas logically, you should decide on a focus, or main idea, for your composition. To think of a main idea, look over your notes and ask yourself what you want to say about your limited subject. Next think again about your purpose. Being aware of why you are writing helps you select the most appropriate main idea for your composition. For the composition on differences between junior high and high school, for example, the student who made the cluster on page 22 wrote three possible main ideas, which are listed on the next page.

- Of the differences between junior high and high school, three have had the greatest effect on me.
- Because of the differences between junior high and high school, I have sometimes felt lost in high school.
- The differences between junior high and high school are all for the best.

The student chose the first idea as the focus because it seemed most meaningful and because it suited the writing purpose (to inform) and the audience (students).

Grouping Your Details When you carefully look over your supporting details, you will often see that they fall naturally into groups, or categories. For example, if you were describing a baby, you might categorize your details in terms of the baby's appearance, movements, and sounds. If you were explaining the similarities and differences between two sports, you might group all the differences together and all the similarities in another group. Presenting your ideas in logical groups will help readers understand what you are trying to say.

Writing Is Thinking

Classifying

When clustering, freewriting, or brainstorming, you generate ideas freely as you think of them. Then, to organize those ideas, you must group them into meaningful categories. When you group your ideas, you will be using a thinking skill called classifying. *Classifying* is a process of grouping items into classes, or categories. The following chart, for example, compares equipment for English-style and Western-style horseback riding. Notice that details are classified under two categories of equipment: Saddle and Bridle.

Horseback Riding Equipment		
	ENGLISH-STYLE	**WESTERN-STYLE**
Saddle	flatter, lighter small saddle pad short stirrups	higher back, horn saddle blanket long stirrups
Bridle	snaffle or double bit single or double reins	curb bit single pair of reins

While classifying, you may add categories as needed to group new details. In the above chart, for example, you could add the category "Other Equipment" to classify any new details about horseback riding equipment—such as spurs, crops, and lariats—that do not fit logically under the existing categories.

Thinking Practice   Create categories to classify details about one of the following subject comparisons or one of your own. Then make a classification chart like the one above.

1. the similarities between ice hockey and field hockey
2. the pros and cons of bringing or buying school lunches
3. the benefits and drawbacks of summer and winter

Ordering Your Ideas   After grouping your details, you should decide on the best order in which to present them. The following box shows three common ways to order information.

Ways to Order Ideas	
CHRONOLOGICAL ORDER	Arranges events according to when they happened
SPATIAL ORDER	Arranges details according to their location (near to far, etc.)
ORDER OF IMPORTANCE, SIZE, OR DEGREE	Arranges details according to degrees of importance, size, etc.

The student writing about differences between junior high and high school made the following list of organized details. Notice that the list includes only those details from the cluster on page 22 that relate to the main idea, and that the details are listed in order of importance. The student used this list as a guide when writing the first draft.

Student Model: *List of Organized Details*

Focus (Main Idea): Of the differences between junior high and high school, three have had the greatest effect on me.

ORDER OF IDEAS	REASONS

1. Different subjects
  — math versus algebra
  — science versus biology
  — foreign languages
	Good to start with because the course schedule is the first you see of high school

2. More homework
  — 1 hour versus 2 hours
  — study halls
	Next in importance and follows logically from above

3. Crowded feeling
  — halls jammed
  — kids I don't know
  — competition
	Save for last as the most important difference; makes my point that you have to get used to high school

WRITING ACTIVITY *Organizing Details*

Explain which method of organization you would use to organize the details for each of the following subjects. Write *chronological, spatial,* or *order of importance* for each item.

1. an explanation of what to pack for a camping trip
2. a description of your school building
3. an account of your first day in high school
4. a story about the first time you used the subway or the bus
5. a comparison between public and commercial TV

WRITING ACTIVITY *Writing on Your Own*

WRITING
ABOUT THE
THEME

Look over your work from Writing Activity 14 on page 24 for your composition on self-confidence. Keeping your purpose for writing in mind, think of a main idea for your subject. Then group your supporting details into categories and decide in what order you want to present them. Using the model on page 27, write your list of organized details. Keep your prewriting work in your writing folder for later use.

Drafting

When you are satisfied that you have some good ideas to work with and a logical organization, you can test out your plan by writing a first draft. Unlike your prewriting notes, which are for your eyes only, your first draft should be aimed to reach your audience. Therefore, you should express your ideas in complete sentences and follow these Strategies for Drafting.

Strategies for Drafting

1. Write an introduction that will capture the reader's interest and express your main idea.
2. After you write your introduction, use your organized prewriting notes as a guide. Depart from those notes, however, when a good idea occurs to you.
3. Write fairly quickly without worrying about spelling or phrasing. You will have the opportunity to go back and fix your writing when you revise.
4. Stop frequently and read what you have written. This practice will help you move logically from one thought to the next as you draft.
5. Return to the prewriting stage whenever you find that you need to clarify your thinking. You can always stop and freewrite, brainstorm, or cluster to collect more ideas.
6. Write a conclusion that drives home the main point of the composition.

Following is a draft written on the subject of three differences between junior high and high school. Notice that the first and last paragraphs serve as an introduction and conclusion, which are important parts of any composition. Also notice that the writing follows the order of ideas that was planned in the student model on page 27. Last, notice that while drafting, the student writer made several mistakes in spelling, grammar, and punctuation. These mistakes will be corrected at a later stage in the writing process.

Student Model: *First Draft*

High school was a real suprise to me. I knew it would be different from junior high, but not this different. There were three things especially that made me realize that high school would never be the same.

One difference you notice write away from junior High is the courses you take. In junior high for example you take science and and math. In high school the courses are definately more avanced. In highschool you take Biology in stead of science and Algebra insteadof math. High school offers also foriegn languages which some junior highs don't, I'm taking spanish.

You also find you have more homework in high school. I I find I have twice as much homework in high school. In junior high I used to spend about an hour every week night doing homework. Now that I'm in high school I spend about two hours a night and sometimes even week ends. It does help that high schools have longer study hall periods. In study halls you can get some of your work do during school hours. There should be some way to keep things quieter in study halls at least some of the time.

High school is also much more crowded than junior high. The halls are jammed with students, and I dont even know alot of them. You sometimes feel lost. The other thing about so many students is that high school has a pretty competative atmosphere. There are more kids trying out for the same spots on sports teams, or in other groups. The added competition is a plus because it keeps you on you toes you really have to do your best at all times.

I guess I'm getting used to the idea that high school is a hole new experience. There are alot of diffrences between junior high and high school and these are only three of them. Such differences can be unsettling at first but you will find that they all have a strong plus side too.

Drafting a Title   You may think of a good title at any stage in the writing process. Whenever you come up with a title, however, consider carefully if it gets the attention of your readers. The title should also be appropriate to your subject, purpose, and audience.

Guidelines for Choosing a Title

1. Choose a title that identifies your subject or relates to your subject focus.
2. Choose a title that is appropriate for your purpose and audience.
3. Choose a title that will capture the reader's interest.

Following are examples of titles for the student draft on page 30. Notice how they meet the Guidelines for Choosing a Title.

Subject: differences between junior high and high school

PURPOSE	AUDIENCE	POSSIBLE TITLES
to inform	classmates	Making a Transition to High School
to create	classmates	Lost in the Crowd and Other Surprises
to describe	junior high students	What to Expect When You Start High School
to persuade	parents	Help Your High School Freshman

WRITING ACTIVITY   17  *Writing on Your Own*

WRITING
ABOUT THE
THEME
    Look over all your prewriting work for your composition on the theme of self-confidence. Then, using the list of organized details you developed in Writing Activity 16 on page 28, write your first draft. Remember to include an introduction and a conclusion. Also remember to pause occasionally and read over what you have written to keep your ideas on track. After you have written your first draft, compose a title for it. Then save all your work in your writing folder for revising.

Revising

Writing Process

Revising means "seeing again." When writers revise, they stand back from their work and look at it again with the eyes of someone reading it for the first time. The heaviest revising is usually done after a first draft is completed, but until you are completely satisfied with your revision, you may write a second, third, or even fourth draft. If you compose your draft on a word processor, the task of revising will be easier and quicker to do.

Before starting to revise your composition, you should put it away for a few days if you can. Then come back to it with a fresh eye and evaluate it objectively—perhaps even reading it aloud to see how it sounds. The following Revision Checklist will help you evaluate your composition.

Revision Checklist

1. Does your composition state your main idea?
2. Did you include enough interesting details to explore your subject in depth and support your main idea?
3. Do all of your sentences relate to the subject or the main idea?
4. Did you present your ideas in a logical order?
5. Does your composition have a strong ending?
6. Is the purpose of your composition clear?
7. Is your writing suited to your audience?
8. Are your sentences smoothly connected?
9. Did you vary your sentences and use specific words?
10. Is your title effective?

Revising on Your Own

After evaluating your composition, you are ready to revise, paying particular attention to the problems you identified. The following strategies will help you rework your draft until you are satisfied that it is the best it can be.

Adding Ideas   Look over your composition. Have you included all aspects of the subject? Are your ideas interesting to you and your audience? Are they fresh, original ideas rather than ones that people have heard over and over? Have you explored the subject in depth? If your answer to any of these questions is no, then you need to think of new ideas by freewriting about the subject or talking about it with others.

Adding Details and Information   As you reread your composition, ask yourself the following questions. Does it seem fully developed? Are your ideas fully supported? If not, you probably need to add more details and information. Brainstorm or use any other prewriting strategies to come up with additional, lively supporting details.

Rearranging   Check the organization of your words, sentences, and ideas. Does one idea lead logically into another? If not, rearrange your sentences or paragraphs so that the reader can easily follow your train of thought.

Deleting Unneeded Words or Details   Deleting means "removing." If you have included any details in your draft that do not really relate to your limited subject and main idea, delete them. Also delete any extra or unneeded words and repetitive sentences. *(See pages 76–77 for information about unneeded words.)*

Substituting Words and Sentences   Reread your draft once more. If any part of it might confuse the reader, think of a clearer way to express the same idea. For any word or phrase that may sound dull and boring, substitute a more interesting, original way to say the same thing. Also vary the structure and length of sentences to keep them from sounding monotonous. *(See pages 66–70 for information about sentence combining.)*

Using a Revision Checklist   The Revision Checklist on page 32 lists important qualities of a composition. When using the Revision Checklist, remember to personalize it by adding or modifying items to suit your own writing style.

WRITING ACTIVITY *Studying a Revision*

Study the following unedited portion of a revised draft on three differences between junior high and high school. Compare the revised draft with the first draft on page 30. Then, based on your comparison of the drafts, write answers to the following questions.

> *Although*
> ∧ High school was a real suprise to me. ⟨I knew it would⟩
> *a change*
> be ~~different~~ from junior high, ⟨~~but not this different~~⟩
> *Three differences*   *surprised me the most and*
> ~~There were three things~~ especially ~~that~~ made me realize that
> *a whole new experience.*
> high school would ~~never~~ be ~~the same.~~
> ∧
>   ℓ
> One difference ~~you~~ notice write away ~~from junior High~~
> *I am taking, which*
> is the courses ~~you take.~~ In junior high for example ~~you~~
> *took courses called*
> ~~take~~ science and and math. ~~In high school the courses~~ ⟨are⟩
> ∧
> ⟨definately more avanced.⟩ In highschool ~~you~~ take Biology
>
> in stead of science and Algebra insteadof math.   High
>   *more subjects than junior high, including*
> school offers also ∧ foriegn languages ~~which some junior high~~
> *I find that all the new courses make the subjects more*
> ~~don't I'm taking spanish.~~
> *interesting.*

1. In the revision which detail was deleted?

2. Which idea was out of place?

3. Point out two places where additional information or new details were added.

4. Point out three examples of rearranging sentences.

5. Point out two examples of replacing a weak expression with a stronger one.

6. Make one suggestion for further revision of this portion of the draft.

WRITING ACTIVITY *Revising a Paragraph*

Use the strategies for revising and the Revision Checklist to revise the following paragraph.

Fifties Fashions

Every decade seems to have its own uniform for teenagers who want to look "in." In the 1950's the look was unmistakable and easy to spot from head to toe. The fashionable girl of the fifties wore her hair in a pony tail, often with a scarf or kerchief around the rubber band. Matching sweater sets were popular too. These included a pullover and a cardigan in a matching color. The fifties girl also usually wore her hair with bangs. Boys in the fifties often wore their hair slicked back, with a wave or two in front. For skirts the big item was a wide circular skirt made out of felt and often embroidered or decorated with a poodle. It was considered very "cool" to wear a sweater clip connecting the two sides of the cardigan, rather than buttoning the sweater. On her feet the fifties girl usually wore ankle socks that she folded down once and two-tone saddle shoes that were mainly white with black or brown sections and ties. Shoes for boys were very pointed. If you ever stage a fifties party, you will know just how to dress.

Revising through Conferencing

At some point during the revising stage, you may wish to have a conference about your writing with one or more readers. A *conference* is a meeting with one or more other people for the purpose of sharing information and ideas or identifying and solving problems. Arranging a conference is as simple as inviting a reader—a friend, relative, classmate, or teacher—to tell you honestly what he or she thinks about your work. Ask for comments about what your reader likes and also for specific suggestions about what could be improved. Afterwards, analyze the comments and suggestions and use those that you think will improve your draft. In addition, you should be prepared to provide feedback to your reader on his or her writing. The following guidelines will help you when you use conferencing.

Guidelines for Conferencing

1. Read your partner's work carefully.
2. Start your comments by saying something positive, such as, "Your introduction really captured my attention."
3. Be specific. Refer to a specific word, sentence, or section of the composition when you comment.
4. Phrase your criticisms as questions. For example, "Could your ending be stronger? Maybe you could end with some kind of example."

WRITING ACTIVITY ⟨20⟩ *Writing on Your Own*

WRITING
ABOUT THE
THEME

Return to the first draft you wrote in Writing Activity 17 on page 31. With your teacher's permission, exchange papers with a peer reader—someone near your own age. Next, use the Guidelines for Conferencing to evaluate and discuss one another's compositions. Then begin revising your draft. Use the strategies for revising to add and rearrange ideas and details and to delete and substitute words and sentences. Remember to refer to the Revision Checklist in this chapter as you prepare your second draft. Save your work in your writing folder.

Editing and Publishing

Writing Process

When you revise, you are concerned mainly with reordering your ideas if necessary and making them clear. In the *editing* stage, you pay more attention to following the rules for correct writing. In *publishing* your work, you present your work in a final, correct form.

Editing a Draft

When you edit, you polish your work, correcting any mistakes you may have made in spelling, grammar, usage, or mechanics. The following strategies will help you edit your work thoroughly.

Using an Editing Checklist One way to look for errors is to use a checklist like the following one. You may also wish to refer to your Personalized Editing Checklist in your journal. (*See page 13.*) Rather than trying to cover all the items on the checklist at one time, read over your composition several times, each time looking for different kinds of errors. Breaking down the task will help you edit more thoroughly.

Editing Checklist

I. Are your sentences free of errors in grammar and usage?
2. Did you spell each word correctly?
3. Did you use capital letters where needed?
4. Did you punctuate each sentence correctly?
5. Did you indent your paragraphs as needed and leave proper margins on each side of the paper? (*See page 42.*)

Using Proofreading Symbols Writers often use a type of shorthand to mark errors they find when they *proofread*, or check for errors. The following proofreading symbols will save you time when you are editing.

Proofreading Symbols

∧	insert	I'll give you a *call* later.
⁄⟩	insert comma	Rosa, Katy, and I planned the dance.
⊙	insert period	Everyone stared at the soaring eagle ⊙
ℓ	delete	Did you hear ~~hear~~ the phone?
⌐⊢	new paragraph	⌐⊢ Another source of fuel is coal.
· · · ·	let it stand	I'll never forget that exciting day!
#	add space	I am studying for a math test.
⌣	close up	Auditions for the play are to morrow.
⌒	transpose	Tyrone recieved the late package.
☰	capital letter	My friend's name is aurora.
⁄	lowercase letter	The Scouts camped along the River.

In the following student model, notice how proofreading symbols were used to edit a portion of the revised draft of "Making a Transition to High School."

Student Model: *Edited Draft*

One ~~difference~~ I notice *d right* ~~write~~ away is the courses I

am taking, which are defin*i*tely more a*d*vanced. In junior

high, for example, I took courses called science and ~~and~~

math, *while* In high school I take ~~b~~iology in stead of science and

Algebra instead of math. High school offers also more

subjects than junior high, including foreign languages⊙ I

find that all the new courses make the subjects more

interesting.

Editing

"Language is man's way of communicating with his fellow man . . ." Mrs. Flowers told Marguerite in *I Know Why the Caged Bird Sings.* Communication in writing can break down, however, if the sentences are filled with errors. For this reason editing is an important stage in the writing process.

When you edit you pull together, or integrate, everything you know about usage and mechanics and other language skills. As you review different language skills in each composition chapter, write them in your Personalized Editing Checklist where you can refer to them when you edit. Then, at the end of the composition section, you will see that you have covered every major language skill in this book.

Sentence Fragments   When editing, you might begin with subjects and verbs, which are the foundation of all sentences. Without a subject and a verb, you have no sentence. Instead you have a *sentence fragment*—only part of a sentence. Therefore, always check for any missing subjects or verbs. *(For other kinds of fragments and practice in correcting them, see pages 695–699.)*

SENTENCE FRAGMENT   In high school, courses like science and math. [The verb is missing. You do not know what is being said about the courses.]

SENTENCE   In high school, courses about science and math are called biology and algebra.

Subject and Verb Agreement   Once you know that each of your sentences has a subject and a verb, your next step is to check to see if the subject and verb in each sentence agree in number. *Number* refers to whether the subject and verb are singular (one) or plural (more than one). To agree, both the subject and the verb must be either singular or plural. *(To review the singular and plural endings of verbs, see pages 754–755.)*

In the following examples, the subject is underlined once and the verb is underlined twice. Notice how they agree in number.

SINGULAR SUBJECT AND VERB   The <u>study hall</u> <u><u>was</u></u> quiet.
PLURAL SUBJECT AND VERB   The <u>study halls</u> <u><u>were</u></u> quiet.

Words Interrupting a Subject and a Verb   Subject and verb agreement is seldom a problem when the subject and verb are side by side. Sometimes, though, words separate the subject from the verb. When this happens you may easily make a mistake by having the verb agree with a nearby word rather than with the subject. *(For more information about subject-verb agreement and practice in correcting it, see pages 752–773.)*

AGREEMENT ERROR
The halls at the high school is jammed with students. [The verb must agree with the subject *halls*, not with *high school*.]

CORRECT AGREEMENT
The halls at the high school are jammed with students. [The plural verb *are* now agrees with the plural subject *halls*.]

When you edit your writing, you are guaranteeing that your words will communicate loudly and clearly to your audience. Therefore, take whatever time you need to edit your writing.

Editing Checklist

1. Are there any sentence fragments? *(See pages 695–698.)*
2. Do the subject and verb in each sentence agree in number? *(See pages 753–769.)*

WRITING ACTIVITY 21 *Writing on Your Own*

WRITING ABOUT THE THEME
As you edit your work from Writing Activity 20, make sure you cover the problems in the checklist above. Also review the Editing Checklist on page 37 and your Personalized Editing Checklist in your journal. Make your editing as easy as possible by remembering to use the proofreading symbols on page 38. Save your work in your writing folder for later use.

Publishing Your Work

Sometimes you write just for yourself to express your feelings. Often, however, you will be sharing your writing with others. Before you share, or publish, your writing, you should prepare the final draft of your composition in correct manuscript form.

Correct Manuscript Form The appearance of your composition may be almost as important as its content because a neat, legible, readable paper makes a positive impression on your readers. For this reason writers follow certain conventions, or customs, for arranging the appearance of a manuscript. Follow your teacher's instructions for preparing your final draft or use the following guidelines for Standard Manuscript Form.

Standard Manuscript Form

1. Use standard-sized, 8½- by 11-inch, white paper. Use one side of the paper only.
2. If handwriting, use black or blue ink. If typing or using a computer printer, use a black ribbon cartridge and double-space the lines.
3. Leave a 1¼-inch margin at the left and a 1-inch margin at the right. The left margin must be even. The right margin should be as even as possible without too many hyphenated words.
4. Put your name, the course title, the name of your teacher, and the date in the upper right-hand corner of the first page.
5. Center the title about 2 inches from the top of the first page. Do not underline or put quotation marks around your title.
6. If handwriting, skip 2 lines between the title and the first paragraph. If typing or using a word processor, skip 4 lines.
7. If handwriting, indent the first line of each paragraph 1 inch. If typing or using a word processor, indent 5 spaces.
8. Leave a 1-inch margin at the bottom of all pages.
9. Starting on page 2, number each page in the upper right-hand corner. Begin the first line 1 inch from the top of the page.

Student Model: *Final Draft*

½ inch

Sandra Diorio

English: Mr. Lee

2 inches

January 11, 1992

Making a Transition to High School

4 lines

5 spaces

Although I knew it would be a change from junior high, high school was a real surprise to me. Three differences especially surprised me the most and made me realize that high school would be a whole new experience.

One difference I noticed right away is the courses I am taking, which are definitely more

1¼ inches

advanced. In junior high, for example, I took courses called science and math, while in high school I take biology instead of science and algebra instead of math. High school also offers more subjects than junior high, including

1 inch

foreign languages. I find that all the new courses make the subjects more interesting.

Another surprise was the amount of homework. I find I have twice as much homework in high school. In junior high I spent about an hour every week night doing homework, but now I spend about two hours a day, sometimes even on weekends. Longer study hall periods, however, help me to get some of my homework done during school hours. Although the homework takes longer and is harder than before, I usually feel like I'm accomplishing things.

1 inch

2

1 inch

1 inch

1¼ inches

When I discovered I was having trouble
concentrating in study hall, I realized how much
more crowded high school is compared to junior
high. The halls are jammed with students, many
of whom I don't even know. With so many
students, high school has a more competitive
atmosphere. Many kids are trying out for the
same spots on sports teams, for example. The
added competition does have a positive side,
however. It keeps me sharp.

   I'm getting used to the idea that high
school is a whole new experience. Although the
differences between junior high and high school
unsettled me at first, I find they all have a
strong plus side. The changes, such as the
different courses, more homework, and a bigger
crowd, become less surprising every day.

Ways to Publish   After you have prepared your final draft in correct manuscript form, you are ready to publish it. One common way to publish your work is to submit it to a teacher. In addition, you have many other options for publishing. For instance, you can post your final draft with visuals on a bulletin board, share your writing in a school literary magazine, contribute to a school poetry or essay contest, or start a writing group with some classmates.

WRITING ACTIVITY   22   *Writing on Your Own*

WRITING
ABOUT THE
THEME

Using Standard Manuscript Form, make a neat final copy of your composition from Writing Activity 21. Then think of an appropriate way to publish your work.

A Writer Writes

A Composition about Personal Goals

PURPOSE: to express your thoughts and feelings
AUDIENCE: close relatives or friends

Prewriting   Brainstorm for ideas for a list of personal goals that hold special meaning for you. These could be short-term goals for this semester or long-term goals for your future. Make a list of 20 goals—as complete and specific as possible. Then choose and limit one goal for the subject of a composition. The goal you select should reflect one of your greatest interests, needs, or desires.

Next, use brainstorming to help you think of supporting details. First describe your goal. Then tell why you have that goal and what you will gain by achieving it. With your brainstorming notes in hand, think about your purpose and audience and determine a way to focus your subject.

After you determine your main idea, think about a logical way to organize your supporting details. First group your details into categories and list them in a logical order. Choose only those supporting details that relate to your main idea.

Drafting   Using your list of organized details, write your first draft. As you write, catch your reader's attention in the introduction and summarize your main idea in the conclusion. Remember to add a title to your composition. Your title should capture your reader's interest and be appropriate to your subject, purpose, and audience.

Revising *Conferencing:*   With your teacher's permission, share your draft with two or three other students in your class. For each composition you read, fill out a separate response sheet that answers the following questions. Then give your response sheet to the writer of each composition.

1. Which sentences and paragraphs, do you think, are particularly well written? What makes those parts good?
2. What words and phrases seem especially good?
3. What qualities of the composition could be improved? How would you improve them?
4. Does the composition have a strong introduction and conclusion? If not, how would you strengthen them?

Using the response sheets from readers and your own self-evaluation, add, delete, substitute, or rearrange material until you are satisfied that your draft is the best you can make it.

Editing and Publishing   Use the Editing Checklist on page 37 and your own Personalized Editing Checklist to find and correct any errors you may have made. Then make a neat final copy, using your teacher's guidelines or those for Standard Manuscript Form on page 41. Publish your work by sharing it with your audience of close relatives or friends.

Independent Writing

In *I Know Why the Caged Bird Sings*, Marguerite finds her own voice by discovering the power of others' voices; that is, she is inspired by the sound of words and sentences in literature. Find a short passage or quotation from literature that you find especially inspiring and write it down. Then write a composition explaining what the quotation means to you, what makes it powerful, and why you find it particularly inspiring.

Creative Writing

Write a poem about one of the following subjects. Let the language and images in your poem capture the feeling the subject stirs in you. Your poem may or may not rhyme, as you choose.

being alone	belonging	changing
being together	feeling left out	winning

 ## Writing about Literature

An *autobiography* is a person's written account of his or her life. When people write their autobiographies, they usually include the people, places, and events that shaped their lives the most. In her autobiography *I Know Why the Caged Bird Sings*, Maya Angelou describes Mrs. Flowers as the person "who threw me my first life line." She means that Mrs. Flowers became her role model, someone she looked up to and wanted to pattern herself after. How was Mrs. Flowers a role model to Marguerite? How have people in your life served as role models for you? Write a composition comparing your experience with the author's.

Writing in Other Subject Areas

Social Studies   Use the skill of observation to write a composition that objectively describes some aspect of group behavior. For example, you might describe the behavior of fans at a soccer match from the point of view of a visitor from another planet. Use vivid details to bring your description to life and make it entertaining for your readers.

Checklist

The Writing Process

Prewriting

✔ Find subjects by exploring your interests and knowledge, freewriting, exploring literature, and keeping a journal. *(See pages 10–13.)*

✔ Choose and limit the subject that you find the most interesting. *(See pages 14–15.)*

✔ Consider your purpose and your audience. *(See pages 16–17.)*

✔ Develop supporting details for your subject by observing, brainstorming, group brainstorming, clustering, or inquiring. *(See pages 18–23.)*

✔ Organize your ideas by grouping your supporting details and ordering your ideas. *(See pages 24–27.)*

Drafting

✔ Write a first draft and give it a title. *(See pages 29–31.)*

Revising

✔ Use self-evaluation, revision strategies, and the Revision Checklist to revise your draft. *(See pages 32–33.)*

✔ Use individual or group conferencing to get ideas for improving your composition. *(See page 36.)*

Editing and Publishing

✔ Edit your composition by correcting any errors in grammar, usage, capitalization, punctuation, and spelling. *(See pages 37–38.)*

✔ Make a neat final copy of your work, following Standard Manuscript Form. *(See pages 41–43.)*

✔ Present your work to readers by publishing your composition. *(See page 43.)*

2 Developing Your Writing Style

Part 1

Reading to Write

THEME: *Environment*

Suppose that you and your family are vacationing in Canada. As you travel north, you notice startling changes in the landscape—fragrant forests of tall firs, crystal rivers and streams, endless stretches of unpeopled countryside. So different is this setting from your home territory that you ask yourself, "What is it like to live in this place?" With that question you have raised a subject that writers have explored many times—the importance of your environment in shaping who you are, how you act, and how you see the world.

The story that opens this chapter adds insight to the theme of the effects of environment on people's lives. As the story unfolds, the author Ray Bradbury reveals his writing style by using unusual words and images and varied, rhythmic sentences. In this chapter you too will explore the theme of environment and develop your *writing style*—the unique way in which you express yourself through the words you choose and the way you shape your sentences. As you read "All Summer in a Day," think about how the setting of the story on another planet affects the characters.

All Summer in a Day

R a y   B r a d b u r y

"Ready?"

"Ready."

"Now?"

"Soon."

"Do the scientists really know? Will it happen today, will it?"

"Look, look; see for yourself!"

The children pressed to each other like so many roses, so many weeds, intermixed, peering out for a look at the hidden sun.

It rained.

It had been raining for seven years; thousands upon thousands of days compounded and filled from one end to the other with rain, with the drum and gush of water, with the sweet crystal fall of showers and the concussion of storms so heavy they were tidal waves come over the islands. A thousand forests had been crushed under the rain and grown up a thousand times to be crushed again. And this was the way life was forever on the planet Venus and this was the schoolroom of the children of the rocket men and women who had come to a raining world to set up civilization and live out their lives.

"It's stopping, it's stopping!"

"Yes, yes!"

Margot stood apart from them, from these children who could never remember a time when there wasn't rain and rain and rain. They were all nine years old, and if there had been a day, seven years ago, when the sun came out for an hour and showed its face to the stunned world, they could not recall.

49

Sometimes, at night, she heard them stir, in remembrance, and she knew they were dreaming and remembering gold or a yellow crayon or a coin large enough to buy the world with. She knew they thought they remembered a warmness, like a blushing in the face, in the body, in the arms and legs and trembling hands. But then they always awoke to the tatting drum, the endless shaking down of clear bead necklaces upon the roof, the walk, the gardens, the forests, and their dreams were gone.

All day yesterday they had read in class about the sun. About how like a lemon it was, and how hot. And they had written small stories or essays or poems about it:

> *I think the sun is a flower.*
> *That blooms for just one hour.*

That was Margot's poem, read in a quiet voice in the still classroom while the rain was falling outside.

"Aw, you didn't write that!" protested one of the boys.

"I did," said Margot. "I *did*."

"William!" said the teacher.

But that was yesterday. Now the rain was slackening, and the children were crushed in the great thick windows.

"Where's teacher?"

"She'll be back."

"She'd better hurry, we'll miss it!"

They turned on themselves, like a feverish wheel, all fumbling spokes.

Margot stood alone. She was a very frail girl who looked as if she had been lost in the rain for years and the rain had washed out the blue from her eyes and the red from her mouth and the yellow from her hair. She was an old photograph dusted from an album, whitened away, and if she spoke at all her voice would be a ghost. Now she stood, separate, staring at the rain and the loud wet world beyond the huge glass.

"What're *you* looking at?" said William.

Margot said nothing.

"Speak when you're spoken to." He gave her a shove. But she did not move; rather she let herself be moved only by him and nothing else.

They edged away from her, they would not look at her. She felt them go away. And this was because she would play no games with them in the echoing tunnels of the underground city. If they tagged her and ran, she stood blinking after them and did not follow. When the class sang songs about happiness and life and games her lips barely moved. Only when they sang about the sun and the summer did her lips move as she watched the drenched windows.

And then, of course, the biggest crime of all was that she had come here only five years ago from Earth, and she remembered the sun and the way the sun was and the sky was when she was four in Ohio. And they, they had been on Venus all their lives, and they had been only two years old when last the sun came out and had long since forgotten the color and heat of it and the way it really was. But Margot remembered.

"It's like a penny," she said once, eyes closed.

"No, it's not!" the children cried.

"It's like a fire," she said, "in the stove."

"You're lying, you don't remember!" cried the children.

But she remembered and stood quietly apart from all of them and watched the patterning windows. And once, a month ago, she had refused to shower in the school shower rooms, had clutched her hands to her ears and over her head, screaming the water mustn't touch her head. So after that, dimly, dimly, she sensed it, she was different and they knew her difference and kept away.

There was talk that her father and mother were taking her back to Earth next year; it seemed vital to her that they do so, though it would mean the loss of thousands of dollars to her family. And so, the children hated her for all these reasons of big and little consequence. They hated her pale snow face, her waiting silence, her thinness, and her possible future.

"Get away!" The boy gave her another push. "What're you waiting for?"

Then, for the first time, she turned and looked at him. And what she was waiting for was in her eyes.

"Well, don't wait around here!" cried the boy savagely. "You won't see nothing!"

Her lips moved.

"Nothing!" he cried. "It was all a joke, wasn't it?" He turned to the other children. "Nothing's happening today. *Is* it?"

They all blinked at him and then, understanding, laughed and shook their heads. "Nothing, nothing!"

"Oh, but," Margot whispered, her eyes helpless. "But this is the day, the scientists predict, they say, they *know*, the sun . . . "

"All a joke!" said the boy, and seized her roughly. "Hey, everyone, let's put her in a closet before teacher comes!"

"No," said Margot, falling back.

They surged about her, caught her up and bore her, protesting, and then pleading, and then crying, back into a tunnel, a room, a closet, where they slammed and locked the door. They stood looking at the door and saw it tremble from her beating and throwing herself against it. They heard her muffled cries. Then, smiling, they turned and went out and back down the tunnel, just as the teacher arrived.

"Ready, children?" She glanced at her watch.

"Yes!" said everyone.

"Are we all here?"

"Yes!"

The rain slackened still more.

They crowded to the huge door.

The rain stopped.

It was as if, in the midst of a film concerning an avalanche, a tornado, a hurricane, a volcanic eruption, something had, first, gone wrong with the sound apparatus, thus muffling and finally cutting off all noise, all of the blasts and repercussions and thunders, and then, second, ripped the film from the projector and inserted in its place a peaceful tropical slide which did not move or tremor. The world ground to a standstill. The silence was so immense and unbelievable that you felt your ears had been stuffed or you had lost your hearing altogether. The children put their hands to their ears. They stood apart. The door slid back and the smell of the silent, waiting world came in to them.

The sun came out.

It was the color of flaming bronze and it was very large. And the sky around it was a blazing blue tile color. And the jungle burned with sunlight as the children, released from their spell, rushed out, yelling, into the springtime.

"Now, don't go too far," called the teacher after them. "You've only two hours, you know. You wouldn't want to get caught out!"

But they were running and turning their faces up to the sky and feeling the sun on their cheeks like a warm iron; they were taking off their jackets and letting the sun burn their arms.

"Oh, it's better than the sun lamps, isn't it?"

"Much, much better!"

They stopped running and stood in the great jungle that covered Venus, that grew and never stopped growing, tumultuously, even as you watched it. It was a nest of octopi, clustering up great arms of fleshlike weed, wavering, flowering in this brief spring. It was the color of rubber and ash, this jungle, from the many years without sun. It was the color of stones and white cheeses and ink, and it was the color of the moon.

The children lay out, laughing, on the jungle mattress, and heard it sigh and squeak under them, resilient and alive. They ran among the trees, they slipped and fell, they pushed each other, they played hide-and-seek and tag, but most of all they squinted at the sun until tears ran down their faces, they put their hands up to that yellowness and that amazing blueness and they breathed of the fresh, fresh air and listened and listened to the silence which suspended them in a blessed sea of no sound and no motion. They looked at everything and savored everything. Then, wildly, like animals escaped from their caves, they ran and ran in shouting circles. They ran for an hour and did not stop running.

And then—

In the midst of their running one of the girls wailed.

Everyone stopped.

The girl, standing in the open, held out her hand.

"Oh, look, look," she said, trembling.

They came slowly to look at her opened palm.

In the center of it, cupped and huge, was a single raindrop. She began to cry, looking at it.

They glanced quietly at the sky.

"Oh, Oh."

A few cold drops fell on their noses and their cheeks and their mouths. The sun faded behind a stir of mist. A wind blew cool around them. They turned and started to walk back toward the underground house, their hands at their sides, their smiles vanishing away.

A boom of thunder startled them and like leaves before a new hurricane, they tumbled upon each other and ran. Lightning struck ten miles away, five miles away, a mile, a half mile. The sky darkened into midnight in a flash.

They stood in the doorway of the underground for a moment until it was raining hard. Then they closed the door and heard the gigantic sound of the rain falling in tons and avalanches, everywhere and forever.

"Will it be seven more years?"

"Yes. Seven."

Then one of them gave a little cry.

"Margot!"

"What?"

"She's still in the closet where we locked her."

"Margot."

They stood as if someone had driven them, like so many stakes, into the floor. They looked at each other and then looked away. They glanced out at the world that was raining now and raining and raining steadily. They could not meet each other's glances. Their faces were solemn and pale. They looked at their hands and feet, their faces down.

"Margot."

One of the girls said, "Well . . . ?"

No one moved.

"Go on," whispered the girl.

They walked slowly down the hall in the sound of cold rain. They turned through the doorway to the room in the sound of the storm and thunder, lightning on their faces, blue and terrible. They walked over to the closet door slowly and stood by it.

Behind the closet door was only silence.

They unlocked the door, even more slowly, and let Margot out. ◆

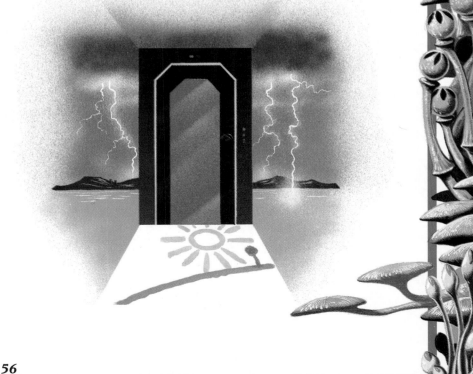

Responding to the Theme

Environment

Responding in Your Journal   In "All Summer in a Day," the physical environment of sunlessness and constant rain has a strong influence on the characters. Think about how your environment— your home, neighborhood, city or town, and region of the country— has influenced you. Perhaps, for instance, you feel a special connection to the desert, the bayou, the prairie, or the sea. Or perhaps you see yourself as a city person or a Southerner. In your journal for the next few days, write about how your environment has influenced your customs, interests, and outlook. Start today by writing about an activity you enjoy, such as fishing or hiking, that reflects the influence of your local environment.

Speaking and Listening   With your teacher's permission, work with four or more classmates to discuss how the story could be continued beyond its present ending. What might Margot, the teacher, William, and the other children say and do after the events in the story? Choose someone in the group to record ideas and then develop a script, incorporating those ideas into a new scene. After writing the script, assign speaking parts and act out your scene for the class.

Critical Thinking: Inferring   Write a paragraph in which you draw a conclusion about the main reasons the children in the story were cruel to Margot. Find sentences in the story that support your conclusion and include them in your paragraph.

Extending Your Vocabulary   "All Summer in a Day" contains many ordinary words that are used in unexpected ways, which is a characteristic of interesting writing. In some instances words ordinarily used as nouns appear as verbs. For example, Bradbury writes, "The world *ground* to a standstill." In other instances words usually used as verbs appear as nouns: "The sun faded behind *a stir* of mist." Write sentences using each of the following words from the story as a noun and then as a verb.

drum	edge	stuff	ground	blush
burn	surge	shake	tag	avalanche

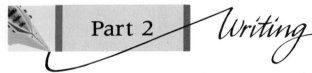

Part 2 / *Writing*

Good writing sparkles like jewelry, catching the reader's eye with vivid words and varied, uncluttered sentences. As you read the following description of an imaginary scene on Mars, notice how the words and sentences are carefully crafted to capture the reader's imagination.

Model: *Vivid Words and Sentences*

Summer burned the canals dry. Summer moved like a flame upon the meadows. In the empty Earth settlement, the painted houses flaked and peeled. Rubber tires upon which children had swung in back yards hung suspended like stopped clock pendulums in the blazing air.

RAY BRADBURY, "Dark They Were and Golden Eyed"

The vivid writing in this paragraph leaves a lasting impression in the reader's mind. The paragraph's words and sentences allow you to picture a parched, motionless setting and may also make you wonder what will happen next in such a place.

Choosing Vivid Words

During the revising stage, writers look for ways to make their writing shine. One way to do this is by choosing words and expressions that express what you mean specifically, colorfully, and clearly.

Writing Tip   When you revise, create clear and vivid images by using **specific words**, rich **connotations**, and **figurative language**.

Specific Words

Specific words help readers visualize what they read. For example, both of the following examples describe the same item on a restaurant menu. However, the first example uses general words that leave only a vague impression. The second uses specific words that whet the appetite.

GENERAL   Cooked meat covered with a good sauce, served with tasty potatoes and cooked fresh vegetables

SPECIFIC   Barbecued spareribs smothered in a tangy sauce, served with sizzling French-fried potatoes and crisp steamed broccoli

General words may mean different things to different people, but specific words leave an exact picture in the reader's mind. The following examples show how you can replace general words with more specific words.

	GENERAL	SPECIFIC	MORE SPECIFIC
NOUNS:	meat	pork	spareribs
	clothes	pants	blue jeans
ADJECTIVES:	uneasy	nervous	jittery
	thin	delicate	fragile
VERBS:	went	walked	strolled
	saw	watched	examined
ADVERBS:	happily	gleefully	exuberantly
	soon	promptly	now

WRITING ACTIVITY *Revising with Specific Words*

Revise the following paragraph by replacing each underlined word or words with more vivid, specific language. The first sentence has been done for you as an example.

After the Movies

Kathy's dad took us out for **(1)** ~~dessert~~ ^ice cream^ after the movie. While we were eating, we **(2)** <u>talked about</u> the movie. Kathy thought the acting was convincing, but the story was **(3)** <u>weak</u>. I thought the scenes with the Martians were **(4)** <u>good</u>. The chase scenes were comical because the four-legged Martians **(5)** <u>walked oddly</u>. Kathy's dad thought the special effects were **(6)** <u>poor</u>. He **(7)** <u>laughed</u> during one scene when you could see the strings that were attached to the spaceship. Before leaving the **(8)** <u>place where we were having dessert</u>, each of us gave the movie a grade. I gave it an **(9)** <u>excellent grade</u>, but Kathy and her dad gave it a D +. Later that night I dreamed that green **(10)** <u>creatures</u> were chasing me with report cards.

Denotation and Connotation

All words convey a literal meaning, the meaning found in a dictionary. This meaning is called *denotation*. Many words, however, also stir up emotions. This extra level of meaning is called *connotation*. The words *trip* and *vacation*, for example, have similar denotations, but *vacation* has an extra level of meaning. It brings many feelings immediately to mind: freedom from the usual routine, fun, relaxation, different surroundings.

Understanding connotations is important when you write because some words have similar denotations but opposite connotations.

POSITIVE CONNOTATION | The city was **bustling** with people during the holiday.

NEGATIVE CONNOTATION | The city was **mobbed** with people during the holiday.

In these examples the words *bustling* and *mobbed* both mean "filled." *Bustling*, however, suggests a positive feeling of energy and excitement, while *mobbed* suggests a negative feeling of overcrowding, noise, and restricted movement. This extra level of meaning offered by a word's connotation helps to stir the readers' emotions. When you revise, add another dimension to your writing by using words with rich connotations.

WRITING ACTIVITY *Using Connotation to Add Meaning*

Write the word in each of the following sentences that has the connotation given in brackets.

EXAMPLE   Ellen is very (frank, blunt). [negative]
ANSWER   blunt

1. Every October the old maple (paints, litters) the lawn with its falling leaves. [positive]
2. The mare ran (courageously, recklessly) into the flaming barn to save her colt. [positive]
3. We walked at a (leisurely, sluggish) pace. [negative]
4. The rabbit (scrambled, scampered) across the lawn. [positive]
5. My sister showed her report card (boastfully, proudly). [positive]

Figurative Language

You can create vivid pictures in your readers' minds not only by using specific words and words with rich connotations but also by using *figurative language*. The two most common types of figurative language are *similes* and *metaphors*.

Similes and Metaphors   These figures of speech stimulate the reader's imagination by expressing a similarity between two things that are essentially different. Similes state a comparison by using the words *like* or *as*. Metaphors, however, imply a comparison by simply saying that one thing *is* another.

SIMILE   Summer moved **like a flame** upon the
meadows.   RAY BRADBURY

METAPHOR   The road was **a ribbon of moonlight.**
                                              ALFRED NOYES

Summer and flame are two different things, but they share the quality of intense heat. Roads and ribbons are not alike, but on a moonlit night a road can share the shiny, winding appearance of a ribbon.

Road Past the View I, Georgia O'Keeffe, 1964.

WRITING ACTIVITY *Identifying Similes and Metaphors*

Write *simile* or *metaphor* to identify each underlined figure of speech in the following sentences.

1. My brother's room <u>is a federal disaster area</u>.
2. With crashing cymbals and booming drums, the symphony was <u>like a thunderstorm</u>.
3. Good friends revolve around Sandra <u>as the planets revolve around the sun</u>.
4. Hope went through me <u>like a faint breeze over a lake</u>.
   ANTOINE DE SAINT-EXUPERY
5. The coach <u>growled</u> when his players quit too soon.
6. Her secret was <u>as dark as her eyes</u>.
7. Hermit crabs, <u>like frantic children</u>, scamper on the bottom sand. JOHN STEINBECK
8. All the strength went out of me, and I toppled forward <u>like an undermined tower</u>. MARK TWAIN
9. Memories <u>poured</u> from every corner of the old house.
10. The <u>black bat, night, has flown</u>. ALFRED, LORD TENNYSON

Clichés Some comparisons that were once clever and striking have become dull with overuse. Such worn-out expressions are called *clichés*. If you find yourself using a simile or metaphor that you have heard before, replace it with a fresh comparison or with specific words.

CLICHÉ	knocked me over with a feather
SPECIFIC WORDS	completely surprised me; made me weak with amazement
CLICHÉ	make a mountain out of a molehill
SPECIFIC WORDS	exaggerate unnecessarily; needlessly make things more difficult
CLICHÉ	as cool as a cucumber
SPECIFIC WORDS	relaxed; nonchalant
FRESH COMPARISON	as unruffled as duck feathers in a still wind; as self-possessed as a snail

WRITING ACTIVITY 4 *Revising to Eliminate Clichés*

Revise the following paragraph by replacing each underlined cliché with a fresh simile or metaphor or with specific words.

Tryouts

Everyone told me the tryouts for the school play would be **(1)** <u>as easy as A, B, C</u>, but when I saw how many juniors and seniors were trying out, I felt **(2)** <u>like a duck out of water</u>. By the time I was called to read my lines, I was **(3)** <u>shaking like a leaf</u>, and my throat was **(4)** <u>as dry as a desert</u>. Somehow I managed to **(5)** <u>spit out</u> the first few lines. Then suddenly my voice became **(6)** <u>a squeaky, old hinge</u>. Mercifully the director stopped me and told me **(7)** <u>to start from scratch</u>. This time I was **(8)** <u>as steady as a rock,</u> and my voice was **(9)** <u>as clear as a bell</u>. When the cast list was announced the next day at school, **(10)** <u>it was music to my ears</u>.

WRITING ACTIVITY 5 *Writing on Your Own*

WRITING
ABOUT THE
THEME

 Look over your brainstorming entries in your journal related to how your environment has influenced you. *(See Responding in Your Journal on page 57.)* Circle the ideas that relate to general conditions of life on Earth, such as geography, climate, plants and animals, and human habitations. Then imagine that you are marooned on some distant, alien planet, like the characters in Ray Bradbury's story "All Summer in a Day." As you watch Earth rise and set, what images and comparisons would you use to describe your longings for your home planet? Brainstorm until you have as many details as possible that describe your feelings.

Draft a composition in which you describe your feelings for your home planet. Include specific details about what you would miss the most about your former Earth environment.

Look for ways to polish your writing by using specific words, words with rich connotations, and figurative language. Explore opportunities to use similes or metaphors. Save your draft in your writing folder for additional revising later.

Developing Vivid Comparisons

When you write a simile or a metaphor, you are using a thinking skill called comparing. When you *compare*, you tell how two things are similar. Thinking of a fresh comparison to use in a simile or metaphor, however, is sometimes difficult to do. The following chart illustrates a thinking strategy that will help you develop vivid comparisons.

QUALITIES OF A STRAWBERRY	THINGS WITH SIMILAR QUALITIES
plump	a marshmallow, a baby's cheek
juicy	a watermelon, an orange
red	a ruby, a clown's nose
rough	a puppy's tongue, cornmeal

To create a comparison chart, first think about what you want to describe. Then make a list of its most important qualities. Next to each quality list some other things that have the same quality. Stretch your imagination and avoid overused comparisons like *red as a rose*. Once you have a list of comparisons, you can select the best one for your simile or metaphor.

SIMILE   Red, ripe strawberries gleamed under the shadowy leaves **like unmined rubies in a gem field.**

Thinking Practice   Use the thinking strategy described above to help you write a fresh simile or metaphor for each of the following items.

I. waves hitting rocks
2. a Ferris wheel at night
3. a stubbornly determined child going up stairs

65

Sentence-Combining Strategies

Do you recall what it is like to read a paragraph that consists only of a string of short, choppy sentences? Too many short sentences in a row make the writing choppy and difficult to read. When you revise your writing, you can improve the flow of short sentences by combining them to make longer, varied ones. The following sentence-combining strategies show you how.

Combining Sentences with Phrases

One way to combine short sentences is to express some of the information in a phrase. The following models show how to combine sentences using three kinds of phrases. *(See pages 633–645 and 649–667 for more information about phrases.)*

A. Handlers can usually train dogs. Training is in basic obedience. Training takes about eight weeks.

Handlers can usually train dogs **in basic obedience in about eight weeks**. [prepositional phrases]

B. Handlers and dogs work together. This strengthens the bond between pet and master.

Handlers and dogs work together, **strengthening the bond between pet and master**. [participial phrase]

C. A training collar helps the handler correct the dog. It is the handler's most important tool.

A training collar, **the handler's most important tool**, helps correct the dog. [appositive phrase]

WRITING ACTIVITY *Combining Sentences with Phrases*

Combine each pair of sentences in the following items, using the above models. The letter in brackets indicates which model to use. Remember to insert commas where needed.

Inner Games

1. Tim Gallwey wrote a book. He wrote about becoming a winner. [A: prepositional phrase]

2. His book captured great attention. His book is *The Inner Game of Tennis.* [C: appositive phrase]

3. Gallwey identifies an "inner game." This is a game between the player's actions and his or her thoughts and feelings. [B: participial phrase]

4. The inner game influences the play between opponents. The inner game tests a player's confidence and powers of concentration. [B: participial phrase]

5. Playing the inner game well brings rewards. The rewards are in concentration. The rewards are in relaxation. The rewards are in success in the game. [A: prepositional phrase]

6. Each player plays two roles that determine his or her skill. These are the director and the doer. [C: appositive phrase]

7. The director is the inner player. The director gives the doer such instructions as, "OK, hit the next volley high." [B: participial phrase]

8. In good players the director and the doer interact. They interact in harmony. [A: prepositional phrase]

9. In weaker players, the doer can become frustrated. The doer tries too hard and fails. [B: participial phrase]

10. Mastering the inner game has value. The value is in life as well as in tennis. [A: prepositional phrase]

Combining Sentences by Coordinating

Another way to smooth out short, choppy sentences is to link ideas of equal importance with a coordinating conjunction. *(See pages 549–550, 685–686, and 824–825 for more information about coordinating.)*

Coordinating Conjunctions						
and	but	for	nor	or	so	yet

The model sentences about dog training on the next page show how to combine sentences with coordinating conjunctions.

A. Kindness is also important. Praise is important too.

Kindness <u>and</u> **praise** are also important. [compound subject]

B. Soon your dog will heel on command. Soon your dog will sit on command.

Soon your dog **will heel** <u>and</u> **sit** on command. [compound verb]

C. The dog should be confined before each session. The place of confinement should be comfortable.

The dog should be confined before each session, <u>but</u> **the place of confinement should be comfortable**. [compound sentence]

WRITING ACTIVITY **7** *Combining Sentences by Coordinating*

Combine each pair of sentences, using the model identified in brackets following each pair. Add punctuation as needed.

The
Alexander
Method

1. F. M. Alexander, who lived in the 1800's, acted. He also gave speeches. [B: compound verb]

2. In the 1880's he suddenly lost his voice. His career ground to a halt. [C: compound sentence]

68

3. He visited doctors. None of them could help him.
   [C: compound sentence]
4. He had little choice but to help himself. He had no medical training. [C: compound sentence]
5. He began observing in the mirror his efforts to speak. He saw something odd about his movements. [B: compound verb]
6. His head moved when he tried to talk. His neck also moved. [A: compound subject]
7. These movements affected his posture. His posture in turn affected his speech. [C: compound sentence]
8. He kept up his observations. He eventually cured himself by relaxing his head and neck. [B: compound verb]
9. Alexander's method became a classic treatment. It is still used to help people solve some medical problems through better posture. [B: compound verb]
10. The treatment stresses simple, everyday exercises, such as walking. Anyone can do them. [C: compound sentence]

Combining Sentences by Subordinating

If the ideas in two short sentences are of unequal importance, you can combine them by subordinating. To subordinate, express the less important idea in an adjective clause that begins with a relative pronoun or in an adverb clause that begins with a subordinating conjunction. The pronouns and conjunctions below are often used to begin clauses. *(For a complete list of subordinating conjunctions, see page 674. See pages 671–681 for more information about subordinating with adjective and adverb clauses.)*

For Adjective Clauses		For Adverb Clauses	
RELATIVE PRONOUNS		**SUBORDINATING CONJUNCTIONS**	
who	which	after	unless
whom	that	although	until
whose		because	whenever

The following model sentences about dog training show how to combine sentences by creating adjective or adverb clauses. *(For information about punctuating subordinate clauses, see pages 676, 680, and 821–833.)*

A. Mother dogs use a barking sound to get their pups to obey. The barking sound resembles the word *out*.

Mother dogs use a barking sound, **which resembles the word** *out*, to get their pups to obey. [adjective clause]

B. Handlers can also use this sound. Dogs have a long memory of their mothers' stern corrections.

Handlers can also use this sound **because dogs have a long memory of their mothers' stern corrections**. [adverb clause]

WRITING ACTIVITY *Combining Sentences*

Combine each pair of sentences, using the method indicated in brackets following each pair. Refer to the examples on pages 66 and 68 and to those above. Add punctuation as needed.

On the Trail

(1) We wanted to do something different on our vacation. We chose backpacking in the wilderness. [compound sentence] **(2)** We walked the entire distance. We had packs on our backs. [prepositional phrases] **(3)** I could carry my own pack. It weighed 50 pounds. [adverb clause] **(4)** The trail was steep and hazardous. It had been a logging road. [adjective clause] **(5)** At one point we came to a lookout tower. It was in good condition. [adjective clause] **(6)** I climbed the tower. I strapped my camera around my neck. [participial phrase] **(7)** Fog had covered the valley. I could barely see. [compound sentence] **(8)** In the distance a river came down from the mountains. It flowed east. [compound verb] **(9)** A footpath followed the river. An old railroad track followed the river. [compound subject] **(10)** That foggy view has stayed in my memory to this day. It was a highlight of the vacation. [appositive phrase]

Creating Sentence Variety

Good writing flows with the natural, varied rhythms of speech. As you read the following passage by Ernest Hemingway, notice how the varied rhythm of his sentences contributes to the pleasure of reading the paragraph.

Model: *Sentence Variety*

Before it was really light, he had his baits out and was drifting with the current. One bait was down forty fathoms. The second was at seventy-five, and the third and fourth were down in the blue water at one hundred and twenty-five fathoms.

ERNEST HEMINGWAY, *The Old Man and the Sea*

Writing Tip   When you revise, create a natural rhythm by **varying** the beginning, length, and structure of your sentences.

Varying Sentence Beginnings

The most natural way to begin a sentence is with the subject. If too many sentences begin in the same way, however, even a gripping story will sound dull. The following examples show how Hal Borland varied the beginning of his sentences in his novel *When the Legends Die*.

SUBJECT   **The boy** caught trout in the pool and watched for his friend, the bear.

ADVERB   **Reluctantly** the boy fastened the collar on the bear cub.

PHRASE   **For days** he watched them. [prepositional phrase]
Driving with one hand, he headed for home. [participial phrase]

CLAUSE   **If he rode the horse with its own rhythm**, he could ride every horse in the herd. [adverb clause]

When you revise, vary the rhythm of your writing by starting your sentences in a variety of ways.

71

WRITING ACTIVITY *Varying Sentence Beginnings*

Vary the beginning of each of the following sentences by using the openers suggested in brackets.

The Milky Way

1. The universe, stretching endlessly beyond the reaches of our imagination, holds many mysteries. [participial phrase]
2. There are 100 billion stars in just our own galaxy, the Milky Way. [prepositional phrase and appositive phrase]
3. However, only the nearest and brightest stars are visible when we gaze into the vast sea of stars. [adverb clause]
4. We can see fewer than 3,000 stars on a clear night. [prepositional phrase]
5. The Milky Way would look like a giant fried egg if we could look down on it. [adverb clause]
6. Our galaxy, bulging in the middle, spans 10,000 light-years at the center. [participial phrase]
7. Orbiting stars in the outer part of the galaxy form graceful spiral arms. [prepositional phrases]

8. One spiral arm extending through the constellations Perseus and Cassiopeia reaches out 7,000 light-years from the sun. [participial phrase]

9. Our solar system travels 250 miles per second, although we do not feel the motion. [adverb clause]

10. One complete orbit around the galaxy nevertheless takes 250 million years. [adverb]

Varying Sentence Structure

Another way to achieve a natural sound and rhythm in your writing is to vary the structure of your sentences. In the following example, Marjorie Kinnan Rawlings describes a part of her stay near a North Carolina orphanage. Notice how she uses a variety of sentence structures to create a flowing rhythm. *(See pages 685–687 for more information about simple, compound, complex, and compound-complex sentences.)*

Model: *Sentence Variety*

SIMPLE	At daylight I was half wakened by the sound of
COMPLEX	chopping. Again it was so even in texture that I
COMPOUND-COMPLEX	went back to sleep. When I left my bed in the cool morning, the boy had come and gone, and a stack
COMPLEX	of kindling was neat against the cabin wall. He came again after school in the afternoon and worked until it was time to return to the orphan-
COMPOUND-COMPLEX	age. His name was Jerry; he was twelve years old, and he had been at the orphanage since he was four.　　MARJORIE KINNAN RAWLINGS "A Mother in Manville"

WRITING ACTIVITY *Revising for Sentence Variety*

The following paragraph contains only simple sentences. Create a variety of simple, compound, complex, and compound-complex sentences by combining the sentences according to the structure indicated in brackets. Use commas where needed.

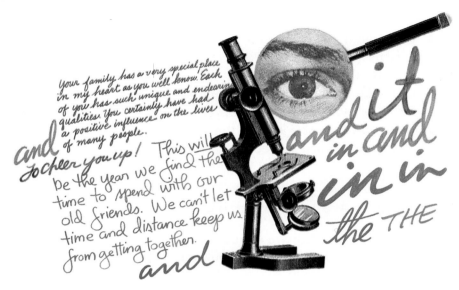

Your family has a very special place in my heart as you well know. Each of you has such unique and endearing qualities. You certainly have had a positive influence on the lives of many people.

and

To cheer you up! This will be the year we find the time to spend with our old friends. We can't let time and distance keep us from getting together.

and

and it in and in in the THE

Handwriting Analysis

(1) Handwriting analysis is not an exact science. Police often seek the opinion of a handwriting expert in cases of forgery. [complex] (2) The handwriting in question is placed under a microscope. A known piece of handwriting is placed beside it. [compound] (3) The handwriting expert analyzes the two samples. The expert does this by comparing significant details. These details include the dots above *i*'s, the crosses through *t*'s, the angle of the pen, and the beginnings and ends of pen strokes. [simple] (4) Experts sometimes disagree. Many people doubt the reliability of handwriting analysis. [complex] (5) Doubts persist. Courts allow handwriting experts to testify. Juries are often persuaded by the testimony of these experts. [compound-complex]

WRITING ACTIVITY *Writing on Your Own*

WRITING
ABOUT THE
THEME

Review the draft you wrote in Writing Activity 5 about your former Earth environment. Do your sentences flow naturally with the varied rhythms of speech? Could you add variety by combining sentences? Revise your draft by varying the beginning, length, and structure of your sentences. Save your draft for additional revising later.

Writing Concise Sentences

Compact cars go farther on a gallon of gasoline than do huge gas-guzzlers. In the same way, concise sentences deliver more meaning from each word than do repetitive, wordy sentences.

Writing Tip   Create **concise** sentences by expressing your meaning in as few words as possible.

Rambling Sentences

A sentence that rambles on too long is dull and hard to understand. In the following description, too many ideas are strung together in one sentence.

RAMBLING   The buzz saw screams as you watch the tree come up the conveyor belt, and as the tree hits the saw, chips fly left and right, and when it reaches the end of the saw, the log folds over into two slabs.

When you revise, eliminate rambling sentences by separating the ideas into a variety of short and long sentences.

REVISED   The buzz saw screams as you watch the tree come up the conveyor belt. As the tree hits the saw, chips fly left and right. When it reaches the end of the saw, the log folds over into two slabs.

WRITING ACTIVITY ◆ 12 *Revising Rambling Sentences*

Revise the following paragraph by breaking up the rambling sentence. Use capital letters and punctuation where needed.

Winchester House

Winchester House is the name of a huge, rambling mansion in San José, California, that was built by Sarah Winchester, who was heir to the Winchester fortune and who believed that she would go on living as long as she was adding to the house, which has 160 rooms, 200 doors, and 47 fireplaces.

Redundancy

Unnecessary repetition is called *redundancy*. In a redundant sentence, the same idea is expressed more than once with no new or different shades of meaning.

REDUNDANT   The **hungry** wolf ate **ravenously**.
  CONCISE   The wolf ate **ravenously**.

REDUNDANT   The **hot, steamy** asphalt shimmered.
  CONCISE   The **steamy** asphalt shimmered.

WRITING ACTIVITY *Revising to Eliminate Redundancy*

Revise each of the following sentences by eliminating the redundancy.

1. Do you have a spare pencil that you are not using?
2. Friday is the final deadline for the report.
3. Each and every member of the class must help.
4. Can you keep this secret confidential?
5. I can begin to get started on the project now.

Wordiness

The use of words and expressions that add nothing to the meaning of a sentence is called *wordiness*. Like redundancy, wordiness is tiresome and distracting to a reader.

Empty Expressions   One way to avoid wordiness is to rid your sentences of empty expressions. Notice how the revisions for conciseness improve the following sentences.

WORDY   I can't go to the movies **due to the fact that** I have my guitar lesson tonight.
CONCISE   I can't go to the movies **because** I have my guitar lesson tonight.

WORDY   **There are** dozens of games that resemble checkers.
CONCISE   Dozens of games resemble checkers.

Empty Expressions to Avoid	
the thing that	due to the fact that
on account of	the reason that
what I want is	the thing/fact is that
in my opinion	there is/are/was/were
It is/was	what I mean is that
It seems as if	I believe/feel/think that

WRITING ACTIVITY *Eliminating Empty Expressions*

Revise each of the following sentences by eliminating the empty expressions. If necessary replace empty expressions with more precise language.

EXAMPLE   The thing that I enjoy is skiing.
POSSIBLE ANSWER   I enjoy skiing.

1. We canceled the game due to the fact that it rained.
2. The reason that I called was to ask if you need help.
3. Because of the fact that he was sick, his report is late.
4. The thing that I really hate is getting up early.
5. There are some places in the river that are dangerous.

Wordy Phrases and Clauses   Another way to avoid wordiness is to shorten wordy phrases and clauses. In many cases a phrase can be reduced to a single word.

WORDY	Archaeologists found ancient tools **made of stone.** [participial phrase]
CONCISE	Archaeologists found ancient **stone** tools. [adjective]
WORDY	Elana spoke to the shy horse **in a gentle tone.** [prepositional phrase]
CONCISE	Elana spoke **gently** to the shy horse. [adverb]
WORDY	**To be tardy** is often a sign of laziness. [infinitive phrase]
CONCISE	**Tardiness** is often a sign of laziness. [noun]

Similarly, a clause can be reduced to a phrase or even to a single word.

WORDY   People **who are in show business** lead a hectic life of rehearsals and performances. [clause]

CONCISE   People **in show business** lead . . . [prepositional phrase]

WORDY   In Yosemite, **which is a national park in California**, cars are forbidden past a certain point. [clause]

CONCISE   In Yosemite, **a national park in California**, cars . . . [appositive phrase]

WORDY   Climates **that are dry** are good for people with allergy problems. [clause]

CONCISE   **Dry** climates are good for . . . [adjective]

WRITING ACTIVITY *Revising Wordy Phrases and Clauses*

Revise each of the following sentences by shortening the underlined wordy phrase or clause.

1. Misha likes chicken <u>cooked with barbecue sauce</u>.
2. Students <u>who are trying out for band</u> should come to school on Saturday morning.
3. An exchange student <u>who came to our neighborhood from France</u> lives with our neighbors.
4. Tamara, <u>who is an accident victim</u>, competed in the marathon in a wheelchair.
5. Games <u>that are in good condition</u> will be accepted for the charity drive.
6. Luis organized his bookshelf <u>in a neat way</u>.
7. The motel had a pool <u>that was heated</u>.
8. The storm <u>that came in from the west</u> left ten inches of snow.
9. Buildings <u>along the riverfront</u> are being torn down to make room for a park.
10. I love to read the novels <u>written by the author Mark Twain</u>.

WRITING ACTIVITY *Applying Revision Techniques*

Revise the following paragraph to eliminate the problems indicated in brackets.

Up in the Air

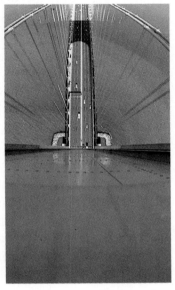

(1) Some people do not like going into skyscrapers. Being so high up makes them feel sick as a dog. [cliché, short and choppy sentences] **(2)** The fact is that acrophobiacs, who are people with a fear of heights, may even suddenly lose their balance and fall. [empty expression, wordy clause] **(3)** The tallest skyscrapers are the most frightening, since the top of one of these buildings can sway as much as three feet in the wind and on a windy day, people who are riding in the elevator can hear it hitting the sides of the shaft. [rambling sentence, wordy clause] **(4)** Because of the fact that skyscrapers sway and move, some people feel airsick when they are on the upper floors. [empty expression, redundancy]

WRITING ACTIVITY *Writing on Your Own*

WRITING
ABOUT THE
THEME

Return to the composition on environment that you partially revised in Writing Activity 11. With your teacher's permission, exchange papers with a classmate and check one another's work for conciseness. Sometimes a different eye can catch something that you may have missed. When your paper is returned, use your classmate's suggestions and the Revision Checklist on page 32 to make any changes that you think will improve your writing. Look for opportunities to apply the revising techniques that you have learned in this chapter.

Editing and Publishing

Grammar in the Writing Process

Describing the sounds that the children in "All Summer in a Day" heard, Ray Bradbury writes, "A boom of thunder startled them and like leaves before a new hurricane, they tumbled upon each other and ran." What a difference the specific nouns *boom* and *hurricane* make in this sentence! As you revise and edit your writing, keep in mind that the nouns you use can bring your writing to life.

Capitalization of Proper Nouns   One way to make nouns more specific is to substitute proper nouns for common nouns. A *common noun* is any person, place, or thing. A *proper noun* is a particular person, place, or thing. Remember that proper nouns always begin with a capital letter. *(For examples of proper nouns and for practice in capitalizing them, see pages 800–808.)*

COMMON NOUNS	After leaving the **city**, we boarded the **spaceship** for another **planet.**
PROPER NOUNS	After leaving **Philadelphia**, we boarded **Spacemet** for **Venus.**

Punctuation with Possessive Nouns   To show ownership, or possession, a singular noun must end with *'s*. To form the possessive of a plural noun, however, you need to do one of two things: add only an apostrophe to a plural noun that ends in *s* or add *'s* to a plural noun that does not end in *s*. *(For examples of possessive nouns and for practice in writing possessive nouns correctly, see pages 857–862.)*

SINGULAR POSSESSIVE	The **spaceship's** ride was comfortable, but the **planet's** climate is not.
PLURAL POSSESSIVE	The **adults'** spacesuits were blue, but the **children's** spacesuits were green.

Punctuation with a Series of Nouns   Three or more nouns in a row are confusing to read if they are not separated by commas. *(For examples of how to use commas with words in a series and for practice in writing them correctly, see pages 821–823.)*

INCORRECT   The aliens had three heads seventeen arms and only one leg.

CORRECT   The aliens had three heads, seventeen arms, and only one leg.

Spelling the Plurals of Nouns   Simply add an *s* to form the plural of most nouns. The endings of a few nouns must be changed, however, before you add an *s*. For example, if a word ends in a consonant and a *y*, you must change the *y* to *i* and add *es*. *(For other spelling rules that affect plural nouns and for practice in writing plural nouns correctly, see pages 487–490.)*

SINGULAR   The **baby** in the space **capsule** slept peacefully.

PLURAL   The **babies** in the space **capsules** slept peacefully.

Editing Checklist

1. Are proper nouns capitalized? *(See pages 800-808.)*
2. Are apostrophes used correctly with possessive nouns? *(See pages 857–862.)*
3. Do commas separate words in a series? *(See pages 821–823.)*
4. Are plural nouns spelled correctly? *(See pages 487–490.)*

WRITING ACTIVITY   18   *Writing on Your Own*

WRITING
ABOUT THE
THEME
   Editing   Read through your revised composition from Writing Activity 17 in which you describe the environment of your former home planet. Then edit your description, using the checklist above, the Editing Checklist on page 37, and your Personalized Editing Checklist in your journal.

Publishing   After producing a final copy, add your composition to a class album or anthology, or share it with classmates in one of the other ways listed on page 43.

A Writer Writes

A Description of a Character

PURPOSE: to describe and evaluate a cartoon character

AUDIENCE: readers of a student newspaper

Prewriting   Write about a popular comic strip character or cartoon character who especially appeals to you. Your description and evaluation of the character will appear in your school newspaper. After choosing your subject, begin listing details about the character's appearance, personality, and typical actions and attitudes. Then think of situations or relationships in the comic strip or cartoon that reveal the character. The character's environment, for example, may reveal something important about the character.

© 1982 DC Comics Inc. Used by permission.

After reviewing your notes, experiment with ways to organize your details and decide on the focus, or main idea, of your composition. For example, you could describe what you like most about the character or show how the character is a hero or a symbol with a message to readers.

Drafting   Use your prewriting work to help you write the first draft of your characterization. Each time you make an evaluative statement about the character, remember to provide specific examples that back up your opinions. Then add a strong conclusion in which you make a generalization or recommend the character to others to enjoy.

Revising   Exchange papers with a classmate. If possible, find someone who chose the same character. After comparing your descriptions and evaluations, comment on each other's writing. Are the words specific? Do they vividly describe the cartoon or comic strip character and related situations? With your partner check for sentence variety, ways to combine sentences, and ways to eliminate redundancies and wordiness. After working with your partner, consult the Revision Checklist on page 32 and revise your draft again on your own.

Editing and Publishing   When you are satisfied with your revised draft, check it for mistakes, using the Editing Checklist on page 37 as a guide. Exchange papers again with your partner and help one another by checking for errors you may have missed. Then prepare a neat copy of your characterization for publication in your school newspaper or in a special publication, such as a class booklet.

WRITING
ABOUT THE
THEME **Independent Writing**

Imagine that one of your favorite places is about to be bulldozed to make room for a new office building. This favorite place could be a building or an outdoor site where you go to be alone, to find inspiration, or to have fun. Write a composition persuading the people in your community not to allow this place to be destroyed. Begin by describing the place and explaining its meaning or importance to you and to others.

Creative Writing

Write a descriptive paragraph or poem about some natural event or condition, such as a sunrise, a frozen pond, the wind, heat, sleep, or hunger. In your paragraph or poem, use specific words and fresh comparisons that will make the readers experience in their imaginations the event or condition you describe. Look for opportunities to create vivid images by using similies and metaphors.

  ## Writing about Literature

Mood is the atmosphere of a piece of writing or the feeling it creates. In "All Summer in a Day," Ray Bradbury creates strong moods of rainy-day gloom and sunny-day bliss. As you reread the story, keep a log of vivid words, words with rich connotations, and figurative language that help create these strong moods. Then, using items in your log as supporting details, write a composition in which you show how Bradbury contrasts the experiences of rain and sun.

Writing in Other Subject Areas

Geography   Use concise, vivid language to describe one of the following environments or another one of your choice. Find information in a textbook or in the library to help you. When you revise your writing, look for ways to make your description clearer and livelier by substituting new words, combining sentences, and varying your sentence constructions.

Antarctica	Amazon Basin	Himalaya Mountains
Nile Delta	Gobi Desert	Great Barrier Reef
Death Valley	Niagara Falls	Strait of Hormuz

Science   Using reference materials or observations, write an explanation of one of the natural phenomena listed below. Make your explanation both accurate and exciting to read.

dew	metamorphosis	cell division
erosion	germination	decay

2 Checklist

Developing Your Writing Style

Choosing Vivid Words

✔ Use specific words to express your meaning exactly. *(See page 59.)*

✔ Choose words with connotations that match the feelings you wish to convey. *(See pages 60–61.)*

✔ Create fresh similes and metaphors to appeal to your reader's imagination. Avoid clichés. *(See pages 62–63.)*

Sentence-Combining Strategies

✔ Combine short sentences into longer, more varied ones by using phrases, coordination, or subordination. *(See pages 66–70.)*

Creating Sentence Variety

✔ Begin your sentences in a variety of ways. *(See page 71.)*

✔ Vary your sentence structure by including simple, compound, complex, and compound-complex sentences. *(See page 73.)*

Writing Concise Sentences

✔ Eliminate rambling sentences by separating your ideas into a variety of short and long sentences. *(See page 75.)*

✔ Eliminate redundancy. *(See page 76.)*

✔ Eliminate empty expressions. *(See pages 76–77.)*

✔ Shorten wordy phrases and clauses. *(See pages 77–78.)*

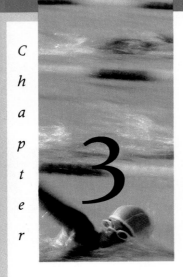

3 Writing Effective Paragraphs

Part 1 Reading to Write

THEME: *Sports*

The United States is clearly a sports-loving country. How many students in your school are members of sports teams? How often do your friends and family members watch football, baseball, or other sports on television? Did you know that millions of people watch the Super Bowl game on television every January? Many people also enjoy sports-related hobbies and respond to sports-related advertising. Every year thousands of collectors of all ages get together to trade baseball cards, and companies hire athletes to help them sell their products through advertising. Examples of the importance of sports in American life seem endless.

Why, do you think, are so many Americans sports fans? Is the reason only that sports are fun? Could the love of sports have something to do with competition? Competition is the rivalry between two or more individuals or teams for rewards, such as prizes, profit, or fame. As you read the following short story, "The Confidence Game," think about the reasons people love sports, including the possibility that fans and players get involved in sports because they enjoy competing and winning.

The Confidence Game

P a t   C a r r

My confidence started draining out my toes the day Angela Brady showed up at the pool for workout. I even started to chew the inside of my cheek, a nervous habit I usually reserve for fighting the fear that clutches at me just before a race. In a way, I guess I knew it *was* a race between Angela and me for the backstroke position on our team relay for National Championship.

I hadn't even seen her swim yet, but the whole team knew she had been swimming for a famous club in California. We were just a small city team, only two years old. But we had a coach whose middle name was motivation. He'd motivated me into swimming a grueling three miles a day, and now I was actually in the running to compete at the Nationals. Or I was until Angela showed up.

"Okay, swim freaks, hit the water for an 800 meter freestyle warm-up!" barked Coach. Then he added in a more human voice, "Angela, why don't you try lane four today?"

Lane four was the fast lane, my lane. I'd had to earn my place in that lane by swimming 400 meters in less than five minutes. Now all Angela had to do was jump in. It wasn't fair.

I didn't think I could pretend friendliness, so I started the 800 before Angela hit the water. But I didn't even have time to settle into my pace when I felt the water agitating behind me. I stroked harder, but I could still feel the churning water of someone closing in on me. I soon felt a light touch on my foot.

In swim workouts, it's one of the rules that when a teammate taps your foot, you move to the right to let that swimmer go ahead of you. I knew that, and I also knew that I was interfering with Angela's pace by not letting her pass me. My conscience told me to move over, but something stubborn kept my body in the middle of the lane.

At the end of the 800, I glanced up and saw Coach staring at me. Realizing that he had seen me refuse to let Angela pass, I took a deep breath and ducked underwater.

When the workout was over, everyone crowded around Angela, asking her if she knew any Olympic swimmers and stuff like that. Finding a quiet corner for myself, I slipped on my warm-up suit, draped a towel over my head and hurried toward my bike.

"Hey, Tobi! Where are you going?" someone shouted.

I didn't answer, just hopped on my bike and pedalled fast.

It was like that for the next two weeks. At every workout Angela was the star of the show; I was an invisible stagehand. Even worse, during time trials she beat me in all four strokes and took my place as lane leader.

I was miserable. And I was scared, too; scared that Angela was taking away my chance at the Nationals, a chance I had earned by a lot of hard work.

I started to show up late to workouts so that I wouldn't have to talk to anyone. I even walked on the bottom of the pool and faked my stroke, a swimmer's cheating trick I'd never used before. It was easy to catch up to Angela that way. And I always managed to be underwater when she gave our lane instructions.

I'll admit I wasn't very happy with my actions. But my jealous feelings were like a current I couldn't swim against.

The day before the Riverdale Meet, Coach called me over. At that moment I would rather have tried to talk to King Kong.

"Tobi, I want to talk to you about sportsmanship," he began.

"Sportswomanship, in this case, Coach," I quipped, hoping to distract him.

"Okay, sportswomanship," he said, taking me seriously. "Or whatever you want to call it when one athlete accepts a better athlete in a spirit of friendly competition."

"Maybe the so-called better athlete is not as good as everyone thinks," I mumbled.

Coach left a big silence for my statement to fall into. I started to chew the inside of my cheek again.

"Let's stop talking about this athlete and that athlete," he said softly, "and talk instead about Tobi and Angela. She has made better time than you, Tobi. And that is an objective fact, not something everyone thinks."

He paused. I stared at my toes, which were curling under my feet as if trying to hide.

"The worst of it, Tobi, is that your attitude is hurting your performance. Do you know that your times have become worse in the last two weeks? Maybe showing up late and walking on the bottom have something to do with that," he said. My face felt as if it had been splashed with hot pink paint.

"Do you have anything you want to say?" he asked. I shook my head. "That's all then, Tobi. I'll see you tomorrow at the Riverdale Meet."

The next morning I was too nervous to eat my special breakfast of steak and eggs. This meet would decide who was going to Nationals.

The early skies were still gray when I arrived at the Riverdale pool for the warm-up session. The other swimmers were screeching greetings at each other like a flock of gulls. I jumped into the water to cut off the sound and mechanically began my stroke.

Half an hour later, I shuddered as the public address system squealed. The meet was about to start. After climbing out of the pool, I quickly searched the heat sheet[1] for my name. Disappointed, I saw that I had just missed making it into the last, and fastest, qualifying heat. Angela's name, of course, was there. She'd taken my place just as she had at the trials.

Better not to think about Angela at all, I told myself, recalling Coach's words. Better to concentrate on my own race. Carefully, I went over Coach's instructions in my mind, shutting out the milling crowd around me, swimming my race perfectly, over and over again in my head, always perfectly.

1. **heat sheet:** A list of athletes who will compete in a preliminary race.

"Would you like an orange?"

Without looking I knew whose voice it was. "It's good for quick energy," continued Angela, holding the orange out to me.

"No thanks," I said. "I've got all I need." I saw that she was about to sit down next to me, so I added, "I don't like to talk before a race."

She nodded sympathetically. "I get uptight, too. The butterflies are free," she said with a nervous laugh.

For a moment I felt a little better toward her, knowing that she had the jitters, too. Then I remembered that she didn't have to worry.

"You'll be an easy winner," I said.

"You never know," she replied uncertainly.

My heat was called. Up on the blocks,[2] I willed my muscles into obedience, alert for the starter's commands. At the gun, I cut into the top of the water smoothly.

2. **blocks:** Platforms on which racers stand at the start of a race.

I swam exactly as I had been imagining it before the race, acting out the pictures in my mind. I felt the water stream past me, smooth, steady and swift. When I finished, I was certain I had done my best in that heat.

Overwhelmed by exhaustion, I sat on the deck for several minutes, eyes closed, totally spent. I knew I was missing Angela's heat, but I was too tired to care.

The sound of the announcer's voice was like a crackling firecracker of hope bursting through my fatigue. Then I heard my name. I'd made it!

I also heard Angela's name, but it was several minutes before I realized that my name had been called last. That meant my time had been better. Figuring there must have been a mistake I checked the official postings, but there were our times with mine four seconds faster.

Heading for the gym, where all the swimmers rest and wait for the heats to be called, I saw Angela sitting with her back against the wall alone. Her shoulders were rounded in a slump.

It could be me, I whispered to myself, remembering what it feels like to mess up a race. There's no worse anger than the kind you feel toward yourself when you've ruined something you care about. I knew how she felt, and I also knew there was no way I could make up for the way I had acted. But I just had to try.

"I don't talk before races, but I do talk after them. Sometimes it helps," I said, knowing Angela had every right to tell me to go drown myself.

"Talk if you want to," she murmured.

"Well, I will, but I was hoping you'd talk, too."

She hesitated, and I saw her trying to swallow. "I will as soon as I'm sure I'm not going to cry," she whispered.

So I babbled on for a few minutes about the meet, some of the other swimmers, the team standings, anything. I knew it didn't matter what I said as long as I kept talking.

All at once, Angela interrupted my opinion of the snack bar's hamburgers. "I do this all the time," she burst out. "I do great at workouts, then comes a meet, and something happens; I just can't do it."

"Maybe you don't know how to play the confidence game," I said. She looked at me suspiciously, but I went on. "How do you psych yourself up for a race?"

"I don't exactly." She was twisting the ends of the towel into tiny corkscrews. "I just try to block it out, not think about it."

"What about during a race?"

"I concentrate on not making mistakes."

"Very negative methods," I commented.

"What do you mean?"

"Well, take my positive approach. First, I think about all the good things I've done in previous races. Then I plan my upcoming race carefully, going over each detail in my mind, picturing myself the perfect swimmer. Then when I'm in the water, I tell myself to do it again, only this time for real."

"And you win," Angela added with a smile. Now I really felt badly, remembering how I had acted when Angela had done better than I in workouts.

"Listen, I have an idea," I said. Maybe I *could* make it up to her. "You swim faster than me, right?" Angela looked doubtful.

"Yes, you do, that's an objective fact," I insisted. "Now my idea is that you use me as a pacer[3] in the backstroke final this afternoon."

At first Angela wasn't sure, but I soon had her convinced, and we were planning our strategy when Coach showed up.

"What's going on here?" He gave me an accusing look.

"We've got it all settled," Angela spoke up. "Tobi and I are going to be a team from now on."

"All right!" he said, giving us a smile usually reserved for winners.

As Angela and I sat together on the ready bench,[4] I had conflicting thoughts about helping her. What was I doing anyway? Handing her my relay position on a silver platter, that's what.

I hadn't time to get worked up over it, though, because the whistle blew, and we stepped up to the blocks. At the sound of the gun I was into the water with barely a splash, skimming the surface like a water bug.

---

3. **pacer:** A racer who sets the pace for others.
4. **ready bench:** A bench on which swimmers sit before the start of a race.

As I reached the wall, I pretended all my strength was in my legs as I flipped and pushed off. Pull hard, hard, hard, I told myself, muscles aching from the effort. Then on the last lap, I concentrated on a single word. Win! I shot through the water and strained for the finish.

Immediately, I looked to Angela's lane. She was there, but it was too close to tell who had won. She gave me the thumbs up sign, and I returned it.

I stared at the electronic scoreboard. Usually it didn't take long for the times to appear, but now it remained blank for so long I was beginning to worry that a fuse had blown.

Please, please let me be the winner, I whispered over and over. Finally, the winning times flashed on. I blinked away the chlorine haze, or maybe tears. Angela had won. I managed to give her a congratulatory hug.

"I couldn't have done it without you, Tobi," she bubbled.

"You did it, girls!" Coach couldn't keep himself from shouting, he was so excited. "You've just raced yourself to the Nationals!"

I had never felt so left out, so disappointed in my whole life. "Well, at least Angela has," I said, struggling to smile.

Coach looked startled. "And you did, too, Tobi."

What was he talking about? "I saw that Angela won the place on our relay team."

"That's right, but you missed something. You both swam so fast that you made qualifying times for the *individual* backstroke event!"

I was stunned. I had concentrated so hard on the relay place I hadn't even thought about the individual events.

"So you'll both go to the Nationals!" Coach couldn't resist doing a couple of dance steps, and I was so ecstatic, I joined him. But a wet concrete swim deck is not an ideal dance floor.

"Look out!" yelled Angela, as we just missed falling into the water. "I don't want my partner to break a leg. We've got a long way to go before the 1980 Olympics."

"What?" I gasped.

"Just doing some positive mental rehearsing," she grinned.

"A little confidence sure goes a long way," I retorted.

Still, maybe that *is* something to think about! ◆

Responding to the Theme

Sports

■ **Responding in Your Journal**   When Tobi discovers that Angela is the stronger swimmer, she loses her enthusiasm for competing. How would you have reacted in Tobi's place? How does competition affect you? What happens when you lose or think you will lose? In your journal record your observations, thoughts, and feelings about competing. Each day add an entry about some form of competition you become involved in—in sports or in other areas of school life.

■ **Speaking and Listening**   With four or five classmates, conduct a group discussion on the subject of friendly competition. Group members should define *friendly competition*, describe its qualities, and give examples. Then contrast friendly competition with the unfriendly kind. On the basis of this discussion, develop a list of five principles, or general rules, for ensuring friendly competition. One person should record the group's ideas to share results with classmates.

■ **Critical Thinking: Analyzing**   Analyze the plot of "The Confidence Game," especially the events leading to Tobi's decision to cooperate with Angela. At what point in the plot does Tobi's attitude toward Angela change? What do you think is the turning point in their relationship? As you answer these questions, find passages in the story that support your conclusions.

■ **Extending Your Vocabulary**   "The Confidence Game" contains several compound nouns—nouns made up of more than one word. The parts of some compound nouns run together as one word (*sportswoman*), while in other compound nouns the parts appear as two separate words (*relay team*). Also, some compound nouns are written with a hyphen (*warm-ups*). Find the following compound nouns in a dictionary and identify the ones that should be written as one word. Then use five of the compound words in a paragraph.

work outs	back stroke	stage hand	cork screws
snack bar	fire cracker	starting gun	heat sheet
ready bench	team mate	water bug	score board

Part 2 / *Writing*

When you write a composition you build sentences into paragraphs. While each sentence *expresses* a complete thought, a paragraph *develops* a thought.

Writing Term

A **paragraph** is a group of related sentences that present and develop one main idea.

Notice that the first sentence of the first paragraph of "The Confidence Game" expresses the main idea of the story. The second sentence then develops that idea by giving an example. The third sentence gives information readers need to follow the story and to make the transition to the next paragraph.

> My confidence started draining out my toes the day Angela Brady showed up at the pool for workout. I even started to chew the inside of my cheek, a nervous habit I usually reserve for fighting the fear that clutches at me just before a race. In a way, I guess I knew it was a race between Angela and me for the backstroke position on our team relay for National Championship.

This chapter will show you how to compose clear, well-developed, effective paragraphs.

Paragraph Structure

In a good paragraph, every sentence plays a role. Notice the role of each sentence in the paragraph that follows.

Model: *Paragraph Structure*

Eskimo Customs

TOPIC SENTENCE: STATES THE MAIN IDEA

The activities of the Eskimo are determined by the seasons and, of course, by the weather. During the dark, stormy winter months, when the sun hardly shows itself above the arctic horizon before it disappears again, hunters are confined to their homes for days at a time. In the summer, during the weeks when the sun does not set at all, the Eskimo lose all sense of time, and hunters often paddle about in their canoes until they are exhausted. People are up at all hours, and there is always noise and laughter outside. Visitors barge in at all hours, too, expecting to be fed and entertained. This constant activity exhausts even the sturdiest and hardiest Eskimo. Many of them confess that although they look forward to the sun and warmth during the severe winter, they feel relieved when the weather begins to turn colder, the sun begins to set, and their lives resume a regular day-and-night routine.

SUPPORTING SENTENCES: DEVELOP THE MAIN IDEA

CONCLUDING SENTENCE: PROVIDES A STRONG ENDING

SONIA BLEEKER, *The Eskimo*

Paragraph structure varies. While the model paragraph begins with a topic sentence and ends with a concluding sentence, you may construct a paragraph differently. For example, you may express your main idea in two sentences rather than in one topic sentence. While the topic sentence appears at the beginning of the model, you may express your main idea in the middle of the paragraph or at the end. Also, your paragraph may not need a concluding sentence if you end with your topic sentence or if your paragraph is part of a longer composition. In a one-paragraph composition, however, you must make clear the main idea, whatever paragraph structure you choose.

Guidelines for a One-Paragraph Composition

1. Make your main idea clear.
2. Develop your main idea fully.
3. Provide a strong ending.

You may accomplish these three goals by including in your paragraph a clear topic sentence, a body of supporting sentences, and an effective concluding sentence.

Topic Sentence

Wherever your topic sentence appears—as the first sentence in the paragraph, the last sentence, or any one of the middle sentences—it serves the same purpose.

Writing Term    A **topic sentence** states the main idea of the paragraph.

Because it states the main idea, a topic sentence is usually more general than the sentences that develop that idea. In the following model, the main idea is general enough for the supporting details to support it. At the same time, the main idea is specific enough to be developed adequately in one paragraph.

Model: *Topic Sentence*

The Heavy Task of Fighting Fires

TOPIC SENTENCE   Fighting a major fire takes tremendous strength and endurance. The protective clothing that a fire fighter wears into a burning building will weigh more than 20 pounds. To protect himself from the smoke, the fire fighter will usually wear an oxygen tank and mask. These self-contained breathing units may weigh as much as 50 pounds. The weight of the hose and other tools that the fire fighter carries will raise the total weight to more than 100 pounds.

WALTER BROWN/NORMAN ANDERSON, *Fires*

As the following example shows, the topic sentence in the model is general enough to cover all the details yet specific enough to develop adequately in one paragraph.

TOO GENERAL   Fire fighting is hard work.
SPECIFIC ENOUGH   Fighting a major fire takes tremendous strength and endurance.

WRITING ACTIVITY *Evaluating Topic Sentences*

Write the letter of the topic sentence that is specific enough to be covered adequately in a single paragraph.

1. **a.** Bats use sonar to locate prey.
   b. Bats are complex animals.
2. **a.** Many medical discoveries were made by accident.
   b. There have been some interesting discoveries.
3. **a.** Folk songs are part of life.
   b. Folk songs reveal a country's values.
4. **a.** Many people like camping.
   b. Pitching a tent is easy if you follow directions.
5. **a.** Dolphins are always friendly to humans.
   b. Dolphins are amazing creatures.

WRITING ACTIVITY *Writing Topic Sentences*

For each general statement below, write a topic sentence that is specific enough to develop adequately in a single paragraph.

1. Life can be difficult at times.
2. Good health is important.
3. Holidays are nice.
4. Movies today are very exciting.
5. Dinner should be eaten in peace.

Writing Is Thinking

Generalizing

When you develop a topic sentence, you often use the thinking skill of generalizing. When you *generalize*, you form an overall rule, or principle, based on specific details. A generalization makes an effective topic sentence because it tells the reader, "Here is the point. Here is what the details add up to."

Suppose, for example, that you are writing a paragraph on the subject of Greek myths and have collected many facts on that subject. To think of a generalization, make a fact list like the one below.

Generalizing from a Fact List

FACTS ABOUT GREEK MYTHS

- Clytie loves the god Apollo and is turned into a sunflower so that she can always watch him.
- Narcissus falls in love with his own reflection and is turned into a riverbank flower.
- Daphne flees the amorous Apollo and is turned, with the help of the gods, into a laurel tree.

POSSIBLE GENERALIZATIONS ABOUT THESE FACTS

1. Many Greek myths tell the origins of different plants.
2. In Greek myths gods intervene to help those in love.
3. Love is a unifying theme of many Greek myths.

Thinking Practice Choose one of the subjects below or another about which you know several facts. Form a generalization by making and analyzing a fact list.

1. how high school students spend their money
2. television role models
3. using leisure time

Supporting Sentences

Alert readers ask questions as they read. Supporting sentences answer those questions and form the body of the paragraph.

Writing Term  **Supporting sentences** explain the topic sentence by giving specific details, facts, examples, or reasons.

The following topic sentence begins a paragraph about Robert Peary's successful return from the North Pole.

Model: *Topic Sentence*

On the sixth of September, 1909, the gallant little *Roosevelt* steamed into Indian Harbor, Labrador, and from the wireless tower on top of a cliff two messages flashed out.

Readers will naturally wonder, "What were the two messages?" The supporting sentences answer that question.

Model: *Supporting Sentences*

The first was to Peary's anxiously waiting wife, more eager, if the truth were known, to hear of her husband's safety than of the discovery of the Pole. This message read: "Have made good at last. I have the Pole. Am well. Love." The second one was to his country, for which he had sacrificed so much. It read: "Stars and Stripes nailed to the North Pole. Peary."

MARIE PEARY STAFFORD, *Discoverer of the North Pole*

When you write supporting sentences, think of the questions readers might ask and then answer those questions.

WRITING ACTIVITY *Writing Supporting Sentences*

Write three sentences that would support each item.

1. Styles of dress may reveal people's personalities.
2. Life without a telephone seems impossible.
3. Old photographs can help you understand history.

Concluding Sentence

A one-paragraph composition often needs a concluding sentence to summarize the ideas presented in the paragraph.

Writing Term    A **concluding sentence** recalls the main idea and adds a strong ending to a paragraph.

Strategies for Ending a Paragraph

1. Restate the main idea using different words.
2. Summarize the paragraph.
3. Add an insight about the main idea.
4. Express how you feel about the subject.

Avoid making your concluding sentence too repetitive or oversimplified. The following paragraph, for example, has a weak concluding sentence that adds no real meaning.

Example: *Weak Concluding Sentence*

An All-Around Player

Although Babe Ruth is best remembered for his home runs, he was also a great pitcher. In 1916, he led the American League in earned-run percentage. He won 23 games that year, including 9 shutouts. The next year he won 24. Until 1961, Ruth held the record for pitching scoreless innings in the World Series. As you can see, Ruth was a great pitcher as well as a home-run king.

Any one of the following sentences would create a stronger ending because they have less repetition and more meaning.

Models: *Strong Concluding Sentences*

Ruth's home runs are remembered in the Hall of Fame, but the pitching of this all-around star should not be forgotten. [restates main idea]

Ruth's impressive pitching statistics show that he was more than a great hitter. [summarizes]

Rare, indeed, are the athletes who, like Ruth, excel at more than one position. [adds an insight]

What a remarkable, all-around champion Ruth was! [shows feeling]

WRITING ACTIVITY *Writing Concluding Sentences*

The following paragraphs have weak concluding sentences. Write two new concluding sentences for each.

I. Chasing Rainbows

Whenever you are standing with a light source behind you and misty water in front of you, you can see a rainbow. The biggest, most complete rainbows are created when the sun is close to the horizon. You can also sometimes see a rainbow in the mist from a waterfall or the spray from a garden hose. Now and then even a full moon on a rainy night will create a faint rainbow. I have just told you about the ways you can see rainbows.

2. Hailstones

Hailstones consist of many onionlike layers of ice. In certain weather conditions, small ice crystals drop into a band of very cold moisture. Some of this moisture freezes onto the crystal, forming the first layer. Updrafts then carry the hailstone back up, and when it drops again, another layer is formed. The process continues until the hailstone is too heavy to be lifted by updrafts, and then it drops to the earth. That is how hailstones are formed.

WRITING ACTIVITY *Writing on Your Own*

WRITING
ABOUT THE
THEME

Review your ideas about the reasons people love sports and your thoughts and feelings about competition that you wrote in your journal. Then group together the ideas that relate best to the question of why people participate in sports. Brainstorm for examples and illustrations from your life or the lives of others to support your ideas.

Draft a paragraph that explains why you think people compete in sports—from high school teams to the major leagues.

Paragraph Development

A topic sentence is like a baseball score. It gives the general idea without the specifics of how the game developed. Readers, like sports fans, want to know the details. They want to see the idea developed play by play.

Methods of Development

You can use a variety of methods to develop a topic sentence.

Strategies for Developing Your Main Idea
• Give descriptive details. • Give facts or examples. • Give reasons. • Relate an incident. • Make a comparison or draw a contrast. • Give directions or explain the steps in a process.

Your topic sentence often suggests the best method for developing your main idea. As you read each topic sentence below, think of the questions each paragraph should answer. Then consider the type of supporting details a reader would need to know to answer those questions.

Models: *Developing a Topic Sentence*

TOPIC SENTENCE	*Everything about the house next door was eerie.*
QUESTION	What did the house look like?
METHOD OF DEVELOPMENT	Give **descriptive details**.
TOPIC SENTENCE	*In the past 50 years, the gorilla population has declined drastically.*
QUESTIONS	How much has it declined? Where has it declined?
METHOD OF DEVELOPMENT	Give **facts** and **examples**.

TOPIC SENTENCE	*People living alone should adopt a pet.*
QUESTION	Why?
METHOD OF DEVELOPMENT	Give **reasons**.
TOPIC SENTENCE	*I learned early in life that temper tantrums don't pay off.*
QUESTION	What experience led you to this conclusion?
METHOD OF DEVELOPMENT	Relate an **incident**.
TOPIC SENTENCE	*Despite their similarities, guitars and banjos are two very different instruments.*
QUESTIONS	What are the similarities? What are the differences?
METHOD OF DEVELOPMENT	**Compare** and **contrast** the two instruments.
TOPIC SENTENCE	*Even an inexperienced gardener can grow healthful, tangy radishes.*
QUESTION	How?
METHOD OF DEVELOPMENT	Give the **steps in the process**.

Writing Tip   Use the **method of development** most appropriate for your topic sentence.

WRITING ACTIVITY *Recognizing Methods of Development*

Use the models on pages 104 and 105 to help you decide how each paragraph is developed. Indicate your answer by writing *descriptive details, facts and examples, reasons, incident, comparison, contrast,* or *steps in a process.*

I. Home Site

Mama had picked the spot for our log house. It nestled at the edge of the foothills in the mouth of a small canyon and was surrounded by a grove of huge red oaks. Beyond our house we could see miles and miles of the mighty Ozarks. In the spring the aromatic scent of wildflowers, redbuds, pawpaws, and dogwoods, drifting on the wind currents, spread over the valley and around our home.

WILSON RAWLS

2. Taking the Plunge

Most experts agree that swimming is the healthiest form of vigorous exercise. Because water offers so little resistance, swimmers are unlikely to experience the muscle strain associated with land sports such as jogging and tennis. Yet swimming strengthens many areas of the body—arms, legs, torso, and neck. Most importantly, if done regularly, it is strenuous enough to condition the heart and lungs. See your doctor before starting any new exercise program, but don't be surprised if he or she tells you to go jump in a lake!

3. Space Junk

If you think roadside litter is a problem, consider some of the junk that is floating around space. About 3,400 pieces of trackable debris are orbiting Earth, according to the North American Defense Command in Colorado, which uses radar to keep tabs on space junk. Everything from spent rocket boosters to broken solar panels is on the list. As long as the debris stays in space or burns up on reentry, it gets little attention from the public. When space junk litters the planet, problems start. NATIONAL WILDLIFE (Adapted)

4. Two Great Leaders

There are many similarities between Mohandas Gandhi and Martin Luther King, Jr. Both believed in nonviolent resistance to laws they felt were unfair. Both were leaders who rallied millions behind their causes. Both leaders struggled for equal rights for oppressed peoples, and both met a tragic end.

5. Upside-Down Painting

Even a museum employee may wonder how to hang an abstract painting. Which edge is the top? Which is the bottom? Henri Matisse's abstract painting *The Boat* hung upside down at the Museum of Modern Art in New York from October 18 to December 11, 1961. More than 100,000 people looked at *The Boat*, and not one of them noticed that it was upside down. Finally, after 47 days, an art expert discovered the mistake, and at least one museum employee had a bad case of embarrassment.

Adequate Development

Insufficiently developed writing makes readers quickly lose interest. Even an interesting idea loses merit if it is not backed up with sufficient information. The following paragraph, for example, lacks adequate development because it does not give enough specific details.

Example: *Poorly Developed Paragraph*

Childhood Treasures

Aunt Sally's cabinet of art supplies was like a toy chest to me. It had all kinds of neat things in it. There was paper and paint and clay. We used these supplies to make things when I went to visit her as a child. I'll always remember that cabinet.

After careful thought, the writer revised the paragraph to illustrate the main idea more fully for the reader. Notice how much richer and clearer the revised paragraph is. Because of the added details, readers can visualize the cabinet's art supplies shelf by shelf.

Model: *Adequate Paragraph Development*

Childhood Treasures

Aunt Sally's cabinet of art supplies was like a toy chest to me. The top shelf, beyond my reach, had an endless supply of paper. There was stiff, brilliant-white paper for watercolors, blank newsprint for charcoals, glossy paper, dull paper, tracing paper. On the second shelf sat oozing tubes of bright-colored oils, bottles of the blackest ink, and cartons of chalk in sunrise shades of pastels. The third shelf—my favorite—held the damp lumps of gray clay, waiting to be shaped into creatures only my aunt and I would recognize. On the bottom shelves were brushes and rags for cleaning up. Despite the thorough cleanups Aunt Sally insisted on, that cabinet was a paradise of play for me on countless Sunday afternoons.

Writing Tip   Use specific details and information to achieve **adequate development** of your main idea.

WRITING ACTIVITY **7** *Recognizing Adequate Development*

After comparing the first and second drafts of the paragraph on Childhood Treasures on page 108, list all the details that were added to provide adequate development.

Unity

In developing a paragraph fully, avoid straying from the main idea, which could confuse the reader. In a well-developed paragraph, all the supporting sentences relate directly to the main idea expressed in the topic sentence. This quality of a well-written paragraph is called *unity*.

Writing Tip Achieve **unity** by deleting any sentences that do not relate directly to the main idea of the paragraph.

In the following example, sentences that detract from the unity of the paragraph are underlined.

Example: *A Paragraph Lacking Unity*

Candlelight

Candles, which go back to prehistoric times, were a chief source of light for 2,000 years. The first candle may have been discovered by accident when a piece of wood or cord fell into a pool of lighted fat. In ancient times crude candles were made from fats wrapped in husks or moss. <u>Early people also used torches.</u> Later a wick was placed inside a candle mold, and melted wax was poured into the mold. Candles could be used to carry light from place to place and could be stored indefinitely. <u>The first lamps used a dish of oil and a wick.</u>

Although the underlined sentences relate to the subject (sources of light in prehistoric times), they do not relate directly to the main idea expressed in the topic sentence (*candles* as a source of light in prehistoric times). As a result these sentences can mislead or confuse readers about the main idea. When you revise your writing, delete any sentences that weaken the unity.

WRITING ACTIVITY *Revising a Paragraph for Unity*

Write the two sentences that destroy the unity of the following paragraph.

The First Cheap Car

Henry Ford was not the first person to build a car, but he was the first to figure out how to make cars cheaply. His assembly-line methods resulted in huge savings and changed the car from a luxury to a necessity. The mass-produced Model T sold for about $400, a price the average wage earner could afford. Ford sold over 15 million cars from 1908 to 1927. Ford reduced the workday for his employees from 9 to 8 hours. He set the minimum wage at $5 a day. By building a cheap, easy-to-operate car, Ford changed the nation.

Coherence

In a coherent paragraph, each idea follows logically and smoothly from one to the next.

Writing Tip   Achieve **coherence** by presenting ideas in logical order and by using transitional words or phrases.

The chart below lists some methods of organization and transitions that you can use to write coherent paragraphs.

Methods of Organization

CHRONOLOGICAL ORDER

Method used with events or stories to tell what happened first, second, third, and so on. Also used to explain a sequence of steps in a process.

TRANSITIONS	first	later	after
	second	then	finally
	third	next	by evening
	before	while	at noon

SPATIAL ORDER

Method used in descriptions to show how objects are related in location.

TRANSITIONS	beside	left	farther
	behind	right	at the top
	above	across	in front of
	below	north	in the center
	beyond	south	at the bottom

ORDER OF IMPORTANCE, INTEREST, OR DEGREE

Method often used in paragraphs that describe, persuade, or explain. Presents ideas in order of least to most (or most to least) important, interesting, or sizable.

TRANSITIONS	also	furthermore	to begin with
	first	moreover	more important
	finally	in addition	most important

WRITING ACTIVITY *Identifying Methods of Organization*

Write *chronological, spatial,* or *order of importance, interest, or degree* to identify the method of organization used in each paragraph.

1. A House in the Woods

The house was on the left side of the lane, a hundred yards back from the gate. It was a wooden house, like most of them in that country, and the paint had mostly disappeared from it. The barn was on the right. The well was a little in front of the house, boxed in with lumber and having a wheel above it for the rope which held the bucket to run through. There were three big oaks around the house; the whole group of buildings, weathered and gray, looked rather desolate and bleak against the dark pine woods that grew behind them.   ROBERT MURPHY

2. Gold Rush

James Marshall started a race for gold. The story begins in 1848 when Marshall was helping Captain John Sutter build a sawmill in California. The mill wheel was not working properly, so Marshall stood in the river that turned the wheel to study the flow of water. Suddenly he noticed gleaming colors in the water. The colors turned out to be nuggets of gold. Soon word of Marshall's discovery had reached far and wide, and the gold rush of 1849 had begun.

3. Endless Speeches

Sometimes to delay an important vote, a U.S. senator will deliver a seemingly endless speech called a filibuster. In 1983, William V. Allen spoke for 14 hours and 45 minutes. In 1925, Senator Huey Long filibustered for 15 hours and 30 minutes. In 1908, Robert LaFollette spoke for 18 hours and 23 minutes against a currency bill. In 1957, Senator Strom Thurmond filibustered for 24 hours and 18 minutes. Since 1959, a two-thirds vote of the Senate can limit the "big talkers" to one hour.

4. Curious Manners

The manners of seventeenth-century French society may strike modern Americans as curious. For example, wearing a hat inside the home was considered the height of good manners. A gentleman was supposed to keep his hat on even during dinner. Offering a sneezing person the use of your handkerchief was considered a great offense. Most curious of all, saying "God bless you!" out loud was considered impolite, while saying it to yourself silently was proper. However curious these manners may seem, like all rules of etiquette, they allowed people to treat one another with respect.

WRITING ACTIVITY **10** *Writing on Your Own*

WRITING
ABOUT THE
THEME
Revising Review the draft of the paragraph you wrote in Writing Activity 5. Check your paragraph for the features listed below and revise as needed. Also consult the Revision Checklist on page 32. After you revise your paragraph, get your teacher's permission to use peer conferencing to help you evaluate your second draft. *(For more information about conferencing, see page 36.)*

- clear structure
- appropriate method of development
- adequate development
- unity
- coherence

Language
Integrating
Skills

Editing and Publishing

Grammar in the Writing Process

"How do you psych yourself up for a race?"

"I don't exactly." She was twisting the ends of her towel into tiny corkscrews. "I just try to block it out, not think about it."

"What about during a race?"

"I concentrate on not making mistakes."

"Very negative methods," I commented.

In the above dialogue between Tobi and Angela from "The Confidence Game," Tobi twice speaks in incomplete sentences. You can understand what she says because of the context of the conversation. However, when you are not writing dialogue, incomplete sentences can be easily misunderstood. Therefore, always check your writing for incomplete sentences.

Sentence Fragments   A *sentence fragment* is a group of words that does not express a complete thought. A common type of fragment is a phrase that has neither a subject nor a verb.

SENTENCE FRAGMENTS   At the end of the championship meet.
Swimming as fast as possible.
To perfect her dive.

One way to detect a fragment is to read your writing aloud. When you finish reading most sentence fragments, your voice will still be pitched high, as if you were expecting more information. *(For other examples of sentence fragments and practice in correcting them, see pages 695–699.)*

SENTENCES   At the end of the championship meet, **we celebrated in the locker room.**
Swimming as fast as possible, **Angela broke her previous record.**
To perfect her dive, **Tobi practiced every day.**

Run-on Sentences   Another common writing mistake is a *run-on sentence.* This mistake happens when one sentence literally runs into another sentence. To correct a run-on sentence, therefore, you have to separate the two sentences. Sentences in a run-on sentence can be separated with a period and a capital letter or with a comma and a conjunction.

RUN-ON
SENTENCE   Amy aimed the ball toward the basket a guard rushed up in front of her.

CORRECTED
SENTENCES   Amy aimed the ball toward the basket**. A** guard rushed up in front of her.

Amy aimed the ball toward the basket**, but** a guard rushed up in front of her.

Another way to correct a run-on sentence is to make one of the sentences into a subordinate clause. *(For information about subordinate clauses, see pages 671–682.)*

CORRECTED
SENTENCE   **As Amy aimed the ball toward the basket,** a guard rushed up in front of her.

(For other examples of run-on sentences and practice in correcting them, see pages 700–702.)

Editing Checklist

I. Are there any sentence fragments? *(See pages 695–698.)*
2. Are there any run-on sentences? *(See pages 700–701.)*

WRITING ACTIVITY ◆❚❚ *Writing on Your Own*

WRITING
ABOUT THE
THEME   **Editing**   Use the items on the checklist above and the Editing Checklist on page 37 to guide you through the editing of your paragraph about sports that you revised in Writing Activity 10.

Publishing   Publish your paragraph by reading it aloud to a small group of classmates. After hearing everyone's paragraph, discuss the similarities and differences among group members' ideas about the reasons people love sports.

115

A Writer Writes

WRITING
ABOUT THE
THEME

A Paragraph about a New Sport

PURPOSE: to explain a new sport and to describe any necessary equipment

AUDIENCE: sports fans

Prewriting   Is there such a thing as a perfect sport? Probably
none exists now, but you could create one by including all the
things you like best in current sports. Begin by jotting down
the names of specific sports you like to play or watch. You may
include anything from dominoes to wrestling. Brainstorm for
a list of what you like most about each sport. Then incorporate
your favorite aspects of your favorite sports into a general plan
for a new sport.

As you think about your new sport, consider what its goal would be and how winners would be determined. Also brainstorm for ideas about any equipment your game would require. You may include standard sporting equipment or unusual items, such as a pogo stick, or you may invent completely new equipment. After you have explored all possibilities, group your ideas and organize them in a logical order. Then think of a name that fits your new sport.

Drafting   Write a first draft of a paragraph that explains your sport. In your topic sentence, make a generalization about the object of your game and the reasons others should enjoy it. Develop this idea in the body of your paragraph by providing specific details about the game. Then add a strong conclusion.

Revising   With your teacher's permission, exchange papers with a classmate and evaluate one another's work in terms of paragraph structure and paragraph development. Consider the strengths and weaknesses of your partner's topic sentence, supporting details, and concluding sentence. Then using your partner's comments, your own evaluation, and the Revision Checklist on page 32, revise your paragraph. Look for opportunities to make changes that will enhance your paragraph's unity, coherence, and clarity.

Editing and Publishing   Check your work for errors, using the editing checklists on pages 37 and 115. Then have your gym teacher, coach, or another sports lover read your paragraph and give her or his opinion of your new sport.

WRITING
ABOUT THE
THEME

 Independent Writing

In "The Confidence Game," Tobi makes the generalization that "There's no worse anger than the kind you feel toward yourself when you've ruined something you care about." Develop Tobi's idea in a composition, using one of the strategies on page 104 for developing a main idea. For example, you might support the generalization by giving reasons or by relating an incident from your own experience.

Creative Writing

Write a description, story, or poem that expresses a general truth about one of the following attitudes or behaviors or another one of your choice. For example, you could write a poem about the general truth that "honesty is the best policy" or a description of fear that shows how that emotion can prevent a person from taking action. Develop your composition by using descriptive details, by relating an incident, or by making a comparison or contrast.

jealousy	fear	loyalty
pride	anger	honesty
cheating	faking	habits

WRITING
ABOUT THE
THEME

Writing about Literature

Conflict is the struggle between opposing forces around which the action of a work of literature revolves. A conflict often occurs between two characters, such as a misunderstanding between two friends, or between people and nature, such as a struggle to survive a natural disaster. However, a conflict can also occur within an individual. Write a paragraph that explains the conflict that took place within Tobi in the story "The Confidence Game."

Writing in Other Subject Areas

Geography   List facts about the effects humans have had on the environment in your region or community. For example, has land use altered the face of the land in your area? Based on your fact list, use the skill of generalizing to make three generalizations. *(See Writing Is Thinking on page 100.)* After choosing one generalization as a topic sentence, write a paragraph in which your facts serve as supporting details.

Mathematics   Write a paragraph beginning with the topic sentence "Percentages are fractions of a whole." Using the "steps in a process" method of development explained on page 105, explain for an audience of sixth graders how to figure percentages.

3

Checklist

Writing Effective Paragraphs

Paragraph Structure

✔ Write a topic sentence that states the main idea of the paragraph. *(See pages 98–99.)*

✔ Include supporting sentences that explain or prove the topic sentence with specific details, facts, examples, or reasons. *(See page 101.)*

✔ Write a concluding sentence that adds a strong ending to the paragraph. *(See pages 102–103.)*

Paragraph Development

✔ Use the method of development most appropriate for your topic sentence. *(See pages 104–105.)*

✔ Use enough specific details and information to develop your main idea adequately. *(See page 108.)*

✔ Achieve unity by deleting any sentences that do not relate directly to your main idea. *(See pages 109–110.)*

✔ Achieve coherence by presenting ideas in logical order and by using transitions. *(See page 111.)*

4 Writing Expository Paragraphs

Part 1 *Reading to Write*

THEME: *Nature's Marvels*

- One kind of eagle in Africa hunts over a territory of 250 square miles in one day.
- The blue whale weighs as much as 30 elephants and is as long as 3 city buses.
- The noseprint of a dog is as unique as the fingerprint of a person.
- Some ants create underground gardens by feeding and cultivating fungi.

If you take the time to read about them, you will find that the creatures in nature are enormously interesting. You will probably even be surprised at some of your discoveries. Did you know, for example, that the eye of the giant squid is as big as a paperback book? Did you know that fleas can jump as high as 100 times their own height? If people could jump as high as a flea, they could leap to the top of a 40-story building. In the following selection from "The Life and Death of a Western Gladiator," you will read about *Crotalus atrox*, surely one of nature's most amazing creatures.

from

The Life and Death of a Western Gladiator

Charles   G.   Finney

He was born on a summer morning in the shady mouth of a cave. Three others were born with him, another male and two females. Each was about five inches long and slimmer than a lead pencil.

Their mother left them a few hours after they were born. A day after that his brother and sisters left him also. He was all alone. Nobody cared whether he lived or died. His tiny brain was very dull. He had no arms or legs. His skin was delicate. Nearly everything that walked on the ground or burrowed in it, that flew in the air or swam in the water or climbed trees was his enemy. But he didn't know that. He knew nothing at all. He was aware of his own existence, and that was the sum of his knowledge.

The direct rays of the sun could, in a short time, kill him. If the temperature dropped too low he would freeze. Without food he would starve. Without moisture he would die of dehydration. If a man or a horse stepped on him he would be crushed. If anything chased him he could run neither very far nor very fast.

Thus it was at the hour of his birth.
Thus it would be, with modifications,
all his life.

But against these drawbacks he had certain qualifications that fitted him to be a competitive creature of this world and equipped him for its warfare. He could exist a long time without food or water. His very smallness at birth protected him when he most needed protection. Instinct provided him with what he lacked in experience. In order to eat he first had to kill, and he was eminently adapted for killing. In sacs in his jaws he secreted a virulent poison. To inject that poison he had two fangs, hollow and pointed. Without that poison and those fangs he would have been among the most helpless creatures on earth. With them he was among the deadliest.

He was, of course, a baby rattlesnake, a desert diamondback, named *Crotalus atrox* by the herpetologists[1] Baird and Girard and so listed in the *Catalogue of North American Reptiles* in its issue of 1853. He was grayish brown in color, with a series of large, dark, diamond-shaped blotches on his back. His tail was white with five black crossbands. It had a button on the end of it.

Little Crotalus lay in the dust in the mouth of his cave. Some of his kinfolk lay there too. It was their home. That particular tribe of rattlers had lived there for scores of years.

The cave had never been seen by a white man.

Sometimes as many as two hundred rattlers occupied the den. Sometimes the numbers shrunk to as few as forty or fifty.

The tribe members did nothing at all for each other except breed. They hunted singly; they never shared their food. They derived some automatic degree of safety from their numbers, but their actions were never concerted toward using their numbers to any end. If an enemy attacked one of them, the others did nothing about it.

Young Crotalus's brother was the first of the litter to go out into the world and the first to die. He achieved a distance of fifty feet from the den when a Sonoran racer, four feet long and hungry, came upon him. The little rattler, despite his poison fangs, was a tidbit. The racer, long skilled in such arts, snatched him up by the head and swallowed him down. Powerful digestive juices in the racer's stomach did the rest. Then the racer,

1. **herpetologists:** Researchers who study reptiles.

appetite whetted, prowled around until it found one of Crotalus's little sisters. She went the way of the brother.

Nemesis[2] of the second sister was a chaparral cock. This cuckoo, or road runner as it is called, found the baby amid some rocks, uttered a cry of delight, scissored it by the neck, shook it until it was almost lifeless, banged and pounded it upon a rock until life had indeed left it, and then gulped it down.

Crotalus, somnolent in a cranny of the cave's mouth, neither knew nor cared. Even if he had, there was nothing he could have done about it.

On the fourth day of his life he decided to go out into the world himself. He rippled forth uncertainly, the transverse plates on his belly serving him as legs.

2. **nemesis** [nem' mə səs]: A victorious rival, from the name of a Greek goddess.

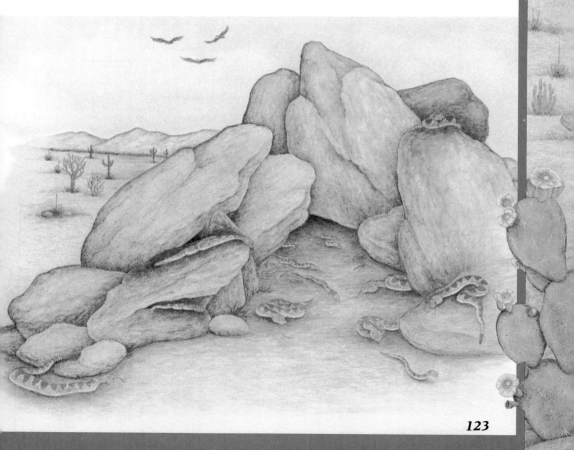

He could see things well enough within his limited range, but a five-inch-long snake can command no great field of vision. He had an excellent sense of smell. But, having no ears, he was stone deaf. On the other hand, he had a pit, a deep pock mark between eye and nostril. Unique, this organ was sensitive to animal heat. In pitch blackness, Crotalus, by means of the heat messages recorded in his pit, could tell whether another animal was near and could also judge its size . . .

The single button on his tail could not, of course, yet rattle. Crotalus wouldn't be able to rattle until that button had grown into three segments. Then he would be able to buzz.

He had a wonderful tongue. It looked like an exposed nerve and was probably exactly that. It was weird, and Crotalus thrust it in and out as he traveled. It told him things that neither his eyes nor his nose nor his pit told him.

Snake fashion, Crotalus went forth, not knowing where he was going, for he had never been anywhere before. Hunger was probably his prime mover.[3] In order to satisfy that hunger, he had to find something smaller than himself and kill it.

He came upon a baby lizard sitting in the sand. Eyes, nose, pit, and tongue told Crotalus it was there. Instinct told him what it was and what to do. Crotalus gave a tiny one-inch strike and bit the lizard. His poison killed it. He took it by the head and swallowed it. Thus was his first meal.

During his first two years, Crotalus grew rapidly. He attained a length of two feet; his tail had five rattles on it and its button. He rarely bothered with lizards any more, preferring baby rabbits, chipmunks, and roundtailed ground squirrels. Because of his slow locomotion,[4] he could not run down these agile little things. He had to contrive instead to be where they were when they would pass. Then he struck swiftly, injected his poison, and ate them after they died.

At two he was formidable. He had grown past the stage where a racer or a road runner could safely tackle him. He had grown to the size where other desert dwellers—coyotes, foxes, coatis, wildcats—knew it was better to leave him alone . . .

3. **prime mover:** The source of motion.
4. **locomotion:** Way of moving from place to place.

He had not experienced death for the simple reason that there had never been an opportunity for anything bigger and stronger than himself to kill him. Now, at two, because he was so formidable, that opportunity became more and more unlikely.

He grew more slowly in the years following his initial spurt. At the age of twelve he was five feet long. Few of the other rattlers in his den were older or larger than he.

He had a castanet[5] of fourteen segments. It had been broken off occasionally in the past, but with each new molting a new segment appeared.

His first skin-shedding back in his babyhood had been a bewildering experience. He did not know what was happening. His eyes clouded over until he could not see. His skin thickened and dried until it cracked in places. His pit and his nostrils ceased to function. There was only one thing to do and that was to get out of that skin.

Crotalus managed it by nosing against the bark of a shrub until he forced the old skin down over his head, bunching it like the rolled top of a stocking around his neck. Then he pushed around among rocks and sticks and branches, literally crawling out of his skin by slow degrees. Wriggling free at last, he looked like a brand-new snake. His skin was bright and satiny, his eyes and nostrils were clear, his pit sang with sensation.

5. **castanet** [kas tə net']: A hand-held musical instrument that makes a clicking sound (Spanish).

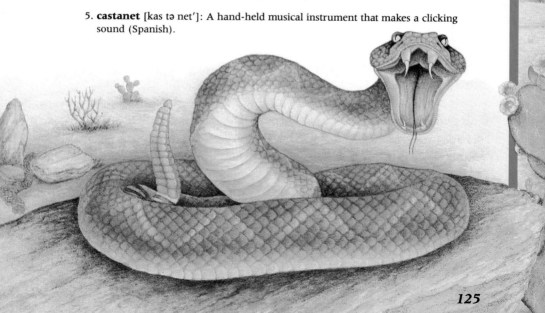

For the rest of his life he was to molt three or four times a year. Each time he did it he felt as if he had been born again.

At twelve he was a magnificent reptile. Not a single scar defaced his rippling symmetry.[6] He was diabolically beautiful, and he was deadly poison.

His venom was his only weapon, for he had no power of constriction. Yellowish in color, his poison was odorless and tasteless. It was a highly complex mixture of proteins, each in itself direly toxic. His venom worked on the blood. The more poison he injected with a bite, the more dangerous the wound. The pain rendered by his bite was instantaneous, and the shock accompanying it was profound. Swelling began immediately, to be followed by a ghastly oozing. Injected directly into a large vein, his poison brought death quickly, for the victim died when it reached his heart.

At the age of twenty, Crotalus was the oldest and largest rattler in his den. He was six feet long and weighed thirteen pounds. His whole world was only about a mile in radius. He had fixed places where he avoided the sun when it was hot and he was away from his cave. He knew his hunting grounds thoroughly, every game trail, every animal burrow.

He was a fine old machine, perfectly adapted to his surroundings, accustomed to a life of leisure and comfort. He dominated his little world.

The mighty seasonal rhythms of the desert were as vast pulsations, and the lives of the rattlesnakes were attuned to them. Spring sun beat down, spring rains fell, and, as the plants of the desert ended their winter hibernations, so did the vipers in their lair. The plants opened forth and budded; the den "opened" too, and the snakes crawled forth. The plants fertilized each other, and new plants were born. The snakes bred, and new snakes were produced. The desert was repopulated.

In the autumn the plants began to close; in the same fashion the snake den began to close. The reptiles returned to it, lay like lingering blossoms about its entrance for a while, then disappeared within it when winter came. There they slept until summoned forth by a new spring.

6. **symmetry** [sim' ə trē]: Balance in size and shape; correspondence of parts.

Responding to the Theme

Nature's Marvels

Responding in Your Journal   To most busy people, many of nature's marvels go unnoticed. When was the last time you traced the progress of a bee from flower to flower or observed a chameleon, waiting patiently for it to move? Even when people do take the time to notice, they often cannot explain what they see. How does a bee know where to go, for example, and why do chameleons remain still for so long? This week in your journal, write about your observations of life forms. For each observation, write at least two questions you could ask that, if answered, would help you explain what you saw.

Speaking and Listening   Interview a person in your community who is knowledgeable about plants or animals. For example, you might interview a biology teacher, veterinarian, farmer, pet shop operator, landscaper, or florist. Ask them what animals or plants they find most fascinating or most enjoy working with. As you listen, record information about the special qualities of the plants or animals and the reasons experts have for choosing them. Your teacher may ask you to share your information with classmates.

Critical Thinking: Generalizing   Based on the information in the selection, write a *generalization*—a general rule or principle— about the life of a rattlesnake. Then find the facts in the selection that support your generalization. Would your generalization about a rattlesnake also be true for a gladiator?

Extending Your Vocabulary   Find the following words in "The Life and Death of a Western Gladiator." Using context clues, write a working definition of each word. Then compare your definition of each word with the dictionary definition. After checking the dictionary, use at least three of the words in a paragraph that describes something other than a snake.

agile *(p. 124)*	formidable *(p. 124)*	transverse *(p. 123)*
automatic *(p. 122)*	somnolent *(p. 123)*	venom *(p. 126)*
diabolically *(p. 126)*	symmetry *(p. 126)*	virulent *(p. 122)*

Setting Sun (Sol Poente), Tarsila do Amaral, 1929.

Part 2   *Writing*

When you write about one of nature's marvels, your purpose may be to explain something about it. For example, you may want to explain the night vision of an owl or the diet of a bat. Whenever your purpose for writing a paragraph on any subject is to explain or to inform, you will be writing an *expository paragraph*.

Writing Term   The purpose of an **expository paragraph** is to explain or to inform.

The subjects of expository paragraphs can range widely—from simple, everyday things to the great puzzles of nature; from blue jeans to black holes in space. You have probably already written many expository paragraphs—in letters to friends, in reports for a club newsletter, or in answers to essay tests. The following models show the two main purposes of expository paragraphs.

Models: *Expository Paragraphs to Explain*

The Birth of an Island

Millions of years ago, a volcano built a mountain on the floor of the Atlantic. In eruption after eruption it pushed up a great pile of volcanic rock, until it had accumulated a mass a hundred miles across at its base. Finally its cone emerged as an island with an area of about 200 square miles. Thousands of years passed, and thousands of thousands. Eventually the waves of the Atlantic reduced the cone to a shoal—all of it, that is, but a small fragment which remained above the water. This fragment we know as Bermuda.   RACHEL CARSON
                                                The Sea Around Us

Orphans from the Wild

A very small baby [mammal] that has no hair or whose eyes are not yet open may be picked up in your bare hands. Gently slide your fingers under the baby, scoop it up, and cradle it in your palms. Most babies, particularly very small ones, will enjoy the warmth of your hands. Adjust your fingers to fit snugly around the baby, so it can absorb the maximum warmth from your fingers, but not so snugly that it can't shift its position. The tiny, hairless baby will become quiet almost at once and will soon drop off to sleep.   WILLIAM J. WEBER
                                                Wild Orphan Babies

Model: *Expository Paragraph to Inform*

Food for Thought

Dr. Wolfgang Koehler did a great many experiments with chimpanzees in which he found that they were able to solve very difficult problems. In one experiment he hung some bananas from the ceiling of a cage. He then placed some boxes around the cage. The chimps stacked the boxes like blocks and got their bananas. Next he placed the bananas outside the cage and gave the chimps two sticks that were not long enough to reach. The chimps fitted the two sticks together and got their bananas. One animal, who could not reach a banana hanging from the ceiling of his cage, took the scientist by the hand, placed him just under the banana and climbed up on his shoulders. Apparently the animal was quite capable of reasoning a solution. It did not need to learn through trial and error.   GLORIA KIRSHNER
                                                From Instinct to Intelligence

Prewriting

Writing Process

When writing an expository paragraph, you already know your writing purpose: to explain or inform. Your first goal during prewriting, then, is to think of subjects suitable for your purpose.

Discovering Subjects to Write About

All of the following strategies will help you think of possible subjects for an expository paragraph. Use the ones that work best for you.

Strategies for Thinking of Expository Subjects

1. Look through your journal, particularly your Learning Log, for ideas you could explain. *(See page 13.)*
2. Think about books or magazine articles you have read lately on subjects of special interest to you.
3. Think about an interesting television show or movie you have seen lately.
4. Think about a conversation you had recently that made you stop and think.
5. Browse through the library.
6. Think about what interests you in your other classes.
7. Talk to friends and family members to find out what they would like to know more about.
8. Start freewriting to see what is on your mind.
9. Brainstorm on your own or in a group.
10. Use the clustering technique, starting with the phrase *things I could explain*.

WRITING ACTIVITY ❶ *Writing on Your Own*

WRITING
ABOUT THE
THEME

Use your journal entries, interview notes, or any of the Strategies for Thinking of Expository Subjects to find at least five possible subjects for writing an expository paragraph about one of nature's marvels. Save your notes.

Choosing a Subject

After you have thought of several possible subjects, the next step is to choose one of them. The following guidelines will help you make that choice.

Choosing an Expository Subject

1. Choose a subject that interests you.
2. Choose a subject that will also interest your audience.
3. Choose a subject you know well enough to explain accurately or can learn enough about.

Knowledge is the basis of all explanations. While some explanations come from firsthand experience and observation, others require research—reading books and magazines and talking with experts. Before choosing a subject for an expository paragraph, measure what you know about it by writing answers to the following questions.

- What do I already know about the subject?
- Do I know enough to explain it thoroughly to others? If not, what else do I need to know?
- Where can I find that information?

WRITING ACTIVITY *Identifying Types of Subjects*

List five subjects that you could write about from firsthand experience. Then list five subjects that you would need to research. Label each list "Experience" or "Research."

WRITING ACTIVITY *Writing on Your Own*

WRITING
ABOUT THE
THEME
Review the possible subjects for an expository paragraph about one of nature's marvels that you chose in Writing Activity 1. Then list what you know about each one. Choose the subject that best follows the above guidelines. Save your work in your writing folder for later use.

Limiting a Subject

After you have chosen a subject, the next step is to limit your subject so that you can treat it thoroughly in one paragraph.

Writing Tip   **Limit your subject** so that it can be covered adequately in one paragraph.

The following chart gives examples of how general subjects may be limited and then limited even further.

Models: *Limiting a Subject*

GENERAL	LIMITED	MORE LIMITED
computers	programs	word processing
science fiction	movie monsters	Godzilla
food	food groups	carbohydrates
Colorado history	explorers	Coronado
sports	basketball	fouls

After you decide on a limited subject, focus your thoughts by expressing the main idea in a phrase. Then write a sentence that contains your main idea.

Model: *Focusing a Limited Subject*

LIMITED SUBJECT	basketball fouls
FOCUS	why players sometimes commit fouls on purpose
MAIN IDEA	Basketball players sometimes commit fouls on purpose for a number of reasons.

WRITING ACTIVITY *Limiting Subjects*

Make three columns on your paper and label them "General Subject," "Limited Subject," and "More Limited Subject." Then list and limit each of the following general subjects by completing the columns. Save your work for Writing Activity 5.

I. music
2. bicycles
3. vitamins
4. track and field sports
5. careers

6. dogs
7. politics
8. deserts
9. fire fighting
10. mass media

WRITING ACTIVITY *Focusing Limited Subjects*

Choose five "More Limited Subjects" from Writing Activity 4 and write a phrase that focuses your thoughts for each one. Then, using that phrase, write a sentence that expresses your main idea.

WRITING ACTIVITY *Writing on Your Own*

WRITING
ABOUT THE
THEME

Limit the subject on one of nature's marvels that you chose in Writing Activity 3. After you write a phrase that focuses your thoughts about the subject, work the phrase into a complete sentence that expresses your main idea. Save your work in your writing folder for later use.

Determining Your Audience

Early in the planning stage, you should also think about your audience—the people who will read your paragraph. Asking yourself the following questions about your readers will help you determine their interests, needs, and attitudes.

- What do my readers already know about my subject? What else might they need to know or want to know?
- What are my readers' attitudes toward my subject? If they differ from mine, how can I address those differences?

133

When thinking about your readers' attitudes, consider how their past experiences with your subject might color their views. For example, if you are writing about football—the great love of your life—keep in mind that all of your readers may not share your enthusiasm. Some may even dislike the game.

When considering your audience, also ask yourself why they will be reading your work. For example, your classmates may read to learn more about an interesting subject. If you are writing for your teacher, keep in mind that often his or her reason for reading is to evaluate what you know and how well you express that knowledge.

WRITING ACTIVITY **7** *Writing on Your Own*

WRITING
ABOUT THE
THEME
 Review the main idea that you wrote in Writing Activity 6 and determine who your audience will be. Then, using the questions on page 17, write a brief audience profile. Save your work in your writing folder for later use.

Developing Supporting Details

Without strong supporting details, the main idea of your paragraph will not be clear to your audience. *(See pages 18–23.)* To support your main idea in an expository paragraph, use one of the following types of supporting details or a combination of them.

Types of Supporting Details		
facts	incidents	steps or stages
examples	causes	directions
reasons	effects	characteristics
parts	differences	similarities

When choosing what type of supporting details to use, you should first consider your main idea and the questions a reader may have about the subject.

Writing Tip List **details** that suit the main idea of your paragraph and that explain the subject clearly.

For a paragraph explaining *why* basketball players sometimes commit fouls on purpose, for example, you would list *reasons* as supporting details. This type of detail would be most suitable for developing your main idea and for answering readers' likely questions.

The focus of your subject, stated as your main idea, often offers a clue to the type of details you should use. In the first model below, for example, the focus calls for *facts* about the heart. In the second model, the focus calls for *examples* of whale spouts.

Model: *Facts as Supporting Details*

LIMITED SUBJECT the heart

FOCUS how hard the human heart works

FACTS
- beats between 60 and 80 times per minute
- pumps a little more than 5 quarts of blood each minute
- in an average lifetime, beats 3 billion times
- work done by heart over a lifetime is equivalent to lifting 70 pounds every minute of your life

Model: *Examples as Supporting Details*

LIMITED SUBJECT whale spouts

FOCUS different spouts of the great whales

EXAMPLES
- blue whale—high and narrow
- gray whale—low and bushy
- right whale—V-shaped, like a heart
- sperm whale—blown sharply forward

Inquiring One way to generate a list of details for an expository paragraph is to think of questions your readers may have and to brainstorm a list of answers. Your list may include a combination of different types of supporting details, such as facts and examples. Although you may not use all your details in your paragraph, you should list as many as you can.

WRITING ACTIVITY 8 *Inquiring*

For each of the following focused subjects, write at least three questions readers may ask about it. Then write one type of supporting detail from the list on page 134 that would be appropriate for answering each question.

EXAMPLE   school spirit at your school

POSSIBLE   • How is school spirit shown at games? (give
ANSWER   examples)

           • How is school spirit shown by club members?
             (relate incidents)

           • What does school spirit mean in your school?
             (describe characteristics)

1. the importance of good nutrition
2. student clubs at your school
3. the benefits of learning to type
4. how to pack for a camping trip
5. comparing and contrasting volleyball and tennis

WRITING ACTIVITY 9 *Writing on Your Own*

WRITING
ABOUT THE
THEME

Review your main idea and the audience profile that you wrote in Writing Activity 7 for your paragraph about one of nature's marvels. Then write a list of questions that your readers may have about your subject and brainstorm a list of answers. Do research to find answers for any questions that you cannot answer from your own knowledge or experience. You may find information in your science book or in the reference section of the library. Jot down any information you think you may need to draft your paragraph.

Next, evaluate your information. When you are sure that you have enough supporting details to develop your subject fully, place your notes in your writing folder for later use.

Writing Is Thinking

Analyzing

To think of supporting details for a paragraph that gives directions, begin by analyzing the process or task you want to explain. *Analyzing* means breaking down a whole into its parts to see *how* the parts fit together to form the whole.

Suppose your focused subject is *planning a costume party*. To analyze the planning of the party, break the planning process down into its different parts. Brainstorm a list of all the steps that you can think of for planning a party. After brainstorming, number the steps in the order that they should be carried out. The result will be a chart like this.

Subject: planning a costume party

Brainstormed Steps	Best Order of Steps
make guest list	1. get permission
put up decorations	2. make guest list
get permission	3. send invitations
get costume	4. plan music and games
send invitations	5. get costume
prepare food and drinks	6. shop for food and drinks
plan music and games	7. put up decorations
shop for food and drinks	8. prepare food and drinks

Thinking Practice Choose one of the following subjects or use one of your own. Make a chart similar to the one above to help you analyze the steps required to accomplish the task.

1. how to organize a car wash
2. how to make the world's best pizza
3. how to make wise consumer choices when buying clothes

Classifying Supporting Details

After listing details about your subject, classify them to find the best way to develop your paragraph. When you *classify,* you group details into categories. The following examples show different ways to explain a main idea and classify the supporting details. Notice that each way of classifying is an appropriate way to explain the main idea. *(For more information about classifying, see page 26.)*

1. MAIN IDEA   Whales' spouts vary in size and shape.

   DETAILS   **Classify** information according to facts about whales' spouts and examples of how they vary.

   METHOD OF DEVELOPMENT   Facts and examples

2. MAIN IDEA   Locating whales is a complex process.

   DETAILS   **Classify** information according to steps in the process of locating whales.

   METHOD OF DEVELOPMENT   Steps in a process

3. MAIN IDEA   After locating a pod of whales, whale watchers must approach cautiously.

   DETAILS   **Classify** information about approaching whales in a set of directions.

   METHOD OF DEVELOPMENT   A set of directions

4. MAIN IDEA   The right whale was the most widely hunted during the nineteenth century.

   DETAILS   **Classify** information according to the characteristics of the right whale.

   METHOD OF DEVELOPMENT   Definition

5. MAIN IDEA   The bottlenose dolphin and killer whale can be trained to perform, but the dolphin is more adaptable to captivity.

   DETAILS   **Classify** information according to similarities and differences between dolphins and killer whales in captivity.

   METHOD OF DEVELOPMENT   Comparison/contrast

6. MAIN IDEA   Early mariners' reports about narwhals were like myths about unicorns.

    DETAILS   **Classify** information according to similar characteristics of unicorns and narwhals.

    METHOD OF DEVELOPMENT   Analogy

7. MAIN IDEA   Whales have bodies that are especially adapted to living in the sea.

    DETAILS   **Classify** information according to the different parts of a whale's body.

    METHOD OF DEVELOPMENT   Analysis

8. MAIN IDEA   Because of commercial whaling practices in the early twentieth century, the number of whales dropped dramatically.

    DETAILS   **Classify** information into causes (whaling practices) and effects (drop in the number of whales).

    METHOD OF DEVELOPMENT   Causes and effects

9. MAIN IDEA   There are two main types of whales.

    DETAILS   **Classify** information according to the two main types.

    METHOD OF DEVELOPMENT   Grouping into types

The following model shows how one student classified details about types of whales by making a chart.

Student Model: *Charting to Classify Details*

MAIN IDEA: There are two main types of whales.

Two Types of Whales	
	I. BALEEN WHALES	**2. TOOTHED WHALES**
DETAILS	• have slats (baleen) instead of teeth • slats grow from upper jaw • baleen strains food out of sea water	• use teeth to catch food • eat fish, squid, small sea mammals • swallow food whole
EXAMPLES	blue whale, right whale, humpback, bowhead	sperm whale, killer whale, narwhal, dolphin

The student writer wrote the following paragraph based on the classification of whales given above. Notice that the writer converted the details and examples listed in the chart into sentences. These sentences make up the body of the paragraph.

Student Model: *An Expository Paragraph*

Two Types of Whales

BODY OF THE PARAGRAPH

The two main types of whales are baleen whales and toothed whales. Baleen whales have slats that grow from their upper jaws instead of teeth. These slats, called baleen, strain food out of sea water. Whales that get their food this way include the blue whale, the right whale, the humpback, and the bowhead. Toothed whales, on the other hand—such as the sperm whale, killer whale, narwhal, and dolphin—use their teeth to catch food. They eat fish, squid, and small sea mammals, which they swallow whole. The main difference between baleen whales and toothed whales, therefore, is the way they get food.

WRITING ACTIVITY *Identifying Methods of Development*

Using the models on pages 138–139, write the best method of development for each of the following main ideas.

1. Athens and Sparta were both founded by Greek tribes but developed strikingly different ways of life.
2. Spartans valued harsh self-discipline in many ways.
3. Ancient Greek armies consisted of two main parts.
4. The Greek *phalanx* was a fearsome fighting force.
5. Because of political reforms in 594 B.C., Athens became a democracy.
6. Voting in ancient Athens was a simple process.
7. The Greeks made lasting contributions in architecture.
8. Constructing a plaster model of Greek columns is fun to do if you know how.
9. Greek theaters presented several types of drama.
10. The presentation of Greek plays was like the competition of athletes in the ancient Olympics.

WRITING ACTIVITY *Classifying Details*

Think of details for an expository paragraph on one of the following main ideas. Decide the best method of development and classify your details in a chart like the one on page 140.

1. Our school offers several types of extracurricular activities.
2. Our school is active in intramural sports.
3. You can reach school in a shorter time by taking this shortcut.
4. Both small schools and large ones have advantages.
5. Poor attitudes can lead to poor grades.

WRITING ACTIVITY *Writing on Your Own*

WRITING
ABOUT THE
THEME

Classify the supporting details you developed in Writing Activity 9 for your paragraph on one of nature's marvels. Use one of the methods of classification shown on pages 138–139. Remember that your main idea helps you decide the best method of development. Save all your work for later use.

Arranging Details in Logical Order

After you have listed and classified your supporting details, you need to arrange your ideas in a logical, understandable order. Arranging your details in a logical order will help make your explanation clear to readers. When organizing details for an expository paragraph, use one of the following strategies. *(For more information about ordering details, see page 27.)*

Strategies for Organizing Details

1. Arrange details in order of importance, interest, size, or degree.
2. Arrange details in sequential, or step-by-step, order.
3. Arrange details in chronological, or time, order.
4. Arrange details in spatial, or place-to-place, order.

When you arrange details in order of importance, you arrange them either from *least to most* or from *most to least* important. In the following paragraph, the main supporting details are underlined. You will see that the writer used facts and examples to develop the main idea that dogs that aid the blind must be trained to overcome some basic fears. Notice that the writer chose to organize those facts and examples in order from the least to the most important.

Model: *Order of Importance*

Training a Seeing-Eye Dog

Dogs who will aid the blind must be trained to overcome some basic fears. To learn how to <u>keep calm in a crowd</u>, the dogs are taken to school playgrounds when students are leaving school. The dogs are sharply corrected if they get excited in all the bustle. To <u>overcome any fear of loud noises</u>, they must hold still while blanks are fired above their heads. Sometimes they are even trained on an airport runway. <u>Especially important is overcoming a fear of heights</u>, for the day may come when a dog will have to lead its master down a fire escape. A well-trained dog is more than a pair of eyes; it can also be a lifesaver.

For an explanation in which you give directions or tell the steps in a process, sequential order is used most commonly. *Sequential order* arranges details in the order in which they take place or are done. The details in the next paragraph, for example, explain a training sequence.

Model: *Sequential Order*

Rope Jumping for Tennis Players

There are very few exercises that really help a tennis player get in shape and stay there. One form of exercise that I strongly urge on a player is to skip rope. It is wonderful for the wind and legs. If it is to do you any good at all, it must be done systematically, and not just now and again. Start slowly for your first week or so. Jump a normal "two-foot" skip, not over ten times without resting, but repeat five separate tens and, if possible, do it morning and evening. Take the ten up to twenty after two days, then in a week to fifty. Once you can do that, begin to vary the type of skipping. Skip ten times on one foot, then ten times on the other. Add a fifty at just double your normal speed. Once that is all mastered, simply take ten minutes in the evening and skip hard, any way you want and at any speed. Let your own intelligence direct you to what gives you the best results. Remember always that stamina is one of the deciding factors in all long, closely contested tennis matches, so work to attain the peak of physical conditioning when you need it most.

BILL TILDEN, *How to Play Better Tennis*

Some subjects call for details to be arranged in chronological or spatial order. *Chronological order* is time order. It places events in the order in which they occurred over time. Chronological order may be appropriate, for example, when you want to explain the causes and effects of an event. *Spatial order,* on the other hand, arranges details according to their location—for example, from near to far, from top to bottom, or from east to west. Spatial order may be appropriate when you want to explain the parts of a whole, such as the different departments of a department store. The models on the next page demonstrate the use of chronological and spatial order.

Model: *Chronological Order*

Cracking an Ancient Code

Although the Rosetta Stone was discovered in 1799, the ancient Egyptian hieroglyphics written on it remained a mystery for 20 more years. The first person to try cracking the code was Silvestre de Sacy. He managed to figure out that some signs referred to proper names, but the rest stumped him. He turned his work over to a Swedish expert, David Akerblad, who made a little more progress. Then Sir Thomas Young, an Englishman, went to work on the code. He discovered that some of the signs stood for sounds as well as ideas. The real honor of cracking the Rosetta code belongs to Jean François Champollion. After years of careful study, he had his first breakthrough in 1821. The puzzle pieces then began to fall swiftly into place. Others may have paved the way, but Champollion deserves the credit for discovering a 1500-year-old secret.

Model: *Spatial Order*

A Formidable Mountain Barrier

The Sierra Nevada is a chain of peaks 400 miles long, longer than any one range of the American Rockies. The range stretches from Tehachapi Pass in the south nearly to Lassen Peak in the north where the Sierra block disappears beneath sheets of younger volcanic rocks. The Sierra's western flank rises gradually from one of the world's richest agricultural areas, the great Central Valley, while to the east the mountains rise in a magnificent abrupt escarpment to soar 7,000 to 10,000 feet above the arid basin of the Owens Valley. With not a single river passing through the range, the Sierra forms a formidable mountain barrier.

FRED BECKEY, *Mountains of North America*

WRITING ACTIVITY *Arranging Details in Logical Order*

Read each of the following subjects and main ideas for expository paragraphs. Then arrange the details in a logical order. Indicate how you ordered the details by writing *sequential order, chronological order, spatial order, order of importance, order of interest,* or *order of size or degree.*

I. FOCUSED SUBJECT   calories burned per hour

MAIN IDEA   In every hour you spend in any form of exercise, you burn calories.

DETAILS
- roller skating—330 calories
- cleaning your room — 70 calories
- running (10 mph) — 900 calories
- bicycling (5 mph) — 200 calories
- sitting and thinking — 5 calories
- touch football — 400 calories
- walking — 110 calories

METHOD OF DEVELOPMENT   facts and examples

2. FOCUSED SUBJECT   getting a driver's license

MAIN IDEA   To get a driver's license, it is best to follow certain steps.

DETAILS
- study manual
- when permit issued, practice
- take road test to get license
- get driver's manual
- get driver's permit by taking eye test and written test

METHOD OF DEVELOPMENT   steps in a process

3. FOCUSED SUBJECT   muscles helped by swimming the front crawl

     MAIN IDEA   Swimming the front crawl is beneficial for developing some muscles.

     DETAILS
- leg muscles in kicking
- arm and chest muscles in reaching
- waist and lower back in side-to-side motion
- neck in breathing motion

     METHOD OF DEVELOPMENT   examples, analysis

4. FOCUSED SUBJECT   famous volcanic eruptions in the twentieth century

     MAIN IDEA   Of volcanic eruptions during the twentieth century, five became the most famous.

     DETAILS
- Mount Pelée—1902
- Mount St. Helens—1980
- Mount Agung—1963
- Mount Kilauea—1990
- Mount Katmai—1912

     METHOD OF DEVELOPMENT   facts

5. FOCUSED SUBJECT   the supply of fresh water

     MAIN IDEA   The world's supply of fresh water comes from several different sources.

     DETAILS
- ground water—22 percent of total
- Arctic ice cap, glaciers—8 percent
- atmosphere—less than 1 percent
- Antarctic ice cap—70 percent

     METHOD OF DEVELOPMENT   facts, analysis

WRITING ACTIVITY   **14**   *Writing on Your Own*

WRITING
ABOUT THE
THEME

Return to the details you listed in Writing Activity 9 and classified in Writing Activity 12 for your paragraph on one of nature's marvels. Then make a list or a chart that shows the most logical arrangement for ordering your ideas and identify the method of organization you used. Save your work in your writing folder for later use.

Drafting

After prewriting you are ready for the next stage of the writing process—writing the first draft. Although the first draft need not be polished, it should contain all the elements of a paragraph. As you learned in Chapter 3, these elements include a topic sentence, supporting sentences, and a concluding sentence. *(To review the structure of a paragraph, see pages 97—103.)*

Drafting a Topic Sentence

When you are ready to write a topic sentence, you already have some prewriting notes that include your focused subject and an organized list of details. Keep in mind that a topic sentence should clearly express the main idea of your paragraph and bind together all the supporting details.

The following example shows how a student developed a topic sentence for a paragraph about whales.

Student Model: *Developing a Topic Sentence*

MAIN IDEA	The spouts of the great whales have different shapes.
DETAILS (EXAMPLES)	• blue whale—high and narrow
	• gray whale—low and bushy
	• right whale—V-shaped, like a heart
	• sperm whale—blown sharply forward
TOPIC SENTENCE	Some whale spouts are low plumes, while others shoot high into the air.

This first attempt at writing a topic sentence, however, does not bind together all the details. Notice how the following revised topic sentence is general enough to cover the V-shaped spout of the right whale and the angled spout of the sperm whale, as well as the low and high spouts of the blue and gray whales.

REVISED TOPIC SENTENCE — Whale watchers can tell one kind of great whale from another by the shape of its spout.

WRITING ACTIVITY *Drafting a Topic Sentence*

Read the following prewriting notes for an expository paragraph. Then write two possible topic sentences.

FOCUSED SUBJECT   things to do in national parks
        DETAILS
- camping
- canoeing
- photographing
- swimming
- hiking
- observing wildlife
- rock climbing
- trail riding

Drafting the Body of an Expository Paragraph

When you are satisfied with your topic sentence, you should write the body of the paragraph. The *body* is made up of the supporting sentences that contain your details. These details support the main idea expressed in your topic sentence. Begin by writing a complete sentence to express information about your first supporting detail. Then use the following strategies to help you draft the body of your paragraph.

Strategies for Drafting the Body

1. Work fairly quickly without worrying about mistakes.
2. Follow the order of details you developed in your prewriting notes.
3. Pause occasionally to read over what you have written. This will help you keep track of the flow of your ideas.
4. Add transitional words and phrases where necessary to make one sentence lead smoothly to the next. *(See page 111.)*

In the student model on the next page, the notes about whales on page 147 were converted into complete sentences to form the body of a paragraph. Notice that the first draft of the body contains some transitional words and phrases to tie the sentences together. Other transitions can be added during the revising stage.

Student Model: *First Draft of an Expository Paragraph*

TOPIC SENTENCE

BODY

  Whale watchers can tell one kind of great whale from another by the shape of its spout. For example, the blue whale has a high, narrow spout. The spout of the gray whale is low and bushy. The right whale has a V-shaped spout. The sperm whale can also be identified by its spout, which is blown forward at a sharp angle.

WRITING ACTIVITY *Drafting a Paragraph*

Using the following prewriting notes, draft the topic sentence and body of an expository paragraph. Notice that the details are arranged in the order of *most to least in size*. Save your work for Writing Activity 17.

MAIN IDEA Although dinosaurs were huge in size, they lacked intelligence.

DETAILS

- Brontosaurus—70 feet long, 40 tons, apricot-sized brain
- Tyrannosaurus—50 feet long, 10 tons, smaller brain than Brontosaurus
- Stegosaurus—10 tons, walnut-sized brain (smallest); first to become extinct

Drafting a Concluding Sentence

  To write a concluding sentence, reread your paragraph. Then use one or more of the following strategies to add a conclusion.

Strategies for Writing a Concluding Sentence

1. Restate the main idea in different words.
2. Summarize the paragraph, emphasizing key ideas or terms.
3. Evaluate the information given in the supporting details.
4. Add an insight that shows some new understanding of the main idea.

Read the following examples of concluding sentences for the paragraph about whale spouts. Any one of them would make an effective ending. Which would you choose? Why?

Models: *Concluding Sentences*

These differences in spouts help whale watchers tell one type of great whale from another. [restates the main idea]

Narrow or angled, V-shaped or bushy, the spouts of the great whales can be clearly identified. [summarizes]

Although recognizing whale spouts takes practice, this method works well as a way for observers to tell one kind of whale from another. [evaluates the details]

Because whales are underwater most of the time, whale watchers at the water's surface rely on the shape of the spout to tell what kind of whale they are watching. [adds an insight]

WRITING ACTIVITY **17** *Concluding a Paragraph*

Write four possible concluding sentences for the paragraph about dinosaurs that you wrote in Writing Activity 16. Identify each concluding sentence as *restating main idea, summarizing, evaluating details,* or *adding an insight.*

WRITING ACTIVITY **18** *Writing on Your Own*

WRITING
ABOUT THE
THEME

With your teacher's permission, form a small discussion group with classmates. Using only your prewriting notes for your paragraph on one of nature's marvels, explain your ideas orally to the group. As you listen to others' explanations, note any questions you have about the subject and make a comment that will help each writer write a first draft. Then draft your own paragraph. When you write the body, remember to use the list or chart that you developed in Writing Activity 14 as a guide. Then save your draft for revising.

Revising

Writing Process

During the revising stage, look for ways to improve your first draft. As you revise, read your paragraph with a fresh eye, as if you were reading it for the first time.

Checking for Adequate Development

When you reread your draft, evaluate the effectiveness of your supporting details. Do you have enough specific facts, examples, or directions to explain your subject fully?

Writing Tip   Achieve **adequate development** by adding any specific information that the reader will need to understand your subject.

WRITING ACTIVITY   *Revising for Adequate Development*

Using a dictionary, find additional details to improve the development of the paragraph below. Then revise the paragraph.

All in a Name

People's names have sometimes become the words for familiar items. One example is the Earl of Sandwich, who supposedly invented the hand-held, stuffed bread that we call the *sandwich*. Another example is *maverick*. Still another example is the *Ferris wheel*. *Sousaphone* also comes from a name. Such words give people's names a permanent place in the English language.

Checking for Unity

A paragraph has *unity* when all the other sentences in the paragraph support the topic sentence. A paragraph with unity is easy to follow because it keeps the reader's attention on the main idea. *(See page 109.)* In the following paragraph, which lacks unity, the sentences that stray from the subject are underlined. In revising, these sentences would be deleted.

Model: *Revising for Unity*

The Real McCoy

Elijah McCoy became famous as the inventor of an oiling system for machines. Granville T. Woods was another black inventor. In the 1870's, factory owners had to turn off all their machines before oiling them. McCoy's system, developed in 1872, allowed the machines to be oiled while they were still running, saving time and money for the factory owners. McCoy also held patents for an "Ironing Table" and a "Lawn Sprinkler." McCoy applied his system to steam engines, including those on locomotives, and to the air brakes on trains. His system was so much better than others' that when people bought new machinery, they always asked, "Is this the real McCoy?" To this day, people use that expression to mean "the real thing."

Writing Tip Achieve **unity** in a paragraph by eliminating any sentences that stray from the main idea.

WRITING ACTIVITY *Checking for Unity*

The following paragraph about dreaming lacks unity. Write the three sentences that should be deleted because they do not support the topic sentence.

Busy Nights

Sleeping is for rest, but parts of your body remain active when you dream. For centuries people have wondered about the meaning of dreams. In the dream state, your closed eyes dart around rapidly, following the action of your dream. Sleep expert Dr. Dement did many experiments to learn about dreams. Your brain waves are also as active as when you are awake. Your breathing is sometimes faster, and your heart rate increases. If people are awakened each time they enter the dream state, they will make up for lost dream time the next night. Although your large muscles are limp and relaxed, your eyes, brain, and breathing system get little rest when you dream.

Checking for Coherence

Coherence is the quality in writing that acts like a glue to bond each sentence to the one before and after it. As a result of such bonds, a paragraph becomes a coherent whole that easily makes sense to the reader. The information below and on pages 154–155 explains several strategies that will help you achieve coherence in expository paragraphs. *(For more information about coherence, see page 111.)*

Using Transitions When writing a first draft, you may not always make clear, smooth connections between your sentences. Therefore, during the revising stage, you need to add transitional words and phrases to connect your ideas. The chart on the next page lists commonly used transitions, including general ones as well as some that relate to particular ways of ordering information. *(For more information about ordering information, see page 27.)*

Commonly Used Transitions			
Order of Importance	**Chronological Order**	**Spatial Order**	**General Transitions**
even more	after	above	also
finally	as soon as	ahead	besides
first	at first	behind	despite
more important	at last	below	for example
most	first, second	higher	however
one reason	later	inside	in addition
to begin with	meanwhile	outside	while

WRITING ACTIVITY *Revising for Coherence*

Revise the following paragraph, adding transitional words and phrases where needed.

Days of Our Lives

Although the calendar we use today is the most accurate one yet devised, it has many irregularities. We have two different types of years: common years and leap years. The number of days in each month varies. April and June have 30 days. May and July have 31, and February 28 or 29. Many holidays fall on a different day each year, which causes considerable confusion. The calendar we use today has been keeping time successfully for more than 400 years.

Rearranging, Repeating, and Substituting During the revising stage, you may need to rearrange the sentences so that all of your ideas follow in a logical order. Aside from using transitions, you can also give your paragraph coherence by occasionally repeating a key word or by replacing a key word with a pronoun, a synonym, or a substitute expression. In a paragraph about bats, for example, instead of always using the word *bats*, you could substitute *creatures*, *animals*, and *mammals*. As you read the following paragraph, notice the nouns and pronouns in heavy type that refer to the key word, *tree*.

Model: *Using Repetition and Substitution for Coherence*

Death of a Tree

For a great **tree** death comes as a gradual transformation. **Its** vitality ebbs slowly. Even when life has abandoned **it** entirely **it** remains a **majestic thing**. On some hilltop a dead **tree** may dominate the landscape for miles around. Alone among living things **it** retains **its** character and dignity after death. Plants wither; animals disintegrate. But a dead **tree** may be as arresting, as filled with personality, in death as **it** is in life. Even in **its** final moments, when the **massive trunk** lies prone and **it** has moldered into a ridge covered with mosses and fungi, **it** arrives at a fitting and noble end. **It** enriches and refreshes the earth. Later, as part of other green and growing things, **it** rises again.

EDWIN WAY TEALE, *Dune Boy*

Other substitutes for the key word *tree* might include references to particular kinds of trees as examples of the main idea, such as *an old oak* or *a fallen birch*. The paragraph "Death of a Tree" illustrates all of the Strategies for Achieving Coherence.

Strategies for Achieving Coherence

1. Organize your ideas logically.
2. Use transitional words and phrases.
3. Occasionally repeat key words.
4. Use synonyms or alternative expressions in place of key words.
5. Use pronouns in place of key words.

Using a Revision Checklist

When you are satisfied that your paragraph is well structured, adequately developed, and clearly organized, you should look for ways to improve your sentence constructions and choice of words. As you revise your sentences, consider adding, deleting, substituting, and rearranging words. *(See page 33.)* Also, refer to the Revision Checklist on the next page when you revise.

Revision Checklist

CHECKING YOUR PARAGRAPH

1. Do you have a clear topic sentence? *(See page 147.)*

2. Is your paragraph adequately developed? *(See page 151.)*

3. Does your paragraph have unity? *(See page 152.)*

4. Does your paragraph have coherence? Did you use transitional words and phrases? *(See pages 153–155.)*

5. Do you have a strong concluding sentence? *(See pages 149–150.)*

CHECKING YOUR SENTENCES

6. Do your sentences have variety? *(See pages 71–73.)*

7. Did you combine sentences that go together? *(See pages 66–70.)*

8. Did you avoid rambling sentences? *(See page 75.)*

9. Did you trim away any unnecessary repetition? *(See page 76.)*

CHECKING YOUR WORDS

10. Did you choose specific words that have appropriate connotations? *(See pages 60–61.)*

11. Did you use descriptive words that bring your subject to life? *(See page 59.)*

WRITING ACTIVITY *Studying a Revision*

Study the following revised draft of the paragraph about whales on page 149. After referring to the Revision Checklist on page 156, explain why each change was made.

Whale Watching

Whale watchers can tell one kind of great whale from

another by the shape of its spout. For example, the blue

, while

whale has a high, narrow spout. The spout of the gray

a   plume   , on the other hand,

whale is low and bushy. The right whale has a V-shaped

that looks like a heart to whale watchers.

spout. The sperm whale can also be identified by its

unusual

spout, which is blown forward at a sharp angle. Although

recognizing whale spouts takes practice,

this method works well as a way for

observers to tell one kind of

whale from another.

WRITING ACTIVITY *Writing on Your Own*

Evaluate your draft from Writing Activity 18 on one of nature's marvels to check for development, unity, and coherence. Revise your paragraph, using the Revision Checklist on page 156. Consider the strategies of adding, deleting, substituting, and rearranging words to improve your writing. After you revise, read your paragraph aloud to check if your explanation sounds logical and clear. Then save your work in your writing folder.

Editing and Publishing

This cuckoo, or road runner as it is called, <u>found</u> the baby amid some rocks, <u>uttered</u> a cry of delight, <u>scissored</u> it by the neck, <u>shook</u> it until it was almost lifeless, <u>banged</u> and <u>pounded</u> it upon a rock until life had indeed left it, and then <u>gulped</u> it down.

In this excerpt from "The Life and Death of a Western Gladiator," all of the underlined words are verbs; they tell what the cuckoo did to the baby snake. Colorful verbs, such as *scissored* and *gulped*, let the reader imagine the scene clearly and vividly. Because of their power to bring events to life, verbs are important in all writing. *(For more information about using verbs and practice in identifying and choosing them, see pages 574–585 and 706–727.)*

Tenses of Verbs   The verbs in "The Life and Death of a Western Gladiator" are written in the *past tense*—to show that the action has already taken place (for example: *crawled*). Two other tenses are *present (crawls)* and *future (will crawl)*. When you edit your writing, always check that you have used the same tense throughout or that necessary shifts in tense are clear. Accidental shifts in tense can confuse the reader about the order of events or about the relationship between events in a sentence. *(For more information about tenses and tense shifts and practice in correcting them, see pages 715–721.)*

CONFUSING TENSE SHIFT	When Crotalus **left** the cave, a rabbit **hops** in front of him. [shifts from the past tense to the present tense]
CONSISTENCY IN TENSE	When Crotalus **left** the cave, a rabbit **hopped** in front of him. [Both verbs are in the past tense.]

Principal Parts of Verbs The tenses are formed from the principal parts of the verb—the *present,* the *present participle,* the *past,* and the *past participle.* The present tense is usually formed by adding *-s* or *-es* to the present while the present participle is usually formed by adding *-ing.* The past tense and the past participle of most verbs are formed by adding *-d* or *-ed* to the present. *(For more information about the principal parts of the verb, see pages 707–708.)*

PRESENT	As friction increases, the rope **fray<u>s</u>.**
PRESENT PARTICIPLE	The **fray<u>ing</u>** rope lost its ability to bear weight. The rope **was fray<u>ing</u>** continually.
PAST	The rope gradually **fray<u>ed</u>** beyond repair.
PAST PARTICIPLE	The **fray<u>ed</u>** rope finally broke and had to be replaced. This type of rope **has fray<u>ed</u>** repeatedly in the past.

Irregular Verbs Some verbs do not form the past tense and past participle in the usual way. For example, the principal parts of the irregular verb *leave* are *leaves, leaving, left,* and *have left. (For lists of the principal parts of irregular verbs and practice in writing them, see pages 708–715.)*

Editing Checklist

1. Have you used the correct tense for each verb? *(See pages 715–720.)*
2. Are there any accidental shifts in tense? *(See page 720.)*
3. Have you used the correct principal parts of verbs for each tense? *(See pages 707–713.)*

WRITING ACTIVITY ▶24 *Writing on Your Own*

WRITING ABOUT THE THEME

Using the checklist above and the Editing Checklist on page 37, edit your expository paragraph about one of nature's marvels. After you write a neat final copy, publish your work in one of the ways listed on page 43.

A Writer Writes

  ## An Explanation of a Behavior

PURPOSE: to explain a behavior or characteristic
AUDIENCE: younger students

Prewriting   Brainstorm, freewrite, or browse through your science book or other books on nature to discover an interesting behavior or characteristic of a plant or animal to explain to younger students. For example, you might explain how oysters form pearls, why some birds can fly underwater, or why some flowers close their petals at night.

When you have three or four good ideas, choose the one that interests you the most. Remember to take into account your audience's knowledge, attitudes, and needs. After you list the details you already know about your subject, find additional details in your science book or in the library. Then choose an appropriate method of development and arrange all of your details in a logical order.

Drafting   Using your prewriting notes, draft your paragraph. To keep your ideas clear as you write, pause occasionally to read aloud what you have written.

Revising   Check your draft for adequate development, unity, and coherence. Then, using the Revision Checklist on page 156 as a guide, revise your draft. You may also want to read your paragraph to a classmate or a younger student to find out if you have left any questions unanswered.

Editing and Publishing   Use the Editing Checklist on page 37 and the proofreading symbols on page 38 to correct any errors in your writing. You may also wish to refer to the Personalized Editing Checklist in your journal. Hand in your work when you have finished editing and have written a clear, final copy. Your paragraph and those of your classmates will be published and presented to a science class of younger students.

Independent Writing

Using the Checklist for Writing Expository Paragraphs on page 163, write an expository paragraph on the steps in a process. A *process* is a series of actions or events that brings about a result. Write about one of the following processes or another of your choice.

how to win at a video game	how a firecracker works
how to adjust bicycle brakes	how food is digested
how to make a plaster cast	how to sew in a sleeve
how to propagate plants	how tree trunks grow
how to make fruit preserves	how glass is made
how stars are formed	how to build a fence

Creative Writing

In a *visual poem,* the shape of the writing, as well as the words, conveys meaning. After you analyze the visual poem below, think of subjects that you could represent visually and write a short visual poem of your own.

To a Brown Spider: *en el cielo*
ANGELA DE HOYOS

Brave arachnid
spinning with star-lit dreams
your daring web
—how precarious is your perch!

I too h
    a
    n
    g by a thread.

WRITING
ABOUT THE
THEME

Writing about Literature

In "The Life and Death of a Western Gladiator," the author enlivens his nonfiction writing by personifying his subject—the rattlesnake. *Personification* is a method that fiction writers use to give human qualities to an animal or object. In his story about the rattlesnake, for example, the author uses the creature's scientific name as its personal name—Crotalus. Write a paragraph that explains some other ways in which the author gives the snake human characteristics.

WRITING
ABOUT THE
THEME

Writing in Other Subject Areas

Physical Science   Write a paragraph explaining one of the following physical processes or another one you know about or can research. Assume that your readers are parents who will be attending a science open house at your school.

the water cycle   internal combustion   nuclear fission
a stellar nova   tectonic plate dynamics   beach erosion

4 Checklist

Writing Expository Paragraphs

Prewriting

✔ Use the Strategies for Thinking of Expository Subjects to develop a list of subjects. *(See page 130.)*

✔ Measure what you know about the subjects that interest you the most and then choose one subject. *(See page 131.)*

✔ Limit and focus your subject. *(See page 132.)*

✔ Determine your audience and analyze their knowledge, attitudes, and needs. *(See pages 133–134.)*

✔ List and classify your supporting details. *(See pages 134–140.)*

✔ Arrange your details in a logical order. *(See pages 142–144.)*

Drafting

✔ Write a topic sentence. *(See page 147.)*

✔ Draft the body of your paragraph. *(See pages 148–149.)*

✔ Add a concluding sentence. *(See pages 149–150.)*

Revising

✔ Using the Revision Checklist, check paragraph structure, development, unity, coherence, sentences, and words. *(See page 156.)*

Editing and Publishing

✔ Using the Editing Checklist, check your grammar, usage, spelling, and mechanics. *(See page 37.)*

✔ Prepare a neat final copy and present it to a reader. *(See pages 41–43.)*

Chapter

5

Writing Other Kinds of Paragraphs

Part 1 · *Reading to Write*

THEME: *Exploration*

The next selection, "A Flag at the Pole," is about the British explorer Robert Scott and his men, who sacrificed everything to be the first to reach the South Pole. As they and their challengers—a Norwegian team headed by Roald Amundsen—raced toward the South Pole in 1911, an era of daring exploration was coming to an end. By 1911, all of Earth's continents had been explored. For Scott and Amundsen, therefore, Antarctica was the last challenge.

Nearly a hundred years after conquering the South Pole, however, explorers still find plenty of challenges to meet. Although all of the continents have been mapped and the highest mountains climbed, many of Earth's mysteries remain to be solved by present-day explorers. Undersea explorers now map the ocean floors, for example, while astronauts and orbiting telescopes push back the frontiers of space.

What would Amundsen and Scott, forging their way through the snow to the South Pole, think of the astronauts of today? As you read "A Flag at the Pole," think about the qualities that explorers in all fields share across the ages.

from

A Flag at the Pole

P a x t o n   D a v i s

It was the first of November before we set out, too late, too late. And almost from the start there were difficulties. The motorized sledges, by which I'd set such store and from which I'd hoped for so much, proved worthless. The horses, despite Oates's miraculous ministrations,[1] faltered and fell. We'd brought too few dogs and handled them poorly. The weather had an unseasonable edge, gray and cutting and with temperatures too low too soon, when in fact it should have been the very mildest time of the year. The wind on the Great Ice Barrier was the worst any of us had ever encountered, so sharp and unrelieved as to be all but unendurable; and, men and beasts alike stuck, bogged, we lost a crucial week waiting for a chance to go forward, decreasing day by day the food and fuel we'd need later on. And always, at the back of my mind, perhaps at the backs of the minds of all sixteen of us, lurked the terrible suspicion that Amundsen might by now be ahead . . . Despite my fear of failure, or maybe because of it, I stirred myself to a heartier show of cheer and confidence than ever, giving encouragement here, a smile of approval there, applauding Wilson's cooking, Bowers's determination to keep up his measurements and records, Oates's soldierly stoicism, Evans's cleverness with gear; and thus I stirred them all, when, it now appears, the wiser course might have been to turn back.

1. **ministrations:** Efforts to help.

165

Yet we didn't and we continued, under my leadership, Day and Hooper turning back at the end of November, Meares and Dimitri and the dog teams at the end of the Ice Barrier, while those remaining, I and eleven more, made our way up the Beardmore Glacier, nearly seven thousand feet high, the hardest task of the journey. Scurvy was beginning to show itself, frost-bite was endemic,[2] the bad weather was worsening; and just before Christmas, at Upper Glacier Depot, I sent back Atkinson, Wright, Cherry-Garrard and Keohane. And I and the four Happy Few, the Band of Brothers—Wilson *(the finest character I ever met)*, Bowers *(a positive treasure, absolutely trustworthy and prodigiously[3] energetic)*, Oates *(a delightfully humorous cheery old pessimist)* and Petty Officer Evans *(a giant worker with a really remarkable headpiece[4])*—were left to face the Pole, now one hundred seventy miles away.

Already well past the moment at which, according to our own exacting calculation, chances for success were greatest, we met the bleakest terrain, the harshest and most nearly impassable snow, the coarsest winds, the ugliest falls in temperature any of us could have imagined; and in a burst of self-indulgence I let myself confess to the journal the misery we all five felt: *This is an awful place.*

Yet no foreboding, however melancholy, could have readied me for the disappointment when it came, too weak a word perhaps, for to my journal at that instant I burst forth: *The worst has happened.* No more than a dozen miles from the Pole, Bowers's sharp eye picked up way ahead a dark speck that he, that we all, at first believed must be a shadow along the snow, a trick of the light, but which, as foot after foot between us fell away, we had to admit, tears freezing along our eyelids and cheeks, could be nothing less than a deliberately moulded mound of snow, topped by a flag, a black flag.

Amundsen's black flag—nothing less, nothing other—and then as the gray day darkened, the signs of Amundsen's priority continued to mount: dog tracks, ski tracks, sledge tracks, foot-

2. **endemic:** Widespread within a group.
3. **prodigiously:** To an extraordinary degree.
4. **headpiece:** Intelligence.

prints, all of them leading, as my own instruments were leading, toward the Pole; which next day, dreaming no longer, not even of it, we reached. Amundsen had pitched his tent there, a tidy affair supported by a single bamboo, Norse flag above, skis upstanding alongside, sextants and spare supplies inside, leaving a courteously deferential[5] note asking me, should I survive instead of himself, to pass on a second note, attached, to King Haakon[6] . . . which I shall, if I can, if I live.

It was only a pretense of cheer and sportsmanship and courage with which I turned toward the haggard, fallen faces of my companions and, with smiles and gestures and words that mocked my emptiness, demanded their spirit. But it worked. So we spent the rest of the day sighting and measuring, allowing ourselves only an instant's rest for a bit of food, and then, at my urging too, we placed the camera on its tripod, lined up before it, myself standing in the center, Oates and Evans on either side, Bowers and Wilson seated in the snow before us, the Union Jack behind, and, Bowers pulling the cable, took our own picture. Someday, I suppose, if our bodies are found, the negative will be developed, the photograph printed. I hope it will not show the depth of the defeat. I asked them to smile.

5. **deferential:** Showing respect.
6. **King Haakon:** The king of Norway in 1911, in whose name Amundsen explored Antarctica.

Will it show we knew ourselves doomed? For though the likelihood of our dying was at that moment a thought still unspoken, to my journal, to myself, I admitted my apprehension: *Now for the run home and a desperate struggle. I wonder if we can do it.* As, a day or two later: *I'm afraid we are in for a bad pull.* And, a day after that: *Things beginning to look a little serious.* It would be, as all of us knew, an eight-hundred-mile job of it, sledge-hauling the entire way, temperatures falling rapidly, winds rising, snow surface at its most unpredictably dangerous, and without—what we'd had most of the way out—the support of a party larger than five tired men who'd just stared into the refuse[7] of their own shattered dreams. *I don't like the look of it.* Evans and Oates were suffering from spreading frostbite, Wilson from snow blindness; and though Bowers continued strong and energetic and I was myself, despite my seniority in age, unaware of serious physical decline, I saw what lay ahead for us both in the faces of our three weakening companions. Still—food dwindling and mysteriously short at the depots, fuel running low as our pace fell—we went on. I scarcely knew how, often lagging behind the mileage I'd calculated we must make to beat the winter. But then, approaching the descent of the Glacier, Evans and I fell into crevasses, Evans's second such spill; and afterward, though to that point the strongest of us all, Evans grew increasingly dull and confused, his cuts and wounds reopening, eyes glazed, needing more and more the help that till then he'd been able to give the rest. We got him down the Glacier, but by then he could no longer assist at night with the tent. But at last, hanging back farther and farther, the poor sick fellow collapsed altogether. Then, we others helplessly watching, he fell into a coma and died.

The first to go, as I myself shall be the last. So at length, now down to four, and Oates noticeably failing, we set forth again, following our own tracks when we could find them, taking bearings and sighting always, weather continuing to worsen . . .

Well, worse was, temperatures now down to thirty or more below zero; fuel at the depots less and less than we'd expected;

---

7. **refuse** [ref' yus] n.: Leavings; rubbish.

food thinning; Wilson in agony from his eyes; all of us frost-bitten; daily mileage falling critically. Then, stricken at having to do so, Oates showed us his feet.

We had no choice, of course, but to urge Oates on, gangrene notwithstanding, and by insisting he ride one of the sledges, we perhaps reduced a little the terrible pain his toes must have been giving him. But that meant both a heavier load and one fewer to haul it; and though Oates went on without complaint, soldier to the end, his withering face and empty eyes told us everything.

He tried to, though; we all did; and if the rest of us could see Oates was dying, unable any longer to walk, taking more and more time in the morning to get into his boots and thus costing us more and more time on the march, he did so without complaint, struggling always to summon some sort of smile to his face.

Yet in the end, moral strength, which we'd all shown, was not quite enough; for not even Oates's supreme courage could heal the corruption of gangrenous frostbite. And at last, admitting both his inability to go on and his recognition that his decay was slowing fatally the progress of his companions, the Soldier, we'd come to call him, begged us to leave him behind, in his sleeping bag. But we couldn't do that, we *couldn't*. And the next morning, after a prolonged battle with his boots, stood suddenly and said, "I am just going outside and may be some time." When he failed to return we staggered into the snow ourselves but of course he was gone; no trace of him remained. Only the seemingly endless snow remained. Snow will always remain.

Oh, another desperate day into the wind, and another, a few miles; but by then there was little to choose between the three of us left. Bowers, perhaps, was in the best condition, though badly frostbitten. Wilson was nearly blind, and his hands and feet useless. As for myself, I mixed a small spoonful of curry with my melted pemmican, got violent indigestion, lay awake all night in pain, saw my bad foot turn black. Well, no matter; no doubt by then nothing could have held off the inevitable.

Which now, at last, came. Each day, for days, Wilson and Bowers readied themselves for the final march on One Ton Depot, now only eleven miles ahead. Each day the blizzard stopped them from leaving the tent. And the fuel gave out. And the last of the food went. And the blizzard continued.

And then they died, Wilson and Bowers, quietly, without a murmur of regret, sleeping away in their sleeping bags so slowly that even I, surviving them, could not say with certainty which had gone first; though from the occasional rise and fall of their chests I believed, as I wanted to, that Wilson was last, clinging, noble heart, to life, to me, to Scott, for as long as he could. So finally, except for the howl of the wind, there was only . . . silence.

Silence; yet knowing I must keep my courage high, I wrote, to the sounds of their expiring breaths: *I do not think we can hope for any better things now. We shall stick it out to the end, but we are getting weaker, of course, and the end cannot be far.*

But that was days ago, I myself scarcely know how many, and in my stiffened hands the journal and the pencil seem almost mute; so I try for a coda and write: *It seems a pity, but I do not think I can write more.* Yet can, after all, and sign my name: *R Scott.*

Perhaps at that I dozed; perhaps not. One task remains. I raise myself, lean across and close their sleeping bags above the faces of my beloved companions. I have strength for nothing more—except, if it is given me, to *know.*

. . . Snow, then: it will be snow; we are all of us flakes of snow, blown willy-nilly[8] through the eternal night.

The bodies of Robert Scott and two of his companions were found in November 1912. They died of cold and exhaustion while returning from the Pole. Also found was the diary Scott had kept until the end— the basis of this story.

8. **willy-nilly:** Randomly, without choice.

Responding to the Theme

Exploration

■ ***Responding in Your Journal*** Stories about the adventures of explorers like Robert Scott are filled with excitement and suspense. Today brainstorm in your journal a list of explorations, discoveries, and challenges on the present-day frontiers of human knowledge. For example, consider explorations in the fields of medicine and science. Include discoveries that you would like to understand better. For each discovery you think of, write your ideas about why it presents a challenge. How is it an adventure? What makes it exciting or suspenseful?

■ ***Speaking and Listening*** With your teacher's permission, form a discussion group with four or five of your classmates. Your goal is to brainstorm a list of possible future scientific discoveries that could have a significant effect on the quality of life in the twenty-first century. As you develop your list, discuss the possible effects of each discovery and any obstacles you can think of to making or using that discovery. When you finish, rank the items in order of importance to people and share your results with classmates.

■ ***Critical Thinking: Evaluating*** "A Flag at the Pole" is a fictional account about real people and true events. By using information in Robert Scott's diary and by writing from Scott's point of view, the author tries to re-create what the explorer actually experienced. Write a paragraph that evaluates the believability of this narrative. Using examples from the story, show what makes the re-creation of Scott's experiences seem real.

■ ***Extending Your Vocabulary*** Many words have interesting origins. For example, *humorous* originally meant "moody" and came from a Latin word for "fluid." In the Middle Ages, people believed that *humors*—imaginary fluids in the body—affected people's moods. Use a dictionary to find the origins of the following words from "A Flag at the Pole."

coda	gangrene	pessimist
coma	melancholy	scurvy
crevasses	pemmican	stoicism

Whalers Active,
Balaena
and Diana
in the Antarctic,
W.G. Burn
Murdoch.

Part 2 — *Writing*

In Chapter 4 you wrote *expository* paragraphs that explain or inform. In this chapter you will explore other kinds of paragraphs: narrative paragraphs, descriptive paragraphs, and persuasive paragraphs. *Narrative* writing tells a real or an imaginary story, while *descriptive* writing vividly depicts a person, object, or scene. *Persuasive* writing expresses an opinion and tries to persuade others, using reasons and facts.

Whatever your writing purpose is, you may decide to use narrative, descriptive, or persuasive writing, or a combination of them. In "A Flag at the Pole," for example, the purpose is to express thoughts and feelings. To achieve this purpose, the author writes both narrative and descriptive paragraphs—telling a story and describing the setting. If you were writing about the dangers of drugs, on the other hand, you might include descriptive and persuasive paragraphs to help achieve your purpose of explaining and informing. In this chapter you will write different kinds of paragraphs for a variety of purposes. You will also write paragraphs of your own by using the writing process. As you write, remember that you can use any stage of the writing process whenever you need to.

Writing Narrative Paragraphs

You will often write stories. They may be about explorers, or they may be about your own adventures. Whatever the subject, if your purpose for writing is to tell a story, you will be writing a *narrative*.

Writing Term   A **narrative paragraph** tells a real or an imaginary story.

"In any story," wrote Malcolm Cowley, "there are three elements: persons, situations, and the fact that in the end something has changed. If nothing has changed, it isn't a story." When you think of ideas for narrative paragraphs, think of times when a situation or character changed. After recalling details about the situation, the people involved, and the change that occurred, then you develop those three elements into the story you want to tell.

In addition to at least three main story elements, a narrative paragraph has three main parts. The following chart shows the function of each part of a narrative paragraph.

Structure of a Narrative Paragraph

1. The **topic sentence** makes a general statement about the story, captures attention, or sets the scene.
2. The **supporting sentences** tell the story, event by event, of how the problem or situation developed, what happened at its height, and how it was resolved.
3. The **concluding sentence** summarizes the story or makes a point about its meaning.

The narrative paragraph on the following page, based on a true story, tells the story event by event. Notice how the topic sentence introduces the main character and captures attention; the supporting sentences tell about the problem, or crisis; and the concluding sentence summarizes the story.

Model: *Narrative Paragraph*

Rescue!

TOPIC SENTENCE

SUPPORTING
SENTENCES

CONCLUDING
SENTENCE

For thirteen-year-old Karen Edwards, July 17, 1972, became a day to remember. She was resting on the side of a motel pool in Duncansville, Pennsylvania, when she saw a young boy struggling in the deep end. Then she saw the boy's father dive in after him and not come up. While others stood by, Karen jumped in and towed the drowning boy to the side. Tired but not waiting to rest, she went back for the father, who was floating face down. As she dragged him to the side, he began struggling, his waving arms splashing water in Karen's eyes. Her chest heaving, she finally made it to the side of the pool, and in a few minutes father, son, and Karen were all well. Karen's quick thinking and heroic effort had saved two lives.

L. B. TAYLOR, JR., *Rescue!*

Like this rescue story, most stories are about some conflict or problem. The topic sentence introduces the subject and prepares the reader for what will happen. The supporting sentences then tell how the problem developed, what happened at its height (the climax), and how it was resolved. In telling the story, the supporting sentences answer the questions *who, what, where, why, when,* or *how.* The concluding sentence brings out the meaning or outcome of the story.

WRITING ACTIVITY *Writing Topic Sentences*

Write three different topic sentences for each of the following subjects for narrative paragraphs. One topic sentence should make a general statement, one should capture attention, and one should set the scene.

1. going to the orthodontist to get braces
2. spotting a tornado in the distance
3. having a narrow escape from danger
4. being lost
5. helping someone in need

WRITING ACTIVITY *Writing on Your Own*

WRITING
ABOUT THE
THEME Review your journal entries about present-day discoveries and explorations. Then use freewriting, brainstorming, and researching to develop a list of discoveries. After you choose the one discovery that you would most like to record in a narrative paragraph, use library resources to find additional details about how that discovery was made. Save your prewriting notes in your writing folder.

Chronological Order and Transitions

Because a story has a beginning, a middle, and an end, the most logical organization for a narrative paragraph is chronological order. In a paragraph organized chronologically, transitions help the reader see how the events are related according to the passage of time.

Writing Term  In **chronological order** (time order), events are arranged in the order in which they happened.

The following chart lists a variety of transitions that you may find useful when arranging details chronologically.

Transitions for Chronological Order			
after	during	afterward	immediately
before	at last	finally	after a while
later	at noon	just as	in December
next	first	meanwhile	last night
when	second	suddenly	the next day
while	until	on Monday	by evening
then	early	as soon as	throughout the day

In the paragraph on the next page, the transitions that show the passage of time are in heavy type. Notice that the story begins one morning and ends the following morning.

Student Model: *Chronological Order and Transitions*

Thirst

I never thought I would prefer a glass of water to birthday cake, but that's what happened when I had my tonsils out. It was **the morning before** I turned 14. I woke up in the recovery room, thinking only of WATER. **Then** a nurse wheeled me to my room, where my mother was waiting. She told us that all I could have was chipped ice, and definitely no water. **Immediately** I asked my mother for a cup of ice, but it melted so slowly that my thirst wasn't quenched. **Throughout the long afternoon,** I dozed in thirsty misery, waking only to get more ice and see my mother patiently reading a book. **At dinnertime** my mother left for 15 minutes, and I **finally** saw my chance to get a good gulp of water. The ice in the pitcher had melted, and **just as** I was pouring a glass of cold, wonderful water, a nurse came in and whisked it away. I was **still** miserable **the next morning until** I heard some voices singing "Happy Birthday" and saw my mom and the nurse enter my room. They had a big pitcher of water with a bright red ribbon around it. That water tasted better than any birthday cake **before or since**.

WRITING ACTIVITY *Using Chronological Order*

Use the following list of events to write a narrative paragraph. First write the events in chronological order, using complete sentences. Then add transitions that show how the events are related in time. Underline each transition.

- teacher told me I should try out for all-state chorus
- couldn't find my good-luck pin to wear to tryouts
- teacher rehearsed me for two weeks before tryouts
- got a letter a few days later saying I had made it
- ran downstairs to show my father
- heard something crack under my running feet
- looked down and saw my pin—smashed
- sang "The Star-Spangled Banner" at audition, wishing I had my pin
- miss the pin but glad to learn success doesn't depend on good-luck charm

WRITING ACTIVITY *Writing on Your Own*

WRITING
ABOUT THE
THEME

 After rereading your prewriting notes about an explorer's discovery from Writing Activity 2, arrange your supporting details in chronological order. Then write a draft of your narrative paragraph, telling the story of how the discovery was made. Remember to include transitions to show the passing of time. Save your work in your writing folder for later use.

Point of View

In a narrative paragraph, the person telling the story is called the *narrator*. The narrator can tell the story from one of two *points of view*. If the narrator participates in the story and uses such personal pronouns as *I, we, our,* and *us,* the story is called a *first person narrative.* The narrator tells his or her own thoughts, feelings, actions, and observations.

Model: *First Person Narrative*

In **my** younger and more vulnerable years, **my** father gave **me** some advice that **I**'ve been turning over in **my** mind ever since.
F. SCOTT FITZGERALD
The Great Gatsby

If, however, the narrator stands back from the action and tells what happened to others, the story is called a *third person narrative.* A third person narrative contains pronouns such as *he, she,* and *they.*

Model: *Third Person Narrative*

Just then the hyena stopped whimpering in the night and started to make a strange, human, almost crying sound. **The woman** heard it and stirred uneasily. **She** did not wake.
ERNEST HEMINGWAY
"The Snows of Kilimanjaro"

As you plan your narrative paragraph, decide which point of view would be better for your story and then use it consistently.

Writing Tip   If you are a character in the story, use **first person point of view.** If your story is about others, use **third person point of view.**

WRITING ACTIVITY *Recognizing Point of View*

Determine the point of view of each of the following excerpts. Indicate your answer by writing *first person* or *third person*.

1. The sled started with a bound, and they flew on through the dusk, gathering smoothness and speed as they went, with the hollow night opening out below them and the air singing by like an organ.

EDITH WHARTON, *Ethan Frome*

2. Before Roger Chillingworth could answer, they heard the clear, wild laughter of a young child's voice, proceeding from the adjacent burial-ground.

NATHANIEL HAWTHORNE, *The Scarlet Letter*

3. There was no shame in his face. He ran like a rabbit.

STEPHEN CRANE, *The Red Badge of Courage*

4. If that staid old house near the green at Richmond should ever come to be haunted when I am dead, it will be haunted, surely, by my ghost.   CHARLES DICKENS
Great Expectations

5. I looked at him steadfastly. His face was leanly composed; his eyes dimly calm.   HERMAN MELVILLE
"Bartleby the Scrivener"

6. She was shown into the breakfast-parlour, where all but Jane were assembled, and where her appearance created a great deal of surprise.   JANE AUSTEN
Pride and Prejudice

7. I went back to the Devon School not long ago, and found it looking oddly newer than when I was a student there fifteen years before.   JOHN KNOWLES
A Separate Peace

8. In this manner we journeyed for about two hours, and the sun was setting when we entered a region infinitely more dreary than any yet seen.

EDGAR ALLAN POE, "Hop-Frog"

WRITING ACTIVITY *Writing on Your Own*

  Look over the narrative you wrote in Writing Activity 4. Most likely you wrote from a third person point of view. As an experiment rewrite your story as a first person narrative. That is, rewrite it from the discoverer's point of view—as if *you* were the discoverer. When you have finished, choose the draft you like best and revise and edit it, using The Process of Writing a Narrative Paragraph on page 181. Then give a neat final copy of it to your science teacher to read.

WRITING ACTIVITY *Writing a First Person Narrative*

Prewriting The firsts in your life are good subjects for narratives because they represent a change or turning point, however modest. Think back to times when you experienced something for the first time, such as your first day in a new school, your first date, your first dance, your first time on a stage, or the first time you won a prize.

- Through brainstorming, freewriting, or clustering, list all the firsts in your life that you can recall.
- Choose the one idea that would make the most interesting narrative.
- Develop a list of details, using the technique of inquiring to answer the questions *who, why, what, when, where,* and *how.*
- Arrange your ideas in chronological order.

Prewriting *Conferencing:* With your teacher's permission, form small groups. Without using your notes, tell your story to the rest of the group. Then ask your listeners to offer comments about any strong or weak points in your narrative.

Drafting   While the words you used to tell your story are still fresh in your mind, draft your narrative paragraph.

Revising   *Conferencing:* If your teacher permits it, exchange papers with a classmate. Comment on your partner's work, noting what might be added, deleted, rearranged, or substituted. Use your reader's comments and The Process of Writing a Narrative Paragraph on page 181 to revise your work.

Editing and Publishing   Edit your work, using the checklist on page 37. Then publish your narrative by adding it to a class collection, or anthology, titled "The Book of Firsts." You may also want to tape it for future enjoyment.

WRITING ACTIVITY *Writing a Third Person Narrative*

Every family has its own stories. These are often repeated at family gatherings as relatives share memories. Think of a relative or ancestor you find particularly interesting. What incident in that person's life has become part of your family's lore? Write that story in a third person narrative paragraph. Use The Process of Writing a Narrative Paragraph on page 181 as a guide. Then tape your story and play it for family members.

Old Father the Story Teller, Pablita Velarde, 1960.

The Process of Writing a Narrative Paragraph

PREWRITING

1. Using various strategies for thinking of subjects, scan your memory for experiences and events that would make a good story. Then choose one and limit it. *(See pages 10–15.)*
2. Consider your purpose and audience. *(See pages 16–17.)*
3. Think back to the first incident that sets the story in motion. Then list all the events in the story, including details of time and place. *(See pages 173–174.)*
4. After arranging your notes in chronological order, delete any details you decide not to use. *(See pages 175–176.)*

DRAFTING

5. Write a topic sentence that makes a general statement about the story, captures attention, or sets the scene. *(See pages 173–174.)*
6. Use your prewriting notes to tell the story from beginning to end—the conflict that developed, the climax or turning point, and the resolution. *(See pages 173–174.)*
7. Add a concluding sentence that summarizes the story or makes a point about its meaning. *(See pages 173–174.)*

REVISING

8. Does your paragraph have all the elements listed in the checklist for narrative paragraphs? *(See page 209.)*
9. Should you add anything to strengthen development? *(See page 108.)*
10. Should you delete anything to strengthen unity? *(See pages 109–110.)*
11. Should you rearrange anything to strengthen coherence? *(See pages 111 and 175–176.)*
12. Do your sentences have variety? *(See pages 71–73.)*
13. Did you avoid rambling sentences? *(See page 75.)*
14. Can you substitute any vivid, specific words for general ones? *(See page 59.)*

EDITING AND PUBLISHING

15. Using the Editing Checklist, check your grammar, usage, spelling, and mechanics. *(See page 37.)*
16. Prepare a neat final copy and publish it in one of the ways suggested on page 43.

Writing Descriptive Paragraphs

When you write to help readers visualize an object, a scene, or a person, you are writing a description. *Descriptive* writing has many uses. For example, you might lose your jacket and have to write a letter to a lost-and-found department describing it. On a literature test, you might be asked to describe a character in a book. In a letter to a friend, you might want to describe the sights and sounds at a concert. In all of these situations, using colorful words and careful organization can make your reader see, hear, smell, taste, and feel what you are describing. This response in readers is the goal of descriptive writing.

Writing Term   A **descriptive paragraph** creates a vivid picture in words of a person, an object, or a scene.

Like a narrative paragraph, a descriptive paragraph has three main parts. The following chart shows the function of each part of a descriptive paragraph.

Structure of a Descriptive Paragraph
1. The **topic sentence** introduces the subject, often suggesting an overall impression of the subject.
2. The **supporting sentences** supply details that bring the subject to life.
3. The **concluding sentence** summarizes the overall impression of the subject.

In the descriptive paragraph on the next page, the writer describes strangely shaped desert trees. As you read the paragraph, notice how the visual details build an impression of twisted shapes. Look for the vivid words, phrases, and comparisons that help you to visualize the cottonwood trees. Also notice how the topic sentence, supporting sentences, and concluding sentence fulfill their functions as parts of a descriptive paragraph.

Model: *Descriptive Paragraph*

Twisted Shapes

TOPIC SENTENCE

Beside the river was a grove of tall, naked cottonwoods . . . so large that they seemed to belong to a bygone age. They grew far apart, and their strange twisted shapes must have come about from the ceaseless winds that bent them to the east and

SUPPORTING SENTENCES

scoured them with sand, and from the fact that they lived with very little water—the river was nearly dry here for most of the year. The trees rose out of the ground at a slant, and forty or fifty feet above the earth all these white, dry trunks changed their direction, grew back over their base line . . . High up in the forks, or at the end of a preposterous length of twisted bough, would burst a faint

CONCLUDING SENTENCE

bouquet of delicate green leaves . . . The grove looked like a winter wood of giant trees, with clusters of mistletoe growing among the bare boughs.

WILLA CATHER
Death Comes for the Archbishop

Notice that Willa Cather's topic sentence suggests an overall impression of the grove, hinting that the cottonwoods make a strange sight. The supporting sentences call on the reader's imagination and senses to picture these trees, detail by detail. Finally, the concluding sentence frames the picture by summarizing the scene in a simile.

WRITING ACTIVITY **9** *Writing Topic Sentences*

For each of the following subjects, write two topic sentences for a descriptive paragraph. In one topic sentence, suggest a positive overall feeling about the subject; and in the other, suggest an overall negative feeling.

EXAMPLE | an old house in the woods

POSITIVE IMPRESSION | The graceful old house, nestled in a grove of young pines, welcomed travelers to the meadow beyond.

NEGATIVE IMPRESSION | The shabby old house, hidden as if abandoned in a menacing stand of pines, discouraged trespassers.

I. a stray dog
2. nightfall on the beach
3. a city park on a Sunday
4. a new acquaintance
5. a car

WRITING ACTIVITY **10** 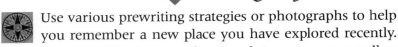 *Writing on Your Own*

  Use various prewriting strategies or photographs to help you remember a new place you have explored recently. That place may be as huge as the Grand Canyon or as small as a box in your closet. Choose the one place on your list that you think would make the best subject for a descriptive paragraph. Then write a topic sentence that expresses the overall impression of your subject that you want to convey. Save your work.

Specific Details and Sensory Words

At the core of every good descriptive paragraph is one main impression. This impression may be scary, peaceful, barren, lush, chilly, warm, comical, sad, or it may suggest any other feeling or mood. The overall impression comes to life when you use your supporting details to *show* the subject rather than merely to *tell* about it. When you *show* readers—by using specific details and sensory words—you make them see, hear, smell, and feel the impression you are creating.

Writing Tip   Use **specific details** and **sensory words** to bring your description to life.

Notice how the word choices in the following paragraph create an overall impression of cool comfort.

Model: *Specific Details and Sensory Words*

Harbored for the Night

In the breeze-cooled cabin of the *Jodi-Lee*, daylight seems ages ago. Outside, the dark, cool waters splash in whispers against the hull in an ageless rhythm. Creaking ropes and mellow clangs of other boats blend in a harbor hush. The musty smell of wet wood is carried by the breeze. All around the harbor, the damp night air cools away the sunburns of the day. In the *Jodi-Lee*, the moon is a comforting night-light.

The following chart shows how the writer used specific details and sensory words to create a cool, comfortable, and peaceful impression of the boat and the harbor.

Specific Details	Sensory Words
cabin of the *Jodi-Lee*	breeze-cooled
water against hull	dark, cool, splash, whispers, rhythm
ropes and other boats	creaking, clangs, hush
wet wood	musty
night air, sunburns	damp, cools
moon	night-light

Using Comparison and Contrast In "Twisted Shapes" on page 183, the concluding sentence contains a simile that compares the cottonwood grove to a wintertime forest with mistletoe. In a similar manner, the concluding sentence of "Harbored for the Night" on page 185 presents a metaphor, comparing the moon to a night-light. A comparison in which you give human qualities to an animal, object, or idea—as if it were a person— is called *personification*. "The waves danced ashore," for example, personifies water. A metaphor, a simile, or personification—figurative language—adds richness to a description by suggesting a striking, fresh comparison.

Direct comparisons and contrasts also enhance descriptive writing. For example, a description of a calm sea could be strengthened through contrast with a stormy one. You could also enhance the description by directly comparing the calm sea with some other thing that shares the same qualities of calmness. Whether you use figurative language or comparison and contrast, remember to avoid clichés. *(See pages 62, 63, and 65.)*

SIMILE As wary as a panther behind a screen of bamboo, she quickly sought an opening among the taller players.

METAPHOR His mustache was a small black bird poised for flight; his beard, its nest.

PERSONIFICATION After the quake the shivering building fought for control, failed to collect its wits, and promptly collapsed.

COMPARISON The lava flow had the consistency of old-fashioned custard, crusted on top and smoothly thick below.

CONTRAST Unlike the uniform ranks of doorways in the nearby housing tract, the cottages on Poole's Lane had cheerfully haphazard shapes.

Writing Tip Use **figurative language** or **comparison and contrast** to enrich your description.

WRITING ACTIVITY *Recognizing Details and Sensory Words*

After reading the following paragraph, make a chart like the one on page 185. Begin by making two columns, labeled "Specific Details" and "Sensory Words." Then fill in the columns with words from the paragraph. Include at least five items in each column.

The Aftermath

By the time the fire had been reduced to smoldering ashes, it was already beginning to get light. The crowd of curious onlookers had mostly dispersed, and the remaining homeless had been swept away by local charity groups. The shrunken, black skeleton of the building looked defeated as it loomed over the awakening city and contrasted with the brightening sky. The dirty firefighters collected near the still shiny engine and, after wiping the soot off their faces and hands, drove away. Finally all was silent, and the orange arms of the sun reached greedily, grabbing and pulling at invisible handholds in the pinkish sky.

CYNTHIA GREEN, (Student Writer)

WRITING ACTIVITY *Recognizing Comparisons*

Identify and write four comparisons that appear in "The Aftermath" above. For each comparison explain what two things the student writer compares and what quality those things have in common.

WRITING ACTIVITY *Writing on Your Own*

WRITING
ABOUT THE
THEME
Review the subject you chose in Writing Activity 10—the location of one of your explorations. Then use brainstorming and clustering—and a visit to the place, if possible—to generate specific details, sensory words, and comparisons that will help you describe that place vividly. Keep in mind the overall impression of the place that you decided on. Save your notes in your writing folder for later use.

Spatial Order and Transitions

Often the most natural way to organize a descriptive paragraph is to use spatial order. Transitions tell how details are located in space.

Writing Term  In **spatial order** details are arranged according to their location. Transitions make clear the spatial relationships among details.

The following chart shows several ways to organize details in spatial order. Also listed are some transitions that are used with each method of organization.

Transitions for Spatial Order	
SPATIAL ORDER	**TRANSITIONS**
near to far (or reverse)	north, south, east, west, beyond, around, in the distance, close by, farther, across, behind
top to bottom (or reverse)	higher, lower, above, below, at the top (bottom)
side to side	at the left (right), in the middle, next to, beside, at one end, at the other end, to the east (west, north, south)
inside to outside (or reverse)	within, in the center, on the outside, at the edge

When you describe a scene, you might use near-to-far order to guide readers from the foreground of the scene to the background, or you might use side-to-side order to show the panorama of a scene from left to right. In the following paragraph, the details are arranged spatially from side to side. The transitions in heavy type make clear the location of each item.

Model: *Side-to-Side Spatial Order and Transitions*

Depending on how you look at it, we live in a wildflower garden or a weed patch. Our dooryard extends **from** the big old barn **on one side to** the vegetable garden **on the other, from** the home pasture **in the back to** the country road and the riverbank **in front**. I keep the grass **around** the house mowed, in season, for a lawn. The garden has a fence only theoretically rabbit- and woodchuck-proof; that fence is thickly twined with vines, and catbirds and cardinals nest **there.** Half a dozen old apple trees are huge bouquets, loud with bees, **in the backyard** each May.   HAL BORLAND, *The Countryman's Flowers*

WRITING ACTIVITY *Identifying Types of Spatial Order*

Identify the type of spatial order used in each of the following paragraphs by writing *near to far, top to bottom, side to side, inside to outside,* or the reverse of any of these.

1. A Writer's Study

The study was a catastrophe. On the floor was a layer of partially typed pages, and near the desk chair, books and magazines lay opened flat. On the chair was an empty glass, resting in a bowl which looked as if it had held tomato soup. The desk lamp was on and lit the countless pages of the writer's work and assorted writing and erasing tools. The shelves above the desk held books positioned at every imaginable angle. Crowning the mess was a stack of newspapers on top of the bookcase. The scene lacked only the writer, who clearly had gone out for air.

2. New Bicycle

Luis's new bike was a beauty, so beautiful in fact that I forgot for a moment to envy him. The gracefully thin, white-walled front wheel was attached to the frame with two sparkling chrome wheel locks. The handlebar turned downward in the racing style and was wrapped in red tape that matched the fire red of the frame. The gear levers were chrome and the seat was soft leather. In the center of the rear wheel was the source of speed—the five black gears and the chrome derailleur. Proud and smug, Luis watched my long gaze, but I was too filled with awe to care.

3. London at Night

The view from the balcony of the Royal Festival Hall could have been photographed for a travel guide. The navy blue tinge of the night sky made a luminous backdrop for the stars. On the far side of the Thames River, seemingly just below the deep blue sky, several old buildings stood like huge guards, positioned shoulder to shoulder to protect the river. An orangish light, which must have come from lights placed on the buildings' lawns, illuminated them. The river itself was black and untraveled. All tourist boats were docked. Along the near riverbank, a lamplit, concrete walk was filled with people in fancy evening dress and a few teenagers in blue jeans. Further from the river on the near bank stood the modern performing arts complex from which others like myself enjoyed the view of London.

4. The Big Game

The most important game of the year was almost under way. José Magarolas of our team crouched at center court, waiting to jump against Tech's big man. Positioned so that the tips of their sneakers nearly touched the white arc of the jump circle, our forwards, Jimmy Jones and Don Fox, stood against Tech's forwards. All four pairs of eyes already looked up into the space where the ball would soon be tossed. Outside the jump circle, behind one pair of forwards, Blake Roberts and a Tech guard of equal height readied themselves. Ken Wan, our captain, and Tech's other guard jogged to their positions at opposite ends of the court, still farther outside the center circle. The lights of the scoreboard showed only "Home 00, Visitor 00." Leaping and shouting along the edges of the court, cheerleaders for both teams stirred the crowd. From every seat around the court, in a multitude of red and green hues, Central and Tech fans screamed their delight that the championship game was about to begin.

WRITING ACTIVITY ◆ **15** *Writing on Your Own*

WRITING
ABOUT THE
THEME

After reviewing the details you listed in Writing Activity 13, think about the best order in which to present those details in your descriptive paragraph. After you arrange the details in the order you decide, write your first draft. Remember to include transitions to make clear the relationship among your details. Then revise your draft, using The Process of Writing a Descriptive Paragraph on page 195 as your guide. Save your work in your writing folder for Writing Activity 19.

WRITING ACTIVITY ◆ **16** *Describing a Setting*

Prewriting   Popular television shows often make viewers feel as familiar with the details of the show's setting as they are with their own living rooms. Describe the set of one of your favorite television shows, following The Process of Writing a Descriptive Paragraph on page 195.

- Begin by listing several television shows you know well. For each one, note the main setting in which the action takes place. For example, if the show is a family comedy, much of the action probably takes place in a living room.
- Choose the setting you know best and would most enjoy re-creating in words. Jot down all the details you remember about the set. If possible, include details that appeal to all five senses.
- Look over your notes and decide which type of spatial order would be best for your description.

Drafting   Use your prewriting notes to write your first draft.

Revising   *Conferencing:* If your teacher permits, share your draft with a classmate. Ask your partner what you could add to make the description even more vivid. Then use your partner's comments, your own evaluation, and The Process of Writing a Descriptive Paragraph on page 195 to revise your first draft. Save your revision for editing in Writing Activity 18.

WRITING ACTIVITY *Describing a Character*

Picture each of the following situations. Choose one and create a character in that situation to describe. Describe your character, including his or her appearance, thoughts, and actions in the situation. Be especially careful to avoid stereotypes. Refer to The Process of Writing a Descriptive Paragraph on page 195 to write and revise your paragraph. Then save your revision in your writing folder for editing in Writing Activity 18.

1. a new teacher teaching for the first time
2. a veteran preparing to march in a parade
3. a candidate running for office
4. a law enforcement officer directing traffic
5. an athlete training for a contest

Editing and Publishing

As you read "A Flag at the Pole," you probably began to feel cold in response to the story's vivid details.

Already well past the moment at which, according to our own <u>exacting</u> calculations, chances for success were <u>greatest</u>, we met the <u>bleakest</u> terrain, the <u>harshest</u> and most nearly <u>impassable</u> snow, the <u>coarsest</u> winds, the <u>ugliest</u> falls in temperature . . .

The underlined words in this passage are *adjectives*, words that describe nouns and pronouns. If you omit all of the adjectives, you will see how much color and exactness they add to the description. *(For more information about adjectives and words used as adjectives, see pages 587–594 and 649–653.)*

Comparison of Adjectives   Adjectives are often used to make a comparison. To compare two people or things, add *-er* to most adjectives that have one or two syllables and add *more* to adjectives with three or more syllables.

ONE OR TWO SYLLABLES	Their bread was **staler** than it had been the week before.
THREE OR MORE SYLLABLES	Dogs were **more beneficial** than horses to Scott and his men.

When you compare three or more people or things, add *-est* to most adjectives with one or two syllables and add *most* to any adjective with three or more syllables. *(For more information about adjectives used in comparison and for practice in using them correctly, see pages 774–785.)*

ONE OR TWO SYLLABLES	They suffered from the **harshest** snow of the whole trip.
THREE OR MORE SYLLABLES	Seeing Amundsen's flag was the **most miserable** part of the trip so far.

Punctuation with Adjectives When you use two adjectives before a noun, often you must separate them with a comma. Sometimes, however, a comma is not needed. To decide, read the sentence as if the two adjectives were joined by *and*. If this wording sounds right, or natural, then you do need a comma between the two adjectives. *(For more information and for practice in punctuating adjectives correctly, see pages 823–824.)*

COMMA NOT NEEDED   They felt the **cold Arctic** winds on their faces.

COMMA NEEDED   They felt the **cold, coarse** winds on their faces.

Editing Checklist
1. Have you used the correct form when using an adjective to make a comparison? *(See pages 775–781.)*   **2.** Are adjectives punctuated correctly? *(See page 823.)*

WRITING ACTIVITY   *Editing Descriptive Paragraphs*

Using the checklist above and the one on page 37, edit your paragraphs from Writing Activities 16 and 17. Ask a classmate to illustrate a copy of your final drafts, based solely on your description. If the illustration generally resembles what you imagined as you wrote, you will know that you have written an effective descriptive paragraph.

WRITING ACTIVITY   *Writing on Your Own*

WRITING ABOUT THE THEME   **Editing** Use the Editing Checklists above and on page 37 to edit the description of a place that you wrote in Writing Activity 15.

Publishing After you make a final copy, share your work by exchanging papers with a writing partner.

The Process of Writing a Descriptive Paragraph

PREWRITING

1. Using various strategies for thinking of subjects, scan your memory for persons, objects, or scenes to describe. Then choose one and limit it. *(See pages 10–15.)*
2. Determine your audience by asking yourself questions about your readers. *(See page 17.)*
3. Form an overall impression of your subject—either positive or negative. Then list all the specific details and sensory impressions you could include to convey that overall feeling. *(See pages 182–186.)*
4. After you arrange your details in spatial order, delete any that do not support the overall impression. *(See page 188.)*

DRAFTING

5. Write a topic sentence that introduces your subject and suggests your overall impression of it. *(See pages 182–183.)*
6. Use your prewriting notes to write supporting sentences that reveal the details one by one. *(See pages 182–183.)*
7. Add a concluding sentence that summarizes the overall impression of the subject. *(See pages 182–183.)*

REVISING

8. Does your paragraph have all the elements listed in the checklist for descriptive paragraphs? *(See page 209.)*
9. Should you add anything to strengthen development? *(See page 108.)*
10. Should you delete anything to strengthen unity? *(See pages 109–110.)*
11. Should you rearrange anything to strengthen coherence? *(See pages 111 and 188–189.)*
12. Do your sentences have variety? *(See pages 71–73.)*
13. Did you avoid rambling sentences? *(See page 75.)*
14. Can you substitute any vivid, specific words for general ones? *(See page 59.)*

EDITING AND PUBLISHING

15. Using the Editing Checklist, check your grammar, usage, spelling, and mechanics. *(See page 37.)*
16. Prepare a neat final copy and publish it in one of the ways suggested on page 43.

Writing Persuasive Paragraphs

When your writing purpose is to persuade others to think or act in a certain way, you will be writing *persuasive* paragraphs. Persuasive writing can be very powerful. For example, you can use persuasion in a letter to demand a refund for a faulty product you bought. You can also use persuasion to defend or criticize viewpoints or actions reported in the news. This section will teach you effective strategies for writing to persuade. In addition to these strategies, you will sometimes be able to use *narrative writing* and *descriptive writing* to achieve your overall purpose of persuading *(See pages 173–189.)*

Writing Term   A **persuasive paragraph** states an opinion and uses facts, examples, and reasons to convince readers.

Like narrative and descriptive paragraphs, persuasive paragraphs have three main parts.

Structure of a Persuasive Paragraph
I. The **topic sentence** states an opinion on a subject.
2. The **supporting sentences** use facts, examples, and reasons to back up the opinion.
3. The **concluding sentence** makes a final appeal to readers.

The following model shows how each sentence in a persuasive paragraph functions. Notice how facts are used to back up the opinion.

Model: *Persuasive Paragraph*

Unidentified Flying Objects

TOPIC SENTENCE   Although the United States Air Force has dismissed reports of UFO's, there is so much evidence that UFO's exist that we should take them seriously. More than 12,000 sightings have been reported to various organizations and authorities.

SUPPORTING SENTENCES

Many of these reports were made by pilots, engineers, air-traffic controllers, and other reliable people. According to a Gallup poll, five million Americans believe they have sighted UFO's, and some have even taken

CONCLUDING SENTENCE

photographs. The great number of sightings warrants an open mind on the subject of UFO's.

WRITING ACTIVITY 20 *Writing Topic Sentences*

Write a topic sentence for a persuasive paragraph on each of the following subjects. Each topic sentence should state an opinion.

1. television commercials
2. fast food
3. the legal driving age
4. computers in schools
5. school awards ceremonies

6. animal rights
7. team selection in sports
8. field trips
9. part-time jobs for students
10. elections of class officers

WRITING ACTIVITY 21 *Writing on Your Own*

WRITING ABOUT THE THEME

When you explored possible subjects for a paragraph about present-day explorations and discoveries, you probably found some subjects that are controversial, such as the splicing of genes to create new organisms. Select one subject to write about in a persuasive paragraph. Choose a subject that you have strong opinions about. Then write a topic sentence that clearly states your opinion. Save your work in your writing folder for use in Writing Activity 23.

Facts and Opinions

The opinion you present in a persuasive paragraph will often conflict with readers' opinions. To win readers over to your viewpoint, therefore, you must present a convincing argument. Because facts, real-life examples, and clear reasons are convincing, they are your most important tools. Few readers will argue with *facts*—statements that can be proven to be true.

Writing Tip As you develop your persuasive paragraph, use **facts and examples** to convince your reader. Do not use **opinions** to support your argument.

WRITING ACTIVITY *Distinguishing Facts and Opinions*

For each of the following statements, write *F* if it states a fact or *O* if it states an opinion. Then, for each factual statement, write an opinion about it.

EXAMPLE Advertising often appeals to the emotions.

POSSIBLE ANSWER F—Consumers should buy products for their usefulness and quality, not for the emotional appeal of their advertising.

1. Fighting in sports such as hockey should be outlawed.
2. The U.S. Constitution contains a Bill of Rights.
3. Not all students want to go on to college.
4. Citizens who are at least eighteen years old can vote.
5. Touring bikes are better than racing bikes.

WRITING ACTIVITY *Writing on Your Own*

WRITING ABOUT THE THEME Reread your opinion about some area of exploration that you stated in Writing Activity 21. Use brainstorming or clustering to develop a list of facts, examples, and reasons you could use to support your opinion. If necessary, gather additional information from the library or discuss the subject with others. Save all your notes for later use.

Order of Importance and Transitions

When you arrange your evidence in a logical order, you may find that order of importance often works best. It is the most common way to organize facts, examples, and reasons in a persuasive paragraph. Saving the most important or most convincing evidence for last is a common strategy.

Writing Term  In **order of importance**, supporting evidence is arranged in the order of least to most (or most to least) important. Transitions show the relationships between ideas.

Transitions for Order of Importance		
also	for this reason	moreover
another	furthermore	more important
besides	in addition	most important
finally	in the first place	similarly
first	likewise	to begin with

In the following model, the transitions are printed in heavy type. Notice that the facts and examples that support the argument are presented in order from the least to the most important.

Model: *Order of Importance and Transitions*

Saving Our History

Although some people support tearing down old buildings, cities should restore them instead. **In the first place,** cities gain a sense of pride when neglected buildings are restored by skillful workers. The work of restoring old landmarks **also** provides many needed jobs. When buildings are improved, **moreover,** the value of property goes up. Seeing the rebuilt homes, other people want to buy and rebuild. **Most important,** restored buildings save a city's history and give people a sense of their roots. A salvaged city is a salvaged history.

WRITING ACTIVITY *Using Transitions*

Revise the following paragraph by adding transitions where needed to show order of importance.

Buckling Up

Drivers should always wear their seat belts. Buckling up is a reminder to drive carefully. With seat belts fastened, drivers are more aware of the potential danger of accidents. Drivers wearing seat belts set a good example, and passengers will follow their lead. Wearing seat belts saves lives and reduces the chances of serious injury. The National Safety Council estimates that wearing seat belts would save more than 14,000 lives in the United States each year. A five-second buckle-up could mean the difference between life and death.

WRITING ACTIVITY *Writing on Your Own*

WRITING ABOUT THE THEME

 Review the facts, examples, and reasons that you listed in Writing Activity 23 to support your opinion. Then make a simple chart that shows how your details can be arranged in the most logical order. Using your chart as a guide, write the first draft of your persuasive paragraph. Remember to add transitions where needed. Save your work for later use.

Persuasive Language

If you present your opinions in reasonable language, your audience will probably keep an open mind about what you have to say. If you use insulting, exaggerated, or overly emotional language, however, readers will not take you seriously.

Writing Tip   Use **precise, reasonable language** that is not exaggerated or loaded with emotion.

Model: *Persuasive Language*

EXAGGERATED   The best suspense story ever written is by Edgar Allan Poe.

PRECISE   "The Fall of the House of Usher" shows that Edgar Allan Poe was a master of suspense.

LOADED   Driving a car in the city is really stupid.

REASONABLE   Using public transportation is preferable to driving a car in the city.

WRITING ACTIVITY 26 *Using Reasonable Language*

Rewrite each of the following sentences, replacing exaggerations and loaded words with reasonable language.

1. People who ride bicycles without wearing a helmet should have their heads examined.
2. The most stupendous, all-around greatest sport is baseball.
3. Rock is the only music worth listening to.
4. Study-hall classes are zoos.
5. Professional wrestling is a joke.

WRITING ACTIVITY 27 *Writing on Your Own*

WRITING
ABOUT THE
THEME   Check the draft you wrote in Writing Activity 25 to make sure you have used reasonable language. Then revise your paragraph, using The Process of Writing a Persuasive Paragraph on page 205. Save your work.

Writing Is Thinking

Evaluating Alternative Arguments

When you write to persuade, you are trying to change readers' minds. To do so, you need to recognize the different positions that your readers may take on an issue. The more you understand these positions, the better you can develop an effective argument that will reach more members of your audience.

For example, suppose you want to write a speech opposing the use of pesticides on food crops. The audience profile chart below shows alternative arguments you might develop, depending on your readers' concerns.

Audience Profile Chart		
	Positions on the Issue	**Alternative Arguments**
City Dwellers	• indifferent; uninformed • fearful of effects of pesticides; want them banned	• People should be concerned. • Pesticides should be classified and harmful ones banned.
Farmers	• concerned about possible ill effects on health • fearful that banning pesticides may lead to crop damage from insects	• Research is needed to assess ill effects of pesticides. • New ways must be found to protect crops and control insects.

Thinking Practice Suppose you want to give a speech to persuade a group to raise money to improve local schools. For each audience below, make an audience profile chart.

1. parents

2. local business people

3. people without school-age children

WRITING ACTIVITY *Appealing to Reason*

Prewriting   Imagine that you have been asked to write a paragraph for the newspaper, persuading people to bring their old newspapers, glass bottles, and metal cans to a new recycling center instead of discarding them.

- Brainstorm or freewrite to develop a list of reasons citizens should take the trouble to recycle their household waste.
- Use your library to find out where your city or town dumps its trash and why a recycling center is a good idea. For more information call the mayor's office or the town hall.
- After gathering the necessary information, organize your details in the order you wish to present them.

Drafting   As you draft, be sure to state your opinion clearly and to provide sufficient evidence to persuade your readers.

Revising *Conferencing:* If your teacher permits, exchange papers with a classmate. Explain why you would or would not be persuaded by what you read and make suggestions for improving your partner's argument. Then use your partner's comments, your own evaluation, and The Process of Writing a Persuasive Paragraph on page 205 to revise your work.

Editing Using the Editing Checklist on page 37, edit your revision to ensure that it is correct in spelling, grammar, punctuation, and usage.

Publishing After you make a neat final copy of your paragraph, submit it to your school or local newspaper for publication. Also consider writing a longer composition to submit in the form of an editorial or letter to the editor. *(For information about writing letters to the editor, see pages 439 – 442.)*

WRITING ACTIVITY **29** *Writing a Persuasive Paragraph*

Write a persuasive paragraph on one of the following subjects or another one of your choice. Use The Process of Writing a Persuasive Paragraph on the next page as a guide.

1. wheelchair access in your community
2. a dangerous intersection
3. physical education as a required subject
4. the availability of bicycle lanes
5. vocational school as an educational alternative

WRITING ACTIVITY **30** *Writing on Your Own*

WRITING
ABOUT THE
THEME

Look over your persuasive paragraph about a controversial exploration, which you revised in Writing Activity 27. Edit it carefully for mistakes, using the Editing Checklist on page 37 as a guide. Use your final paragraph as the basis for a letter to a local newspaper or for a speech at a school assembly or public meeting. *(For information about giving a speech, see pages 450 – 456.)*

The Process of Writing a Persuasive Paragraph

PREWRITING

1. Using various strategies for thinking of subjects, explore your opinions on a variety of subjects. Then choose one opinion you feel strongly about and limit it. *(See pages 10–15.)*
2. Determine your audience by asking yourself questions about your readers' opinions. *(See page 17.)*
3. Gather whatever information you need to persuade people that your opinion is worthwhile. As you gather evidence, also note opposing views. *(See pages 196–198 and 202.)*
4. Arrange your ideas in a logical order. *(See page 199.)*

DRAFTING

5. Write a topic sentence that states your opinion. *(See pages 196–197.)*
6. Use your prewriting notes to provide facts, examples, and reasons that support your opinion. *(See pages 196–197.)*
7. Add a concluding sentence that makes a final appeal to your readers. *(See pages 196–197.)*

REVISING

8. Does your paragraph have all the elements listed in the checklist for persuasive paragraphs? *(See page 209.)*
9. Should you add anything to strengthen development? *(See page 108.)*
10. Should you delete anything to strengthen unity? *(See pages 109–110.)*
11. Should you rearrange anything to strengthen coherence? *(See pages 111 and 199.)*
12. Do your sentences have variety? *(See pages 71–73.)*
13. Did you use precise, reasonable language? *(See page 201.)*

EDITING AND PUBLISHING

14. Using the Editing Checklist, check your grammar, usage, spelling, and mechanics. *(See page 37.)*
15. Prepare a neat final copy and present it to a reader. *(See pages 41–43.)*

A Writer Writes

Paragraphs for Different Purposes

Many subjects can be developed in a number of different ways. Using the same general subject, for example, you can write a narrative paragraph, a descriptive paragraph, or a persuasive paragraph. Examining a subject with different writing purposes in mind is a good way to explore the subject in depth.

WRITING
ABOUT THE
THEME

1. Writing a Narrative Paragraph

PURPOSE: to tell a story about an imaginary discovery
AUDIENCE: newspaper readers

Recall stories about the adventures of European explorers during the Age of Discovery, when daring navigators found new continents. Then refer to The Process of Writing a Narrative Paragraph on page 181 to write a fictional narrative about the discovery of an imaginary new land.

from *THE HOBBIT or There and Back Again* © 1966, J.R.R. Tolkien.

WRITING
ABOUT THE
THEME

2. Writing a Descriptive Paragraph

PURPOSE: to describe an imaginary land

AUDIENCE: newspaper readers

Review the fictional narrative that you were asked to write on the previous page. Then decide on an overall impression of the newly discovered land that you wish to convey and brainstorm a list of specific details and sensory impressions. Using The Process of Writing a Descriptive Paragraph on page 195, write a paragraph in which you describe the new land.

WRITING
ABOUT THE
THEME

3. Writing a Persuasive Paragraph

PURPOSE: to persuade people to support or oppose an imaginary exploration

AUDIENCE: newspaper readers

Following The Process of Writing a Persuasive Paragraph on page 205, write a paragraph in which you urge people to support or to oppose the exploration for oil and ores in the new land that you have discovered and explored in your narrative and descriptive paragraphs on page 206 and above.

Independent Writing

Write a narrative, descriptive, or persuasive paragraph on one of the following subjects or another one of your choice.

1. student lockers
2. a television commercial
3. skateboarding
4. school cafeteria food
5. the celebration of Martin Luther King Day
6. a horse show event
7. the American flag
8. the dangers of drunk driving
9. forest fire prevention
10. school spirit

Creative Writing

Combine narration and description to write a three-paragraph short story. Base your story on the scene shown in the photograph above.

  ## Writing about Literature

"A Flag at the Pole" is written from the *first person point of view*. That is, the story is told by a narrator who participates in the story, using the pronouns *I* and *we*. Reread the selection and imagine how the story would change if it were written from the *third person point of view,* using the pronouns *he* and *they.* Then write a paragraph that explains the advantages of using the first person point of view in a story.

Writing in Other Subject Areas

Civics   Write a persuasive paragraph in which you use facts to argue for or against one of the following opinions.

- Certain books should be banned from the school library.
- People should be required by law to donate their organs when they die.
- Men and women should be paid the same for the same work.

Writing Other Kinds of Paragraphs

Narrative Paragraphs

✔ Does your topic sentence make a general statement, capture attention, or set the scene? *(See pages 173–174.)*

✔ Do the supporting sentences tell the story event by event? *(See pages 173–174.)*

✔ Did you use chronological order with transitions? *(See pages 175–176.)*

✔ Is your point of view consistent? *(See pages 177–178.)*

✔ Does your concluding sentence summarize the story or make a point about its meaning? *(See pages 173–174.)*

Descriptive Paragraphs

✔ Does your topic sentence introduce your subject and suggest your overall impression of it? *(See pages 182–183.)*

✔ Do the supporting sentences supply specific details and sensory words that bring the picture to life? *(See pages 182–185.)*

✔ Did you use striking comparisons? *(See page 186.)*

✔ Did you use spatial order with transitions? *(See pages 188–189.)*

✔ Does your concluding sentence summarize the overall impression? *(See pages 182–183.)*

Persuasive Paragraphs

✔ Does your topic sentence state an opinion about a subject of interest? *(See pages 196–197.)*

✔ Do the supporting sentences use facts, examples, and reasons to back up the opinion? *(See pages 196–198.)*

✔ Did you use order of importance with transitions? *(See page 199.)*

✔ Did you use reasonable language? *(See page 201.)*

✔ Does your concluding sentence make a final appeal to your readers? *(See pages 196–197.)*

Chapter

6 Writing
Effective Essays

Part 1 *Reading to Write*

THEME: *Television*

"When before in human history has so much humanity collectively surrendered so much of its leisure to one toy, one mass diversion?" To what "toy" or "diversion," do you think, does this quotation refer? According to Robert MacNeil, the author of the next selection, the answer is *television*. In his essay, "The Trouble with Television," MacNeil claims that television holds its viewers hostage to thoughtlessness.

People's attitudes toward television were quite different in the 1950's, when this amazing invention first became available to the general public. Many viewers predicted then that television would become one of the most effective educational tools ever created.

What is the truth about television? Has it become an effective educational tool? How has it affected people's lives—the way they find entertainment, the way they get their news? Does television foster illiteracy and violence? Has it brought the world closer together? As you read "The Trouble with Television," form your own opinions.

The Trouble with Television

R o b e r t   M a c N e i l

It is difficult to escape the influence of television. If you fit the statistical averages, by the age of 20 you will have been exposed to at least 20,000 hours of television. You can add 10,000 hours for each decade you have lived after the age of 20. The only things Americans do more than watch television are work and sleep.

Calculate for a moment what could be done with even a part of those hours. Five thousand hours, I am told, are what a typical college undergraduate spends working on a bachelor's degree. In 10,000 hours you could have learned enough to become an astronomer or engineer. You could have learned several languages fluently. If it appealed to you, you could be reading Homer[1] in the original Greek or Dostoevski[2] in Russian. If it didn't, you could have walked around the world and written a book about it.

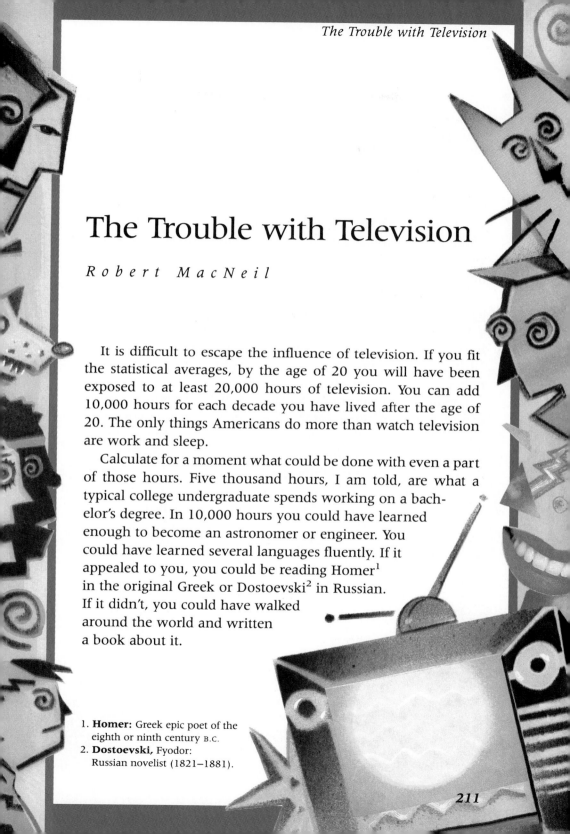

1. **Homer:** Greek epic poet of the eighth or ninth century B.C.
2. **Dostoevski,** Fyodor: Russian novelist (1821–1881).

The trouble with television is that it discourages concentration. Almost anything interesting and rewarding in life requires some constructive, consistently applied effort. The dullest, the least gifted of us can achieve things that seem miraculous to those who never concentrate on anything. But television encourages us to apply no effort. It sells us instant gratification. It diverts us only to divert, to make the time pass without pain.

Television's variety becomes a narcotic, not a stimulus.[3] Its serial, kaleidoscopic exposures force us to follow its lead. The viewer is on a perpetual guided tour: thirty minutes at the museum, thirty at the cathedral, then back on the bus to the next attraction—except on television, typically, the spans allotted are on the order of minutes or seconds, and the chosen delights are more often car crashes and people killing one another. In short, a lot of television usurps[4] one of the most precious of all human gifts, the ability to focus your attention yourself, rather than just passively surrender it.

Capturing your attention—and holding it—is the prime motive of most television programming and enhances its role as a profitable advertising vehicle. Programmers live in constant fear of losing anyone's attention—anyone's. The surest way to avoid doing so is to keep everything brief, not to strain the attention of anyone but instead to provide constant stimulation through variety, novelty, action and movement. Quite simply, television operates on the appeal to the short attention span.

It is simply the easiest way out. But it has come to be regarded as a given, as inherent[5] in the medium itself: as an imperative,[6] as though General Sarnoff, or one of the other august[7] pioneers of video, had bequeathed to us tablets of stone commanding that nothing in television shall ever require more than a few moments' concentration.

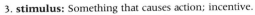

3. **stimulus:** Something that causes action; incentive.
4. **usurps:** Takes away without right.
5. **inherent:** Part of the basic nature of something.
6. **imperative** n.: An order that must be obeyed.
7. **august** adj.: Respected.

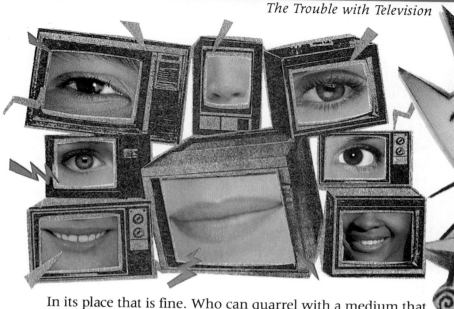

In its place that is fine. Who can quarrel with a medium that so brilliantly packages escapist entertainment as a mass-marketing tool? But I see its values now pervading this nation and its life. It has become fashionable to think that, like fast food, fast ideas are the way to get to a fast-moving, impatient public.

In the case of news, this practice, in my view, results in inefficient communication. I question how much of television's nightly news effort is really absorbable and understandable. Much of it is what has been aptly described as "machine gunning with scraps." I think its technique fights coherence. I think it tends to make things ultimately boring and dismissable (unless they are accompanied by horrifying pictures) because almost anything is boring and dismissable if you know almost nothing about it.

I believe that TV's appeal to the short attention span is not only inefficient communication but decivilizing as well. Consider the casual assumptions that television tends to cultivate: that complexity must be avoided, that visual stimulation is a substitute for thought, that verbal precision is an anachronism. It may be old-fashioned, but I was taught that thought is words, arranged in grammatically precise ways.

There is a crisis of literacy in this country. One study estimates that some 30 million adult Americans are "functionally illiterate" and cannot read or write well enough to answer a want ad or understand the instructions on a medicine bottle.

Literacy may not be an inalienable human right, but it is one that the highly literate Founding Fathers might not have found unreasonable or even unattainable. We are not only not attaining it as a nation, statistically speaking, but we are falling further and further short of attaining it. And, while I would not be so simplistic as to suggest that television is the cause, I believe it contributes and is an influence.

Everything about this nation—the structure of the society, its forms of family organization, its economy, its place in the world—has become more complex, not less. Yet its dominating communications instrument, its principal form of national linkage, is one that sells neat resolutions to human problems that usually have no neat resolutions. It is all symbolized in my mind by the hugely successful art form that television has made central to the culture, the thirty-second commercial: the tiny drama of the earnest housewife who finds happiness in choosing the right toothpaste.

When before in human history has so much humanity collectively surrendered so much of its leisure to one toy, one mass diversion? When before has virtually an entire nation surrendered itself wholesale to a medium for selling?

Some years ago Yale University law professor Charles L. Black, Jr. wrote: ". . . forced feeding on trivial[8] fare is not itself a trivial matter." I think this society is being force fed with trivial fare, and I fear that the effects on our habits of mind, our language,

our tolerance for effort, and our appetite for complexity are only dimly perceived.

If I am wrong, we will have done no harm to look at the issue skeptically and critically, to consider how we should be resisting it. I hope you will join with me in doing so.

8. **trivial:** Unimportant.

Responding to the Theme

Television

■ **Responding in Your Journal**   As you watch and listen to television this week, record the number of hours you watch TV and keep a list of the programs you watch. Note what you like and dislike about those programs. Also note what you learn when you learn something new. Then use this information to begin writing in your journal about television. Also record your views on issues concerning television— such as ratings and censorship—and your evaluations of the programs you watch. Begin today by writing your reactions to "The Trouble with Television." In what ways do you agree or disagree with the author and why?

■ **Speaking and Listening**   With your teacher's permission, meet in small discussion groups to brainstorm ways in which television affects your life. For example, how does television viewing and programming affect your family life, social life, mealtimes, and bedtimes? How does television affect you as a student, a consumer, and a citizen? How much do the programs you watch influence what you think, do, and want? End the discussion by summarizing the points that were raised.

■ **Critical Thinking: Classifying**   Organize information in "The Trouble with Television" to show how the author supports his argument. Start with the following three categories, which are based on reasons the author gives for his views. Then make a chart by listing the supporting facts or examples that fit under each category.

Television as a Waste of Time
Television as a Narcotic
Television as Inefficient Communication

■ **Extending Your Vocabulary**   In "The Trouble with Television," the following words are used to express negative aspects of television. In a dictionary or thesaurus, find an antonym for each word. Then use each antonym in a paragraph to describe positive aspects of television.

| typical | decivilizing | narcotic |
| anachronistic | simplistic | passively |

Part 2 *Writing*

In "The Trouble with Television," Robert MacNeil criticizes television for seldom including programs that require "more than a few moments' concentration." He believes that brief, superficial treatment of complex ideas results in ineffective communication. His observation could also be applied to writing, because effective communication in writing usually involves more than just a quick paragraph. On many subjects you will probably need the fuller space of an essay to communicate what you think and know.

Writing Term An **essay** is a composition that presents and develops one main idea in three or more paragraphs.

You can use the essay form for any of the writing purposes: to explain or inform, to describe, to create, to persuade, and to express your thoughts and feelings. As the novelist and essayist Aldous Huxley once wrote, "The essay is a literary device for saying almost everything about almost anything."

Analyzing Essay Structure

An essay has three main parts—an introduction, a body, and a conclusion. As the following chart shows, these three parts of an essay parallel the three-part structure of a paragraph.

Paragraph Structure	Essay Structure
INTRODUCTION	
topic sentence that introduces the subject and expresses the main idea	introductory paragraph that introduces the subject and expresses the main idea in a thesis statement
BODY	
supporting sentences	supporting paragraphs
CONCLUSION	
concluding sentence	concluding paragraph

Notice the three-part structure in the following essay.

Model: *Essay*

Cat Lovers, Dog Lovers

INTRODUCTION One controversy in this highly controversial era is that between those who love only cats and those who love only dogs. "I love dogs, but I can't stand cats" is a statement I often hear; or "I hate dogs, but I adore cats."

THESIS STATEMENT I stand firmly on my belief that both dogs and cats give richness to life, and both have been invaluable to humankind down the ages.

PARAGRAPHS OF THE BODY Historians agree that dogs moved into humans' orbit in primitive days when they helped hunt, warned of the approach of enemies, and fought off marauding wildlife. In return, bones and scraps were tossed to them, and they shared the warmth of the first fires. Gradually they became part of the family clan.

217

As for cats, it was cats who saved Egypt from starvation during a period when rats demolished the grain supplies. Cats were imported from Abyssinia and became so valuable that they moved into palaces. At one time a man who injured a cat had his eyebrows shaved off. When the cats died, they were embalmed and were put in the tombs of the Pharaohs along with jewels, garments, and stores of food to help masters in their journey to the land of the gods. There was even a cat goddess, and a good many bas-reliefs picture her.

CONCLUSION

So far as service to humankind goes, I do not see why we should discriminate between dogs and cats. Both have walked the long roads of history with humankind. As for me, I do not feel a house is well-furnished without both dogs and cats, preferably at least two of each. I am sorry for people who limit their lives by excluding either. I was fortunate to grow up with kittens and puppies and wish every child could have that experience.

GLADYS TABER, *Country Chronicle*

WRITING ACTIVITY *Analyzing Essay Structure*

Write answers to the following questions about "Cat Lovers, Dog Lovers." If necessary, reread all or part of the essay.

1. What is the main idea expressed in the introduction?
2. How does each paragraph of the body relate to the thesis statement?
3. What is the conclusion?
4. How does the conclusion relate to the main idea expressed in the introduction?

WRITING ACTIVITY *Writing on Your Own*

WRITING
ABOUT THE
THEME

What, do you think, are the positive and negative aspects of television and its effects on people? After you review your journal entries about television, use clustering to explore the negative effects and positive value of television. (*See page 22 for a model of clustering.*) Save your notes for later use.

The Essay Introduction

Like the topic sentence of a paragraph, the introduction of an essay prepares the reader for what will follow. When you write a short essay, you can usually complete the introduction in one paragraph.

Functions of the Essay Introduction

1. It introduces the subject of your essay.
2. It states or implies your purpose for writing.
3. It presents the main idea of your essay in a thesis statement.
4. It establishes your tone.
5. It captures your readers' interest.

The introduction of "Cat Lovers, Dog Lovers" performs very well the functions of an essay introduction. It introduces the subject—the controversy between cat lovers and dog lovers—and establishes a serious tone. The thesis statement then presents the main idea that both cats and dogs have been important to people throughout history. The writer's purpose, clearly implied in the introduction, is to persuade the reader that people should love both dogs and cats. With strongly worded, eye-catching quotes, the introduction also captures the reader's attention.

Ancient Egyptian Cat, 600 B.C.
collection of the British Museum

Writing the Thesis Statement

The *thesis statement* is usually a single sentence. It may appear anywhere in your first paragraph, although it often has the strongest impact when it is the first or the last sentence.

Writing Term The **thesis statement** states the main idea and makes the purpose of the essay clear.

In the following examples, each thesis statement is underlined. The implied purpose of each model is, in order, to inform, to express thoughts and feelings, and to persuade. *(For information about the purposes for writing, see page 16.)*

Models: *Thesis Statements*

1.

The name "Indian Summer" has no valid relationship to the Indians that I can discover. There was no such season on the Indian calendar, which reckoned time by the moon and not the weather. The moons were named for the weather or for the seasonal occupation, but I can find no Indian Summer moon.

HAL BORLAND, *An American Year*

2.

My coming to America in 1979 was not very pleasant. When I was twelve, my parents had to leave my homeland, Vietnam. We lived near My Tho all my years and I did not want to leave, but they said we must. My two sisters were younger, four and seven, and they did not know what it meant to leave. My mother said that we must not tell any of our friends, that our going was a secret. It was hard for me to think I would never see my home or some of my family again. Some of my story I tell here I remember well, but some is not clear and is from stories my family tells.

HIEU HUYNH (STUDENT WRITER)
"Coming to America"

3.

Nowhere is modern thinking more muddled than over the question of whether it is proper to debate moral issues. Many argue it is not, saying it is wrong to make "value judgments." This view is shallow. If such judgments were wrong, then ethics, philosophy, and theology would be unacceptable in a college curriculum—an idea that is obviously silly. <u>As the following cases illustrate, it is impossible to avoid making value judgments.</u>

VINCENT RYAN RUGGIERO
"Debating Moral Questions"

WRITING ACTIVITY *Recognizing Thesis Statements*

Read each of the following introductory paragraphs and write the thesis statement. Then below each thesis statement, identify the purpose for writing that is stated or implied. Indicate the purpose by writing *to describe, to express thoughts and feelings, to explain or inform,* or *to persuade.*

I.

The difference between "a place in the country" and a farm is chiefly a matter of livestock. It is in New England, anyway. You can own 200 acres, you can pick your own apples, you can buy a small tractor—and you're still just a suburbanite with an unusually large lot. But put one cow in your pasture, raise a couple of sheep, even buy a pig, and instantly your place becomes a farm.

NOEL PERRIN, "Raising Sheep"

2.

Running is the sport of the people. If it is not the largest participant sport already in terms of numbers, it no doubt is in terms of time devoted to it. It requires little in the way of skills or money, and no particular body type or age or location. It doesn't discriminate. Even at competitive levels it thrives on friendship. Where has it been all this time?

ROBERT E. BURGER, *Jogger's Catalogue*

3.

Analysts have had their go at humor, and I have read some of this interpretive literature, but without being greatly instructed. Humor can be dissected, as a frog can, but the thing dies in the process and the innards are discouraging to any but the pure scientific mind.

E. B. WHITE, "Some Remarks on Humor"

4.

Opponents of day care will call for women to return to home and hearth, but the battle is really over. Now the question is: Will day care continue to be inadequately funded and poorly regulated, or will public policy begin to put into place a system that rightly treats children as our most valuable national resource?   MAXINE PHILLIPS

"Needed: A Policy for Children When Parents Go to Work"

5.

While most of the northern European immigrants who came to America prior to the Civil War were farmers, many city dwellers came to the new land as well. These newcomers were attracted to the bustling urban centers of the New World, and as a result, American cities expanded enormously. New York, for example, which had a population of only sixty thousand in 1800, grew to a city of more than one million people by 1860. As urban settlers moved west, they helped to change cities like St. Louis, Chicago, and Cincinnati from minor frontier outposts to major metropolitan centers. For a time St. Louis doubled its population every nine years; Cincinnati every seven years.

ALBERT ROBBINS, *Coming to the City*

The City of St. Louis, 1874. Color lithography by Parsons & Atwater.

Writing Is Thinking

Drawing Conclusions

Before you write a thesis statement, you should first draw conclusions about your subject. When you *draw a conclusion,* you make a reasoned judgment, based on all the information you have about the subject. That is, you reach a logical conclusion that accounts for all the facts you have gathered. The following chart shows, for example, how Robert MacNeil drew some conclusions about television in his essay "The Trouble with Television." Notice that the first conclusion became the thesis statement in his introductory paragraph.

INFORMATION
- Americans watch 20,000 hours of television by the age of twenty.
- Sleeping and eating are the only activities that consume more time.

CONCLUSIONS BASED ON THE INFORMATION
1. It is impossible to escape the influence of television.
2. Watching television is the primary leisure activity for many Americans.

Thinking Practice Analyze the information given below and write three possible conclusions you could draw from it.

SUBJECT the Louisiana Purchase of 1803

FACTS
- western territory of North America that belonged to France
- Napoleon unexpectedly offered it for sale
- purchase price was only $15 million
- Jefferson almost passed up the opportunity because he thought the Constitution did not give a president the right to buy territory
- purchase doubled the size of the United States
- provided valuable waterways and natural resources

WRITING ACTIVITY *Writing a Thesis Statement*

For each of the following subjects, write a thesis statement. Base each one on the ideas and information provided.

EXAMPLE:

SUBJECT global warming

IDEAS AND
INFORMATION
- leads to rise in sea level
- lengthens growing seasons in temperate zones
- contributes to spread of deserts
- changes rainfall patterns
- concentrates pollution in the atmosphere

POSSIBLE
ANSWER: Global warming could have dramatic effects on planet Earth.

1. SUBJECT Brasília

IDEAS AND
INFORMATION
- became capital of Brazil in 1960
- was built from scratch in Brazil's interior to open up the frontier to settlers
- has buildings with unique, modern design
- is a source of national pride
- is isolated from older cities on coast
- has problems: overpopulation, poverty

2. SUBJECT   savings accounts

IDEAS AND INFORMATION
- Anyone can open one by making a deposit.
- Each deposit is added to the balance.
- Deposits and withdrawals are recorded in a passbook.
- Banks pay interest on the balance.
- When interest is compounded daily, interest is paid on the interest and added to the balance.
- Banks may pay higher interest rates on an account that keeps a high minimum balance.

3. SUBJECT   the communications industry

IDEAS AND INFORMATION
- includes videotape recording, communications satellites, and computer links
- speeds up and improves communication
- recent breakthroughs: use of lasers and fiber optics
- new technology: cordless telephones and fax machines
- makes the world increasingly smaller

WRITING ACTIVITY ⑤ *Writing on Your Own*

WRITING ABOUT THE THEME

 On the basis of your prewriting work from Writing Activity 2, develop ideas for a thesis for your essay on television. Before you consider any possibilities, however, first see if you can draw some conclusions from your notes about the negative effects and the positive value of television. *(See Writing Is Thinking on page 223.)* For example, you might conclude that television plays a positive role in the education of young children or that network news is often biased.

After making a list of conclusions, choose one to be the main idea for your essay. The main idea you choose will be expressed in your thesis statement when you draft your introduction. Write your main idea in the form of a complete sentence. Then save all your notes in your writing folder.

Setting the Tone

Your *tone* in writing is like your tone of voice when you speak. That is, the way you express yourself reveals your attitudes—positive, negative, or neutral—toward a subject.

Writing Term   Set the **tone** of an essay by making your attitude toward your subject clear.

Your word choices and sentence constructions should make clear to readers what they should expect and how they should interpret what you say. Your tone could be personal or impersonal, serious or humorous, angry or sympathetic. Whatever tone you decide to set, it should suit your subject, purpose, and audience.

Writing Tip   Choose a tone that is appropriate for your subject, your writing purpose, and your audience.

In "Cat Lovers, Dog Lovers," for example, the tone is serious, persuasive, and enthusiastic. In contrast, the essay on "The Trouble with Television" has a negative, even angry, tone.

WRITING ACTIVITY ◆ **6** *Recognizing Tone*

Write two or more adjectives that describe the tone of the following introductory paragraph.

Industry blasted the ore out of the earth and Ontonagon developed under the settling dirt. The ore held out for ten years; then the blasting stopped. Production closed and big industry moved on, leaving behind a loading platform and four empty Northern Iron freight cars. The townspeople stayed on; they had nowhere to go or couldn't summon up the interest to leave. They opened five-and-dime stores, hardware, and live bait shops. Some worked in the paper mill by the tracks; others joined the logging crews.

KRISTEN KING BIBLER, "Ontonagon"

Capturing the Reader's Interest

You can capture your readers' interest in many ways. For example, in her introduction to "Cat Lovers, Dog Lovers," Gladys Taber uses two eye-catching quotations. In "The Trouble with Television," Robert MacNeil peppers his introduction with attention-getting statistics. Below are several strategies for starting an introduction.

Strategies for Capturing the Reader's Interest

1. Start with an interesting quotation.
2. Start with a question.
3. Present an unusual or little-known fact.
4. Present an idea or image that is unexpected.
5. Cite a statistic that is alarming or amusing.
6. Lead in with a line of dialogue from a conversation.
7. Give an example or illustration of the main idea.
8. Relate an incident or personal experience.

WRITING ACTIVITY *Analyzing Introductions*

Briefly explain how the following introduction captures the reader's interest.

> Merely as an observer of natural phenomena, I am fascinated by my own personal appearance. This does not mean that I am pleased with it, mind you, or that I can even tolerate it. I simply have a morbid interest in it.
>
> ROBERT BENCHLEY, "My Face"

WRITING ACTIVITY *Writing on Your Own*

WRITING ABOUT THE THEME   After checking the Functions of the Essay Introduction on page 219, draft the introductory paragraph of your essay about the value of television. When you are satisfied that your thesis statement clearly states your main idea, experiment with placing it at the beginning or the end of the introduction. Save the introduction you like best in your writing folder.

The Essay Body

Following the introduction, the body of an essay explains the thesis statement by developing the main idea in supporting paragraphs. An essay body, therefore, is much like the body of a paragraph.

Paragraph Body	Essay Body
The body consists of **sentences** that support the **topic sentence**.	The body consists of **paragraphs** that support the **thesis statement**.
All the sentences relate to the **main idea** expressed in the topic sentence.	All the paragraphs relate to the **main idea** expressed in the thesis statement. At the same time, each **paragraph** has a topic sentence, a body, and a conclusion of its own.
Each sentence develops a **supporting detail** that supports the main idea.	Each paragraph develops a **supporting idea** that supports the main idea. At the same time, each supporting idea contains **supporting details**.

Supporting Paragraphs

The information in the body of your essay may come from your own experience and observations or from research. Wherever it comes from, the information proves or supports your thesis by serving as the supporting paragraphs in the body of your essay.

Writing Tip Each paragraph in the **body of an essay** supports the thesis statement by developing an idea contained within it.

The topic sentence of each supporting paragraph supports the thesis statement of the essay. The sentences in each paragraph then develop that paragraph's topic sentence by giving supporting details. As you read the following model, notice how each paragraph of the body develops the main idea that is expressed in the thesis statement. Also notice how each paragraph has its own structure, with a topic sentence and a body of supporting sentences.

Student Model: *Supporting Paragraphs*

The Anza-Borrego Desert

INTRODUCTION

We approach the Anza-Borrego Desert in southern California from the west, driving through lush, velvety green mountains, forested and thriving with life. Suddenly, as we leave the mountains behind us, the landscape takes on the character of a planet long ago deserted of all life. In the Anza-Borrego Desert, every detail for miles around adds to the sense of desolation.

THESIS STATEMENT

TOPIC SENTENCE OF THE FIRST PARAGRAPH IN THE BODY

In such a setting, our eyes search in vain for a sign of the life we saw thriving on the other side of the mountains. The barren, sandy land is mostly flat, but craggy hills, worn into strange shapes by the wind-driven sand, lurch up from the desert floor in scattered patterns. Cacti contorted into menacing human shapes cast gray shadows over the sand and scraggly desert grasses. Colors are faded; the sand is a dull beige or a bleached-out white. Only the leathery green of the cacti and the blue of the cloudless sky serve as reminders that the bright colors of life even exist.

TOPIC SENTENCE OF THE SECOND PARAGRAPH IN THE BODY

Not only is the sight of the desert desolate, but sounds seem too weirdly nonexistent. There are no sounds of natural life, no calling birds or rustling leaves. There are also no sounds of human life, no whir of cars down the hot asphalt road that seems forgotten. So complete is the silence of the desolate area that we speak in the whispers of an unbelieving awe.

229

The body of this model can be presented in a simple outline that shows how the main idea of each paragraph supports the thesis statement of the whole essay.

THESIS STATEMENT   In the Anza-Borrego Desert, every detail for miles around added to a sense of desolation.

    I. Our eyes searched in vain for a sign of the life we saw thriving on the other side of the mountain.

    II. Not only did the sight of the desert seem desolate, but sounds too seemed weirdly nonexistent.

WRITING ACTIVITY 9 *Listing Supporting Ideas*

For each of the following thesis statements, list at least two supporting ideas that could be developed into two supporting paragraphs for the body of an essay. After you write each supporting idea, add at least two details you could use to develop that paragraph.

EXAMPLE   Hobbies can lead to money-making ventures.

POSSIBLE ANSWERS   I. Some hobbies produce salable goods.
Gardeners can sell their vegetables.
Knitters can sell their sweaters.
Jewelry makers can sell their creations.

    II. Some hobbies involve salable services.
Photographers can take pictures at weddings.
Musicians can perform at dances.
Mechanics can fix cars.

1. Going to the country [or city] is my idea of a perfect outing.
2. Holidays have important meanings in American life.
3. Everyone should have a hero—someone they can look up to and emulate.
4. The neighborhood I live in could stand some improvements.
5. Our state played a role in U.S. history.

Unity, Coherence, and Clarity

Like a paragraph, an essay should keep to the subject, read smoothly and logically from one idea to the next, and make sense to the reader. These three qualities of a composition are called unity, coherence, and clarity.

Unity   An essay has *unity* if none of the ideas wanders off the subject. Every sentence in each paragraph of the body should develop the main idea expressed in the paragraph's topic sentence. At the same time, every paragraph in the essay should develop the thesis statement. In the body of "The Anza-Borrego Desert" on page 229, for example, the paragraphs develop the details of sight and sound that are needed to support the thesis statement. The topic of the first supporting paragraph is the sights of the desert, and the topic of the second supporting paragraph is the sounds of the desert. The essay has unity because both of these paragraphs develop the thesis and neither paragraph contains any details that are not related to its topic sentence. That is, there is no paragraph about weather in the desert, and the paragraph about desert sounds does not contain details about desert colors. *(For more information about unity, see pages 109–110.)*

Coherence   An essay has *coherence* if the ideas follow in a logical order and if transitions are used to connect those ideas. In the body of "The Anza-Borrego Desert," for example, the first supporting paragraph describes only the sights that give the impression that the desert lacks signs of life, while the second supporting paragraph describes only the sounds that give that impression. Transitional words and phrases connect all the supporting details within each paragraph. At the same time, a transition between the two supporting paragraphs is provided by the sentence that begins, "Not only is the sight of the desert desolate, but also . . . " If the essay mixed up the sights and sounds and lacked transition between the paragraphs, then it would not have coherence. *(For more information about coherence, see page 111.)*

Clarity An essay has *clarity* if the meaning of the paragraphs, sentences, and words is clear. One way you can achieve clarity is by writing sentences that are not wordy or rambling. You can also add clarity to your paragraphs by making sure they are adequately developed. Using specific words and precise images also helps you make your writing clear. In the introduction of "The Anza-Borrego Desert," the writer's negative attitude toward the unfamiliar desert is clear. In the body, crisp sentences and specific details make the meaning clear. For example, in the sentence "There are no sounds of natural life, no calling birds or rustling leaves," the meaning of "sounds of natural life" is made clear by adding specific examples of those sounds. *(For more information about clarity and adequate development, see pages 108 and 276.)*

WRITING ACTIVITY *Analyzing the Body of an Essay*

Reread the introduction and the body of the essay "Cat Lovers, Dog Lovers" on pages 217–218. Then develop an outline that shows the relationships between the thesis statement and the supporting paragraphs. Follow the model of an outline on page 230. When you have finished, think about how your outline illustrates the unity and coherence of the essay.

WRITING ACTIVITY *Writing on Your Own*

WRITING ABOUT THE THEME Review all your prewriting notes about the positive or negative value of television and reread the introductory paragraph that you wrote in Writing Activity 8. List all the ideas you will use to support your thesis statement. Then, under each idea, group all the details that you will use to support it.

As you work, arrange your notes in a simple outline like the one on page 230. Then, using your outline as a guide, write the body of your essay by developing each group of supporting ideas and details into a separate paragraph. As you write, remember that each paragraph should have its own topic sentence. Save your draft in your writing folder.

The Essay Conclusion

In the conclusion of an essay, you should summarize your supporting ideas and recall the main idea that is expressed in your thesis statement. As in the conclusion of a paragraph, you may also want to add an insight in the concluding paragraph of an essay. This concluding paragraph may be long or short, but it should end with a memorable sentence—the *clincher*. As the last sentence in your essay, the clincher sentence should leave as strong an impression as does the opening line of your introduction.

Writing Tip   The **concluding paragraph** completes the essay and reinforces the main idea.

The paragraph starting on the next page is the conclusion to the model essay about the Anza-Borrego Desert. Notice how it reinforces the main idea stated in the introduction: "In the Anza-Borrego Desert, every detail for miles around adds to the sense of desolation."

Model: *Conclusion*

As if to make up for the emptiness all around, our imaginations fill with fears and threats. What seems to be the hiss of some venomous snake turns out to be the gentle fizz of the just-opened soft drink. What we thought was a permanently ruined car that would leave us stranded forever has cooled down and starts up easily. Not until we cross the mountains once again do our thoughts turn from snakes and sunstrokes to the everyday worries of ordinary life.

The clincher sentence in this paragraph captures the reader's attention by referring to snakes and sunstrokes. These references leave a memorable impression because readers can imagine the relief the travelers must have felt as they drove out of the desert.

WRITING ACTIVITY *Analyzing a Conclusion*

The following concluding paragraph is from "We'll Never Conquer Space," an essay about the limits of space travel. Read the concluding paragraph. Then answer the questions that follow it.

When you are next outdoors on a summer night, turn your head toward the zenith. Almost vertically above you will be shining the brightest star of the northern skies— Vega of the Lyre. It is twenty-six years away at the speed of light, near enough the point of no return for us short-lived creatures. Past this blue-white beacon, fifty times as brilliant as our sun, we may send our minds and bodies, but never our hearts. For no people will ever turn homewards from beyond Vega, to greet again those they knew and loved.   ARTHUR C. CLARKE
"We'll Never Conquer Space"

1. Arthur Clarke's concluding paragraph reinforces the main idea of his essay. What is the main idea?
2. The clincher sentence in Arthur Clarke's concluding paragraph leaves a lasting impression in the reader's mind. What image does the clincher sentence create?

WRITING ACTIVITY *Writing a Clincher Sentence*

Write a clincher for the following concluding paragraph.

> Despite their fearsome looks and formidable sting, mud wasps are gentle creatures. Their lives are devoted to collecting balls of wet earth for their intricate constructions. You can observe them at work whenever the hot sun begins to bake a rain puddle. While gathering mud, a wasp will barely notice an observer. Tread carefully, however.

WRITING ACTIVITY *Writing on Your Own*

WRITING
ABOUT THE
THEME

Add a strong conclusion to the introduction and body that you wrote in Writing Activities 8 and 11 for your essay about the value of television. As you write the conclusion, remember to refer back to your main idea and to add a good clincher sentence at the end. Also add a title. No essay is complete without one. *(For more information about writing a title, see page 31.)*

Before you write a final copy of your essay, check that the introduction, body, and conclusion have unity, coherence, and clarity. Then refer to the Revision Checklist on page 32 to revise your writing further. When you are pleased with your work, place your revision in your writing folder.

Language Integrating Skills

Editing and Publishing

Grammar in the Writing Process

In "The Trouble with Television," Robert MacNeil says he believes that television corrupts the way people think and express themselves.

> Consider the casual assumptions that television tends to culti-vate: that complexity must be avoided, that visual stimulation is a substitute for thought, that verbal precision is an anachronism. It may be old-fashioned, but I was taught that thought is words, arranged in grammatically precise ways.

Most high school teachers, college professors, and employers would probably agree with the author about communicating "in grammatically precise ways." Resources in this textbook that will help you write with grammatical precision include "A Writ-er's Glossary of Usage," which begins on page 786. In this glos-sary you will find a list of commonly made writing errors, arranged alphabetically. Following are a few examples of what you will find. As you study the examples, you will notice expressions that are referred to as standard or nonstandard. In formal communication, such as in writing an essay, you should choose standard English usage and avoid nonstandard usages. *(For more information on standard and nonstandard English, see page 786. For other glossary entries and practice in writing them correctly, see pages 786–797.)*

among, between *Among* is used when referring to three or more people or things. *Between* is used when referring to two people or things.

AMONG   Jean and her friends discussed the TV show **among** themselves.

BETWEEN   **Between** TV and radio, I prefer TV for getting the news.

double negative Words such as *but* (when it means "only"), *hardly, never, no, none, no one, nobody, not* (and its contraction *n't*), *nothing, nowhere, only, barely,* and *scarcely* are all negatives. Do not use two negatives to express one negative meaning.

NONSTANDARD	I do**n't hardly** know why I watch so much TV.
STANDARD	I do**n't** know why I watch so much TV.
STANDARD	I **hardly** know why I watch so much TV.

fewer, less *Fewer* is plural and refers to things that can be counted. *Less* is singular and refers to quantities and qualities that cannot be counted.

FEWER	This fall TV had **fewer** new programs.
LESS	I watched **less** television this month than last month.

Editing Checklist

1. Is your composition written in standard English? *(See page 786.)*
2. Have you checked your writing using "A Writer's Glossary of Usage"? *(See pages 786–797.)*

WRITING ACTIVITY ⑮ *Writing on Your Own*

WRITING
ABOUT THE
THEME

Editing Use the Editing Checklist on page 37 as a guide to editing your essay about the value of television. You may find it helpful to go over your paper several times—each time looking for a different kind of error. Then turn in your textbook to "A Writer's Glossary of Usage" on page 786 and skim through the items. When you see any words you used in your essay, check them against the glossary entries to make sure that you have written them with grammatical precision.

Publishing With your teacher's permission, exchange essays with classmates and comment on each other's work. Are others' views about the negative effects or positive value of television the same as yours or different?

237

A Writer Writes

A Proposal to Solve a Problem

PURPOSE: to describe a new television program and explain
its value

AUDIENCE: television executives

Prewriting   What kind of shows would you create for television if you had the opportunity? What clever new ideas could you propose for making television better than it is now? Imagine that you have been hired as a program director at one of the network television companies. Because there has been so much criticism in recent years about the emptiness and lack of value of TV shows, you have been asked to come up with ideas for a new program.

Use freewriting and brainstorming to think of a program that would be worthwhile but would still hold the interest of the viewers. Looking through your recent journal entries about television programming may give you some ideas.

Peer Conferencing: With your teacher's permission, meet in small groups and discuss the ideas you generated by freewriting and brainstorming. As you share ideas, try to anticipate any reasons people may have for not liking your new programs. At the end of the discussion, use your notes to outline an essay in which you present ideas for one new program that would help solve the problems for which network television has been criticized.

Drafting   Use your outline to draft a problem-solving essay in which you describe your program and explain why it would be worthwhile. Remember to include your thesis statement in your introductory paragraph. When you are ready to write your concluding paragraph, summarize your supporting ideas and end with a clincher sentence.

Revising   Revise your essay, using the Revision Checklist on page 32 as a guide. Add, delete, substitute, or rearrange any words or examples that will improve your essay.

Editing   Using the Editing Checklists on pages 37 and 237, edit your essay and then write a final copy.

Publishing   Write a cover letter to go with your essay and send it to the Programming Department of one of the national or cable networks. Ask the librarian to help you find the address.

WRITING
ABOUT THE
THEME   **Independent Writing**

Write an essay about some aspect of animated cartoon serials on television. For example, what makes some better than others? How are they produced? What role do they play in the lives of children and youths? What ones have you enjoyed and why? Use brainstorming and clustering to develop ideas for an essay subject. Then choose one subject and follow the checklist for Writing Effective Essays on page 241.

Creative Writing

Write a script for a television documentary about your school or another subject of your choice that would interest members of your community. In addition to writing the narrative or dialogue, include a brief description of each scene that would appear on camera and the sounds that would be heard. For example, one of your scenes may show students at basketball practice. Viewers would see the action, listen to a narrator comment about the scene, and hear sounds in the background of the basketball bouncing and hitting the basket. Form a production team to help plan the details of your documentary and—if possible—produce it, using a portable video camera from home, school, or your local cable television station. If possible, air your documentary on closed-circuit television or a video-cassette player.

  ## Writing about Literature

An *anachronism* is a device often used in literature to refer to anything that seems to be out of its proper place in history—either outdated or before its time. For example, the mention of a computer in a story about Robin Hood would be an anachronism. How does Robert MacNeil use the term *anachronism* in "The Trouble with Television"? Write a paragraph in which you answer this question and add fresh examples of anachronisms that you have read or invented.

  ## Writing in Other Subject Areas

History   Write an essay on one of the following subjects or a similar one of your choice. Use reference materials or periodicals in the library to find the information you need.

1. how the astrolabe helped navigators in the 1400's
2. how the invention of the cannon changed warfare
3. how the first refrigerator was invented
4. how radium was discovered
5. how automatic teller machines have changed banking
6. how the invention of the zipper changed clothing styles

6 Checklist

Writing Effective Essays

Prewriting

✔ List possible subjects and choose one. *(See pages 10–14.)*
✔ After you consider your purpose and audience, limit and focus your subject. *(See pages 15–17.)*
✔ Make a list of supporting details. *(See pages 18–23.)*
✔ Organize your details into a simple outline. *(See page 230.)*

Drafting

✔ Write a thesis statement. *(See pages 220–221.)*
✔ Draft an introduction that includes your thesis statement and captures the reader's interest. *(See pages 219–227.)*
✔ Using your outline as a guide, draft the paragraphs for the body of your essay. *(See pages 228–230.)*
✔ Use transitions to connect your supporting paragraphs. *(See page 111.)*
✔ Add a concluding paragraph. *(See pages 233–234.)*
✔ Add a title. *(See page 31.)*

Revising

✔ Check your essay for unity, coherence, and clarity. *(See pages 231–232.)*
✔ Check your paragraphs for adequate development. *(See page 108.)*
✔ Check your paragraphs for varied sentences and vivid, precise words. *(See pages 71–73 and 59–65.)*

Editing and Publishing

✔ Using the Editing Checklist on page 37 and the proofreading symbols on page 38, correct any errors in grammar, spelling, and mechanics.
✔ Publish your polished final draft. *(See pages 41–43.)*

Unit 2
Achieving the Writer's Purpose

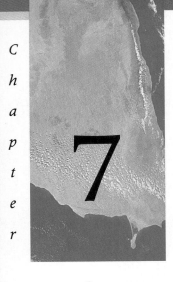

7 Writing Essays to Inform

Part 1 *Reading to Write*

THEME: *Space*

Can you answer the following questions about the American space program? Take out a sheet of paper and a pencil and answer as many questions as you can.

1. Who was the first American astronaut to orbit the earth?
2. In what year did an astronaut first walk on the moon?
3. What was the name of the first American space station?
4. In what year was the space shuttle first used?
5. What is the name of the first American woman astronaut to travel in space?

How many answers did you know? Does learning about space and space travel excite your imagination? Sally Ride, the first American woman astronaut to travel on a space shuttle, believes that traveling through space is a truly extraordinary experience. In her essay, "Single Room, Earth View," she describes what it was like orbiting Earth, and she concludes that viewing Earth from space is completely different from any earthbound experience. As your read Sally Ride's account, imagine yourself looking down on Earth from a 200-mile vantage point.

from

Single Room, Earth View

S a l l y   R i d e

Everyone I've met has a glittering, if vague, mental image of space travel. And naturally enough, people want to hear about it from an astronaut: "How did it feel . . . ?" "What did it look like . . . ?" "Were you scared?" Sometimes, the questions come from reporters, their pens poised and their tape recorders silently reeling in the words; sometimes, it's wide-eyed, ten-year-old girls who want answers. I find a way to answer all of them, but it's not easy.

Imagine trying to describe an airplane ride to someone who has never flown. An articulate traveler could describe the sights but would find it much harder to explain the difference in perspective provided by the new view from a greater distance, along with the feelings, impressions, and insights that go with the new perspective. And the difference is enormous: Space flight moves the traveler another giant step farther away. Eight and one-half thunderous minutes after launch, an astronaut is orbiting high above the Earth, suddenly able to watch typhoons form, volcanoes smolder, and meteors streak through the atmosphere below.

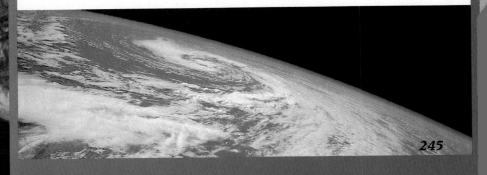

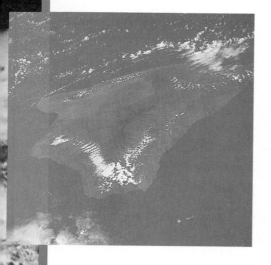

While flying over the Hawaiian Islands, several astronauts have marveled that the islands look just as they do on a map. When people first hear that, they wonder what should be so surprising about Hawaii looking the way it does in the atlas. Yet, to the astronauts it is an absolutely startling sensation: The islands really *do* look as if that part of the world has been carpeted with a big page torn out of Rand-McNally,[1] and all we can do is try to convey the surreal quality of that scene.

In orbit, racing along at five miles per second, the space shuttle circles the Earth once every 90 minutes. I found that at this speed, unless I kept my nose pressed to the window, it was almost impossible to keep track of where we were at any given moment—the world below simply changes too fast. If I turned my concentration away for too long, even just to change film in a camera, I could miss an entire land mass. It's embarrassing to float up to a window, glance outside, and then have to ask a crewmate, "What continent is this?"

We could see smoke rising from fires that dotted the entire east coast of Africa, and in the same orbit only moments later, ice floes jostling for position in the Antarctic. We could see the Ganges River dumping its murky, sediment-laden water into the Indian Ocean and watch ominous hurricane clouds expanding and rising like biscuits in the oven of the Caribbean.

Mountain ranges, volcanoes, and river deltas appeared in salt-and-flour relief, all leading me to assume the role of a novice geologist. In such moments, it was easy to imagine the dynamic upheavals that created jutting mountain ranges and the internal wrenchings that created rifts and seas. I also became an instant believer in plate tectonics;[2] India really *is* crashing

1. **Rand-McNally:** An atlas.
2. **plate tectonics:** Movements and collisions of pieces of the earth's crust.

into Asia, and Saudi Arabia and Egypt really *are* pulling apart, making the Red Sea wider. Even though their respective motion is really no more than mere inches a year, the view from overhead makes theory come alive . . .

From space shuttle height, we can't see the entire globe at a glance, but we can look down the entire boot of Italy, or up the East Coast of the United States from Cape Hatteras to Cape Cod. The panoramic view inspires an appreciation for the scale of some of nature's phenomena. One day, as I scanned the sandy expanse of Northern Africa. I couldn't find any of the familiar landmarks—colorful outcroppings of rock in Chad, irrigated patches of the Sahara. Then I realized they were obscured by a huge dust storm, a cloud of sand that enveloped the continent from Morocco to the Sudan.

Since the space shuttle flies fairly low (at least by orbital standards; it's more than 22,000 miles lower than a typical TV satellite), we can make out both natural and manmade features in surprising detail. Familiar geographical features like San Francisco Bay, Long Island, and Lake Michigan are easy to recognize, as are many cities, bridges, and airports. The Great Wall of China is *not* the only manmade object visible from space.

The signatures of civilization are usually seen in straight lines (bridges or runways) or sharp delineations (abrupt transitions from desert to irrigated land, as in California's Imperial Valley). A modern city like New York doesn't leap from the canvas of its surroundings, but its straight piers and concrete runways catch the eye—and around them, the city materializes. I found Salina, Kansas (and pleased my in-laws, who live there) by spotting its long runway amid the wheat fields near the city. Over Florida, I could see the launch pad where we had begun our trip, and the landing strip, where we would eventually land.

Some of civilization's more unfortunate effects on the environment are also evident from orbit. Oil slicks glisten on the surface of the Persian Gulf, patches of pollution-damaged trees dot the forests of central Europe. Some cities look out of focus, and their colors muted, when viewed through a pollutant haze.

Not surprisingly, the effects are more noticeable now than they were a decade ago. An astronaut who has flown in both Skylab and the space shuttle reported that the horizon didn't seem quite as sharp, or the colors quite as bright, in 1983 as they had in 1973.

Of course, informal observations by individual astronauts are one thing, but more precise measurements are continually being made from space: The space shuttle has carried infrared film to document damage to citrus trees in Florida and in rain forests along the Amazon. It has carried even more sophisticated sensors in the payload bay. Here is one example: sensors used to measure atmospheric carbon monoxide levels, allowing scientists to study the environmental effects of city emissions and land-clearing fires.

Most of the Earth's surface is covered with water, and at first glance it all looks the same: blue. But with the right lighting conditions and a couple of orbits of practice, it's possible to make out the intricate patterns in the oceans—eddies and spirals become visible because of the subtle differences in water color or reflectivity.

Observations and photographs by astronauts have contributed significantly to the understanding of ocean dynamics, and some of the intriguing discoveries prompted the National Aeronautics and Space Administration to fly an oceanographic observer for the express purpose of studying the ocean from orbit. Scientists' understanding of the energy balance in the oceans has increased significantly as a result of the discoveries of circular eddies tens of kilometers in diameter, of standing waves hundreds of kilometers long, and of spiral eddies that sometimes trail into one another for thousands of kilometers . . .

Believe it or not, an astronaut can also see the wakes of large ships and the contrails[3] of airplanes. The sun angle has to be just right, but when the lighting conditions are perfect, you can follow otherwise invisible oil tankers on the Persian Gulf and trace major shipping lanes through the Mediterranean Sea.

---

3. **contrails:** Visible trails of water vapor that form in the wake of aircraft.

Similarly, when atmospheric conditions allow contrail formation, the thousand-mile-long condensation trails let astronauts
trace the major air routes across the northern Pacific Ocean.

Part of every orbit takes us to the dark side of the planet. In
space, night is very, very black—but that doesn't mean there's
nothing to look at. The lights of cities sparkle; on nights when
there was no moon, it was difficult for me to tell the Earth from
the sky—the twinkling lights could be stars or they could be
small cities. On one nighttime pass from Cuba to Nova Scotia,
the entire East Coast of the United States appeared in twinkling
outline . . .

Of all the sights from orbit, the most spectacular may be the
magnificent displays of lightning that ignite the clouds at night.
On Earth, we see lightning from below the clouds: in orbit, we
see it from above. Bolts of lightning are diffused by the clouds
into bursting balls of light. Sometimes, when a storm extends
hundreds of miles, it looks like a transcontinental brigade is
tossing fireworks from cloud to cloud.

As the shuttle races the sun around the Earth, we pass from
day to night and back again during a single orbit—hurtling into
darkness, then bursting into daylight. The sun's appearance
unleashes spectacular blue and orange bands along the horizon,
a clockwork miracle that astronauts witness every 90 minutes.
But, I really can't describe a sunrise in orbit. The drama set
against the black backdrop of space and the magic of the materializing colors can't be captured in an astronomer's equations
or an astronaut's photographs.

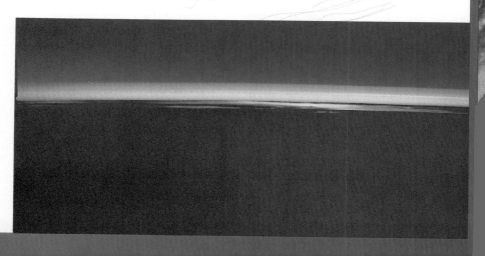

I once heard someone (not an astronaut) suggest that it's possible to imagine what space flight is like by simply extrapolating[4] from the sensations you experience on an airplane. All you have to do, he said, is mentally raise the airplane 200 miles, mentally eliminate the air noise and the turbulence, and you get an accurate mental picture of a trip in the space shuttle.

Not true. And while it's natural to try to liken space flight to familiar experiences, it can't be brought "down to Earth"—not in the final sense. The environment is different, the perspective is different. Part of the fascination with space travel is the element of the unknown—the conviction that it's different from earthbound experiences. And it is. ◆

4. **extrapolating:** Estimating or inferring the unknown, based on the known.

space

E v a n g e l i n a   V i g i l - P i ñ ó n

privacy that no one owns
a silent moment
outdoors, in the city
the shade of a tree at a park
a vacant table at a library
your own office window with your own view
beaches and sea
body-free
your own breath of air
an expansive horizon
viewed by many
but singularly

Responding to the Theme

Space

Responding in Your Journal   In your journal this week, explore your ideas about space, space travel, and the American space program. How has the space program affected your life? What, do you think, is the value of knowing about the history of the space program and the adventures of astronauts like Neil Armstrong and John Glenn? In addition, write about your impressions of space. What fascinates you most about the universe beyond Earth? What one place in space would you most like to visit?

Speaking and Listening   Imagine that you and a classmate have been assigned to interview Sally Ride on a television talk show. What would you like to know about her experience that she does not explain in her essay? With your teacher's permission, work with your partner to prepare an in-depth interview. After you develop at least ten main questions, conduct an interview by taking turns playing the roles of Sally Ride and a talk show host.

Critical Thinking: Comparing   In "Single Room, Earth View," Sally Ride describes her view of Earth from space. In her poem "space," Evangelina Vigil-Piñón describes a similar experience on a smaller scale. Compare these two different meanings of space and then compare the specific images and ideas in the poem with those in the essay. Write a brief explanation of how the two experiences of "space" are different and how they are alike.

Extending Your Vocabulary   Each of the following words from "Single Room, Earth View" has a root word on which the rest of the word is based. For example, the root word in *singularity* is *single*. As you might expect, all the words based on *single* have meanings that relate to the idea of oneness. Using a dictionary, write each root word and its basic meaning. Then write one other example of a word that is based on that root.

aeronautics	emissions	signatures
civilization	indivisibility	surreal

Part 2 *Writing*

In her essay Sally Ride answers the following questions that readers commonly ask about the experience of space travel.

- What does Earth look like from space?
- What does the view from space show about Earth's weather?
- Can signs of civilization be seen from space?

Anticipating readers' questions is a key to writing an *expository essay*—an essay that explains or informs.

Writing Term An **expository essay** explains or informs.

In her essay Sally Ride uses several different types of writing. For example, she uses *narrative writing* to explain the shuttle's speed: "I found that at this speed . . . it was almost impossible to keep track of where we were at any given moment." She uses *descriptive writing* to explain what the earth looks like from space: "From space shuttle height, we . . . can look down the entire boot of Italy."

In expository essays you can use narrative writing and descriptive writing. *(See pages 173–192.)* You can also use *classification* and *evaluating. (See pages 138–140 and 261.)*

Prewriting

The prewriting stage of the writing process helps you discover possible subjects for an expository essay, develop your ideas, and shape those ideas into an organized plan for an essay. Planning and writing an expository essay on a subject that interests you can lead you to new knowledge and understanding.

Discovering and Choosing a Subject

Subjects for expository essays may come from your own interests and knowledge or from your reading or research. The first step in discovering subjects for expository essays is to identify those subjects you already know about from your own experiences. For example, in school you may have learned about metrics well enough to explain the metric system. In a hobby or job, you may have learned enough about various dances, weaving, model trains, or pigeons to write about them in an essay to inform.

Strategies for Finding Subjects for Essays to Inform

1. Brainstorm or freewrite to list subjects you know well enough to explain.
2. Ask yourself questions about your interests and skills.
3. Review your journal entries to find possible subjects that are suitable for explaining or informing.
4. Skim books, newspapers, or magazines for subjects that interest you.
5. Read your notes from courses in other subject areas to find possible subjects.
6. View television programs that explain or inform—such as documentaries or educational programs—to discover subjects that you would like to explore in writing.

After you think of a number of possible subjects, the next step is to choose one. Choose a subject that you know enough about to explain or can learn about through reading or research.

The subject you choose should also be one that you will enjoy writing about and that your audience will enjoy reading about.

Determining Your Audience

Sometimes your choice of a subject will depend in part on who will be reading your essay. A classmate, a teacher, and a yearbook editor, for example, may prefer to read about quite different subjects. At other times, however, you will be able to choose both your subject and the audience you wish to write for. For example, you may decide to write an essay about synthesizers for an audience of musicians and others who are interested in electronic keyboards.

Whether you choose a subject to suit your audience or choose an audience for the subject you want to write about, you will need to take the interests, knowledge, opinions, and needs of your audience into account. *(For more information about analyzing an audience, see pages 16–17.)*

WRITING ACTIVITY ◆ **1** *Writing on Your Own*

WRITING ABOUT THE THEME Review your journal entries about space and the American space program and list ten possible subjects for an expository essay. You could, for example, write about an astronaut, a particular spacecraft or spaceflight, a first in the space program, a benefit of space technology, a space-related industry or agency—such as NASA—or a theory about matter in space or space itself. After listing possible subjects, choose the best one. Then write a brief explanation of why you think that subject is a good one and what audience you would write for. Save your work in your writing folder for later use.

Limiting and Focusing a Subject

Many expository subjects—like the subject of space exploration—may be too broad to be developed adequately in a short essay. After you choose a subject, therefore, you usually need to narrow, or limit, it. To limit a subject, think of specific aspects or examples of it. If your new subjects are still too broad, continue the process of limiting by thinking of specific aspects or examples of your narrower subjects. The model below shows how a writer might limit the subject of space exploration to arrive at subjects suitable for a short essay.

Model: *Limiting a Subject*

Subject   space exploration

LIMITED SUBJECTS	MORE LIMITED SUBJECTS
early spaceflights	moon probes
firsts in space	first moon landing
Soviet achievements	*Sputnik*
spaceflight projects	*Skylab*
space encounters	*Vega's* encounter with Halley's Comet

After you have limited a subject, your next step is to find a focus for your thoughts. One way to find a focus is to make a preliminary survey of your subject by reading about it in a reference book. Another way is to brainstorm general questions you could ask about the subject, based on what you know about it. For example, if you chose moon probes as your limited subject, you might decide to focus on the adventures of *Surveyor I* as an example of an early moon probe, or you might focus on the question of what new facts scientists learned from moon probes before the astronauts' first moon landing.

Strategies for Focusing a Subject

1. Focus on a specific event or incident.
2. Focus on a specific time and place.
3. Focus on one example that best represents your subject.
4. Focus on one person or group that represents your subject.

The example on the next page shows how a limited subject may have more than one possible focus.

LIMITED SUBJECT   *Sputnik*

POSSIBLE
SUBJECT FOCUSES
- how *Sputnik* started a space race between the U.S. and the U.S.S.R.
- the story of Laika, first dog in space on *Sputnik II*
- the effect of *Sputnik* on education in the United States
- how *Sputnik II* differed from *Lunik I*— the first missile to reach the moon
- why putting an object into orbit for the first time was so difficult

WRITING ACTIVITY *Limiting and Focusing a Subject*

Limit each of the following general subjects. Then write two phrases that could serve as a focus for each limited subject.

1. astronomy
2. planets
3. weather

4. space movies
5. geography

WRITING ACTIVITY ❸ *Writing on Your Own*

WRITING
ABOUT THE
THEME

Review the subject you chose in Writing Activity 1 for your expository essay about space. Then make a list of limited subjects. Continue to limit your subjects until each one is narrow enough to be developed adequately in a short essay. Use reference materials, if necessary, to find ideas. After you choose one limited subject, think of ways to focus it. Then save your list of focused subjects in your writing folder.

Gathering Information

Once you have a focused subject, you should then gather more information that will help you explain it clearly to your reader in an essay of three or more paragraphs. Use brainstorming, freewriting, clustering, inquiring, or researching to explore your subject and find details that will help you to inform others about it. *(For more information about gathering information, see pages 368–372.)*

Collect as much information as possible so that you will be able to choose the details that will best explain your subject. Your list may include any of the types of details shown in the box below. Remember that the type of detail often indicates the best method of development for your paragraphs. *(For more information about methods of development in expository writing, see pages 138–140.)*

Types of Details Used in Expository Essays		
facts and examples	analogies	similarities
reasons	incidents	differences
steps in a process	definitions	causes and effects

The prewriting notes on the next page, for example, list facts and examples for an essay about firsts in space exploration. As you read the notes, notice that the information is not yet arranged in any logical order.

Student Model: *Gathering Information*

SUBJECT
FOCUS
firsts in space exploration

FACTS AND
EXAMPLES
AS DETAILS

- 1983—first U.S. woman in space (Sally Ride)
- Alan Shepard first American in space—1962
- 1969—first manned moon landing (U.S.)
- June 1965—first American space walk
- first space walk (U.S.S.R., March 1965)
- Yuri Gagarin first Soviet in space—1961
- 1963—first Soviet woman in space
- *Explorer I*—first U.S. satellite (1958)
- *Sputnik*—first satellite (U.S.S.R., 1957)

WRITING ACTIVITY *Identifying Types of Details*

Each sentence is from a paragraph in Sally Ride's essay. Use the chart on page 257 to identify the type of details used.

1. Sometimes, when a [lightning] storm extends hundreds of miles, it looks like a transcontinental brigade is tossing fireworks from cloud to cloud.
2. It was almost impossible to keep track of where we were at any given moment—the world below simply changes too fast.
3. I also became an instant believer in plate tectonics; India really *is* crashing into Asia, and Saudi Arabia and Egypt really *are* pulling apart, making the Red Sea wider.

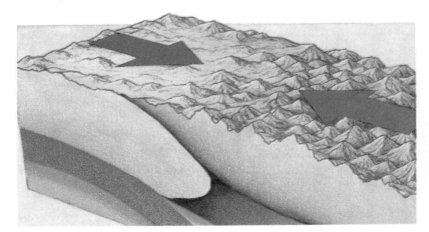

4. While flying over the Hawaiian Islands, several astronauts have marveled that the islands look just as they do on a map.

5. Some cities look out of focus, and their colors muted, when viewed through a pollutant haze.

WRITING ACTIVITY *Writing on Your Own*

WRITING
ABOUT THE
THEME
Review your work from Writing Activity 3. After you choose one focus for your subject, gather information for your essay. Save your work for later use.

Developing a Working Thesis

As you gather information, a main idea for your essay will begin to emerge. At this point you should express this emerging main idea as a *working thesis*—a preliminary statement of what you think the main idea will be. For example, as you look over the details on page 258 about firsts in space exploration, you see that the United States achieved many firsts. Therefore, you could write the working thesis below.

WORKING THESIS   The United States achieved many firsts in the development of its space program.

This working thesis would guide you in selecting information to use in your essay. That is, you would select details from the list only about firsts in the United States space program. You would not, however, use the information that refers to the Soviet space program. If you wanted to include information about achievements in space by both the United States and the Soviet Union, you could broaden your working thesis.

WORKING THESIS   The United States and the Soviet Union both achieved firsts in space exploration.

As you can see, a list of details can lead to several different theses. As you gather and think about information, you may wish to modify your working thesis. You may find the following steps helpful in developing a working thesis.

Steps for Developing a Working Thesis

1. Look over the information you have gathered.
2. Express the main idea you plan to convey.
3. Select the details you will use to support your main idea.
4. Check that the working thesis takes into account *all* of the information you selected to include in your essay.

WRITING ACTIVITY *Developing a Working Thesis*

Study the following information and cross out any items that would not help you to explain the focused subject. Then use the remaining items to develop a working thesis for an essay.

SUBJECT   the effects of *Sputnik* on education in the U.S.

INFORMATION
- *Sputnik*—first artificial satellite, launched by Soviets in 1957
- caused Americans to worry that the Soviets were more advanced in science education
- $4 billion spent on rocket research in 1958
- news media reported "crisis in education"
- 1958—United States launches *Pioneer 1*
- Congress voted National Defense Education Act in 1958
- government spent $1 billion to teach science in the schools
- NASA established in 1958

WRITING ACTIVITY *Writing on Your Own*

WRITING ABOUT THE THEME Review the list of information that you gathered in Writing Activity 5. After you have developed a working thesis, select the relevant ideas and details from your list that best support it. Then, if necessary, find more information or discard information that does not relate to your thesis. *(See Writing Is Thinking on page 261.)* Save your list of supporting details.

Writing Is Thinking   **Critical Thinking**

Evaluating Information for Relevance

To decide which ideas and details to include in an essay, evaluate the information for *relevance* by asking yourself the following questions: Is it appropriate for my purpose in writing? Does it relate directly to my working thesis? Will it help me support or prove my thesis? Study the following prewriting notes. Which ideas and information, do you think, lack relevance to the given thesis?

THESIS STATEMENT	The chambered shell of the nautilus has long fascinated marine biologists.
1. SUPPORTING IDEA	The nautilus is a marine mollusk.
DETAILS	• soft-shelled sea animal • lives in warm waters of South Pacific
2. SUPPORTING IDEA	The nautilus grows a unique shell with many chambers.
DETAILS	• adds chambers to shell as it grows • moves into new chamber and closes off the old one, leaving airtight cavity
3. SUPPORTING IDEA DETAILS	Fascinating features of nautilus • eye works like a pin-hole camera • swims by siphoning water
4. SUPPORTING IDEA	Oliver Wendell Holmes was inspired to write a poem about the nautilus.

The first idea and its details are relevant because they describe the subject. The second idea and details are also clearly relevant because they are about the shell of the nautilus. The third and fourth ideas, however, are not directly relevant.

Thinking Practice   Explain why items 3 and 4 on the outline are not directly relevant. Then refine the thesis statement to make these items relevant to an essay about the nautilus.

Organizing an Essay

In planning an expository essay, you will usually be handling a great deal of information, so you will have to organize the information by developing an outline. Before you start an outline, you should group your information into categories and then arrange those categories in a logical order.

Grouping Information into Categories A *category* is a group, or class, of related pieces of information. In the list of firsts in space exploration on page 258, for instance, the information could be grouped into two categories: the United States space program and the Soviet space program.

To group information, write your categories at the top of a sheet of paper and beneath each category, list the information that belongs. Use the thinking skill of classifying to help you create categories. *(See Writing Is Thinking on page 26.)* The following examples show how Sally Ride might have categorized some of the information in her essay, "Single Room, Earth View."

CATEGORY 1   CATEGORY 2

Geography seen from space   *Signs of Civilization*

1. Antarctic ice floes   1. Great Wall of China

2. Ganges River   2. irrigated land

3. Caribbean Sea   3. airports

4. mountain ranges   4. fires in Africa

5. "boot" of Italy   5. oil slicks

6. Sahara Desert   6. city lights at night

WRITING ACTIVITY *Creating Categories*

Study the following groups of details from "Single Room, Earth View" to determine what they have in common. Then write a word or phrase that creates a specific category name for each group.

1. space shuttle
   Skylab
   satellite
   planetary probe

3. plate tectonics
   ocean dynamics
   volcanic activity
   desertification

2. reflectivity
   infrared
   ultraviolet
   color

4. atlas map
   star chart
   photograph
   computer image

WRITING ACTIVITY *Grouping Details*

Using the essay "Single Room, Earth View" by Sally Ride as a guide, group the following list of details under each of the three categories.

1. Instruments for precise observations and measurement
2. Ocean dynamics viewed from space
3. Evidence of transportation systems seen from space

contrails
carbon monoxide sensors
spiral eddies
bridges

infrared film
standing waves
ships' wakes
runways

WRITING ACTIVITY *Writing on Your Own*

WRITING
ABOUT THE
THEME Organize the list of details that you selected in Writing Activity 7 for your expository essay about space. First group related details together. Then develop categories and arrange your groups of details under those categories. These groupings of ideas and information will later form the supporting paragraphs of your essay. Save your work.

Arranging Categories in Logical Order   Once you have grouped your information into categories, you should then arrange those categories in the order in which you want to include them in your essay. The following chart lists some commonly used types of logical order. The examples show how Sally Ride used several of these types of order to develop her essay.

Types of Order	
CHRONOLOGICAL ORDER	Information is presented in the order in which it occurred.
EXAMPLE	**first,** the launch; **then,** reaching orbit; **finally,** making one complete orbit of Earth
SPATIAL ORDER	Information is given according to location.
EXAMPLE	**on** the launch pad; **in** orbit; **inside** the spacecraft; **over** Hawaii
ORDER OF IMPORTANCE	Information is given in order of importance, interest, size, or degree.
EXAMPLE	personal observation **(most interesting to Ride),** television pictures, data from previous flights **(least interesting to Ride)**
DEVELOPMENTAL ORDER	Information of equal importance is arranged to lead up to a conclusion.
EXAMPLE	Damaged forests, spreading deserts, oil slicks, and pollutant haze are evidence of human destruction. **(conclusion)**
COMPARISON/ CONTRAST	Information is arranged to point out similarities and differences.
EXAMPLE	Details of Earth were not as sharp in 1983 as they were in 1973. **(contrast)**

The type of order you choose for an expository essay will depend partly on your subject and partly on your thesis. For example, the thesis that radioactivity is more common in nature than most people think lends itself to an organization based on order of importance or developmental order. The thesis that radioactivity was an important discovery in the history of science, on the other hand, suggests chronological order.

Sally Ride chose the following order of ideas for the first half of her essay. Notice that Ride uses mainly developmental order to organize her essay. That is, she orders ideas and information to build an impression of the view from space and to prove her main point that such a view is completely different from any earthbound experience.

1. It's not easy to describe something that most people have never seen.
2. Spaceflight is different from airplane travel.
3. From space Earth looks like an atlas map.
4. It's hard to keep track of where you are because the world changes too fast.
5. You can see all kinds of geographic features.
6. You can see only portions of continents and large-scale phenomena.
7. You can see manmade features in surprising detail.
8. Signatures of civilization are seen in straight lines.
9. You can see the unfortunate effects of civilization on the environment.
10. Precise instruments measure what astronauts cannot see.

WRITING ACTIVITY *Ordering Information*

Review the list of details on page 258 about firsts in space exploration. Select the details that are relevant to the American space program and then arrange those details in chronological order.

Organizing Comparison and Contrast If you have chosen to organize your essay to compare and contrast two subjects, you have two ways to organize your information. One way is to write about one subject of comparison or contrast first and then to write about the other subject. For example, if you were comparing Mercury (subject *A*) to Mars (subject *B*), you would first write all your information about subject *A* (Mercury). Then you would write all your information about subject *B* (Mars). For convenience this is called the *AABB pattern* of comparison and contrast.

You could use the *AABB* pattern within a paragraph by discussing subject *A* in the first half of the paragraph and subject *B* in the second half. As an alternative you could use the *AABB* pattern in two paragraphs by discussing subject *A* in the first paragraph and subject *B* in the second one. The following portion of an essay shows how the *AABB* pattern works.

Model: *AABB Pattern of Organization*

Conflict between the North and the South

As Americans pushed westward during the early 1800's, conflict grew between the North [subject *A*] and the South [subject *B*]. Since the nation's early days, the northern and southern parts of the United States had followed different ways of life. Each section wanted to extend its own way of life to the western lands.

(A)The North had a diversified economy with both farms and industry. **(A)Northern farmers** raised a variety of crops that fed the thriving northern cities. **(A)Mills and factories in the North** competed with Britain in making cloth, shoes, iron, and machinery. For both its farms and factories, **(A)the North** depended on free workers. Such workers could move from place to place to meet the needs of industry. They could also be laid off when business slumped.

(B)The South depended on just a few cash crops, mainly cotton. To raise cotton, **(B) planters in the South** needed a large labor force year-round. They relied on slave labor. **(B)Southerners** traded their cotton for manufactured goods from Europe, especially from Great Britain. **(B)The South** had little industry of its own.

In the second paragraph above, the writer makes several points about the economy of subject *A*—the North. In the third paragraph, the writer turns to subject *B*—the South—and explains several ways in which the economy of the South was different from that of the North.

The second way to organize comparison and contrast is called the *ABAB* pattern. As you might expect, in the *ABAB pattern*, instead of discussing subject *A* and subject *B* separately, you discuss them together. That is, first you compare both *A* and *B* in terms of one similarity or difference and then you compare both of them in terms of another similarity or difference. The following continuation of the essay on the conflict that led to the Civil War switches to the *ABAB* pattern.

Model: *ABAB Pattern of Organization*

The economic differences between the two sections soon led to political conflicts. The bitterest of these conflicts arose over slavery. **(A)Many people in the North** considered slavery morally wrong. They wanted laws that would outlaw slavery in the new western territories. Some wanted to abolish slavery altogether. **(B)Most white southerners, on the other hand,** believed slavery was necessary for their economy. They wanted laws to protect slavery in the West so that they could raise cotton on the fertile soil there.

(A)Northerners had great political power in the national government. **(B)Southerners** feared the North's rising industrial power and growing population. Soon, they reasoned, the North would completely dominate the federal government. The election of 1860 seemed to confirm their worst fears. Abraham Lincoln, a northern candidate who opposed the spread of slavery, was elected president.

In the passage, the writer discusses the differences between the North and the South regarding attitudes toward slavery. Then the writer discusses differences between the North and South on political power at the federal level.

WRITING ACTIVITY *Organizing Comparison and Contrast*

For three of the following pairs of subjects, list similarities and differences. Use reference materials if necessary. Then organize your information according to the *AABB* or the *ABAB* pattern.

1. microscope/telescope
2. pinball machine/video game
3. lobster/shrimp
4. calendar years/light years
5. tape/compact disc

6. knitting/crocheting
7. volleyball/table tennis
8. science fiction/fantasy
9. silver/gold
10. credit card/cash

Making an Outline

When you select and group details, you probably write simple outlines to keep track of your decisions. You might number the points you want to make, for example. By developing an even more detailed outline, you can plan the whole body of your essay. The first two supporting paragraphs of the essay on page 266 were written from the following outline.

Model: *Making an Outline*

WORKING THESIS   Conflict grew as northerners and southerners followed different ways of life.

MAIN TOPIC   I.   The way of life in the North

SUBTOPIC   A. Had a diversified economy

SUPPORTING POINTS
              1. Had farms and industry
              2. Had a variety of crops
              3. Fed thriving cities

SUBTOPIC   B. Had industry

SUPPORTING POINTS
              1. Had mills and factories
              2. Competed with Britain in making goods such as cloth, shoes, iron, and machinery

SUBTOPIC   C. Depended on free workers

SUPPORTING POINTS
              1. Could move from place to place to meet the needs of industry
              2. Could be laid off when business slumped

MAIN TOPIC   II. The way of life in the South

SUBTOPIC   A. Depended on a few cash crops

SUPPORTING POINTS
              1. Grew mainly cotton
              2. Needed a large labor force year-round
              3. Depended on slave labor

SUBTOPIC   B. Depended on trade with Europe

SUPPORTING POINTS
              1. Traded cotton for manufactured goods
              2. Traded mainly with Great Britain
              3. Had little industry of its own

Notice that when you write a formal outline for the body of your essay, you use Roman numerals for each idea that supports your thesis. Each idea becomes the *main topic* of a supporting paragraph. You then use capital letters for each *subtopic*—a category of information that comes under a topic. Then, under each subtopic, you use numbers to list the supporting details or points. When you draft the body of your essay, all the information under a Roman numeral will go together to make up one paragraph.

Guidelines for Making an Outline

1. Use Roman numerals for topics.
2. Use capital letters for subtopics and indent them under the topic. If you use subtopics, always include at least two of them.
3. Use Arabic numerals (numbers) for supporting points and indent them under the subtopic. If you use supporting points, always include at least two of them.
4. Use lowercase letters for any additional details and indent them under the supporting point to which they refer. If you use supporting details, always include at least two of them.

Model: *Outline Form*

I. (Main topic)
    A. (Subtopic)
        1. (Supporting point)
        2. (Supporting point)
           a. (Detail)
           b. (Detail)
    B. (Subtopic)
        1. (Supporting point)
           a. (Detail)
           b. (Detail)
        2. (Supporting point)
II. (Main topic)
    Etc.

WRITING ACTIVITY *Making an Outline*

Outline the third and fourth supporting paragraphs of "Conflict between the North and the South" on page 267. These paragraphs—Roman numerals III and IV of the outline for the essay body—are about political conflicts between northerners and southerners before the Civil War.

WRITING ACTIVITY *Writing on Your Own*

WRITING
ABOUT THE
THEME

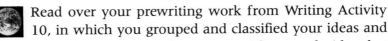

Read over your prewriting work from Writing Activity 10, in which you grouped and classified your ideas and information for your essay about space. After you decide what your topics, subtopics, and supporting points will be, organize them in a logical order. *(See page 264.)* Then follow the Guidelines for Making an Outline to write an outline of the body of your essay. Change your outline as often as you need to—until you are satisfied with its content, logical order, and form. When you have finished, save your outline.

Drafting

During the drafting stage of the writing process, you will use your prewriting notes and outline to write an introduction, a body, and a conclusion. Before you draft your introduction, however, you should refine your working thesis into a thesis statement.

Writing a Thesis Statement

The *thesis statement*, which expresses your main idea, should appear somewhere in the essay introduction. Thesis statements are often most effective when they appear at the beginning or at the end of the introduction.

Writing Term   The **thesis statement** makes the main idea of the essay clear to readers.

In an expository essay, the most important feature of a thesis statement is that it accurately cover all of the information you include in the essay. The following guidelines suggest the steps you should take to refine your working thesis into an effective thesis statement.

Drafting a Thesis Statement

1. Look over your outline and revise your working thesis so that it covers all of your main topics.
2. Express your working thesis in a complete sentence.
3. Check your thesis statement for clarity; use peer conferencing to check that the thesis is clearly stated.
4. Look over all your information again to make sure it is relevant to the thesis statement. *(See Writing Is Thinking on page 261.)*
5. Continue to refine your thesis statement as you develop your essay, taking into account any changes you make in the main idea or in the information you include.

Drafting the Introduction

In an essay to inform, the introduction has several functions other than stating the thesis. For example, in the introduction you also set the tone of your essay and capture the reader's interest. Because the purpose in writing an expository essay is to inform or to explain, a candid, matter-of-fact tone is usually appropriate. Common ways to attract the reader's attention in an expository essay are listed below.

Writing Introductions for Essays to Inform

1. Tell about an incident that shows how you became interested in your subject.
2. Give some background information.
3. Cite an example that illustrates your thesis.
4. Cite a startling statistic about the subject.
5. Define or describe the subject.
6. Quote an expert on the subject.

The following model presents an introduction for the essay on page 266 about conflicts between the North and the South that led to the Civil War. Notice how this introduction introduces the subject, captures interest, and sets the tone. Also the main idea is clearly expressed in a refined thesis statement.

Model: *Introduction of an Expository Essay*

As Americans pushed westward during the early 1800's, conflict grew between the North and the South. The main reason for this conflict was the contrast between the different ways of life that had developed in the North and the South ever since colonial times. As each section tried to extend its own way of life to the new western lands, those different ways of life began to threaten the nation's unity. By the 1860's, differences between the ways of life in the North and the South brought the nation to the brink of war.

REFINED
THESIS
STATEMENT

WRITING ACTIVITY *Writing on Your Own*

Writing about the theme   Review all your prewriting notes for your essay about space. Then refine your working thesis and draft an introduction with a thesis statement. Experiment with placing your thesis statement at the beginning and at the end of the introduction. Then choose the introduction you like best and save your work in your writing folder.

Drafting the Body

When you draft the body of your essay, you should follow your outline. Each main topic, with some or all of the subtopics and supporting points, will become at least one paragraph. If you have a number of supporting details, you may need two or more paragraphs to cover each topic adequately. *(For more information about the body of an essay and its relationship to the introduction, see pages 228–230.)*

Guidelines for Adequately Developing an Essay

1. Include enough supporting ideas to explain your thesis statement fully.
2. Leave no question unanswered that you would expect readers to ask.
3. Include enough information to explain each topic and subtopic fully.
4. Use specific details and precise language to explain each piece of information fully.

As you draft the body from your outline, connect your words, sentences, and paragraphs with transitions to make the essay read smoothly and to give it unity, coherence, and clarity. Strategies for achieving coherence while drafting are listed on the next page. *(For a list of transitions, see page 154. For more information about adequate development and about unity, coherence, and clarity, see pages 151 and 231–232.)*

Strategies for Achieving Coherence

1. Use transitional words and phrases.
2. Repeat a key word from an earlier sentence.
3. Use synonyms for key words from earlier sentences.
4. Use a pronoun in place of a word used earlier.

WRITING ACTIVITY *Writing from an Outline*

Convert the following outline into a short introduction and body of an essay. As you write, refer to the guidelines on page 273 and to the strategies above.

THESIS STATEMENT   The launching of the satellite *Sputnik* by the Soviets caused a revolution in American education.

  I.   *Sputnik* launch was a worldwide sensation
    A. Launched by Soviets in October 1957
    B. First artificial Earth satellite
  II.   *Sputnik's* success troubled Americans
    A. In 1950's, Americans and Soviets were rivals
    B. Americans feared Soviets were ahead in science and education
    C. Magazines began to publish articles about a "crisis in education"
  III.   United States government responded by funding education
    A. Congress voted National Defense Education Act
      1. In 1958, after December 1957 launch of American Vanguard Rocket failed
      2. $1 billion to teach more science in public schools
    B. School improvements included modern science labs, science fairs, and teacher training in sciences

WRITING ACTIVITY *Writing on Your Own*

WRITING ABOUT THE THEME   Working from the outline you developed in Writing Activity 14, draft the paragraphs of the body for your essay about space. Save your work in your writing folder.

Drafting the Conclusion

An expository essay is not complete without a conclusion. The concluding paragraph sums up your information and reinforces your thesis. You might also add an interesting detail from your notes that you did not previously include. *(For more information about the conclusion of an essay, see pages 233–234.)*

Strategies for Writing a Conclusion

1. Summarize the body of the essay.
2. Restate the thesis in new words.
3. Draw a conclusion based on the body of the essay.
4. Add an insight about the thesis.
5. Write a memorable clincher sentence.

The following paragraph concludes the essay on page 266 about conflicts that led to the Civil War. Notice that the conclusion adds interesting details about the start of the Civil War and also restates the thesis in a memorable clincher sentence.

Model: *Conclusion of an Expository Essay*

> After Lincoln's election, 11 southern states made the fateful decision to withdraw from the United States. They established a separate nation called the Confederate States of America. On April 12, 1861, Confederate guns opened fire on Fort Sumter, a fort in South Carolina held by soldiers of the federal government. This event marked the beginning of the Civil War—a tragic clash between Americans following different ways of life.

CLINCHER
SENTENCE

WRITING ACTIVITY *Writing on Your Own*

WRITING
ABOUT THE
THEME Reread the introduction and body of your essay about space and draft a strong concluding paragraph. Then write two or three possible titles for your essay. Choose the best title and save your draft in your writing folder.

Revising

Writing Process

The purpose of revising is to make your final draft as clear and readable as possible. If time allows, put away your draft for a day or two so you can revise it with a fresh eye. Also read your draft aloud to notice parts that need improvement. A peer reader can tell you whether your explanations are clear.

Checking for Unity, Coherence, and Clarity

In revising, as in drafting, you should be alert for ways to improve the unity, coherence, and clarity of your essay. The following questions will help you to check for these qualities.

Checking for Unity, Coherence, and Clarity

CHECKING FOR UNITY

1. Does every idea and piece of information relate to the subject?
2. Does every paragraph support the thesis statement?
3. Does every sentence in each paragraph support its topic sentence?

CHECKING FOR COHERENCE

4. Did you follow a logical order of ideas or topics?
5. Did you follow a logical order of supporting points or details?
6. Did you use transitions to connect the introduction, body, and conclusion?
7. Did you use transitions between paragraphs?
8. Did you use transitions between sentences within each paragraph?

CHECKING FOR CLARITY

9. Does each word express clearly and precisely what you want to say?
10. Does the introduction make your subject, purpose, tone, and thesis clear to readers?
11. Does the body clearly support the thesis and lead to the conclusion?
12. Does the conclusion make clear to readers how the body supports the thesis?

Using a Revision Checklist

A general revision checklist also helps you keep track of all the points you should check when you revise. As you use the following Revision Checklist, read through your essay several times, focusing on a different point each time.

Revision Checklist

CHECKING YOUR ESSAY

1. Do you have a strong introduction?
2. Does your thesis statement make your main idea and purpose clear?
3. Do you have enough details to support your thesis fully?
4. Does your essay have unity? Does the topic sentence of each paragraph relate directly to the thesis?
5. Does your essay have coherence?
6. Does your essay have clarity?
7. Do you have a strong conclusion?
8. Did you add an interesting and appropriate title?

CHECKING YOUR PARAGRAPHS

9. Does each paragraph have a topic sentence? *(See pages 98–99.)*
10. Does each paragraph have adequate development? *(See pages 108–109.)*
11. Does each paragraph have the qualities of unity, coherence, and clarity?

CHECKING YOUR SENTENCES AND WORDS

12. Did you vary your sentences and sentence beginnings? *(See pages 71–74.)*
13. Are your sentences concise? *(See pages 75–79.)*
14. Did you use words that are specific and precise? *(See pages 59–60.)*
15. Did you use vivid words and rich connotations? *(See pages 59–61.)*

WRITING ACTIVITY *Writing on Your Own*

WRITING
ABOUT THE
THEME

Use Checking for Unity, Coherence, and Clarity on page 276 and the Revision Checklist above to revise your essay on space. Keep your revised draft in your writing folder.

Editing and Publishing

Grammar in the
Writing Process

Prepositional phrases help a writer describe even the indescribable, as shown in Sally Ride's closing remarks in her essay "Single Room, Earth View."

I really can't describe a sunrise *in orbit*. The drama set *against the black backdrop of space* and the magic *of the materializing colors* can't be captured *in an astronomer's equations or an astronaut's photographs.*

Ride's use of prepositional phrases in this passage helps the reader imagine the magnificence of a sunrise in orbit.

Prepositional Phrases A *prepositional phrase* is a group of words that has no subject or verb and that modifies, or describes, other words in the sentence. It is useful for adding important information to a sentence. In the following examples, each prepositional phrase adds information by answering a question. *(For more information about kinds of prepositional phrases and practice in recognizing them, see pages 633–638.)*

WHERE? **From space shuttle height,** we couldn't see the entire globe. (From *where* couldn't they see?)

WHEN? The lightning ignites the clouds **at night.** (*When* does lightning ignite the clouds?)

HOW? The land was obscured **by a huge dust storm.** (*How* was the land obscured?)

WHAT KIND? Patches **of pollution-damaged trees** dotted the European forests. (*What kind* of patches dotted the forests?)

WHICH ONES? The astronauts traced the major air routes **across the northern Pacific Ocean.** (*Which* major air routes did the astronauts trace?)

Punctuation with Prepositional Phrases When a long prepositional phrase comes at the beginning of a sentence, you should put a comma after it. *(For other examples of commas with prepositional phrases and practice in using them correctly, see pages 826–827.)*

Combining Sentences with Prepositional Phrases As the following examples show, you can use prepositional phrases to combine two short sentences into one sentence. *(For more examples and practice in combining sentences with prepositional phrases, see pages 66–67.)*

SEPARATE SENTENCES	Bolts of lightning are diffused by the clouds. The lightning bursts into balls of light.
COMBINED SENTENCE	Bolts of lightning are diffused by the clouds into bursting balls of light.

Editing Checklist

1. Have you used prepositional phrases to incorporate additional information into a sentence? *(See pages 633–638.)*
2. Are all prepositional phrases punctuated correctly? *(See pages 826–827.)*
3. Could you use prepositional phrases to combine any sentences? *(See pages 66–67.)*

WRITING ACTIVITY 20 *Writing on Your Own*

WRITING ABOUT THE THEME

Editing Use the checklist above and the Editing Checklist on page 37 to edit your essay on space from Writing Activity 19. You will edit most effectively if you read through your paper several times, looking for different kinds of errors each time.

Publishing When you have written a neat final copy, include it with classmates' essays in a compiled publication called *Space*. You can refer to this booklet at any time to find writing ideas for other courses, such as science or history.

A Writer Writes

WRITING
ABOUT THE
THEME

An Essay to Inform

PURPOSE: to explain an aspect of outer space that would
interest and enlighten children

AUDIENCE: students in the fourth or fifth grade

Prewriting   Look over your journal entries in which you
described the things that fascinate you the most about space
and brainstorm for more ideas. For example, you might want
to find out how heat from the sun can travel 93,000,000 miles
to Earth and still be warm when it gets there. On the other
hand, you might be interested in Mars, especially since there
has been some discussion of a joint American-Soviet landing
on Mars. You might want to know, for instance, what commercial value Mars might have or what would be required before
people could colonize that planet.

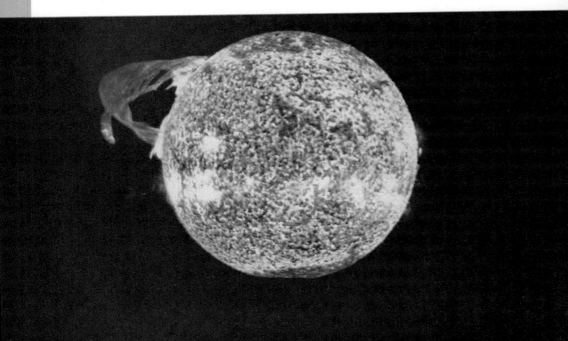

After choosing and limiting a subject for an expository essay, brainstorm for all the facts you already know about that subject. Then find any additional information you need, using your science book or reference books. Based on the information you gather, develop a working thesis, group your details, and arrange them in a logical order. Then develop an outline from your notes.

Drafting   Keeping in mind your purpose and audience, refine your thesis and work your thesis statement into an introduction. Then draft the body of your essay and the conclusion. Be sure to add a title.

Revising   Read your essay aloud to find places where you can improve your wording or flow of ideas. Also use the Revision Checklist on page 277 to make changes that will improve the quality and style of your essay. Before you edit, also check your essay for unity, coherence, and clarity.

Editing and Publishing   Use the Editing Checklists on pages 37 and 279 to prepare a neat and error-free final copy. Then submit your essay to a fourth- or fifth-grade teacher to read to his or her students or to give to the students to read on their own. You can check the effectiveness of your explanation by finding out what questions the students have about it.

Independent Writing

Using one of the following focused subjects or one of your choice, develop an outline for an essay to explain or inform. Begin by gathering information and developing a working thesis. Then organize and order your information and ideas. Before you write your outline, refer to the Guidelines for Making an Outline on page 269 and the models on pages 268–269.

1. how baboons differ from other apes
2. why the Aztecs and the Incas built pyramids
3. how an abacus [or some other instrument] works
4. what is distinctive about Norway [or some other country]
5. where place-names in your community came from

Creative Writing

Examine maps of your county, city, or town. Then imagine what you might see if you were viewing your community from the air. What could you tell about life in your community from an aerial view of the natural and human environment? For example, perhaps you would see smokestacks with smoke, cotton fields, roads converging on a town common, people at the beach, or a river with rafts of logs. For additional writing ideas, explore your community to make firsthand observations. When you have gathered ideas and information, write them in an essay to inform. Assume that—like Sally Ride—you are explaining a view of your community that is unfamiliar to your readers.

WRITING
ABOUT THE
THEME

Writing about Literature

Find examples of *figures of speech* in Sally Ride's essay, including both similes and metaphors. A *simile* uses the word *like* or *as* to compare two different things, while a *metaphor* makes a comparison by referring to a thing as something else that it resembles. After you have found at least two examples of each kind of figure of speech, invent some on your own, based on Ride's descriptions of the view from space. The following simile, for example, is based on Ride's description of ocean waves viewed from space.

> Waves scrawl across the surface of the sea, like the handwriting of a child.

Writing in Other Subject Areas

Home Economics   Write an expository essay on one of the following subjects and submit it to a teacher of health or home economics.

1. food poisoning and how to avoid it
2. synthetic and natural fibers and how to tell the difference
3. household hazards and how to prevent them
4. potatoes and how to use them in cooking or crafts
5. food packaging labels and how to read them

Checklist

Writing Essays to Inform

Prewriting

✔ Find subjects by drawing on your experience and reading. *(See page 253.)*

✔ Choose and limit your subject. *(See pages 253–256.)*

✔ Focus your ideas by asking yourself questions about your subject, purpose, and audience. *(See page 255.)*

✔ Gather information and develop a list of supporting ideas. *(See pages 257–259.)*

✔ Develop a working thesis. *(See pages 259–260.)*

✔ Group together, categorize, and order your ideas and information. *(See pages 262–267.)*

✔ Make an outline. *(See pages 268–270.)*

Drafting

✔ Write an introduction that includes your refined thesis statement. *(See pages 271–272.)*

✔ Use your outline as you write the paragraphs of the body. *(See pages 273–274.)*

✔ Use transitions to connect your ideas. *(See pages 153–154.)*

✔ Add a concluding paragraph. *(See page 275.)*

✔ Add a title. *(See page 31.)*

Revising

✔ Check for unity, coherence, and clarity. *(See page 276.)*

✔ Refer to the Revision Checklist on page 277.

Editing and Publishing

✔ Use the Editing Checklist on page 37 to check your grammar, spelling, mechanics, and manuscript form.

✔ Publish your essay in one of the ways listed on page 43.

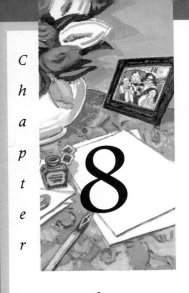

8 Writing Personal Essays

THEME: *Family*

You experience the world in a way that is peculiarly your own. You have your own perceptions, beliefs, and values. No one else is quite like you or experiences life just as you do. Although each person lives uniquely, however, there are some life experiences—such as being part of a family—that most people share in some way.

Each family is also unique. You may be part of a traditional or a nontraditional family—large or small. You may live in a single-parent family or with foster parents. You may be an only child or one of many. The author of the next literature selection grew up in an extended family—one that included relatives other than parents and siblings, such as grandparents, aunts, uncles, cousins, and even family friends.

In the following selection from *Barrio Boy*, Ernesto Galarza shares the experiences of his extended family during a time in his youth. As you read the selection, think about the adjustments he and his family had to make in moving to a new home in a different community.

from

Barrio Boy

Ernesto Galarza

To make room for a growing family it was decided that we should move, and a house was found in Oak Park, on the far side of town where the open country began. The men raised the first installment for the bungalow on Seventh Avenue even after Mrs. Dodson explained that if we did not keep up the monthly payments we would lose the deposit as well as the house.

The real estate broker brought the sale contract to the apartment one evening. Myself included, we sat around the table in the living room, the gringo[1] explaining at great length the small print of the document in a torrent of words none of us could make out. Now and then he would pause and throw in the only word he knew in Spanish: "Sabee?"[2] The men nodded slightly as if they had understood. Doña[3] Henriqueta was holding firmly to the purse which contained the down payment, watching the broker's face, not listening to his words.

1. **gringo** [grēn′ gō]: An English-speaking foreigner, especially from North America.
2. **Sabee?** [sä′ bē]: You know?
3. **Doña** [dō′ nyä]: Respectful term of address, used before women's first names.

She had only one question. Turning to me she said: "Ask him how long it will take to pay all of it." I translated, shocked by the answer: "Twenty years." There was a long pause around the table, broken by my stepfather: "What do you say?" Around the table the heads nodded agreement. The broker passed his fountain pen to him. He signed the contract and after him Gustavo and José. Doña Henriqueta opened the purse and counted out the greenbacks. The broker pocketed the money, gave us a copy of the document, and left.

The last thing I did when we moved out of 418 L was to dig a hole in the corner of the backyard for a tall carton of Quaker Oats cereal, full to the brim with the marbles I had won playing for keeps around the *barrio*.[4] I tamped the earth over my buried treasure and laid a curse on whoever removed it without my permission.

Our new bungalow had five rooms, and porches front and back. In the way of furniture, what friends did not lend or Mrs. Dodson gave us we bought in the secondhand shops. The only new item was an elegant gas range, with a high oven and long, slender legs finished in enamel. Like the house, we would be paying for it in installments.

It was a sunny, airy spot, with a family orchard to one side and a vacant lot on the other. Back of us there was a pasture. With chicken wire we fenced the back yard, turned over the soil, and planted our first vegetable garden and fruit trees. José and I built a palatial rabbit hutch of laths and two-by-fours he gathered day by day on the waterfront. A single row of geraniums and carnations separated the vegetable garden from the house. From the vacant lots and pastures around us my mother gathered herbs and weeds which she dried and boiled the way she had in the pueblo.[5] A thick green fluid she distilled from the mallow that grew wild around us was bottled and used as a hair lotion. On every side our windows looked out on family orchards, platinum stretches of wild oats and quiet lanes, shady and unpaved.

---

4. **barrio** [bär′ ryō]: District of a large town or city.
5. **pueblo** [pwe′ blō]: Village.

We could not have moved to a neighborhood less like the *barrio*. All the families around us were Americans. The grumpy retired farmer next door viewed us with alarm and never gave us the time of day, but the Harrisons across the street were cordial. Mr. Harrison loaned us his tools, and Roy, just my age but twice my weight, teamed up with me at once for an exchange of visits to his mother's kitchen and ours. I astounded him with my Mexican rice, and Mrs. Harrison baked my first waffle. Roy and I also found a common bond in the matter of sisters. He had an older one and by now I had two younger ones. It was a question between us whether they were worse as little nuisances or as big bosses. The answer didn't make much difference but it was a relief to have another man to talk with.

Some Sundays we walked to Joyland, an amusement park where my mother sat on a bench to watch the children play on the lawn and I begged as many rides as I could on the roller coaster, which we called in elegant Spanish "The Russian Mountain." José liked best the free vaudeville because of the chorus girls who danced out from the stage on a platform and kicked their heels over his head.

Since Roy had a bicycle and could get away from his sister by pedaling off on long journeys I persuaded my family to match my savings for a used one. Together we pushed beyond the boundaries of Oak Park miles out, nearly to Perkins and the Slough House. It was open country, where we could lean our wheels against a fence post and walk endlessly through carpets of golden poppies and blue lupin. With a bike I was able to sign on as a carrier of the *Sacramento Bee*, learning in due course the art of slapping folded newspapers against people's porches instead of into the bushes or on their roofs. Roy and I also became assistants to a neighbor who operated a bakery in his basement, taking our pay partly in dimes and partly in broken cookies for our families.

For the three men of the household as well as for me the bicycle became the most important means for earning a living. Oak Park was miles away from the usual places where they worked and they pedaled off, in good weather and bad, in the early morning. It was a case of saving carfare.

I transferred to the Bret Harte School, a gingerbread two-story building in which there was a notable absence of Japanese, Filipinos, Koreans, Italians, and the other nationalities of the Lincoln School. It was at Bret Harte that I learned how an English sentence could be cut up on the blackboard and the pieces placed on different lines connected by what the teacher called a diagram. The idea of operating on a sentence and rearranging its members as a skeleton of verbs, modifiers, subject, and prepositions set me off diagraming whatever I read, in Spanish and English. Spiderwebs, my mother called them, when I tried to teach her the art.

My bilingual library had grown with some copies of old magazines from Mexico, a used speller Gustavo had bought for me in Stockton, and the novels my mother discarded when she had read them. Blackstone was still the anchor of my collection and I now had a paperback dictionary called *El Inglés sin Maestro.*[6] By this time there was no problem of translating or interpreting for the family I could not tackle with confidence.

6. **El Inglés sin Maestro** [el en glēs' sen mä es' trō]: *English without a Teacher.*

It was Gustavo, in fact, who began to give my books a vague significance. He pointed out to me that with diagrams and dictionaries I could have a choice of becoming a lawyer or a doctor or an engineer or a professor. These, he said, were far better careers than growing up to be a *camello,*[7] as he and José always would be. *Camellos,* I knew well enough, was what the *chicanos*[8] called themselves as the worker on every job who did the dirtiest work. And to give our home the professional touch he felt I should be acquiring, he had a telephone installed.

It came to the rest of us as a surprise. The company man arrived one day with our name and address on a card, a metal tool box and a stand-up telephone wound with a cord. It was connected and set on the counter between the dining room and the parlor. There the black marvel sat until we were gathered for dinner that evening. It was clearly explained by Gustavo that the instrument was to provide me with a quick means of reaching the important people I knew at the Y.M.C.A., the boy's band, or the various public offices where I interpreted for *chicanos* in distress. Sooner or later some of our friends in the *barrio* would also have telephones and we could talk with them.

"Call somebody," my mother urged me.

With the whole family watching I tried to think of some important person I could ring for a professional conversation. A name wouldn't come. I felt miserable and hardly like a budding engineer or lawyer or doctor or professor.

Gustavo understood my predicament and let me stew in it a moment. Then he said: "Mrs. Dodson." My pride saved by this ingenious suggestion, I thumbed through the directory, lifted the earpiece from the hook, and calmly asked central for the number. My sisters, one sitting on the floor and the other in my mother's arms, never looked less significant, but they, too, had their turn saying hello to the patient Señora[9] Dodson on the other end of the line. ◆

___

7. **camello** [käme' yō]: Camel.
8. **chicanos** [chē kä' nōs]: Mexican Americans.
9. **Señora** [se nyō' rä]: Mrs.

Lineage

M a r g a r e t   W a l k e r

My grandmothers were strong.
They followed plows and bent to toil.
They moved through fields sowing seed.

They touched earth and grain grew.
They were full of sturdiness and singing.
My grandmothers were strong.

My grandmothers are full of memories
Smelling of soap and onions and wet clay
With veins rolling roughly over quick hands
They have many clean words to say.
My grandmothers were strong.
Why am I not as they?

Responding to the Theme

Family

Responding in Your Journal This week in your journal write about changes in your family and family life. Include changes in the family as a unit and also changes to which individual family members have had to adjust. Perhaps you and your family are newcomers to a neighborhood, for example, as Ernesto Galarza was. Perhaps you erected a basketball hoop in your driveway or your mother found a new job or your sister went to college or your grandfather came to live with you. No change is too great or too small to write about in your journal. As you write, include as many specific details as you can remember—bits of conversation, how you learned of a change, the effects of that change, and how you and others responded.

Speaking and Listening In the selection from *Barrio Boy*, the family decided to move to a new neighborhood, to buy a home, and to acquire a telephone. With your teacher's permission, form a group with classmates to discuss family decision making. List major and minor decisions that families face and the different ways in which families may reach those decisions. As you share your views, have one classmate keep a record of the ideas that emerge. End the discussion by drawing conclusions about family decision making.

Critical Thinking: Inferring In his autobiography Ernesto Galarza refers to several people by name without explaining their relationship to him. As you reread the selection, list characters by name and add any clues you find about their identities. Then make inferences about who all the people are in relation to the author.

Extending Your Vocabulary The following words from *Barrio Boy* may be less widely used today than when Ernesto Galarza was growing up in California. Using a dictionary, find each word's meaning as it is used in the story. Then write a brief description of the object or quality that the word names.

bungalow	gingerbread	laths	range
carfare	hutch	parlor	vaudeville

Two Figures at Desk,
Milton Avery, 1944.

Part 2   *Writing*

In *Barrio Boy* Ernesto Galarza expresses his memories and feelings about a great change in his family's life—a change that deeply influenced his own life, both as a youth and as an adult. Like Galarza you have in your memory a host of subjects that involve your personal experiences. Writing a personal essay is a way to interpret and share those experiences.

The purpose in writing personal essays is to express feelings and insights about yourself and the people and events in your life. This process may require some deep thought. It may mean checking facts in an old newspaper or talking with other family members who shared that experience or choosing a humorous or a serious tone. It may even mean using other kinds of paragraphs in addition to expressive writing—such as paragraphs of description, explanation, narration, and persuasion. Whatever kinds of paragraphs you include, however, in a personal essay you will be writing about your own life experiences.

Writing Term   A **personal essay** expresses the writer's personal point of view on a subject drawn from the writer's own experience.

Prewriting

During prewriting, your mind should be free to roam through your memories and reflections about experiences you have had. As you think freely, you will discover ideas that could be developed as the subjects of personal essays. For example, you may recall an important conversation, a surprise or a disappointment, an observation that affected you deeply, or a decision that had fateful consequences. In the following excerpt from her autobiography, Jamaica Kincaid recalls how she learned her personal history as a child.

Model: *Subject of a Personal Essay*

From time to time, my mother would fix on a certain place in our house and give it a good cleaning. If I was at home when she happened to do this, I was at her side, as usual. When she did this with the trunk, it was a tremendous pleasure, for after she had removed all the things from the trunk, and aired them out, and changed the camphor balls, and then refolded the things and put them back in their places in the trunk, as she held each thing in her hand she would tell me a story about myself. Sometimes I knew the story first hand, for I could remember the incident quite well; sometimes what she told me had happened when I was too young to know anything; and sometimes it happened before I was even born. Whichever way, I knew exactly what she would say, for I had heard it so many times before, but I never got tired of it.   JAMAICA KINCAID, *Annie John*

Jamaica Kincaid with her children.

Drawing on Personal Experience

When you write from personal experience, essay subjects may sometimes seem inexhaustible. At other times, however, you may need to stir your memories and emotions. To think of subjects for a personal essay, look through your journal entries and use freewriting, inquiring, or brainstorming to stimulate your thinking. You may also find the following sources helpful in jogging your memory.

Idea Sources for Subjects of Personal Essays

- letters
- photographs
- family stories
- personal heroes
- school yearbooks
- newspapers
- magazines

- albums or scrapbooks
- souvenirs or mementos
- articles of clothing
- favorite times
- favorite places
- old toys or games
- favorite things

WRITING ACTIVITY *Writing on Your Own*

WRITING
ABOUT THE
THEME

Use your journal entries, discussion ideas from Speaking and Listening on page 291, and Idea Sources for Subjects of Personal Essays above to create a list of ten possible subjects for a personal essay about a decision or change in your family. One subject you might list, for example, is a family event that was an important milestone in your life. Another subject might be a decision that you or another family member made that had some effect on everyone in the family. You might also include a welcome or unwelcome change that occurred independently of your family's decisions—for example, a change caused by changes in the community or wider society. After you have listed ten possible subjects, narrow the choice to five and think back to remember the details surrounding each decision or change. Then choose the one subject that you can recall most clearly that is also the most meaningful to you. Save your subject idea for your personal essay in your writing folder.

Deciding on the Meaning of an Experience

American novelist John Irving wrote, "Every writer uses what experience he or she has. It's the translating, though, that makes the difference." Translating means finding meaning in an experience. For instance, suppose you recall a summer you spent with an aunt in a distant city. That summer had special meaning for you because you felt more mature when you returned home. That insight could be the main idea of a personal essay. The expression of your main idea then serves the same function as the thesis statement in other kinds of essays.

The following paragraph, for example, continues Jamaica Kincaid's reflections on her childhood experience of hearing "stories from the trunk." Notice how she makes the meaning of this experience clear to the reader.

Model: *Expressing the Meaning of an Experience*

As she told me the stories, I sometimes sat at her side, leaning against her, or I would crouch on my knees behind her back and lean over her shoulder. As I did this, I would occasionally sniff at her neck, or behind her ears, or at her hair. She smelled sometimes of onions, sometimes of sage, sometimes of roses, sometimes of bay leaf. At times I would no longer hear what it was she was saying; I just liked to look at her mouth as it opened and closed over words, or as she laughed. How terrible it must be for all the people who had no one to love them so and no one whom they loved so, I thought.   JAMAICA KINCAID
Annie John

As Kincaid makes clear, her experience taught her the importance of loving and being loved. This insight is the main idea of her essay.

WRITING ACTIVITY ◆ 2 *Writing on Your Own*

WRITING
ABOUT THE
THEME   Think about the change or decision that you chose as your subject in Writing Activity 1. In a sentence or two, write what the experience meant to you—what made it important. Save your work in your writing folder.

Writing Is Thinking

Interpreting Experience

Think about an event in your life that seems important to you now. Why was it important? What was the meaning of this event for you? Such questions may be hard to answer because when you are experiencing events, it is often difficult to stand back from them to see their significance. Only after some time has passed can you gauge their meaning.

When you reexamine an experience to interpret its meaning, you might begin by completing a checklist like the one below.

Model: *Interpreting an Experience*

Experience: when I unexpectedly received an award in sixth grade for showing the greatest improvement.

This experience is important to me now because it
- ☐ helped me see something in a new way.
- ☐ changed the way I feel about someone.
- ☑ changed the way I feel about myself.

I will always remember this experience because it
- ☐ strongly affected my emotions.
- ☐ gave me new knowledge or understanding.
- ☑ had important consequences.

This experience is worth writing about because
- ☑ it will be familiar to many readers.
- ☐ it is unique or extraordinary.
- ☐ writing will help me to understand it better.

Meaning: This event boosted my self-confidence. It sticks in my mind as the first time I realized that I might amount to something. I became a better student because of it.

Thinking Practice   Think of any memorable past experience and interpret it by developing a checklist like the one above.

Deciding on Purpose and Audience

When you have decided on a subject for your personal essay and its meaning, you need to think about your purpose in writing and your audience. Personal essays are usually written to express your thoughts and feelings in a way that will interest readers and win their appreciation. To accomplish this purpose, however, you may include different kinds of paragraphs to combine the overall purpose with specific purposes. The following examples illustrate how a specific purpose may call for a specific kind of paragraph. *(For more information about other kinds of paragraphs, see pages 172–205.)*

Model: *Purpose*

Overall Purpose: To express thoughts and feelings

EXAMPLES OF SPECIFIC PURPOSES	KINDS OF PARAGRAPHS
to explain why I felt ashamed	expository
to tell a funny story	narrative
to warn against taking dares	persuasive
to help readers see the mountain I climbed	descriptive

Considering your audience is just as important as deciding on your purpose and goals. You should take into account the interests and knowledge of your readers so that you can make sure they will understand your experience and its meaning. Because you reveal yourself in a personal essay, you should also decide how much you want to share. Whether you write for family members and friends, for classmates and teachers, or for wider audiences, your audience will partly determine the kinds of details you select to include in your essay.

WRITING ACTIVITY **3** *Writing on Your Own*

WRITING
ABOUT THE
THEME

Reread the interpretation of your subject that you wrote in Writing Activity 2. Then refine your interpretation by making a checklist like the one in Writing Is Thinking on page

297

296. After you write a few sentences explaining the meaning of your experience, make some notes on your purpose and your audience. Save all your notes in your writing folder.

Discovering Appropriate Details

When you write a personal essay, you want your readers to understand what is happening and to share your feelings about it as if they were there. For this sharing to happen, you need to give your readers factual details of time and place that will make your experience clear. Details of sight, sound, smell, taste, and touch are especially important because they will bring your experience to life.

In the following excerpts, for example, Jamaica Kincaid uses *descriptive details* to help her readers see the contents of her mother's keepsake trunk and to visualize the events they commemorate. Maxine H. Kingston uses *sensory details* to help her readers hear children reciting their lessons, and Russell Baker gives *background details* to provide a context for telling his experience as a news carrier.

Model: *Descriptive Details*

. . . there was the dress I wore when I first went to school, and the first notebook in which I wrote; there were the sheets for my crib and the sheets for my first bed; there was my first straw hat, my first straw basket—decorated with flowers—my grandmother had sent me from Dominica; there were my report cards, my certificates of merit from school, and my certificates of merit from Sunday School.　　　Jamaica Kincaid, *Annie John*

Model: *Sensory Details*

After American school, we picked up our cigar boxes, in which we had arranged books, brushes, and an inkbox neatly, and went to Chinese school from 5:00 to 7:30 P.M. There we chanted together, voices rising and falling, loud and soft, some boys shouting, everybody reading together, reciting together and not alone with one voice.　　　Maxine H. Kingston
The Woman Warrior

Night Intersection,
Don Williams,
1989.

Model: *Background Details*

At my twelfth birthday my mother had got me a job delivering the *Baltimore News-Post* and *Sunday American.* The *News-Post* was an afternoon paper, but the *American* didn't come off the presses until long after midnight and had to be delivered before dawn on Sunday. Usually I set my alarm clock for two A.M. on Sundays and tiptoed out of the house to avoid waking my mother and Doris. 　　　　　　　　　　　　RUSSELL BAKER, *Growing Up*

WRITING ACTIVITY *Finding Examples of Details*

Reread parts of *Barrio Boy* on pages 285–289 and find details that the author used to make his experience real to you. List five examples under each of the following categories: Descriptive Details, Sensory Details, and Background Details.

WRITING ACTIVITY *Writing on Your Own*

WRITING
ABOUT THE
THEME
After you read your prewriting notes from Writing Activity 3, use brainstorming or clustering to list details that you could include in your personal essay about your family. Think of background details that readers may need to understand the time and place of your experience. Also look for descriptive details and sensory details that appeal to all five senses. Keep your notes in your writing folder.

Selecting Details

Once you have a list of details, you should select the ones you will use and then arrange them in a logical order. Not every detail will be relevant to the meaning of your experience, and if you include a flood of details that are interesting but not relevant, your readers will not understand your main idea. You may find the following guidelines helpful in selecting the most effective details.

Guidelines for Selecting Details

1. Choose details that develop your main idea.
2. Choose details that are appropriate for your purpose.
3. Choose details that are appropriate for your audience.
4. Use factual details to provide background information.
5. Use vivid descriptive and sensory details to bring your experience to life.

WRITING ACTIVITY *Choosing Effective Details*

Suppose you were writing a personal essay about an interview that you had at a corner store for a part-time job helping out on Saturday mornings. You want to include details that would set the stage for the incident and help your readers visualize the setting. Choose the five details from the following list that you think would be the most effective. Be prepared to defend your choices.

cashier behind counter	three refrigerated cases
electronic cash register	10:00 A.M., Saturday
two customers just leaving	day-old bread on sale
display of motor oil by door	candy in jars
stack of grocery bags	blinking fluorescent light
owner wearing red tie	tiny office in the rear
dusty window display	unpriced goods in cartons
rack full of magazines	pay phone near rear entrance

Organizing Details

After you select your details, you then group them into categories and decide on an appropriate order. As in expository essays, each category becomes the basis of a supporting paragraph. The following examples show common ways of organizing details in personal essays. *(For more information about types of order, see pages 264–265.)*

Model: *Organizing Details*

KIND OF DETAILS   events in a story, narrated from beginning to end

TYPE OF ORDER   chronological order

KIND OF DETAILS   descriptive details to help readers visualize a person, object, or scene

TYPE OF ORDER   spatial order

KIND OF DETAILS   background details and details explaining the meaning of an experience

TYPE OF ORDER   order of importance or interest

KIND OF DETAILS   sensory details and details leading up to an impression or interpretation of an experience

TYPE OF ORDER   developmental order

WRITING ACTIVITY *Organizing Details*

Arrange the following details into logical groupings for the supporting paragraphs of a personal essay.

MAIN IDEA   My brother and I are different in most ways.

DETAILS

He enjoys working out.   I have a best friend.
I get better grades.   He's darker-skinned.
He's athletic.   I'm heavier.
I have longer hair.   We play cards together.
He's more social.   I love movies.
I'm clumsier.   He's tall and slim.
He's good in math.   We like the same music.

WRITING ACTIVITY *Identifying Types of Order*

Identify the type of order used in each of the following passages from *Barrio Boy*. Answer by writing *chronological order, spatial order, order of importance,* or *developmental order.*

1.

Our new bungalow had five rooms, and porches front and back. In the way of furniture, what friends did not lend or Mrs. Dodson gave us we bought in the secondhand shops. The only new item was an elegant gas range, with a high oven and long, slender legs finished in enamel . . .

2.

It was a sunny, airy spot, with a family orchard to one side and a vacant lot on the other. Back of us there was a pasture. With chicken wire we fenced the back yard, turned over the soil, and planted our first vegetable garden and fruit trees . . . A single row of geraniums and carnations separated the vegetable garden from the house . . . On every side our windows looked out on family orchards, platinum stretches of wild oats and quiet lanes, shady and unpaved.

3.

For the three men of the household as well as for me the bicycle became the most important means for earning a living. Oak Park was miles away from the usual places where they worked and they pedaled off, in good weather and bad, in the early morning. It was a case of saving carfare.

WRITING ACTIVITY *Writing on Your Own*

WRITING
ABOUT THE
THEME
Follow the guidelines on page 300 to select the details for your essay about a family change or decision. Then organize those details by grouping them into categories and deciding how you will order those groupings. To show how you have categorized and ordered your details, write a simple cluster or outline. Save your notes for later use.

Drafting

Writing the first draft of your essay is a matter of transforming the information in your cluster or outline into sentences and paragraphs. As you write, remember that a personal essay is less formal than other kinds of essays. Unlike an expository essay, for example, it is written from the first person point of view and does not have a formal thesis statement. Like all essays, however, a personal essay should have a clear main idea, an attention-getting introduction, a well-organized body, and a strong conclusion.

Drafting the Introduction

In a personal essay, the introduction lets readers know what they are about to hear, who you are, and how you feel about your subject. The introduction also should interest readers enough so that they want to continue reading about your experience. *(For more information about introductions, see page 219.)*

The Introduction of a Personal Essay

1. It introduces the subject and purpose of the essay.
2. It makes clear the main idea of the essay.
3. It sets the tone to reveal the writer's point of view.
4. It captures the readers' interest.

Tone in Personal Essays   The tone of an essay reveals the writer's attitudes toward the subject and the audience. The words and expressions you use clue readers in to your intentions. In setting the tone of an essay, therefore, you need to decide how you want readers to feel. Do you want them to laugh, cry, feel nostalgic or reflective, or become angry? You also have to decide if you want them to feel sympathetic toward you and the insight you gained through your experience. *(For more information about tone, see page 226.)*

The following models show how a student experimented with tone in four different introductions on the same subject. Keep in mind, however, that once you choose a tone, you should maintain it throughout your entire essay.

Student Models: *Tone*

SYMPATHETIC

Life in a big family can be hectic. Someone is always playing with the dog, usually riling him up to a fever pitch of barking and jumping. Someone else is always watching television, and in the same room two people might be listening to two different radio stations. When I need an escape, I go up to the roof of our apartment building and play my guitar. I lose the rest of the world when I play the guitar, but I find myself.

HUMOROUS

It was four o'clock on a humid afternoon and the household was in an uproar. J.C. was riling up the dog, which had reached a fever pitch of hysterical barking. My sisters in the next room were each listening to a different rock station on their radios, and Gramps had raised the volume on the television set to compensate for all the noise. Amidst the nerve-racking roar of sports fans, the brain-numbing basses of the two rock numbers, and the dog's pandemonium, I grabbed my guitar and headed for the roof. Peace at last, peace at last, peace at last!

ANGRY

Life in a big family does not have to be hectic if only everyone would be considerate of one another's basic needs. This is not the case at my house, where the rule seems to be everyone for oneself. People don't think twice about making the dog bark, turning up the television, or playing their music too loud—often all at the same time. I can take it only for so long before I have to escape to the roof with my guitar. If it weren't for my guitar, there would be far more arguments at my house about peace and quiet.

REFLECTIVE

I remember the time I first left my hectic family behind and escaped to the roof to play my guitar. It had been a humid afternoon, and everyone seemed to be in a contrary mood—even the dog. The result was more noise than I could stand. The dog was barking, my sisters were listening to two different, loud radio stations, and my grandfather had turned up the volume on the television set to hear the ball game. I can still sense the sudden relief my guitar and I felt as we let our first gentle chords float down from the quiet rooftop.

WRITING ACTIVITY *Experimenting with Tone*

Add a paragraph to each of the four models on page 304 and above that continues the same tone that has been set. Then think about the tone that you would choose for this subject if you were writing this essay from your own experience. State the reason for your choice in a sentence or two.

WRITING ACTIVITY *Writing on Your Own*

WRITING
ABOUT THE
THEME

Review your prewriting notes and draft possible introductions for your essay about your family. Experiment with setting different tones. You may use the tones illustrated in the student models on page 304 and above or other tones of your choice. As you write your introduction, also remember to refine and clearly express your main idea and to begin in a way that will capture the readers' interest. Save your drafts in your writing folder.

Drafting the Body

After you have introduced the subject and set a tone appropriate for your purpose, you are ready to draft the body of your essay. Use your cluster diagram or outline to convert the details of your experience into paragraphs. As you write, make your interpretation of your experience clear and use vivid, well-organized details to hold your readers' attention to the end. You may find the following guidelines helpful.

Guidelines for Drafting the Body

1. Make sure that each supporting paragraph has a topic sentence that supports the main idea.
2. Write your ideas and details in a logical order.
3. Use transitions between sentences and paragraphs to give your essay coherence.
4. Include vivid details and sensory words to bring your experience to life.
5. As you write, add any new ideas and details you discover, if they will help you develop your main idea.

The student who wrote the introductions on pages 304 and 305 chose the one with a sympathetic tone and then drafted the following body for a short personal essay.

Student Model: *The Body of a Personal Essay*

My escape to the rooftop always works for me because I am listening only to my sounds for a change. As I sing along with my guitar, I can hear my own voice—however weak it may be. If I finger the wrong strings or frets, then at least they are my mistakes. Whatever mistakes I make, my music always sounds good to me, because when I concentrate on playing the right notes and chords, the rest of the world seems far away.

306

The greatest value of escaping with my guitar, however, is the chance it gives me to express my feelings. The tunes I play depend on my mood. Sometimes I play simple, quiet ballads or sad, bluesy refrains. Other times I strum loud sets, joyous or angry, until my fingertips sting. After each session on the roof with my guitar, I feel as if I have had a good long talk with an understanding friend.

WRITING ACTIVITY 12 *Writing on Your Own*

WRITING
ABOUT THE
THEME

Choose the introduction you like best that you wrote in Writing Activity 11. Then, keeping the same tone, draft the body of your personal essay about your family. Be sure to include the most effective details that you selected in Writing Activity 9. When you have finished, save your draft in your writing folder.

Drafting the Conclusion

The conclusion of your personal essay should emphasize in some way the meaning of your experience. You might give your readers a sense of completion and make your last sentence as memorable as your first. You might also end your essay in any of the ways below or a combination of them.

Ways to End a Personal Essay

1. Summarize the body.
2. Restate the main idea in new words.
3. Add an insight that shows a new or deeper understanding of the experience.
4. Add a striking new detail or memorable image.
5. Refer to ideas in the introduction to bring your essay full circle.
6. Appeal to the readers' emotions.

The conclusion below ends the student essay, which was entitled "My Guitar and I." This conclusion refers back to the introduction on page 304 and restates the main idea.

Student Model: *Conclusion of a Personal Essay*

By the time I come down from the roof, the television does not seem so loud anymore, and the dog seems like his old self again. I even smile when I hear my sisters' noisy radios. Although I have come back to reality, I am glad to know that my guitar is there for me the next time I need to escape.

WRITING ACTIVITY ⑬ *Writing on Your Own*

WRITING
ABOUT THE
THEME

Reread the introduction and body of your personal essay about your family. Then draft at least two possible conclusions. Also think of three or four possible titles. Then choose the conclusion and title that best suit your essay. When you have finished your first draft, lay it aside for a day or two, if possible, before you reread it.

Revising

Once you have turned the raw materials of your personal perceptions and reflections into a rough draft of your essay, you can turn to the important task of revision. Revising a personal essay involves attention to three important points.

- Have you developed your essay in sufficient detail?
- Have you made your ideas and feelings clear?
- Have you maintained a consistent tone?

Revising for Adequate Development

Part of the success in writing a personal essay comes in making the reader clearly see and hear what you want to share. Therefore, you should check to make sure you have included enough specific supporting details to give substance to your ideas. Notice in the following example from *Barrio Boy* how details are used to build an adequately developed paragraph.

Model: *Adequate Development*

LACKS ADEQUATE DEVELOPMENT	Before we moved, I buried my marbles in the backyard.
ADEQUATELY DEVELOPED	The last thing I did when we moved out of 418 L was to dig a hole in the corner of the backyard for a tall carton of Quaker Oats cereal, full to the brim with the marbles I had won playing for keeps around the *barrio*. I tamped the earth over my buried treasure and laid a curse on whoever removed it without my permission.

The details that Galarza provides help readers to feel the way he did when he buried his treasured marbles. To evaluate whether you have achieved this effect, check your essay for vivid and interesting details. The strategies on the next page will help you think of additional details as you revise your essay.

Strategies for Revising for Adequate Development	
EVENTS	Close your eyes and slowly visualize the experience that you are writing about. Write down the details as you "see" them in your mind's eye.
PEOPLE	Visualize each person you are writing about. Start by visualizing the head and face of each person and slowly move down to the feet. Write down details as you "see" them.
PLACES	Visualize the place you are describing. Start at the left of the setting and visualize slowly to the right. Also visualize from the foreground to the background.
FEELINGS	Imagine yourself repeating the experience that you are writing about. Focus on your thoughts and feelings as you relive the experience.

Using a Revision Checklist

After you have revised your writing to be sure that you have developed your ideas adequately, check your essay for unity, coherence, and clarity. *(See pages 231–232.)* Especially, look for places where you can add transitions to help your writing flow smoothly. The following Checklist for Revision will help you identify other areas for improvement when you revise a personal essay.

Checklist for Revision
1. Does your introduction capture the readers' interest? If not, can you make a better beginning?
2. Are there any parts of the essay where your reader's attention might wander? If those parts are needed to achieve your purpose, how can you add interest to them?
3. Does your feeling about your subject come through? If not, how can you make the point more clearly?
4. Does your ending give the readers a sense of completion? If not, how might you make it more effective?

WRITING ACTIVITY *Revising for Adequate Development*

Revise the following paragraphs by adding details that would capture the readers' interest and fully develop the experience. Consider what questions the writers leave unanswered and what details are missing that would help readers to visualize or understand the experience.

1.

Seeing my uncle in the parade gave me a lump in my throat. Just as I recognized his familiar face, he winked at me as he passed. He was marching with the veterans of the Vietnam War. They looked really impressive. The first time I saw my uncle marching in the parade, he became a real hero to me.

2.

We slowed down to see the alligator. It was in the road, sunning itself with its mouth wide open. As we drove past, it lunged forward and bit the tail pipe. Who would have thought that a gator would try to take a bite out of a car.

WRITING ACTIVITY *Writing on Your Own*

WRITING
ABOUT THE
THEME

Return to the personal essay on the theme of family that you have written and revise it, using the Checklist for Revision on page 310 as a guide. Also be sure to check for adequate development, clarity, and consistency in tone.

311

Editing and Publishing

In *Barrio Boy*, Ernesto Galarza writes the following.

It was at Bret Harte [School] that I learned how an English sentence could be cut up on the blackboard and the pieces placed on different lines connected by what the teacher called a diagram. The idea of operating on a sentence and rearranging its members as a skeleton of verbs, modifiers, subject, and prepositions set me off diagraming whatever I read, in Spanish and English.

Galarza was learning about the extraordinary versatility of the English language, in which the same thought may be expressed in a variety of ways simply by rearranging the parts of a sentence. An example of versatile parts of a sentence is the kind of modifier called the appositive phrase.

Appositive Phrases   An *appositive phrase* is a group of words with no subject or verb that adds information about another word in the sentence. The added information usually identifies a person, place, or thing that may be unknown to the reader. In the following sentences, for example, the readers would not know who the Harrisons are or what Joyland and "The Russian Mountain" are without the appositive phrases. Notice that appositive phrases are set off by commas. *(For more information about appositive phrases and practice in punctuating them correctly, see pages 640–647 and 830–831.)*

APPOSITIVE PHRASES   The Harrisons, **the people across the street,** were cordial to us.

Some Sundays we walked to Joyland, **an amusement park,** where my mother sat on a bench to watch the children play on the lawn . . .

Combining Sentences with Appositive Phrases Often you can make your writing more concise by using an appositive phrase to combine two sentences. *(For more examples and for practice in combining sentences, see pages 66 and 643.)*

TWO SENTENCES	I transferred to Bret Harte School. It was a gingerbread two-story building.
COMBINED SENTENCE	I transferred to Bret Harte School, **a gingerbread two-story building.**
TWO SENTENCES	The telephone was a communications tool. It would connect me with important people.
COMBINED SENTENCE	The telephone, **a communications tool,** would connect me with important people.

Editing Checklist

I. Did you use appositive phrases to add important information about another word in the sentence? *(See page 640.)*

2. Did you punctuate appositive phrases correctly? *(See pages 642 and 830.)*

3. Did you use appositive phrases to combine sentences where possible? *(See pages 66 and 643.)*

WRITING ACTIVITY   16   *Writing on Your Own*

WRITING
ABOUT THE
THEME

Editing   Share your personal essay about your family with classmates, friends, or family members. To hear places where you could improve your writing, read your essay aloud. Then edit your essay, using listeners' comments and the Editing Checklists above and on page 37.

Publishing   When your essay is the best it can be, make a neat final copy. Then publish it in one of the ways listed on page 43. If possible, tape-record your essay as a remembrance of this time in your life.

A Writer Writes

  ## A Personal Experience Essay

PURPOSE: to express thoughts and feelings about a family relationship

AUDIENCE: your classmates and teacher

Prewriting The people you are most closely related to can be the greatest source of strength when you are facing a challenge. Sometimes, however, it is a more distant relative or an

The Boating Party, Mary Cassatt, 1893/1894.

extended family member or friend who offers special under-standing. Decide on a particularly close or meaningful relation-ship in your past that you will write about in a personal essay. Use freewriting, inquiring, clustering, or brainstorming to recall important details of the relationship, the person with whom you shared it, and the context in which it became meaningful to you. Next write a statement explaining why you found this relationship so meaningful.

Drafting   Write a first draft of your personal essay, including an introduction that states or suggests your main idea, a body of supporting paragraphs, and a conclusion.

Revising   Have you included enough descriptive, sensory, and background details to develop your main idea sufficiently? Is the tone of your essay consistent from beginning to end? Will the essay hold your readers' attention to the end? Make any necessary revisions and add transitions that will help your essay flow more smoothly.

Editing and Publishing   Use the Editing Checklists on pages 37 and 313 to edit your essay. Copy your corrected essay neatly onto a spirit duplicating master or reproduce it in some other way so that all your classmates can read a copy. You may wish to make a class anthology of personal-experience essays, enti-tled "Relationships." You may also wish to share your work, if possible, with the person who is the subject of your essay.

Independent Writing

Search Idea Sources for Subjects of Personal Essays on page 294, your journal entries, and your memory for a personal experience you can develop into a humorous essay. You might write about a childhood experience that seems humorous to you now, even though you did not find it funny at the time. Before you plan your essay, examine the experience for its meaning to you. Maintain a humorous tone throughout the essay, at the same time making it clear to readers how you felt at the time of the experience.

Creative Writing

In her poem "Lineage," Margaret Walker identifies the strengths that she admires in her grandmothers—in contrast to herself. She bases this contrast on her observations of her grandmothers in the simple tasks of daily life. Write a poem that expresses an observation you have made about your family life or about a particular family relationship. You may choose to base your writing on fictional rather than real observations. Your poem may be unrhymed, like "Lineage," or rhymed, like the following poem by Miriam Hershenson.

Husbands and Wives

Husbands and wives
With children between them
Sit in the subway;
So I have seen them.

One word only
From station to station;
So much talk for
So close a relation.

  ## Writing about Literature

Tone, as you have already learned in this chapter, is the writer's attitude toward his or her subject. Write a paragraph that explains what you think is Ernesto Galarza's tone in the selection from *Barrio Boy.*

  ## Writing in Other Subject Areas

Social Studies   Ask members of your family to tell you about a period or event in history that had a significant effect on their thoughts and feelings. As you interview your respondents, list details about the period or event, the respondent's experience in it, and the meaning of that experience. For example, your respondent may talk about his or her feelings during the civil rights movement of the 1960's or during the spread of democracy to Communist countries in the 1990's. Based on the information you have gathered, choose one experience to develop into a personal essay. Using the first person point of view, write from the respondent's viewpoint—as if you were the one who had had the experience.

C
h
a
p
t
e
r

8 Checklist

Writing Personal Essays

Prewriting

✔ Search your memory for personal experiences and insights to share with readers. *(See page 294.)*

✔ Choose one subject that interests you most and interpret its meaning. *(See pages 295–296.)*

✔ Decide on your specific purpose in writing, your main idea, and your audience. *(See page 297.)*

✔ List background details of time and place and vivid descriptive and sensory details. *(See pages 298–300.)*

✔ Group your details and organize them in a logical order. *(See page 301.)*

Drafting

✔ Introduce your subject in a way that captures the reader's interest and sets the tone of the essay. *(See pages 303–305.)*

✔ Build the body of your essay, using the most effective details for accomplishing your purpose. *(See pages 306–307.)*

✔ Add a conclusion that clearly expresses the idea or feeling that you want to convey. *(See page 308.)*

✔ Choose a title that is consistent with the tone of your essay. *(See page 31.)*

Revising

✔ Revise your essay for adequate development. *(See pages 309–310.)*

✔ Revise your essay for unity, coherence, and clarity. *(See pages 231–232.)*

Editing and Publishing

✔ Use the Editing Checklists to polish your grammar, usage, spelling, and mechanics. *(See pages 37 and 313.)*

✔ Publish your final draft. *(See pages 41–43.)*

9 Writing Essays about Literature

Part 1 *Reading to Write*

THEME: *Choices*

You face many choices in your life. When you make important decisions, you apply a variety of standards for what is best. In trying to decide on the best choice, you may consider the convenience of a particular course of action or its costs and benefits to you and to others. You may also consider the rightness of a choice in terms of your religious beliefs or moral values and your family's or community's standards.

Throughout your life these standards for making choices will often conflict. Doing the right thing, for example, will sometimes be inconvenient or costly. Sometimes you will find that you must choose between the lesser of two evils. Each time such conflicts occur, you will have to decide whether or not to change or lower your standards.

In the following story, "Say It with Flowers," the main character faces just such a conflict. As you read, look for the standards that formed the basis of Teruo's decision. After you read the story, you will be making some choices about the best way to interpret it and to respond to it in writing.

Say It with Flowers

T o s h i o   M o r i

He was a queer one to come to the shop and ask Mr. Sasaki[1] for a job, but at the time I kept my mouth shut. There was something about this young man's appearance which I could not altogether harmonize with a job as a clerk in a flower shop. I was a delivery boy for Mr. Sasaki then. I had seen clerks come and go, and although they were of various sorts of temperaments and conducts, all of them had the technique of waiting on the customers or acquired one eventually. You could never tell about a new one, however, and to be on the safe side I said nothing and watched our boss readily take on this young man. Anyhow we were glad to have an extra hand because the busy season was coming around.

Mr. Sasaki undoubtedly remembered last year's rush when Tommy, Mr. Sasaki and I had to do everything and had our hands tied behind our backs from having so many things to do at one time. He wanted to be ready this time. "Another clerk and we'll be all set for any kind of business," he used to tell us. When Teruo[2] came around looking for a job, he got it, and Morning-Glory Flower Shop was all set for the year as far as our boss was concerned.

When Teruo reported for work the following morning Mr. Sasaki left him in Tommy's hands. Tommy had been our number one clerk for a long time.

1. **Sasaki** [sä sä′ ki].
2. **Teruo** [tə rū′ ō].

"Tommy, teach him all you can," Mr. Sasaki said. "Teruo's going to be with us from now on."

"Sure," Tommy said.

"Tommy's a good florist. You watch and listen to him," the boss told the young man.

"All right, Mr. Sasaki," the young man said. He turned to us and said, "My name is Teruo." We shook hands.

We got to know one another pretty well after that. He was a quiet fellow with very little words for anybody, but his smile disarmed a person. We soon learned that he knew nothing about the florist business. He could identify a rose when he saw one, and gardenias and carnations too; but other flowers and materials were new to him.

"You fellows teach me something about this business and I'll be grateful. I want to start from the bottom," Teruo said.

Tommy and I nodded. We were pretty sure by then he was all right. Tommy eagerly went about showing Teruo the florist game. Every morning for several days Tommy repeated the prices of the flowers for him. He told Teruo what to do on telephone orders; how to keep the greens fresh; how to make bouquets, corsages, and sprays. "You need a little more time to learn how to make big funeral pieces," Tommy said. "That'll come later."

In a couple of weeks Teruo was just as good a clerk as we had had in a long time. He was curious almost to a fault, and was a glutton for work. It was about this time our boss decided to move ahead his yearly business trip to Seattle. Undoubtedly he was satisfied with Teruo, and he knew we could get along without him for a while. He went off and left Tommy in full charge.

During Mr. Sasaki's absence I was often in the shop helping Tommy and Teruo with the customers and the orders. One day Teruo learned that I once worked in the nursery and had experience in flower-growing.

"How do you tell when a flower is fresh or old?" he asked me. "I can't tell one from the other. All I do is follow your instructions and sell the ones you tell me to sell first, but I can't tell one from the other."

I laughed. "You don't need to know that, Teruo," I told him. "When the customers ask you whether the flowers are fresh, say yes firmly. 'Our flowers are always fresh, madam.'"

Teruo picked up a vase of carnations. "These flowers came in four or five days ago, didn't they?" he asked me.

"You're right. Five days ago," I said.

"How long will they keep if a customer bought them today?" Teruo asked.

"I guess in this weather they'll hold a day or two," I said.

"Then they're old," Teruo almost gasped. "Why, we have fresh ones that last a week or so in the shop."

"Sure, Teruo. And why should you worry about that?" Tommy said. "You talk right to the customers and they'll believe you. 'Our flowers are always fresh? You bet they are! Just came in a little while ago from the market.'"

Teruo looked at us calmly. "That's a hard thing to say when you know it isn't true."

"You've got to get it over with sooner or later," I told him. "Everybody has to do it. You too, unless you want to lose your job."

"I don't think I can say it convincingly again," Teruo said. "I must've said yes forty times already when I didn't know any better. It'll be harder next time."

"You've said it forty times already so why can't you say yes forty million times more? What's the difference? Remember, Teruo, it's your business to live," Tommy said.

"I don't like it," Teruo said.

"Do we like it? Do you think we're any different from you?" Tommy asked Teruo. "You're just a green kid. You don't know any better so I don't get sore, but you got to play the game when you're in it. You understand, don't you?"

Teruo nodded. For a moment he stood and looked curiously at us for the first time, and then went away to water the potted plants.

In the ensuing weeks we watched Teruo develop into a slick salesclerk but for one thing. If a customer forgot to ask about the condition of the flowers Teruo did splendidly. But if someone should mention about the freshness of the flowers he wilted right in front of the customers. Sometimes he would splutter. He would stand gaping speechless on other occasions without a comeback. Sometimes, looking embarrassedly at us, he would take the customers to the fresh flowers in the rear and complete the sales.

"Don't do that any more, Teruo," Tommy warned him one afternoon after watching him repeatedly sell the fresh ones. "You know we got plenty of the old stuff in the front. We can't throw all that stuff away. First thing you know the boss'll start losing money and we'll all be thrown out."

"I wish I could sell like you," Teruo said. "Whenever they ask me, 'Is this fresh?' 'How long will it keep?' I lose all sense about selling the stuff, and begin to think of the difference between the fresh and the old stuff. Then the trouble begins."

"Remember, the boss has to run the shop so he can keep it going," Tommy told him. "When he returns next week you better not let him see you touch the fresh flowers in the rear."

On the day Mr. Sasaki came back to the shop we saw something unusual. For the first time I watched Teruo sell some old stuff to a customer. I heard the man plainly ask him if the flowers would keep good, and very clearly I heard Teruo reply, "Yes, sir. These flowers'll keep good." I looked at Tommy, and he winked back. When Teruo came back to make it into a bouquet he looked as if he had a snail in his mouth. Mr. Sasaki came back to the rear and watched him make the bouquet. When Teruo went up front to complete the sale Mr. Sasaki looked at Tommy and nodded approvingly.

When I went out to the truck to make my last delivery for the day Teruo followed me. "Gee, I feel rotten," he said to me. "Those flowers I sold to the people, they won't last longer than tomorrow. I feel lousy. I'm lousy. The people'll get to know my word pretty soon."

"Forget it," I said. "Quit worrying. What's the matter with you?"

"I'm lousy," he said, and went back to the store.

Then one early morning the inevitable happened. While Teruo was selling the fresh flowers in the back to a customer Mr. Sasaki came in quietly and watched the transaction. The boss didn't say anything at the time. All day Teruo looked sick. He didn't know whether to explain to the boss or shut up.

While Teruo was out to lunch Mr. Sasaki called us aside. "How long has this been going on?" he asked us. He was pretty sore.

"He's been doing it off and on. We told him to quit it," Tommy said. "He says he feels rotten selling old flowers."

"Old flowers!" snorted Mr. Sasaki. "I'll tell him plenty when he comes back. Old flowers! Maybe you can call them old at the wholesale market but they're not old in a flower shop."

"He feels guilty fooling the customers," Tommy explained.

The boss laughed impatiently. "That's no reason for a businessman."

When Teruo came back he knew what was up. He looked at us for a moment and then went about cleaning the stems of the old flowers.

"Teruo," Mr. Sasaki called.

Teruo approached us as if steeled for an attack.

"You've been selling fresh flowers and leaving the old ones go to waste. I can't afford that, Teruo," Mr. Sasaki said. "Why don't you do as you're told? We all sell the flowers in the front. I tell you they're not old in a flower shop. Why can't you sell them?"

"I don't like it, Mr. Sasaki," Teruo said. "When the people ask me if they're fresh I hate to answer. I feel rotten after selling the old ones."

"Look here, Teruo," Mr. Sasaki said. "I don't want to fire you. You're a good boy, and I know you need a job, but you've got to be a good clerk here or you're going out. Do you get me?"

"I get you," Teruo said.

In the morning we were all at the shop early. I had an eight o'clock delivery, and the others had to rush with a big funeral order. Teruo was there early. "Hello," he greeted us cheerfully as we came in. He was unusually highspirited, and I couldn't account for it. He was there before us and had already filled out the eight o'clock package for me. He was almost through with the funeral frame, padding it with wet moss and covering it all over with brake fern, when Tommy came in. When Mr. Sasaki arrived, Teruo waved his hand and cheerfully went about gathering the flowers for the funeral piece. As he flitted here and there he seemed as if he had forgotten our presence, even the boss. He looked at each vase, sized up the flowers, and then cocked his head at the next one. He did this with great deliberation, as if he were the boss and the last word in the shop. That was all right, but when a customer soon came in, he swiftly attended him as if he owned all the flowers in the world. When the man asked Teruo if he was getting fresh flowers Teruo without batting an eye escorted the customer into the rear and eventually showed and sold the fresh ones. He did it with so much grace, dignity and swiftness that we stood around like his stooges. However, Mr. Sasaki went on with his work as if nothing had happened.

Along toward noon Teruo attended his second customer. He fairly ran to greet an old lady who wanted a cheap bouquet around fifty cents for a dinner table. This time he not only went back to the rear for the fresh ones but added three or four extras. To make it more irritating for the boss, who was watching every move, Teruo used an extra lot of maidenhair because the old lady was appreciative of his art of making bouquets. Tommy and I watched the boss fuming inside of his office.

When the old lady went out of the shop Mr. Sasaki came out furious. "You're a blockhead. You have no business sense. What are you doing here?" he said to Teruo. "Are you crazy?"

Teruo looked cheerful. "I'm not crazy, Mr. Sasaki," he said. "And I'm not dumb. I just like to do it that way, that's all."

The boss turned to Tommy and me. "That boy's a sap," he said. "He's got no head."

Teruo laughed and walked off to the front with a broom. Mr. Sasaki shook his head. "What's the matter with him? I can't understand him," he said.

While the boss was out to lunch Teruo went on a mad spree. He waited on three customers at one time, ignoring our presence. It was amazing how he did it. He hurriedly took one customer's order and had him write a birthday greeting for it; jumped to the second customer's side and persuaded her to buy Columbia roses because they were the freshest of the lot. She wanted them delivered so he jotted it down on the sales book, and leaped to the third customer.

"I want to buy that orchid in the window," she stated without deliberation.

"Do you have to have orchid, madam?" Teruo asked the lady.

"No," she said. "But I want something nice for tonight's ball, and I think the orchid will match my dress. Why do you ask?"

"If I were you I wouldn't buy that orchid," he told her. "It won't keep. I could sell it to you and make a profit but I don't want to do that and spoil your evening. Come to the back, madam, and I'll show you some of the nicest gardenias in the market today. We call them Belmont and they're fresh today."

He came to the rear with the lady. We watched him pick out three of the biggest gardenias and make them into a corsage. When the lady went out with her package a little boy about eleven years old came in and wanted a twenty-five-cent bouquet for his mother's birthday. Teruo waited on the boy. He was out in the front, and we saw him pick out a dozen of the two-dollar-a-dozen roses and give them to the kid.

Tommy nudged me. "If he was the boss he couldn't do those things," he said.

"In the first place," I said, "I don't think he could be a boss."

"What do you think?" Tommy said. "Is he crazy? Is he trying to get himself fired?"

"I don't know," I said.

When Mr. Sasaki returned, Teruo was waiting on another customer, a young lady.

"Did Teruo eat yet?" Mr. Sasaki asked Tommy.

"No, he won't go. He says he's not hungry today," Tommy said.

We watched Teruo talking to the young lady. The boss shook his head. Then it came. Teruo came back to the rear and picked out a dozen of the very fresh white roses and took them out to the lady.

"Aren't they lovely?" we heard her exclaim.

We watched him come back, take down a box, place several maidenhairs and asparagus, place the roses neatly inside, sprinkle a few drops, and then give it to her. We watched him thank

her, and we noticed her smile and thanks. The girl walked out.

Mr. Sasaki ran excitedly to the front. "Teruo! She forgot to pay!"

Teruo stopped the boss on the way out. "Wait, Mr. Sasaki," he said. "I gave it to her."

"What!" the boss cried indignantly.

"She came in just to look around and see the flowers. She likes pretty roses. Don't you think she's wonderful?"

"What's the matter with you?" the boss said. "Are you crazy? What did she buy?"

"Nothing, I tell you," Teruo said. "I gave it to her because she admired it, and she's pretty enough to deserve beautiful things, and I liked her."

"You're fired! Get out!" Mr. Sasaki spluttered. "Don't come back to the store again."

"And I gave her fresh ones too," Teruo said.

Mr. Sasaki rolled out several bills from his pocketbook. "Here's your wages for this week. Now, get out," he said.

"I don't want it," Teruo said. "You keep it and buy some more flowers."

"Here, take it. Get out," Mr. Sasaki said.

Teruo took the bills and rang up the cash register. "All right, I'll go now. I feel fine. I'm happy. Thanks to you." He waved his hand to Mr. Sasaki. "No hard feelings."

On the way out Teruo remembered our presence. He looked back. "Good-bye, Good luck," he said cheerfully to Tommy and me. He walked out of the shop with his shoulders straight, head high, and whistling. He did not come back to see us again.

Responding to the Theme

Choices

■ ***Responding in Your Journal*** Reserve a section of your journal for responding to literature or start a separate reader's journal in which you can write your thoughts, reactions, and feelings about any literary work you read. Then use the entries in your reader's journal as ideas for essays about literature or for your own creative writing. Start your reader's journal today by responding to the following questions about "Say It with Flowers."

1. What did you like or dislike about the story?
2. What events in the story puzzled you or left a particularly strong impression?
3. How did characters change and why?
4. Who or what in your life did the story remind you of?
5. What are your ideas about the theme of "choices"?

■ ***Speaking and Listening*** Imagine that you are another coworker in the Morning-Glory Flower Shop. What might you say to Mr. Sasaki, Tommy, and the narrator to persuade them to take a different point of view? With your teacher's permission, work with three classmates to discuss Teruo's behavior. Take turns playing each character, including the imaginary coworker. Listen carefully to each player's complete argument before you respond.

■ ***Critical Thinking: Predicting*** At the end of the story, Teruo is happy to leave his job when Mr. Sasaki fires him. What consequences do you imagine Teruo's decision will have after the end of the story— for himself and for the other characters? What are some choices that Mr. Sasaki, Tommy, and the narrator might make because of Teruo's decision?

■ ***Extending Your Vocabulary*** The following words in "Say It with Flowers" all relate to doing business. Using a dictionary, write the origins of five of the following words.

business	clerk	market	transaction
cash	delivery	profit	wages

The New York Times

Arts & Leisure

'Our Town' and Our Towns

Fifty years ago the first performances of Thornton Wilder's "Our Town" captured a now-vanished time in American life. On the occasion of the anniversary, the Pulitzer Prize-winning playwright Lanford Wilson, whose works include "Talley's Folly" and the current "Burn This," reflects on the meaning of the play today. On page 36, Mel Gussow reviews the current production at the Long Wharf Theater in New Haven and discusses the place of "Our Town" in the American theater.

By LANFORD WILSON

GROVER'S CORNERS, NEW HAMPSHIRE, IS 50 years old and holding up considerably better than most of our towns. Whole neighborhoods in our cities are being restored, prettied up and made profitable but it only takes a trip to the

Part 2 · *Writing*

"Say It with Flowers" is a literary work of the type known as the short story. Some other *genres* [zhon' rə]—literary forms— include novels, poems, essays, and plays. These genres have the following characteristics. Understanding these characteristics will help you prepare to write a critical essay about a work of literature.

Characteristics of Literary Genres

SHORT STORY   A short work of narrative fiction. The story usually occurs within a short period of time and involves few characters and settings. Readers rely mainly on the writer's descriptions and on dialogue to understand the plot, characters, setting, and theme.

NOVEL   A long work of narrative fiction with a plot that is unfolded by the actions, speech, and thoughts of the characters. Like most short stories, a novel presents a central conflict and its resolution or outcome.

POEM   A highly structured composition, which presents images concretely using condensed, vivid language that is chosen for the way it sounds as well as for its meaning. Characteristics commonly include the use of meter, rhyme, and figurative language.

ESSAY   A short composition on one subject, on which the writer expresses his or her opinions, thoughts, and feelings. A *critical essay* is a short composition in which the writer presents an interpretation or review of a performance or of a work of literature, music, or art.

PLAY   A composition written for dramatic performance on the stage. Like a short story, a play usually tells a story that has few characters and settings and takes place within a short period of time. The audience relies on dialogue, stage sets, and action to understand the setting, plot, characters, and theme.

During your years in school, you will read many literary works in a variety of genres from poems to plays. In many cases you will also be asked to write about what you have read. From time to time, for example, you may be asked to write an essay in which you express your personal response—your feelings about the literary work you have read. At other times you may be asked to write a critical essay, in which you evaluate a literary work and share your understanding of it.

Writing about a literary work will help you understand it better and see meanings that you might otherwise miss. Writing your thoughts and feelings also gives you time to savor the words, images, and ideas that you will find as you read a literary work. The famous writer Vladimir Nabokov even drew an analogy between studying literature and digesting food.

Literature, real literature, must not be gulped down . . .
Literature must be taken and broken into bits, pulled
apart, squashed . . . [T]hen, and only then, its rare flavor
will be appreciated . . . and the broken and crushed
parts will come together again in your mind . . .

Prewriting

Reading is more than appreciating a literary work's "rare flavor." Like writing, reading is a creative process. That is, as a reader you help create the meaning of a literary work. Because each reader brings personal meanings to a work, a story or poem affects different readers in different ways, and no work has a single, correct meaning. Instead, the meaning grows out of the relationship between the writer's words and each reader's response. That response comes from several sources.

Sources of a Reader's Response to Literature
1. Individual characteristics—such as age, sex, and personality **2.** Cultural or ethnic origins, attitudes, and customs **3.** Personal opinions, beliefs, and values **4.** Life experiences and general knowledge **5.** Knowledge of literature and literary genres **6.** Knowledge of the historical and cultural context of a work **7.** Reading and language skills

All of these sources combine to affect your response to anything you read. Who you are, where you live, and what your life has been like so far, for example, may enable you to identify with a character, situation, or feeling in a work. When you *identify* with characters, you put yourself in their shoes; you see

what they see and feel what they feel. The more closely you can identify, the more enjoyment and meaning you will usually find in reading and writing about a literary work.

Responding from Personal Experience

One of the reasons you may enjoy reading and writing about a particular work is the pleasure you get from recalling your past. A story, play, or poem will often trigger memories of your own feelings and experiences. You use these memories to identify closely with characters.

In the process of identifying, you remember times in your life when you were in similar situations and how you felt at those times. For example, if you identified with Tobi in "The Confidence Game" on page 87, you may have remembered a time in your life when fear of losing made you a poor sport temporarily. This memory may then have given the story a deeper meaning for you. The following strategies will help you explore your personal responses to a literary work.

Personal Response Strategies

1. In your reader's journal, freewrite answers to the following questions.
   a. What character do you identify with? Do the other characters remind you of people you know?
   b. How does the work make you feel? Why?
   c. If you were a character in the work, would you have behaved differently? What behaviors in the story puzzle you?
   d. What experiences from your own life came to your mind as you read this work? How did you feel about those experiences?
2. Write a personal response statement in which you summarize what the work means to you.
3. In small discussion groups, share your responses to the work. As you listen to your classmates' reactions, refine your ideas about the work. Afterward, write freely about how, if at all, your ideas about the work have changed.

WRITING ACTIVITY *Responding from Personal Experience*

Complete the following activity in your reader's journal.

1. Based on your first reading of "Say It with Flowers" by Toshio Mori, write answers to the questions in item 1 in the Personal Response Strategies on page 331.

2. Next, reread the story up to the last paragraph on page 321, and stop to write your reactions. What do you think of the characters? What do you think of Teruo's approach to learning his job? When you first read the story, what did you think was going to happen next?

3. Continue rereading, this time stopping before the last paragraph on page 323. Again write your reactions. Have your feelings about any of the characters changed? What does Teruo mean by saying, "I'm lousy"? What is he trying to do when he defies his boss? Did your predictions about the ending change at this point? Why or why not?

4. Finish rereading the story and write about whether your predictions were accurate. Then write freely about any memories you had from your own life as you read the story. Conclude by writing a personal response statement that explains what this story means to you.

Responding from Literary Knowledge

As a reader, you not only respond to each work on the basis of your past experience and background, but you also apply your knowledge of other stories, poems, or plays that you have read. This knowledge helps you interpret a work and appreciate a writer's skill. When you respond to literature on the basis of your literary knowledge, you analyze its *elements*.

The following chart describes the main elements of three literary genres—fiction, poetry, and drama. Because drama has most of the same elements as other works of fiction, the elements listed under drama show only how reading a dramatic work differs from reading other kinds of fiction.

Elements of Literature

FICTION

plot—the events in a story that lead to a *climax* (high point) and to an outcome that resolves a central *conflict*

setting—when and where the story takes place

characters—the people in the story who advance the plot through their thoughts and actions

dialogue—conversations among characters that reveal their personalities, actions, and *motivations,* or reasons for behaving as they do

tone—the writer's attitude toward his or her characters

point of view—the "voice" telling the story—*first person (I)* or *third person (he* or *she)*

theme—the main idea or message of the story

POETRY

persona—the person whose "voice" is saying the poem, revealing the character the poet is assuming

meter—the rhythm of stressed and unstressed syllables in each line of the poem

rhyme scheme—the pattern of rhymed sounds, usually at the ends of lines

sound devices—techniques for playing with sounds to create certain effects, such as *alliteration* and *onomatopoeia.*

figures of speech—imaginative language, such as *similes* and *metaphors,* which create images by making comparisons

shape—the way the poem looks on the printed page, which may contribute to meaning

theme—the overall feeling or underlying meaning of the poem, which expresses the poet's thoughts and feelings

DRAMA

setting—Stage directions describe all aspects of the setting.

characters—A cast of characters identifies the characters, and stage directions describe their appearance.

plot—Stage directions describe action, which is divided into acts and scenes. The plot is usually developed only through action and dialogue.

theme—The meaning of a play is revealed only through characters' words and actions.

How Literary Elements Contribute to Meaning The elements of each genre contribute to the meaning of a work. In fiction, for example, a writer uses plot, setting, and characters to reveal his or her message. One way to find meaning in a work of literature, therefore, is to analyze the author's treatment of the elements and their interrelationships. The following strategies list questions to ask as you explore the meaning of a poem, a play, or a short story or novel.

Questions for Finding Meaning in a Poem

1. What is the poet's persona? How does the persona relate to the subject, mood, and theme of the poem?
2. How does the meter affect the rhythm of the poem? How does that rhythm express the mood?
3. How does the rhyme scheme affect the expression of thoughts and feelings?
4. What sounds do sound devices like alliteration and onomatopoeia create? What images do those sound devices create in the reader's mind?
5. What images do the figures of speech create? What feelings do those images suggest?
6. How does the shape of the poem relate to the subject, mood, or theme?
7. What effect did the poem have on you? How effectively does the poem achieve this effect? What meaning does the poem have for you?
8. What feeling, theme, or message does the poem express?

Questions for Finding Meaning in a Play

1. What details of setting and character do the stage directions emphasize? How do those details contribute to the meaning?
2. What are the key relationships among the characters? How do those relationships reveal the central conflict? What changes in the relationships help resolve the conflict?
3. How does the dialogue alone advance the plot? What developments in the plot occur with each change of act and scene?
4. What subject and theme does the play treat? What meanings does the play have for you?

Questions for Finding Meaning in Fiction

PLOT

1. What is the significance of each main event in the development of the plot? How does each event in the plot affect the main characters?
2. What do details in the plot reveal about the narrator's attitude toward the central conflict? What do the climax and the ending reveal about the theme?

SETTING

3. How does the setting contribute to the tone or mood of the story? How do details of the setting help define the characters?
4. Which details of the setting are most important in the development of the plot? How do details of the setting relate to the theme?

CHARACTERS

5. How do the characters respond to their setting?
6. How does each character contribute to the development of the plot? Who or what does each character represent? How do the details of characterization reveal personalities?
7. What does the dialogue reveal about the characters' personalities and motivations? How does the point of view of the story affect the characterization? What does the point of view contribute to the theme?

THEME

8. What passages and details in the story best express the main theme? Are there other recurring ideas that contribute to the meaning?
9. How effectively does the author communicate the theme through the development of setting, characters, and plot? How does this theme have meaning for you? What else have you read that has the same or a similar theme?

Evaluating a Literary Work Analyzing the elements in a story or a poem helps you make judgments about the work. Because there are many different standards of evaluation, however, your personal judgment and the judgments of literary critics, historians, biographers, teachers, and classmates will not always be in agreement. You may find it helpful, however, to know the criteria by which any great work of literature, or classic, is usually judged. When you evaluate a literary work, consider the following standards.

Some Characteristics of Great Literature

1. Explores great themes in human nature and the human experience that many people can identify with—such as growing up, family life, or war
2. Expresses universal meanings—such as truth or hope— that people from many different backgrounds and cultures can appreciate
3. Conveys a timeless message that remains true for many generations of readers
4. Creates vivid impressions of characters and settings that many generations of readers can treasure

Whether or not a literary work you are reading is regarded as a classic, you can apply other standards of evaluation. When

you are making judgments about a work, ask yourself the following questions.

Questions for Evaluating Literature

1. How inventive and original is the work?
2. How vividly and believably are the characters, settings, dialogue, actions, and feelings portrayed? In fiction, how well-structured is the plot? Does it have a satisfying resolution of the central conflict?
3. How strongly did you react to the work? Did you identify with a character, situation, or feeling? Did the work touch your memories and emotions?
4. Did the work have meaning for you? Will you remember anything about it a year from now?

WRITING ACTIVITY *Responding from Literary Knowledge*

Express your opinions about "Say It with Flowers" on pages 319–326 by answering the following questions in your reader's journal.

1. What are the five most important events in the plot and what is the importance of each one? How do the events relate to the central conflict in the story?
2. Why does Teruo behave the way he does when he is working at the flower shop? Do his actions change much from the beginning of the story to the end? Explain how and why his actions do or do not change.
3. How do the other characters react to Teruo's actions? Do their opinions of him change? On what grounds do they conclude that Teruo would not succeed in business?
4. What details in the setting bring the story to life?
5. What is the theme of the story—that is, what thought or message does the story convey?
6. From what point of view is the story told? Who is the "I"? How would the story have changed if it were told from Teruo's point of view?

Writing Is Thinking

Making Inferences about Characters

Making inferences, or *inferring*, means filling in the gaps in your knowledge on the basis of what you know. The following chart shows you how to make inferences about a character from his appearance, behavior, and speech.

Character Chart

Question: In "Say It with Flowers," why does Teruo give away flowers?

TYPE OF CLUE	CLUE
DESCRIPTION OF CHARACTER	Teruo's appearance did not "harmonize with a job as a clerk in a flower shop"; he was "a quiet fellow with very little words for anybody, but his smile disarmed a person."
STATEMENTS ABOUT THE CHARACTER'S ACTIONS	He added extra flowers "because the old lady was appreciative of his art of making bouquets"; gave roses to a child with 25 cents to spend for his mother's birthday; gave a dozen roses to a pretty girl.
CHARACTER'S OWN WORDS	"I just like to do it that way, that's all." "I gave it to her because she admired it, and she's pretty enough to deserve beautiful things, and I liked her."

Logical inferences about Teruo's motives, based on these clues: In giving away flowers, Teruo bases his decisions on personal values of honesty and generosity. He gives away flowers to people he thinks deserve them. His actions represent his decision not to compromise his values, even if it means getting fired.

Thinking Practice   Make a chart to help you infer an answer to the question: In "The Confidence Game" on page 87, what made Tobi change her mind about Angela?

Choosing and Limiting a Subject

As you respond to a work by using both your personal experience and your literary knowledge, you will develop some definite ideas about the meaning of the work. Your understanding will then become the basis for choosing a subject for a critical essay.

Unless your teacher has assigned you a specific subject for a critical essay, you will have a wide choice of possible subjects. When choosing a subject, first read over what you have already written about the work in your reader's journal. Then narrow your choice by asking yourself the following questions.

Questions for Choosing a Subject

1. What parts or elements of the work would you like to understand better?
2. What parts of the work do you find especially moving? Why?
3. What images or details made a strong impression on you? What do they contribute to the overall work?
4. With which character do you identify the most and why?
5. How do the characters relate to one another? How do their relationships seem to affect the plot?
6. What feeling, meaning, or message does the work convey to you? What insight or understanding have you gained?

Synthesizing Personal and Literary Responses Another strategy for choosing a subject is to *synthesize*, or combine, your personal responses with responses based on your literary knowledge. For example, in your personal response statement to "Say It with Flowers," you may have expressed disapproval of dishonest business practices. Perhaps you once had an unpleasant experience as a consumer in which you were a victim of dishonesty. To synthesize that personal reaction with a literary response, you might discuss the central conflict in the story, which relates to the issue of dishonesty in business. By synthesizing your personal and literary responses in this way, you can best focus your thoughts for a critical essay.

339

Finding a Subject Focus   Whatever strategy you use for choosing a subject, check to make sure the subject is suitably limited and focused. Ask yourself, "What do I want to say about my subject?" When you can answer that question in a phrase or sentence, you have suitably focused your subject.

Model: *Focusing a Subject*

GENERAL SUBJECT	The character Teruo
LIMITED SUBJECT	Teruo's response to the central conflict
QUESTION	What about Teruo's response to the central conflict in the story do you want to say?
POSSIBLE ANSWER	Teruo's refusal to compromise his high principles does not necessarily mean that he would be unsuccessful in business.
FOCUSED SUBJECT	Qualities Teruo has that would contribute to his success in business

WRITING ACTIVITY *Choosing and Limiting Subjects*

For each of the following elements of literature, think of a possible subject for a critical essay on "The Confidence Game." *(See pages 87–94.)* Then limit and focus each subject by expressing it in a phrase or a sentence.

1. character   **3.** setting   **5.** theme
2. plot   **4.** point of view

WRITING ACTIVITY *Writing on Your Own*

WRITING ABOUT THE THEME   Review the personal and literary responses to "Say It with Flowers" that you wrote in your reader's journal. Also review the Questions for Choosing a Subject on page 339. Then list ideas for possible subjects on the theme of choices, such as Mr. Sasaki's decision to fire Teruo. After you choose one limited subject, write a phrase or sentence that expresses your focus. Save your work in your writing folder.

Developing Your Thesis

When you clearly focus your subject, you will discover the thesis, or main idea, for your critical essay. By expressing your main idea in a complete sentence, you will have a working thesis statement on which to build. Your specific purpose in writing a critical essay is to prove that your thesis is true. The example below shows the thesis statement for the focused subject from page 340. Notice that the thesis statement is carefully worded. In a critical essay, a thesis statement should be specific enough to be proven conclusively.

FOCUSED SUBJECT Qualities Teruo has that would contribute to his success in business

WORKING THESIS Despite his experience in Mr. Sasaki's shop, Teruo has qualities that would make him successful in business without having to compromise his high principles.

WRITING ACTIVITY *Writing a Working Thesis Statement*

Write one working thesis statement for each of the following focused subjects from "The Confidence Game."

1. details of the setting that contribute to the impression of a tense, competitive atmosphere
2. the effect of the first person point of view in making the story believable
3. Angela's response to the central conflict

WRITING ACTIVITY *Writing on Your Own*

WRITING ABOUT THE THEME Review your work from Writing Activity 4 and use the main idea in your focused subject to develop a thesis for your critical essay about "Say It with Flowers." After you express your thesis in a complete sentence, keep your work in your writing folder.

Gathering Evidence

To prove the truth of your thesis, you must supply the reader of your critical essay with evidence. You automatically gather evidence when you read, whether you are aware of it or not. Each detail fits into some pattern of ideas that you develop as you read. This pattern of ideas leaves you with an overall impression of a work and leads you to your thesis.

After you have stated your thesis, however, you should reread the work and look for the specific details that will help you prove it. The kinds of details you will use include specific examples of dialogue, description, action, and thoughts.

Model: *Kinds of Evidence in Literature*

BACKGROUND DETAILS	We were glad to have an extra hand [in the flower shop] because the busy season was coming around.
DESCRIPTIVE DETAILS	Teruo came back to the rear and picked out a dozen of the very fresh white roses.
NARRATIVE DETAILS	He told Teruo what to do on telephone orders; how to keep the greens fresh; how to make bouquets, corsages, and sprays.
DIALOGUE	Teruo looked at us calmly. "That's a hard thing to say when you know it isn't true." "You've got to get it over with sooner or later," I told him.
ACTION	He hurriedly took one customer's order and . . . jumped to the second customer's side and persuaded her to buy Columbia roses . . .

To develop a list of supporting details, skim the work from start to finish, looking for any and all details that will directly contribute to proving your thesis. As you skim, jot down each supporting detail you find—either on a note card or on a separate sheet of paper.

The following models show how a student writer gathered evidence on note cards to support the proposition that Teruo has qualities that would help him succeed in business. Notice that each card has a page reference for easily locating the passage used. In addition, each card includes a brief note reminding the writer of why the detail helps support the thesis.

Student Model: *Gathering Evidence*

TEXT PORTIONS

We soon learned that he knew nothing about the florist business. He could identify a rose when he saw one . . . but other flowers and materials were new to him. "You fellows teach me something about this business and I'll be grateful. I want to start from the bottom," Teruo said.

In a couple of weeks Teruo was just as good a clerk as we had had in a long time. He was curious almost to a fault, and was a glutton for work.

When I went out to the truck . . . Teruo followed me. "Gee, I feel rotten," he said to me. "Those flowers I sold to the people, they won't last longer than tomorrow. I feel lousy. I'm lousy. The people'll get to know my word pretty soon."

NOTE CARDS

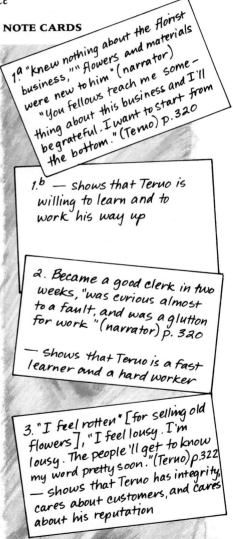

1.ᵃ "knew nothing about the florist business," "flowers and materials were new to him" (narrator) "You fellows teach me something about this business and I'll be grateful. I want to start from the bottom." (Teruo) p. 320

1.ᵇ — shows that Teruo is willing to learn and to work his way up

2. Became a good clerk in two weeks, "was curious almost to a fault, and was a glutton for work." (narrator) p. 320
— shows that Teruo is a fast learner and a hard worker

3. "I feel rotten" [for selling old flowers], "I feel lousy. I'm lousy. The people'll get to know my word pretty soon." (Teruo) p.322
— shows that Teruo has integrity, cares about customers, and cares about his reputation

"You've been selling fresh flowers and leaving the old ones go to waste . . ." Mr. Sasaki said. "Why don't you do as you're told? We all sell the flowers in the front . . . Why can't you sell them?"

"I don't like it, Mr. Sasaki," Teruo said. "When the people ask me if they're fresh I hate to answer. I feel rotten after selling the old ones."

Teruo was there early. "Hello," he greeted us cheerfully as we came in . . . He was there before us and had already filled out the eight o'clock package . . . When Mr. Sasaki arrived, Teruo waved his hand and cheerfully went about gathering the flowers . . . As he flitted here and there he seemed as if he had forgotten our presence . . .

He looked at each vase, sized up the flowers, and then cocked his head at the next one. He did this with great deliberation, as if he were the boss and the last word in the shop . . . [W]hen a customer soon came in, he swiftly attended him as if he owned all the flowers in the world . . . He [sold the fresh flowers] with so much grace, dignity and swiftness . . .

4ª "Why don't you do as you're told?" (Mr. Sasaki) "I don't like it . . . When the people ask me if they're fresh I hate to answer. I feel rotten after selling the old ones." (Teruo) p. 323

4.ᵇ — shows that Teruo cares about customers, values honesty, and does not easily obey orders that go against his moral principles

5.ª "Teruo was there early," "greeted us cheerfully," "had already filled out the eight o'clock package," "cheerfully went about gathering the flowers," "flitted here and there" (narrator) pp. 323 - 324

5.ᵇ — shows that Teruo is prompt, cheerful, and industrious

6.ª Worked "with great deliberation, as if he were the boss and the last word in the shop," "swiftly attended [a customer] as if he owned all the flowers in the world," "[worked with]

6.ᵇ grace, dignity and swiftness." (narrator) p. 324

— shows that Teruo can take charge and is self-confident and efficient

. . . Mr. Sasaki came out furious. "You're a blockhead. You have no business sense . . ."

Tommy nudged me. "If he was the boss he couldn't do those things," he said.

"In the first place," I said, "I don't think he could be a boss."

7ª "You have no business sense." (Mr. Sasaki) p. 324
"If he was the boss he couldn't do those things [give away flowers]." (Tommy) p. 325
"I don't think he could be a boss." (narrator) p. 325

7.ª — Shows that the others don't understand that Teruo has what it takes to succeed in business. As a boss, Teruo could give up some profits in exchange for customer goodwill and could insist on selling only quality products

WRITING ACTIVITY *Gathering Evidence*

Find text portions in "The Confidence Game" on pages 87–94 that support the thesis that self-confidence is a result of a conscious choice by an individual. As you find evidence for this thesis, write each supporting detail on a note card or a separate sheet of paper. Gather at least five details. Remember to include page references and brief explanations of how the details prove the thesis. Save your work for later use.

WRITING ACTIVITY *Writing on Your Own*

WRITING ABOUT THE THEME

Gather evidence on note cards to support the thesis statement you wrote in Writing Activity 6 for a critical essay about "Say It with Flowers." Save your work for later use.

Organizing Details into an Outline

For your critical essay—as for other kinds of essays—you should group your details into categories. Then you can arrange your ideas and information in a logical order. If you skim a story from start to finish looking for evidence for a thesis, you will probably arrange your details in the order in which they appear in the work. In some cases you will be able to keep this chronological order for your essay. For example, if you were showing how a character changed or grew over time, you would logically follow a chronological order. The following chart shows examples of how different types of order may be appropriate for proving different kinds of theses.

Ordering Evidence	
KIND OF THESIS	**TYPE OF ORDER**
To show how a character or elements of a plot changed or developed over time	Chronological order *(See page 264.)*
To show similarities and differences between characters or to compare two different works of literature	Comparison/contrast, using the *AABB* or the *ABAB* pattern of development *(See pages 264–267.)*
To analyze a character's motivation or to explain the significance of the setting	Order of importance or cause and effect *(See pages 264 and 139.)*
To draw conclusions about the theme	Developmental order *(See page 264.)*

After you decide how to organize your ideas and evidence, you should make a list, chart, or outline to use as a guide for writing your critical essay. When outlining, you may use either an informal outline—a simple listing, in order, of the points you wish to cover—or a formal outline like the ones on pages 268–269.

Following is a simple outline for a critical essay about "Say It with Flowers." Notice that the student included ideas for the introduction and the conclusion. Also, because the details have equal importance in proving the thesis, the student arranged them in developmental order. In developmental order information is arranged to lead up to a conclusion.

Student Model: *Outline for a Critical Essay*

INTRODUCTION   Background details about Teruo's experience

Thesis statement: Despite his experience in Mr. Sasaki's shop, Teruo has qualities that would help him succeed in business without having to compromise his high principles.

BODY   Qualities Teruo has for success in business:
  I. Willingness to learn and to work hard (note cards 1, 2, and 5)
  II. Positive attitudes and the ability to take charge (note cards 5 and 6)
  III. Honesty and integrity (note cards 3 and 4)

CONCLUSION   Why the other characters thought that Teruo could not succeed in business (note card 7)

How my evidence shows that they were wrong

WRITING ACTIVITY 9 *Developing an Outline*

Using your notes from Writing Activity 7, develop a simple outline for a critical essay on "The Confidence Game." Be sure to organize your details in a way that will best prove your thesis. *(To use your prewriting work on "The Confidence Game" for a critical essay, see Independent Writing at the end of this chapter.)*

WRITING ACTIVITY 10 *Writing on Your Own*

WRITING ABOUT THE THEME Review your work from Writing Activity 8. Then decide on an appropriate order for your supporting details and create an outline as a plan for your critical essay on "Say It with Flowers." Save your prewriting work in your writing folder.

347

Drafting

Writing Process

When you are ready to draft your critical essay, you may find the following guidelines helpful.

Guidelines for Drafting a Critical Essay

1. In the introduction identify the title and author of the work you are discussing and include your thesis statement.
2. In the body of your essay, include your clearly organized supporting details, using transitions to show how one detail relates to another. Using quotation marks, include direct quotes from the work wherever they strengthen the points you are making.
3. In the conclusion reinforce the main idea of your essay by explaining how the details that you included prove your thesis.
4. Add a title that suggests the focus of your essay.

The following student model was written from the outline on page 347 and the note cards on pages 343–345. Notice how the model, which has already been revised and edited, follows the above Guidelines for Drafting a Critical Essay.

Student Model: *A Critical Essay*

Teruo in Business

INTRODUCTION   In the story "Say it with Flowers," author Toshio Mori explores the potential conflict between succeeding in business and preserving one's integrity. For Teruo, the eager young clerk in the flower shop, preserving his integrity means selling only the freshest flowers. He even gives flowers away to customers. For his actions he earns the scorn of his coworkers and of his boss, Mr. Sasaki, who eventually fires him. Like them, readers might conclude that Teruo would be a failure in business

THESIS
STATEMENT   unless he learns to "play the game." Despite his experience in Mr. Sasaki's shop, however, Teruo has many qualities that would help him succeed

in business without having to compromise his high principles.

When Teruo first comes to work at the shop, he asks his coworkers—Tommy and the narrator of the story—to teach him about the florist business. "You fellows teach me something about this business and I'll be grateful. I want to start from the bottom," he explains, implying that he might someday like to run his own flower shop. In only two weeks, Teruo becomes a good clerk who is "curious almost to a fault" and "a glutton for work." This behavior shows that Teruo is willing to learn and to work his way up. He is also a fast learner and a hard worker. These are all qualities that are needed for success in business.

Teruo has positive attitudes that would contribute to any person's success in business. Descriptions of his work in the Morning-Glory Flower Shop, for example, show that he is prompt, conscientious, cheerful, and industrious. In addition, he works "with great deliberation, as if he were the boss and the last word in the shop." He swiftly attends to customers "as if he owned all the flowers in the world." His coworkers are awed by his "grace, dignity, and swiftness" as he works. These observations show that Teruo can take charge and can use his initiative. He is clearly self-confident and efficient in his work.

When Teruo is forced to go against his principles by lying and selling flowers that are not fresh, he says, "I feel rotten . . . I'm lousy. The people'll get to know my word pretty soon." Even after Mr. Sasaki confronts him and tells him to do as he's told, Teruo insists, "When the people ask me if they're fresh I hate to answer. I feel rotten after selling the old ones." This quote shows that Teruo values his honesty and integrity—qualities that certainly contribute to success in business. He cares about his customers and about his reputation. He risks losing his job rather than going against his moral values.

CONCLUSION   The other characters in the story do not understand that Teruo has what it takes to succeed in business. "You have no business sense," Mr. Sasaki accuses. "If he was the boss he couldn't do those things," Tommy says. "I don't think he could be a boss," the narrator replies. As a boss, however, Teruo could choose to give up some of his profits in exchange for customer goodwill, more customers, and more business. He could insist on selling only the best quality products and still afford to be generous toward his customers. When viewed in this way, everything about Teruo's character suggests that he could become a successful businessman— without compromising his high principles.

WRITING ACTIVITY *Writing on Your Own*

WRITING
ABOUT THE
THEME

Using the guidelines on page 348 and your outline from Writing Activity 10, write a first draft of your critical essay on "Say It with Flowers." Remember to stop every now and then and read over what you have written to keep your ideas on track. Save your draft for revising later.

350

Revising

Writing Process

After completing your first draft, you may want to share your essay with a peer reader. Using your partner's comments and the following checklist, you should then revise your essay.

Revision Checklist

CHECKING YOUR ESSAY

1. Do you have a strong introduction that identifies the author and the work you will discuss? *(See page 348.)*
2. Does your introduction contain a clearly worded thesis statement? *(See page 341.)*
3. Does the body of your essay provide ample details from the work to support your thesis? *(See pages 342–345.)*
4. Did you use quotations from the work to strengthen your points?
5. Does your conclusion summarize the details in the body and reinforce your thesis statement?
6. Does your whole essay have unity, coherence, and clarity? *(See pages 231–232.)*
7. Did you add a title that suggests the focus of your essay?

CHECKING YOUR PARAGRAPHS

8. Does each paragraph have a topic sentence? *(See page 228.)*
9. Does each paragraph have unity, adequate development, coherence, and clarity? *(See pages 108–111.)*

CHECKING YOUR SENTENCES AND WORDS

10. Are your sentences varied and concise? *(See pages 71–78.)*
11. Did you use vivid, precise words? *(See pages 59–63.)*

WRITING ACTIVITY

WRITING
ABOUT THE
THEME

If your teacher permits, exchange critical essays on "Say It with Flowers" with a partner and comment on the strengths and weaknesses of your partner's paper. How effectively do the supporting details prove the thesis? Use your partner's comments and the Revision Checklist above to improve your draft. Then save it for editing.

Editing and Publishing

Grammar in the Writing Process

"Tommy and I watched the boss fuming inside of his office." The words *fuming inside of his office* in this sentence from "Say It with Flowers" form a phrase. Like all phrases, it lacks a subject and a verb. Because this phrase begins with a verb form—*fuming*—it is called a *verbal phrase.*

There are three kinds of verbal phrases: participial phrases, gerund phrases, and infinitive phrases. *Fuming inside of his office is a participial phrase. (For information about the other kinds of verbal phrases, see pages 654–656 and 658–660.)*

Participial Phrases A *participle* is a verb form that is used as an adjective to describe nouns and pronouns. *Present participles* end in *-ing*, and *past participles* end in *-ed, -n, -t,* and *-en.* In the following sentences, you can see how participial phrases can not only add liveliness to your writing but also provide variety in your sentence structure. *(For other examples of participial phrases and practice in using them correctly, see pages 649–652.)*

PARTICIPIAL **Ignoring us,** Teruo waited on customers.
PHRASES   We watched Teruo **talking to the young lady.**

Punctuation with Participial Phrases Like the first example above, a comma follows an introductory participial phrase. Commas also enclose a *nonessential participial phrase*—one that can be removed without changing the meaning of the rest of the sentence. *(For more information about nonessential phrases and practice in writing them correctly, see pages 653–654.)*

NONESSENTIAL   Sometimes, **looking embarrassedly at us,**
PARTICIPIAL   he would sell the fresh flowers first. (Commas
PHRASE   needed because removing the phrase does not change the meaning of the sentence.)

ESSENTIAL
PARTICIPIAL
PHRASE

We watched Teruo **talking to the young lady.** (Comma not needed because removing the phrase changes the meaning.)

Combining Sentences with Participial Phrases

You can eliminate choppiness in your writing by using verbal phrases to combine sentences. Combining sentences also helps to show the relationship between ideas. *(For other examples of sentence combining with phrases and for practice in combining sentences, see pages 664–665.)*

TWO SENTENCES   I was often in the shop. I helped Tommy and Teruo with the customers and the orders.

COMBINED   I was often in the shop, **helping Tommy and Teruo with the customers and the orders.**

TWO SENTENCES   I sat in the back. I could watch Teruo.

COMBINED   **Sitting in the back,** I could watch Teruo.

Editing Checklist

1. Have you used verbal phrases for liveliness and sentence variety? *(See pages 649–660.)*
2. Are all of the verbal phrases punctuated correctly? *(See pages 653 and 832–833.)*
3. Could you use verbal phrases to combine any sentences? *(See pages 664–665.)*

WRITING ACTIVITY   13   *Writing on Your Own*

WRITING
ABOUT THE
THEME

Editing Read aloud your critical essay about "Say It with Flowers." Listen especially for any verbal phrases. Then use the checklist above and the one on page 37 to edit your essay.

Publishing After you write a neat final copy, publish your critical essay by submitting it to your teacher or by adding it to a class anthology.

A Writer Writes

A Critical Essay

PURPOSE: to explain your understanding of "All Summer in a Day," by Ray Bradbury

AUDIENCE: peer readers

Prewriting   Often when you write about a story or a poem, you rediscover the enjoyment you felt when you read it for the first time. You also bring a new perspective or greater understanding of the work. Test this idea by writing a critical essay about a story you have already read, "All Summer in a Day" on pages 49–56. As you reread this story, keep in mind the theme, choices. What choices did the characters in Bradbury's story make, for example, and what were the implications of those choices?

When you have finished rereading "All Summer in a Day," record your personal reactions to it in your reader's journal and use the strategies on page 335 to respond in writing on the basis of your literary knowledge. Then choose, limit, and focus a subject relating to choices. After you write a thesis statement, follow the steps for gathering evidence to support your proposition. Then arrange your supporting details in logical order in an outline.

Drafting   Using your outline and your prewriting notes as a guide, draft your critical essay. You may want to review the guidelines on page 348 before you begin to write.

Revising: *Conferencing*   With your teacher's permission, exchange papers with a classmate. Then answer the following questions about your partner's paper. After you hear your partner's responses, use the Revision Checklist on page 351 to revise your essay so that it is the best you can make it.

1. Is the thesis statement clear?
2. Are there enough examples and quotations? Do these details all support the thesis?
3. Does the essay contain a clear introduction, body, and conclusion?
4. Does the essay have unity, coherence, and clarity? *(See pages 231–232.)*
5. Does the title suggest the focus of the essay?

Editing and Publishing   Use the checklists on pages 37 and 353 as guides to edit your essay. Then make a neat final copy and enter your essay in a literary contest. For information write to the National Council of Teachers of English, 1111 Kenyon Road, Urbana, IL 61801.

WRITING
ABOUT THE
THEME

Independent Writing

Using the outline you wrote in Writing Activity 9 and the evidence you gathered in Writing Activity 7, write a critical essay about "The Confidence Game" on pages 87–94. When you have finished your essay, get your teacher's permission to form a discussion group with several of your classmates. Within your group each student should read his or her essay aloud. After each reading, the participants respond with questions and ideas of their own.

Creative Writing

Write a letter to one of the characters in "All Summer in a Day" on pages 49–56. In your letter accomplish one or more of the following goals.

1. Tell the character how you feel about him or her and explain why.
2. Give the character advice on how to resolve a problem or prevent a situation from recurring.
3. Explain what you would have done in the same situation.

WRITING
ABOUT THE
THEME

 ## Writing about Literature

A *protagonist* is the principal character in a story. The story focuses on this character's efforts to resolve a conflict or his or her struggles to overcome an obstacle. Most often the protagonist triumphs in some way. In "Say It with Flowers," Teruo is the protagonist. Write a paragraph that explains in what ways Teruo fits the definition of a protagonist.

Writing in Other Subject Areas

Social Studies   Write a critical review of an essay on some subject in the social sciences and submit it to your social studies teacher. For example, you could respond to an article on the economy, an editorial on politics, or a persuasive essay—such as "The Trouble with Television" on pages 211–214.

Art   Think of the works of art in any form that you enjoy the most. For example, you could choose a work from music, dance, theater, film, painting, sculpture, or literature. Select one work of art and write a critical essay about that work or a performance of it.

9

Checklist

Writing Essays about Literature

Prewriting

✔ Read the literary work carefully and respond to it from both personal experience and literary knowledge. *(See pages 330–337.)*

✔ By synthesizing your personal and literary responses, choose and limit a subject for your essay. *(See pages 339–340.)*

✔ Think of a subject focus and shape it into a statement of your thesis. *(See page 341.)*

✔ Skim the work again, looking for details to use as evidence to support your thesis. On a separate sheet of paper or card, note each detail, its page reference, and its significance. *(See pages 342–345.)*

✔ Organize your ideas and supporting details into an outline. *(See pages 346–347.)*

Drafting

✔ Use the guidelines on page 348 to help you draft your critical essay.

Revising

✔ After conferencing, use the Revision Checklist on page 351 to revise your essay.

Editing and Publishing

✔ Use the Editing Checklists to check your grammar, spelling, usage, and mechanics. *(See pages 37 and 353.)*

✔ Prepare a neat final copy of your work and publish it in one of the ways listed on page 43.

10

Writing Reports

Part 1 *Reading to Write*

THEME: *Traditions*

Traditions are activities, collective memories, and ways of thinking that are passed down orally and by example from generation to generation. Families, groups, communities, and nations all have traditions. In fact, traditions are an important part of the cultural, national, social, and spiritual life of people everywhere.

The literature selection in this chapter, "Rancho Buena Vista," by Fermina Guerra, reports on family traditions that reflect the local history of ranchers in southern Texas.

The traditions pertaining to Buena Vista that have been told over and over among the children and grandchildren of Florencio Guerra and his wife, Josefa Flores, are the kind of traditions to be heard all up and down the Border country.

As you read "Rancho Buena Vista," think about traditions—how they start, how they persist, and how they affect people's lives. You might also think of some of the traditions in your family, at school, and in your community.

Rancho Buena Vista

Fermina Guerra

In the northeastern part of Webb County, fifty miles from Laredo[1] and twenty-one miles from Encinal, lies the Buena Vista Ranch. It is not large as ranches go, only about three thousand acres; but it has its share in the traditions of the ranch country. . . .

The traditions pertaining to Buena Vista that have been told over and over among the children and grandchildren of Florencio Guerra and his wife, Josefa Flores, are the kind of traditions to be heard all up and down the Border country.[2]

Some of them, perhaps a majority of them, treat of actual happenings, and are folklore only in that they are traditional and that they are hardly important enough for history. The stories are of Indians, floods, captives, sheepherders, buried treasure, violent death, happenings when the bishop came or the wool went to town. When a fire burns on a winter night or when it is raining and the water in Becerra Creek is high, people at Buena Vista tell and hear these traditions of the land.

1. **Laredo:** City in Texas.
2. **Border country:** Lands bordering the Rio Grande.

Ever-present in the minds of ranch people is the question of water. The foremost topic of conversation among them is the condition of the range, the prospect of rain, the water of the tanks. This part of the country has never found good well water to pump up with windmills, and tanks are depended on for stock water.

In the old days there were no tanks. The cattle watered at the two or three creeks in the country. In time of drouth they were driven the eighteen miles to the Nueces River. There was never trouble over water rights. Through the years these ranchmen kept the peace among themselves; the struggle with Nature occupied their chief energies. The first fence went up in 1891. Don Florencio's son, Donato, used to go out of his way before and after school to watch the fence-building operations being carried on by the Callaghan Ranch hands, who were erecting a fence between Buena Vista Ranch and theirs.

Three times in the history of Buena Vista Ranch, La Becerra Creek has been half a mile wide—in 1878, 1903, and 1937. Of course, the oldest flood is the most romantic. Don Justo and his wife were still living then, old and set in their ways. Their ranch house was of mesquite poles and adobe, thatched with grass and set on the very banks of La Becerra Creek.

One day it started to rain; torrents poured down. As the creek began to rise and there was no abatement of the downpour, the other members of the family grew frightened. Not Don Justo. He had seen rain before; nothing ever came of it. But the rain poured all night and a second day; the creek continued to rise.

Now it was up to the corral, adjoining the house. No matter; it would go down presently. A second night, and a third day, the rain continued pouring. At dusk of the third day, the water began to enter the house. A young matron, wife of Don Carmen, holding her child in her arms, told her husband to take her to higher ground. She feared remaining in the house another night with that constantly rising water. Gladly enough, he complied. Before leaving, he begged his aged father and mother to accompany him, but they laughed. "You will get all wet for nothing," they said. "We have a roof over our heads. What if there is a little water in the house?"

But the young mother set out for the hill to the east. Before she reached it, she was obliged to swim to save herself and child, her husband aiding her. The rain was still pouring so hard that they got lost in the brush, but they went on eastward.

Eventually they found themselves on a well-known hill. Don Florencio's ranch was just a mile to the northwest. The mother asked her husband to go down there and ask for some dry clothing for the baby, as the night was cold and it was still raining hard. Willingly enough, Don Carmen set out.

On reaching the house, he told Don Florencio what had happened at the upper ranch. Hurriedly the latter saddled his best horse and set out to see what he could do to persuade his parents to leave their house and take to the hills. The water was not so high at Buena Vista, though it was at the door of the main house.

About daybreak, he reached the shore opposite his parents' ranch. There was a raging torrent between him and them. From afar off, barely to be seen among the treetops, he could discern the roof of the house and two people perched on it. He could hardly hear their feeble cries, so great was the distance.

Like most ranchmen of his time, Don Florencio could not swim. He depended upon his horse to carry him across streams. This task his present mount refused to perform. Time after time he forced the animal into the water, only to have it turn back. At length he returned to his own ranch for a fresh mount. This horse, too, refused to venture out into the flood. So Florencio was forced to flounder at the edge of the current and watch those faraway forms, fearing to see them disappear from sight. But towards evening, the waters began to recede, and the next day he was able to go out and rescue the exhausted old people from their predicament.

The flood of 1903 was unusual in that no rain accompanied it. One hot, sunny morning Don Florencio noticed what appeared to be a cloud of mist rising rapidly from the bushes south of the house along the creek. It was coming fast, with a rushing sound. Suddenly he realized that a wall of water, far wider than the creek banks, was bearing down upon him. One of his laborers was down the creek bed driving some goats to higher ground.

Racing his horse, he hurried to get within calling distance of the man, Carlos. The laborer saw Don Florencio and heard his call, but not realizing that the danger was so close, went leisurely on with his work. Suddenly the turbulent water was upon him, and he was borne along with it as it swirled among the bushes. Fortunately, after his first fright, he was able to collect his wits sufficiently to grasp at an overhanging limb and so save his life.

The flood of 1937 was more prosaic;[3] the creek itself did no particular damage, but the water destroyed all but three tanks in a radius of twenty miles and left the range worse off than before the rain.

Such is the life of the ranchmen of Southwest Texas; drouth and flood; too much water or not enough; then, now, and always. ◆

3. **prosaic** [prō zā′ ic]: Ordinary.

Responding to the Theme

Traditions

Responding in Your Journal   This week in your journal, write about traditions that you have followed or observed. Begin now by brainstorming for a list of the traditions that are important to you and your family. Then explore the many others, including cultural and social traditions and national, state, and local traditions. After brainstorming, write freely about your feelings toward particular traditions and toward traditional behavior and ideas. How important are traditions? In your opinion what function do they serve in modern society? You also may want to research the origins of certain traditions in your own or another society.

Speaking and Listening   Because many traditions are passed down as stories, telling and hearing those stories is important for keeping those traditions alive. Tape-record or transcribe at least two family traditions told by other family members and then record a personal tradition of your own. When you have finished, share your results with family members by playing your tape or by reading your stories aloud.

Critical Thinking: Organizing   In her report "Rancho Buena Vista," Fermina Guerra uses chronological order to organize her information about the floods that have become a major part of the folklore in the Texas ranch lands. Think about other types of order that would suit the details in her report. Then write a paragraph in which you propose an alternative method of organization. Include your reasons for ordering details in the way you chose.

Extending Your Vocabulary   The first word in each of the following word pairs appears in "Rancho Buena Vista." Use a dictionary to investigate and explain the relationship between the words in each pair. For example, the words may be similar or different in origin, meaning, usage, or spelling.

prosaic/prose	matron/patron	drouth/drought
folklore/lore	flounder/founder	turbulent/turbo

Part 2 Writing

Fermina Guerra's report includes information about events that she could not have experienced directly because they occurred in the distant past. Often in your studies you will write about subjects that are not part of your personal experiences and knowledge. By researching those subjects, you will be exploring the knowledge and experience of others. The composition you write, based on your findings, will be a research paper, or report.

Writing Term   A **report** is a composition based on research drawn from books, periodicals, and interviews with experts.

Both in school and in many workplaces, you will need to be able to do research and state your findings in a written report. Because the main purpose of reports is to explain or inform, you will use the skills and techniques of expository writing. You will also use library skills to find the information you need for your report. *(For more information about library skills, see pages 495–504.)*

Prewriting

Part of the challenge of writing a report is being able to keep track of the information that you have gathered from several different sources. The first step that you should take, therefore, is to gather the supplies that you will need to organize your research. These supplies usually include a folder with pockets, index cards, paper clips, and rubber bands. With your materials in hand for organizing your information, you will be prepared to begin your research. The next step is to decide on a subject that is limited enough to allow you to cover it adequately in your report.

Choosing and Limiting a Research Subject

Sometimes teachers assign research subjects or list alternatives for you to choose among. Often, however, a choice of subjects is left entirely to you. You may easily be able to think of subjects that you would like to know more about. If not, you may find the following suggestions helpful when you are searching for a good research subject.

Finding Ideas for Reports

1. Using the Dewey decimal system, find a section of the library that interests you. Then walk up and down the aisles, looking for titles that catch your eye.
2. Skim through magazines and other periodicals.
3. Skim through any volume of an encyclopedia.
4. Ask others—your potential readers—what they would like to know more about.
5. Check the assignments in your other courses to see if any of them require a research paper.

After you have listed five to ten possible subjects for a report, choose one for which the statements in the box at the top of the next page hold true.

Choosing a Research Subject

1. I would like to know more about this subject.
2. My audience would like to know more about this subject.
3. This subject is appropriate for my purpose; that is, I can explain it well in a short (three to five pages) research report.
4. I can find enough information on this subject in the library and other sources.

Once you have chosen a subject, the next step is to limit it. One way to limit a subject is to break it down into its different aspects or elements. Suppose, for example, that you decided to write a report on the movie *The Wizard of Oz*. Realizing that this subject is too broad for a short research report, you might then list the following aspects of the movie as possible limited subjects.

SUBJECT	*The Wizard of Oz*
LIMITED SUBJECTS	the story the cast the music the special effects the sets the costumes

Writing Tip Limit a subject for a report by listing elements, or aspects, of the subject and by selecting one of them to research.

WRITING ACTIVITY *Limiting Research Subjects*

Decide which of the following subjects are suitable for a short report of two to five pages and which ones are too broad. Answer each item by writing *limited enough* or *too broad*. Then, using reference materials if necessary, limit each subject that is too broad by listing three aspects of it that could serve as possible limited subjects.

1. the history of Mexico
2. types of helicopters
3. the novel *Moby Dick*
4. how the Big Bang theory was first proposed
5. formations in square dancing
6. World War II
7. the life cycle of a tarantula
8. how sandstone forms
9. the main duties of a senator
10. the brain

WRITING ACTIVITY *Writing on Your Own*

WRITING
ABOUT THE
THEME

After you reread your journal entries about traditions, apply the suggestions on page 365 to find ideas for a report. For example, you could find the section in the library that contains books about traditions and read the titles or look through a few of the books. Explore all kinds of traditions and their origins and meanings—from the celebration of Mardi Gras to graduation week at your school.

After you have listed at least five possible subjects, use the criteria on page 366 to help you choose one subject. Then limit it by listing as many aspects or elements of that subject as you can think of. When you have finished, save all your prewriting notes in your writing folder for later use.

Gathering Information

After you have limited your subject, first recall what you already know about it. Then, on the basis of what you already know, pose questions about what more you would like to find out. These questions will serve as a guide in gathering information. By summarizing your questions into one general research question, you can focus your efforts and thoughts. The chart below shows how this questioning process works.

Limited Subject: *special effects in The Wizard of Oz*

FOCUS QUESTIONS	POSSIBLE ANSWERS
WHAT DO I ALREADY KNOW ABOUT THESE SPECIAL EFFECTS?	• saw the movie • remember the tornado, the flying monkeys, and the melting witch • saw a program on how the special effects for another movie were made
WHAT MORE DO I WANT TO FIND OUT?	• What other special effects are in *The Wizard of Oz?* • How were the tornado, flying monkeys, melting witch, and other special effects created? • Which effects were easiest to make and which hardest and costliest? • What is the background of the movie: when was it made, who created the special effects, etc.? • How do the special effects in *The Wizard of Oz* compare with those in that other movie?
GENERAL RESEARCH QUESTION	How were the special effects in *The Wizard of Oz* created?

With your research questions clearly in mind, you can begin gathering the information you need to answer those questions. As you find answers, be alert for possible main ideas that you could use as the thesis of your report. *(For more information about developing a thesis, see pages 259–260.)*

Use the following steps to help you use books, magazines, and other sources to gather the information you need to answer your research questions.

Steps for Gathering Information

1. Consult a general reference work, such as an encyclopedia, to find an overview of your subject, some references to other books on that subject, and cross-references to related topics.

2. Use the subject cards in the card catalog to find more books on your subject. *(See page 498.)*

3. Consult the *Readers' Guide to Periodical Literature* and a news index, such as *Facts on File*, to find magazine and newspaper articles on your subject.

4. Make a list of all your sources. For each book write the author, title, copyright year, publisher's name and location, and call number. For each periodical include the date (month, day, and year), the volume, the issue number, and pages.

5. Assign each source on your list a number that you can use to refer to that source in your notes.

Following is a list of sources for the student report on the special effects in *The Wizard of Oz*.

Student Model: *List of Sources*

Books

Down the Yellow Brick Road, by Doug McClelland, 1976, Pyramid Books, New York 791.437 W792M (1)

The Making of The Wizard of Oz, by Aljean Harmetz, 1977, Alfred A. Knopf, New York 791.437 W792H (2)

Magazines

Newsweek, August 21, 1939, pp. 23–24 (3)

Senior Scholastic, September 18, 1939, p. 32 (4)

Good Housekeeping, August 1939, pp. 40+ (5)

Newspapers

The New York Times, February 5, 1939, Section IX, page 5, column 6 (6)

The New York Times, July 11, 1939, page 28, column 4 (7)

WRITING ACTIVITY **3** *Gathering Information*

Make charts like the one on page 368 for posing research questions, using three of the following subjects. Then use the library to list four sources for each of the subjects you chose. At least one of the sources for each subject should be a magazine article. Follow all the Steps for Gathering Information on page 369.

1. blues singers
2. dieting fads
3. fencing
4. zoo habitats
5. National Football League
6. wildebeest migration
7. Japanese theater
8. noise pollution
9. Walt Disney films
10. uses of laser light

WRITING ACTIVITY **4** *Writing on Your Own*

WRITING
ABOUT THE
THEME

 Review your work from Writing Activity 2. For your limited subject for a report on a tradition, generate a list of facts you already know and a list of questions you would like to answer through your research. After you pose a basic research question, use the library to find five sources on your subject, including at least one magazine article. Then follow all the Steps for Gathering Information on page 369 and save all your notes in your writing folder for later use.

Taking Notes and Summarizing

After you have developed a list of sources, gather the books and periodicals and bring them to the place you plan to work. Then skim each source, looking for the information you need for your report. You will find the table of contents and the index of a book especially helpful in your search. Once you have located the relevant portion of a source, take a note card and in the upper right-hand corner of the card, write the identifying number you gave that source. This number should appear on each note card you use to record the information from that source. Keep the following goals in mind as you read the source and begin taking notes.

Writing Tip The goals of **note-taking** for a report are to summarize the main points in your own words and to record quotations that you might use in your report.

When you *summarize,* you write information in a condensed, concise form, touching only on the main ideas. To *record direct quotations,* you copy the words exactly and enclose them in quotation marks. Always write the name of the person who made the statement you are quoting and the page number where you found the statement in the source.

Example: *Quoting and Summarizing*

QUOTATION "Three times in the history of Buena Vista Ranch, La Becerra Creek has been half a mile wide—in 1878, 1903, and 1937." (Fermina Guerra, p. 360)

SUMMARY La Becerra Creek flooded in 1878, 1903, and 1937.

The excerpt below is from page 244 of the book *The Making of The Wizard of Oz.* The note card on the next page shows how this information can be summarized.

Student Model: *Taking Notes from a Source*

Basically, what Gillespie [the special-effects director] knew about tornados in 1938 was that "we couldn't go to Kansas and wait for a tornado to come down and pick up a house." Everything beyond that was an experiment . . . "I was a pilot for many years and had an airplane of my own. The wind sock they used in airports in the old days to show the direction of the wind has a shape a little bit like a tornado and the wind blows through it. I started from that. We cast a cone out of thin rubber. We were going to whirl the rubber cone and rotate it. But tornados are called twisters and the rubber cone didn't twist. So that was rather an expensive thing down the drain. We finally wound up by building a sort of giant wind sock out of muslin." The giant thirty-five-foot muslin tornado was—technically—a miniature.

Sample Note Card

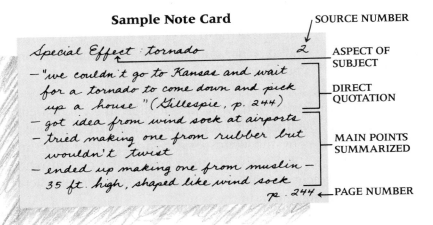

SOURCE NUMBER

Special Effect : tornado 2

ASPECT OF SUBJECT

— "we couldn't go to Kansas and wait for a tornado to come down and pick up a house" (Gillespie, p. 244)

DIRECT QUOTATION

— got idea from wind sock at airports
— tried making one from rubber but wouldn't twist
— ended up making one from muslin — 35 ft. high, shaped like wind sock

MAIN POINTS SUMMARIZED

p. 244

PAGE NUMBER

WRITING ACTIVITY 5 *Taking Notes and Summarizing*

The excerpt below is from page 165 of *The Making of Star Trek— The Motion Picture*. Assume the book is your third source and make a note card for the excerpt.

Alex's most spectacular effects were prepared in connection with [the movie's] only exterior set built at Paramount—the planet Vulcan. Location scenes had already been shot at Yellowstone [National Park], and it was up to Alex to find a way of duplicating the swirling pools of milky steam with a look of authenticity. Both dry ice and steam machines were used . . . To match the appearance of the swirling pools of water in the real Yellowstone, Alex used evaporated milk and white poster paint, mixed with water and poured into the set's pools. The pressure of the steam caused just the proper amount of movement in the pale white whirlpools and eddies duplicated in this enormous outdoor set.

WRITING ACTIVITY 6 *Writing on Your Own*

WRITING ABOUT THE THEME

Follow the model of note-taking above to take notes from your sources for your report on a tradition. Keep all your note cards together in your writing folder.

Developing a Thesis

During your research you will likely discover what you want to say about your subject. Consequently, after you have gathered information and have taken notes from many sources, your next step is to pull together your ideas and information to form a working thesis. A *working thesis* is a statement that expresses a possible main idea of your report. In a report, as in a critical essay, you may frame your thesis as a statement that you intend to prove is true. You then give the information you researched as evidence to support your thesis.

Keep in mind that you may change your working thesis as you continue to develop your report. When organizing your notes to write a first draft, you may even think of new ideas that lead you to change your thesis and do additional research. You may modify your working thesis at any stage in the process of planning, drafting, and revising your report.

To create your working thesis, think about what you have discovered about your subject. For instance, the writer of the report on *The Wizard of Oz* gathered information about how the special effects in that film were made. One example was how the filmmakers used a 35-foot wind sock to create the impression of a tornado. From this and similar examples, the writer concluded that the special-effects creators had used great ingenuity. A working thesis based on this conclusion was easy to write.

Student Model: *Working Thesis*

LIMITED SUBJECT	special effects in *The Wizard of Oz*
WORKING THESIS STATEMENT	Much wizardry went into creating the special effects in *The Wizard of Oz*.

WRITING ACTIVITY ⑦ *Writing on Your Own*

WRITING ABOUT THE THEME

 Using all your notes from Writing Activity 6, develop three or four possible theses for your report on a tradition. Select the one you like best as a working thesis and save your notes for later use.

Organizing Your Notes

As you take notes, you will begin to notice closely related ideas that could be grouped together into a single category. Building a system of categories is the first step in organizing your notes into an outline.

To create meaningful categories, review the information in your note cards, looking for ideas that are closely related. Then think of a category that would cover each group of related ideas. Once you have determined your categories, you can easily sort through your notes and clip together all the cards that belong in each category. If some of your notes do not fit into any of the categories, clip them together separately for possible use in your introduction or conclusion. After you have arranged your categories in a logical order, wrap the whole bundle of note cards together with a rubber band to prevent losses or mix-ups.

The student reporting on the special effects in *The Wizard of Oz* initially sorted notes into the following categories.

CATEGORY 1   general information: cost, year of release, quotations from reviews, name of special-effects director

CATEGORY 2   the tornado

CATEGORY 3   the melting witch

CATEGORY 4   Glinda's arrival in the glass bubble

CATEGORY 5   the flying monkeys

CATEGORY 6   the horse-of-a-different-color

CATEGORY 7   the crystal ball

CATEGORY 8   the lifting and dropping of the house

After reviewing all of the information in the eight categories, the student decided to combine some categories to create a smaller number of them to serve as main topics in an outline. For example, the special effects in categories 3, 4, 7, and 8 had something in common; they were all simple tricks that were easy to achieve. The revised organization, shown on the next page, consists of only four categories, which are broad enough to cover all the information.

CATEGORY 1 general information
CATEGORY 2 hardest effect to achieve—tornado
CATEGORY 3 simple tricks—house being picked up and
            dropped, crystal ball, glass bubble, melting witch
CATEGORY 4 tricks that should have been simple but proved
            difficult—flying monkeys, horse-of-a-different-
            color

Based on these categories, the student writer chose to arrange the information in order of importance. For a memorable effect, the student decided to place the more interesting information at both the beginning and the end of the report.

Writing Tip Group your notes into three to five main categories that are broad enough to include all
your information.

WRITING ACTIVITY 8 *Classifying Information*

Think of three main categories into which the following tourist attractions could be grouped for a report on "Tourist Attractions in San Diego." Then under each category write the letters of the attractions that fit into the category. Save your work for Writing Activity 10.

a. Point Loma,
   historic lighthouse
b. Wild Animal Park
c. Old Town,
   historic mission
d. ocean

e. San Diego Zoo
f. nearby mountains
g. Sea World aquarium
h. palm trees
i. nearby desert
j. *Star of India,* historic ship

WRITING ACTIVITY 9 *Writing on Your Own*

WRITING
ABOUT THE
THEME

Classify your information for your report about a tradition by developing three to five broad categories that cover all your notes. After you organize your categories in a logical order, arrange your note cards and keep them banded together in your writing folder. Save your notes for later use.

Critical Thinking *Writing Is Thinking*

Synthesizing Information

Often in your research projects, you will need to *synthesize*, or merge together, information from different kinds of sources. For example, you may use both published sources and findings from your own observations or experiments to answer a research question. The following diagram shows the steps you can take to synthesize information.

Synthesizing Information from Different Sources

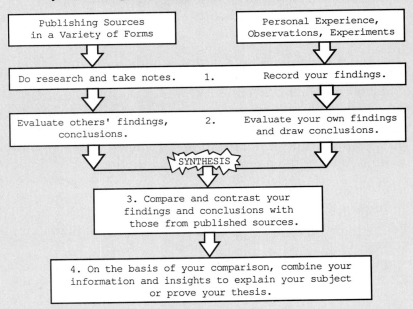

Publishing Sources in a Variety of Forms

Personal Experience, Observations, Experiments

1. Do research and take notes.

Record your findings.

2. Evaluate others' findings, conclusions.

Evaluate your own findings and draw conclusions.

SYNTHESIS

3. Compare and contrast your findings and conclusions with those from published sources.

4. On the basis of your comparison, combine your information and insights to explain your subject or prove your thesis.

Thinking Practice Choose one of the research questions below. Then write a two-page report in which you synthesize information from both published sources and personal study.

1. How can common kinds of dreams be classified?

2. How intelligent are ants?

3. How does the pH of water affect microorganisms?

Outlining

The final step in the prewriting stage is to develop an outline as a guide to drafting your report. Your outline will be based on the categories and the order of categories that you have already created for your notes. In your outline each main category becomes a *main topic* with a Roman numeral, as in the following outline of the main topics for the body of the student report on special effects in *The Wizard of Oz*.

Student Model: *Topic Outline for the Body of a Report*

SUBJECT	Special Effects in <u>The Wizard of Oz</u>
MAIN TOPICS	I. Hardest special effect: tornado
	II. Simple tricks
	III. Simple tricks made difficult by unexpected problems

When you are satisfied with the organization of your main topics, study the information in your note cards again and add *subtopics* with capital letters under the Roman numerals. Then add *supporting points* with numbers under the subtopics and if necessary to cover all the facts you gathered, add *supporting details* with lowercase letters under each point.

MAIN TOPIC	I. Hardest special effect: tornado
SUBTOPIC	A. First attempt
SUPPORTING POINTS	1. Cost and materials
	2. Why it failed
SUBTOPIC	B. Attempt that succeeded
SUPPORTING POINTS	1. Cost and materials
	2. How it moved
	3. Related effects
SUPPORTING DETAILS	a. Storm clouds
	b. Dark sky

 *Writing Tip* Convert your note-card categories into the main topics of an outline. Then use your notes to add subtopics, supporting points, and additional details to the outline.

Use the outline below as a model when you outline a report.

Student Model: *Expanded Outline for the Body of a Report*

MAIN TOPIC   I. Hardest special effect: tornado

SUBTOPIC   A. First attempt

SUPPORTING
POINTS
        1. Cost and materials
        2. Why it failed

SUBTOPIC   B. Attempt that succeeded

SUPPORTING
POINTS
        1. Cost and materials
        2. How it moved
        3. Related effects

SUPPORTING
DETAILS
          a. Storm clouds
          b. Dark sky

MAIN TOPIC   II. Simple tricks

     A. House's lifting and dropping
     B. Crystal ball
     C. Glinda's glass bubble

MAIN TOPIC   III. Simple tricks made difficult by unexpected problems

     A. Flying monkeys
        1. Technique
        2. Problems
     B. Horse-of-a-different-color
        1. Technique
        2. Problems
          a. Objection of ASPCA
          b. Horses' licking off Jell-O

WRITING ACTIVITY **10** *Outlining*

Outline the information about tourist attractions in San Diego in Writing Activity 8. Show three main topics with at least three subtopics under each one.

WRITING ACTIVITY **11** *Writing on Your Own*

WRITING
ABOUT THE
THEME
   Review the categories and notes from Writing Activity 9 for your report about a tradition and write an outline for the body of the report. Save your outline for drafting.

Drafting

Writing Process

Your main goal in writing the first draft is to use your thesis statement, outline, and notes to write a well-structured report. Like an essay, a report has three main parts: an introduction, a body, and a conclusion. In addition, a report usually contains some form of references—such as parenthetical citations or footnotes—and a works cited page that, like a bibliography, lists all the sources you used. The following chart shows the function of each part of a report.

The Structure of a Report	
PARTS	**PURPOSE**
TITLE	• suggests the subject of the report
INTRODUCTION	• captures the readers' attention • provides necessary background information related to the subject • contains the thesis statement
BODY	• supports the thesis statement • has paragraphs that each cover one topic or subtopic
CONCLUSION	• brings the report to a close, often by restating the thesis in different words
CITATIONS	• give credit to other authors for their words and ideas
WORKS CITED	• lists all the sources that you have cited in the report • appears at the end of the report

Notice that in the structure of a report, the introduction makes your thesis clear to readers. As you draft your introduction, therefore, you should refine your working thesis into an appropriate thesis statement.

Guidelines for Refining a Thesis Statement

1. Make the thesis statement specific enough so the main point of your report is clear to the readers.
2. Make the thesis statement general enough to include all the main topics in your outline.

WRITING ACTIVITY *Refining Thesis Statements*

Rewrite each thesis statement to include all the main topics in the outline.

1. Some lifesaving techniques are simple enough for anyone to learn.
   I. Heimlich maneuver
   II. Cardiopulmonary resuscitation (CPR)
   III. Techniques only doctors should use
2. Dogs are beneficial to their masters' lives.
   I. Lower blood pressure in master
   II. Feeling of being needed
   III. Experiments letting prisoners have birds and hamsters
3. The Constitution of the United States grew out of the Articles of Confederation.
   I. Summary of Articles of Confederation
   II. Changes from Articles to Constitution
   III. Constitution as model for other countries

Signing of the Constitution, Louis Glanzman.

Using Sources

As you consult your note cards for the details you will need to draft the body of your report, think of ways to work your source materials smoothly into your own writing. The following tips may help you to incorporate source quotations and borrowed ideas into your draft.

Tips for Using Sources

1. Use a quotation to finish a sentence you have started.
2. Quote a whole sentence. If you omit words from a quoted sentence, indicate the omission with an ellipsis (. . .).
3. Quote only a few words from the source as part of one of your sentences.
4. Paraphrase information from a source. When you *paraphrase,* you reword a passage of text, using your own words. When you summarize information on note cards, you are often paraphrasing.

Example: *Paraphrasing*

ORIGINAL SOURCE   "To match the appearance of the swirling pools of water in the real Yellowstone, Alex used evaporated milk and white poster paint, mixed with water and poured into the set's pools. The pressure of the steam caused just the proper amount of movement in the pale white whirlpools and eddies duplicated in this enormous outdoor set."

PARAPHRASE   Using evaporated milk, poster paint, and steam on the set, Alex duplicated the swirling pools of water in the real Yellowstone.

WRITING ACTIVITY *Using Sources*

The following paragraph is an explanation of how fire fighters classify fires into four groups. Read the explanation carefully.

Then use it as a source for completing the four items that follow the paragraph.

Classifying Fires

Fire fighters classify fires into four groups. Class A fires are those in which such things as wood or paper are burning. These fires can usually be put out with water. Class B fires are caused by burning liquids, such as gasoline, oil, or alcohol. Putting water on fires of this type usually results in spreading the fire, since the fuel will float on the water. Only carbon dioxide or dry chemical extinguishers can be safely used on these fires. The same type of chemicals can be used on Class C fires. These are caused by electrical wires or equipment that becomes overheated. If the current is still on, the person trying to put out the fire might be electrocuted if he put water onto the blaze. Class D fires are those rare ones in which certain metals burn. These special chemical fires require specific types of chemicals to put out the fires. WALTER R. BROWN, BILLYE W. CUTCHEN, AND NORMAN D. ANDERSON *Catastrophes*

1. Write a sentence about Class B fires that ends with a quotation.
2. Write three sentences about Class C fires, using one of the sentences as a direct quotation from the source.
3. Write a sentence about fires that includes only a few words that are quoted from the source.
4. Write a sentence paraphrasing the information about Class D fires.

WRITING ACTIVITY *Paraphrasing*

Write a sentence paraphrasing the following passage.

Class B fires are caused by burning liquids, such as gasoline, oil, or alcohol. Putting water on fires of this type usually results in spreading the fire, since the fuel will float on the water. Only carbon dioxide or dry chemical extinguishers can be safely used on these fires.

Studying a Model Draft of a Report

Following is the final draft of the student report on special effects in *The Wizard of Oz*. As you read the report, notice how it follows both The Structure of a Report on page 379 and the outline on page 378. You will also see how the student writer added transitions—such as *although, instead, first,* and *meanwhile*—to connect the parts of the outline into coherent paragraphs.

As you read, notice too how the student incorporated source material, with quotes and paraphrases worked into the sentences and paragraphs. You will see that sources are cited in parentheses in the body of the report. The student chose this method of citing sources, called *parenthetical citation,* instead of using footnotes at the bottom of each page. A parenthetical citation briefly identifies the source and page number within each sentence in which the source of information must be credited. When you finish reading the model report, you will learn more about citing sources.

Student Model: *Draft of a Report*

TITLE

The Wizardry of Oz

<u>The Wizard of Oz</u> was released in 1939 after two years in production at a cost of three million dollars. One motion-picture reviewer remarked that "the wizards of Hollywood have turned on their magic full force in the making of this film" (Rev. of <u>The Wizard of Oz</u> 32). The "magic" referred

INTRODUCTION

to the movie's special effects, such as the "realistically contrived cyclone" praised by <u>Newsweek</u> ("The Fabulous Land of Oz" 23). Other reviewers raved about the Good Witch's arriving in a golden bubble, the Wicked Witch's skywriting and her later melting away to nothing, the monkeys' flying, the trees' talking, and the horse's changing colors. The movie won an Oscar in 1939 for these creative effects by special-effects director A. Arnold (Buddy) Gillespie. Although these effects looked effortlessly magical, much real wizardry went into creating the special effects in <u>The Wizard of Oz</u>.

The most challenging effect was the twister. Gillespie knew he "couldn't go to Kansas and wait for a tornado to come down and pick up a house" (Harmetz 244). Instead, he got an idea from watching cone-shaped wind socks used at airports to indicate wind direction. First he made a similar cone out of rubber at a cost of $8,000; but when the rubber did not twist properly, he had to start over. After several experiments he built a 35-foot miniature cyclone out of muslin. He attached it to a machine that moved along a track and blew a dusty substance through the model twister to create a dust cloud. The $12,000 machine moved and twisted the muslin cone in a convincing way. Meanwhile a worker perched above the machine made huge clouds of yellowish-black smoke from carbon and sulfur. In front of the cameras, glass panels covered with gray cotton gave the tornado scene a dark, menacing quality on film and at the same time hid all the machinery (Harmetz 247-48).

A much simpler effect was the illusion that the cyclone lifted Dorothy's house off the ground. Gillespie's crew filmed a three-foot-high model of the house falling onto a floor painted like the sky. Then the film was simply run in reverse. The crystal ball in the witch's castle was also a simple trick. It was a big glass bowl placed over a small screen. Film shot earlier was projected onto the screen, giving the illusion of real images appearing in the crystal ball. Another simple effect was the glass bubble that transports Glinda into Munchkinland. Gillespie's crew first filmed a silver ball, "just like a Christmas tree ornament, only bigger," by moving the camera closer and closer, making the ball seem to grow larger (Harmetz 254-55). Then, by layering the films, they added the scene of Munchkinland and Billie Burke, the actress playing Glinda.

THIRD PARAGRAPH IN BODY (Roman numeral III in outline

Some effects that should have been simple became complicated because of unexpected problems. The flying monkeys, for example, were models suspended from a trolley, attached by 2,200 piano wires that moved them and their wings (McClelland 92). The wires kept breaking, however, which forced the crew to reshoot the scene repeatedly. Another problem was the horse-of-a-different-color, the creature that keeps changing hues. Six matching white horses were used for the trick photography--each colored a different shade. When the crew proposed to paint the horses to achieve the desired effect, however, the American Society for the Prevention of Cruelty to Animals protested. As a creative solution, the horses were "painted" with Jell-O, but the crew had to work fast because the horses kept licking it off (McClelland 92-3)!

CONCLUSION

While the cyclone was the most difficult effect, the melting disappearance of the Wicked Witch was the simplest of all. "As for how I melted," said Margaret Hamilton, the actress playing the witch, "I went down

385

through the floor on an elevator . . . leaving
some fizzling dry ice and my floor length
costume" (McClelland 96-7). While the demise
of the Wicked Witch was truly effortless, the
other tricks and illusions in <u>The Wizard of Oz</u>
required both effort and skill. Every bit of
"magic," from the cyclone to the electric tail
wagger in the Cowardly Lion's costume (Hall
137), was created by Gillespie's wizards of
special effects.

Works Cited

"The Fabulous Land of Oz: Dream World via
     Cyclonic Ride Recreated in Technicolor."
     <u>Newsweek</u> 21 Aug. 1939: 23-4.
Hall, Jane. "The Wizard of Oz." <u>Good</u>
     <u>Housekeeping</u> Aug. 1939: 40-1+.
Harmetz, Aljean. <u>The Making of The Wizard of</u>
     <u>Oz</u>. New York: Alfred A. Knopf, 1977.
McClelland, Doug. <u>Down the Yellow Brick</u>
     <u>Road: The Making of The Wizard of Oz</u>.
     New York: Pyramid Books, 1976.
Rev. of <u>The Wizard of Oz</u>, dir. Victor
     Fleming. <u>Senior Scholastic</u> 18 Sept.
     1939:32-33.

WRITING ACTIVITY **15** *Writing on Your Own*

WRITING
ABOUT THE
THEME

Following your outline, write a first draft of your report
on a tradition. Be sure your thesis statement achieves the
goals outlined on page 380. Add a parenthetical citation every
time you include a quotation or an idea that is not your own.
Simply identify the source and page number in parentheses, as
in the model. As long as you know which source you mean,
you can rewrite each citation in the proper form if necessary
when you revise your draft.

Citing Sources

Laws protect authors and publishers whose materials have been copyrighted. Using another person's words or ideas without giving proper credit is called *plagiarism*, a serious offense. Whenever you use source materials, therefore, you must give credit to the authors—even if you only paraphrase. You have already taken steps to avoid plagiarism by taking notes in your own words and by recording the author, the page number, and the exact words of any quotation you plan to use. The chief methods of citing sources are parenthetical citations, as you have seen, and footnotes or endnotes.

Parenthetical Citations The following guidelines and examples will help you use parenthetical citations correctly. Keep in mind that the citations in parentheses are intentionally brief. Their purpose is to provide the reader with only enough information to identify the source of the material you have borrowed. Readers then refer to the works cited page at the end of your report for complete information about each source.

Models: *Parenthetical Citations*

BOOK BY ONE AUTHOR	Give author's last name and a page reference: (Harmetz 244).
BOOK BY TWO OR MORE AUTHORS	Give both authors' names and a page reference: (Morella and Epstein 27).
ARTICLE	Give author's last name and a page reference: (Hall 40).
ARTICLE; AUTHOR UNNAMED	Give shortened form of title of article and page reference: ("The Fabulous Land of Oz" 24).
ARTICLE IN A REFERENCE WORK; AUTHOR UNNAMED	Give title (full or shortened) and page number, unless title is entered alphabetically in an encyclopedia: ("Special Effects").

Parenthetical citations should be placed as close to the words or ideas being credited as possible. To avoid interrupting the flow of the sentence, place them at the end of a phrase, a clause, or a sentence. If a parenthetical citation falls at the end of a sentence, place it before the period. If you are using quotation marks, the citation goes after the closing quotation mark but before the period.

Footnotes and Endnotes   If your teacher directs you to use footnotes or endnotes instead of parenthetical citations, you will use a different form. For either footnotes or endnotes, you put a small number halfway above the line immediately after the borrowed material. This number is called a *superscript*. It refers readers to a note at the bottom, or foot, of the page. Your teacher will tell you whether to number your notes consecutively throughout your report or to begin the first note on each page with the number *1*. Endnotes are the same as footnotes, except that they are listed at the end of the report.

Model: *Correct Form for Footnotes and Endnotes*

GENERAL REFERENCE WORKS
[1]Frederick J. Hoffman, "L. Frank Baum," World Book Encyclopedia, 1983 ed.

BOOKS BY ONE AUTHOR
[2]Aljean Harmetz, The Making of The Wizard of Oz (New York: Alfred A. Knopf, 1977) 244.

BOOKS BY TWO OR MORE AUTHORS
[3]Joe Morella and Edward Epstein, The Films and Career of Judy Garland (New York: Citadel Press, 1969) 34.

ARTICLES IN MAGAZINES
[4]Jane Hall, "The Wizard of Oz," Good Housekeeping, Aug. 1939 137.

ARTICLES IN NEWSPAPERS
[5]Frank S. Nugent, "A Critic's Adventure in Wonderland," New York Times 5 Feb. 1939, sec. 9: 5.

Whenever you cite a work that you previously cited in full, you can use a shortened form of footnote for all repeated references to that work.

FIRST REFERENCE
[2]Aljean Harmetz, The Making of The Wizard of Oz (New York: Alfred A. Knopf, 1977) 244.

LATER REFERENCE
[6]Harmetz 247.

Preparing a Works Cited Page The sources you cited in your report should be listed on a works cited page at the end of the report. In the report on *The Wizard of Oz,* for example, the student writer added a works cited page to give a complete list of references for the parenthetical citations in the report. *(See page 386.)*

Writing Term A **works cited page** is an alphabetical listing of sources cited in a report.

On a works cited page, sources are listed alphabetically by the author's last name or by the title if no author is given. Page numbers are given for articles but usually not for books. The following examples show the correct form for works cited entries. In each example note the order of information, the indentation, and the punctuation.

Model: *Correct Form for a List of Works Cited*

GENERAL REFERENCE WORKS	Hoffmann, Frederick J. "L. Frank Baum." <u>World Book Encyclopedia</u>. 1983 ed.
BOOKS BY ONE AUTHOR	Harmetz, Aljean. <u>The Making of The Wizard of Oz</u>. New York: Alfred A. Knopf, 1977.
BOOKS BY TWO OR MORE AUTHORS	Morella, Joe, and Edward Epstein. <u>Judy: The Films and Career of Judy Garland</u>. New York: Citadel Press, 1969.
ARTICLES IN MAGAZINES— AUTHOR NAMED	Hall, Jane. "The Wizard of Oz." <u>Good Housekeeping</u> Aug. 1939: 40–1 +.
ARTICLES IN MAGAZINES— AUTHOR UNNAMED	"The Fabulous Land of Oz: Dream World via Cyclonic Ride Recreated in Technicolor." <u>Newsweek</u> 21 Aug. 1939: 23-4.
ARTICLES IN NEWSPAPERS	Nugent, Frank S. "A Critic's Adventure in Wonderland." <u>New York Times</u> 5 Feb. 1939, sec. 9: 5.
REVIEWS	Rev. of <u>The Wizard of Oz</u>, dir. Victor Fleming. <u>Senior Scholastic</u> 18 Sept. 1939: 32–33.

Sometimes your teacher may ask you to include a works consulted page—often called a bibliography—on which you include all the works you consulted but did not necessarily cite in your report. A works consulted page or bibliography uses the same form as the works cited page.

WRITING ACTIVITY **16** *Preparing a Works Cited Page*

The following sources for a report on Titan (Saturn's largest moon) do not have the correct form for a works cited page. Following the examples given on page 389, rewrite each entry correctly and place it in the correct order. Save your work for Writing Activity 17.

Randall Black. *Science Digest*, "Blimp on Titan," Aug. 1983, 14–15.

Ridpath, Ian, "The Living Void," *Encyclopedia of Space Travel and Astronomy*, 1979, p. 112–113.

Isaac Asimov, *The Universe: From Flat Earth to Quasar* Avon Books, New York, 1966, 38.

"Titan's Sea," *Omni*, by Patrick Moore July 1983: 28–31.

New York Times: "The Gases of Titan," June 21, 1983, sec. 4, pp. 2–4.

WRITING ACTIVITY *Using Parenthetical Citations*

Write a parenthetical citation for each of the following references to the works cited page about Titan that you prepared in Writing Activity 16.

EXAMPLE   Information from the article by Patrick Moore in *Omni* magazine

ANSWER   (Moore 28)

1. A quote from the article in *Science Digest*
2. A fact from the book by Isaac Asimov called *The Universe: From Flat Earth to Quasar*
3. A reference to information in the article in the *New York Times*
4. A quote from "The Living Void" article in the *Encyclopedia of Space Travel and Astronomy*

WRITING ACTIVITY *Writing on Your Own*

WRITING ABOUT THE THEME

After you review what you have learned about citing sources correctly, reread the first draft of your report on a tradition and write the parenthetical citations in the proper form. Then prepare a works cited page to add at the end of your report. If you have a source that does not fit one of the categories described on page 389, refer to the *MLA Handbook for Writers of Research Papers*, third edition, by Joseph Gibaldi and Walter S. Achtert, for information on how to cite it correctly. Save your completed draft for revising.

Revising

Writing Process

Drafting your report is like stitching together a quilt. You assemble and join the various pieces of information you have collected through your research. Your time and effort are rewarded when you have the finished product in your hands. Once the whole quilt is finished, you can stand back from it and check to make sure you have no missed stitches or wrong patterns. Two qualities of a report are especially important to check for—adequate development and accuracy.

Checking for Adequate Development   As you read over your draft, check the development of your main ideas. Did you use sufficient supporting details to back up your thesis? Have you adequately covered all the main points on your outline? Have you consulted enough sources to write authoritatively about your subject? If your answer to any of these questions is *no*, consider doing additional research to improve the content of your report.

Checking for Accuracy   Check for accuracy in your use of sources by examining all the quotes in your report. Have you accurately represented each source? Have you quoted any source out of context, thus distorting the author's real meaning? Have you used a number of sources so that you are not relying too heavily on one viewpoint? The more accurate and balanced your report is, the greater will be its power to explain or inform.

Conferencing to Revise   A second opinion is valuable when you are preparing the final draft of your report. If possible, therefore, ask a reader to review and critique your work. Specifically, ask your reviewer to summarize in his or her own words the main idea of your report and to point out any words, sentences, or paragraphs that seem unclear. Then, as you revise, take into account the reader's specific comments and suggestions. If your reviewer cannot summarize your main idea, you may need to make your focus or thesis more clear.

Using Revision Checklists   Use the Revision Checklist on page 32 and the following checklist to revise your draft.

Checklist for Revising a Report
1. Does your report include an introduction with a thesis statement?
2. Does the body adequately develop and support the thesis statement and main points?
3. Is your report accurate and balanced?
4. Does your report and the paragraphs within it have unity, coherence, and clarity?
5. Are your sentences concise and your words precise?
6. Did you use and cite sources correctly?
7. Did you add a suitable conclusion?
8. Did you include a works cited page?
9. Did you add an appropriate title?
10. Did you follow standard manuscript form? *(See page 41.)*

WRITING ACTIVITY 19 *Writing on Your Own*

WRITING
ABOUT THE
THEME

Evaluate your report on a tradition and do more research if necessary to develop your ideas adequately. Then, using the Revision Checklists on this page and on page 32, thoroughly revise your report and save it for editing.

Editing and Publishing

Grammar in the Writing Process

A *clause* is a group of words that has a subject and a verb. In the following example, the clause in bold type is a *subordinate clause* because it cannot stand alone as a complete sentence. It is attached to an *independent clause*.

CLAUSE   **As the creek began to rise,** the other members of the family grew frightened.

There are two types of subordinate clauses: adverb clauses and adjective clauses.

Adverb Clauses   An *adverb clause* is a subordinate clause that acts as a single adverb, usually describing a verb. You can vary your sentences by beginning some of them with an adverb clause. *(For more examples of adverb clauses and for practice in using them correctly, see pages 673–676.)*

ADVERB   **As the rain continued,** the creek rose higher.
CLAUSES   [The clause tells when the action of the verb *rose* took place.]
           The horse swam **as if its life depended on it.**
           [The clause tells how the action of the verb *swam* took place.]

Adjective Clauses   An *adjective clause* is a subordinate clause that acts as a single adjective, describing a noun or a pronoun. *(For more examples of adjective clauses and for practice in using them correctly, see pages 676–681.)*

ADJECTIVE He watched the workers **who were erecting a**
CLAUSES   **fence.** [The clause describes *workers*.]
           The flood of 1903, **which was not caused by rain,** was the most severe. [The clause describes *flood*.]

394

Punctuation with Clauses Always place a comma after an introductory adverb clause. Also use commas to separate a nonessential adjective clause from the rest of the sentence. A *nonessential adjective clause* can be removed without changing the meaning of the sentence. *(For more information about punctuating nonessential adjective clauses, see page 680.)*

NONESSENTIAL CLAUSE   The wall of water, **which was far wider than the creek banks,** bore down upon him. [The clause is nonessential because the sentence makes sense without it.]

Combining Sentences with Clauses With an understanding of clauses, you can combine short, choppy sentences to form more interesting sentences that read smoothly. *(For other examples of sentences combined with clauses and for practice in combining sentences, see pages 69–70.)*

TWO SENTENCES   The sun rose. He reached his home.
COMBINED   **As the sun rose,** he reached his home.
TWO SENTENCES   He watched the torrent. It raged before him.
COMBINED   He watched the torrent **that raged before him.**

Editing Checklist

1. Are all clauses punctuated correctly?
2. Did you use subordinate clauses to combine any sentences?

WRITING ACTIVITY ⟨20⟩ *Writing on Your Own*

WRITING ABOUT THE THEME   **Editing** Edit your report, using the checklist above and the one on page 37. Then produce two final copies, using standard manuscript form, outlined on page 41.

Publishing Bind each copy of your finished report within a plastic or cardboard cover to protect it. Then give one copy to your teacher and keep one for your future reference.

A Writer Writes

A Research Report

PURPOSE: to explain and inform
AUDIENCE: your teacher and classmates

Prewriting   Choose a cultural tradition that is practiced by some members of your community that you would like to know more about. For example, you might research a festival, a religious practice, or a custom. After you have chosen your subject, compile a list of sources. Your sources should include individuals to interview as well as published materials. Begin by gathering information and taking notes from books, periodicals, and any available audio-visual sources. Then, on the basis of your research, develop a working thesis about your subject. Your thesis may relate to the meaning, origin, history, or significance of a tradition.

The better informed you are about your subject, the better you will be able to conduct interviews. Before interviewing respondents, however, you should develop a set of questions that you hope to answer through interviews. List questions that relate to your subject and that will help you to refine and support your thesis. Be sure to record the name of each respondent, the date of the interview, and the information you gained. After you have gathered all your notes, use synthesizing to combine information from the different kinds of sources you consulted. *(See Writing Is Thinking on page 376.)*

Drafting   After you decide the best order in which to write what you have learned, draft your report. Begin with an introduction that will capture your reader's attention, perhaps by explaining what is intriguing about the tradition. Also include your thesis statement. Then draft the body of your report by following your outline. Conclude with a restatement of your thesis.

Be sure to document all your sources in the proper form, using parenthetical citations. For an interview, give the last name of the respondent and the date of the interview in parenthesis before the end of a sentence (Domenico 1992). Then, on your works cited page, include interview sources in alphabetical order in the following form.

Domenico, Allessandra. Personal interview. 15 Mar. 1992.

Revising   When you have finished your first draft, check the structure and content of your report for unity, coherence, accuracy, and adequate development. Then look for ways to improve the clarity and interest of your paragraphs, sentences, and words.

Editing and Publishing   Use the Editing Checklists on pages 37 and 395 to polish your final draft and to catch any mistakes you may have made. Give a neatly bound copy of your report to your teacher, who may ask you to share your research results with your classmates by using your paper as the basis of an oral report. If possible and appropriate, send a copy of your report to the people you interviewed.

Independent Writing

Write a research report on one of the following subjects or on one of your own. Use the checklist on page 399 as a guide.

1. rodeos
2. ozone
3. black holes in space
4. Lewis Carroll's poetry
5. nuclear energy
6. mummies
7. the ocean floor
8. Israel
9. computer viruses
10. African art

Creative Writing

Use your report-writing skills to write about a period of history. First, research one of the following events or another one of your choice. Then, writing from the point of view of a participant or an observer, draft a short fictional memoir. Make your memoir as historically accurate as you can.

1. the celebration of the first U.S. Independence Day
2. the White House in the War of 1812
3. the building of the Brooklyn Bridge
4. Julius Caesar's conquest of Gaul
5. the trial of Socrates

WRITING
ABOUT THE
THEME

Writing about Literature

Style is the characteristic way in which a writer writes. Some writers, for example, write precisely and straightforwardly; others use long sentences and many figures of speech. Write a paragraph that describes the author's style in "Rancho Buena Vista." How is her style appropriate to her purpose?

Writing in Other Subject Areas

Civics   Write a report on a current issue in your community. For example, you might write an investigative report about a plant's closing, a new water-treatment plan, or a safety problem. Wherever possible, apply the thinking skill of synthesizing to combine information and ideas from published sources, interviews, and your own experiences and observations.

Checklist

Writing Reports

Prewriting

✔ Use a variety of strategies to discover ideas to write about that require research. *(See page 365.)*

✔ Make a list of possible subjects for a research report. Then choose one and limit it. *(See pages 366–367.)*

✔ Gather information and take notes on notecards. *(See pages 368–372.)*

✔ Develop a working thesis. *(See page 373.)*

✔ Organize your notes into categories and create an outline for your report. *(See pages 374–378.)*

Drafting

✔ Include your refined thesis statement in the introduction and then write the body and conclusion. *(See pages 379–380.)*

✔ Avoid plagiarism by using and citing sources carefully. *(See pages 381–382 and 387.)*

✔ Prepare the citations and a works cited page. *(See pages 387–391.)*

✔ Add a title.

Revising

✔ Check your report for adequate development and accuracy. *(See page 392.)*

✔ Use the Revision Checklists to edit your report. *(See pages 32 and 393.)*

Editing and Publishing

✔ Use the Editing Checklists to edit your report. *(See pages 37 and 395.)*

✔ Share your finished work with an interested reader.

11

Creative Writing

Part 1 | Reading to Write

THEME: *The Unexpected*

Life is full of unexpected twists and turns and surprises. For example, you may have met your best friend by accident, or you may have acquired your pet unintentionally when it chose you out of all the people in your neighborhood. Have you ever started out for one place, become lost, and as a result unexpectedly found a better or more interesting place than your original destination?

The unexpected is often an element in many stories, such as humorous stories and stories of suspense. Surprising, curious, scary, or unexplainable events trigger the plots of many tales. In fact, what makes a good story entertaining to read is that you do not know what to expect—and are therefore surprised when the unexpected happens.

The following story by Saki, "The Open Window," begins by telling about ordinary characters in an ordinary situation in England during the early 1900's. The story ends unexpectedly, however. As you read "The Open Window," see if you can predict the ending.

The Open Window

S a k i

"My aunt will be down presently, Mr. Nuttel," said a very self-possessed young lady of fifteen; "in the meantime you must try and put up with me."

Framton Nuttel endeavored to say the correct something that should duly flatter the niece of the moment without unduly discounting the aunt that was to come. Privately he doubted more than ever whether these formal visits on a succession of total strangers would do much towards helping the nerve cure which he was supposed to be undergoing.

"I know how it will be," his sister had said when he was preparing to migrate to this rural retreat; "you will bury yourself down there and not speak to a living soul, and your nerves will be worse than ever from moping. I shall just give you letters of introduction to all the people I know there. Some of them, as far as I can remember, were quite nice."

Framton wondered whether Mrs. Sappleton, the lady to whom he was presenting one of the letters of introduction, came into the nice division.

"Do you know many of the people round here?" asked the niece, when she judged that they had had sufficient silent communion.

"Hardly a soul," said Framton. "My sister was staying here, at the rectory, you know, some four years ago, and she gave me letters of introduction to some of the people here."

He made the last statement in a tone of distinct regret.

"Then you know practically nothing about my aunt?" pursued the self-possessed young lady.

"Only her name and address," admitted the caller. He was wondering whether Mrs. Sappleton was in the married or widowed state. An undefinable something about the room seemed to suggest masculine habitation.

"Her great tragedy happened just three years ago," said the child; "that would be since your sister's time."

"Her tragedy?" asked Framton; somehow in this restful country spot tragedies seemed out of place.

"You may wonder why we keep that window wide open on an October afternoon," said the niece, indicating a large French window that opened on to a lawn.

"It is quite warm for the time of the year," said Framton; "but has that window got anything to do with the tragedy?"

"Out through that window, three years ago to a day, her husband and her two young brothers went off for their day's shooting. They never came back. In crossing the moor to their favorite snipe-shooting ground they were all three engulfed by a treacherous piece of bog. It had been that dreadful wet summer, you know, and places that were safe in other years gave way suddenly without warning. Their bodies were never recovered. That was the dreadful part of it." Here the child's voice lost its self-possessed note and became falteringly human. "Poor aunt always thinks that they will come back some day, they and the little brown spaniel that was lost with them, and walk in that window just as they used to do. That is why the window is kept open every evening till it is quite dusk. Poor dear aunt, she has often told me how they went out, her husband with his white waterproof coat over his arm, and Ronnie, her youngest brother, singing 'Bertie, why do you bound?' as he always did to tease her, because she said it got on her nerves. Do you know, sometimes on still, quiet evenings like this, I almost get a creepy feeling that they will all walk in through that window—"

She broke off with a little shudder. It was a relief to Framton when the aunt bustled into the room with a whirl of apologies for being late in making her appearance.

"I hope Vera has been amusing you?" she said.

"She has been very interesting," said Framton.

"I hope you don't mind the open window," said Mrs. Sappleton briskly; "my husband and brothers will be home directly from shooting, and they always come in this way. They've been out for snipe in the marshes today, so they'll make a fine mess over my poor carpets. So like you menfolk, isn't it?"

She rattled on cheerfully about the shooting and the scarcity of birds, and the prospects for duck in the winter. To Framton it was all purely horrible. He made a desperate but only partially successful effort to turn the talk on to a less ghastly topic; he was conscious that his hostess was giving him only a fragment of her attention, and her eyes were constantly straying past him to the open window and the lawn beyond. It was certainly an unfortunate coincidence that he should have paid his visit on this tragic anniversary.

"The doctors agree in ordering me complete rest, an absence of mental excitement, and avoidance of anything in the nature of violent physical exercise," announced Framton, who labored under the tolerably widespread delusion that total strangers and chance acquaintances are hungry for the least detail of one's ailments and infirmities, their cause and cure. "On the matter of diet they are not so much in agreement," he continued.

"No?" said Mrs. Sappleton, in a voice which only replaced a yawn at the last moment. Then she suddenly brightened into alert attention—but not to what Framton was saying.

"Here they are at last!" she cried. "Just in time for tea, and don't they look as if they were muddy up to the eyes!"

Framton shivered slightly, and turned towards the niece with a look intended to convey sympathetic comprehension. The child was staring out through the open window with dazed horror in her eyes. In a chill shock of nameless fear Framton swung round in his seat and looked in the same direction.

In the deepening twilight three figures were walking across the lawn towards the window; they all carried guns under their arms, and one of them was additionally burdened with a white coat hung over his shoulders. A tired brown spaniel kept close at their heels. Noiselessly they neared the house, and then a hoarse young voice chanted out of the dusk:

"I said, Bertie, why do you bound?"

Framton grabbed wildly at his stick and hat; the hall door, the gravel drive, and the front gate were dimly noted stages in his headlong retreat. A cyclist coming along the road had to run into the hedge to avoid imminent collision.

"Here we are, my dear," said the bearer of the white mackintosh, coming in through the window; "fairly muddy, but most of it's dry. Who was that who bolted out as we came up?"

"A most extraordinary man, a Mr. Nuttel," said Mrs. Sappleton; "could only talk about his illnesses, and dashed off without a word of goodbye or apology when you arrived. One would think he had seen a ghost."

"I expect it was the spaniel," said the niece calmly; "he told me he had a horror of dogs. He was once hunted into a cemetery somewhere on the banks of the Ganges[1] by a pack of pariah[2] dogs, and had to spend the night in an newly dug grave with the creatures snarling and grinning and foaming just above him. Enough to make anyone lose his nerve."

Romance at short notice was her speciality. ◆

1. **Ganges:** River in India.
2. **pariah** [pə rī′ yä]: Outcast.

Responding to the Theme

The Unexpected

Responding in Your Journal   This week in your journal write about things in your life that have caught you by surprise—events or phenomena that you were not expecting to turn out the way they did. What stories, for example, could you tell about life's little surprises, surprise endings, strange or unexplained phenomena, and jokes that people sometimes play on each other for fun? Start today by writing about unexpected turns of events that you have observed or have experienced in your own life. Then write about any unexpected happenings that you have read or heard about. As you write about each example of the unexpected, include as many details about it as you know or can remember. You might also think of imaginative explanations for each unexplained event you write about.

Speaking and Listening   With your teacher's permission, join with classmates in taking the parts of the characters in "The Open Window" and reading aloud the dialogue as if the story were a play. Volunteer for the parts of Vera, Framton, all the supporting characters, and the narrator. The narrator's job is to read aloud the lines that are not part of the dialogue. Your group might enjoy adapting the story as a play and performing it for other students.

Critical Thinking: Analyzing   In "The Open Window," Vera— for her own amusement—decides to play a practical joke on a nervous, self-absorbed stranger who has come to visit her aunt, Mrs. Sappleton. Trace the steps Vera takes to set up this joke and to ensure its effect on Framton Nuttel. Then describe in your own words the sequence of these steps.

Extending Your Vocabulary   Use a dictionary or a thesaurus to find synonyms for the following words from "The Open Window." Then indicate whether the connotation of each synonym is positive, negative, or neutral.

bog	duly	mackintosh	rectory
delusion	ghastly	moor	romance

405

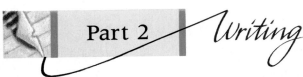

Part 2 *Writing*

Sometimes writing fulfills a practical purpose, as when you write an expository essay or a report. However, at other times, your purpose will be more like the author's of "The Open Window." You will want to delight, or even surprise, your readers by expressing yourself creatively.

Most creative writing—including stories, novels, plays, and poems—takes the form of fiction with imaginary characters, events, and settings. This chapter focuses on the creative writing of a short story.

Writing Term A **short story** is a fictional account of characters resolving a conflict or situation.

While a short story may be based on actual people or events, it is nevertheless fictional because it is a product of the writer's imagination. This chapter will give you practice in using your imagination to write stories.

The Elements of a Short Story

All short stories have three main sections: a beginning, a middle, and an end. Usually in the beginning of a story, the writer provides all the necessary background information that readers will need to understand and to enjoy the story. For example, readers will find out where the story takes place, who the main characters are, and what problem, or conflict, the main character has to solve or overcome. The middle of the story then develops the plot; that is, the writer relates—usually chronologically—what happens to the characters as a result of the conflict and how the characters react to those events. The ending of the story tells the outcome or shows how the central conflict is resolved. *(For information about how the elements of a short story contribute to its meaning, see pages 334–335.)*

The Plot and the Central Conflict

The *plot*, the sequence of events leading to the outcome or point of the story, is the story's core. The plot tells what happens as the characters meet and struggle to resolve a *central conflict*. This conflict can come from within a character, such as a con-flict of conscience; between characters, such as a conflict between friends; or between characters and the outside world, such as a struggle against the forces of nature. The plot usually begins with an event that triggers the central conflict. Once the central conflict is revealed, the plot develops more quickly, bringing the story to a *climax*, or high point, when the conflict is greatest. After resolving the conflict (or explaining why it remains unre-solved), the story rapidly comes to an end.

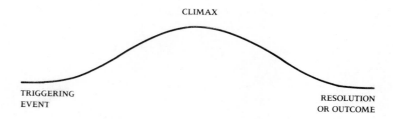

CLIMAX

TRIGGERING
EVENT

RESOLUTION
OR OUTCOME

407

The Characters

Most short stories focus on one main character, who has or faces the conflict, or on two main characters, whose relationship is often the source of the conflict. The other characters in the story, the minor, or supporting, characters, either help or hinder the main character in resolving the crisis. In the best short stories, characters are colorful, authentic, and memorable to readers in some way. Authors develop characters through narration, description, and dialogue.

The Setting

The setting of a story is the environment in which the action takes place. It is like the backdrop of scenery and the props on a stage set. The setting also includes the time during which the story occurs.

One of the functions of a setting is to create a *mood*—the overall feeling that the story conveys. The mood of the setting might reflect the story's theme. A neglected park at dusk, for instance, might make a tale of suspense more suspenseful. An author might also plan settings that either match or contrast with the main character's mood. For example, a confused character might be lost at sea in a dense fog or wandering around in a perfectly ordered formal garden.

The Narrator

The person who tells a story is the *narrator*. Readers see the events of a story through the eyes of the narrator, or from the narrator's *point of view*. The following chart describes the different points of view from which a story can be told.

Point of View	Narrator's Role in the Story
FIRST PERSON	Participant in the action; relates the events as he or she sees them; uses pronouns such as *I, me, we, us,* and *our*
THIRD PERSON OBJECTIVE	Does not participate in the action; relates the words and actions of characters but not thoughts or feelings; uses pronouns such as *he, she, they, him, her,* and *them*
THIRD PERSON OMNISCIENT ("ALL KNOWING")	Does not participate in the action; relates the thoughts and feelings of all the characters as well as their words and actions

Each point of view has certain advantages. For example, the third person objective narrator can relate two events happening simultaneously in different places. The omniscient narrator can relate not only simultaneous events but also all the characters' thoughts and feelings; that is, the inner life of the characters as well as the outer action. In the excerpt below, the narrator reports the characters' thoughts and feelings.

Model: *Third Person Omniscient*

Neither [Mr. nor Mrs. Delahanty] wanted, in the midst of their sorrow for the good man whose life was ending, to enter into any discussion of Cress [their daughter]. What was the matter with Cress? What happened to her since she went away to college? She, who had been open and loving? And who now lived inside a world so absolutely fitted to her own size and shape that she felt any intrusion, even that of the death of her own grandfather, to be an unmerited invasion of her privacy . . .

JESSAMYN WEST, *Sixteen*

The Theme

Most short stories have a theme, or main idea, of some kind, such as the healing power of love, the rewards of showing courage, or the wastefulness of despair. The outcome of the story may then imply some lesson or moral about the theme, or it may affirm some meaningful observation or conclusion about life. However, some short stories aim chiefly to surprise or entertain readers rather than to give a message.

A Sample Short Story

Studying a good short story can help you with your own writing. The following short story by Ernest Hemingway contains all the elements of a short story described on pages 407–410. As you read it, look for the central conflict and the development of the plot, the descriptions of the setting and characters, the point of view of the narrator.

A Day's Wait

SETTING, CHARACTERS, TRIGGERING EVENT, FIRST PERSON POINT OF VIEW

He came into the room to shut the windows while we were still in bed and I saw he looked ill. He was shivering, his face was white, and he walked slowly as though it ached to move.

"What's the matter, Schatz?"

"I've got a headache."

"You better go back to bed."

"No. I'm all right."

"You go to bed. I'll see you when I'm dressed."

But when I came downstairs he was dressed, sitting by the fire, looking a very sick and miserable boy of nine years. When I put my hand on his forehead I knew he had a fever.

"You go up to bed," I said, "you're sick."

"I'm all right," he said.

CENTRAL CONFLICT

When the doctor came he took the boy's temperature.

"What is it?" I asked him.

"One hundred and two."

Downstairs, the doctor left three different medicines in different colored capsules with instructions for giving them. One was to bring down the fever, another a purgative, the third to overcome an acid condition. The germs of influenza can only exist in an acid condition, he explained. He seemed to know all about influenza and said there was nothing to worry about if the fever did not go above one hundred and four degrees. This was a light epidemic of flu and there was no danger if you avoided pneumonia.

Back in the room I wrote the boy's temperature down and made a note of the time to give the various capsules.

"Do you want me to read to you?"

THOUGHT SHOWN THROUGH DESCRIPTION

"All right. If you want to," said the boy. His face was very white and there were dark areas under his eyes. He lay very still in the bed and seemed very detached from what was going on.

I read aloud from Howard Pyle's *Book of Pirates*; but I could see he was not following what I was reading.

"How do you feel, Schatz?" I asked him.

"Just the same, so far," he said.

I sat at the foot of the bed and read to myself while I waited for it to be time to give another capsule. It would have been natural for him to go

THOUGHT SHOWN THROUGH ACTION

to sleep, but when I looked up he was looking at the foot of the bed, looking very strangely.

"Why don't you try to go to sleep? I'll wake you up for the medicine."

"I'd rather stay awake."

THOUGHT SHOWN THROUGH DIALOGUE

After a while he said to me, "You don't have to stay in here with me Papa, if it bothers you."

"It doesn't bother me."

"No, I mean you don't have to stay if it's going to bother you."

I thought perhaps he was a little light-headed and giving him prescribed capsules at eleven o'clock I went out for a while.

411

CHARACTER
REVEALED
THROUGH ACTION
AND SENSORY
DETAILS

It was a bright, cold day, the ground covered with a sleet that had frozen so that it seemed as if all the bare trees, the bushes, the cut brush and all the grass and the bare ground had been varnished with ice. I took the young Irish setter for a little walk up the road and along a frozen creek, but it was difficult to stand or walk on the glassy surface and the red dog slipped and slithered and I fell twice, hard, once dropping my gun and having it slide away over the ice.

We flushed a covey of quail under a high clay bank with overhanging brush and I killed two as they went out of sight over the top of the bank. Some of the covey lit in trees, but most of them scattered into brush piles and it was necessary to jump on the ice-coated mounds of brush several times before they would flush. Coming out while you were poised unsteadily on the icy, springy brush they made difficult shooting and I killed two, missed five, and started back pleased to have found a covey close to the house and happy there were so many left to find on another day.

At the house they said the boy had refused to let anyone come into the room.

"You can't come in," he said. "You mustn't get what I have."

PLOT ADVANCED
THROUGH
DIALOGUE

I went up to him and found him in exactly the position I had left him, white-faced, but with the tops of his cheeks flushed by the fever, staring still, as he had stared, at the foot of the bed.

I took his temperature.

"What is it?"

"Something like a hundred," I said. It was one hundred and two and four tenths.

"It was a hundred and two," he said.

"Who said so?"

"The doctor."

"Your temperature is all right," I said. "It's nothing to worry about."

"I don't worry," he said, "but I can't keep from thinking."

CLUE TO THE
THEME

"Don't think," I said. "Just take it easy."

"I'm taking it easy," he said and looked straight ahead. He was evidently holding tight onto himself about something.

"Take this with water."

"Do you think it will do any good?"

"Of course it will."

I sat down and opened the *Pirate* book and commenced to read, but I could see he was not following, so I stopped.

CLIMAX

"About what time do you think I'm going to die?" he asked.

"What?"

"About how long will it be before I die?"

"You aren't going to die. What's the matter with you?"

"Oh, yes, I am. I heard him say a hundred and two."

"People don't die with a fever of one hundred and two. That's a silly way to talk."

"I know they do. At school in France the boys told me you can't live with forty-four degrees. I've got a hundred and two."

CLUE TO THE
THEME

He had been waiting to die all day, ever since nine o'clock in the morning.

RESOLUTION

"You poor Schatz," I said. "Poor old Schatz. It's like miles and kilometers. You aren't going to die. That's a different thermometer. On that thermometer thirty-seven is normal. On this kind it's ninety-eight."

"Are you sure?"

"Absolutely," I said. "It's like miles and kilometers. You know, like how many kilometers we make when we do seventy miles in the car?"

"Oh," he said.

OUTCOME

But his gaze at the foot of the bed relaxed slowly. The hold over himself relaxed too, finally, and the next day it was very slack and he cried very easily at little things that were of no importance.

ERNEST HEMINGWAY
"A Day's Wait"

WRITING ACTIVITY *Understanding Short Story Elements*

Write answers to the following questions about "The Open Window," on pages 401–404.

1. What is the plot of "The Open Window"? Briefly outline the main events.
2. What is the central conflict? Briefly describe it.
3. Who are all the characters in the story? Which one is the main character and how do you know that?
4. What is the setting? Describe it in a few sentences.
5. From what point of view is the story told? How do you think that point of view affects the story?
6. What do you think the theme of the story is? Express the theme in a few sentences in your own words.

Prewriting

Author Kurt Vonnegut once compared writing fiction to making a movie, saying, "All sorts of accidental things will happen after you've set up the cameras . . .You set the story in motion, and as you're watching this thing begin, all these opportunities will show up. Keeping your mind open to opportunities will help you imagine your story fully. Unless you think through the basic elements of your story, however, it may remain only as bits of "footage." For this reason your prewriting work should include building a plot.

Building a Plot

Many of your best ideas for a plot will come from your own experiences and observations, while others will come from your imagination. The following strategies may stimulate your thinking for story ideas.

Strategies for Thinking of Plots

1. Brainstorm for a list of story ideas based on conflicts you have experienced or observed firsthand. Then use clustering or inquiring to develop plot details. For each conflict you think of, identify the triggering event and describe the resolution or outcome.
2. Scan newspaper headlines and news items for an event you could build into a fictional story. Some items might suggest a comic or a tragic tale, for example, or might report a discovery or a mystery that you could explore in fiction.
3. Think of conflicts or events in history—including your family history and local history—that might be interesting to develop in fiction writing.
4. Observe people and events in your life. Sometimes even small events or snatches of conversation will suggest a conflict on which to build a plot. An incident that you noticed in a mall, for example, could become the basis of a story.

Once you have a story idea and a conflict, you can build the plot around it. A plot usually unfolds from the event that triggers the conflict to the event that resolves it. Therefore, you will need to arrange the details of your plot so that they naturally unfold as the story progresses. The following chart shows some steps for revealing a plot, along with examples.

Strategies for Developing a Plot

1. Introduce the event or circumstance that triggers the action. Include descriptive details about the triggering event, making the source of the conflict clear.

FROM WITHIN A CHARACTER	• the desire to change one's circumstances
FROM THE OUTSIDE WORLD	• the receipt of a letter or phone call
	• an accident

2. Develop details describing the nature of the conflict.

CONFLICT WITH SELF	• one's conscience
CONFLICT WITH OTHERS	• friends or family members
	• enemies or strangers
CONFLICT WITH NATURE	• severe weather conditions
	• disease or disability

3. Develop details about the obstacles the characters will struggle against or overcome to resolve the central conflict.

WITHIN A CHARACTER	• fears or other emotions
IN THE OUTSIDE WORLD	• other characters
	• trials of nature

4. Develop details about how the main character might overcome the obstacles.

BY THE CHARACTER	• strength of character
	• perseverance
THROUGH OUTSIDE EVENTS	• luck or chance
	• new knowledge or understanding

5. Develop details about how the conflict will be resolved and how the story will end.

OBSTACLES OVERCOME	• new wisdom
	• success or satisfaction
OBSTACLES NOT OVERCOME	• acceptance of shortcomings
	• decision to try again

WRITING ACTIVITY *Developing Plots for Stories*

Using the chart on the previous page, briefly describe a possible plot based on each of the following triggering events.

1. A boy loses his wallet, which contains money he has saved to buy his mother a birthday present.
2. After some students have climbed a mountain, they realize that it will be dark before they can get down.
3. A girl discovers that her friend has been untruthful.
4. A man starts getting strange messages on the computer he is working on.
5. Two friends discuss dropping out of school.

WRITING ACTIVITY  *Writing on Your Own*

WRITING
ABOUT THE
THEME

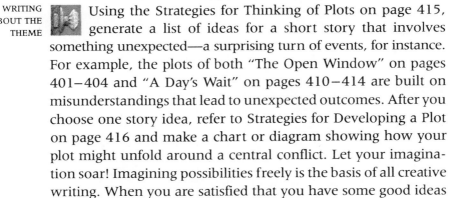 Using the Strategies for Thinking of Plots on page 415, generate a list of ideas for a short story that involves something unexpected—a surprising turn of events, for instance. For example, the plots of both "The Open Window" on pages 401–404 and "A Day's Wait" on pages 410–414 are built on misunderstandings that lead to unexpected outcomes. After you choose one story idea, refer to Strategies for Developing a Plot on page 416 and make a chart or diagram showing how your plot might unfold around a central conflict. Let your imagination soar! Imagining possibilities freely is the basis of all creative writing. When you are satisfied that you have some good ideas for a plot, save your notes in your writing folder.

Sketching Characters

Readers usually enjoy and remember stories that have interesting, believable characters. As you plan your story, therefore, you should visualize the characters who will appear in it. You could, for example, write a brief sketch of each one by brainstorming for the following kinds of details: the character's name, age, physical appearance, voice, mannerisms, background, and personality traits.

The more completely you visualize your characters, the more independent they can become in your imagination. Many fiction writers report that the characters themselves seem to come alive during writing, directing the plot and dictating the dialogue. In a sense, therefore, visualizing your characters gives them life. Notice how the following writer uses details that allow you to visualize the character.

Model: *Characterization*

In the smallest of these huts lived old Berl, a man in his eighties . . . Old Berl was one of the Jews who had been driven from their villages in Russia and had settled in Poland. In Lentshin, they mocked the mistakes he made while praying aloud. He spoke with a sharp "r." He was short, broad-shouldered, and had a small white beard, and summer and winter he wore a sheepskin hat, a padded cotton jacket, and stout boots. He walked slowly, shuffling his feet. He had a half acre of field, a cow, a goat, and chickens.

ISAAC BASHEVIS SINGER
"The Son from America"

WRITING ACTIVITY   **4**   *Sketching Characters*

Imagine characters for each of following scenes from short stories. Then, for three of the scenes, write brief sketches of the characters you invented.

1. two men fishing from the end of a pier
2. a child bullying another child
3. two students doing their homework together
4. a couple dancing
5. two women visiting a gift shop

WRITING ACTIVITY   **5**   *Writing on Your Own*

WRITING
ABOUT THE
THEME

Review your prewriting notes from Writing Activity 3 for your short story on the unexpected. After visualizing the characters that will appear in your story, write a brief character sketch of each one. Save your sketches in your writing folder for use in drafting.

418

Imaging

To create characters and events, fiction writers often use *imaging*—visualizing and feeling what it would be like to be a character and to experience an imaginary event. If you take time for imaging as you plan, later you will more easily find the right words to express yourself when you draft your story. The following passages from "The Open Window" on pages 401–404 are evidence of the author's imaging.

FOCUS FOR IMAGING: how a character like Framton Nuttel might feel about visiting strangers and how he might act

Results of Imaging	Written Expression
anxious to be polite	"Framton Nuttel endeavored to say the correct something that should duly flatter the niece of the moment without unduly discounting the aunt that was to come."
mildly curious	"He was wondering whether Mrs. Sappleton was in the married or widowed state."
boring	"[He] labored under the tolerably widespread delusion that total strangers and chance acquaintances are hungry for the least detail of one's ailments and infirmities, their cause and cure."

Thinking Practice   For ten minutes use imaging to visualize the encounter Framton might have had with Mr. Sappleton if he had not fled. With your teacher's permission, describe to your classmates what you saw during your imaging.

Creating a Setting

When you have your plot and characters in mind, you can more fully visualize the main setting of your story, because the setting may mirror the feelings of the main character. By relating the setting to the central conflict and to the characters' feelings, you can create the mood you want for your story. In a sketch of your setting, you might note details you could use to describe the indoor or outdoor location where the action of the story takes place. For example, you might visualize objects, dimensions, terrain, the time of day, the weather, or the season of the year. Notice how the following description of a setting creates a suspenseful mood. *(For more information about descriptive writing, see pages 182–192.)*

Model: *Details of a Setting*

At the most remote end of the crypt there appeared another . . . Its walls had been lined with human remains, piled to the vault overhead, in the fashion of the great catacombs of Paris . . . From the fourth side the bones had been thrown down . . . forming at one point a mound of some size. Within the wall thus exposed by the displacing of the bones, we perceived a still interior crypt or recess, in depth about four feet, in width three, in height six or seven.   EDGAR ALLAN POE, "The Cask of Amontillado"

WRITING ACTIVITY 6 *Sketching Settings*

Choose three of the following imaginary situations. Then write a brief sketch of an appropriate setting for each one.

1. An exasperated Inspector Jyllka finally finds the murder weapon in a woodchuck hole.
2. While waiting, fifteen-year-old Cara suddenly feels insignificant and small.
3. Humming with satisfaction, old Mrs. Santos arranges flowers for the church.
4. Hunched tensely in concentration, a small boy enters the world of his action figures.
5. Drained of energy, Michael sinks to the ground.

WRITING ACTIVITY *Writing on Your Own*

WRITING
ABOUT THE
THEME

Determine the mood you want to convey in your short story about the unexpected and imagine an appropriate setting in detail. After writing a sketch of the setting in the form of a summary or list of details, save it in your writing folder.

Choosing a Point of View

As you have learned on page 409, you can choose among three different points of view for telling your stories: first person, third person objective, and third person omniscient. If you are writing a story with a narrator who is a participant, the first person point of view is probably the most natural. If the narrator is writing about other characters and is not a participant in the story, use third person objective or omniscient. Use the same point of view throughout your story.

WRITING ACTIVITY ⬧ 8 *Writing from Different Points of View*

The following portion of a narrative is written from a first person point of view. Rewrite it from either the third person objective or the third person omniscient point of view.

> We might have drowned if it hadn't been for Rhonda. She rooted us out of bed just in time to get from our bunk beds to the big old willow. How Rhonda knew there was a wall of water rolling down the valley, I'll never know. Craig, who always said that even pet pigs belong in a pen, had put Rhonda out after I was asleep. I don't know what Craig has against pigs, but for once I was glad he'd acted behind my back. It was Rhonda's frantic efforts to get back in that saved us.

WRITING ACTIVITY **9** *Writing on Your Own*

WRITING
ABOUT THE
THEME

Review your prewriting notes for your story on the unexpected that you have been developing. Imagine how your story would read if it were told from the point of view of your main character and from that of each of the other characters. Next, imagine how your story would sound if it were told from the first person, the third person objective and the third person omniscient point of view. Finally, choose the best point of view for your story, make a note of your decision, and save it in your writing folder.

Ordering Events

When you have developed the central conflict, plot, characters, and setting, and have chosen the narrator's point of view, you are almost ready to begin drafting. First, however, you should visualize all the events you want to include in your story and arrange them in chronological order. You may later decide to deviate from this order. For instance, you could start your story at the end and then go back to the beginning, or you could start in the middle and remember back to the beginning in a *flashback* before ending your story. "The Open Window" is an example of a story that begins in the middle, gives background information in a flashback, and then proceeds chronologically to the end. Whatever order you decide to use when you draft, you will find it helpful to have a chronological list of all the events you plan to include.

WRITING ACTIVITY **10**  *Writing on Your Own*

WRITING
ABOUT THE
THEME

After you list all the events you plan to include in your story on the unexpected, arrange them in chronological order. As you study your list, think of other possible ways to order the events that would make sense to readers and would capture their interest. Then save your organized list of events and your ideas for other possible ways to order them in your writing folder to use when drafting your story.

Drafting

As you write your story, keep in mind your reasons for writing and your audience. While the purpose of all creative writing is to create, you may have particular writing goals. For example, you may want your readers to laugh or cry, or you may want them to identify in a positive way with your main character. To achieve these purposes, you have available a variety of types of writing. For instance, you can use *narrative writing* to advance the plot. *(See pages 173–181.)* You can use *descriptive writing* to create the settings and characters' appearances. *(See pages 182–192.)* *Expository writing* allows you to explain background information about the plot or characters. *(See pages 128–157.)* In addition to these basic types of writing, you can use the following strategies, which are specific to fiction writing.

Strategies for Drafting a Short Story

1. Use vivid language and interesting details to introduce the characters and the central conflict.
2. Use sensory details to create a mood.
3. Use background details to set the time and place of the story and to capture your readers' interest.
4. Aim for originality in your writing by avoiding stereotypes and by using vivid words to bring the story to life.
5. Start the plot early in the story by introducing the triggering event.
6. Reveal the characters and unfold the plot through a combination of description; narration, or action; and dialogue.
7. Maintain a clear and consistent point of view.
8. Include only those events that have a direct bearing on the plot and the central conflict. Connect the events in your story by showing how each event in the plot relates naturally and logically to the central conflict.
9. Use chronological order and transitions to show the passing of time and to build up tension.
10. End your story in a way that makes the outcome clear and that leaves a strong emotional impression on your readers.

Using Dialogue

In many cases you can use dialogue to develop your characters and to advance your plot. The following examples from "The Open Window" show how the author used dialogue for a variety of purposes.

Model: *Using Dialogue*

TO GIVE BACKGROUND INFORMATION	"I know how it will be," his sister had said . . . "[You] will bury yourself down there and not speak to a living soul . . . I shall just give you letters of introduction to all the people I know there . . ."
TO ADVANCE THE PLOT	"Do you know many of the people round here?" asked the niece . . . "Hardly a soul," said Framton . . . "Then you know practically nothing about my aunt?" . . . "Only her name and address," admitted the caller . . . "Her great tragedy happened just three years ago," said the child; "that would be since your sister's time." "Her tragedy?" asked Framton . . .
TO REVEAL CHARACTERS' FEELINGS	"Their bodies were never recovered. That was the dreadful part of it . . . Do you know, sometimes on still, quiet evenings like this, I almost get a creepy feeling that they will all walk in through that window—"
TO EXPRESS THE CLIMAX	"Here they are at last!" she cried. "Just in time for tea . . ."
TO TELL THE OUTCOME	"A most extraordinary man, a Mr. Nuttell," said Mrs. Sappleton; "could only talk about his illnesses, and dashed off without a word of goodbye . . . One would think he had seen a ghost."

WRITING ACTIVITY *Writing Dialogue*

Imagine each of the following situations. Then select one of the situations or another of your choice and write a dialogue about

12 lines long between the characters. You may want to review the correct form for writing dialogue on pages 844–853.

1. A stranger asks for directions to the police station.
2. A hurried shopper seeks help from a sales clerk.
3. A student has a conference with his or her advisor.
4. Two teenagers discuss someone else's problem.
5. Two friends argue over what movie to see.

WRITING ACTIVITY  *Writing on Your Own*

WRITING
ABOUT THE
THEME

After you review all your prewriting notes, write the first draft of the short story you have been developing. Use the Strategies for Drafting a Short Story on page 423, but as you write, let your imagination roam freely. Add fresh details and new ideas for unexpected turns of plot as you think of them. If you get stuck, skip that part and continue writing on another part that you have visualized more fully. Although you should try to get all the way to the end of your story, you may go back and work on any part of it at any time. With your teacher's permission, use peer conferencing to test your ideas or to get help with trouble spots. However, keep writing until you have a workable first draft.

425

Revising

Writing Process

Many fiction writers report that they often keep only the few best parts of a first draft and drop all the rest. When you revise, therefore, be ready to give up ideas or details that weaken your short story or that rob it of life. Look especially for ways of strengthening your plot, enhancing your descriptions, and sharpening your characterizations.

Revising Strategies for Short Stories

STRENGTHENING THE PLOT
- Add background details and transitions to ensure adequate development and coherence.
- Delete any plot details that do not relate to the central conflict and its resolution.
- Check for clarity to ensure that readers will understand the story's meaning, point, or theme.

ENHANCING DESCRIPTIONS
- Add or substitute sensory details to enliven descriptions of characters, settings, and actions.
- Use imaging to visualize your descriptions again so you can improve them.
- Enrich your descriptions by using figurative language.

SHARPENING CHARACTERIZATIONS
- Add or eliminate details to sharpen the characterization of your main character.
- Look for ways to reveal characters and their motivations through dialogue and action.
- Rewrite dialogue until it sounds as natural as real-life conversations.

Using a Revision Checklist

After you have applied the revising strategies above, review the structure and content of your story, using the following revision checklist.

Revision Checklist

1. Does the beginning of your story describe the setting, capture the readers' attention, introduce characters, and include the triggering event? *(See pages 408, 410, and 416 – 420.)*
2. Does the middle develop the plot by making the central conflict clear and by including events that are directly related to that conflict? *(See pages 407, 410, and 415 – 416.)*
3. Are events in the plot arranged in chronological order or in an order that makes the chronology of events clear? *(See page 422.)*
4. Does the story build until the action reaches a climax? *(See pages 407, 413, and 415 – 416.)*
5. Did you use dialogue and description to bring your characters to life? *(See pages 411 – 412 and 424.)*
6. Does the ending show how the conflict was resolved and bring the story to a close? *(See pages 407 and 414 – 416.)*
7. Did you choose an appropriate point of view and stick to it throughout the story? *(See pages 409, 410, and 421.)*
8. Does the story have a theme or express your reasons for writing it? Does it accomplish your specific purpose for creative writing? *(See page 410.)*

WRITING ACTIVITY *Sharpening Characterization*

Add, eliminate, and rearrange details in the following passage to sharpen the characterization and to enhance the description. Provide transitions as you write.

> She sat in the tree with her journal. She had black hair and was not unpretty. She wore a blouse and jeans. She was barefoot. From her serious expression, you could see she had something important to write about. She liked hiking and playing the flute.

WRITING ACTIVITY *Writing on Your Own*

WRITING
ABOUT THE
THEME

 Revise your story, using the Revising Strategies for Short Stories on page 426 and the Revision Checklist above. Then save it for editing.

Editing and Publishing

Grammar in the Writing Process

In fiction, writers find many uses for dialogue— written conversations between two or more characters. For example, dialogue can advance the plot, reveal character traits, and add realism to a story. To write dialogue clearly, you will need to understand how to choose the right pronouns and how to use quotation marks correctly.

Cases of Pronouns A *pronoun* is a word that takes the place of a noun. Knowing which pronoun to use in a line of dialogue involves understanding the different cases of pronouns. *Nominative case* pronouns, used as subjects and predicate nominatives, are *I, you, he, she, it, we,* and *they. Objective case* pronouns, used as objects, are *me, you, him, her, it, us,* and *them. Possessive case* pronouns, used to show ownership or possession, are *my, mine, your, yours, his, her, hers, its, our, ours, their,* and *theirs. (For more information about pronouns and practice in using them correctly, see pages 566–571 and 728–751.)*

NOMINATIVE CASE	**"I will write letters of introduction,"** she had said.
OBJECTIVE CASE	The girl told **him** to sit down.
POSSESSIVE CASE	**Her** aunt would be down any minute.

Quotation Marks with Dialogue When writing dialogue, use quotation marks to enclose a person's exact words. Put the opening quotation marks before the first word a person says and the closing quotation marks after the last word.

"Do you know many people around here?" she asked.
Framton answered, "Hardly a soul."

Capitalization and Indentation with Dialogue Begin each sentence of a direct quotation with a capital letter. Also begin a new paragraph each time the speaker changes, using indentation to show that the speaker has changed.

> **S**he said, "**H**er great tragedy happened three years ago. **T**hat was before your sister's time."
> "**H**er tragedy?" asked Framton.

Commas and End Marks with Dialogue   Use a comma to separate a direct quotation from the speaker tag—the words that identify the speaker—for example, *she said* or *replied Framton*. If the speaker tag comes at the end of the sentence, place the comma inside the closing quotation marks. If the quotation ends the sentence, place the end marks inside the closing quotation marks. *(For more information about dialogue and practice in writing direct quotations correctly, see pages 844–855.)*

> "I hope Vera has been amusing you," Mrs. Sappleton said to Mr. Framton.
> He said**,** "She has been very interesting."

Editing Checklist

1. Have you used the correct case of each pronoun? *(See pages 729–743.)*

2. Have you correctly punctuated, capitalized, and indented all dialogue? *(See pages 844–853.)*

WRITING ACTIVITY ⬢**15** *Writing on Your Own*

WRITING
ABOUT THE
THEME

Editing   Use the checklist above and the one on page 37 to edit your story. When you are so pleased with your story that you are eager to read it to someone else, write a final copy.

Publishing After writing a title page and possibly illustrating your story, publish it by giving it to your teacher and classmates to read. Consider making your story available to a wider audience through your school's newspaper or literary journal.

A Writer Writes

A Short Story

PURPOSE: To entertain

AUDIENCE: Your classmates

Prewriting   Use your imagination to create a "why" story that explains the origin of a phenomenon of nature, such as thunder and lightning or the changing of the seasons. A "why" story explains how and why such a phenomenon came into being—and usually does so in an unexpected and imaginative way.

Throughout history people have made up "why" stories. The Greeks and Romans created stories about gods to explain every important process of nature, such as the rising and setting of the sun. The Indians of the southeastern United States told a "why" story to explain the origins of Spanish moss. According to the story, a young Indian mother and her two children were caught by surprise in a hurricane that sent floodwaters rising. To escape drowning, the mother climbed the nearest tree, carrying her babies. After the storm, the air turned sharply colder and the mother feared that she and her children would die from the cold. Despite the cold, however, they slept. When they awoke, they were wrapped in a furry gray blanket, which had kept them warm and saved their lives. According to the story, a loving spirit of nature had provided this blanket—Spanish moss— which has hung on trees throughout the South ever since.

Plan your "why" story by looking through your journal and brainstorming for any wonders of nature that you find fascinating. After choosing one, plan the plot of your story, including a central conflict, a triggering event, a climax, and a resolution. After planning the plot, sketch your characters, establish your setting, and decide on the point of view.

Drafting   Using your prewriting work, draft a version of your "why" story. Follow a chronological order to unfold the plot from its triggering event to its resolution. Unlike the simple summary of the story about Spanish moss, take the time during drafting to fully develop your story. Add details that bring the characters and setting to life. Use dialogue, description, and narration.

Revising   Read your story aloud, listening particularly for the natural sound of the dialogue. Then use the Revision checklists on pages 32, 426, and 427 to revise your draft.

Editing and Publishing   Use the Editing Checklist on page 37 to go over your final draft, looking for mistakes. After preparing a neat final copy, add it to a classroom anthology of "why" stories. Consider illustrating your story and putting a copy on file in the library.

Independent Writing

"Mostly, we authors must repeat ourselves," wrote F. Scott Fitzgerald. "We have two or three great moving experiences in our lives—experiences so great and moving that it doesn't seem at the time that anyone else has been caught up and pounded and dazzled and astonished and beaten and broken and rescued and illuminated and rewarded and humbled in just that way ever before." Using fictional characters, write a short story about one of the "great moving experiences" of your life.

Creative Writing

Write a short story on any of the following subjects or one of your own. Use the checklist on page 433 as a guide.

1. true meaning of friendship	**6.** the supernatural
2. the championship game	**7.** a daring escape
3. a lie	**8.** true definition of success
4. a family crisis	**9.** poverty and wealth
5. trust	**10.** a crime

WRITING
ABOUT THE
THEME

Writing about Literature

Empathy is the act of sharing the feelings or even some physical sensations of a character in a work of literature. Write a paragraph that states which character in "The Open Window" you feel empathy with and explain why.

Writing in Other Subject Areas

Science Write a science-fiction story based on factual information that you have learned in science. Begin by reviewing your science notes or by skimming a text to list scientific phenomena on which a central conflict could be based. For example, you might write a story about repairing Earth's ozone layer or discovering a strange new tube worm. Develop characters for your story and research your subject to get the technical information you will need to make your story believable. Share your finished story with your science teacher.

11 Checklist

Creative Writing

Prewriting

✔ Draw on your own experiences or imagination to think of a conflict. *(See pages 415–416.)*

✔ Write a brief character sketch for each person in your story. *(See pages 417–419.)*

✔ Create a setting appropriate to the mood of your story. *(See page 420.)*

✔ Choose an appropriate point of view. *(See page 421.)*

✔ List in chronological order the plot events. *(See page 422.)*

Drafting

✔ At the beginning of your story, introduce the characters, the setting, and the triggering event. *(See page 423.)*

✔ In the middle of your story, build on the conflict at the heart of your plot, bringing the action to a climax. Use dialogue and description to bring the events and characters to life. *(See pages 423–424.)*

✔ Write the ending. Tell how the conflict is resolved and bring the story to a close. *(See page 423.)*

Revising

✔ Check your story carefully for any and all ways you can strengthen your plot, enhance your descriptions, and sharpen your characterizations. *(See page 426.)*

✔ Use the Revision Checklist on page 427 to check all the elements in your story.

Editing and Publishing

✔ Use the Editing Checklist on page 37 to polish your final draft. Then share your work with an interested reader.

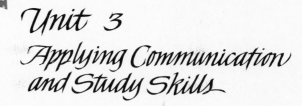

Unit 3
Applying Communication and Study Skills

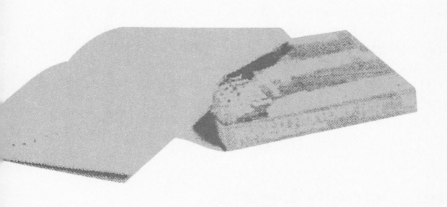

12 Letters and Applications

In some kinds of writing, you need to think carefully about your writing purpose. In other kinds, however, the purpose is clear from the start. Writing letters and filling out applications carry within them a clear-cut practical purpose.

When you write a letter, for example, you usually have a specific purpose in mind. You know why you are writing and who will be reading your letter. Whether you are inviting a friend to a party, ordering something from a catalog, or registering a complaint to a company, you can shape your letter to suit your purpose and the receiver. In this chapter you will learn the correct form for friendly letters and business letters written for a variety of purposes. This chapter will also give you practice in filling out applications for employment—another very practical form of writing to help you accomplish specific purposes.

Writing Friendly Letters

Some friendly letters are written as part of a regular correspondence between friends and relatives to share news and keep in touch. Other friendly letters serve such special purposes as making, accepting or declining invitations, expressing congratulations or sorrow, or thanking someone for a thoughtful gift or act.

Whatever their purpose, friendly letters have five main parts: a heading, a salutation, a body, a closing, and a signature. These five parts are shown in the following model. Each part of a friendly letter is explained in the chart shown on the next page.

Correct Form for a Friendly Letter

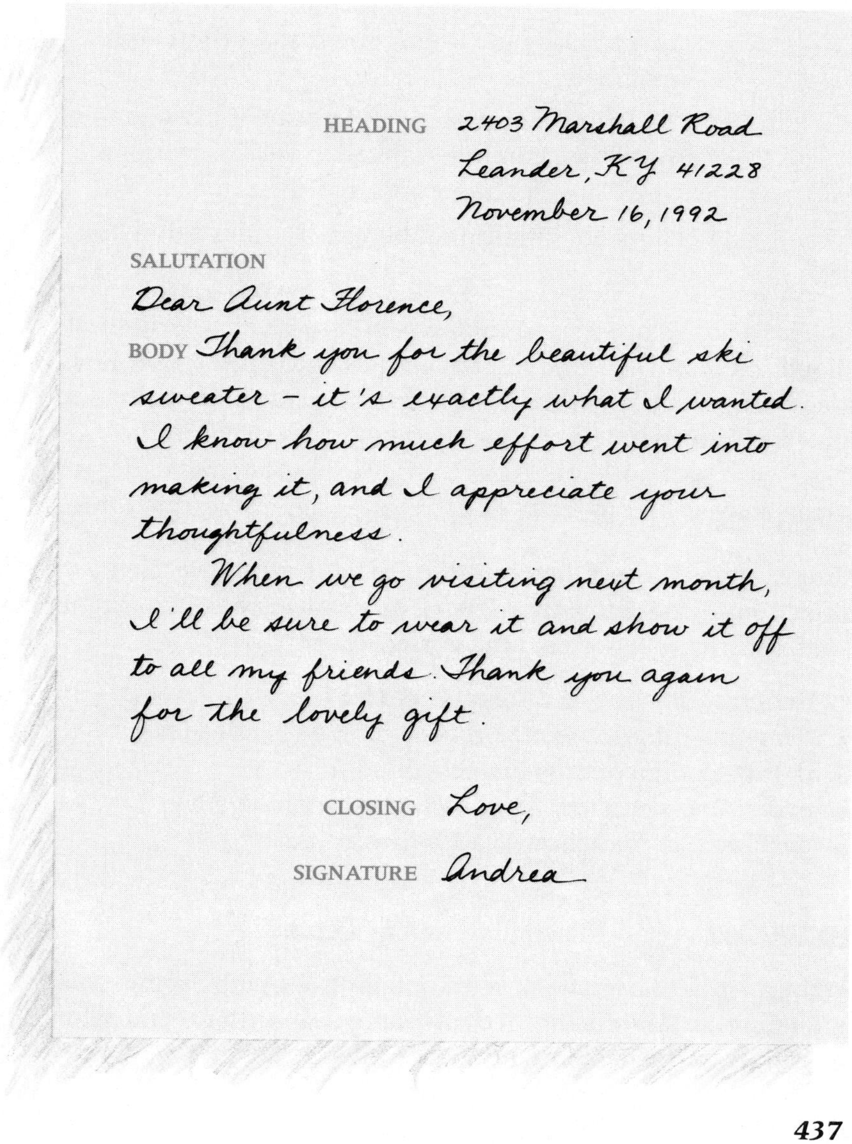

HEADING   2403 Marshall Road
Leander, KY 41228
November 16, 1992

SALUTATION

Dear Aunt Florence,

BODY   Thank you for the beautiful ski sweater — it's exactly what I wanted. I know how much effort went into making it, and I appreciate your thoughtfulness.

    When we go visiting next month, I'll be sure to wear it and show it off to all my friends. Thank you again for the lovely gift.

CLOSING   Love,

SIGNATURE   Andrea

HEADING The heading includes your full address with the ZIP code. Write out the name of your state or abbreviate it. Always include the date after your address.

SALUTATION The salutation is your friendly greeting and is followed by a comma. Capitalize the first word and any proper nouns.

BODY In the body of the letter, include your conversational message. Indent the first word in each paragraph.

CLOSING End your letter with a brief personal closing, followed by a comma. Capitalize the first word of the closing.

SIGNATURE Your signature should be handwritten below the closing.

Note: The envelope for a friendly letter may be handwritten. It should contain the same information as that on the envelope for a business letter. *(See pages 441–442.)* Be sure both addresses are clear and complete.

EXERCISE **1** *Writing a Friendly Letter*

Choose one of the following purposes for writing a friendly letter. Write the letter to a friend or relative. Make sure that your completed letter uses the correct form.

1. inviting someone to a surprise party
2. congratulating someone on becoming a cheerleader
3. thanking someone for a weekend visit
4. expressing sympathy for someone who broke a leg
5. declining an invitation to a Halloween party

EXERCISE **2** *Writing a Friendly Letter*

Write a letter to a friend or relative telling about the things that are going on in your life. To encourage an answer, end with questions to the person who will receive the letter.

Writing Business Letters

Most of the business letters you write will call for some action on the part of the receiver. You may write to request information, to order merchandise, or to ask for a refund or exchange on faulty merchandise. To make sure busy companies understand your point, keep your letters simple and direct.

You may wish to write a draft of your main message to make sure you have included all necessary information. Then you can prepare a neat final version that follows the correct form for business letters.

Business Letter Form

Because a business letter is more formal than a friendly letter, it requires a more precise form. One of the most common forms is called *modified block form*. The examples in this chapter follow this form.

When writing a business letter, use white stationery, preferably 8 1/2 by 11 inches in size. Whenever possible, type the letter, leaving margins at least one inch wide.

HEADING   The heading of a business letter is the same as the heading of a friendly letter. Include your full address, and on the line below, the date.

INSIDE ADDRESS   A business letter has a second address, called the *inside address*. Start the inside address two to four lines below the heading. Write the name of the person who will receive the letter, if you know it. Use *Mr., Ms., Mrs., Dr.,* or other appropriate title before the name. If the person has a title, such as *Personnel Director* or *Manager*, write it on the next line. Write the receiver's address, using the same method of identifying the state that you used in the heading.

SALUTATION Start the salutation, or greeting, two lines below the inside address. Use "Dear Sir or Madam" if you do not know the name. Otherwise, use the person's last name preceded by *Mr., Ms., Mrs., Dr.,* or other title. You should follow the salutation with a colon.

BODY Two lines below the salutation, begin the body or main message of the letter. Single-space each paragraph, skip a line between paragraphs, and indent each new paragraph.

CLOSING In a business letter, use a formal closing, such as *Sincerely, Sincerely yours, Very truly yours,* or *Yours truly.* Start the closing two or three lines below the body. Line up the closing with the left-hand edge of the heading. Capitalize only the first letter and place a comma after the closing, as you did in the friendly letter.

SIGNATURE In the signature of a business letter, your name appears twice. First type (or print if your letter is handwritten) your name four or five lines below the closing. Then sign your name in the space between the closing and your typed name. Do not refer to yourself as *Mr., Ms.,* or the like in the signature.

Make a copy of the business letter for yourself in case you do not receive a reply in a reasonable amount of time and need to follow up by writing a second letter. You can make copies with carbon paper or on the copying machines that are available in most libraries.

When you are writing a business letter, always make sure it is clearly written, has a neat appearance, and follows the correct form. A sample business letter, with each part labeled, appears on the next page.

Correct Form for a Business Letter

HEADING   1411 Vista Drive
Oakland, CA 94611
July 16, 1992

INSIDE
ADDRESS
Customer Service Department
Silvertone Tapes, Inc.
352 Rosemont Avenue
Olympia, WA 98502

SALUTATION
Dear Sir or Madam:

BODY   Recently I bought four Silvertone blank tapes.
Three of them work fine. The fourth one, however,
is defective. When I played back a recording I had
made on it, the sound was garbled, and I could not
make out the voices.

    I have enclosed the defective tape, which I
would like you to replace. I would appreciate it
if you would send a new tape as soon as possible.

CLOSING   Yours truly,

SIGNATURE   *Robert Tessler*

Robert Tessler

The Envelope

If you type the letter, also type the envelope. Place your name and address in the upper left-hand corner. The receiver's address is centered on the envelope. Use the postal abbreviations for the state and include the ZIP code.

Correct Form for Business Envelopes

Robert Tessler
1411 Vista Drive   YOUR NAME
Oakland, CA 94611   AND ADDRESS

RECEIVER'S   Customer Service Department
ADDRESS   Silvertone Tapes, Inc.
             352 Rosemont Avenue
             Olympia, WA 98502

Using Commas in Dates and Addresses   When you write the date in the heading of a letter, use a comma to separate the month and day from the year.

March 21, 1991

Also use commas to separate parts of addresses (the city from the state, for example). Note these exceptions, however.

1. Do not use a comma at the end of a line, but do separate parts of an address on the same line.

EXAMPLE   455 Wilmington Drive, Apartment 2-C

2. Do not use a comma between the state and ZIP code.

EXAMPLE   Wethersfield, CT 06109

Write this heading and inside address correctly.

HEADING   26 Longmeadow Avenue Rockford IL
          61101 June 13 1992

INSIDE ADDRESS   Order Department Wearever Shoe Company 4000 Lake Avenue Ames IA 51101

Letters of Request

When writing a letter of request, be as specific as possible about the information you want and state your request politely. Notice how the business form of the letter is used to request information.

Letter of Request

3412 Falcon Road
Mobile, Alabama 36619
May 29, 1992

Dr. Alan Morley
Membership Director
National Science Club
8880 Wilton Drive
Cooperstown, New York 13326

Dear Dr. Morley:

I learned about the National Science Club in a magazine and am eager to know more about it. Please send me information on activities the club sponsors, rules for membership, and annual dues. If a membership application is required, please send me the necessary form.

I would also be interested in learning whether there is a local chapter somewhere in the Mobile area. Thank you for your assistance.

Sincerely,

Carla Rodriquez

Carla Rodriquez

Order Letters

A business letter to order merchandise should give complete information, including the description, size, order number, price, and quantity of the items. If you enclose payment for your order, the letter should state the amount enclosed.

Order Letter

142 Harper Drive
Buffalo Gap, TX 79508
November 11, 1992

Capital Music Store
6554 Northwest Highway
Austin, TX 78756

Dear Sir or Madam:

Please send me the following items from your 1992 catalog.

1 Starlite music notebook, size 8 1/2" x 11", Order #267-C	$ 1.35
1 music stand, Olympia model, Order #383-F	$24.95
Shipping and handling	$ 3.70
TOTAL	$30.00

I have enclosed a money order for $30.00 to cover the cost of the merchandise and shipping and handling.

Sincerely yours,

Raymond Stevenson

Raymond Stevenson

Letters of Complaint

If you have a complaint about a product, express yourself courteously in a letter of complaint to the company. The following letter uses a polite but firm tone, which is appropriate for a letter of complaint.

Letter of Complaint

```
                              313 Lavender Way
                              Millville, PA 17846
                              September 7, 1992

Subscription Department
Sky and Stars Magazine
36 Parkway Drive
Evanston, IL 60201


Dear Sir or Madam:

     On August 4, I mailed an order form and a
check for $12.50 to cover the cost of receiving
your magazine for one year.  Two weeks later I
received a card indicating that my first issue
would arrive by September 1.  So far I have not
received a magazine.

     Please check into this problem and notify me
as soon as possible about your findings.

     Thank you for your cooperation.

                         Very truly yours,

                         Michael Chin

                         Michael Chin
```

EXERCISE *Writing a Letter of Request*

Use the following information to write a letter of request. Be sure that you clearly state the information being requested.

INSIDE ADDRESS   Arna Silverstein, 364 Willow Street, Hainesburg, New Jersey 07832, January 10, 1992.

HEADING   Ms. Sandra Hanson, Quality Computer, Inc. 1167 Sequoia Boulevard, Belmont, California 94002

REQUEST   The writer, Arna Silverstein, is considering buying a home computer and has heard that the company's model #453-A has all the features that she needs. She is writing to request a brochure and information about the price of the computer.

EXERCISE *Writing an Order Letter*

Use the following information to write an order letter. Be sure the ordering information is clearly shown, as in the model on page 444.

ADDRESS   Order Department, The Cycle City, 4212 Emerson Street, Emporia, Kansas 66801

ORDER   2 rolls of Ace handlebar tape, ½ inch, Order #33, $1.00 each; 4 Nite-Glow reflectors, Order #48, $2.49 each; $1.00 for shipping and handling

EXERCISE *Revising a Letter of Complaint*

Rewrite the body of the following letter of complaint so that the tone is polite but firm.

I can't understand how anyone can be so careless! I ordered a kit for building a model of a bird feeder (kit #34-SS) from your fall catalog, and you sent me a kit that does not include instructions. How do you expect a person to know how to put it together? I demand my money back or a set of instructions.

Completing a Job Application

When you apply for a job, you may be asked to fill out an application form. Application forms vary, but most of them ask for similar kinds of information. You may wish to prepare your information ahead of time so that you will be ready to complete the form when you apply for a job. The following is a list of items you will most likely need to know to complete a job-application form.

- the current date
- your complete name, address, and telephone number including the area code
- your date and place of birth
- your Social Security number
- names and addresses of schools you have attended, dates attended, and year of graduation
- any special courses or advanced degrees
- names and addresses of employers for whom you have worked and the dates you were employed
- any part-time, summer, and volunteer jobs
- names and addresses of references (Obtain permission beforehand from each person you intend to list as a reference.)

When you fill out a job application, use the following general guidelines.

Completing a Job Application

1. Print all the information requested neatly and accurately. Try, if possible, to type the information on the form.
2. Be sure your answers are accurate and complete.
3. Do not leave blanks. If a section does not apply to you, write *N/A* ("not applicable").
4. List schools attended and work experience in order, giving the most recent first.
5. If you mail the application form, include a brief cover letter stating the job you are applying for. The cover letter should follow the Correct Form for a Business Letter on page 441.

Job Application

BARTOW'S DEPARTMENT STORE
EMPLOYMENT APPLICATION

Date _September 1, 1992_

Name _Paula_ _Jane_ _Samuels_
      FIRST   MIDDLE   LAST

Address _414 Broad Street, Garfield, Pennsylvania 19015_
      STREET   CITY   STATE   ZIP CODE

Phone _(215) 874-3198_   Social Security Number _181-98-0945_

Have you ever been employed here before? ___ Yes _✓_ No   If so, when? _N/A_

Date of Birth _November 15, 1979_   Place of Birth _Evanston, Illinois_
    MONTH DAY YEAR   CITY   STATE

Work Permit Number (if under 18) _8754_

Married? ____ Yes _✓_ No Number of Children _N/A_

EDUCATION

College or University _N/A_   From _N/A_   to _N/A_

Vocational Training _N/A_   From _N/A_   to _N/A_

Senior High School _N/A_   From _N/A_   to _N/A_

Junior High School _Wilson Junior High_   From _1991_   to _present_

Elementary School _Bradford School_   From _1985_   to _1991_

PREVIOUS WORK EXPERIENCE

Year	Employer	Address	Position
1991 – present	Bart's Drug Store	211 Main Street, Garfield	Stock clerk
1990 – 1991	PA Red Cross	22 Third Avenue, Garfield	Volunteer aid
1989 – 1990	Reese Family	45 Durand Road, Garfield	Baby-sitter

REFERENCES

1. _Carl Smith, Wilson Junior High, 14 Main Street, Garfield, Principal_

2. _Jane Bart, Bart's Drug Store, 211 Main Street, Garfield, Manager_

3. _Michael Reese, 45 Durand Road, Garfield, Accountant_

Applicant's Signature _Paula Jane Samuels_

12 Review

A **Letters about a Lost Wallet** Imagine that you have lost your wallet. Write three letters about the experience, as described below. Make up the names and addresses but be sure to use the correct form for each letter.

1. Write one letter requesting information about your lost wallet. Direct the letter to the lost-and-found director at the store where you last had your wallet.

2. Write a thank-you note expressing your appreciation to the stranger who found your wallet.

3. Write a friendly letter to a cousin, in which you tell the harrowing story of losing your wallet.

B **Starting a Regular Correspondence** Start a correspondence with a friend or relative who lives far away. Maybe you have an aging grandmother or grandfather who would love to hear from you. Maybe you have a distant cousin or friend who shares the same interests as you. Write and mail a friendly letter to the person of your choice and then keep up the correspondence!

C **Writing to a Business of the Future** Imagine you are living in the twenty-third century. Write a business letter to a company or some other organization to request information, order merchandise, or make a complaint. Use your imagination to create the company name and address and the kind of information or merchandise that might be available in the future. Use the correct form for a business letter.

D **Writing a Letter of Complaint** Imagine that you have just eaten dinner at a restaurant that was highly recommended by the newspaper. To your surprise, however, everything seemed to go wrong. The food was cold, the service was surly, and the surroundings seemed unclean. Write a letter of complaint to this imaginary restaurant.

13 Speaking and Listening

Think about a time you listened to a good speaker communicate ideas to an audience. Perhaps you listened to a tape of Dr. Martin Luther King's powerful "I Have a Dream" speech given before 200,000 people in 1963. Perhaps a local politician delivered an eloquent speech about the importance of an environmental project such as recycling.

True communication occurs when a speaker presents his or her ideas in a clear, organized, and forceful way and the listeners are able to comprehend and respond to the speaker's message. In this chapter you will learn effective strategies for speaking and listening to help you become a better communicator.

Preparing a Speech

Preparing and giving speeches for a variety of purposes is similar to preparing and writing a report, a persuasive essay, or a short story. The steps in preparing a speech are similar to the prewriting steps in the process of writing. In both speaking and writing, you choose and limit your subject, gather supporting ideas, develop a thesis, and organize your ideas into an outline. In an oral presentation, however, instead of editing and publishing a written composition, you practice your speech and then deliver it orally to your listeners.

Knowing Your Audience and Purpose

Who is going to hear your speech? You may have an opportunity to speak formally to an audience made up of parents or voters, or you may be asked to speak informally to a group of your classmates. The following strategies will help you think about your audience and your purpose as you limit the subject of your speech.

Strategies for Considering Audience and Purpose

1. If possible, find out the interests of your audience. Then limit your subject to match your listeners' interests.
2. Try to determine what your audience already knows about the subject you plan to talk about. Consider what your audience may expect to hear.
3. Decide whether your purpose is to inform, to persuade, or to entertain by expressing your thoughts or by telling a story. *(See pages 128–159, 172–205, and 252–279 for more information about these purposes for written and oral compositions.)*

The following examples illustrate three ways to limit the subject of skiing according to the purpose of your speech.

Purposes of Speeches

PURPOSE	EXAMPLE
to inform	explaining the similarities and differences between downhill and cross-country skiing
to persuade	convincing students to take up cross-country skiing
to entertain	telling about your experiences the first time you went downhill skiing

---

EXERCISE *Recognizing Purpose*

For each of the three purposes—to inform, to persuade, and to entertain—write an example of a subject for a speech.

Choosing and Limiting a Subject

The first step in preparing a speech is to choose an interesting subject. Then limit it so that you can cover it fully for a given audience and within a given time period. For a ten-minute speech, for example, narrow your subject enough to cover it completely in that time. As a rule of thumb, it takes about as long to deliver a ten-minute speech as it does to slowly read aloud four pages of a typed double-spaced report.

Strategies for Choosing and Limiting a Subject

1. Choose a subject that interests you and is likely to interest your audience.
2. Choose a subject that you know well or can research thoroughly.
3. Limit the subject by choosing one aspect of it. For example, for a ten-minute speech on the planet Mars, you could limit the subject to weather on Mars.

EXERCISE *Finding a Subject*

For each item, write a subject for a speech.

1. personal experience
2. experiences of others
3. current events or issues
4. past events or people
5. how to do something
6. how to make something

EXERCISE *Limiting a Subject*

Write limited subjects for five of the following broad subjects. Limit them enough for a ten-minute speech.

1. pollution
2. gorillas
3. country music
4. American Revolution
5. sports
6. Canada
7. famous tourist attractions
8. wildlife
9. explorers
10. public transportation

Gathering and Organizing Information

After choosing and limiting your subject, you should begin to gather information. First, brainstorm for and list any information you already know about your subject. *(See page 20.)* Think of knowledgeable people you might interview, but before interviewing, prepare the questions you will ask. Another excellent source is the library, where you may find useful articles in encyclopedias, other reference books, and periodicals. As you locate information, write it on note cards. *(See pages 370–371.)*

While gathering information, collect or create visual materials such as pictures, maps, tape recordings, charts, slides, or props to make your presentation more interesting. When you have finished gathering information, begin organizing your speech.

Strategies for Organizing a Speech

1. Arrange your note cards in the order you intend to present your information. Use the cards to make a detailed outline of your speech and then draft an introduction.

2. To catch the interest of your audience, begin your speech with an anecdote, an unusual fact, a question, or an interesting quotation. Be sure you have a thesis statement that makes clear the main point and the purpose of your speech.

3. The body of your speech should include several ideas with facts or examples to support each idea. Arrange the ideas in a logical order and think of the transitions you will use.

4. Write a conclusion for your speech that summarizes your important ideas. Try to leave your audience with a memorable sentence or phrase.

EXERCISE *Gathering and Organizing Information*

Choose and limit a subject for a ten-minute speech in which the purpose is to inform. Write what you know about the subject on note cards. Then find information in the library for at least four more note cards. Organize your cards and write a detailed outline of your speech. Save your cards and outline for Exercise 5.

Practicing Your Speech

Although you need to rehearse your speech, in most cases you should not attempt to write it out or to memorize it. Instead, use your outline or convert your outline and note cards into cue cards. Cue cards help you remember your main points, your key words and phrases, and any quotations you plan to use in the speech.

Strategies for Practicing a Speech

1. Practice in front of a long mirror so that you will notice your facial expressions, gestures, and posture.
2. As you practice, look around the room as if you were looking at your audience.
3. Time your speech. If necessary, add or cut information.
4. As you practice, use your cue cards and any audiovisual aids or props that are part of your speech.
5. Practice over a period of several days. Your confidence will grow each time you practice, and as your confidence grows, your nervousness will decrease.

Revise your speech as you practice. You can do this by experimenting with your choice of words or adding and deleting information to make your main points clearer. In addition, if you practice your speech with a classmate or a friend, that listener's comments may help you revise and improve your speech before you deliver it.

EXERCISE *Practicing and Revising Your Speech*

Prepare cue cards for the speech you started preparing in Exercise 4. Then, using the Strategies for Practicing a Speech, practice in front of a friend or a classmate. Use your listener's comments to make improvements and then practice your revised speech in preparation for Exercise 6.

Delivering Your Speech

If you have followed the strategies for preparing and rehearsing, you should feel confident when the time comes to stand up in front of your audience and deliver your speech.

Strategies for Delivering a Speech
1. Have ready all the materials you need, such as your outline or cue cards and visual aids or props.
2. Wait until your audience is quiet and settled.
3. Take a deep breath and begin your introduction.
4. Stand with your weight evenly divided between both feet. Avoid swaying back and forth.
5. Look directly at the people in your audience, not over their heads. Try to make eye contact.
6. Speak slowly, clearly, and loudly enough to be heard.
7. Be aware of using correct grammar and well-formed sentences.
8. Use appropriate gestures and facial expressions to emphasize your main points.
9. Remember to use your audiovisual aids, making sure everyone in your audience can see them.
10. After finishing your speech, return to your seat without making comments to people in the audience.

Evaluating an Oral Presentation   After you have finished delivering your speech, evaluate it yourself as your audience evaluates it. The Oral Presentation Evaluation Form on page 456 may be useful.

Oral Presentation Evaluation Form

Subject: _____

Speaker: _____

Date: _____

Content
Is the subject appropriate for the audience?
Is the main point clear?
Are there enough details and examples?
Do all the ideas clearly relate to the subject?
Is the length appropriate (not too long or too short)?

Organization
Does the speech begin with an interesting introduction?
Do the ideas in the body follow a logical order?
Are transitions used between ideas?
Does the conclusion summarize the main points?

Presentation
Does the speaker use good word choice?
Does he/she speak loudly and clearly enough?
Is the rate appropriate (not too fast or too slow)?
Does the speaker make eye contact with the audience?
Does he/she use gestures and pauses effectively?
Are audiovisual aids or other props used effectively?
Are cue cards or an outline used effectively?

Comments: _____
_____
_____
_____
_____

EXERCISE *Delivering and Evaluating Your Speech*

With your teacher's permission, deliver the speech you prepared and practiced in Exercise 5. Then listen to the speeches of your classmates. Be sure to follow the Strategies for Delivering a Speech. After each speech, including your own, complete an Oral Presentation Evaluation Form. Each speaker should then collect and read the listeners' evaluations of his or her speech.

Listening

Listening usually involves much more than simply hearing the words that are spoken. When listening to directions, a speech, or a lecture, you must comprehend, evaluate, organize, and remember the information.

Listening to Directions

When you are assigned a task, listen carefully to the instructions. Do not assume you know what to do or what the speaker will say. Then follow the strategies below for understanding directions.

Strategies for Listening to Directions

1. Write down directions as soon as the speaker gives them. You may not remember them as well as you think.
2. Ask specific questions to clarify the directions.
3. When you have finished an assignment, briefly review the directions once more to make sure you have followed them correctly.

Listening to and Writing Directions   To practice giving and following directions, think of a simple task that can be completed in the classroom, such as making a book cover out of a paper bag or putting new laces in a pair of sneakers. Write step-by-step directions for completing the task. Then read your directions to a classmate and have the classmate follow them using the Strategies for Listening to Directions.

Listening for Information

When you listen to a speech or a lecture, pay close attention so that you can understand and evaluate what you hear. Listening for the purpose of learning requires extra concentration. You may find the following strategies helpful.

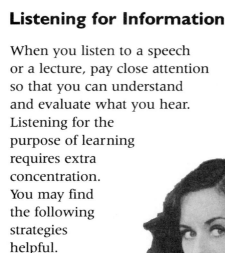

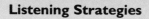

Listening Strategies

1. Sit comfortably but stay alert. Try to concentrate on what the speaker is saying without being distracted by people and noises.
2. Determine whether the speaker's purpose is to inform, to persuade, or to express thoughts and feelings.
3. Listen for verbal clues to identify the speaker's main ideas. Often, for example, a speaker emphasizes important points by using such words and phrases as *first . . . , finally . . . , also consider . . . , most importantly . . . , remember that . . . ,* or *in conclusion . . .*
4. Watch for nonverbal clues such as gestures, pauses, or changes in the speaking pace. Such clues often signal important ideas.
5. Determine the speaker's point of view about the subject. For example, is the speaker expressing positive or negative attitudes or arguing for or against an issue?
6. Take notes to organize your thoughts and to help you remember details. Your notes provide a basis for further discussion. You may also want to use your notes to outline the speech or write a summary of it. If the speech is a course lecture, notes will help you study for a test on the subject. *(See pages 516–518 for information on how to take notes.)*

EXERCISE *Listening and Taking Notes*

With your teacher's permission, organize a classroom experiment. Prepare a short speech for the purpose of informing. Then write a few key questions you think your listeners should be able to answer after listening to your talk. Next, deliver the speech, having half the class listen and the other half listen and take notes. Afterward, have all the students answer the questions you wrote. The test results will show how well you communicated, how well your audience listened, and to what extent note-taking helped.

Recognizing Propaganda

As a critical listener, you evaluate the content or message of a speech and make judgments about what you hear. To make sound judgments, you must be able to recognize propaganda devices, which people may use to mislead you.

The aim of propaganda is to get you to accept a point of view or to take some action. Rather than provide facts and examples as evidence, however, speakers who use propaganda distort or misrepresent information or disguise opinions as facts. Propaganda techniques also appeal to people's emotions by using emotional language, stereotypes, and exaggerations. By listening critically, you can learn to detect the following propaganda techniques.

Confusing Fact and Opinion   A *fact* is a statement that can be proved to be true or accurate. An *opinion* is a personal feeling or judgment about something. Knowing the difference is important in being able to detect opinions that are disguised as facts.

FACT   I ate tacos for dinner last night.
OPINION   Tacos make the best meal.

FACT   Dogs are members of the canine family.
OPINION   Dogs make the most loving and intelligent pets.

EXERCISE *Distinguishing between Fact and Opinion*

Label each of the following statements with an *F* for *fact* or an *O* for *opinion*.

 1. Charles Dickens wrote *Great Expectations*.
 2. Dogs are more fun than cats.
 3. The sun will set at 7:02 this evening.
 4. My brother plays basketball on the high school team.
 5. All roller-coaster rides are dangerous.
 6. Dickens was the best writer of all time.
 7. I had my first roller-coaster ride when I was five.
 8. My brother should be captain of the basketball team.
 9. A German shepherd is larger than a cocker spaniel.
 10. Fall is the most beautiful season of the year.

Bandwagon Appeals   A *bandwagon appeal* is an invitation to do or think the same thing as everyone else. Advertisements that use bandwagon appeals often try to make consumers feel inferior if they do not conform. A political campaign may use bandwagon appeals to make voters feel useless if they do not vote on the winning side. Common slogans associated with this propaganda device include *Get on board! Join the crowd! Everyone enjoys* . . . and *Don't be left out!*

> The with-it generation drinks Vita-Juice. If you don't drink Vita-Juice, you're not with it; you're out of it!

Testimonials   A *testimonial* is a statement, usually given by a famous person, that supports a product, a candidate, or a policy. A testimonial can be misleading because it suggests that a famous person's opinions must be right or that a product must be excellent if a celebrity endorses it.

> Hi! I'm Greg Husky, quarterback for the Longhorns. Since getting to each game on time is important, I depend on my Leopard convertible to get me there. If you need a dependable car the way I do, get yourself a Leopard.

Unproved Generalizations   A *generalization* is a conclusion that is based on many facts or examples. However, a generalization that is based on only one or two facts or examples is unsound, or unproved. Unsound generalizations are misleading when they are used as if they were proven facts that apply to all cases. Unproved generalizations usually contain words such as *always, never, all,* or *none.*

UNPROVED
GENERALIZATIONS

If I stay up too late, I always get up late the next day.

Television makes children violent.

Watching a movie is never as good as reading the book.

ACCURATE
GENERALIZATIONS

Sometimes if I stay up too late, I get up late the next day.

Some children behave violently after watching violent programs on television.

Watching a movie is **usually** not as good as reading the book.

EXERCISE *Identifying Propaganda Techniques*

Label each statement *B* for *bandwagon*, *T* for *testimonial*, or *U* for *unproved generalization.*

1. As United States senator, I urge you to reelect Governor Smith in your state election. My long experience in office tells me that he is your best choice.

2. Not a single flea will survive in your home after just one application of extra-strength Flea Bomb.

3. Don't be a misfit. Now you can fit in with our Good-Fit jeans. Everybody's wearing them!

4. We asked the students at Town High School to test our Deluxe pencils for one week. They all agree that Deluxe pencils are the best writing instruments they have ever used.

5. Don't be old-fashioned! Join the new generation of health-conscious people and drink a delicious Yummy Yogurt every day.

Group Discussion

A group discussion provides an opportunity for you to share your ideas and learn from others. In both formal and informal group discussions, you communicate ideas, exchange opinions, solve problems, and reach decisions.

Discussing ideas with your classmates plays an important role in the learning process. When you are writing, the technique of group brainstorming can help you in the prewriting stage— particularly in generating ideas for subjects. Peer conferencing can help you in the revising stage, when you are looking for ways to improve a composition. In addition, you may use discussion skills in practicing a speech or an oral report or in preparing for a test.

Learning group discussion skills will help you to state your own ideas effectively and to listen carefully to others' ideas. *(See pages 450 – 456 and 458.)*

Strategies for Participating in Group Discussions

1. Listen carefully and respond respectfully to others' views.
2. Ask questions to make sure you understand others' views and information.
3. Keep in mind that everyone in the group should have an equal opportunity to speak.
4. Make sure your contributions to the discussion are clear, constructive, and relevant to the subject.

Discussion Leaders

While all members of a discussion group should follow the same guidelines, the discussion leader has extra responsibilities. A leader, sometimes called a moderator, may be chosen by the group or by the teacher to guide a discussion. If you are chosen to lead a group discussion, use the following strategies to meet your new responsibilities.

Strategies for Discussion Leaders

1. Introduce the topic, question, or problem.
2. With the group's help, state the purpose or the goal of the discussion.
3. Keep the discussion on track to help the group accomplish its goals.
4. Make sure that everyone has an equal opportunity and equal time to participate.
5. Keep a record of the group's main points and decisions or assign this task to a group member.
6. At the end of the discussion, summarize the main points and restate any conclusions the group reached.

EXERCISE *Conducting a Group Discussion*

With your teacher's permission, form small groups and conduct a group discussion. Begin by choosing a subject or issue related to your school. Then choose a discussion leader and establish a goal. During the discussion take turns practicing the responsibilities of a discussion leader.

Cooperative Learning

A special kind of discussion group is the *cooperative learning* group, sometimes called a task group. In a cooperative learning group, you work with others to achieve a particular goal. Tasks connected with the goal are divided among the members of the group. Then, with the help of a leader, members coordinate the results of their individual efforts.

For example, members of a cooperative learning group in a social studies class may work together to prepare an oral presentation on Saudi Arabia. One member of the group may research the geography and economy of Saudi Arabia, another member may concentrate on the history and government of that country, a third member may explore the religion and art, and so on.

In addition to performing a task, you might have a particular role in the group, such as acting as the group leader. Besides being a discussion leader, the leader of a cooperative learning group helps to coordinate the group's efforts.

Strategies for Cooperative Learning

1. Observe the Strategies for Participating in Group Discussions. *(See page 462.)*
2. Participate in planning the project and in assigning tasks.
3. When you have been assigned a task, do not let your group down by coming to meetings unprepared.
4. Cooperate with others in the group to resolve conflicts, solve problems, reach conclusions, or make decisions.
5. Help your group achieve its goals by taking your fair share of responsibility for the group's success.

EXERCISE *Organizing a Cooperative Learning Group*

With your teacher's permission, form cooperative groups of five to seven members and plan a presentation on the subject of deserts. Define your goals, choose a leader, and divide the work into manageable tasks. Then assign tasks, following the Strategies for Cooperative Learning. Next, gather and share information, meeting several times to coordinate your efforts. Finally, make your presentation to the class. Remember to follow the steps for an oral presentation. *(See pages 450–456.)*

13 Review

A **Giving a Speech** Prepare a ten-minute speech about one of the following subjects or one of your own. Decide whether the purpose of your speech will be to inform, to persuade, or to entertain.

1. the importance of school sports
2. younger (or older) brothers and sisters
3. the life of a reptile

B **Listening for Directions** Work with a partner or in a small group. Each group member should first draw a simple design on a piece of paper without showing it to the other group members. Then give directions to the group members that explain how to draw your design. The group members should follow the directions and then compare drawings.

C **Recognizing Propaganda** Brainstorm ideas for a new product that you think is needed. After you have given the product a name, design a magazine or newspaper advertisement for it. Use one or more of the following propaganda techniques in your ad: opinion presented as fact, bandwagon appeal, testimonial, and unproved generalization.

D **Group Discussion** Find examples of propaganda used in advertising on television or in magazines. With your teacher's permission, form small groups and discuss the propaganda techniques used in the ads. Select a leader who will direct the discussion and summarize its findings at the end.

E **Cooperative Learning** Form a task group with the goal of preparing a presentation on propaganda techniques. Decide how you will achieve this goal. Then assign tasks and choose a leader to help coordinate your efforts.

14

Vocabulary

The saddest words of tongue or pen
Are those you didn't think of then.

BETTY PILLIPP

How can you be sure that you think of the right word when the situation demands it? When you are engaged in an argument or debate, how do you think of words to answer your opponent's arguments? When you write a story, how do you think of the right words for your characters to say? Having a rich vocabulary will help you select the word that is most effective and precise in communication situations like these.

In this chapter you will learn a variety of strategies for expanding your storehouse of words. First, though, you will see how English developed into a language that is both rich and varied.

The History of English

More than 300 million people throughout the world speak English as their native language. This language that so many people speak today began to develop more than 1,500 years ago, in about A.D. 450. During this period England was part of the Roman Empire, and Latin was the written language. At that time three Germanic tribes—the Angles, the Saxons, and the

Jutes—invaded England from the shores of the North Sea. After conquering the Celts who lived there, they stayed and settled on the land. These tribes discarded the older Celtic and Roman cultures and made their own language the language of the land.

The language those Germanic tribes spoke is now called Old English, although to English-speaking people today it would sound like a foreign language. Nevertheless, some Old English words are still part of the language. They include common nouns and verbs: *man, child, house, mother, horse, knee, eat, sing, ride, drink,* and *sell.* They also include most of the modern numbers such as *one, five, nine;* the pronouns such as *you, he, they, who;* the articles *a, an,* and *the;* and prepositions such as *at, by, in, under, around,* and *out.*

Middle English

Old English began its change into Middle English when William the Conqueror invaded England from northwestern France in 1066 and made French the official language. Although the royal court and the upper classes spoke French, the common people continued to speak Old English. Nevertheless, English might eventually have faded out if the parliament had not started to use it in 1392. By 1450, Middle English, which included hundreds of French words, had evolved. At this time Geoffrey Chaucer, a famous writer, wrote his works in Middle English. In addition, the first books printed in England were in Middle English.

Modern English

Modern English started to evolve out of Middle English in the middle of the 1400's. During that time writers and scholars borrowed numerous words from Latin. In fact, it has been estimated that about half of the present words in English have a Latin origin. By the time Shakespeare was writing in the last half of the 1500's, English was a versatile language that is understandable to modern speakers of English.

Word Origins

Modern English words are derived from many languages, old and new. The *etymology* of a word is the history of that word from its earliest recorded use to the present. Many dictionaries use brackets at the beginning or end of an entry to show the etymology of a word, as in the following example.

oc·to·pus \ 'äk-tə·pəs \ *n, pl* **-pus·es** *or* **-pi** : any of various cephalopod sea mollusks having eight muscular arms [Greek *oktōpous* "having 8 feet," from *oktō* "eight" + *pous* "foot"]

ETYMOLOGY

By permission. From Webster's School Dictionary © 1980 by Merriam-Webster® Inc., publishers of the Merriam-Webster Dictionaries.

Dictionaries commonly use the following abbreviations to indicate languages of origin. A complete list of abbreviations is given at the front of most dictionaries.

L	Latin	OE	Old English	Sp	Spanish
Gk	Greek	ME	Middle English	It	Italian
Ar	Arabic	OF	Old French	G	German
Skt	Sanskrit	F	French	D	Dutch

EXERCISE *Discovering Word Origins*

Using a dictionary, write the language or languages of origin of each of the following words.

1. noodle
2. macaroni
3. waffle
4. career

5. apple
6. asparagus
7. macaroon
8. buckaroo

9. crouton
10. pickle
11. spinach
12. pecan

American Dialects

Today more than 600,000 words make up the English language. Not all of these words are spoken exactly the same way by all English-speaking people. People in different countries and even different regions of the same country often have their own way of pronouncing certain words. These different ways of speaking are called *dialects*. In the United States, for example, New Englanders are said to speak with a twang and Southerners with a drawl.

American English varies among three main regional dialects: Eastern, Southern, and General American. Each of these dialects contains many subdialects. For instance, the Southern dialect includes distinctive subdialects spoken in Texas and Louisiana.

Dialects can be different from one another in vocabulary, pronunciation, and even grammar. In Columbus, Ohio, for instance, a green pepper may be called a *mango*, and in New York City, many local residents pronounce *birds* as *boids*. Although dialects vary across the country, none are so different that one group cannot understand another. In fact, dialects add color and richness to American English.

Dialects have appropriate uses in informal conversation and in creative writing. In a formal speech or in expository writing, however, you should use standard English, which is the correct form of English used in newspapers and on television.

EXERCISE *Understanding Dialects*

With your teacher's permission, form small groups and discuss the dialect that is spoken in your region. Brainstorm for examples of the vocabulary, pronunciation, and grammar that characterize the dialect. For example, do speakers of the dialect use the term *sofa, lounge, davenport, couch,* or *settee?* Do they use the word *soda, pop,* or *tonic?* After you have developed a list of examples of the dialect, compare and contrast them with standard English. You may wish to publish your findings in the form of a chart, an index, or a dictionary of words that introduces people from other parts of the country to your regional dialect.

Idioms, Colloquialisms, Slang, and Jargon

Besides dialect, another source of the richness of the English language is found in the idioms, colloquialisms, and slang of everyday conversation. Because these three types of expressions are informal, they are usually not appropriate in your writing. *(See page 786 about levels of usage.)*

Idioms An *idiom* is a phrase or expression that has a meaning different from what the words suggest in their usual meanings. Idioms often do not make sense when taken literally, yet they are still meaningful to most people who speak a particular language.

> Elise was **beside herself with worry** [very concerned] because she had not heard from Barbara.

> We didn't want to **put up with** [tolerate] the barking of the neighbor's dog.

Colloquialisms A *colloquialism* is an informal phrase or expression that is appropriate for conversation but not for formal writing.

> As soon as Dan and Luis met, they **hit it off** [got along well together].

> For dinner the Hendersons certainly **put on a spread** [served a generous amount of food].

Slang *Slang* expressions are nonstandard English expressions that are developed and used by particular groups. Such expressions are highly colorful, exaggerated, and often humorous. Although most slang goes out of fashion quickly, a few slang expressions—such as those that follow—have become a permanent part of the language.

> Simone earned ten **bucks** [dollars] by mowing Mr. Henshaw's lawn.

> Sitting in an airport and waiting for someone can be **a real drag** [tiresome].

Jargon *Jargon* is the specialized vocabulary that scientists, engineers, lawyers, doctors, and other specialists use to communicate precisely and efficiently with one another. Using jargon to communicate with other experts, such as in an article for a scientific journal, is appropriate. However, using jargon to communicate with a general audience can cause lack of understanding. The second sentence below would be much clearer to a general audience than the first sentence.

JARGON   There is no locality similar to a structure that is used exclusively for a permanent residential and noncommercial purpose.

TRANSLATION   There is no place like home.

EXERCISE *Using Appropriate English*

Substitute words or phrases in standard English for the underlined colloquialisms, idioms, and slang expressions in the following sentences.

1. The gymnastics coach told Midori to <u>go all out</u> in her next routine.
2. Some adventurous types of people get <u>a kick</u> out of hang gliding.
3. You should see Beth's car. What a <u>heap</u>!
4. <u>To come by</u> a part-time summer job can be difficult and time-consuming.
5. Maria asked her little brother to please stop <u>bugging</u> her while she tried to read.
6. Roberto told Larry, "I've got to <u>plow through</u> the rest of that book before we have the test on it tomorrow."
7. The explorers trying to scale Mount Everest have had a <u>tough time of it</u>.
8. Julia would <u>jump at the chance</u> to work for the newspaper during the summer.
9. The library has <u>tons of</u> books, articles, and pamphlets about volcanoes.
10. Are you going to <u>see them off</u> at the train station tomorrow afternoon?

471

Determining Word Meaning

Often you may hear or read words that are new to you. One way to learn their meanings is to look up the words in a dictionary. However, the rest of this chapter will explain meanings of unfamiliar words.

Using Context Clues

One of the best ways to learn the meaning of a word is through context clues. The *context* of a word is the sentence, the surrounding words, or the situation in which the word occurs. The following examples show the four most common kinds of context clues.

Four Types of Context Clues	
DEFINITION OR RESTATEMENT	During the storm travelers took a detour because the *isthmus*, **a narrow strip of land connecting the two larger landmasses**, was flooded. [The word *isthmus* is defined within the sentence.]
EXAMPLE	You may find a *fossil* here, perhaps **like the one in our science lab that has an imprint of a leaf.** [The word *fossil* is followed by an example that is known to the readers or listeners.]
COMPARISON	The mayor said that tax *revenues*, **like personal income**, should be spent wisely. [The word *like* compares *revenues* to its synonym *income*.]
CONTRAST	*Contemporary* students learn more about computers **than did students of a few years ago.** [A contrast is drawn between today's students (*contemporary* students) and students of the past.]

EXERCISE *Using Context Clues*

Write the letter of the word or phrase that is closest in meaning to each underlined word. Then identify the type of context clue that helped you determine that meaning by writing *definition* or *restatement, example, comparison,* or *contrast.*

1. The team members gathered in a huddle but <u>dispersed</u> when the coach blew her whistle.
  (A) cheered   (B) scattered   (C) exercised
  (D) planned   (E) answered

2. Because ferns, orchids, and bromeliads are <u>indigenous</u> to the tropics, they must be grown in hothouse conditions in the North.
  (A) unknown   (B) exotic   (C) warlike
  (D) unemployed   (E) native

3. Louise Nevelson, a famous sculptress, <u>salvaged</u> useless scraps of metal and wood and transformed them into beautiful works of art.
  (A) built   (B) created   (C) rescued
  (D) destroyed   (E) judged

4. Ms. Ord thought that the impatient <u>patron</u> should wait her turn in line, like others in the local grocery store.
  (A) owner   (B) speaker   (C) prisoner
  (D) customer   (E) hypnotist

5. We were fascinated by the strange, large, green insect that was climbing up the wall, but Matthew seemed <u>oblivious</u> to it.
  (A) devious   (B) clear   (C) unaware
  (D) pale   (E) superior

6. The dogwood in our garden is a <u>perennial</u> source of delight, beautiful at every season of the year.
  (A) perfect   (B) timid   (C) slippery
  (D) victorious   (E) lasting

7. The politician accused his opponents of <u>contriving</u> to defeat his proposal.
  (A) scheming   (B) refusing   (C) electing
  (D) grieving   (E) answering

8. The idea was <u>infamous</u>, a scheme that no fair or honest person could accept.

(A) disgraceful   (B) unknown   (C) childlike

(D) diseased   (E) well-known

9. My <u>hypothesis</u>, the way I explain it, is that Shana made the phone call.

(A) mistake   (B) theory   (C) dream

(D) publicity   (E) thanks

10. Her <u>graphic</u> description enabled her readers to picture each object in the room in detail.

(A) musical   (B) vague   (C) geometric

(D) vivid   (E) exaggerated

11. National parkland cannot be <u>exploited</u> for resorts, industries, or other money-making projects.

(A) explored   (B) defended   (C) observed

(D) increased in value   (E) abused for profit

12. Have an expert <u>appraise</u>, or estimate the worth of, a major purchase before you buy it.

(A) record   (B) buy   (C) evaluate

(D) announce   (E) glorify

13. Winning the blue ribbon is her <u>incentive</u> to practice daily for the race.

(A) excuse   (B) reward   (C) payment

(D) idea   (E) motivation

14. Heavy rain fell continuously for four days, ending the drought and <u>saturating</u> the soil.

(A) dissolving   (B) soaking   (C) drying

(D) planting   (E) mixing

15. Although city streets are <u>congested</u> during the rush hour, traffic decreases between 6:00 P.M. and 7:00 A.M.

(A) clogged   (B) deserted   (C) paved

(D) wide   (E) narrow

Prefixes and Suffixes

Words in English often have Latin or Greek roots, prefixes, and suffixes. These word parts offer clues to help you unlock the meanings of words. A *root* is the part of a word that carries

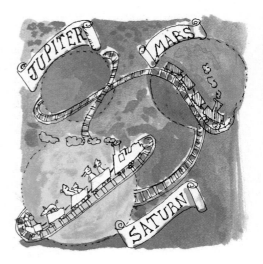

the basic meaning. A *prefix* is one or more syllables placed in front of the root to modify the meaning of the root or to form a new word. A *suffix* is one or more syllables placed after the root to change its part of speech. In the following examples, notice how the meaning of each word part is related to the meaning of the word as a whole.

Using Word Parts to Determine Meanings

WORD	PREFIX	ROOT	SUFFIX
dissimilarity (state of being unlike)	dis- (not)	-similar- (alike)	-ity (state of)
independence (state of not relying)	in- (not)	-depend- (to rely)	-ence (state of)
intergalactic (relating to area between galaxies)	inter- (between)	-galaxy- (star system)	-ic (relating to)
transporter (one who carries across)	trans- (across)	-port- (to carry)	-er (one who)
resourceful (able to use ways and means again)	re- (again)	-source- (ways and means)	-ful (full of)

Because word meanings in any language often change over years of use, you will not always find a perfect match between words and the meanings of their Latin and Greek word parts. Even so, a knowledge of prefixes, roots, and suffixes can help you figure out the meanings of thousands of words.

Common Prefixes and Suffixes

PREFIX	MEANING	EXAMPLE
com-, con-	with, together	con + form = to become the same shape
dis-	not, lack of	dis + harmony = a lack of agreement
extra-	outside, beyond	extra + curricular = outside the regular school courses
in-, il-, im-	in, into, not	im + migrate = to come into a country, il + legal = not lawful
inter-	between, among	inter + state = among or between states
post-	after	post + date = to give a later date
re-	again	re + occur = to happen again
sub-	under	sub + standard = under the standard
trans-	across	trans + Atlantic = across the Atlantic

SUFFIX	MEANING	EXAMPLE
-ance, -ence	state of	import + ance = state of being important
-er	one who or that	foreign + er = one who is foreign
-ful	full of	hope + ful = full of hope
-ic	relating to	atom + ic = relating to atoms
-ite	resident of	Milford + ite = resident of Milford
-ity	state of	active + ity = state of being active
-less	without, lack of	pain + less = without pain

EXERCISE *Understanding Prefixes and Suffixes*

Write the prefix or the suffix that has the same meaning as the underlined word or words. Then write the complete word defined after the equal sign. Your teacher may also ask you to use each word in a sentence.

EXAMPLE under + marine = beneath the water
ANSWER sub—submarine

1. <u>among</u> + stellar = taking place among the stars
2. <u>together</u> + press = to squeeze together
3. depend + <u>state of</u> = the state of relying on someone or something for support
4. patriot + <u>relating to</u> = relating to love of country
5. <u>across</u> + plant = to lift from one place and to reset in another
6. <u>not</u> + similar = not like
7. actual + <u>state of</u> = state of being real
8. speech + <u>without</u> = without conversation
9. <u>after</u> + game = following a game
10. <u>not</u> + frequent = not often
11. <u>again</u> + examine = to inspect again
12. Brooklyn + <u>resident</u> = one who lives in Brooklyn
13. contend + <u>one who</u> = one who strives in a competition
14. meaning + <u>full</u> = full of meaning or purpose
15. solid + <u>condition</u> = state of being solid

EXERCISE *Using Prefixes*

Write the letter of the phrase that is closest in meaning to each word in capital letters. Use the prefixes as clues to meaning.

1. DISUNITY: (A) agreement with (B) agreement between (C) lack of agreement
2. INTERVENE: (A) come into (B) come together (C) come between
3. TRANSPOLAR: (A) extending across a polar region (B) moving out of a polar region (C) extending under a polar region

4. SUBMERGE: (A) put underwater (B) place together
(C) float across
5. EXTRAORDINARY: (A) after what is usual (B) beyond
what is usual (C) among what is usual
6. CONJUNCTION: (A) joining together (B) not joining
(C) joining across
7. POSTPONE: (A) delay to a future time (B) move
across a barrier (C) place under
8. IMPLODE: (A) fly across at a high speed (B) burst out
of (C) collapse inward
9. REACTIVATE: (A) give energy again (B) be energetic
with (C) take away energy
10. IMPARTIAL: (A) lacking parts (B) not favoring one
side (C) after each part

Synonyms and Antonyms

A *synonym* is a word that has nearly the same meaning as
another word. An *antonym*, on the other hand, is a word that
means the opposite of another word. Knowing synonyms and
antonyms of words can help you choose the best words when
you write or speak.

SYNONYMS   affable:friendly   terminate:finish

ANTONYMS   affable:hostile   terminate:begin

Your dictionary contains information on synonyms and often
explains the slight differences among the synonyms for a given
word. A *thesaurus* is a kind of specialized dictionary for synonyms. It lists words and their synonyms alphabetically or provides an index of words for finding synonyms easily. *(See page
502.)*

EXERCISE   7   *Recognizing Synonyms*

Write the letter of the word that is closest in meaning to the
word in capital letters. Then check your answers in the dictionary.

1. ACUTE: (A) lovely   (B) mountainous   (C) sharp
(D) prior   (E) hasty

2. COMPREHEND: (A) write   (B) bother   (C) lose
(D) collect   (E) understand

3. COURIER: (A) spy   (B) gentleman   (C) pilot
(D) employer   (E) messenger

4. DEBRIS: (A) ruins   (B) corruption   (C) debt
(D) poverty   (E) confidence

5. EXASPERATE: (A) depart   (B) irritate   (C) increase
(D) reduce   (E) evaporate

6. EXEMPT: (A) perfect   (B) empty   (C) required
(D) excused   (E) important

7. GENTEEL: (A) real   (B) selfish   (C) polite
(D) nonspecific   (E) lifeless

8. INTEGRITY: (A) honesty   (B) cleverness   (C) wealth
(D) annoyance   (E) fame

9. KNOLL: (A) holiday   (B) noise   (C) mound
(D) forest   (E) merrymaker

10. LUDICROUS: (A) fortunate   (B) questionable
(C) laughable   (D) happy   (E) shy

11. MUTUAL: (A) active   (B) changed   (C) deep
(D) shared   (E) solitary

12. NARRATE: (A) tell   (B) judge   (C) notch
(D) separate   (E) believe

13. OBSOLETE: (A) outdated   (B) lost   (C) hidden
(D) wrecked   (E) reversed

14. OBSTRUCT: (A) teach   (B) disagree   (C) build
(D) hinder   (E) watch

15. PHENOMENAL: (A) lucky   (B) remarkable   (C) hasty
(D) musical   (E) unemotional

EXERCISE ◆8◆ *Recognizing Antonyms*

Write the letter of the word that is most nearly opposite in
meaning to the word in capital letters.

1. ABSTRACT: (A) hazy   (B) total   (C) honest
(D) concrete   (E) theoretical

2. ADJACENT: (A) distant   (B) acceptable   (C) vague
   (D) accidental   (E) near
3. ADVERSE: (A) unreliable   (B) favorable   (C) clever
   (D) hostile   (E) risky
4. BIZARRE: (A) crowded   (B) familiar   (C) odd
   (D) commercial   (E) unreasonable
5. BREVITY: (A) briefness   (B) wittiness   (C) dullness
   (D) wordiness   (E) slowness
6. COMPRESS: (A) expand   (B) point   (C) accuse
   (D) squeeze   (E) impress
7. CRUCIAL: (A) unimportant   (B) required   (C) stern
   (D) unbelievable   (E) refined
8. DISSIMILAR: (A) truthful   (B) different   (C) prompt
   (D) genuine   (E) alike
9. ESSENTIAL: (A) unnecessary   (B) secret
   (C) incorrect   (D) tall   (E) easy
10. EXEMPT: (A) taxed   (B) dependent   (C) excused
    (D) perfect   (E) obligated
11. HACKNEYED: (A) thoughtful   (B) overused
    (C) skilled   (D) original   (E) wide
12. IMPROVISE: (A) disprove   (B) react   (C) increase
    (D) plan   (E) stop
13. INFAMOUS: (A) pleasant   (B) untrustworthy
    (C) honorable   (D) huge   (E) shady
14. OBSTRUCT: (A) refuse   (B) assist   (C) improve
    (D) suggest   (E) obtain
15. PHENOMENAL: (A) poisonous   (B) brilliant
    (C) ordinary   (D) pitiful   (E) generous

Analogies

One type of standardized test that often calls upon your knowledge of synonyms and antonyms is analogies. *Analogies* ask you to identify relationships between pairs of words.

REMEDY:CURE   ::   (A) simple:fancy   (B) wet:dry
(C) lessen:reduce

To answer this test question, first identify the relationship between the two words in capital letters. In the test item on the previous page, the words are synonyms because *remedy* and *cure* have similar meanings. Then, from the possible answers, you need to find the other pair of words that has the same relationship as the words in capital letters. Choice *A* is not correct because the two words, *simple* and *fancy*, are antonyms, not synonyms. Choice *B* is not correct because those two words, *wet* and *dry*, are also antonyms. Choice *C* is the correct one because the two words, *lessen* and *reduce*, are synonyms. *(See pages 528–530 for more about analogies.)*

EXERCISE *Recognizing Analogies*

Write the letter of the word pair that has the same relationship as the word pair in capital letters. Then identify the type of relationship by writing *synonym* or *antonym*.

EXAMPLE   WILD:TAME : :   (A) sleepy:tired
(B) empty:full   (C) loud:noisy

ANSWER   B—antonyms

1. COLD:HOT : :   (A) high:low
   (B) kind:gentle   (C) fast:quick
2. SLIM:THIN : :   (A) young:old
   (B) open:closed   (C) careful:cautious
3. LATE:EARLY : :   (A) round:circular
   (B) right:wrong   (C) distant:far
4. SOAR:GLIDE   : :   (A) raise:lower
   (B) watch:observe   (C) arrive:depart
5. REASON:LOGIC : :   (A) courage:bravery
   (B) fantasy:reality   (C) joy:sorrow
6. VALID:LEGAL : :   (A) certain:sure   (B) tall:short
   (C) rough:smooth
7. QUALIFIED:ELIGIBLE   : :   (A) hopeful:discouraged
   (B) fair:just   (C) tidy:messy
8. FOREIGN:ALIEN : :   (A) peaceful:calm   (B) wet:dry
   (C) soft:hard

9. GENUINE:AUTHENTIC : : (A) real:imaginary
(B) hungry:full (C) fortunate:lucky

10. WEAKNESS:STAMINA : : (A) box:carton
(B) car:automobile (C) beginning:conclusion

11. COMPETITION:RIVALRY : : (A) safety:danger
(B) cooperation:teamwork (C) top:bottom

12. CURE:REMEDY : : (A) cause:effect
(B) guilt:innocence (C) value:worth

13. USEFUL:FUTILE : : (A) wicked:evil (B) true:false
(C) prompt:punctual

14. THOUGHTFUL:PENSIVE : : (A) hazy:bright
(B) necessary:essential (C) wide:narrow

15. DOUBTFUL:DUBIOUS : : (A) tart:sweet
(B) alert:watchful (C) shiny:dull

Language *Integrating* Skills

Recording Unfamiliar Words Build your vocabulary by writing in your writer's notebook any unfamiliar words you read or hear. Look up new words in a dictionary. Then include a brief definition of each word and an example of its appropriate context or use.

Begin by listing any of the words in the following list that are unfamiliar to you. Then, whenever you are revising your work, look over your list and include in your writing as many new words as possible. Use your word list as a resource for choosing words that are vivid, appropriate, and precise.

actuality	deduce	improvise	random
acute	disperse	indigenous	skeptical
affable	dubious	knoll	stamina
cajole	exploit	ludicrous	superfluous
connoisseur	genteel	mentor	valiant
contrive	hilarity	pensive	versatile

14 Review

A **Using Context Clues** Write the letter of the answer that is closest in meaning to each underlined word.

1. Marty's <u>ambivalence</u> was frustrating him. He was divided equally between two good choices.
   (A) temper (B) uncertainty (C) decisiveness

2. The angry man uttered a <u>feral</u> snarl, sounding like a savage animal.
   (A) beastlike (B) primitive (C) timid

3. The hikers felt the storm was <u>imminent</u>. At any moment the clouds could burst into rain.
   (A) foreboding (B) threatening (C) angry

4. The victim believed the only way he could <u>redress</u> his wrongs was to take the matter to court.
   (A) correct (B) provide (C) move

5. Unlike the first description, which included unnecessary details, the last description included only the <u>salient</u> details.
   (A) colorful (B) useless (C) striking

B **Understanding Analogies** Write the letter of the word pair that has the same relationship as the given pair in capital letters. Then identify the type of relationship by writing *synonym* or *antonym*.

1. LIGHT:DARK : : (A) compact:loose (B) flip:toss
   (C) hate:detest

2. FANCY:ORNATE : : (A) spicy:bland (B) merge:unite
   (C) reveal:conceal

3. BRINK:EDGE : : (A) leader:follower
   (B) impromptu:prepared (C) jest:joke

4. HITCH:DISCONNECT : : (A) hire:fire (B) gift:present
   (C) horse:wagon

5. FABRICATE:DISMANTLE : : (A) eerie:mysterious
   (B) efficient:wasteful (C) despondent:depressed

15

Spelling

While spelling is easier for some people than for others, everyone can learn some techniques for spelling more accurately.

Recognizing Commonly Misspelled Words In your journal write the commonly misspelled words from the following list that are difficult for you. Then always refer to this personal spelling list as you edit your written work.

Spelling Demons

absence	defendant	license	prejudice
achieve	discipline	loneliness	probably
acquaintance	eighth	maintenance	pronunciation
already	embarrass	marriage	psychology
analyze	exaggerate	mileage	restaurant
attendance	foreign	muscle	secretary
beginning	fourth	necessary	separate
cemetery	handkerchief	occasionally	succeed
committee	immediately	omitted	thorough
conscience	interesting	parallel	tomorrow
courageous	interfere	particularly	truly
courteous	irrelevant	permanent	unnecessary
curiosity	laboratory	possess	weird

Spelling Improvement

Apply these strategies to help improve your spelling skills.

Strategies for Improving Your Spelling

1. In a section of your journal, list the words you find difficult.
2. When writing, use a dictionary to check the spelling of words you are unsure of. Guessing is unreliable.
3. Always proofread your writing carefully.
4. Sound out each syllable to avoid dropping letters.
   math • e • matics   Feb • ru • ary   tem • per • a • ture
5. Use memory tricks for words you frequently misspell.
   committee: 2 *m's*, 2 *t's*, 2 *e's*

EXERCISE *Recognizing Misspelled Words*

Number your paper from 1 to 10. Write the letter of each misspelled word and then write the word correctly.

1. (A) abbreviation   (B) boulevard   (C) extream
   (D) incident   (E) insistence

2. (A) bureau   (B) confer   (C) forgery
   (D) honorary   (E) literture

3. (A) fasinating   (B) guarantee   (C) illustrate
   (D) limousine   (E) manipulate

4. (A) irritate   (B) luxury   (C) mischeif
   (D) organic   (E) presence

5. (A) authentic   (B) brillance   (C) disguise
   (D) interview   (E) miniature

6. (A) mysterious   (B) ocasionally   (C) prestige
   (D) prosperous   (E) reasonable

7. (A) legislasure   (B) merchandise   (C) notch
   (D) rebel   (E) referee

8. (A) punctual   (B) resign   (C) resteurant
   (D) similarity   (E) speculate

9. (A) ridicilous   (B) sizable   (C) thesaurus
   (D) unanimous   (E) veteran

10. (A) coupon   (B) chrystal   (C) dissatisfied
   (D) melancholy   (E) orchestra

Spelling Rules

Knowing common spelling rules can help you to spell hundreds of words. Some of these rules are based on spelling patterns, such as the choice between *ie* or *ei*. Other rules concern forming plurals and adding prefixes and suffixes.

Spelling Patterns

Understanding certain common word patterns can help take the guesswork out of spelling many words.

Words with *ie* and *ei*   The following rule helps you spell words with the *ie* or *ei* pattern.

Put *i* before *e*	believe	field
except after *c*	ceiling	receipt
or when		
sounded like *a*	neighbor	weigh

Although this rule applies in most cases, the following words are exceptions.

ancient	efficient	either	leisure
conscience	species	neither	seize
sufficient	foreign	height	weird

Notice that the rules for spelling the *ie/ei* pattern apply only when the *ie* or *ei* combination appears in the same syllable of a word. The rules do not apply in the following examples, where the *i* and *e* appear in separate syllables.

be ing	re imburse	sci ence	soci ety

Words with *-sede, -ceed,* and *-cede*   Other words that often cause confusion are those ending with a "seed" sound. Keep in mind that only one word in English is spelled with a *-sede* ending and only three words are spelled with a *-ceed* ending.

All other words that end in the "seed" sound are spelled with a *-cede* ending.

-sede   supersede
-ceed   exceed   proceed   succeed
-cede   concede   precede   recede   secede

EXERCISE *Using Spelling Patterns*

Write each word, adding either *ie* or *ei*.

1. th__f	**6.** bel__f	**11.** p__ce	**16.** br__f
2. n__ce	**7.** c__ling	**12.** r__ns	**17.** rec__ve
3. y__ld	**8.** rec__pt	**13.** n__ther	**18.** retr__ve
4. w__gh	**9.** gr__ve	**14.** dec__ve	**19.** n__ghbor
5. h__ght	**10.** __ght	**15.** rel__ve	**20.** l__sure

EXERCISE *Using Spelling Patterns*

Write each word, adding *-sede, -ceed,* or *-cede.*

1. re__	**3.** ac__	**5.** suc__	**7.** pre__	**9.** super__
2. ex__	**4.** se__	**6.** con__	**8.** pro__	**10.** inter__

Plurals

Forming the plural of a noun is no mystery when you use the following guidelines.

Regular Nouns   To form the plural of most nouns, simply add *s*. If a noun ends in *s, ch, sh, x,* or *z*, add *es* to form the plural.

SINGULAR	artist	symbol	maze	sardine
PLURAL	artist**s**	symbol**s**	maze**s**	sardine**s**
SINGULAR	loss	chur**ch**	dish	fox
PLURAL	loss**es**	church**es**	dish**es**	fox**es**

Nouns Ending in *y*   Add *s* to form the plural of a noun ending in a vowel and *y*.

SINGULAR	day	display	journey	toy
PLURAL	days	displays	journeys	toys

Change the *y* to *i* and add *es* to a noun ending in a consonant and *y*.

SINGULAR	memory	trophy	lady	society
PLURAL	memories	trophies	ladies	societies

EXERCISE *Forming Plurals*

Write the plural of each of the following nouns.

1. theme	**6.** reflex	**11.** ability	**16.** galaxy
2. valley	**7.** theory	**12.** stitch	**17.** effect
3. crash	**8.** tomboy	**13.** holiday	**18.** trolley
4. comedy	**9.** waltz	**14.** apology	**19.** issue
5. virus	**10.** image	**15.** trapeze	**20.** vacancy

Nouns Ending in *o*   Add *s* to form the plural of a noun ending in a vowel and *o*.

SINGULAR	ratio	studio	rodeo	igloo
PLURAL	ratios	studios	rodeos	igloos

The plurals of nouns ending in a consonant and *o* do not follow a regular pattern.

SINGULAR	echo	veto	silo	ego
PLURAL	echoes	vetoes	silos	egos

Add *s* to form the plural of a musical term ending in *o*.

SINGULAR	alto	duo	piano	cello
PLURAL	altos	duos	pianos	cellos

When you are not sure about how to form a plural, consult a dictionary. If the dictionary does not give a plural form, the plural usually ends in *s*. *(See pages 504–511 for more information about using a dictionary.)*

Nouns Ending in *f* or *fe* To form the plural of some nouns ending in *f* or *fe,* simply add *s.*

SINGULAR	belief	gulf	chef	**fife**
PLURAL	belie**fs**	gul**fs**	che**fs**	fi**fes**

For other nouns ending in *f* or *fe,* change the *f* to *v* and add *es.*

SINGULAR	hal**f**	shel**f**	lea**f**	kni**fe**
PLURAL	hal**ves**	shel**ves**	lea**ves**	kni**ves**

Because there is no sure way to tell which method you should use, consult a dictionary to check the plural of these words.

EXERCISE 5 *Forming Plurals*

Write the plural of each noun, checking a dictionary.

1. radio   **6.** soprano   **11.** roof   **16.** elf
2. stereo   **7.** hero   **12.** chief   **17.** calf
3. shampoo   **8.** potato   **13.** gulf   **18.** self
4. solo   **9.** taco   **14.** giraffe   **19.** thief
5. trio   **10.** yo-yo   **15.** tariff   **20.** wife

Other Plural Forms Following is a list of examples of nouns that do not form the plural by adding *s* or *es.*

Irregular Plurals		
tooth, teeth	child, children	ox, oxen
foot, feet	woman, women	mouse, mice
goose, geese	man, men	die, dice

Same Form for Singular and Plural		
Chinese	sheep	scissors
Japanese	moose	headquarters
Swiss	salmon	series
Sioux	species	politics

Compound Nouns Most compound nouns are made plural in the same way as other nouns: *men/snowmen, ways/hallways,* and *boxes/music boxes.* In some compound nouns, however, the main word appears in the first part of the compound. In such cases the first part is made plural.

SINGULAR	son-in-law	attorney-at-law	passerby
PLURAL	sons-in-law	attorneys-at-law	passersby

EXERCISE *Forming Plurals*

Write the plural of each of the following words.

1. bedroom	**6.** mouse	**11.** deer	**16.** pen pal
2. eyeglass	**7.** louse	**12.** salmon	**17.** trout
3. runner-up	**8.** foot	**13.** Swiss	**18.** woman
4. fire fighter	**9.** tooth	**14.** pliers	**19.** Chinese
5. mother-in-law	**10.** child	**15.** corps	**20.** passerby

Prefixes and Suffixes

A *prefix* is one or more syllables placed in front of a root to form a new word. When you add a prefix to a root, do not change the spelling of the root.

in + accurate = inaccurate   re + set = reset
pre + arrange = prearrange   over + load = overload
dis + satisfy = dissatisfy   mis + spell = misspell
re + evaluate = reevaluate   over + rate = overrate
ir + regular = irregular   il + legal = illegal

A *suffix* is one or more syllables placed after a root to change its part of speech and possibly its meaning as well. The suffixes *-ness* and *-ly* are simply added to the root.

open + ness = openness   cruel + ly = cruelly
plain + ness = plainness   real + ly = really

When you add other suffixes, you sometimes change the spelling of the root. Following are some rules for adding suffixes.

Words Ending in e Drop the final *e* before a suffix that begins with a vowel.

drive + ing = driving   isolate + ion = isolation
sane + ity = sanity   tone + al = tonal

Keep the final *e* before a suffix that begins with a consonant.

care + ful = careful   price + less = priceless
like + ness = likeness   state + ment = statement

Some common exceptions to the spelling rules for adding suffixes to words ending in *e* include the words *courageous, pronounceable, argument,* and *truly.*

EXERCISE *Adding Suffixes*

Write each word, adding the suffix shown. Remember to make any necessary spelling changes.

I. lone + some   **6.** slide + ing   **11.** love + ly
2. move + ment   **7.** create + ed   **12.** close + est
3. like + ness   **8.** sure + ly   **13.** peace + ful
4. note + able   **9.** one + ness   **14.** stare + ing
5. true + est   **10.** wire + ed   **15.** hope + ful

Words Ending in y To add a suffix to most words ending in a vowel and *y,* keep the *y.*

enjoy + able = enjoyable   stay + ing = staying
convey + ed = conveyed   joy + ful = joyful

To add a suffix to most words ending in a consonant and *y,* change the *y* to *i* before adding the suffix.

easy + ly = easily   happy + ness = happiness
rely + ance = reliance   worry + ed = worried

Some exceptions to the spelling rules for adding suffixes to words ending in *y* include the following words.

ONE-SYLLABLE WORDS   daily, shyness
SUFFIXES BEGINNING WITH *i*   studying, denying

EXERCISE *Adding Suffixes*

Write each word, adding the suffix shown. Remember to make any necessary spelling changes.

1. fly + ing	**6.** busy + ness	**11.** shy + est
2. try + ed	**7.** worry + ed	**12.** pay + ing
3. deny + al	**8.** play + ful	**13.** dry + ly
4. dense + ity	**9.** ply + able	**14.** rely + ed
5. glory + ous	**10.** defy + ant	**15.** boy + ish

Doubling the Final Consonant   Sometimes the final consonant in a word is doubled before a suffix is added. This happens when the suffix begins with a vowel and the word satisfies both of the following conditions.

- The word has only one syllable or is stressed on the final syllable.
- The word ends in one consonant preceded by one vowel.

ONE-SYLLABLE WORD	stop + ing sto**pp**ing	grin + ed gri**nn**ed	red + est re**dd**est
FINAL SYLLABLE STRESSED	refer + al refe**rr**al	begin + er begi**nn**er	prefer + ing prefe**rr**ing

EXERCISE *Adding Suffixes*

Write each word, adding the suffix shown. Remember to make any necessary spelling changes.

1. hot + est	**6.** flip + ant
2. sad + en	**7.** regret + ed
3. drop + ed	**8.** spoil + age
4. trim + ing	**9.** clear + ing
5. swim + ing	**10.** smart + est

15 Review

Applying Spelling Rules Write the letter of the misspelled word in each group. Then write the word, spelling it correctly.

1. (A) niece (B) ratios (C) happyness
2. (A) intercede (B) foriegn (C) innumerable
3. (A) embarass (B) seize (C) engagement
4. (A) offered (B) criticize (C) atheletics
5. (A) conceit (B) branches (C) niether
6. (A) accidentally (B) thinness (C) payed
7. (A) peaceful (B) immediatly (C) misstep
8. (A) twentieth (B) rideing (C) argument
9. (A) journies (B) rained (C) proceed
10. (A) trapped (B) knives (C) permited
11. (A) mispell (B) relieve (C) patios
12. (A) immobile (B) occuring (C) betrayal
13. (A) forcible (B) spying (C) mathmatics
14. (A) surprised (B) reign (C) ridiculeous
15. (A) realy (B) stepping (C) valleys
16. (A) passersby (B) leafs (C) holidays
17. (A) caring (B) decieve (C) studying
18. (A) receipt (B) beliefs (C) easyly
19. (A) echos (B) misguided (C) geese
20. (A) joyful (B) seperate (C) interfere
21. (A) biggest (B) delaying (C) liesure
22. (A) generaly (B) boxes (C) roofs
23. (A) pettiness (B) disatisfied (C) writer
24. (A) anonymous (B) likeness (C) dayly
25. (A) editors-in-chief (B) grammer (C) eighth
26. (A) bushes (B) sadness (C) nieghbor
27. (A) pianoes (B) worrying (C) succeed
28. (A) waltzes (B) babys (C) diaries
29. (A) inaccurate (B) secede (C) hopful
30. (A) insincere (B) peachs (C) deceit

16 Reference Skills

Libraries contain reference materials that include both printed matter, such as books and magazines, and nonprint materials, such as tapes and films. This chapter reviews these different kinds of reference resources, including dictionaries. You will find all of the resources helpful in preparing to write or to make a formal speech. They are particularly useful for writing reports. *(See pages 358–399 for more information about reports.)*

Creating a Writer's Warehouse Warehouses stock things such as television sets, tires, and clothes. When those things are needed in stores, they can be retrieved quickly from a warehouse. You can use this same storage principle to collect interesting pieces of information you find in reference materials. In a section of your journal, write any information you find that is interesting to you. The information you store in this way could range from facts about baseball to data about the amount of rainfall in your area. Then, when you need a subject to write about, look in your "writer's warehouse" and use one or more of your stored items.

The Library

A library is the best place to go when you are gathering information for a report. In the library you will find a section for fiction, one for nonfiction, one for reference books, and one for periodicals.

Finding Fiction

In the fiction section, books are shelved alphabetically by the author's last name according to the following rules.

- Two-part names are alphabetized by the first part of the name—for example, **La**Rosa, **Mac**Donald, **O**'Connor
- Names beginning with *Mc* and *St.* are alphabetized as if they began with *Mac* and *Saint.*
- Books by authors with the same last name are alphabetized by the authors' first names.
- Books by the same author are alphabetized by title, not including *a, an,* or *the* at the beginning of the titles.

Finding Nonfiction

Most libraries use the Dewey decimal classification system to arrange nonfiction books. Each book has a number that identifies its subject. Books are then shelved in numerical order.

Dewey Decimal Classification	
000–099	General Works (reference books)
100–199	Philosophy
200–299	Religion
300–399	Social Science (law, education, economics)
400–499	Language
500–599	Science (mathematics, biology, chemistry)
600–699	Technology (medicine, inventions)
700–799	Fine Arts (painting, music, theater)
800–899	Literature
900–999	History (biography, geography, travel)

Because there are many books about each general subject, the Dewey decimal system divides each of its ten main subjects into smaller categories.

800–899 Literature			
800–809	General	850–859	Italian
810–819	American	860–869	Spanish
820–829	English	870–879	Latin
830–839	German	880–889	Greek
840–849	French	890–899	Other

Because ten numbers are not enough to cover the many books about American literature, one or more decimal numbers may also be used.

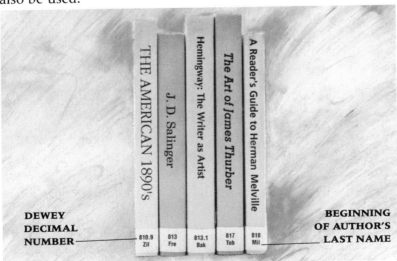

DEWEY
DECIMAL
NUMBER

BEGINNING
OF AUTHOR'S
LAST NAME

Biographies and Autobiographies Biographies and autobiographies are usually in a separate section and are shelved in alphabetical order by the subject's last name rather than by the author's last name. Each book is labeled *B* for *biography* or *92* (a shortened form of *920*), followed by the first letters of the subject's last name. A biography of George Washington, for instance, is labeled on the spine of the book in one of the following ways.

BIOGRAPHY	B	92
BEGINNING OF SUBJECT'S LAST NAME	WAS	WAS

EXERCISE *The Dewey Decimal System*

Using the chart on page 495, write the range of numbers and the general category for each of the following titles.

1. *The Joy of Music*
2. *All About Language*
3. *Basic Biology*
4. *The Making of a Surgeon*
5. *You and the Law*

6. *Chemistry Today*
7. *Trial by Jury*
8. *Shakespeare's Plays*
9. *To a Young Dancer*
10. *The European Middle Ages*

The Card Catalog

The *card catalog* is a cabinet of small file drawers that contain cards for all books, record albums, tapes, and filmstrips in the library. Each drawer is labeled to show what part of the alphabet it contains. The card catalog contains three cards for every book. You may find a book by looking under (1) the author's last name, (2) the title, or (3) the subject of the book.

Author Cards   To find books by a particular author, look for the author's last name in the card catalog. To find books by Melvin Berger, for example, find *Berger* in the drawer marked *B*. Following is the author card for the book *Computers in Your Life* by Melvin Berger.

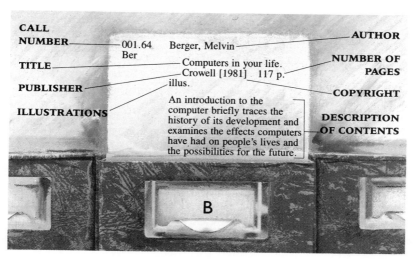

CALL NUMBER — 001.64 Ber

AUTHOR — Berger, Melvin

TITLE — Computers in your life.

PUBLISHER — Crowell [1981]   117 p.   illus.

NUMBER OF PAGES

COPYRIGHT

ILLUSTRATIONS

An introduction to the computer briefly traces the history of its development and examines the effects computers have had on people's lives and the possibilities for the future.

DESCRIPTION OF CONTENTS

B

Title Cards When you know the title but not the author, you can find out if the library has the book by looking up the title card. Title cards are alphabetized by the first word in the title (except *a, an,* and *the*).

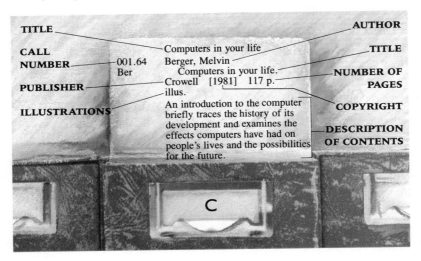

Subject Cards When you gather information, you may use subject cards. If you look up *computers* in the drawer that holds the *C*'s, for example, you will find cards for all the books about computers that the library has.

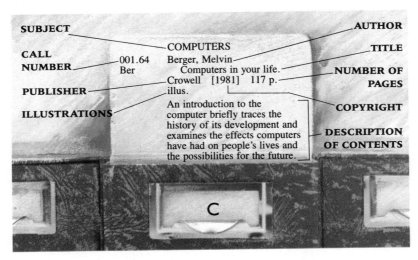

Notice that the author, title, and subject cards for *Computers in Your Life* all provide the same information. Any one of these cards can tell you how to find the book on the library shelves.

Strategies for Finding Books

1. Look for the book you want by finding the appropriate card.
2. Read the card to determine if the book is likely to contain the information you need. Check the copyright date to see how current the information is.
3. On a slip of paper, copy the call number, the title, and the name of the author for each book you want to find.
4. Use the call number, located on the book's spine, to find each book. The first line of the call number tells which section of the library to look in. Then find each book on a library shelf by looking for its call number.

F or FIC	fiction section
B or 92	biography section
Dewey number	nonfiction section

Cross-Reference Cards   A card catalog also contains *See* and *See also* cards. A *See* card tells you that the subject is listed under a different heading. A *See also* card lists other subjects you could look up for more information on your topic.

CARS

see

AUTOMOBILES

AUTOMOBILES

see also

SPORTS CARS
TRUCKS

Your library may also contain computer terminals, which help you or the librarian locate books by searching a database that is arranged like a card catalog. Instead of looking through file drawers, you type the subject, author, or title on a computer keyboard. The terminal then shows you where in the library the material you want is located. The computer may even show you other nearby libraries that have the material.

EXERCISE *Locating Catalog Cards*

Identify the type of card—author, title, or subject—you would use to find each item. Then write the first three letters that you would look under to find each item.

EXAMPLE   S. E. Hinton
ANSWER   Author—Hin

1. popular music
2. Scott O'Dell
3. *A Single Light*
4. moons of Jupiter
5. John Le Carré
6. *A Tree Grows in Brooklyn*
7. forms of transportation
8. *The Double Planet*
9. nineteenth-century inventions
10. *The Milky Way*

Reference Materials

Most libraries have a separate area called a *reference room.* This room contains encyclopedias, dictionaries, atlases, almanacs, and reference books on specific subjects. The following section discusses the kinds of reference works available in most libraries.

Encyclopedias Because encyclopedias provide basic information on a variety of subjects, you can start with an encyclopedia when you are gathering information for a report. Subjects are arranged in alphabetical order, and letters on the spine of each volume show what part of the alphabet that volume covers. A volume labeled *Nel-O,* for example, would contain information on the North Pole, the octopus, and the Olympic Games.

Within each volume, *guide words* at the top of each page tell you at a glance which entries are on that page.

Many encyclopedias provide an index in a separate volume or at the end of the last volume. The index tells you if a subject is discussed under more than one heading. Cross-references to other entries may also be provided at the end of an article. After the article on *sky,* for example, one encyclopedia says, *"See also:* Astronomy, Horizon, and Light."

Specialized Encyclopedias   Hundreds of specialized encyclopedias are available on every subject, from auto racing to weaving. Because they concentrate on a specific subject, specialized encyclopedias provide more information than general encyclopedias do. Some examples of specialized encyclopedias are the *Encyclopedia of World Art* and *The Baseball Encyclopedia.*

Biographical References   To find information about famous people, past and present, use biographical references. Some biographical references contain only a paragraph or a list of facts about each person in the volume, while others contain long articles. All biographical references, however, include important statistics—such as date of birth, education, and occupation—and an explanation of why the person is famous. *Who's Who,* published every year, and *Who's Who in America,* published every other year, are among the most widely used biographical references. Other helpful biographical references are *Current Biography, Dictionary of American Biography, Dictionary of National Biography, Webster's Biographical Dictionary,* and *American Men and Women of Science.*

References about Literature   Have you ever wondered where a quotation came from and who said it? A book of quotations can provide the answers. It can also give you the complete quotation and other quotations on the same subject. Books of quotations are arranged either by subject or by author. An index of first lines or key words leads you to the correct page. Two well-known books of quotations are *Bartlett's Familiar Quotations* and *The Oxford Dictionary of Quotations.*

Another kind of literary reference is the handbook, also called a companion. Some handbooks give plot summaries or describe characters. Others explain literary terms, such as *imagery* or *plot*, or give information about authors. Two helpful handbooks are *The Oxford Companion to American Literature* and *The Reader's Encyclopedia*.

Atlases An atlas, or book of maps, provides information about cities, countries, continents, mountains, lakes, and other geographical features. Some atlases also give information about population, climate, natural resources, industries, and transportation networks. Historical atlases show you maps of the world during different times in history. Commonly used atlases include the *Rand McNally International World Atlas* and the *Times Concise Atlas of the World*. An historical atlas is *Rand McNally Atlas of World History*.

Almanacs Almanacs contain up-to-date facts and statistics about subjects such as population, weather, government, business, and sports. In an almanac you can find out which countries have had earthquakes, what movies made the most money, and who won Most Valuable Player awards in different sports. Almanacs also contain historical facts and geographic information. Most almanacs are published yearly. *Information Please Almanac* and *World Almanac and Book of Facts* are two popular almanacs.

Specialized Dictionaries A library has many specialized dictionaries that provide information about specific fields—such as medicine, music, and computer science. Two examples of specialized dictionaries are the *Harvard Dictionary of Music* and the *Concise Dictionary of American History*.

Another kind of specialized dictionary lists synonyms. A dictionary of synonyms, also known as a *thesaurus*, can help you make exact word choices. *Roget's Thesaurus in Dictionary Form* and other synonym and antonym dictionaries are found in most libraries.

EXERCISE *Using Specialized References*

Number your paper 1 to 10. Then list one kind of reference book other than a general encyclopedia that would contain information about each of the following subjects.

1. famous Americans
2. records in sports
3. countries in Asia
4. Spanish phrases
5. synonyms for *run*

6. the source of a quotation
7. the location of the Alps
8. the life of Thomas Edison
9. dates of past hurricanes
10. twentieth-century art

The Vertical File Pamphlets, catalogs, and newspaper clippings on a variety of subjects are also available in most libraries. These materials are stored in a filing cabinet called the *vertical file*. Items are kept in folders and arranged alphabetically by subject on a variety of subjects.

Readers' Guide to Periodical Literature Magazines and journals are among the best sources of current information. An index called the *Readers' Guide to Periodical Literature* can help you find magazine and journal articles on almost any subject. The complete *Readers' Guide*—which indexes articles, stories, and poems published in more than 175 magazines—is issued in paperback form twice a month during most months. A quarterly issue comes out every three months, and a hardbound volume comes out at the end of each year. Many schools subscribe to the abridged *Readers' Guide,* which indexes about 60 magazines.

Articles indexed in the *Readers' Guide* are listed alphabetically by subject and by author. Each entry, such as the one below, provides all the information you need to locate the articles you want.

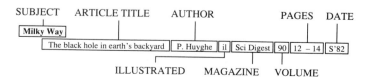

To save space, abbreviations are used. For example, in the entry on the previous page, the abbreviation *S* stands for *September*. A list of abbreviations is provided at the front of every volume of the *Readers' Guide*.

EXERCISE *Locating Articles in the* Readers' Guide *to Periodical Literature*

Using the *Readers' Guide to Periodical Literature,* list two recent magazine articles on four of the following subjects. List the title of the article, the name of the magazine in which each article can be found, the date of publication, and the pages on which the article may be found.

I. astronomy
2. gymnastics
3. journalism
4. law
5. youth

6. pollution
7. music
8. nuclear power
9. marine biology
10. medical costs

The Dictionary

Most people use the dictionary more often than they use any other reference book. Whether you refer to a huge unabridged dictionary or a shortened student dictionary, you will find a wealth of information. This information includes pronunciations, definitions, and usages of words. In this section you will review the kinds of information that are available in a dictionary and learn how to use this resource efficiently to find that information.

Word Location

Dictionaries are organized to help you locate quickly the information you need.

Guide Words   A pair of guide words, printed at the top of each page, identifies the first and last words defined on that page. The guide words *attain/auction*, for example, show you that *attorney* and *auburn* are among the words that appear on that page.

Alphabetical Order   From beginning to end, the dictionary is a single, alphabetical list. Words beginning with the same letters are alphabetized by the first subsequent letter that is different: *face*, for example, comes before *facet*. Compound words, abbreviations, prefixes, suffixes, and proper nouns also appear in alphabetical order.

SINGLE WORD	acrobatics
HYPHENATED COMPOUND	across-the-board
TWO-WORD COMPOUND	acute angle
PREFIX	ad-
ABBREVIATION	AFL (American Federation of Labor)
PROPER NOUN	Alaska Standard Time
SUFFIX	-ally

Note: Compound words are alphabetized as if there were no space or hyphen between each part. Abbreviations are alphabetized letter by letter, not by the words they stand for.

EXERCISE   5   *Alphabetizing Words*

Make three columns on your paper and number the columns *1, 2,* and *3.* Then list each group of words to show how they would be alphabetized in a dictionary.

I. glaze, glow, glimpse, glimmer, glossy, glacier, glance, glisten, glamour, gloomy
2. hiccup, hi-fi, hike, hgt., hickory, high-pitched, hilarious, hibernate, hide, high jump
3. beehive, bee tree, bee, beeline, beetle-browed, bd., beech, beetle, beet, bazaar

Information in an Entry

All of the information given for a word is called an *entry*. Each entry usually provides the spelling, pronunciation, parts of speech, definitions, and origins of the word.

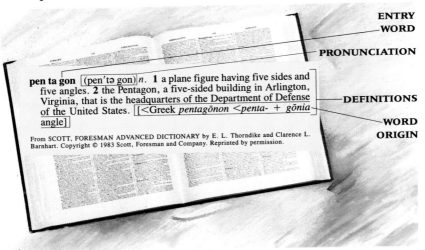

pen ta gon (pen′tə gon) *n.* **1** a plane figure having five sides and five angles. **2** the Pentagon, a five-sided building in Arlington, Virginia, that is the headquarters of the Department of Defense of the United States. [<Greek *pentagōnon* <*penta-* + *gōnia* angle]

From SCOTT, FORESMAN ADVANCED DICTIONARY by E. L. Thorndike and Clarence L. Barnhart. Copyright © 1983 Scott, Foresman and Company. Reprinted by permission.

ENTRY WORD
PRONUNCIATION
DEFINITIONS
WORD ORIGIN

Entry Word The entry word in heavy type tells you (1) how to spell a word, (2) whether to capitalize it, and (3) where to divide it at the end of a line.

First, in addition to showing the correct spelling of a word, an entry also shows any alternative spellings. The more common spelling, called the *preferred spelling,* is usually listed first.

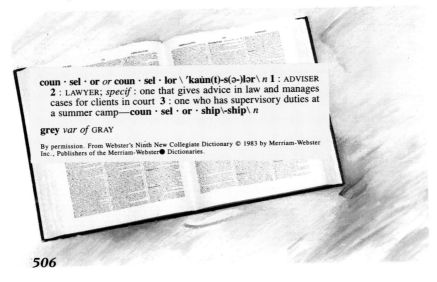

coun · sel · or *or* **coun · sel · lor** \ ′kaun(t)-s(ə-)lər\ *n* **1** : ADVISER **2** : LAWYER; *specif* : one that gives advice in law and manages cases for clients in court **3** : one who has supervisory duties at a summer camp—**coun · sel · or · ship**\-ship\ *n*

grey *var of* GRAY

By permission. From Webster's Ninth New Collegiate Dictionary © 1983 by Merriam-Webster Inc., Publishers of the Merriam-Webster● Dictionaries.

Plural nouns, comparatives and superlatives of adjectives, and principal parts of verbs are also given if their spellings are irregular.

PRINCIPAL PARTS

chime (chīm), *n.,* [*v.,* **chimed, chim ing.**] —*n.* **1** set of bells tuned to a musical scale and played by hammers or simple machinery. **2** the musical sound made by a set of tuned bells. —*v.i.* **1** ring out musically: *The bells chimed at midnight.* **2** agree; be in harmony.

NOUN PLURAL

chi na ber ry (chī′nə ber′ē), [*n., pl.*-**ries.**] **1** tree native to Asia and widely cultivated in warm regions for its purplish flowers and yellow, berrylike fruits.

PRINICIPAL PARTS

choose (chüz); [*v.,* **chose, cho sen, choos ing.**] —*v.t.* **1** pick out; select from a number. **2** prefer and decide; think fit. —*v.i.* make a choice. [Old English *cēosan*]

COMPARATIVE AND SUPERLATIVE

chop py (chop′ē), *adj.,* [**-pi er, -pi est.**] **1** making quick, sharp movements; jerky. **2** moving in short, irregular, broken waves: *The sea is choppy today.*

From SCOTT, FORESMAN ADVANCED DICTIONARY by E. L. Thorndike and Clarence L. Barnhart. Copyright © 1983 Scott, Foresman and Company. Reprinted by permission.

Second, the entry word is printed with a capital letter if it is capitalized. If it is capitalized only in certain uses, it will appear with a capital letter near the appropriate definition.

Milky Way, 1 a broad band of faint light that stretches across the sky at night. It is made up of countless stars too far away to be seen separately without a telescope. **2** the galaxy in which these countless stars are found; Galaxy. The sun, earth, and the other planets around the sun are part of the Milky Way.

mar a thon (mar′ə thon), *n.* **1** a footrace of 26 miles, 385 yards (42.2 kilometers). **2** any race over a long distance. **3** any activity that calls for endurance. **4** Marathon, plain in Greece about 25 miles (40 kilometers) northeast of Athens. After the Athenians defeated the Persians there in 490 B.C., a runner ran all the way to Athens with the news of the victory.

From SCOTT, FORESMAN ADVANCED DICTIONARY by E. L. Thorndike and Clarence L. Barnhart. Copyright © 1983 Scott, Foresman and Company. Reprinted by permission.

Third, when writing, you sometimes need to divide a word at the end of a line. Because a word may be divided only between syllables, use a dictionary to check where each syllable ends. In addition, follow the rules for dividing words on page 873.

sus • pense • ful   char • ac • ter   per • fec • tion

EXERCISE *Using a Dictionary for Editing*

Copy the following paragraph, using a dictionary to help you correct the errors in spelling and capitalization. Then underline each correction.

Starlit Skies

At night thosands of stars appear accross the sky. Over the centurys, stargazers have observed that some stars form particular shapes. These star clusters are called constellations. Two of the most familar are ursa major, "great bear," and ursa minor, "little bear." Within these constellations are the big dipper, the little dipper, and the bright north star. Some constellations can be observed only durring certain seasons. Leo the Lion appears in Spring. During the winter, orion the Hunter is visable. At present more than 80 constellations have been identifyed in the night sky.

Pronunciation   To learn how to pronounce a word, look up the phonetic spelling of the word in the dictionary. The phonetic spelling directly follows the entry word, as in these examples.

clang (klang)   **knack** (nak)

A *pronunciation key* at the front of the dictionary shows what sound each phonetic symbol stands for. Most dictionaries also place a partial key on every other page.

PARTIAL PRONUNCIATION KEY

a hat	**i** it	**oi** oil	**ch** child		**a** in about
ā age	**ī** ice	**ou** out	**ng** long		**e** in taken
ä far	**o** hot	**u** cup	**sh** she	**ə** =	**i** in pencil
e let	**ō** open	**ù** put	**th** thin		**o** in lemon
ē equal	**ô** order	**ü** rule	**ŦH** then		**u** in circus
ėr term			**zh** measure	**<** = derived from	

From SCOTT, FORESMAN ADVANCED DICTIONARY by E. L. Thorndike and Clarence L. Barnhart. Copyright 1983, 1979, 1974 by Scott, Foresman & Company. Reprinted by permission.

To learn to pronounce a word, compare the phonetic spelling to the symbols in the key. For example, the key shows that *zh* stands for the *s* sound in *measure*. The *s* in the following words is also pronounced *zh*.

pleas•ure (plezh′ ər)   **treas•ure** (trezh′ ər)

In the key on the previous page, marks over vowels indicate different vowel sounds. For example, the different sounds of *o* are represented in the following ways.

hot   ōpen   ôrder

The marks over *open* and *order* are called *diacritical marks*. To find out how a vowel with a diacritical mark is pronounced, you refer to the pronunciation key.

odd (od)   [*o* as in *hot*]
ode (ōd)   [*o* as in *open*]
off (ôf)   [*o* as in *order*]

In some words the vowels *a, e, i, o,* and *u* are pronounced *uh*, as in the second syllables of *pleasure* and *treasure*, above. Most dictionaries use a *schwa* (ə) to represent this sound if it comes in an unaccented syllable.

a•bout (ə bout′)   **lem•on** (lem′ ən)   **li•bel** (lī′ bəl)

In many words one syllable receives more emphasis than the other syllables in the word. An *accent mark* indicates a syllable that should be stressed.

lob•ster (lob′ stər)   **de•sign** (di zīn′)

In *lobster*, the first syllable receives emphasis. In *design*, the second syllable should receive emphasis.

If two syllables should be stressed, the syllable receiving more stress is marked with a *primary accent* (′). The less emphasized syllable is marked with a *secondary accent* (′). In the following example, the third syllable receives the most stress in pronunciation.

PRIMARY ACCENT ⟶

en•er•get•ic (en′ ər jet′ ik)

SECONDARY ACCENT ⟶

EXERCISE ⟨7⟩ *Marking Pronunciation*

Number your paper. Then, using a dictionary, write the phonetic spelling of each word.

1. mocha
2. discus
3. nova
4. hedge
5. kiwi
6. kayak
7. hydrophobia
8. equestrian
9. jerboa
10. catamaran

Definitions A dictionary is a handy reference for finding the meanings of a word. At the end of some entries, the dictionary will also list synonyms, or words that have similar definitions.

The following entry for *train* shows the kind of information provided to make each meaning clear.

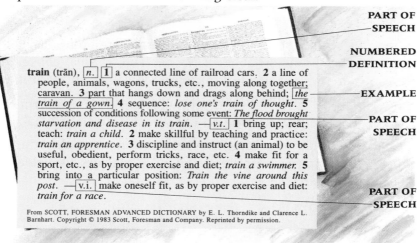

train (trān), *n.* **1** a connected line of railroad cars. **2** a line of people, animals, wagons, trucks, etc., moving along together; caravan. **3** part that hangs down and drags along behind; *the train of a gown.* **4** sequence: *lose one's train of thought.* **5** succession of conditions following some event: *The flood brought starvation and disease in its train.* —*v.t.* **1** bring up; rear; teach: *train a child.* **2** make skillful by teaching and practice: *train an apprentice.* **3** discipline and instruct (an animal) to be useful, obedient, perform tricks, race, etc. **4** make fit for a sport, etc., as by proper exercise and diet; *train a swimmer.* **5** bring into a particular position: *Train the vine around this post.* —*v.i.* make oneself fit, as by proper exercise and diet: *train for a race.*

PART OF SPEECH
NUMBERED DEFINITION
EXAMPLE
PART OF SPEECH
PART OF SPEECH

From SCOTT, FORESMAN ADVANCED DICTIONARY by E. L. Thorndike and Clarence L. Barnhart. Copyright © 1983 Scott, Foresman and Company. Reprinted by permission.

In the entry for *train*, the abbreviations *n.* and *v.* show that *train* can be used as a noun or a verb. Dictionaries use the following abbreviations for the eight parts of speech.

n. noun	*pron.* pronoun	*prep.* preposition
v. verb	*adj.* adjective	*conj.* conjunction
	adv. adverb	*interj.* interjection

When you look up a word, consider which meaning and part of speech apply in the context of the particular sentence.

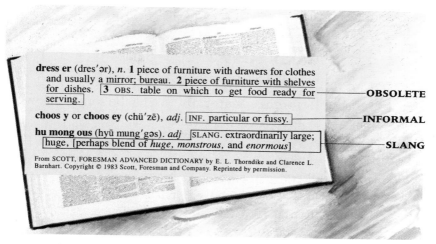

dress er (dres′ər), *n.* **1** piece of furniture with drawers for clothes and usually a mirror; bureau. **2** piece of furniture with shelves for dishes. **3** OBS. table on which to get food ready for serving. — **OBSOLETE**

choos y or **choos ey** (chü′zē), *adj.* INF. particular or fussy. — **INFORMAL**

hu mong ous (hyū mung′gəs). *adj* SLANG. extraordinarily large; huge, [perhaps blend of *huge, monstrous,* and *enormous*] — **SLANG**

From SCOTT, FORESMAN ADVANCED DICTIONARY by E. L. Thorndike and Clarence L. Barnhart. Copyright © 1983 Scott, Foresman and Company. Reprinted by permission.

A dictionary also indicates the present usage of words by including labels such as *obsolete, informal, colloquial,* and *slang.* The abbreviation *obs.* means that the third definition of *dresser* is obsolete, or no longer in use. *Informal, colloquial,* and *slang* indicate words that are used only in informal situations.

EXERCISE 8 *Choosing the Appropriate Definition*

Using the dictionary entry for *train* on the previous page, write the number of the appropriate definition of *train*.

1. Julie had trained her dog Lilypad to jump two feet.
2. I lost my train of thought during my speech!
3. Peter trained for two years to be an electrician.
4. Sara trained the horse's mane to curl.
5. The king tripped over the train of the queen's gown.

EXERCISE 9 *Finding the Meaning of a Word*

Using a dictionary, write the definition that best fits the use of the underlined word in each sentence.

1. The plane gathered speed as it raced down the runway.
2. He gathered from the evidence that they were guilty.
3. I want to review my notes before the final exam.
4. The new movie received a disappointing review.
5. The sign on the fence warned us not to poach.

A **Choosing Reference Materials** Write the source below you would use to answer each question.

card catalog	book of quotations
general encyclopedia	index to poetry
specialized encyclopedia	atlas
specialized dictionary	almanac
biographical reference	*Readers' Guide*

1. What are the titles of three books about horses?
2. Explain the meaning of the symbol of the Olympic Games.
3. What are four synonyms for *laugh?*
4. What is Louis Fabian Bachrach, Jr., famous for?
5. What is a Tasmanian wolf?
6. Who wrote the poem "Miniver Cheevy"?
7. Why was Vladimir Horowitz famous?
8. What are the names of five towns in Newfoundland?
9. How does calligraphy differ from handwriting?
10. Who wrote the line "The world is too much with us"?
11. What is the history of candles?
12. What magazine articles were written about recreational vehicles last year?
13. What is the distance in miles between Los Angeles and Tokyo?
14. Who wrote the line "I ought; therefore I can"?
15. What is Art Buchwald famous for?
16. At what longitude and latitude is Dallas located?
17. What is the meaning of *closure* in math?
18. Why was Jack Dempsey famous?
19. What is the most recently published article on helicopters?
20. What was the lowest temperature ever recorded in Michigan?

B **Finding Information** Using the reference section of your library, find the answers to the first ten questions in Part A.

C **Using the Dictionary** Use the dictionary entries to answer each question.

can ta loupe or **can ta loup** (kan′tl ōp), *n.* kind of muskmelon with a hard, rough rind and sweet, juicy, orange flesh. [<French *cantaloup* < Italian *Cantalupo* papal estate near Rome where first cultivated]

can tan ker ous (kan tang′kər əs), *adj.* hard to get along with because of a nature that is ready to make trouble and oppose anything suggested; ill-natured; quarrelsome. [Middle English *contecker* contentious person < *conteck* strife, quarreling < Anglo-French] —**can tan′ker ous ly,** *adv.*

can ter (kan′tər), *v.t., v.i.* gallop gently. –*n.* a gentle gallop. [short for *Canterbury (gallop)*]

can to (kan′tō), *n., pl.* **-tos.** one of the main divisions of a long poem. [<Italian <Latin *cantus* song]

cap., **1** capacity. **2** capital. **3** capitalize. **4** *pl.* caps. capital letter.

cap il lar y (kap′ə ler′ē), *n., pl.* **-lar ies,** *adj.* —*n.* a blood vessel with a very slender, hairlike opening. Capillaries join the end of an artery to the beginning of a vein. —*adj.* **1** of or in the capillaries. **2** like a hair; very slender [<Latin *capillaris* of hair, hairlike < *capillus* hair]

Cap ri corn (kap′rə kôrn), *n.* **1** tropic of Capricorn. **2** a southern constellation seen by ancient astronomers as having the rough outline of a goat. **3** the 10th sign of the zodiac. [<Latin *capricornus* < *caper* goat + *cornu* horn]

cap ti vate (kap′tə vāt), *v.t.,* **-vat ed, -vat ing.** hold captive by beauty, talent, or interest; charm; fascinate: *The children were captivated by the story.*

1. Which entry word has two accepted spellings?
2. Which entry word should be capitalized?
3. Which entry words have four syllables?
4. Show where *canter* should be divided if it comes at the end of a line.
5. Which syllable in *capillary* should be stressed most? Which syllable should be stressed slightly?
6. What does *cantankerous* mean?
7. How many meanings are given for *Capricorn?*
8. Which entry contains an example sentence?
9. Which entry word can be used as a noun or a verb?
10. Which entry word can be a noun or an adjective?
11. How do you spell the plural of *canto?*
12. How do you spell the plural of *capillary?*
13. How do you spell the principal parts of *captivate?*
14. What part of speech is *cantankerously?*
15. Which entry is an abbreviation?

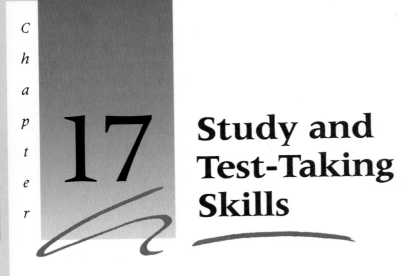

17 Study and Test-Taking Skills

Achieving a high score on a test is much like playing a game well. You must know the strategies of the game and must be prepared. If you know strategies for studying effectively and for taking different kinds of tests, you will be better able to perform successfully on important tests.

Study Skills

In this section you will learn about three important study skills: adjusting your reading rate to suit your purpose, using the "SQ3R" technique for reading textbooks, and taking notes to help you remember important information.

Adjusting Reading Rate to Purpose

Your reading rate is the speed at which you read. Depending on your purpose for reading certain material, you may decide to read quickly or slowly. If your purpose is to get a general impression of what the material is about, for example, you may quickly read only parts of a page, letting your eyes skip over other parts. You read this way when you *scan* headlines in a newspaper. If your purpose is to find the main point of a selection, you read more thoroughly, as when you *skim* an article.

When you are reading to learn specific information, on the other hand, you slow your reading rate considerably to allow for *close reading* of facts and details. Following are some suggestions for adjusting your reading rate according to your purpose for reading the material.

Reading Rates	
SCANNING	Read the title, headings, subheadings, picture captions, words and phrases in boldface or italics, and any focus questions. You can quickly determine what the material is about and what questions to keep in mind. Scanning is reading to get a general impression and to prepare for learning about a subject.
SKIMMING	After scanning a chapter, section, or article, quickly read the introduction, the topic sentence and summary sentence of each paragraph, and the conclusion. Skimming is reading quickly to identify the purpose, thesis, main ideas, and supporting ideas of a selection. Skimming is useful for reading supplementary material and for reviewing material previously read.
CLOSE READING	After scanning a selection, read it more slowly, word for word. Close reading is for locating specific information, following the logic of an argument, or comprehending the meaning or significance of information. Most of your assignments for school will require close reading.

Reading a Textbook

In studying a textbook, the techniques of scanning, skimming, and close reading are combined in steps known as the SQ3R study technique. This method helps you to become more thoughtfully involved with your reading and therefore helps you to understand and remember what you read. *S* in *SQ3R* stands for *Survey*, *Q* for *Question*, and *3R* for *Read, Recite,* and *Review.*

The SQ3R Study Strategy

SURVEY	First get a general idea of what the selection is about. Do this by scanning titles, subtitles, and words set off in a different type or color. Also look at maps, tables, charts, and other illustrations. Then read the introduction.
QUESTION	List questions you think you should be able to answer after reading the selection. Also read any study questions in the book.
READ	Now read the selection. As you read, think about your questions and try to answer them. In addition, find the main idea in each section. During or after reading, take notes.
RECITE	Answer each of your questions in your own words by reciting or writing the answers.
REVIEW	Answer the questions again without looking at your notes or at the selection.

EXERCISE *Using the SQ3R Study Strategy*

Apply the SQ3R study strategy as you read a textbook assignment for one of your classes. First, survey the assigned section. Next, write five or more questions that you expect the chapter to answer. Then, read the assignment and take notes on it. Finally, review your answers without looking at your notes.

Taking Notes

Taking notes helps you to identify and remember the essential information in a textbook or lecture. Two methods of taking notes are the modified outline and the summary.

In a *modified outline*, you use words and phrases to record main ideas and important details. This method is especially useful when you are studying for a multiple-choice test because it allows you to see the most important facts.

In a *summary* you use sentences to express important ideas in your own words. A good summary should do more than restate the information. It should express relationships among the ideas and draw conclusions. For this reason summarizing is a good way to prepare for an essay test.

Whether you are taking notes in modified outline form or in summary form, include only the main ideas and important details. In the following passage from a science textbook, the essential information is underlined.

Model: *Recognizing Important Information*

Characteristics of Fish

All fish have certain characteristics in common. For example, all fish have backbones and are cold-blooded. In addition, most fish breathe through gills. The gills, which are found on either side of a fish's head, take up oxygen that is dissolved in water. As a fish opens its mouth, water enters and passes over the gills, where oxygen molecules diffuse from the water into the fish's blood. At the same time, carbon dioxide passes out of its blood into the water.

Other characteristics of most fish include scales, which cover and protect their bodies, and fins, which aid fish in swimming. Certain fins act as steering guides, while others help a fish to keep its balance in the water. Another aid in swimming that most fish have is a streamlined body, one in which the head and tail are smaller and more pointed than the middle part of the fish. This streamlined body shape helps fish to swim by making it easier for them to push water aside as they propel themselves through the water.

The following examples of note-taking are based on the excerpt about fish.

Characteristics of Fish

MODIFIED OUTLINE
1. Have backbones and are cold-blooded (all)
2. Breathe through gills (most)
3. Have scales, fins, and streamlined bodies (most)

Characteristics of Fish

SUMMARY All fish share two common characteristics: back-bones and cold-bloodedness. Most fish breathe through gills and have scales for protection. Most fish also have fins and streamlined bodies for efficient swimming.

No matter which note-taking method you use, the following strategies will help you make your notes clear, useful, and well-organized.

Strategies for Taking Notes

1. Label your notes with the title and page numbers of the chapter or the topic and date of the lecture.
2. Record only the main ideas and important details using key words and phrases.
3. Use the titles, subtitles, and words in special type or color to help you select the most important information.
4. Use your own words; do not copy word for word.
5. Use as few words as possible.

MODIFIED OUTLINE

- Use words and phrases.
- Use main ideas for headings.
- List any supporting details under each heading.

SUMMARY

- Write complete sentences, using your own words.
- Show the relationships between ideas, using only the essential facts given in the textbook or lecture.
- Organize your ideas logically.

EXERCISE 2 *Taking Notes*

Read the selection "The Trouble with Television," by Robert MacNeil, on pages 211–214. Then take notes on this selection in modified outline or summary form. If time permits, compare your notes with those of a classmate.

Taking Classroom Tests

Preparations for taking a test should begin long before the test day. To be well-prepared, keep up with your assignments, take good notes, review material regularly, and ask questions promptly to clarify anything you do not fully understand.

Objective Tests

A common type of classroom test is an *objective test.* This type of test calls for short answers, such as true-false, matching, fill-in-the-blank, or multiple choice. To prepare for an objective test, follow these strategies.

Strategies for Preparing for an Objective Test

1. Study the notes you took in class and those you took on assigned reading.
2. Try to anticipate the questions that will be asked on the test. Focus on topics that were discussed in class or were stressed by the teacher.
3. Review the questions at the end of main sections in your textbook. Write an answer to each question to organize your thoughts and to recall important details.
4. Review any tests or quizzes you took previously that cover the material on which you will be tested.
5. Get together with classmates to quiz each other on the factual details you are expected to know for the test.
6. Before a test make an appointment with your teacher to discuss anything you still do not fully understand.

Essay Tests

An essay test requires an answer in the form of one or more paragraphs. This type of test measures your understanding of important ideas and your ability to organize material and write clearly.

Strategies for Writing an Essay Answer

1. **Plan your time and strategy.** Begin with the items you find easiest to answer and spend more time on the items that are worth the most points. If you have a choice of items, read each one carefully before choosing.

2. **Carefully read and interpret the question or directions.** Look for the following key direction words.

Analyze	Separate into parts and examine each part.
Compare	Point out similarities.
Contrast	Point out differences.
Define	Clarify the meaning.
Discuss	Examine in detail.
Evaluate	Give your opinion.
Explain	Tell how, what, or why.
Summarize	Briefly review the main points.

3. **Watch your time, but follow the steps in the writing process.** Brainstorm for your main ideas, organize them in a simple outline, and write your essay.

   - Write an introductory paragraph that states the main idea of your essay.
   - Write one paragraph for each main point in your outline, beginning each paragraph with a topic sentence.
   - Back up each main point with specific facts, examples, and other supporting details.
   - Write a concluding paragraph that summarizes the main idea of your essay.
   - Proofread your essay, correcting any grammar, usage, punctuation, or spelling errors.

Classroom afflictions

Math anxiety

Physics floundering

Latin convulsions

Wood shop apathy

Chemistry conniptions

Basic stupidity

The Far Side © 1986 Universal Press Syndicate. Reprinted with permission.

EXERCISE *Interpreting Essay Test Questions*

Write the key direction word in each of the following test items. Add a sentence that explains what each question requires you to do.

EXAMPLE   Explain the eruptions of Old Faithful in Yellowstone National Park.

ANSWER   Explain: Tell what Old Faithful is and how and why it erupts.

1. What are some important ways the Andes Mountains of South America contrast with the Appalachian Mountains of North America?
2. In three paragraphs summarize the plot of Jack London's novel *The Call of the Wild.*
3. Explain the process of photosynthesis.
4. Using the book *Tom Sawyer,* compare the personality of Tom Sawyer with that of Huckleberry Finn.
5. In your own words, define *tropical rain forest.*
6. Contrast Amaroq with Jello in *Julie of the Wolves.*
7. Analyze Carl Sandburg's poem "Limited."
8. In a brief essay, evaluate the contributions of Benjamin Franklin to science.
9. John Ruskin wrote, "The most beautiful things in the world are the most useless." Do you agree or disagree? Discuss his idea.
10. Summarize the causes of the rise of civilization in the Nile Valley.
11. Compare and contrast the plant and animal kingdoms in terms of their biological characteristics.
12. Define and illustrate the economic concept of supply and demand.
13. Present a detailed analysis of the digestive system in an earthworm.
14. In your opinion are supercomputers smart enough to replace people in jobs that require decision making?
15. What is a critical velocity and why must an object from the earth achieve it in order to reach space?

Timed Writing

Throughout your school years, you will be tested on your ability to organize your thoughts quickly and to express them in a limited time. Your essay will then be judged on how well you cover the topic and how clearly you organize your essay.

Writing a timed essay is similar to taking a classroom essay test. In addition, follow the strategies below.

Strategies for Timed Writing

1. Listen carefully to instructions. Find out if you may write notes or an outline to aid you in writing.
2. Find out if you should erase mistakes or should cross them out by neatly drawing a line through them.
3. Plan your time, keeping in mind your time limit.

Practicing a Timed Writing Test   When taking a timed writing test, you will find that following the steps in the writing process will help you make the best use of your time. For example, suppose you were given 20 minutes to write on the following topic:

Explain one change in your town that you would make if you were mayor for a day.

You might organize your time in the following way:

 8 minutes: Brainstorm and organize ideas.
12 minutes: Write a draft.
 5 minutes: Revise and edit your work.

Using the topic above or another topic your class chooses, follow these guidelines as you practice taking a timed writing test.

Preparing Subject-Area Assignments

The strategies you have learned for reading textbooks, taking notes, and preparing for tests can be applied to assignments in any subject area. In addition, you will find that each subject area has specialized aids that help you study and prepare assignments for that subject.

Strategies for Preparing Subject-Area Assignments

1. Carefully read and follow directions before beginning any assignment. *(See page 520.)*

2. As you read, adjust your reading rate to suit your purpose. *(See pages 514–515.)*

3. As you read your textbook, use the SQ3R method. *(See page 516.)*

4. Take notes as you read and listen to a lecture. Label your notes with the date, pages, and subject of the assignment or the date and topic of the lecture. As you review your notes, highlight important information. *(See pages 516–518.)*

5. Be organized. Keep your reading notes and lecture notes about a topic together in your notebook.

6. Keep a separate list of vocabulary, key terms and concepts, or rules and equations.

7. Keep a running list of questions you think of as you read, listen, or review. Seek answers promptly. If there is anything you do not understand, ask for help.

8. Participate in study groups to prepare long-term assignments or review for tests. Follow the principles of cooperative learning. *(See pages 463–464.)*

9. Leave ample time to study for tests. Anticipate the questions you think will be asked on the test and be able to answer them.

10. Practice using any specialized learning aids and skills for specific subject areas, such as formulas in chemistry or maps in history.

Mathematics, geometry, algebra, and science textbooks often list rules, formulas, equations, or models. In these subjects, therefore, you must focus on learning the rules and applying them to solve particular problems. When studying science, think of specific examples that show how a scientific rule or principle works. For social studies courses, on the other hand, you will need to develop your skills in reading and interpreting maps, charts, graphs, chronologies, time lines, documents, and statistical data.

As an example, if you were preparing for a history test on the American Civil War, you might include in your study plan one or more of the following strategies.

- Make a time line of key events in the Civil War.
- Draw a flowchart to show the causes and effects of events leading up to the war.
- Draw graphs to compare the economic resources of the North and the South at the start of the war.
- Evaluate the war from the point of view of a southerner and from the point of view of a northerner.
- Label a map to show the locations of key Civil War battles.
- Develop a chart to name the generals of the North and the South and to compare their roles in the war.
- Analyze a primary source document, such as Lincoln's Gettysburg Address.
- Write an outline for an essay on the significance of the Civil War in the history of the United States.

EXERCISE *Preparing a Subject-Area Assignment*

Develop a study plan for a current or forthcoming unit or assignment in any one of your courses other than English. Your study plan should include some of the strategies discussed in this section. State the subject and purpose of the unit or assignment. Then list the strategies you will follow to complete it successfully. After you have completed the unit or assignment, evaluate in your journal how well your planned strategies helped you with this task.

Taking Standardized Tests

Standardized tests measure your skills, progress, and achievement in such a way that the results can be compared with those of other students in the same grade. Standardized tests that measure your verbal or language skills are divided into three broad categories: vocabulary tests, analogy tests, and tests of writing ability.

The best way to prepare for standardized tests is to work consistently at your subjects during the school year, read widely, and use the following strategies.

Strategies for Taking Standardized Tests

1. Read the test directions carefully. Answer sample questions to be sure you are following the instructions.
2. Try to relax. You can expect to be a little nervous, but concentrate on doing your best.
3. Skim the entire section to get an overview of the kinds of questions you will be asked.
4. Plan your time carefully. Be aware of how much time you are allotted for each part of the test.
5. Answer first those questions you find easiest. Skip questions you find too difficult but come back to them later if you have time.
6. Read all the choices before selecting the best answer. If you are not sure of an answer, eliminate choices that are obviously incorrect. Educated guessing often helps.
7. If you have time, check your answers. Be sure you have correctly marked your answer sheet.

Vocabulary Tests

Two kinds of items, or questions, appear frequently on standardized vocabulary tests. One kind asks you to recognize an antonym—a word opposite to another in meaning. A second kind asks you to recognize a synonym—a word similar in meaning to another word.

Antonyms Antonym items test your ability to recognize words that are most nearly opposite in meaning. An antonym for *strength*, for example, is *weakness*. In the following item, the answer is *(B) open*, which is the opposite of *secretive*.

> SECRETIVE: (A) shady (B) open (C) content
> (D) nominated (E) mysterious

A person who is secretive is not open. The other answer choices are incorrect for various reasons. *Shady* and *mysterious* are synonyms of *secretive*, not antonyms. While someone who is secretive may be content, *content* is not an opposite of *secretive*. Finally, the word *nominated* has no relevance at all to *secretive*.

Synonyms Synonym items have the same format as antonym items, but instead you choose a word with the same meaning as the word in capital letters. For example, in the following item, the answer is *(B) barren*, which means the same as *desolate*.

> DESOLATE: (A) quiet (B) barren (C) teeming
> (D) angry (E) ordinary

Although you may be unfamiliar with some words in an antonym or synonym test, you can nevertheless find ways to figure out the answers. A prefix, root, or suffix can sometimes provide a clue to the meaning of an unfamiliar word. The word *convocation*, for example, contains the prefix *con-* (with), the root *vocare-* (to call), and the suffix *-tion* (an act or a process). Knowledge of any of these parts gives you a clue to figuring out the meaning of the word: *the act or process of calling together.*

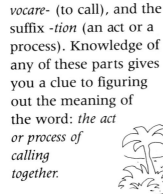

ROGET'S BRONTOSAURUS

Drawing by M. Stevens © 1985 The New Yorker Magazine, Inc.

EXERCISE *Recognizing Antonyms*

Write the letter of the word that is most nearly opposite in meaning to the word in capital letters.

1. PASSIVE: (A) thoughtful   (B) glum   (C) sporty
  (D) active   (E) cooperative
2. ALIEN: (A) familiar   (B) strange   (C) foreign
  (D) agreeable   (E) dull
3. COMPLEX: (A) mysterious   (B) complicated
  (C) simple   (D) fancy   (E) harmless
4. MONOTONOUS: (A) double   (B) noisy   (C) boring
  (D) difficult   (E) unpredictable
5. ANIMATED: (A) inactive   (B) bold   (C) open
  (D) outstanding   (E) irritable
6. INNOCENCE: (A) kindliness   (B) guilt   (C) victory
  (D) greed   (E) sadness
7. LOITER: (A) delay   (B) repair   (C) shrink
  (D) hasten   (E) increase
8. SOMBER: (A) mournful   (B) simple   (C) damp
  (D) cheerful   (E) healthful
9. CAUTIOUS: (A) suspicious   (B) superstitious
  (C) foolhardy   (D) challenging   (E) stern
10. INDIFFERENT: (A) alike   (B) similar   (C) unique
  (D) concerned   (E) amused

EXERCISE *Recognizing Synonyms*

Write the letter of the word that is closest in meaning to the word in capital letters.

1. DESCEND: (A) agree   (B) climb   (C) struggle
  (D) defend   (E) fall
2. IMPRISON: (A) parole   (B) arrange   (C) free
  (D) hide   (E) punish
3. INDULGE: (A) splurge   (B) annoy   (C) keep
  (D) discipline   (E) empty
4. UNKEMPT: (A) orderly   (B) disorganized   (C) polite
  (D) respectful   (E) harmful

5. IMPULSIVE: (A) courageous   (B) spontaneous
   (C) awkward   (D) deliberate   (E) bold
6. POTENT: (A) weak   (B) dangerous   (C) logical
   (D) false   (E) powerful
7. TRIVIAL: (A) daring   (B) meaningless   (C) evil
   (D) shared   (E) important
8. EQUIVALENT: (A) certain   (B) different   (C) sturdy
   (D) synonymous   (E) noisy
9. MINUTE: (A) festive   (B) tiny   (C) gigantic
   (D) ordinary   (E) active
10. INCREDIBLE: (A) extraordinary   (B) normal
   (C) annoying   (D) believable   (E) motivated

Analogies

Analogy questions test your skill at figuring out relationships between words. The first step in answering this kind of question is to determine how the two words in capital letters are related. The second step is to read several other pairs of words and decide which pair has the same relationship as the words in capital letters.

The punctuation in an analogy question stands for the words *is to* and *as*.

CLOCK:TIME   : :   thermometer:temperature

The above example reads, "A clock *is to* time *as* a thermometer *is to* temperature." That is, a clock has the same relationship to time as a thermometer has to temperature. A clock *measures* time *as* a thermometer *measures* temperature.

When you take an analogy test, try to explain to yourself in one sentence the relationship between the two words in capital letters. In the following example, you might say, "Handlebars are part of a bicycle."

HANDLEBARS:BICYCLE   : :   (A) moose:antlers
(B) tire:fender   (C) carpenter:hammer   (D) steering
wheel:automobile   (E) golf:sport

The correct answer is *(D) steering wheel:automobile* because the relationship between these two words is that of part to whole; a steering wheel is part of an automobile. The other choices are incorrect for a variety of reasons. *Moose:antlers* shows a whole-to-part relationship rather than a part-to-whole. *Tire:fender* refers to two parts of an automobile, not to a whole automobile. *Carpenter:hammer* shows the relationship of a worker to a tool, not of a part to a whole. Finally, the relationship in *golf:sport* is item-to-category because *golf* is an item in the category of *sports*.

Remember that the words in the answer must be in the same order as the words in the given analogy. If the given pair of words expresses a cause-to-effect relationship, the words in the correct answer should also be in the order of cause to effect.

Common Types of Analogies	
ANALOGY	**EXAMPLE**
word:synonym word:antonym part:whole cause:effect worker:tool worker:product item:purpose item:category	plain:simple hasten:delay lens:camera burn:pain secretary:typewriter cobbler:shoes pencil:write chipmunk:rodent

EXERCISE *Recognizing Analogies*

Write the letter of the word pair that has the same relationship as the word pair in capital letters.

1. DENTIST:DRILL : : (A) calendar:date
   (B) sculptor:chisel (C) lumberjack:forest
   (D) eyeglasses:sight (E) hammer:carpenter
2. HORSE:MAMMAL : : (A) insect:beetle
   (B) beaver:fish (C) snake:reptile (D) trout:halibut
   (E) animal:tiger

3. HASTEN:HURRY : : (A) laugh:talk (B) trust:doubt
(C) stammer:whisper (D) attempt:try
(E) explain:understand

4. RANCH:CATTLE : : (A) people:city
(B) chickens:coop (C) garden:vegetables
(D) automobiles:garage (E) clowns:circus

5. CALM:RESTLESS : : (A) vague:indefinite
(B) tiny:small (C) colorless:transparent
(D) loud:noisy (E) gloomy:brilliant

6. DAISY:FLOWER : : (A) rye:grain (B) fish:trout
(C) violet:rose (D) yellow:petal (E) garden:soil

7. FOUNDATION:BASE : : (A) handle:door
(B) shoes:belt (C) ruler:inch (D) guest:visitor
(E) top:bottom

8. DIRECTOR:MOVIE : : (A) doctor:patient
(B) cook:diet (C) conductor:symphony
(D) teacher:school (E) building:architect

9. COWARD:BRAVERY : : (A) judge:law
(B) criminal:honesty (C) politician:power
(D) samaritan:kindness (E) hero:courage

10. ARCHERY:TARGET : : (A) bowling:pins
(B) tennis:shoes (C) basketball:swimming
(D) golf:clubs (E) horses:polo

11. ICE:FREEZE : : (A) mixture:stir (B) study:book
(C) debate:argument (D) chill:frost (E) steam:boil

12. BRIGHTEN:LAMP : : (A) sit:chair
(B) cool:refrigerator (C) number:count
(D) plan:calendar (E) handle:open

13. CLIENT:CUSTOMER : : (A) dial:clock
(B) salesperson:purchaser (C) computer:typewriter
(D) peak:summit (E) square:circle

14. BATON:CONDUCTOR : : (A) ship:captain
(B) animal: zoologist (C) banker:money
(D) camera:photographer (E) carpenter:saw

15. TAILOR:JACKET : : (A) designer:illustration
(B) stone:mason (C) case:lawyer (D) review:critic
(E) stitch:seamstress

"We had a word test today . . . I was ignominiously defeated."

Tests of Standard Written English

Tests of standard written English are multiple-choice tests that ask you to identify sentence errors. The tests usually contain sentences with three or more underlined parts. You must decide if there is an error in grammar, usage, word choice, punctuation, or capitalization in any one of the underlined parts. For example, study the sentence below and identify the sentence error.

Some scientists <u>believe</u> that the first <u>dog's</u> <u>were</u> tamed
               A   B   C

over 10,000 years ago<u>.</u> <u>No error</u>
                 D   E

The answer is *B*. The word *dogs* should not have an apostrophe, because it is a plural, not a possessive.

Following are a few common errors you should look for on a test of standard written English.

- lack of agreement between the subject and verb of a sentence
- lack of agreement between a pronoun and the verb in the sentence
- lack of agreement between a pronoun and its antecedent
- incorrect spelling or use of a word
- missing, misplaced, or unnecessary punctuation
- missing or unnecessary capitalization

Some sentences on tests of standard written English have no errors. Before you choose the answer *E (No error)*, however, be sure that you have carefully studied every part of the sentence. The correct parts of the sentence may help you to locate errors in the underlined parts.

EXERCISE   8   *Recognizing Errors in Writing*

Write the letter that is below the underlined word or punctuation mark that is incorrect. If the sentence contains no error, write *E*.

1. Temperatures on summer nights <u>are</u> often <u>cooler</u> in the sub-
                                A   B

     urbs <u>then</u> <u>in</u> the city. <u>No error</u>
          C   D   E

2. One reason for the difference <u>is</u> <u>that</u> suburbs have <u>less</u> build-
                              A   B   C

     ings <u>than</u> the city has. <u>No error</u>
          D   E

3. During the day city streets, sidewalks<u>,</u> and <u>buildings</u> <u>absorb</u>
                               A   B   C

     the <u>Summer</u> heat. <u>No error</u>
          D   E

4. At night the suburbs <u>cool</u> down<u>,</u> but<u>,</u> the city <u>does</u> not.
                      A   B   C   D

     <u>No error</u>
      E

5. Buildings and streets <u>release</u> the heat absorbed during the
                        A

     day<u>,</u> this heat <u>keeps</u> the city warmer throughout the night<u>.</u>
      B   C   D

     <u>No error</u>
      E

6. The suburbs <u>have</u> more trees_and grass that <u>hold</u> rainwater
                 A   B   C

     near the surface<u>.</u> <u>No error</u>
                  D   E

7. The water <u>evaporates</u> in the heat, and <u>cools</u> down the tem-
               A   B   C
perature. <u>No error</u>
      D   E

8. Furthermore, the trees, <u>like</u> a fan, <u>keeps</u> a breeze blow-
                       A B   C D
ing. <u>No error</u>
     E

9. Tall and unbending, the buildings in the city <u>retain</u> the
                A   B
warm air <u>as</u> an oven <u>does</u>. <u>No error</u>
        C   D   E

10. <u>Its</u> easy to understand why <u>people</u> often <u>try</u> to leave the
    A   B   C
city to visit the countryside on a hot <u>July</u> weekend.
<u>No error</u>   D
  E

11. Bottle-nosed dolphins <u>are</u> highly <u>intelligent</u> mammals with
                       A   B
keen eyesight_ and hearing. <u>No error</u>
         C   D   E

12. If we <u>had</u> left home sooner, we could <u>of</u> climbed to the top
        A   B   C
of the <u>mountain</u>. <u>No error</u>
      D   E

13. Which <u>was</u> the <u>larger</u> dinosaur—the Triceratops, or the
        A   B   C
Apatosaurus? <u>No error</u>
       D   E

14. Both my <u>brother</u>-in-<u>law</u> <u>subscribe</u> to the magazine
           A   B   C
Inventions every year. <u>No error</u>
  D   E

15. The techniques in <u>James</u> <u>Whistler's</u> paintings <u>was</u> influ-
                  A   B   C
enced by <u>Japanese</u> woodcuts. <u>No error</u>
        D   E

17 Review

A **Understanding Antonyms** Write the letter of the word that means the opposite of the word in capital letters.

1. FORBID: (A) trespass   (B) inquire   (C) allow
   (D) whisper   (E) prohibit
2. MOBILE: (A) stationary   (B) movable   (C) expensive
   (D) crowded   (E) dangerous
3. MODERATE: (A) mysterious   (B) windy   (C) short
   (D) forgiving   (E) extreme
4. PROHIBIT: (A) ban   (B) permit   (C) warn
   (D) display   (E) sell
5. LOATHE: (A) threaten   (B) hate   (C) adore
   (D) scold   (E) advise

B **Understanding Analogies** Write the letter of the word pair that contains the same relationship as the word pair in capital letters.

1. NICKEL:COIN   : :   (A) valuables:gold
   (B) duck:goose   (C) insect:bites   (D) table:chair
   (E) hammer:tool
2. CONTENT:DISSATISFIED   : :   (A) lazy:happy
   (B) hungry:sleepy   (C) grateful:thankful
   (D) stable:dependable   (E) friendly:hostile
3. RASH:MEASLES   : :   (A) sniffles:influenza
   (B) doctor:illness   (C) throat:tonsillitis
   (D) bone:fracture   (E) bronchitis:coughing
4. CARDIOLOGIST:HEARTS   : :   (A) police:patrol
   (B) plants:biologist   (C) doctors:patients
   (D) computer:operator   (E) dentist:teeth
5. TURNTABLE:RECORD   : :   (A) grape:bunch
   (B) size:color   (C) car:garage   (D) recorder:cassette
   (E) rain:snow

6. STATE:GOVERNOR   : :   (A) laws:people
(B) king:land   (C) teacher:school   (D) tree:forest
(E) city:mayor

7. FOUNDATION:HOUSE   : :   (A) base:statue
(B) chair:legs   (C) valley:river   (D) peak:mountain
(E) forest:tree

8. CAT:FELINE   : :   (A) carrot:orange   (B) kitten:yarn
(C) rabbit:hop   (D) dog:canine   (E) equine:horse

9. PAINTINGS:MUSEUM   : :   (A) sea:ships
(B) play:actors   (C) books:library   (D) key:lock
(E) typewriter:keys

10. ARGUE:DEBATE   : :   (A) think:speak   (B) interest:show
(C) catch:trap   (D) hinder:help   (E) free:enslave

C Understanding Tests of Standard Written English
Write the letter that is below the incorrect underlined word or
punctuation. If the sentence contains no error, write *E*.

1. Hunting their <u>prey</u> at dusk or after dark<u>,</u> <u>owls</u> are <u>bird's</u> of
　　　　　A　　　　　　　　　　　　 B　C　　　　D
the night. <u>No error</u>
　　　　　　 E

2. All members of the owl <u>family</u> <u>have</u> short necks, large heads<u>,</u>
　　　　　　　　　　　　 A　　　 B　　　　　　　　　　　　　 C
and very<u>,</u> keen hearing. <u>No error</u>
　　　 D　　　　　　　　 E

3. Barn owls, more <u>than</u> any <u>others,</u> are the subject of
　　　　　　　　　　 A　　　　 B　C
<u>stories</u> about haunted houses. <u>No error</u>
　 D　　　　　　　　　　　　　　 E

4. <u>These</u> owls <u>sometimes</u> roost in barns<u>;</u> belfries<u>,</u> or aban-
　　 A　　　　　 B　　　　　　　　　　 C　　　 D
doned houses. <u>No error</u>
　　　　　　　　 E

5. All owls, but <u>especially</u> barn owls, <u>can</u> <u>accurately</u> be called
　　　　　　　　 A　　　　　　　　　 B　　 C
<u>winged</u> mousetraps. <u>No error</u>
　 D　　　　　　　　 E

Unit 4
Language Skills Resource

Grammar

Usage

Mechanics

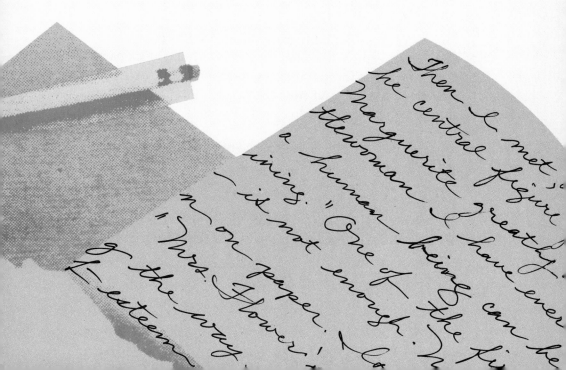

18 **The Sentence**

Diagnostic Test

Number your paper 1 to 10. Then write the subjects and the verbs in the following sentences.

EXAMPLE   Pat and I are going to Boston today.
ANSWER   Pat, I—are going

1. The tusks of an elephant grow throughout its life.
2. The guests seemed tired after the neighborhood block party.
3. Carmen waited for ten minutes and then left.
4. Haven't you done your homework yet?
5. Into the bowl of punch splashed the ball.
6. Here are the pens.
7. The cherries and the grapes should be washed and put into the fruit salad.
8. Trucks and cars roared through the tunnel at the end of the highway.
9. Did you read the newspaper this morning?
10. Melissa should never have loaned Anthony her compact discs.

Recognizing Sentences

In casual conversation people sometimes express their ideas incompletely.

KIM: "Do you want to go for a walk?"
ALLEN: "In this weather? No way!"

Kim easily understood Allen's reply, even though he used only parts of a sentence to answer her. Although Allen's remarks might be effective in conversation, written words should express complete thoughts. Before you can write sentences, however, you first must be able to recognize them.

> **Rule 18a**   A **sentence** is a group of words that expresses a complete thought.

The following groups of words are incomplete thoughts.

The man in the black suit.   Running in the hall.
Ate all the grapes.   When the race was over.

Groups of words that express incomplete thoughts are called *sentence fragments*. To change these fragments into sentences, you must add the missing information. *(For more information about sentence fragments, see pages 695–699.)*

The man in the black suit **is my teacher.**
My brother ate all the grapes.
Running in the hall **is forbidden.**
When the race was over, **we held a party for the winner.**

EXERCISE *Recognizing Sentences*

Number your paper 1 to 10. Then label each group of words *S* if it is a sentence or *F* if it is a fragment.

1. The fans at the hockey game cheered wildly.

2. Because the weather turned cold.
3. Sent the package to her yesterday.
4. A history teacher at the middle school.
5. Roberto works on Saturday afternoons.
6. Skiing down a mountain for the first time.
7. Since we are going out for dinner.
8. George does 20 push-ups each morning.
9. Laughed at Antonia's jokes.
10. After the corn is planted in the far field.

EXERCISE *Completing Sentences*

Add the information needed to make each fragment in Exercise 1 a sentence. Use a capital letter and correct punctuation in your sentences.

Subjects and Predicates

A complete sentence needs a subject and a predicate. A *subject* names the person, place, thing, or idea that the sentence is about. The *predicate* tells something about the subject.

Rule 18b A sentence has two main parts: a **subject** and a **predicate.**

	SUBJECT	PREDICATE
PERSON	Our science teacher	organized the fair.
PLACE	Florida's beaches	attract many tourists.
THING	Jamie's car	is ten years old.
IDEA	His courage	was remarkable.

Complete and Simple Subjects

The *complete subject* of a sentence usually contains more than one word.

Rule 18c A **complete subject** includes all the words used to identify the person, place, thing, or idea that the sentence is about.

To find a complete subject, ask yourself *Whom?* or *What?* the sentence is about.

> **The salesperson in the store** explained the computer. [Whom is this sentence telling about? Who explained the computer? *The salesperson in the store* is the complete subject.]

> **The bananas on the table** aren't ripe yet. [What is this sentence telling about? What isn't ripe yet? *The bananas on the table* is the complete subject.]

EXERCISE *Finding Complete Subjects*

Number your paper 1 to 10. Then write the complete subject in each sentence.

Animal Oddities

1. A huge grizzly bear has the speed of an average horse.
2. The largest elephant in Africa may weigh over 14 thousand pounds.
3. The ancient Egyptians trained baboons as waiters.
4. The opossum dates back 45 million years.
5. A panda weighs four ounces at birth.
6. The greyhound can run over 40 miles per hour.
7. The one-ton African rhinoceros is easily tamed.
8. Cattle branding was practiced 4,000 years ago.
9. Herds of camels roamed Alaska 12,000 years ago.
10. The ancestors of the modern horse were only a foot tall.

Simple Subjects Within each complete subject, one word directly answers the question *Who?* or *What?*

Rule 18d　A **simple subject** is the main word in the complete subject.

In the following examples, the simple subjects are printed in heavy type.

┌——complete subject——┐
The **athletes** on the field stood at attention.

┌—complete subject—┐
The lone gray **horse** galloped across the field.

Sometimes a complete subject and a simple subject are the same.

> **Luis Sanchez** will sing a solo at the concert.
> [*Luis Sanchez* is the simple subject. Both words are
> considered one name.]

> **He** will return my science book.

Note: Throughout the rest of this book, the simple subject will
be called the *subject.*

EXERCISE *Finding Complete and Simple Subjects*

Number your paper 1 to 10. Write the complete subject in each
sentence. Then underline each simple subject.

EXAMPLE   Wild animals in the forest are moving to the city.
ANSWER   Wild <u>animals</u> in the forest

City Critters   **1.** Many people live in busy cities today.
2. This next fact will surprise you.
3. Some wild animals make their homes in cities as well.
4. Geese from Canada have spent many summers on the tenth
floor of an office building in St. Louis.
5. Dave Tylka studies wildlife in cities.
6. He explains the birds' strange behavior.
7. The geese in St. Louis nest on cliffs over the Mississippi.
8. Large balconies on buildings look like cliffs to them.
9. Raccoons in New York City live quite successfully in sewers,
chimneys, and Central Park.
10. Residents in Boulder, Colorado, see deer in their yards.

EXERCISE *Finding Simple Subjects*

Write the simple subject in each sentence.

Farming
Pearls   **1.** Genuine pearls are accidents of nature.
2. A foreign object gets inside an oyster's shell.
3. The irritated oyster immediately produces calcium.
4. This natural substance gradually coats the piece of shell or
grain of sand.

5. A beautiful round pearl is then formed.

6. Japanese people now operate pearl farms.

7. Oysters live their first three years under bamboo rafts.

8. Workers then insert an object inside each shell.

9. The oysters are returned to the water.

10. A great harvest is collected two years later.

Application to Writing

Write a paragraph that describes something unusual you might see during a walk down the main street of your city or town. Be prepared to identify the simple subject in each sentence.

Complete and Simple Predicates

Besides a subject, every sentence needs a predicate.

Rule 18e A **complete predicate** includes all the words that tell what the subject is doing or that tell something about the subject.

To find a complete predicate, first find the subject. Then ask, *What is the subject doing?* or *What is being said about the subject?*

The wild horses **roamed across the prairie.** [The subject is *horses*. What did the horses do? They roamed across the prairie. *Roamed across the prairie* is the complete predicate.]

EXERCISE *Finding Complete Predicates*

Number your paper 1 to 10. Then write the complete predicate in each sentence.

The Statue of Liberty

1. The Statue of Liberty stands in New York Harbor.

2. The tablet in her left hand reads "July 4, 1776."

3. Seven rays surround her head.

4. Broken chains lie at her feet.

5. She weighs 225 tons.
6. Her index finger extends eight feet.
7. The French people gave the statue to the United States as a birthday present.
8. The formal presentation occurred in 1886.
9. One million sightseers visit the statue each year.
10. She remains the best-known statue in the world today.

Simple Predicates   A predicate has one main word or phrase that tells what the subject is doing or tells something about the subject. This key word or phrase is always the verb.

> **Rule 18f**   A **simple predicate,** or **verb,** is the main word or phrase in the complete predicate.

In the following examples, the verb is in heavy type.

> ┌─complete predicate─┐
> Everyone in the audience **enjoyed** the play.

> ┌──── complete predicate ────┐
> The airplane **landed** safely in the field.

> ┌──complete predicate──┐
> My brother **is** a fine soccer player.

Verbs that tell something about a subject are sometimes hard to find because they do not show action. Following is a list of common verb forms used to make a statement about a subject.

Verbs That Make Statements							
am	is	are	was	were	be	being	been

EXERCISE *Finding Complete Predicates and Verbs*

Number your paper 1 to 10. Write the complete predicate in each sentence. Then underline each verb.

EXAMPLE   His coat hangs on that hook.
ANSWER   <u>hangs</u> on that hook

1. Hank Aaron hit 755 home runs during his career.
2. My cat chases the neighbors' dog every morning.
3. That camera is the least expensive model.
4. The United States paid Russia only two cents an acre for Alaska.
5. A cow gives less milk in hot weather.
6. The school board met for five hours last night.
7. Both Washington and Jefferson were six-footers.
8. The principal conducted the first assembly.
9. The temperature fell ten degrees last night.
10. Luther Crowell invented the paper bag in 1867.

EXERCISE 8 *Finding Verbs*

Number your paper 1 to 10. Then write the verb in each sentence.

1. The United States issued the first patent in 1790.
2. I started a savings account last month.
3. Evenings in the fall are quite cool.
4. Otters always entertain the visitors at Sea World.
5. The color on the television needs some adjustment.
6. The lifeguard shouted a warning to the swimmers.
7. My parents insulated our house this year.
8. Edgar Rice Burroughs was the creator of Tarzan.
9. The dog eagerly ate its dinner.
10. The elephant's tusks weighed over 200 pounds.

EXERCISE 9 *Cumulative Review*

Number your paper 1 to 20. Then write the subject and the verb in each sentence.

A Joint
Venture

1. This true story tells about a cat and Eli Whitney.
2. Together they changed the course of history.
3. The man, with the cat's help, invented the cotton gin.
4. As a result the South gained great wealth.
5. In colonial days people removed the seeds from cotton.
6. They pulled the cotton apart by hand.
7. One person cleaned only a few pounds each day.

8. This manual labor was very expensive.

9. Cotton planters wanted a cheaper method.

10. Whitney knew their problems.

11. On a sleepless night, he hunted for a solution.

12. He went to the window for some fresh air.

13. He saw a stray cat in the alley.

14. It clawed at a dead chicken through the slots of a wooden crate.

15. Its sharp claws raked only some feathers through the narrow slots.

16. The space between the slots was very narrow.

17. The chicken remained inside the crate.

18. Suddenly Whitney thought of an idea for his invention!

19. In his machine, sharp teeth pull cotton fibers through narrow openings.

20. That nameless cat helped Whitney with the invention of the cotton gin.

Verb Phrases

The main verb in the following example is *mow.* However, to show that Tom's action will take place in the future, the word *will* must be added to the verb.

Tom **will mow** the lawn tomorrow.

Words such as *will* are called auxiliary verbs, or *helping verbs.* The main verb plus any helping verbs make up a *verb phrase.* The helping verbs in the following examples are in heavy type.

┌─verb phrase┐
Eva **is** watching the football game now.

┌── verb phrase ──┐
Those seeds **can be** planted next month.

┌────── verb phrase ──────┐
You **should have been** warned about the penalty.

Note: As you can see from the examples above, a verb phrase can include as many as three helping verbs plus the main verb.

Common Helping Verbs	
be	am, is, are, was, were, be, being, been
have	has, have, had
do	do, does, did
others	may, might, must, can, could, shall, should, will, would

EXERCISE *Finding Verb Phrases*

Number your paper 1 to 10. Then write the verb phrase in each sentence.

EXAMPLE   Greg will be working on weekends now.
ANSWER   will be working

1. The first photograph was taken in 1826.
2. The freshman class election results will be announced on Monday.
3. Dandelion leaves can be eaten raw like lettuce.
4. Their sneakers are drying in the sun.
5. The invitation must have given the time.
6. You should have spoken to me first.
7. The Girl Scouts was founded on March 12, 1912.
8. American Indians could make beads from shells.
9. The award should have gone to her.
10. With help babies can swim at an early age.

Interrupted Verb Phrases   Verb phrases are often interrupted by other words.

A bloodhound **can** easily **follow** a day-old scent.
Betsy **has** never **seen** the ocean.

In a question the subject sometimes comes in the middle of a verb phrase.

Is Tony **running** in the marathon on Saturday?

Although *not* and its contraction *n't* are never part of a verb phrase, they often interrupt a verb phrase.

Dan **is** not **going** with us to the movies.
Beth **doesn't like** ice cream.

Note: Throughout the rest of this book, the term *verb* will refer to the whole verb phrase.

EXERCISE *Finding Verbs*

Number your paper 1 to 15. Then write the verb in each sentence. Remember that words can interrupt a verb phrase.

1. I must have lost the keys to the house.
2. Some parts of Brazil have never been explored.
3. The roses in our garden haven't bloomed yet.
4. Would you like corn instead of peas?
5. Isn't she wanted in the office?
6. Valuable antiques can sometimes be found at flea markets.
7. Have you eaten your lunch yet?
8. Did you join the track team this year?
9. Platinum was first discovered in Colombia.
10. Cats were not tamed until about 5,000 years ago.
11. The oldest hat in the world may well be the familiar chef's hat.
12. A person can now travel over 9,000 miles in 8 hours.
13. A regular lead pencil can write about 50,000 words.
14. The English didn't invent the umbrella.
15. How often does Halley's comet make an appearance?

EXERCISE *Cumulative Review*

Number your paper 1 to 10. Then write the subject and the verb in each sentence.

An
Accidental
Discovery

1. Long ago, Egyptians would mix hippo fat with moldy bread crumbs.
2. This mixture was then used as a medicine.
3. The moldy bread contained a medicine—penicillin.

4. In 1928, Alexander Fleming was growing bacteria for an experiment.

5. His helper didn't cover the dish of bacteria.

6. Some mold blew in the window.

7. It fell on the bacteria.

8. The next morning, Fleming noticed the dead bacteria.

9. He eventually named the mold penicillin.

10. Since then, penicillin has saved millions of lives.

 Application to Writing

Write a paragraph that describes a young child who is just learning to ride a two-wheeled bicycle. Be prepared to identify the verb in each sentence.

Compound Subjects

Many subjects have a single subject. Others have two or more subjects joined by a conjunction such as *and* or *or.*

Rule 18g   A **compound subject** is two or more subjects in one sentence that have the same verb and are joined by a conjunction.

In the following examples, each subject is underlined once, and each verb is underlined twice.

ONE SUBJECT   <u>Janice</u> <u>spent</u> the day at the beach.

COMPOUND SUBJECT   <u>Janice</u> and <u>Kate</u> <u>spent</u> the day at the beach.

COMPOUND SUBJECT   <u>Janice</u>, <u>Kate</u>, and <u>Sue</u> <u>spent</u> the day at the beach.

The conjunctions *and, or,* and *nor* are used to connect compound subjects. Pairs of conjunctions, such as *either/or, neither/nor, not only/but also,* and *both/and* may also be used.

Either <u>chicken</u> or <u>fish</u> <u>will be served</u> at the banquet.

EXERCISE *Finding Compound Subjects*

Write the subjects in each sentence.

EXAMPLE   Both Otis and Wilma went to the game.
ANSWER   Otis, Wilma

1. Hikers and cyclists often camp by the brook.
2. Neither Gladys nor Rosalie can baby-sit for us.
3. The best baseballs and footballs are made of leather.
4. Shells, starfish, and driftwood are among her souvenirs.
5. Insects and disease are the major enemies of trees.
6. My family and I will fly to Arizona next week.
7. *Jane, Jean,* and *Joan* are forms of the same ancient name.
8. Both basketball and volleyball were first played in the state of Massachusetts.
9. Carnations and zinnias last a long time.
10. Breakfast, lunch, and dinner were included in the price.

Compound Verbs

Just as some sentences have compound subjects, some sentences may have compound verbs. Conjunctions such as *and, or, nor,* and *but* are used to connect the verbs.

Rule 18h   A **compound verb** is two or more verbs in one sentence that have the same subject and are joined by a conjunction.

In the following examples, each subject is underlined once, and each verb is underlined twice.

ONE VERB   Jeff milks the cows.
COMPOUND VERB   Jeff milks the cows and gathers the eggs.
COMPOUND VERB   Jeff milks the cows, gathers the eggs, and feeds the chickens.

A sentence can include both a compound subject and a compound verb.

Nancy and Peg went to Orlando and visited Disney World.

EXERCISE *Finding Compound Verbs*

Write the subjects and the verbs in the following sentences.

Save Those
Cans!

1. Many people drink the last sip of a soda and throw the can away.

2. You should save your cans and deliver them to a recycling center.

3. An employee will take the cans and give you some money.

4. Trucks collect the old cans and unload them at a recycling plant.

5. Machines at the plant flatten the cans and dump them onto conveyor belts.

6. The cans are then shredded and cleaned.

7. Next, workers load the pieces into a hot furnace and soften them.

8. The soft metal is made into long sheets and cooled.

9. Beverage companies buy the sheets and make new cans out of them.

10. These new cans have prevented extra waste and thereby have saved everyone money.

EXERCISE *Cumulative Review*

Write the subjects and the verbs in the following sentences.

Twins: A
Case Study

1. Jim Lewis and Jim Springer are twins but were adopted by different parents.

2. They had neither met nor talked to each other for 30 years.

3. Some unusual facts were then discovered.

4. Their wives were both named Betty.

5. James Allen and James Alan were the names of their first sons.

6. Math and woodworking were hobbies of both the brothers.

7. The twins drove the same make of car and had vacationed at the same beach in Florida.

8. These similarities sound like coincidences.

9. Some researchers don't think so.

10. They have now found identical brain-wave patterns in twins.

Position of Subjects

In most sentences the subject comes before the verb. Sometimes, however, the normal subject-verb order is changed to create sentence variety.

When the verb or part of a verb phrase comes before the subject, the sentence is in *inverted order.* To find the subject and the verb, put the sentence in its natural order. In the following examples, each subject is underlined once, and each verb is underlined twice.

INVERTED ORDER Onto the football field <u>marched</u> the <u>band</u>.
NATURAL ORDER The <u>band</u> <u>marched</u> onto the football field.

INVERTED ORDER Directly overhead <u>flew</u> the <u>helicopter</u>.
NATURAL ORDER The <u>helicopter</u> <u>flew</u> directly overhead.

Finding the subject in an inverted sentence is sometimes easier if you first find the verb. After finding the verb, ask who or what is doing the action, or about whom or what a statement is being made.

Around the corner raced a blue car. [The verb is *raced.* What raced? *Car* is the subject.]

Questions One type of inverted order occurs in a question. Quite often part of a verb phrase will come before the subject. To find the subject in a question, turn the question around so that it makes a statement.

QUESTION <u>Did</u> <u>José</u> <u>bring</u> his camera?
STATEMENT <u>José</u> <u>did bring</u> his camera.

QUESTION <u>Should</u> <u>Peg</u> <u>go</u> to the meeting?
STATEMENT <u>Peg</u> <u>should go</u> to the meeting.

Sentences Beginning with *There* and *Here* Inverted order can also occur in a sentence that begins with the word *there* or *here.* When a sentence begins with one of these words, the verb will come before the subject.

To find the subject of this kind of sentence, drop the word

there or *here*. Then put the rest of the words in their natural order. Just remember that *there* or *here* can never be the subject of a sentence.

INVERTED ORDER   Here <u>comes</u> the <u>plane</u> down the runway.
NATURAL ORDER   The <u>plane</u> <u>comes</u> down the runway.

INVERTED ORDER   There <u>are</u> two <u>cardinals</u> at the feeder.
NATURAL ORDER   Two <u>cardinals</u> <u>are</u> at the feeder.

EXERCISE *Finding Subjects in Inverted Order*

Number your paper 1 to 10. Then write the subject and the verb in each sentence.

1. There are four taste sensations: sweet, bitter, sour, and salty.
2. Over the waves roared the speedboat.
3. High on the mountain stood the hikers.
4. Can you see her in the crowd?
5. There goes the last hamburger.
6. Why can't Cara or Lee bring the records?
7. Here are the muffins and bagels.
8. Did your teacher give you a choice of subjects?
9. Around the track raced the motorcycles.
10. Between Las Vegas and Barstow lies a great desert.

Understood Subjects

Sometimes the subject of a sentence is not stated. It is understood. This happens when a command is given or a request is made.

Look at the beautiful sunset.

If you ask who should look at the sunset, the answer is *you*—the person (or persons) receiving the command. Notice that *you* is the understood subject of each of the following sentences.

(you) Turn down the radio!
(you) Put the cat outside.
Virginia, (you) please come here.

Note: In the last example, the person receiving the request is called directly by name. Nevertheless, *you* is still the understood subject.

EXERCISE *Finding Subjects*

Number your paper 1 to 10. Then write the subject and the verb in each sentence. If the subject is an understood *you,* write it in parentheses.

EXAMPLE   Lower your voice.
ANSWER   (you) Lower

 1. Take the dog for a walk.
 2. Lend me your notes from math class.
 3. Michael, carry these packages for me.
 4. Here comes dinner right now.
 5. Get some milk at the store.
 6. Leave the keys on the table.
 7. Has Roger spoken to you about the meeting?
 8. Carly, meet me at three o'clock.
 9. Answer the questions very carefully.
10. Into the gym raced the eager players.

EXERCISE *Cumulative Review*

Number your paper 1 to 10. Then write the subjects and the verbs in the following sentences.

 1. Has the countdown for the space shuttle begun?
 2. Near the water hole were many animal tracks.
 3. There will be food, games, and prizes at the picnic.
 4. What do you remember about the accident?
 5. Mail the package at the post office.
 6. Here is the Sunday newspaper.
 7. The horse galloped fast and jumped the corral fence easily.
 8. Which job should we give to Susan?
 9. On the walls hung colorful paintings of birds.
10. Tulips and crocuses bloom during the spring and last for weeks.

USING YOUR TEXT

*Brainstorming
(20–21)
Expository Paragraphs
(120–163)*

Grammar: Combining Sentences

To avoid a choppy style in your writing, combine some of your shorter sentences. Besides making your writing smoother, doing so will help you drop unnecessary words. For example, you can combine two sentences that have the same verb but different subjects. You can also combine two sentences that have the same subject but different verbs.

TWO SENTENCES	Inez plays soccer. Rachel plays too.
COMPOUND SUBJECT	**Inez and Rachel** play soccer.
TWO SENTENCES	The dog awoke. It barked a warning.
COMPOUND VERB	The dog **awoke and barked** a warning.

Checking Your Understanding   Number your paper 1 to 5. Then combine each pair of sentences into one sentence with a compound subject or a compound verb. Use *and* or *but*.

1. The eagle circled the ridge. It landed on its nest.
2. Rain fell last night. Sleet also fell.
3. Dogs make good pets. Cats make good pets.
4. Beth left at seven. She still missed her bus.
5. I read Isaac Asimov's latest book. I enjoyed it.

Writing an Expository Paragraph   Brainstorm to think of a person or an event that you think should be celebrated with a holiday. When you have finished, choose the most interesting one that came to mind. Then list details and examples to explain why that person or event deserves to be honored.

Write the first draft of a paragraph that explains the reasons for the holiday you are proposing.   ***Application:*** As you revise your paragraph, combine sentences—where possible—by using a compound subject or a compound verb. Then edit your paragraph for any errors and write a final draft.

Diagraming Subjects and Verbs

A *sentence diagram* is a picture made up of lines and words. It can help you clearly see the different parts of a sentence.

Subjects and Verbs   All sentence diagrams begin with a baseline. A straight, vertical line then separates the subject (or subjects) on the left from the verb (or verbs) on the right. Notice in the following diagram that the capital letter in the sentence is included, but not the punctuation. Also notice that the whole verb phrase is included on the baseline.

She has remembered.

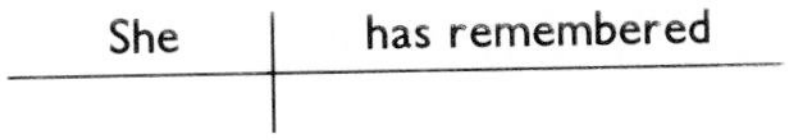

She	has remembered

Inverted Order   A sentence in inverted order, such as a question, is diagramed like a sentence in natural order.

Were you talking?

you	Were talking

Understood Subjects   When the subject of a sentence is an understood *you*, put parentheses around it in the subject position. When a name is included with the understood subject, place it on a horizontal line above the understood subject.

Ted, listen.

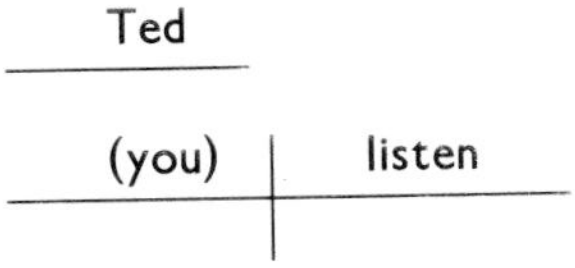

Ted

(you)	listen

Compound Subjects and Verbs   Place compound subjects and verbs on parallel lines. Put the conjunction connecting them on a broken line between them. Notice in the following example that two conjunctions are placed on either side of the broken line.

Both cameras and computers were displayed.

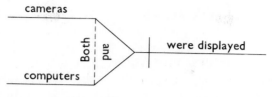

Jan has gone but will return.

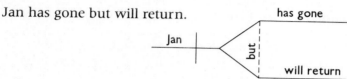

Balloons, streamers, and horns were bought but have been lost.

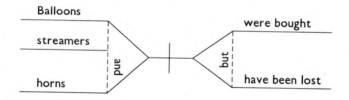

EXERCISE *Diagraming Subjects and Verbs*

Diagram the following sentences or copy them. If you copy them, draw one line under each subject and two lines under each verb. If the subject is an understood *you,* write it in parentheses.

 1. Crickets were chirping.
 2. Hurry!
 3. Both seeds and bulbs have sprouted.
 4. Were you sleeping?
 5. Pepe swung but missed.
 6. Lilacs are blooming.
 7. Sue and Cathy have arrived and are rehearsing.
 8. Roy, wait.
 9. Have tornadoes been spotted?
10. Reports were given and have been discussed.

18

Review

A **Finding Subjects and Verbs**   Number your paper 1 to 10. Then write the subjects and the verbs in the following sentences. If the subject is an understood *you,* write the word *you* in parentheses.

1. Bob has stacked the shelves in the den with books.
2. The children raked the leaves and put them into bags.
3. How many cassettes do you own?
4. Angie and Martin can operate a computer.
5. Here are your glasses.
6. Alberto shouldn't have worked all day.
7. Will Shirley go to Texas with you?
8. Dave, please fix the faucet for me.
9. On Saturday my brother bowled in the afternoon and went to a concert in the evening.
10. At the top of the hill stood a statue.

B **Finding Subjects and Verbs**   Number your paper 1 to 10. Then write the subjects and the verbs in the following sentences. If the subject is an understood *you,* write it in parentheses.

1. The tibia is located in the lower leg.
2. Peru was once ruled by the Incas.
3. The Nile and the Amazon are the two longest rivers in the world.
4. There are no fish in the Dead Sea.
5. Do arteries carry blood from the heart or to the heart?
6. The only perfect game in the World Series was pitched by Don Larsen.
7. Mississippi floods can usually be predicted six months in advance.
8. Look at that spectacular red sunset!
9. The water supply on Earth neither increases nor diminishes.
10. Traffic lights didn't appear until 1914.

C **Finding Subjects and Verbs** Number your paper 1 to 10. Then write the subjects and the verbs in the following sentences. If the subject is an understood *you,* write the word *you* in parentheses.

1. Have you noticed your dog's tail lately?
2. Take a careful look at it sometime.
3. That long, fluffy tail may be telling you something.
4. Dogs' tails wag for happiness but point downward in fear or shame.
5. Here is another example.
6. In a dangerous situation, white-tailed deer will always raise their tails like flags.
7. Beavers see danger and slap the water with their heavy broad tails.
8. Squirrels and monkeys use their tails for balance.
9. Kangaroos couldn't jump all over Australia without the help of their tails.
10. Cows and horses, on the other hand, only flick away insects with their tails.

Mastery Test

Number your paper 1 to 10. Then write the subjects and the verbs in the following sentences.

1. The warm bread melted in my mouth.
2. Candy and soda can cause cavities.
3. Vicky's watch has never lost a minute.
4. They might not have known our address.
5. Under the cupboard ran the tiny mouse.
6. Jim thought for a while and then made a decision.
7. The men remained friends for 30 years.
8. There goes my last dollar.
9. Why can't you go to the dance next Saturday?
10. The Gregsons and the Smiths own that boat and use it each summer.

19 Nouns and Pronouns

Number your paper 1 to 10. Make two columns on your paper. Label the first column *nouns* and the second column *pronouns*. Then, in the proper column, write each noun and pronoun.

EXAMPLE   I asked Fred for his slide rule.

ANSWER   <u>nouns</u>   <u>pronouns</u>
          Fred, slide rule   I, his

1. Our short but relaxing vacation in Florida ended on Labor Day.
2. On their anniversary the Hendersons celebrated.
3. Everyone at the dance had a wonderful time.
4. What happened during halftime at the game?
5. Some of the students play chess every day.
6. I like both of these very much.
7. Who led the parade down Main Street?
8. We enjoyed seeing the monkeys and the elephants at the zoo.
9. Jill built herself shelves for her books.
10. I could learn nothing about the accident.

Nouns

A classroom dictionary lists thousands of words, and an unabridged dictionary includes even more. All of these words, however, can be divided into eight groups called the *parts of speech.* A word's part of speech is determined by the job it does in a sentence.

The Eight Parts of Speech	
noun [names]	**preposition** [relates]
pronoun [replaces]	**conjunction** [connects]
verb [states action or being]	**interjection** [expresses
adjective [describes, limits]	strong feeling]
adverb [describes, limits]	

In English there are more nouns than any other part of speech.

Rule 19a A **noun** is the name of a person, place, thing, or idea.

Nouns that name people, places, and things are usually quite easy to spot. Nouns that name ideas and qualities are often harder to recognize.

PEOPLE	sailor, brother, Dr. Adams, senators, Ed
PLACES	forest, North Carolina, rooms, England, building, beach, White House, home, amusement park
THINGS	rug, explosion, piano, bird, rain, trucks, minutes, wind, flu, chipmunk, colors
IDEAS AND QUALITIES	freedom, happiness, fun, love, inflation, bravery, anger, honesty, sickness, faith, democracy, thought, honor, excitement

EXERCISE *Finding Nouns*

Number your paper 1 to 30. Then write the nouns in the following paragraph.

What a Car!   A car totally run by a computer now exists. A key has been replaced by a card made of plastic. The driver inserts it into a slot in the dashboard. The seat and the mirrors are automatically adjusted first. Then a device uses radar to sense vehicles and objects ahead and puts on the brakes if necessary. If rain begins, the wipers turn on by themselves. A map gives instructions on the best route to follow. The carburetor checks itself to ensure the best mileage from a tank of gas. The car can even follow commands given by voice. To own such an amazing car is the dream of many people.

Compound and Collective Nouns

Some nouns include more than one word. *Office* is one noun, but *post office* is also one noun. A noun that includes more than one word is called a *compound noun*. Compound nouns can take one of three forms.

SEPARATE WORDS	living room, home run, record player
HYPHENATED	break-in, attorney-at-law, bird-watcher
COMBINED	birdhouse, headband, flashlight

Note: It is not always easy to know how a particular compound noun should be written. The best way to find out is to check in a dictionary.

Collective Nouns   A noun can also name a group of people or things. This kind of noun is called a *collective noun*.

COLLECTIVE NOUNS   team, family, herd, choir, jury

EXERCISE ◆2◆ *Finding Nouns*

Number your paper 1 to 10. Then write the nouns in each sentence.

1. The pilot pulled the plane out of the nosedive.
2. Last summer Mark went to a dude ranch for two weeks.
3. Our class will meet with the mayor at city hall.

4. The new high school will open next week.
5. My sister went to school at night to study speed-reading.
6. The private detective compared the fingerprints.
7. Ken and I spent the day doing a jigsaw puzzle.
8. My brother-in-law lost his credit cards recently.
9. Will you give me a rain check on that invitation?
10. The prizewinner was surrounded by a group of fans.

Common and Proper Nouns

All nouns are either common nouns or proper nouns. A *common noun* names any person, place, or thing. A *proper noun* names a particular person, place, or thing. All proper nouns begin with a capital letter.

COMMON NOUNS	PROPER NOUNS
man	Mr. Henry Collins
city	Chicago
building	World Trade Center
team	Dallas Cowboys

Note: A proper noun sometimes includes more than one word. For example, even though *World Trade Center* is three words, it is considered one noun. It is the name of *one* place.

EXERCISE 3 *Finding Common and Proper Nouns*

Number your paper 1 to 10. Make two columns on your paper. Label the first column *common nouns* and the second column *proper nouns*. Then, in the proper column, write each noun.

EXAMPLE   Ronald Taylor from California thinks that most bugs make tasty treats.

ANSWER

common nouns	proper nouns
bugs, treats	Ronald Taylor, California

Foods of the Future

1. In Colombia ants are sold as snacks from pushcarts.
2. Fried worms are eaten in Mexico.
3. People in Uganda crush flies and shape them into pancakes.

4. In other parts of Africa, termites are munched like pretzels.
5. Certain spiders are roasted in New Guinea.
6. These insects taste like peanut butter.
7. Restaurants in New York City serve ants and grasshoppers dipped in chocolate.
8. In recent years the North American Bait Farms have held a bake-off using worms.
9. In some cookbooks you can find a recipe for green peppers stuffed with earthworms.
10. Actually, insects give people protein and vitamins.

EXERCISE *Cumulative Review*

Number your paper 1 to 10. Then write the nouns in each sentence. (There are 33 nouns.)

How Did
Houdini Do
It?

1. How did Houdini escape from jails, straitjackets, and strange containers?
2. Sometimes he kept keys in his throat.
3. He used the same method sword-swallowers use.
4. Once when escaping from a jail in New York, he hid a piece of metal in a callus in the heel of one foot.
5. He attached it to a wire that he had hidden in his hair to make a key.
6. He also designed trick cabinets with locks and hinges in secret places.
7. This magician also had great strength and agility.
8. Like a professional athlete, he kept his body and mind fit.
9. Moreover, he had a great gift; he could dislocate his joints.
10. His skill enabled him to mystify audiences throughout the world.

Application to Writing

Write a paragraph that describes what you might find in an old trunk in the attic or basement of your home. Be prepared to identify the nouns in your paragraph.

USING YOUR TEXT

*Commas with a Series
(821–822)
Letters
(436–446)*

Grammar: Using Specific Nouns

Words create certain pictures in the minds of readers. The nouns you choose can make these pictures dull and fuzzy or clear and exact. Vague, general nouns should almost always be replaced with specific nouns. In that way, you will bring your word pictures into sharp focus.

GENERAL   On a **holiday** we went to a **lake.**
SPECIFIC   On **Labor Day** we went to **Ryan Lake.**

Checking Your Understanding   Number your paper 1 to 5. For each underlined word or words, substitute a specific noun.

1. The boy made a dessert for dinner.
2. Appliances were on sale at the store.
3. I play a musical instrument in the senior string orchestra at school.
4. The girl ordered flowers from the florist.
5. The tree was covered with insects.

Writing a Letter   Imagine that you have just won first prize in a writing contest. Your prize is an all-expenses-paid, two-week vacation at a space station resort near Mars. Make a list of all the things you would want to take along with you on your trip.

Next write a letter to your Uncle Frederick and Aunt Lenore who have been living at the space station for the past two years. Tell them about the things you are planning to take with you and ask them what else you should take. *Application:* Read over the first draft of your letter, looking for any vague, general nouns that you can replace with more informative, specific nouns. Look in a dictionary or a thesaurus for exact nouns to substitute. Then edit your letter for any errors and make a neat final copy.

Pronouns

Holly took Holly's books with Holly.

Speaking and writing would be very repetitious if there were no words to take the place of nouns. *Pronouns* do this job. When pronouns are substituted for nouns, the example above reads more smoothly and is easier to understand.

Holly took **her** books with **her.**

Rule 19b   A **pronoun** is a word that takes the place of one or more nouns.

Pronoun Antecedents

The noun that a pronoun refers to or replaces is called its *antecedent.* In the following examples, an arrow has been drawn from the pronoun to its antecedent. Notice that the antecedent usually comes before the pronoun.

Dion said that **he** couldn't go.

Lynn asked **Sandy,** "Did **we** miss a turn?"

EXERCISE **5** *Finding Antecedents*

Number your paper 1 to 10. Then write the antecedent for each underlined pronoun.

1. Ellen carried <u>her</u> umbrella to school.
2. Walter said, "<u>I</u> like mashed potatoes best."
3. Steve asked Anita to go to the dance with <u>him</u>.
4. Randy and Margo said <u>they</u> were going to the movies.
5. Sandy told Robert that <u>she</u> was having a party.
6. The sky has a rosy tint to <u>it</u>.
7. Did Clara and Ann wear <u>their</u> uniforms?
8. Jeff asked Leda, "Are <u>you</u> leaving now?"
9. Albert said that <u>he</u> was going to play hockey.
10. The coach asked the team, "Are <u>you</u> ready to win?"

Personal Pronouns

All the pronouns in Exercise 5 are *personal pronouns*. These pronouns can be divided into the following three groups.

Personal Pronouns		
FIRST PERSON	(The person speaking)	
SINGULAR	I, me, my, mine	
PLURAL	we, us, our, ours	
SECOND PERSON	(The person spoken to)	
SINGULAR	you, your, yours	
PLURAL	you, your, yours	
THIRD PERSON	(The person or thing spoken about)	
SINGULAR	he, him, his, she, her, hers, it, its	
PLURAL	they, them, their, theirs	

The following sentences use personal pronouns.

FIRST PERSON PRONOUNS	**I** want to take **my** dog with **me.** **We** think **our** way is best for **us.**
SECOND PERSON PRONOUNS	Did **you** clean **your** room? Are these sneakers **yours?**
THIRD PERSON PRONOUNS	The reporter took **his** camera with **him.** **They** like **their** soup very hot.

Reflexive Pronouns These pronouns are formed by adding *-self* or *-selves* to certain personal pronouns.

Reflexive Pronouns	
SINGULAR	myself, yourself, himself, herself, itself
PLURAL	ourselves, yourselves, themselves

Miguel bought **himself** a new notebook.

The guests served **themselves** at the buffet.

EXERCISE *Finding Personal and Reflexive Pronouns*

Number your paper 1 to 10. Then write each personal or reflexive pronoun and its antecedent.

1. The Harrisons bought themselves a video recorder.
2. "Tell me what you heard," Mark told Michele.
3. Doris gives herself a good workout every afternoon.
4. The cat tossed its toy mouse into the air and caught it.
5. The students wrote their reports and turned them in.
6. "Did you teach yourself to ski?" Anne asked David.
7. "I will help myself by walking more," Barbara said.
8. Rick took his turn at the computer after Paula took hers.
9. "Can you tell me if Pedro is here?" Bruce asked Mary.
10. "The Morrisons spoke highly of you when they were here," Audrey told Chris.

Other Kinds of Pronouns

Besides personal pronouns, three other kinds of pronouns will be discussed in this section. A fourth kind, *relative pronouns*, will be covered in Chapter 26.

Indefinite Pronouns   Indefinite pronouns very often refer to unnamed people or things. They usually do not have definite antecedents as personal pronouns do.

Several have qualified for the contest.
Many attended the school concert.
I've heard **everything** now!

Common Indefinite Pronouns			
all	both	few	nothing
another	each	many	one
any	either	most	several
anybody	everybody	neither	some
anyone	everyone	none	someone
anything	everything	no one	something

EXERCISE 7 *Finding Indefinite Pronouns*

Number your paper 1 to 10. Then write each indefinite pronoun.

1. The invitation was extended to everyone.
2. Both of you know everything that happened.
3. No one saw anyone from the other school at the sophomore dance.
4. Each of the four eye-witnesses knew something about the accident.
5. Some arrived early, but many came late.
6. All except Mary attended the class meeting.
7. One of my friends will go with me.
8. None of the dinner had been eaten.
9. Did you tell anybody about either of our ideas for the reunion party?
10. Most of my friends sent me a card or phoned me on my birthday.

Demonstrative Pronouns   These pronouns are used to point out people, places, and objects.

This is Mary's coat on the hanger.
Are **these** John's glasses?

Demonstrative Pronouns			
this	that	these	those

Interrogative Pronouns   These pronouns are used to ask questions.

What is known about the case?
Who is coming to the party?

Interrogative Pronouns				
what	which	who	whom	whose

EXERCISE *Finding Demonstrative Pronouns and Interrogative Pronouns*

Number your paper 1 to 10. Then write each demonstrative and interrogative pronoun in the following sentences.

1. What is the starting time of the championship basketball game?
2. If that is true, who will help us?
3. Bob can't decide between these or those.
4. Whom did Alex meet at the dance?
5. That is my sweater.
6. These are Mike's gloves on the table, and those are Anne's on the desk.
7. If Mom has the keys, then whose are these?
8. This is Amy's first trip to the East.
9. Which of those does Lucy want?
10. What does Ruth think this could be?

EXERCISE *Cumulative Review*

Number your paper 1 to 10. Then write all the pronouns in each sentence. (There are 25 pronouns.)

1. After the party, most of the guests said they enjoyed it very much.
2. What is Tom doing in our garage?
3. Meg thinks she found the missing birthday candles and their holders.
4. Teresa cooked herself and her brother scrambled eggs for breakfast.
5. Everyone donated something to the fund.
6. The judge asked the jury, "Is this your verdict?"
7. Both of the girls took their skates with them to the nearby rink.
8. What does that mean to you?
9. One of the parakeets got out of its cage.
10. When George finished his homework, he put it into his notebook.

USING YOUR TEXT

*Sensory Details
(184–185)
Descriptive Paragraphs
(182–195)*

Grammar: Substituting Pronouns for Nouns

As you have learned in this chapter, pronouns provide short-cuts in writing by referring to nouns. These shortcuts create a smoother flow to your writing by preventing the dull repetition of nouns.

Checking Your Understanding   The following paragraph repeats some nouns too often. Rewrite the paragraph by replacing nouns with pronouns where they are needed. Then underline your changes.

Gorillas Are
Smart
Investigations into the intelligence of gorillas show that gorillas are much smarter than people once thought gorillas were. Gorillas will stack boxes to help gorillas reach bananas that are too high to pick. Gorillas will use sticks as tools to pull food into gorillas' cages. One scientist, Dr. James White, trained a female gorilla named Congo to perform various actions. When the scientist returned some years later, Congo remembered the scientist. Congo also repeated some of the actions the scientist had taught Congo. Her behavior in these instances helped convince scientists of gorillas' intelligence.

Writing a Description   Think about yesterday. What did you see that was unusual? Brainstorm for a list of out-of-the-ordinary persons, places, or things. Then choose one idea from your list and write the first draft of a paragraph that describes the unusual person, place, or thing. In your paragraph use details that appeal to the five senses.   *Application:* As you revise your paragraph, replace any general nouns with proper nouns or specific common nouns. Then check to see if you have repeated any nouns too often. Would substituting a pronoun for a noun make your writing smoother or clearer? Make these and any other needed changes and write a final draft.

19

Review

A **Identifying Nouns and Pronouns** Number your paper 1 to 20. Make two columns on your paper. Label the first column *nouns* and the second column *pronouns*. In the correct column, write each noun and pronoun. Then underline each proper noun.

EXAMPLE   Pat and I skied in Aspen last winter.

ANSWER   <u>nouns</u>   <u>pronouns</u>

Pat, <u>Aspen</u>, winter   I

1. After Alaska, the state with the smallest population is Wyoming.
2. The newspaper praised Rhoda for her calmness and courage after the accident.
3. The long snout and tongue of the anteater enable it to burrow in the ground for its dinner.
4. Tim just bought himself something at the mall.
5. Lee had his hair cut for the wedding on Sunday.
6. Some of your books from the library are due next week.
7. A ring around the moon is a sign of rain or snow.
8. Lynn bought herself a painting of a flock of geese.
9. Harvey Kennedy became a multimillionaire because he invented the shoelace.
10. The first person in history to swim the English Channel was Matthew Webb.
11. Everyone goes to the new shopping center in Newton.
12. I heard Mary say that last night at the game.
13. At any given moment, there are about 2,000 thunderstorms brewing in the atmosphere.
14. If this doesn't fit me, do you want it?
15. After most of the guests had arrived, Sheila came in.
16. Steve bought his mother a music box for her birthday.
17. My family and many of our relatives held a reunion.

18. These are the ones you should buy.

19. Which of the girls from the group was chosen?

20. He explained to me everything about the concert in Melbourne Auditorium.

B **Recognizing Pronouns and Their Antecedents**

Number your paper 1 to 10. Then write each personal pronoun and its antecedent.

1. Because Jamie was absent, he missed the field trip.

2. When the twins dress alike, they look identical.

3. An anteater can extend its tongue about two feet.

4. Linda told Andrew, "If you own a tennis racket, we can play a game on Saturday."

5. Ken took his raincoat with him to the baseball game.

6. Mr. Ash told Nancy, "You should give your report now."

7. Bill and Ron rode their bicycles to school today.

8. "I didn't see you at the mall," Pam told Terry.

9. Linda said she is making her own dinner tonight.

10. "My grandparents asked me to visit them in Florida," Daniel told his friend.

Mastery Test

Number your paper 1 to 10. Make two columns on your paper. Label the first column *nouns* and the second column *pronouns*. Then in the proper column, write each noun and pronoun.

1. Are you playing tennis on Saturday?

2. I have lived in Washington for five years now.

3. Animals usually show loyalty to their owners.

4. What is that on the edge of the table?

5. Pat wants to buy the small, portable radio.

6. Who will help Ralph with a hard problem in math?

7. We thought the special effects in the movie were amazing.

8. Do you think this is a good price for them?

9. Something is wrong with your brakes.

10. Crowds gathered on Lake Street to watch the parade.

20
Verbs

Diagnostic Test

Number your paper 1 to 10. Write the verb or the verb phrase in each sentence. Then label each one *action* or *linking*.

EXAMPLE Has her temperature remained high?
ANSWER has remained—linking

1. Egyptians built the first zoo almost 3,500 years ago.
2. Your radio is too loud.
3. You should have known the answer.
4. Mr. Jenkins will become the new police chief next November.
5. The snow has been falling very heavily for three hours now.
6. Tad did drive through the snowstorm.
7. Ken carefully tasted the hot soup.
8. Mrs. Davidson has lived in that yellow house for seventeen years.
9. Do you feel warm?
10. Lincoln was the 16th president of the United States.

Action Verbs

Verbs breathe life into sentences. One kind of verb gives a subject action and movement. Another kind of verb tells something about a subject. It can state the condition of the subject or state the fact that the subject exists. This chapter will explain these kinds of verbs. You will also learn how to choose the best verbs when you write.

The most frequently used kind of verb is the *action verb*.

Rule 20a An **action verb** tells what action a subject is performing.

Most action verbs show physical action.

Dad **plants** tulip bulbs every fall.
Karen **skated** across the frozen pond.

Some action verbs show mental action. Others show ownership or possession.

José **remembered** the formula.
Toby **has** a new friend.

In Chapter 18 you learned that *helping verbs* are often used with an action verb to form a *verb phrase*.

Rule 20b A **verb phrase** is a main verb plus one or more helping verbs.

Notice in the following examples that a verb phrase may contain more than one helping verb. It may also be interrupted by other words. *(See page 547.)*

John **should have announced** the contest in homeroom today.
Barbara **will** surely **help** you with your math before the test tomorrow.
Shouldn't Robin **go** with us?

On the following page is a list of the most common helping verbs.

Common Helping Verbs	
be	am, is, are, was, were, be, being, been
have	has, have, had
do	do, does, did
others	may, might, must, can, could, shall, should, will, would

EXERCISE *Finding Action Verbs*

Number your paper 1 to 10. Then write the verb or the verb phrase in each sentence.

The Amazing Dolphins

1. Dr. Lilly, a scientist from California, has been experimenting with dolphins for many years.
2. He has made some curious claims about them.
3. Dolphins have larger brains than humans.
4. Their language contains at least 50,000 words.
5. Their brains can handle four conversations at one time.
6. They can also judge between right and wrong.
7. Dolphins can remember sounds and series of sounds.
8. They can even communicate among themselves.
9. They use a series of clicks, buzzes, and whistles.
10. Dolphins have discharged some of these sounds at the rate of 700 times a second.

EXERCISE *Finding Verb Phrases*

Number your paper 1 to 15. Then write the verb phrase in each sentence.

1. The party should have started an hour ago.
2. A diamond will not dissolve in acid.
3. An average person's liver can weigh three and a half pounds.
4. Mark has had a coin collection for ten years.
5. Chewing gum had first appeared in 1848.
6. Some tortoises can live about 100 years.
7. Steve couldn't stay for lunch.

8. Larry must have just finished his chores.
9. Didn't you sleep well last night?
10. Pigs actually do exhibit great intelligence.
11. The Romans had originally named the Colosseum the Flavian Amphitheater.
12. Didn't you see the red light?
13. In Houston you can visit the first domed stadium.
14. A storm had never caused such severe damage before.
15. A mother bird may feed its fledglings over 1,200 times in a given day.

Application to Writing

Think about the last time you passed a construction site. What were the workers doing? Write a paragraph describing some of the action involved in constructing a building, a bridge, or a road. Be prepared to identify the verbs in your sentences.

Transitive and Intransitive Verbs

All action verbs can be either transitive or intransitive. To decide whether a verb is transitive or intransitive, say the subject and the verb. Then ask the question *What?* or *Whom?* A word that answers either question is called an *object.* An action verb that has an object is *transitive.* An action verb that does not have an object is *intransitive.*

TRANSITIVE   Josh always **eats** dinner late. [Josh eats what? *Dinner* is the object. Therefore, *eats* is a transitive verb.]

INTRANSITIVE   The car **skidded** on the icy road. [The car skidded what? The car skidded whom? Since there is no object, *skidded* is an intransitive verb.]

EXERCISE *Transitive and Intransitive Verbs*

Number your paper 1 to 10. Write the action verb in each sentence. Then label each one *transitive* or *intransitive*.

1. Eagles keep the same nests throughout their lives.
2. Hummingbirds sometimes fly backward.
3. The dog buried its bone in the backyard.
4. My family eats fresh vegetables every day.
5. The papers scattered all over the lawn.
6. A human eye winks in one fortieth of a second.
7. Suddenly lightning struck the massive tree.
8. Strawberries contain more vitamin C than oranges.
9. The trees blew gently in the breeze.
10. The Empire State Building has 6,400 windows.

Transitive or Intransitive?   The same verb can be transitive in one sentence and intransitive in another sentence.

TRANSITIVE   Carrie **sang** a song for us. [Carrie sang what?
Song is the object.]

INTRANSITIVE   Carrie **sang** at the Civic Center. [Carrie sang
what? There is no object.]

EXERCISE *Transitive or Intransitive Verbs*

Number your paper 1 to 10. Write the action verb in each sentence. Then label each one *transitive* or *intransitive*.

1. Jeff quickly turned the pages.
2. My mother often speaks at school meetings.
3. On Fridays Ann plays at Symphony Hall.
4. My brother always drives carefully.
5. Kim speaks English, French, and Spanish.
6. The birdhouse hung from a rope on the oak tree.
7. They turned down the dark alley.
8. Anne drives her car to school.
9. We hung new curtains in my bedroom.
10. Rob usually plays tennis on the weekends.

Linking Verbs

Verbs that link or join the subject with another word in the sentence are called *linking verbs*.

Rule 20c A **linking verb** links the subject with another word in the sentence. The other word either renames or describes the subject.

Tim **is** my brother. [*Is* links *brother* and the subject *Tim*. *Brother* renames the subject.]

Have you **been** sad lately? [Turn a question into a statement: *You have been sad lately.* Then you can easily see that *have been* links *sad* and the subject *you*. *Sad* describes the subject.]

Following is a list of common linking verbs. They are all forms of the verb *be*. Any verb phrase ending in *be* or *been* is a form of *be* and can be used as a linking verb.

Common Forms of *Be*		
be	shall be	have been
is	will be	has been
am	can be	had been
are	could be	could have been
was	should be	should have been
were	would be	may have been
	may be	might have been
	might be	must have been

The forms of the verb *be* are not always linking verbs. To be a linking verb, a verb must link the subject with another word in the sentence that renames or describes it. In the following examples, the verbs simply make statements and are not linking verbs.

I **was** there. They **will be** in the library.

EXERCISE *Finding Linking Verbs*

Number your paper 1 to 20. Write the linking verb in each sentence. Then write the two words that the verb links.

EXAMPLE   The roses were a gift.
ANSWER   were roses—gift

I. The comforter was very warm.
2. The Minakos will be our new neighbors.
3. Alex should have been the captain.
4. The elephant is the only animal with four knees.
5. The light here should be brighter.
6. In China the dragon is a symbol of good luck.
7. You might be the winner.
8. Is the butter too hard?
9. Some fish are smaller than ants.
10. Lenny may be correct about the score.
11. The owner of the car is Mr. Borg.
12. No two fingerprints are exactly alike.
13. That road may have been the turnoff to Route 6.
14. This holiday should be happy for everyone.
15. The inventor of the thermometer was Galileo.
16. The Taylors have been our neighbors for 15 years.
17. Would you be my lab partner?
18. The largest desert in the world is the Sahara.
19. Baseball will always be my favorite sport.
20. Lincoln was the 16th president of the United States.

Additional Linking Verbs

A few other verbs besides *be* can be linking verbs.

Additional Linking Verbs			
appear	grow	seem	stay
become	look	smell	taste
feel	remain	sound	turn

These verbs link the subject with a word that renames or describes.

Burt **remained** captain of the team for two years. [*Captain* renames the subject.]

The weather **will turn** colder tomorrow. [*Colder* describes the subject.]

EXERCISE ◆ **6** *Finding Linking Verbs*

Number your paper 1 to 10. Write each verb or verb phrase. Then write the two words that the verb links.

1. That hat looks ridiculous on you!
2. Hector has grown braver.
3. Judy became the new treasurer of the club.
4. The rabbit's fur felt extremely soft.
5. My mother appears quite content.
6. Her hands remained steady throughout her speech.
7. His voice sounded very stern.
8. The grapefruit tasted unusually sour.
9. Does Betsy seem sad to you?
10. The roasting turkey smelled delicious.

Linking Verb or Action Verb?

Most linking verbs can also be action verbs.

LINKING VERB   The medicine **tasted** very bitter. [*Bitter* describes the subject.]

ACTION VERB   Marvin nervously **tasted** the lobster. [*Tasted* shows action. It tells what Marvin did.]

To decide whether a verb is a linking verb or an action verb, ask two questions. *Does the verb link the subject with a word that renames or describes the subject? Does the verb show action?*

LINKING VERB   Your costume **looks** perfect.

ACTION VERB   She **looks** in the mailbox each day.

EXERCISE *Distinguishing between Linking Verbs and Action Verbs*

Number your paper 1 to 10. Write the verb or the verb phrase in each sentence. Then label each one *linking* or *action*.

1. Did you turn the record over?
2. The evening breeze felt cool.
3. My neighbor grows tomatoes in her backyard.
4. Peggy looked everywhere for Penny.
5. Have you felt the material on the sofa?
6. Melinda's voice sounds so pleasant over the phone.
7. Our cat always grows hungry at night.
8. Those shoes look very comfortable.
9. The bugle sounded the start of the race.
10. The photographs turned dull with age.

EXERCISE *Writing Sentences*

Write a sentence using each verb as a linking verb. Then use it as an action verb. Label each *linking* or *action*.

1. taste   **2.** look   **3.** smell   **4.** appear   **5.** grow

EXERCISE *Cumulative Review*

Number your paper 1 to 10. Write the verb or the verb phrase in each sentence. Then label each one *linking* or *action*.

The
Study of
Cold

1. Cryogenics is the study of cold.
2. At very cold temperatures, your breath will turn to a liquid.
3. At colder temperatures, it actually freezes into a solid.
4. Cold steel becomes very soft.
5. A frozen banana can serve as a hammer.
6. Shivers can raise the body temperature seven degrees.
7. People with a low body temperature feel lazy.
8. One should wear layers of clothing for protection from cold.
9. Chipmunks have found a good solution to the cold.
10. They hibernate all winter long.

USING YOUR TEXT

*Clustering
(21–22)
Expository Essays
(244–283)*

Grammar: Using Colorful Verbs

At the beginning of this chapter, you read that verbs can breathe life into a sentence. This is true. However, some verbs can breathe more life into a sentence than other verbs. A dictionary and a thesaurus usually provide colorful alternatives to dull, lifeless verbs such as *say* and *walk*. These colorful alternatives will add life to your writing.

LIFELESS VERB The roller coaster **went** down the steep slope.

COLORFUL VERB The roller coaster **roared** (thundered, crashed, hurtled) down the steep slope.

Checking Your Understanding Number your paper 1 to 10. Then write at least two colorful verbs that have about the same meaning as each of the following overused verbs. Use a thesaurus if possible.

1. tell	**3.** sit	**5.** throw	**7.** go	**9.** speak
2. walk	**4.** eat	**6.** look	**8.** move	**10.** hurry

Writing a Newspaper Article Think about a storm you have seen firsthand or on TV—a snowstorm, a heavy rainstorm, or even a hurricane. Make a cluster diagram with the name of the storm in the center. On connecting lines, write everything you associate with that particular storm. Next, write a newspaper article that tells vividly about the storm and how it affected your community. *Application:* As you revise your article, ask yourself the following questions. Does your opening sentence catch the reader's attention? Have you used fresh, colorful verbs to describe the storm? Then add a title to your article, edit your work for errors, and make a final copy to present to your class.

20 Review

A Identifying Verbs and Verb Phrases   Number your paper 1 to 25. Write the verb or the verb phrase in each sentence. Then label each one *action* or *linking*.

1. Hollywood has made 19 films about Dracula.
2. Ms. Edwards will become the school's new track coach.
3. The flowers still look very fresh.
4. Have you gone to the new science museum?
5. A female condor lays a single egg every two years.
6. For two weeks they have been looking for a job.
7. A human can detect the smell of a skunk a mile away.
8. Daisies have always been my favorite flower.
9. They should have telephoned the restaurant first.
10. Rice is the chief food for half the people of the world.
11. Lettuce is the world's most popular green vegetable.
12. It can be colder in winter in New York than in Iceland.
13. Didn't you sing in the chorus last year?
14. I have always attended the meetings.
15. Rico remains my best friend.
16. Turn right at the next intersection.
17. Guinea pigs are not members of the pig family.
18. At first the exercise appeared very difficult.
19. Some turtles do not breathe at all during the winter.
20. Have you ever seen a meteor?
21. A honeybee can carry an object 300 times its own weight.
22. You should have called him last night.
23. The three primary colors are red, yellow, and blue.
24. I felt dizzy after the roller-coaster ride.
25. A camel's hump does not store water.

B **Understanding Transitive and Intransitive Verbs**

Number your paper 1 to 10. Write the verb or the verb phrase in each sentence. Then label each one *transitive* or *intransitive*.

1. Most of the apples fell from the tree during the storm.
2. Spiders have transparent blood.
3. Dad is reading on the porch.
4. Most American horns beep in the key of F.
5. I usually answer the phone on the second ring.
6. Did you read this book for your book report?
7. Cut the grass tomorrow.
8. The robot will always answer politely.
9. Thomas Jefferson invented the calendar clock.
10. The fire engine rushed through the red light.

Mastery Test

Number your paper 1 to 10. Write the verb or the verb phrase in each sentence. Then label each one *action* or *linking*.

1. An owl can rotate its head in a full circle.
2. Anita will be happy with your decision.
3. Are you going to the game on Saturday?
4. The sky turned dark in the afternoon.
5. You should have told me that sooner.
6. Is Sue your best friend?
7. An orange tree may produce oranges for more than a hundred years.
8. The storm has delayed my flight.
9. The portrait of Martha was very flattering.
10. Have you tasted her homemade chili?

21 Adjectives and Adverbs

Diagnostic Test

Number your paper 1 to 10 and make two columns. Label the first column *adjectives* and the second column *adverbs*. Then in the proper column, write each adjective and adverb. Do not include articles.

EXAMPLE   The three yellow-breasted birds flew away.

ANSWER   <u>adjectives</u>   <u>adverbs</u>
         three, yellow-breasted   away

1. Jeff carefully read the long instructions.
2. Alan spoke briefly but convincingly before the entire faculty.
3. The unusually smart horse could do many tricks.
4. Unsteadily the very nervous actor read his lines.
5. A Sunday brunch of waffles is always delicious.
6. During a two-week vacation, we visited the islands.
7. Amanda received three books as a present.
8. The Mexican dancers whirled swiftly around the large hats.
9. One rose remained in the rather large glass vase.
10. Haven't these books been returned to the library?

Adjectives

A sentence with only nouns or pronouns and verbs would be very short and dull.

Dogs bark.

However, you use *adjectives* and *adverbs* to give color and sharper meaning to a sentence.

Those three huge dogs **constantly** bark **loudly.**

Adjectives and adverbs are called *modifiers* because they modify or change the meaning of other parts of speech.

Adjectives modify, or make more precise, the meanings of nouns and pronouns. For example, what was your day like yesterday? Was it *pleasant, busy, happy, sad,* or *hectic?* All of these possible answers are adjectives because they all make the meaning of *day* clearer or more precise.

Yesterday was a **hectic** but **pleasant** day.

| Rule 21a | An **adjective** is a word that modifies a noun or a pronoun. |

To find an adjective, first find each noun and pronoun in a sentence. Then ask yourself, *What kind? Which one(s)? How many?* or *How much?* about each one. The answers will be adjectives.

WHAT KIND?   The **old** car needs to be painted.

Do you like **fresh** broccoli?

WHICH ONE(S)?   **These** boots belong to Stacy.

I like the **white** one.

HOW MANY?   **Thirty** people attended the meeting.

He owns **many** tapes.

HOW MUCH?   **Little** room was left in the suitcase.

She deserves **much** praise for her work.

Note: *A, an,* and *the* form a special group of adjectives called *articles. A* comes before words that begin with a consonant sound, and *an* before words that begin with a vowel sound. You will not be asked to list articles in the exercises in this book.

EXERCISE *Finding Adjectives*

Number your paper 1 to 10. Then write the adjectives in the following sentences. There are 25 adjectives.

Mini-Cows
 1. For 17 years, two men, named José Villalobos and Angel Castrillón, have been raising cows.
 2. Each year, however, large cows become smaller cows.
 3. The average cow in this strange herd now stands 28 inches from the ground.
 4. Compare this size with that of a normal cow of 67 inches.
 5. Nevertheless, these men are successful scientists.
 6. Villalobos and Castrillón have been breeding these tiny cows especially for farmers in poorer parts of the world.
 7. The cows need little space, but they produce much milk.
 8. These unusual animals also yield delicious steaks.
 9. There is one tiny problem, however.
10. A steak is the same size as a hamburger.

EXERCISE **2** *Supplying Adjectives*

Write an adjective that completes each sentence.

 1. The _____ building will be torn down soon.
 2. I counted _____ birds in that tree yesterday.
 3. Do you want a _____ sweater for your birthday?
 4. I enjoyed eating the _____ cereal.
 5. _____ time was given for the assembly.
 6. There weren't _____ people left when I arrived.
 7. Ellen's _____ choice for a vacation was California.
 8. She could easily be seen in her bright _____ coat.
 9. Kent thought the book was very _____.
10. The _____ flowers decorated the table.

Position of Adjectives

Adjectives can modify different nouns or pronouns, or they can modify the same noun or pronoun.

DIFFERENT NOUNS   Buy **six** pears and a **big** watermelon.

THE SAME NOUN   I just bought **six big** tomatoes.

Usually an adjective comes in front of the noun or the pronoun it modifies. However, an adjective can also follow a noun or a pronoun, or it can follow a linking verb.

BEFORE A NOUN   Her **soft** voice couldn't be heard.

AFTER A NOUN   The dog, **sad** and **wet,** whined.

AFTER A LINKING VERB   Ron looks quite **cheerful** today.

EXERCISE 3 *Finding Adjectives*

Write the adjectives in each sentence. Then beside each adjective, write the word it modifies. There are 30 adjectives.

Fancy Dressers

1. For many years men dressed with more color and greater style than women.
2. During the 1600's, men wore lacy collars and fancy jackets with shiny buttons.
3. Long curly hair reached the shoulder.
4. Men even carried small purses on huge belts.
5. After all, there were no pockets in the warm, colorful tights they wore.
6. By 1850, clothing had become drab and conservative.
7. Gone were elegant white silk shirts, purple vests, lacy cuffs, and stylish black boots.
8. Clothing stayed colorless and dreary until the popular Beatles came along in the 1960's.
9. The way they dressed, bright and informal, created a new style for men.
10. Today people don't follow one style; everyone dresses to suit personal taste.

Proper and Compound Adjectives

You have learned that a proper noun is the name of a particular person, place, or thing—*Mexico* and *Northeast*. A *proper adjective* is an adjective that is formed from a proper noun—*Mexican* food and *Eastern* states. Like a proper noun, a proper adjective begins with a capital letter.

PROPER NOUNS	PROPER ADJECTIVES
England	**English** countryside
Shakespeare	**Shakespearean** dramas

Some proper adjectives keep the same form as the proper noun.

New York	**New York** skyline
Monday	**Monday** traffic

Compound Adjectives   You have also learned that compound nouns are nouns made up of two or more words. *Compound adjectives* are adjectives that are made up of two or more words.

COMPOUND ADJECTIVES   **rooftop** apartment
far-off horizon

EXERCISE *Finding Proper and Compound Adjectives*

Write the proper adjective and the compound adjective in each sentence. Beside each adjective, write the word it modifies.

EXAMPLE   The farsighted investor purchased Mexican art.
ANSWER   farsighted—investor, Mexican—art

1. Francisco lives in a seafront cottage on a Hawaiian island.
2. The topic of Tuesday's after-school discussion will be the American economy.
3. Japanese people enjoy fast-food restaurants.
4. The blue-eyed girl was from a Scandinavian country.
5. A Republican senator spoke of widespread poverty.
6. The pint-sized car is a French import.
7. The all-star team will play the Australian team next.

8. The reporter's straightforward questions pleased the Russian diplomat.

9. Canadian friends of ours met us this morning at the waterfront hotel.

10. Third-class mail is sent by boat to European countries.

Adjective or Noun?

The same word can be an adjective in one sentence and a noun in another sentence.

ADJECTIVE   Her editorial appeared in the **school** paper.
[*School* tells what kind of paper.]

NOUN   I've gone to this **school** for three years. [*School* is the name of a place.]

ADJECTIVE   Did you buy **plant** food?

NOUN   The **plant** is doing very well here.

Note: *Plant* can also be used as a verb.

Plant the evergreen here.

EXERCISE *Distinguishing between Adjectives and Nouns*

Number your paper 1 to 10. Write the underlined word in each sentence. Then label each word *adjective* or *noun*.

1. Have you seen the <u>garden</u> tools?
2. The <u>television</u> series was canceled after two shows.
3. We need two panes of <u>glass</u> to repair the broken picture window.
4. Don't touch the hot <u>oven</u>!
5. I need to buy a <u>picture</u> frame for this snapshot.
6. Margo planted irises in her <u>garden</u>.
7. When was that <u>picture</u> of you taken?
8. Jane received a tiny <u>glass</u> owl as a present.
9. Do they own an <u>oven</u> thermometer?
10. Did you see the special on <u>television</u>?

EXERCISE *Writing Sentences*

Write two sentences for each of the following words. In the first sentence, use the word as an adjective. In the second sentence, use the word as a noun. Label the use of each one.

I. birthday   **2.** rose   **3.** bicycle   **4.** top   **5.** paper

Adjective or Pronoun?

The following words can be either adjectives or pronouns.

Words Used as Adjectives or Pronouns			
DEMONSTRATIVE	**INTERROGATIVE**	**INDEFINITE**	
that	what	all	many
these	which	another	more
this		any	most
those		both	neither
		each	other
		either	several
		few	some

All these words are adjectives if they come before a noun and if they modify a noun. They are pronouns when they stand alone.

ADJECTIVE   I bought **this** bread yesterday.

PRONOUN   Do you like **this?**

ADJECTIVE   **What** time is it?

PRONOUN   **What** did the choir sing?

ADJECTIVE   We phoned you **several** times.

PRONOUN   **Several** of the students received awards.

Note: The possessive pronouns *my, your, his, her, its, our,* and *their* are sometimes called *pronominal adjectives* because they answer the question *Which one?* Throughout this book, however, they will be considered pronouns.

EXERCISE **7** *Distinguishing between Adjectives and Pronouns*

Number your paper 1 to 10. Write the underlined word in each sentence. Then label each word *adjective* or *pronoun*.

1. <u>This</u> is my coat on the chair.
2. <u>Which</u> of the bridesmaids should come first?
3. <u>Both</u> of you will make magazine racks.
4. May I have <u>some</u> peace and quiet?
5. <u>These</u> are the perfect curtains for my room.
6. I like <u>this</u> course the most.
7. John will take <u>both</u> suitcases with him.
8. <u>Which</u> record do you want to play first?
9. Can you tell me the price of <u>these</u> scarves?
10. Mr. Kent spoke with <u>some</u> of Peg's teachers.

EXERCISE **8** *Writing Sentences*

Write two sentences for each word. In the first, use the word as an adjective and in the second, as a pronoun.

1. many   **2.** each   **3.** what   **4.** several   **5.** that

EXERCISE **9** *Cumulative Review*

Write each adjective and the word it modifies.

A Helping Hand

A Russian athlete named Nikolai helped the American team win the Olympic ice-hockey championship in 1960. The Americans had beaten the Canadian team and the Russian team. Now all they had to do was defeat the Czechs in the final game. After two periods the Americans were losing. The thin air in the California mountains was slowing them down. Between the second period and the third period, Nikolai visited the weary Americans. Unfortunately he didn't speak any English. Through many gestures, however, he told them to inhale some oxygen. The team immediately felt lively and energetic. For the first time an American team won the title.

Grammar: Vivid Adjectives

Adjectives should make your writing more colorful and interesting. Some adjectives, however, are used so often that they lose their meaning. Look for fresh adjectives in a thesaurus when you revise your writing.

OVERUSED ADJECTIVE   The movie that is playing now at the Plaza was **great.**

FRESH ADJECTIVE   The movie that is playing now at the Plaza was **hilarious** (matchless, extraordinary).

Checking Your Understanding   Number your paper 1 to 5. Then write at least two fresh adjectives for each of the underlined adjectives.

1. The picnic lunch tasted <u>good</u>.
2. The music at the concert was <u>loud</u>.
3. We enjoyed the <u>nice</u> mountain view.
4. Your puppy is <u>playful</u>.
5. Their house is always <u>clean</u>.

Writing an Advertisement   Imagine that your dog has had puppies or that your cat has had kittens. You need to find these small animals good homes. How can you make someone else want one of them? Make a list of descriptive details, appealing characteristics, and endearing types of behavior the animals show.

Next, write an advertisement for your local newspaper, asking readers to adopt one of the pets.   *Application:* As you read over your advertisement, check for fresh, vivid adjectives that will get readers' attention. Using a thesaurus for help, find precise replacements for any dull, overused adjectives. Then edit your work for errors and write a final copy.

Adverbs

Adjectives add more information about nouns and pronouns. *Adverbs* make verbs, adjectives, and other adverbs more precise.

Rule 21b An **adverb** is a word that modifies a verb, an adjective, or another adverb.

Many adverbs end in *-ly*.

> **Recently** Congress voted **unanimously** for the bill.
> **Absentmindedly** Carl strolled **casually** into the wrong classroom.

Following is a list of common adverbs that do not end in *-ly*.

Common Adverbs			
again	ever	often	somewhere
almost	here	perhaps	soon
alone	just	quite	then
already	later	rather	there
also	never	seldom	today
always	not	so	too
away	now	sometimes	very
even	nowhere	somewhat	yet

Note: *Not* and its contraction *n't* are always adverbs.

> She is **not** answering her phone.
> I could**n't** find the broom.

Adverbs That Modify Verbs

Most adverbs modify verbs. To find these adverbs, first find the verb. Then ask yourself, *Where? When? How?* or *To what extent?* about the verb. The answers to these questions will be adverbs. The adverbs in the following examples are in heavy type. An arrow points to the verb each adverb modifies.

WHERE?   Look **everywhere** for the watch.

Put the newspapers **there.**

WHEN?   I **frequently** visit my grandparents.

Sometimes I wax the car.

HOW?   He **quickly** and **accurately** threw the ball to third base.

Roy has **carefully** read the contract.

TO WHAT
EXTENT?   Stan **completely** enjoyed the dinner.

I have **almost** finished my report.

An adverb can come before or after a verb. It can also come in the middle of a verb phrase.

EXERCISE *Finding Adverbs That Modify Verbs*

Number your paper 1 to 10. Write the adverbs in each sentence. Then next to each one, write the verb it modifies.

EXAMPLE   Pearl suddenly laughed heartily.
ANSWER   suddenly—laughed, heartily—laughed

1. The old train slowly chugged forward.
2. The huge watchdog growled fiercely and angrily at the stranger.
3. I haven't seen that movie yet.
4. He often makes decisions quickly.
5. Julio will soon call his relatives in Mexico.
6. Our cat seldom goes outside.
7. The small plane landed smoothly and safely.
8. Old houses are rapidly being remodeled.
9. We have already hung decorations everywhere.
10. Was the moon shining then?

EXERCISE *Finding Adverbs That Modify Verbs*

Write the adverbs in each sentence. Then next to each one, write the verb it modifies. There are 15 adverbs.

Detour:
Quills
Ahead!

1. Porcupines never shoot their quills.
2. Usually the quills catch on something.
3. Then they fall out.
4. Porcupines always use their quills for protection.
5. Occasionally another animal will greatly disturb a porcupine.
6. The porcupine's quills will immediately stand upright.
7. Often the porcupine will bump the other animal.
8. The quills do not miss.
9. They stick swiftly and securely in the animal's skin.
10. An animal rarely bothers a porcupine twice.

 Application to Writing

Most home movies are entertaining, but even dull ones can seem humorous if they are run backward or forward at a fast speed. Write a paragraph describing a home movie being shown at a fast speed. Include as many details as you can think of. Be prepared to identify the adverbs in your paragraph.

Adverbs That Modify Adjectives and Other Adverbs

A few adverbs modify adjectives and other adverbs.

MODIFYING AN ADJECTIVE   The coat was **too** long.

MODIFYING AN ADVERB   Dennis talks **very** fast.

To find adverbs that modify adjectives or other adverbs, first find the adjectives and the adverbs. Then ask yourself, *To what extent?* about each one. Notice in the preceding examples that the adverbs that modify adjectives or other adverbs usually come before the word they modify.

EXERCISE *Finding Adverbs That Modify Adjectives and Other Adverbs*

Number your paper 1 to 15. Write each adverb that modifies an adjective or another adverb. Then beside each adverb, write the word it modifies.

1. The exceptionally long walk exhausted me.
2. The extremely nervous center fumbled the ball.
3. That was a rather funny speech.
4. The old bike works surprisingly well.
5. Read the directions very carefully.
6. The river near our house seems unusually high.
7. The undertow was alarmingly strong.
8. The job at the supermarket is just right for me.
9. They were sitting somewhat close to the front.
10. David arrived much later than Scott.
11. The temperature is falling rather quickly.
12. My poison ivy is extremely itchy.
13. Was the movie very funny?
14. His predictions were quite accurate.
15. I almost never see my grandparents who live in Southern California.

Adverb or Adjective?

As you have seen in the previous section, many adverbs end in -*ly*. You should, however, be aware that some adjectives also end in -*ly*. Always check to see how a word is used in a sentence before you decide what part of speech it is.

ADVERB   Ralph receives the magazine **monthly.**

ADJECTIVE   He pays on a **monthly** basis.

ADVERB   Tom whacked the ball quite **hard.**

ADJECTIVE   The test was very **hard.** [an adjective that follows a linking verb]

EXERCISE *Distinguishing between Adverbs and Adjectives*

Number your paper 1 to 10. Write the underlined word in each sentence. Then label each one *adverb* or *adjective*.

  1. My <u>early</u> appointment was canceled.
  2. The music was too <u>lively</u> for me.
  3. Their large historic house is located <u>high</u> on the knoll overlooking the town.
  4. We <u>carelessly</u> locked the keys in the car.
  5. Our new microwave oven works <u>well</u>.
  6. Bears are definitely not <u>friendly</u>.
  7. Car prices are very <u>high</u> right now.
  8. Don't speak so <u>loudly</u> in the library.
  9. The snowstorm arrived <u>early</u>.
 10. You should feel <u>well</u> again in a day or two.

EXERCISE *Cumulative Review*

Number your paper 1 to 20. Write the adverbs in the following paragraphs. Then beside each adverb, write the word or words it modifies.

The First Roller Skates

The first pair of roller skates appeared in 1760. They were unsuccessfully worn by Joseph Merlin. Merlin had unexpectedly received an invitation to a very large party. Quite excitedly he planned a grand entrance. The night finally arrived. Merlin rolled unsteadily into the ballroom on skates as he played a violin. Unfortunately he couldn't stop. Joseph Merlin crashed into an extremely large mirror. The mirror broke into a million pieces. Merlin also smashed his violin and hurt himself severely.

Roller skates were never used again until 1823. Robert Tyers eventually made another attempt. His skates had a single row of five very small wheels. In 1863, James Plimpton finally patented the first pair of four-wheel skates. With these skates, people could keep their balance easily. They could even make very sharp turns.

Grammar: Using Adverbs for Sentence Variety

Sentence variety is important in effective writing. To give your writing added variety, begin some sentences with an adverb.

REGULAR ORDER   The group of hikers **wearily** trudged into camp.

VARIATION   **Wearily** the group of hikers trudged into camp.

Checking Your Understanding   Choose five of the following adverbs and include each one in a different sentence. Then rewrite the sentences, beginning each one with that adverb.

1. twice	**6.** today
2. suddenly	**7.** soon
3. closer	**8.** happily
4. clumsily	**9.** silently
5. loudly	**10.** slowly

Writing a Testimonial   In TV commercials, famous people sometimes tell why they like a certain product. Their statements are called testimonials. What product could you give a testimonial about? Choose one and brainstorm for facts and examples to include in your testimonial. You might, for example, answer these questions: How often do you use the product? How easy is it to use? How does the product benefit you? Why do you like it?

Use the questions you have answered to write one persuasive paragraph that is a testimonial to the product you have chosen. *Application:* As you revise your paragraph, make sure it has enough adverbs to add precision to your writing. Also read your testimonial aloud and listen for smoothness. Then edit it and make a final copy.

Diagraming Adjectives and Adverbs

Adjectives and adverbs are diagramed on slanted lines below the words they modify.

My small but strong brother swam fast and skillfully.

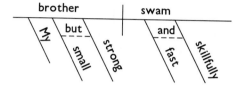

An adverb that modifies an adjective or another adverb is written on a line parallel to the word it modifies.

The extremely smart child won.   She ate too quickly.

EXERCISE *Diagraming Adjectives and Adverbs*

Diagram the following sentences or copy them. If you copy them, draw one line under each subject and two lines under each verb. Then label each modifier *adjective* or *adverb*.

1. The brick wall collapsed.
2. A large silver trophy has disappeared.
3. The happy cat purred softly.
4. The weary but happy winner grinned.
5. You should never swim alone.
6. A rather large yacht sailed past.
7. The colorful new uniforms have arrived.
8. The children were playing very noisily.
9. A cheetah can run rapidly and gracefully.
10. Those little red ants bite.

21 Review

A **Identifying Adjectives and Adverbs** Number your paper 1 to 10 and make two columns. Label the first column *adjectives* and the second column *adverbs*. In the proper column, write each adjective and adverb.

EXAMPLE   Afterward everyone watched an adventure film.
ANSWER   <u>adjectives</u>   <u>adverbs</u>
          adventure   afterward

  1. The Siamese cat was chosen first.
  2. Have you read that book yet?
  3. The car stopped abruptly at the red light.
  4. Canadian bacon tastes delicious.
  5. The first face-to-face meeting between the two opponents was extremely awkward.
  6. Cautiously the young man climbed the ladder.
  7. Lee complained of too much homework.
  8. We completely filled the large basket with beets.
  9. The sneakers were worn-out and dirty.
  10. Didn't you answer the question correctly?

B **Identifying Adjectives and Adverbs** Make two columns on your paper. Label the first column *adjectives* and the second column *adverbs*. In the proper column, write each adjective and adverb.

  1. Have you eaten any good molds lately?
  2. Usually people throw moldy food away.
  3. This information will then sound rather unusual.
  4. Several molds are grown specifically for certain cheeses.
  5. These molds, of course, are totally harmless.
  6. A French cheese called Roquefort always has blue veins.
  7. These veins are an especially delicious mold.
  8. This mold produces the uniquely distinctive taste of Roquefort.

9. A thick, grayish-white mold grows uniformly on the surface of Camembert, another cheese from France.
10. Some people wouldn't eat the cheese without the mold.

C **Distinguishing among Different Parts of Speech**
Number your paper 1 to 10. Write the underlined words in each sentence. Then label each one *noun, pronoun, adjective,* or *adverb*.

1. Your <u>apple</u> pie tastes much better than <u>this</u>.
2. <u>Both</u> of my brothers went to the <u>play</u> rehearsal.
3. <u>Most</u> drivers couldn't see the <u>street</u> sign.
4. <u>Some</u> of the fawns stood <u>close</u> to their mothers.
5. I have waited a long time to see <u>this</u> <u>play</u>.
6. The <u>car</u> roared down the <u>street</u>.
7. The <u>kindly</u> gentleman offered <u>some</u> good advice.
8. <u>Most</u> of the <u>car</u> dealers are holding sales.
9. <u>Apples</u> were given to <u>both</u> children.
10. She spoke <u>kindly</u> of her <u>close</u> friend.

Mastery Test

Number your paper 1 to 10 and make two columns. Label the first column *adjectives* and the second column *adverbs*. Then in the proper column, write each adjective and adverb. Do not include articles.

1. The large American flag waved gently in the breeze.
2. She spoke softly and tenderly to the baby.
3. Noreen and Pat wrapped the expensive presents beautifully.
4. Which test schedule did you just see?
5. The gentleman from the German embassy, in the light-blue suit, seemed very friendly.
6. The market will soon receive the Idaho potatoes.
7. These tomatoes were grown here in the backyard.
8. The black-and-white dog doesn't have a home.
9. The math test was extremely long and hard.
10. Sally dreamed of visiting a far-off land.

22 Other Parts of Speech and Review

Diagnostic Test

Number your paper 1 to 10. Write the underlined words in each sentence. Then beside each word, write its part of speech: *noun, pronoun, verb, adjective, adverb, preposition, conjunction,* or *interjection.*

EXAMPLE   <u>Someone</u> left an <u>empty</u> kettle on the stove.
ANSWER   someone—pronoun, empty—adjective

1. <u>Which</u> brand of tennis racket on the market <u>is</u> the best buy for the money?
2. Usually I <u>fish</u> in <u>Moon Lake</u> on the weekends.
3. The <u>top</u> of the mountain is <u>exactly</u> two miles from the town of Bentleyville.
4. Allen could <u>not</u> find a single pencil <u>or</u> pen.
5. <u>Oh!</u> We can't leave without the <u>dog</u>.
6. Did <u>you</u> catch many <u>fish</u> today?
7. <u>Which</u> of the paintings is <u>for</u> sale?
8. The jar <u>of</u> peanut butter is on the <u>top</u> shelf.
9. We are <u>completely</u> out of <u>dog</u> food.
10. Peter wrote his report <u>and</u> typed <u>it</u> carefully.

Prepositions

This chapter will cover three parts of speech: prepositions, conjunctions, and interjections. A *preposition* shows relationships between words. A *conjunction* connects words. An *interjection* shows strong feeling.

The three words in heavy type in the following sentence are *prepositions*. Each of these prepositions shows a different relationship between Lorraine and the letter. As a result, changing just one preposition will alter the meaning of the whole sentence.

The letter $\begin{cases} \textbf{to} \\ \textbf{from} \\ \textbf{about} \end{cases}$ Lorraine was lost.

Rule 22a A **preposition** is a word that shows the relationship between a noun or a pronoun and another word in the sentence.

Following is a list of the most common prepositions.

Common Prepositions				
aboard	before	down	off	till
about	behind	during	on	to
above	below	except	onto	toward
across	beneath	for	opposite	under
after	beside	from	out	underneath
against	besides	in	outside	until
along	between	inside	over	up
among	beyond	into	past	upon
around	but (except)	like	since	with
as	by	near	through	within
at	despite	of	throughout	without

A preposition that is made up of two or more words is called a *compound preposition*.

Common Compound Prepositions		
according to	by means of	instead of
ahead of	in addition to	in view of
apart from	in back of	next to
as of	in front of	on account of
aside from	in place of	out of
because of	in spite of	prior to

EXERCISE *Supplying Prepositions*

Number your paper 1 to 10. Then write two prepositions that could fill each blank in the following sentences.

  1. The bushes _____ the house need trimming.
  2. Frank should go _____ the store.
  3. The package _____ the chair is mine.
  4. We cannot go _____ the storm.
  5. Ken hid _____ the boat.
  6. Gloria will attend the meeting _____ Howard.
  7. The ball rolled _____ the street.
  8. Janet walked _____ the water.
  9. Carl sat _____ Marcy at the game.
 10. The plane flew _____ the storm clouds.

Prepositional Phrases

A preposition is always part of a group of words called a *prepositional phrase*. A prepositional phrase begins with a preposition and ends with a noun or pronoun called the *object of the preposition*. Any number of modifiers can come between a preposition and its object.

Margaret missed the train **by two minutes.**
The birds flew **between the old wooden beams.**

A sentence can have several prepositional phrases, and the phrases can come anywhere in the sentence.

Without a moment's hesitation, the cat leaped **through the open window.**

***In* view *of* the memo *from* the office *of* the principal,** afternoon classes will be canceled tomorrow.

EXERCISE *Finding Prepositional Phrases*

Number your paper 1 to 10. Then write each prepositional phrase. There are 20 phrases.

Agatha
Christie
Saves a Life

1. A nurse at a London hospital had a young girl in her ward.
2. None of the doctors could find a cure for her.
3. Before work the nurse began reading another chapter in a mystery by Agatha Christie.
4. After several pages she put the book into her bag and hurried to the hospital.
5. According to the book, someone had taken a rare poison called thallium.
6. The description of the victim's symptoms matched the symptoms of the young girl.
7. The nurse placed the book in front of the doctors.
8. She told them about her suspicions.
9. Within minutes the doctors prescribed a new series of treatments for the girl.
10. Because of a mystery by Agatha Christie, a young girl's life was saved.

Preposition or Adverb?

The same word can be a preposition in one sentence and an adverb in another sentence. Just remember that a preposition is always part of a prepositional phrase. An adverb stands alone.

PREPOSITION ***Below** the stairs* is extra storage space.
ADVERB The sailor climbed **below.**

PREPOSITION The children slid ***down** the hill.*
ADVERB Don't put your books **down** on the floor.

EXERCISE *Distinguishing between Prepositions and Adverbs*

Number your paper 1 to 10. Write the underlined word in each sentence. Then label it *preposition* or *adverb*.

1. Walk the pony <u>around</u> the rink.
2. "Be careful that you don't fall <u>off</u>," he shouted.
3. Everyone sang as the flag went <u>up</u>.
4. George did his exercises <u>before</u> breakfast.
5. If you go <u>outside</u>, take your key.
6. <u>Up</u> the hill raced the boys on their bikes!
7. All the marbles rolled <u>off</u> the table.
8. We looked <u>around</u> but couldn't find them.
9. Haven't I met you <u>before</u>?
10. A blizzard was raging <u>outside</u> our warm house.

EXERCISE *Cumulative Review*

Number your paper 1 to 15. Then write the prepositional phrases in the following paragraph.

A Tasty Meal

    In the Beartooth Mountains of Montana, there is a most unusual glacier. Within the ice of the glacier are frozen millions of grasshoppers. According to scientists, an immense swarm of grasshoppers made a forced landing on the glacier two centuries ago! They were then quickly frozen by a snowstorm. Today the grasshoppers are still well preserved. During the warm weather, birds and animals throughout the region flock to the glacier in addition to their normal sources of food. When the ice melts, the grasshoppers provide them with a most unusual meal.

Application to Writing

Write directions for making something simple—such as a paper airplane, a homemade greeting card, or a scrambled egg. List the directions in a series of steps. Then be prepared to identify the prepositional phrases in your directions.

USING YOUR TEXT

*Expository
Paragraphs
(120–163)*

Grammar: Creating Sentence Variety

You can create sentence variety by starting some sentences with prepositional phrases.

REGULAR ORDER   The sick child coughed **throughout the night.**

VARIATION   **Throughout the night** the sick child coughed.

Checking Your Understanding   Choose five of the following prepositions and include each one in a different sentence. Then rewrite the sentences, beginning each one with the prepositional phrase.

I. in place of
2. because of
3. in back of

4. through
5. next to
6. from

7. inside
8. beyond
9. across

Explaining an Invention   Many inventions have been created to meet a need or solve a problem. Make a list of your own needs or problems. Choose one and brainstorm for ideas for an invention that would take care of it. For example, when the weather seemed too hot, people invented air conditioners.

Write a paragraph that describes your invention and explains how it would meet your need or solve your problem. As you revise, make sure your paragraph begins with a topic sentence that describes your need or problem. Then, with your teacher's permission, have a classmate read your explanation. Ask that person to check whether or not your paragraph is clear and easy to follow. *Application:* Make any necessary changes. Check for variety at the beginnings of your sentences, especially for the use of prepositional phrases. Then edit your paragraph and make a final copy.

Conjunctions

A word that connects is called a *conjunction*.

Rule 22b **A conjunction** connects words or groups of words.

There are three kinds of conjunctions. A *coordinating conjunction* is a single connecting word.

Coordinating Conjunctions						
and	but	for	nor	or	so	yet

WORDS

Her *ring* **and** *bracelet* were lost. [nouns]

She **or** *he* will be elected. [pronouns]

Greg *came* to the party **but** *left* early. [verbs]

Wear the *white* **or** *red* gloves. [adjectives]

He joins us *now* **and** *then.* [adverbs]

GROUPS OF WORDS

The dog ran *through the door* **and** *into the kitchen.* [prepositional phrases]

The spring water tasted especially good, **for** we were very thirsty. [sentences]

Correlative conjunctions are pairs of connecting words.

Correlative Conjunctions		
both/and	either/or	neither/nor
not only/but also	whether/or	

Both dogs **and** cats can get fleas.
You should take **either** Route 2 **or** Fowler Highway.

Note: A *subordinating conjunction* is the third kind of conjunction. It will be covered in Chapter 26, "Clauses."

EXACTLY

EXERCISE *Finding Conjunctions*

Number your paper 1 to 10. Then write the coordinating or correlative conjunctions in each sentence.

1. Neither Mercury nor Venus has a natural satellite.
2. We looked for her keys in the house and on the lawn.
3. Linda raised her hand and answered the question.
4. The alarm didn't go off, so I was late for school.
5. I will go with either Nancy or her sister.
6. Sam not only played the piano but also sang.
7. The story was both interesting and informative.
8. Pierre spoke only French, yet we became good friends.
9. Swiftly but carefully he ran the course.
10. The Bucks or the Hornets will win the tournament.

Interjections

Some words show strong feelings or emotions, such as joy or anger. These words are *interjections*.

Rule 22c An **interjection** is a word that expresses strong feeling or emotion.

Interjections usually come at the beginning of a sentence. Since they are not related to the rest of the sentence, they are separated from it by an exclamation point or a comma.

What! Are you sure?	**Surprise!** It's a party.
Wow! That sounds great.	**Great!** We finished on time.
Oh, I'm locked out!	**Well!** Who ate my dessert?

EXERCISE *Writing Sentences*

Number your paper 1 to 10. Then write a sentence for each of the following interjections.

1. Oops! **3.** Aha! **5.** Great! **7.** Ugh! **9.** Whew!
2. Hurrah! **4.** Ouch! **6.** Alas! **8.** Wow! **10.** Gee!

Parts of Speech Review

How a word is used in a sentence determines its part of speech. For example, the word *near* can be used as four different parts of speech.

VERB	She will **near** the halfway point soon.
ADJECTIVE	I will join the club in the **near** future.
ADVERB	The date of her interview drew **near.**
PREPOSITION	Plant the bushes **near** the house.

To find out what part of speech a word is, ask yourself, *What is each word doing in this sentence?*

NOUN   Is the word naming a person, place, thing, or idea?
Tom bought **milk** at the **store.**

PRONOUN   Is the word taking the place of a noun?
This is **my** favorite brand of soup.

VERB   Is the word showing action?
Greg **jogged** four miles.

Does the word link two words in a sentence?

Ellen **is** the captain of the team.

ADJECTIVE   Is the word modifying a noun or pronoun? Does it answer the question *What kind? Which one(s)? How many?* or *How much?*

Three yellow tulips bloomed today.

You can have **these** few.

ADVERB   Is the word modifying a verb, an adjective, or another adverb? Does it answer the question *How? When? Where?* or *To what extent?*

He drove **too fast** on a **very** dark road.

PREPOSITION   Is the word showing a relationship between a noun or pronoun and another word in the sentence? Is it a part of a phrase?

> *Because of their length,* I finished both *of the chapters.*

CONJUNCTION   Is the word connecting words or groups of words?

> Jim **and** I like **neither** rice **nor** peas.
> I turned the key, **but** the car didn't start.

INTERJECTION   Is the word expressing strong feelings?
> **Hurray!** We won the championship.

EXERCISE *Determining Parts of Speech*

Number your paper 1 to 25. Write the underlined words. Then beside each word, write its part of speech: *noun, pronoun, verb, adjective, adverb, preposition, conjunction,* or *interjection.*

The Magic of Music

(1) <u>Caution</u>! Music may wilt (2) <u>your</u> leaves. In 1969, (3) <u>Dorothy Retallack</u> (4) <u>ran</u> some experiments with plants (5) <u>and</u> music. (6) <u>She</u> proved that music affects the growth of plants. (7) <u>In</u> one test (8) <u>loud</u> rock music (9) <u>greatly</u> stunted the growth of (10) <u>corn</u>, squash, and (11) <u>several</u> flowers. In another test (12) <u>several</u> of the plants (13) <u>grew</u> tall, (14) <u>but</u> their leaves (15) <u>were</u> extremely (16) <u>small</u>. Also, they (17) <u>needed</u> water, and (18) <u>their</u> roots were (19) <u>very</u> short. (20) <u>Within</u> several weeks (21) <u>all</u> of the marigolds in (22) <u>one</u> experiment died. Identical healthy flowers, however, bloomed (23) <u>nearby</u>. These (24) <u>flowers</u> had been listening (25) <u>to</u> classical music!

EXERCISE *Writing Sentences*

Number your paper 1 to 5, skipping a line between each number. Then write two sentences for each direction.

1. Use *light* as a verb and a noun.
2. Use *that* as a pronoun and an adjective.
3. Use *below* as a preposition and an adverb.
4. Use *these* as a pronoun and an adjective.
5. Use *secret* as an adjective and a noun.

22 Review

A **Identifying Prepositions, Conjunctions, Interjections, and Prepositional Phrases** Number your paper 1 to 20, skipping a line after each number. After you write each sentence, label each preposition *(prep.)*, conjunction *(conj.)*, and interjection *(interj.)*. Then underline each prepositional phrase.

EXAMPLE   Both Ellie and Cheryl went to Maine.

ANSWER
conj.   conj.   prep.
Both Ellie and Cheryl went <u>to Maine.</u>

1. Without a pause Paul threw the ball quickly and accurately.
2. Because of the heat, Mae and Allison went swimming.
3. Neither our dog nor our cat likes food from a can.
4. For her lunch Glenda ordered soup and a salad.
5. Between you and me, she is the right person for the job.
6. The test in science was hard, yet I did very well.
7. Our trip throughout Alaska was long but exciting.
8. Seriously! Either some of your books or some of your records must go.
9. Wayne can't come until noon, so the game will be delayed.
10. She not only has won meets but also has set records in the broad jump.
11. Are we going to an Italian or Chinese restaurant?
12. Incredible! After a poor season, the team won 20−0.
13. Both Juanita and Maureen applied for the job.
14. Either Steve or Mary Ellen will meet you at the airport.
15. Instead of driving, Chris and he walked across town.
16. Congratulations! You are the winner of the contest.
17. Beneath the murky water, the divers swam toward the sunken ship.
18. Mia not only plays the piano but also studies the harp.
19. Please park the car within the white lines.
20. In spite of the efforts of many people, the candidate lost the election by a few votes.

B **Determining Parts of Speech** Number your paper 1 to 25. Write the underlined words. Then beside each word, write its part of speech: *noun, pronoun, verb, adjective, adverb, preposition, conjunction,* or *interjection.*

Great Finds

In 1928, a farmer was planting (1) <u>horseradishes</u> in a field (2) <u>in</u> Petersburg, (3) <u>West Virginia</u>. He noticed a greasy, (4) <u>shiny</u> stone. He picked it (5) <u>up</u> and brought (6) <u>it</u> home as a curiosity (7) <u>piece</u>. (8) <u>Ten</u> years later (9) <u>he</u> made a startling (10) <u>discovery</u>. The stone (11) <u>was</u> a (12) <u>32-carat</u> diamond. (13) <u>Wow!</u> (14) <u>Imagine</u> how (15) <u>he</u> felt.

Diamonds, however, are (16) <u>not</u> necessarily (17) <u>rare</u> in the United States. The Eagle diamond (18) <u>weighs</u> 16 carats and was found in Wisconsin a (19) <u>few</u> years ago. (20) <u>Other</u> large stones have (21) <u>also</u> been discovered in Ohio, Illinois, (22) <u>and</u> Indiana. The (23) <u>largest</u> diamond found in the United States weighs 40 (24) <u>carats</u>. It was mined (25) <u>near</u> Murfreesboro, Arkansas.

Mastery Test

Number your paper 1 to 10. Write the underlined words in each sentence. Then beside each word, write its part of speech: *noun, pronoun, verb, adjective, adverb, preposition, conjunction,* or *interjection.*

1. Have you <u>ever</u> seen a British <u>stamp</u>?
2. <u>Everyone</u> at the <u>concert</u> had a wonderful time.
3. Did <u>you</u> see the <u>stop</u> sign at the corner?
4. Jerry has <u>just</u> started a <u>stamp</u> collection.
5. Her birthday <u>is</u> on Saturday <u>or</u> Sunday.
6. <u>No!</u> You cannot go <u>into</u> that office now.
7. <u>Because of</u> the <u>storm</u>, school was closed.
8. The <u>concert</u> tickets were very <u>expensive</u>.
9. <u>Stamp</u> your feet <u>and</u> clap your hands for warmth.
10. <u>Recently</u> all the lights in our house <u>went</u> out.

23

Complements

Diagnostic Test

Number your paper 1 to 10. Write the underlined complement in each sentence. Then label each one *direct object, indirect object, predicate nominative,* or *predicate adjective.*

EXAMPLE   Janice received a <u>trophy</u> at the banquet.

ANSWER   trophy—direct object

1. Some starfish have 25 <u>arms</u>.
2. Send <u>me</u> a copy of your editorial.
3. Mr. Reynolds was a <u>sergeant</u> in the Royal Air Force during World War II.
4. The milk in the refrigerator has turned <u>sour</u>.
5. The squeak in the bicycle was very <u>loud</u>.
6. Mr. Dolan offered <u>Keith</u> an after-school job at the dry cleaners.
7. Will you drive <u>me</u> to school this morning?
8. Nearly one third of the earth's land is <u>desert</u>.
9. Do you and Daniel want a big or little <u>piece</u> of watermelon for dessert?
10. Is your toast <u>cold</u> too?

Complements

Sometimes a complete thought can be expressed with just a subject and a verb. At other times a subject and a verb need another word to complete the meaning of the sentence.

Greg likes.   Ruth seems.

To complete the meaning of these subjects and verbs, a completer, or *complement,* must be added.

Greg likes **pears.**   Ruth seems **unhappy.**

There are four common kinds of complements. *Direct objects* and *indirect objects* complete the meaning of action verbs. *Predicate nominatives* and *predicate adjectives,* which are both called *subject complements,* complete the meaning of linking verbs. Together a subject, a verb, and a complement are called the *sentence base.*

Direct Objects

Direct objects complete the meaning of action verbs.

Rule 23a   A **direct object** is a noun or pronoun that receives the action of the verb.

To find a direct object, first find the subject and the action verb in a sentence. Then ask yourself *What?* or *Whom?* after the verb. The answer to either question will be a direct object. In the following sentences, subjects are underlined once, and verbs are underlined twice.

d.o.
<u>Jean</u> <u><u>borrowed</u></u> my English **book** yesterday. [Jean borrowed what? She borrowed a book. *Book* is the direct object.]

d.o.
<u>Kenneth</u> <u><u>invited</u></u> **Penny** to the dance. [Kenneth invited whom? *Penny* is the direct object.]

Verbs that show ownership are action verbs and take direct objects.

d.o.

<u>Mom</u> <u>owns</u> a 1980 **Ford.**

Sometimes two or more direct objects, called a *compound direct object,* will follow a single verb. On the other hand, each part of a compound verb may have its own direct object.

d.o.   d.o.

<u>Have</u> <u>you</u> <u>done</u> your **math** and **science** yet? [one verb]

d.o.   d.o.

<u>I</u> <u>took</u> the **pictures** and <u>developed</u> the **film.** [two verbs]

A direct object can *never* be part of a prepositional phrase.

d.o.

<u>Nancy</u> <u>took</u> only **one** of the puppies. [*One* is the direct object. *Puppies* is part of the prepositional phrase *of the puppies.*]

<u>Marjorie</u> <u>walked</u> through the park. [*Park* is part of the prepositional phrase *through the park.* Even though this sentence has an action verb, it has no direct object.]

EXERCISE *Finding Direct Objects*

Number your paper 1 to 20. Then write each direct object. If a sentence does not have a direct object, write *none* after the number.

1. Rattlesnakes periodically shed their fangs.
2. Philip thanked his father for all his help with the wood-working project.
3. The energetic students raced into the school yard before the bell.
4. The meadowlark can sing 50 different songs.
5. I ripped the wrapping paper off the box and slowly opened the lid.
6. Gorillas eat fruits and vegetables.
7. John emptied the contents of the box onto the floor.

8. Did you see her at the dance last night?
9. A grapefruit tree can bear 1,500 pounds of fruit each year.
10. Nathan went to the shopping mall.
11. Susan placed the clean sheets and pillowcases on the bed in the guest room.
12. Ecuador gets its name from the equator.
13. Have you ever had a parrot for a pet?
14. Joel cut the apple into quarters and then ate it.
15. Heat may damage the film in a camera.
16. We jogged on the path by the pond.
17. He bought two posters for his room and hung them up on the wall.
18. The flounder has both of its eyes on the right side of its body.
19. Robin drove slowly down the dark road.
20. Make your bed and clean your room.

Indirect Objects

If a sentence has a direct object, it also can have another complement, called an *indirect object.*

Rule 23b An **indirect object** answers the questions *To* or *for whom?* or *To* or *for what?* after an action verb.

To find an indirect object, first find the direct object. Then ask yourself, *To whom? For whom? To what?* or *For what?* about each direct object. The answer to any of these questions will be an indirect object. An indirect object always comes before a direct object in a sentence.

                               i.o.   d.o.
Gordon sent his **mother** flowers on her birthday.
[*Flowers* is the direct object. Gordon sent flowers to whom? *Mother* is the indirect object.]

                             i.o.   d.o.
Jennifer gave her **story** a title. [*Title* is the direct object. Jennifer gave a title to what? *Story* is the indirect object.]

A verb in a sentence can have two or more indirect objects, called a *compound indirect object.*

                    i.o.   i.o.   d.o.

The <u>teacher</u> <u>read</u> her **boys** and **girls** a story. [To whom?]

                    i.o.   i.o.   d.o.

<u>Mrs.</u> <u>Samuels</u> <u>gives</u> **dogs** and **cats** obedience training. [To what?]

Keep in mind that an indirect object is *never* part of a prepositional phrase.

                    i.o.   d.o.

The guide showed **us** a map of the trail. [*Us* is the indirect object. It comes between the verb and the direct object, and it is not a part of a prepositional phrase.]

                    d.o.

The guide showed a map of the trail to us. [*Us* is *not* an indirect object. It does not come between the verb and the direct object. It follows the direct object and is part of the prepositional phrase *to us.*]

Note: You cannot have an indirect object without a direct object in a sentence.

EXERCISE ◢2◣ *Finding Indirect Objects*

Number your paper 1 to 10. Then write each indirect object. If a sentence does not have an indirect object, write *none.*

  1. Will you lend me your umbrella?
  2. Tad gave the fence a fresh coat of paint.
  3. We will visit them during our school vacation.
  4. Please read that article to us.
  5. Mrs. Jenkins showed our class a film.
  6. We loaned Tony and Maria our skis.
  7. Show Sam the pictures of your trip to Alabama.
  8. My sister sent him a card on his birthday.
  9. Show me your new watch.
10. I gave the essay to my teacher.

EXERCISE *Finding Direct Objects and Indirect Objects*

Number your paper 1 to 10. Write each direct object and each indirect object. Then label each one *direct object* or *indirect object*.

A Star Is Born

 1. Pal, the first Lassie, worried his owners.
 2. He barked fiercely, chased cars, and chewed things.
 3. In desperation his owners gave him obedience lessons.
 4. Two brothers owned the obedience school.
 5. After a few lessons, they gave Pal a screen test.
 6. Pal got the role of Lassie in the film *Lassie Come Home.*
 7. People throughout the world loved the dog.
 8. Millions sent him fan mail.
 9. A producer made Pal's owners an offer of a TV series.
 10. Since then audiences have seen seven other Lassies.

Predicate Nominatives

Direct objects and indirect objects follow action verbs. Two other kinds of complements follow linking verbs. They are called *subject complements* because they either rename or describe the subject. One subject complement is a *predicate nominative*.

Rule 23c A **predicate nominative** is a noun or a pronoun that follows a linking verb and identifies, renames, or explains the subject.

To find a predicate nominative, first find the subject and the verb. Check to see if the verb is a linking verb. *(See page 622 for a list of linking verbs.)* Then find the noun or the pronoun that identifies, renames, or explains the subject. This word will be a predicate nominative. Notice in the second example that a predicate nominative can be compound.

Melba has become my best **friend.** [friend = Melba]
p.n.

George will be a **reporter** or an **announcer.**
p.n. *p.n.*
[reporter = George, announcer = George]

Following is a list of common linking verbs.

Common Linking Verbs	
BE VERBS	is, am, are, was, were, be, being, been, shall be, will be, can be, should be, would be, may be, might be, has been, etc.
OTHERS	appear, become, feel, grow, look, remain, seem, smell, sound, stay, taste, turn

Like a direct object and an indirect object, a predicate nominative cannot be part of a prepositional phrase.

p.n.
Peggy is **one** of the leaders. [*One* is the predicate nominative. *Leaders* is part of the prepositional phrase *of the leaders.*]

EXERCISE *Finding Predicate Nominatives*

Number your paper 1 to 20. Then write each predicate nominative.

1. "Amethyst" is another name for purple quartz.
2. Last night the rain became sleet.
3. The best hitters on the team are she and Sally.
4. The two countries have remained allies for over two centuries.
5. A white potato is a swollen stem.
6. Pure water is an odorless and tasteless liquid.
7. The bus was his only means of transportation.
8. Many stamps today are also beautiful pictures.
9. His present should be a book or a record.
10. The Siberian tiger is the largest member of the cat family.
11. The chief authors of *The Federalist* were Alexander Hamilton, James Madison, and John Jay.
12. Igor Sikorsky was the inventor of the helicopter.
13. Illinois became a state in 1818.
14. Chippendale is a unique style of furniture.

15. For many years the most popular dog in America was the poodle.

16. New York City has always been the headquarters of the United Nations.

17. Harvard was the first American college.

18. Willie and Roy became friends last year during Roy's visit to Willie's school.

19. These linen tablecloths might be the ones on sale this week.

20. Is New Orleans the home of the Sugar Bowl?

Predicate Adjectives

The second kind of subject complement is a *predicate adjective.*

Rule 23d A **predicate adjective** is an adjective that follows a linking verb and modifies the subject.

Notice the difference between a predicate nominative and a predicate adjective in the following examples.

Some <u>dinosaurs</u> <u>were</u> small **animals.** [A predicate nominative renames the subject.]

Some <u>dinosaurs</u> <u>were</u> **small.** [A predicate adjective modifies the subject.]

To find a predicate adjective, first find the subject and the verb. Check to see if the verb is a linking verb. Then find an adjective that follows the verb and describes the subject. This word will be a predicate adjective. Notice in the second example that there can be a compound predicate adjective.

<u>Does</u> the lemonade <u>taste</u> **sour** to you? [*Sour* describes the lemonade.]

The <u>weather</u> tomorrow <u>will be</u> **warm** and **humid.** [*Warm* and *humid* describe the weather.]

Do not confuse a regular adjective with a predicate adjective. Remember that a predicate adjective must follow a linking verb and describe the subject of a sentence.

REGULAR ADJECTIVE   Henry <u>was</u> an **excellent** speaker.

PREDICATE ADJECTIVE   Henry <u>was</u> **excellent** as a speaker.

EXERCISE *Finding Predicate Adjectives*

Number your paper 1 to 10. Write each predicate adjective. If a sentence does not have a predicate adjective, write *none*.

1. Human beings are taller every century.
2. Was Lian nervous before her piano recital?
3. A piece of watermelon is a refreshing snack.
4. Pure seawater is colorless.
5. The cereal tasted too sweet.
6. Diamonds can be totally black.
7. The winter day grew dark and dreary.
8. Today was the best day of my life!
9. The trail up the mountain was steep and rocky.
10. Dinosaurs became extinct for many reasons.

EXERCISE *Finding Subject Complements*

Number your paper 1 to 10. Write each subject complement. Then label each one *predicate nominative* or *predicate adjective*.

1. The photographer was an expert in her field.
2. The elm remains an endangered tree.
3. The actor seemed nervous and scared.
4. Isn't Russ allergic to seafood?
5. Sirius is the brightest star.
6. Our blackberries will be ripe very soon.
7. Opals are beautiful but soft stones.
8. The movie was very long and tiresome.
9. The female cheetah is a tender parent but an effective hunter.
10. The storm became more and more intense.

EXERCISE ◆ **7** ◆ *Cumulative Review*

Write each complement. Then label each one *direct object, indirect object, predicate nominative,* or *predicate adjective.*

The Sixties

1. In 1960, Chubby Checker started a new dance craze.
2. Dancers loved the twist.
3. The most popular rock group was the Beatles.
4. At that time the Beatles' hair was fairly short.
5. The Beach Boys were also popular.
6. In 1961, parents bought their children Garloo.
7. He was a green robot-monster doll.
8. Teenagers used expressions like *tough toenails.*
9. The miniskirt became the leading fashion.
10. Elephant jokes were the rage in the early 1960's.
11. For example, why do elephants wear green sneakers?
12. Their blue ones are dirty.
13. A fifteen-year-old conducted the London Symphony.
14. Eleven-year-old Mike Grost became a college freshman.
15. Everyone watched more and more television.
16. *Sesame Street* taught boys and girls letters and numbers.
17. Howdy Doody and Soupy Sales were popular on TV.
18. Someone always threw a pie in Soupy Sales's face.
19. Other popular television programs were *Captain Video* and *Captain Midnight.*
20. Kids immediately loved *Mr. Rogers' Neighborhood.*
21. In 1963, Lyndon Johnson became the 36th president.
22. Los Angeles also beat New York in the World Series.
23. Christiaan Barnard transplanted a human heart.
24. Olympics officials gave Peggy Fleming a gold medal for figure skating.
25. At the end of the decade, the problem of inflation became serious.

Application to Writing

Write a paragraph about 1990's facts, fads, and your favorite 1990's things. Then be prepared to identify each complement.

USING YOUR TEXT

Creative Writing
(400 – 433)
Quotation Marks
(844 – 853)

Grammar: Using Sentence Patterns

The boy ran.

The four-year-old boy ran frantically down the street.

Both of these sentences are exactly alike in one respect. They both follow the same subject-verb sentence pattern. Even though there are an endless number of sentences that can be written, there are only a few basic sentence patterns.

PATTERN 1: S-V (subject-verb)

    S   V   S   V

Everyone cheered.   Everyone at the game cheered wildly.

PATTERN 2: S-V-O (subject-verb-direct object)

  S   V   O   S   V   O

Birds eat insects.   Many birds eat harmful insects.

PATTERN 3: S-V-I-O (subject-verb-indirect object-direct object)

    S   V   I   O

Grandfather sends me coins.

          S   V   I   O

My grandfather from Ohio always sends me coins from foreign

countries.

PATTERN 4: S-V-N (subject-verb-predicate nominative)

     S   V   N

The chair is an antique.

                S   V   N

The blue velvet chair is an antique belonging to my aunt.

PATTERN 5: S-V-A (subject-verb-predicate adjective)

    S   V   A

The siren sounds frightening.

    S   V   A

The siren on the fire truck always sounds very frightening.

Checking Your Understanding Write the sentence pattern that each sentence follows.

EXAMPLE   The jacket with the hood is the one for me.
ANSWER   S-V-N

1. The Japanese have developed a half-inch camera.
2. The action in a hockey game is fast and furious.
3. My radio alarm doesn't work anymore.
4. A guppy is a small tropical fish.
5. At the student assembly, the principal gave the athlete a trophy.
6. The holiday catalogue was large and colorful.
7. The scholarship award was a check for five hundred dollars.
8. My grandparents from Iowa travel extensively throughout the United States.
9. Pure radium resembles ordinary table salt.
10. The computer gave us the answer to the question.

Writing a Short Story If you had to become a piece of food, what would you be—a bunch of grapes, a piece of cheese, a turkey leg? Make a list of your favorite foods and choose one. Then imagine what it would be like to be that piece of food for a day. Write freely for several minutes.

Write a story about one day, or one incident, in your life as a piece of food. Write the story from the first-person point of view. *(See pages 177–180.)* **Application:** When you have finished, read over your story and make sure that your sentences have followed a variety of different sentence patterns. Check your ending. Is it as interesting or unexpected as it could be? Revise your story until it is the best it can be. If you have included any dialogue, edit it for correct punctuation. Then edit the rest of your story for any other errors. Finally, write a clean copy.

Diagraming Complements

Together a subject, a verb, and a complement are called the *sentence base*. Since complements are part of the sentence base, they are diagramed on or below the baseline.

Direct Objects A direct object is placed on the baseline after the verb. It is separated from the verb by a vertical line that stops at the baseline.

Some sharks have no natural enemies.

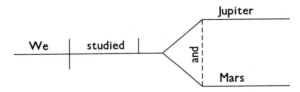

We studied Jupiter and Mars.

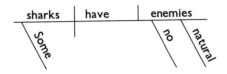

Indirect Objects An indirect object is diagramed on a horizontal line that is connected to the verb.

Give Bart and Ken this message.

Phil prepared his friends a big dinner.

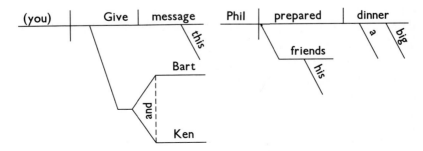

Subject Complements Both subject complements are diagramed in the same way. They are placed on the baseline after the verb. They are separated from the verb by a slanted line that points back toward the subject.

This tree is an oak.   The painting is very old.

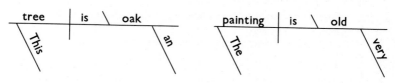

The winners are two freshmen and one senior.

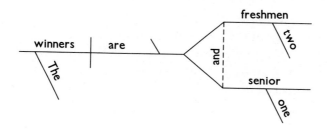

EXERCISE *Diagraming Complements*

Diagram the following sentences or copy them. If you copy them, draw one line under each subject and two lines under each verb. Then label each complement *d.o., i.o., p.n.,* or *p.a.*

 1. My soft sculpture won first prize.
 2. Don gave me a new notebook.
 3. The director is a wonderful man.
 4. I have visited Cypress Gardens and Disney World.
 5. That flower looks so delicate.
 6. Will you show Jan and me your coin collection?
 7. Haven't you given him your answer yet?
 8. The books were very old and dusty.
 9. Sing us another song.
10. My favorite sports are basketball and baseball.

23 Review

A **Identifying Complements** Number your paper 1 to 20. Write each complement. Then label each one *direct object, indirect object, predicate nominative,* or *predicate adjective.*

1. Matt promised me some help with my homework.
2. The moon looked hazy behind the thick clouds.
3. Before his retirement Mr. Berger had been a teacher.
4. The loud crash of thunder frightened our dog and cat.
5. Ricardo is the captain of the soccer team and the president of the National Honor Society.
6. Have you seen Claire in the school play?
7. Eric is only one of the contestants in the show.
8. The receptionist greeted Mary and me at the door.
9. The crowd at City Hall sounded loud and angry.
10. Send your grandmother and grandfather a card for their anniversary.
11. I offered Lalia a slice of freshly baked bread.
12. The first prize is a silver cup.
13. Hand me the scissors.
14. Whales can hold their breath for more than two hours.
15. Baby-sitting is a pleasure to Sarah.
16. The coach shouted encouraging words to the team.
17. Cornelius van Drebbel invented the submarine.
18. The librarian is ill today.
19. The fall asters in the vase were brilliant purple.
20. The concert was a great success.

B **Identifying Complements** Number your paper 1 to 15. Write each complement. Then label each one *direct object, indirect object, predicate nominative,* or *predicate adjective.*

1. I will tell you an unusual story.
2. During World War I, a Canadian pilot was flying a small military plane over Germany.

3. Of course, in those days, military planes were open.
4. Captain J. H. Hedley was the other person in the plane.
5. Suddenly an enemy plane attacked their plane.
6. The situation seemed hopeless.
7. However, the pilot took the plane into a nearly vertical dive.
8. The quickness of this movement gave Hedley a sudden jolt.
9. It literally shot him out of his seat and into the air.
10. Several hundred feet lower the plane was finally level again.
11. Then, incredibly, Hedley grabbed the tail of the plane.
12. Apparently the suction of the steep dive had been extremely powerful.
13. It had pulled Hedley back to the plane.
14. Eventually he reached his seat on the plane.
15. Later, on the ground, Hedley was the happiest man in the world.

Mastery Test

Number your paper 1 to 10. Write the underlined complement in each sentence. Then label each one *direct object, indirect object, predicate nominative,* or *predicate adjective.*

1. Frank Epperson is the <u>inventor</u> of the Popsicle.
2. Can you tell <u>me</u> the assignment?
3. The coats on the rack are not very <u>expensive</u>.
4. The recent documentary on television was very <u>educational</u>.
5. The new play on Broadway will be a big <u>hit</u>.
6. I couldn't carry the large <u>box</u> of books.
7. Did you give <u>Luis</u> your address?
8. On Saturday Meg raked the <u>leaves</u> around her house.
9. The first song on the record sounds <u>familiar</u>.
10. A cat's tail has more <u>muscles</u> than a person's hand and wrist together.

24

Phrases

Diagnostic Test

Number your paper 1 to 10. Write the prepositional phrases and the appositive phrases in the following sentences. Then label each one *adjective, adverb,* or *appositive.*

EXAMPLE   Pat, my young cousin, is moving to Texas.
ANSWER   my young cousin—appositive
            to Texas—adverb

1. A colony of termites may build its nest over an eight-year period.
2. Throw the newspapers by the door into the recycling bin.
3. Our dog, a golden retriever, barks at strangers.
4. Do you know the contents of the box on the table?
5. Several of my friends work on weekends.
6. The mud from your boots stained the carpet in the living room.
7. After the game everyone gathered at Pam's house.
8. The editor of our school newspaper interviewed Mr. Cruz, the town poet.
9. The spare set of keys to the house is missing.
10. Eva seems content with her new job at the college radio station.

Prepositional Phrases

In Chapter 22 you were introduced to phrases.

Rule 24a A **phrase** is a group of related words that function as a single part of speech. A phrase does not have a subject and a verb.

In Chapter 22 you learned that a prepositional phrase begins with a preposition and ends with a noun or a pronoun called the *object of the preposition.*

The sweater **in the box** is a present **from Sue.**

Following is a list of common prepositions. *(See pages 605 and 606 for additional prepositions.)*

Common Prepositions			
above	beside	inside	over
across	between	instead of	past
after	by	into	to
ahead of	down	next to	toward
among	during	of	under
around	for	on	until
at	from	on account of	up
before	in	out	with
behind	in addition to	out of	within
below	in back of	outside	without

EXERCISE *Finding Prepositional Phrases*

Number your paper 1 to 10. Then write the prepositional phrases in the following paragraph.

Tight Going   In 1859, Charles Blondin walked across Niagara Falls on a tightrope. He was high above the water. Later he crossed with a blindfold over his eyes. Then he crossed on stilts. Finally he really amazed everyone. Halfway across the falls, he stopped for breakfast. He cooked some eggs, ate them, and continued to the other side.

Adjective Phrases

A prepositional phrase can be used as an adjective to modify a noun or a pronoun. When it does, it is called an *adjective phrase*.

SINGLE ADJECTIVE   The **library** book is due.
ADJECTIVE PHRASE   The book **from the library** is due.

Rule 24b   An **adjective phrase** is a prepositional phrase that is used to modify a noun or a pronoun.

Like a single adjective, an adjective phrase answers the question *Which one(s)?* or *What kind?* about a noun or a pronoun.

WHICH ONE(S)?   The dog **with short legs** is a dachshund.

WHAT KIND?   Please empty this bag **of groceries.**

An adjective phrase usually modifies the noun or the pronoun directly in front of it. Occasionally an adjective phrase will modify a noun or a pronoun in another phrase.

The movie *about* creatures *from* space was scary.

Two adjective phrases can also modify the same noun or pronoun.

The glass *of* milk *on* the table is yours.

EXERCISE 2 *Finding Adjective Phrases*

Number your paper 1 to 20. Write each adjective phrase. Then beside each phrase, write the word it modifies. Some sentences have more than one adjective phrase.

EXAMPLE   The preserves in that jar are homemade.
ANSWER   in that jar—preserves

1. The radio in the kitchen doesn't work.
2. The last 20 minutes of the movie at Cinema I were dull.
3. None of the Pilgrims on the *Mayflower* had a middle name.

4. The captain of the debating team met the principal.
5. A tablespoon of butter contains 100 calories.
6. The article about animals without a home was sad.
7. Edgar Allan Poe is regarded as the father of the detective story.
8. The little boat with the two masts is a yawl.
9. The pot of soup on the stove should be removed.
10. The car in front of the school is illegally parked.
11. One of my brothers joined the varsity tennis team at the high school.
12. He accidentally dropped the last carton of milk.
13. I took a picture of my grandparents from Utah.
14. Twenty-six species of insects have become extinct.
15. Parrots usually have a vocabulary of only 20 words.
16. I need the box of nails in the top drawer.
17. The wettest city in the United States is Miami, Florida.
18. The tallest species of tree in the world is a kind of eucalyptus.
19. Some of these trees reach a height of almost 400 feet.
20. Each human being has a total of 46 chromosomes.

Application to Writing

Write a paragraph that gives directions from your school to one of your favorite places in town. Make the directions clear and easy to follow by mentioning landmarks wherever possible. Be prepared to identify any adjective phrases in your paragraph.

Adverb Phrases

A prepositional phrase can also be used as an adverb. It can modify a verb, an adjective, or an adverb. When it does, it is called an *adverb phrase*.

Rule 24c   An **adverb phrase** is a prepositional phrase that is used to modify a verb, an adjective, or an adverb.

The following examples show how adverb phrases may be used to modify verbs.

SINGLE ADVERB The baseball whizzed **by.**

ADVERB PHRASE The baseball whizzed **by the batter.**

SINGLE ADVERB Everyone came **here.**

ADVERB PHRASE Everyone came **to my house.**

Like a single adverb, an adverb phrase answers the question *Where? When? How? To what extent?* or *To what degree?* Most adverb phrases modify the verb. Notice that an adverb phrase modifies the whole verb phrase, just as a single adverb does.

WHERE? Next June the Ryans will drive **to California.**

WHEN? We should meet **during intermission.**

HOW? John answered the questions **with confidence.**

Adverb phrases also modify adjectives and adverbs.

MODIFYING
AN ADJECTIVE Sam was happy **with his report card.**

The material was rough **against her skin.**

MODIFYING
AN ADVERB The meeting ran late **into the night.**

The kite soared high **into the sky.**

An adverb phrase does not necessarily come next to the word it modifies. Also several adverb phrases can modify the same word.

On Saturday meet me *at ten o'clock at Harvey's.*

EXERCISE 3 *Finding Adverb Phrases*

Number your paper 1 to 15. Write each adverb phrase. Then beside each phrase, write the word or words it modifies. Some sentences have more than one adverb phrase.

1. Hockey pucks are kept in a refrigerator before a game.
2. A blue whale may weigh 5,000 pounds at birth.
3. Since Wednesday we have been rehearsing the play.
4. The band performed on the field during halftime.
5. A small boy on the riverbank fished for trout.
6. During the winter a person cannot catch a cold at the North Pole.
7. I am very happy about your promotion.
8. A bird sees everything at once in total focus.
9. During the marathon we sat on the curbstone.
10. Some lizards can run on their hind legs.
11. Within the week give your report to Mr. Robertson.
12. The Mexican hedgehog cactus can live five years without any water.
13. On Thursday Pedro's photograph will appear in the local paper.
14. At certain times snow falls in the Sahara.
15. After English class I went to the cafeteria with Sue and Maynard.

 ## *Application to Writing*

Write a paragraph that vividly describes the last few moments of a recent game or sports event at your school. Be prepared to identify all the prepositional phrases in your paragraph.

Punctuation with Adverb Phrases

If a short adverb phrase comes at the beginning of a sentence, usually no comma is needed. You should, however, place a comma after an introductory adverb phrase of four or more words or after several introductory adverb phrases.

NO COMMA   **After dinner** we went to a movie.

COMMA   **Because of the heavy traffic on Route 2,** we were late for dinner.

EXERCISE 4 *Cumulative Review*

Number your paper 1 to 20. Write each prepositional phrase. Then label each one *adjective* or *adverb*.

Louis Braille
1. The Braille family lived in a village near Paris, France, in the early 1800's.
2. As a young boy, Louis Braille played in his father's leather shop.
3. On one fateful afternoon, young Louis was playing with an awl.
4. His father made holes in leather with this sharp tool.
5. Without any warning the awl accidentally went into Louis's left eye.
6. After several days an infection in his injured eye spread to his good eye.
7. Because of the accident, Louis became totally blind.
8. Louis later entered the school in his neighborhood.
9. He could listen to his teacher's words, but he couldn't learn from books.
10. At ten he entered a school for the blind in Paris.
11. Children at that school were reading from special books.
12. Letters of the alphabet were pressed into thick, heavy paper.
13. This pressing created raised outlines on the other side of the paper.
14. The students would feel the outlines with their fingers, and they could read.
15. All the books were extremely large and heavy because of the huge letters.
16. One day a retired army captain came to the school with a secret code.
17. His system of dots and dashes ultimately proved too difficult for everyone.
18. By the age of fifteen, Braille developed a new system of only dots.
19. Now on the door of Braille's home appears a tribute to his accomplishments.
20. The tribute reads, "He opened the doors of knowledge to so many."

Misplaced Modifiers

Because a prepositional phrase is used as a modifier, it should be placed as close as possible to the word it describes. If a phrase is too far away from the word it modifies, the result may be a *misplaced modifier.* Misplaced modifiers create confusion and misunderstanding for readers.

MISPLACED   The puppy belongs to the man with long ears.

CORRECT   The puppy **with long ears** belongs to the man.

MISPLACED   Under the bed Dad could see the cat.

CORRECT   Dad could see the cat **under the bed.**

EXERCISE *Correcting Misplaced Modifiers*

Rewrite the following sentences, placing each misplaced modifier closer to the word it modifies.

1. With a screech Mr. Reynolds stopped the car.
2. Inside the cereal box I looked for the coupons.
3. Charles told us about his vacation in the kitchen.
4. On the ocean floor the professor described sea life to the class.
5. We looked for a cat in the want ads.
6. Behind the bars of the cage John waved to the lion.
7. We heard that the President was ill on television.
8. On top of the cake Elizabeth counted 14 candles.
9. The bird flew to the girl with red feathers.
10. The passengers sighted whales on the deck of the ship.
11. Tonight on the shelf in the closet we will use the new tablecloth.
12. At the age of two my mother taught my little brother to count.
13. On the stage the audience applauded the performers.
14. The realtor is looking for a house for the Rogers family with four bedrooms.
15. The acrobats bowed to the crowd in sequined tights.

Appositives and Appositive Phrases

Sometimes a noun or a pronoun is followed immediately by another noun or pronoun that identifies or explains it.

My sister **Pat** is coming home in June.

In the restaurant he ordered his favorite drink, **milk.**

This identifying noun or pronoun is called an *appositive.*

Rule 24d An **appositive** is a noun or a pronoun that identifies or explains another noun or pronoun in the sentence.

Most of the time, an appositive is used with modifiers to form an *appositive phrase.*

Our car, **a small compact,** gets great gas mileage.

The award went to Mrs. Kenny, **Sue's mother.**

Note: A prepositional phrase can be part of an appositive phrase.

Jack made dinner, **chicken with rice.**

EXERCISE **6** *Finding Appositives and Appositive Phrases*

Number your paper 1 to 15. Write the appositive or the appositive phrase in each sentence. Then beside each one, write the word or words it identifies or explains.

 1. My sister plays the cornet, a wind instrument.
 2. I just finished reading a story by the famous science-fiction writer Isaac Asimov.
 3. *Voyager I* photographed Jupiter, our largest planet, in 1979.
 4. My dog Fred is never late for a meal.
 5. Nora's brother, an Explorer Scout, will attend an Outward Bound program this summer.
 6. Have you seen the play *The Diary of Anne Frank?*

7. Juanita would like to take up the popular sport wind surfing.
8. The first man to drive a vehicle on the moon was David Scott, an American.
9. Juneau, the capital of Alaska, has a deep harbor.
10. The dingo, an Australian dog, must be taught to bark.
11. According to Herodotus, a Greek historian, it took 400,000 men 20 years to build the Great Pyramid in Egypt.
12. Let's meet at Kim's, the new restaurant on Main Street.
13. Tidi Relt, a town in the Sahara, once went ten years without any rainfall.
14. Lynn and Ted danced to the song "Blue Velvet."
15. Babe Ruth, one of the greatest hitters in baseball history, began his career as a pitcher.

EXERCISE *Finding Appositives and Appositive Phrases*

Number your paper 1 to 10. Write the appositive or the appositive phrase in each sentence. Then beside each one, write the word or words it identifies or explains.

1. American artist Norman Rockwell selected scenes from everyday life.
2. Have you ever read the poem "The Road Not Taken" by Robert Frost?
3. We discussed *Moby Dick*, the classic tale of a man's quest for a white whale.
4. July was named after Julius Caesar, a Roman ruler.
5. August was named after Augustus, Caesar's nephew.
6. At the Mardi Gras, a famous carnival in New Orleans, people wear costumes.
7. The organist Franz Gruber wrote the music for "Silent Night."
8. My sister has mastered calligraphy, the art of beautiful handwriting.
9. Eating a meal with chopsticks, two narrow wooden sticks, is an oriental custom.
10. The herbs parsley, mint, and rosemary grow well indoors at a sunny window.

Punctuation with Appositives and Appositive Phrases

If the information in an appositive is essential to the meaning of a sentence, no commas are needed. The information is essential if it identifies a person, place, or thing. However, a comma is needed before and after an appositive or an appositive phrase if the information is not essential to the meaning of a sentence.

ESSENTIAL   Tuesday we watched the play **Romeo and Juliet** on television. [Commas are not used. The appositive is needed to identify the play.]

NOT ESSENTIAL   *Romeo and Juliet*, **a play by Shakespeare,** can be seen on television Tuesday. [Commas are used because the appositive could be dropped from the sentence.]

EXERCISE *Cumulative Review*

Number your paper 1 to 10. Write the prepositional phrases and the appositive phrases in the following sentences. Then label each one *adjective, adverb,* or *appositive.*

Food Facts

1. In a year you eat a total of two and a half tons of food.
2. In parts of China, roast pig was a gourmet's delight.
3. Truffles, a subterranean fungus, is the most expensive food in the world.
4. In the eastern part of Texas, a rich spinach-growing area, farmers have erected a statue of Popeye.
5. A 220-pound wheel of cheese can require a ton of milk.
6. The apple had spread throughout Europe before the dawn of recorded history.
7. In addition to caffeine, chocolate contains *theobromine*, a mild stimulant.
8. Many Americans caught their first glimpse of the banana at the 1876 Exposition in Philadelphia.
9. Rennet, a common substance in cheese, is taken from the inner lining of a calf's stomach.
10. Throughout the United States, consumption of green and yellow vegetables has decreased since the 1940's.

USING YOUR TEXT

Creative Writing
(400–433)

Grammar: Combining Sentences

To avoid a choppy style in your writing, you can combine sentences by using various kinds of phrases. Doing so will make your writing smoother.

TWO SENTENCES Mary had her picture taken.
She wore a red dress.

ONE SENTENCE Mary had her picture taken **in a red dress.**
[prepositional phrase]

TWO SENTENCES Our car needs new tires.
It is an '85 Ford.

ONE SENTENCE Our car, **an '85 Ford,** needs new tires.
[appositive phrase]

Checking Your Understanding Number your paper 1 to 5. Combine each pair of sentences, putting some information into a prepositional phrase or an appositive phrase. Add commas if needed.

1. I called you last night. It was seven o'clock.
2. Cid is a gray mare. She is the fastest horse on the ranch.
3. Dad bought Mom a necklace. He bought it in New Mexico.
4. Have you read this book? It is by Mark Twain.
5. Mount Vernon was the home of George Washington. It is 15 miles south of Washington, D.C.

Rewriting a Fable Think of a familiar fable like Aesop's "The Hare and the Tortoise" or "The Fox and the Crow." Choose a fable the moral of which would still apply today. Then rewrite the fable by setting it and its characters in modern times. *Application:* As you revise your modern fable, combine sentences wherever possible. Then edit your work and write a final copy.

Diagraming Phrases

In a diagram a prepositional phrase is connected to the word it modifies. The preposition is placed on a connecting slanted line. The object of a preposition is placed on a horizontal line that is attached to the slanted line.

Adjective Phrase An adjective phrase is connected to the noun or pronoun it modifies. Notice that sometimes a phrase modifies the object of a preposition of another phrase.

The squirrel with the fluffy tail gathered acorns from the ground under the oak tree.

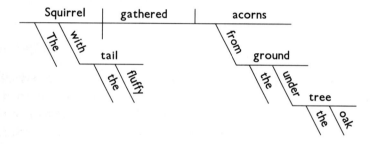

Adverb Phrases An adverb phrase is connected to the verb, adjective, or adverb it modifies.

We drove to the park on Saturday.

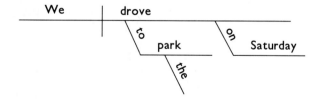

Notice in the next example that an adverb phrase that modifies an adjective or an adverb needs an additional line.

The score was tied early in the inning.

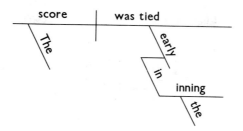

Appositives and Appositive Phrases An appositive is diagramed in parentheses next to the word it identifies or explains.

I bought a new calendar, one with pictures of horses.

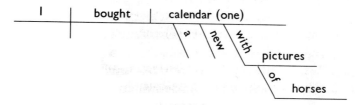

EXERCISE 9 *Diagraming Phrases*

Diagram the following sentences or copy them. If you copy them, draw one line under each subject and two lines under each verb. Then put parentheses around each phrase and label it *adj., adv.,* or *appos.*

1. Many children can swim at an early age.
2. I just bought a new radio, a small portable one.
3. The posters for the dance are beautiful.
4. I went to Mexico with my sister.
5. My friend Bert collects stamps from foreign countries.
6. The tips of the daffodils showed through the snow.
7. Meg left the store with the groceries.
8. Wendy, my best friend, went to the horse show.
9. At the signal every swimmer dived into the water.
10. The summit of Mount McKinley is always covered with snow.

24 Review

A **Identifying Phrases** Number your paper 1 to 10. Write the prepositional phrases and the appositive phrases in the following sentences. Then label each one *adjective, adverb,* or *appositive.*

1. Diamonds sometimes fall from the sky in meteorites.
2. Mr. Leonard, our principal, sings in the church choir.
3. A grasshopper's sense of hearing is centered in its front knees.
4. The Chinese New Year always begins during the period between January 20 and February 20.
5. Silk material from India is very soft to the touch.
6. The lead guitarist in that band is Rufo Ortiz, my next-door neighbor.
7. I now work after school at the supermarket.
8. Some members of the dinosaur family were only the size of rabbits.
9. My father, the man in the blue suit, will be the speaker at the assembly.
10. Musicians tune instruments to the pitch of middle A.

B **Identifying Kinds of Phrases** Number your paper 1 to 15. Write the prepositional phrases and the appositive phrases in the following sentences. Then label each one *adjective, adverb,* or *appositive.*

1. Daylight savings time was begun by Benjamin Franklin.
2. The average adult elephant is covered with approximately one ton of skin.
3. Oysters on trees can be seen on many islands in the Caribbean Sea.
4. The Abyssinian, a beautiful short-haired feline, developed entirely from the African wildcat.
5. The ZIP in *ZIP code* stands for *zone improvement plan.*

6. The center of the earth, a ball of solid iron and nickel, has a temperature of 9,000° F.
7. The largest member of the python family grows to a length of 25 feet.
8. Robert E. Lee was the son of George Washington's cavalry leader.
9. A cheetah can jump from a standstill to a 45-mph run in two seconds.
10. John Tyler, the tenth president of the United States, served from 1841 to 1845.
11. Lungfish of Africa sleep out of water for an entire summer.
12. The center of the United States is located in South Dakota.
13. Ferdinand Magellan, a Spanish explorer, made the first trip around the world.
14. The first sheep were brought to the United States in 1609.
15. In 1891, basketball was invented by James Naismith, a YMCA instructor in Massachusetts.

Mastery Test

Number your paper 1 to 10. Write the prepositional phrases and the appositive phrases in the following sentences. Then label each one *adjective, adverb,* or *appositive*.

1. A famous art museum in New York City has a collection of 200,000 baseball cards.
2. Trees in our backyard are pruned in the spring.
3. Cirrus clouds, the thin feathery type, are always made of ice crystals.
4. Most of the streets in our town have been repaved.
5. Pam arrived with her present, a music box.
6. Everything is buried under two feet of snow.
7. The cars on the parkway crawled for miles.
8. The assembly on Friday lasted for an hour.
9. The stamps in her collection are valued at two thousand dollars.
10. A completely blind chameleon will still change to the color of its environment.

25 Verbals and Verbal Phrases

Diagnostic Test

Number your paper 1 to 10. Write the verbal phrase in each sentence. Then label it *participial, gerund,* or *infinitive.*

EXAMPLE Running swiftly, he caught the football.
ANSWER running swiftly—participial

1. Cultivated over 5,000 years ago, soybeans are still a popular farm crop.
2. Remember to call Sue after dinner.
3. They had hoped to find John's wallet.
4. It is easy to swim in salt water.
5. Do you enjoy flying in a plane?
6. We heard Tommy hammering in the basement.
7. Reaching high notes was easy for Ellen.
8. Finding her house was difficult.
9. They planned the party before sending out the invitations.
10. Her jacket, covered with mud, was finally found.

Verbals and Verbal Phrases

You are already familiar with some of the information presented in this chapter. For example, you already know that the words *exhausted* and *cheering* in the following sentence are used as adjectives.

The **exhausted** singer bowed before the **cheering** fans.

What you may not know is that they belong to a special group of words called *verbals*. A verbal is a verb form that is used as some other part of speech. In the example above, for instance, *exhausted* and *cheering* look like verbs but are actually used as adjectives.

There are three kinds of verbals: *participles, gerunds,* and *infinitives.* All of these verbals are important writing tools. They add variety when placed at the beginning of a sentence, and they add conciseness when they are used to combine two simple sentences.

Participles

The words *exhausted* and *cheering* in the example above are participles.

Rule 25a A **participle** is a verb form that is used as an adjective.

To find a participle, ask the adjective question *Which one?* or *What kind?* about each noun or pronoun. If a verb form answers one of these questions, it is a participle. The participles in the following examples are in heavy type. An arrow points to the noun or the pronoun each participle modifies.

The **starving** hikers gobbled up Mom's **baked** ham.

The teddy bear, **worn** and **frayed,** lay beside the

sleeping child.

There are two kinds of participles. *Present participles* end in -*ing*. *Past participles* usually end in -*ed*, but some have irregular endings, such as -*n*, -*t*, or -*en*.

PRESENT PARTICIPLES   starving, sleeping, missing

PAST PARTICIPLES   baked, frayed, worn, bent, fallen

Everyone enjoyed the smell of the **burning** leaves.

The **defrosted** hamburgers are ready to cook.

EXERCISE *Finding Participles*

Number your paper 1 to 10. Write each participle that is used as an adjective. Then beside each one, write the word it modifies.

1. No one answered the ringing doorbell.
2. The flag of Denmark is the oldest unchanged national flag in existence.
3. The meeting, noisy and disorganized, was a waste of time.
4. The redwoods are the tallest living things on our planet.
5. The speeding car almost crashed.
6. Please empty the overflowing trash.
7. The hikers, hungry and exhausted, returned to their base camp.
8. The barking dog kept me awake all night.
9. Don't step on the broken glass on the floor.
10. Those nails, rusted and bent, are a hazard.

Participle or Verb?

Because a participle is a verb form, you must be careful not to confuse it with the main verb in a verb phrase. A participle in a verb phrase must have a helping verb.

PARTICIPLE   The **injured** bird lay still.

VERB   Sandra **was** not **injured** in the accident.

PARTICIPLE   The **winning** team held a victory party.

VERB   Barbara **is winning** the race right now.

EXERCISE *Distinguishing between Participles and Verbs*

Number your paper 1 to 10. Write the underlined word in each sentence. Then label it *participle* or *verb*.

1. A <u>talking</u> doll was one of Thomas Edison's many clever inventions.
2. Are you <u>caring</u> for a sick squirrel?
3. Maria <u>discarded</u> her old sneakers.
4. The dog <u>buried</u> its bone in the backyard.
5. Our <u>reserved</u> seats were located beside a window.
6. Why are you <u>talking</u> so softly?
7. Have you ever hunted for <u>buried</u> treasure?
8. Jennifer is such a <u>caring</u> person.
9. Have you <u>reserved</u> the book from the library?
10. The <u>discarded</u> lamp was soon missed.

Participial Phrases

Because a participle is a verb form, it can have modifiers or a complement. A participle plus any modifiers or complements form a *participial phrase*.

Rule 25b A **participial phrase** is a participle with its modifiers and complements—all working together as an adjective.

The following examples show three variations of the participial phrase. Notice that a participial phrase can come at the beginning, the middle, or the end of the sentence.

PARTICIPLE WITH AN ADVERB	**Flying low,** the plane circled the airport.
PARTICIPLE WITH A PREPOSITIONAL PHRASE	The elm **growing in our yard** is 20 years old.
PARTICIPLE WITH A COMPLEMENT	The grand prize will go to the person **giving the right answer.**

Note: Once in a while, an adverb will precede a participial phrase. That adverb is still considered part of the phrase.

Quickly raising his hand, Joe was called on first.

EXERCISE *Finding Participial Phrases*

Number your paper 1 to 10. Write the participial phrase in each sentence. Then underline the participle.

Facts and Figures

1. James Zaharee, using a fine pen and a microscope, printed the Gettysburg Address on a human hair.
2. The largest jigsaw puzzle, made in 1954, contained over 10,000 pieces.
3. One of the oldest games, played since prehistoric times, is marbles.
4. Living off the coast of Japan, the largest crabs in the world stand 3 feet high and weigh 30 pounds.
5. Bloodhounds, often used in detective work, can detect a ten-day-old scent.
6. Swimming rapidly, John Sigmund traveled 292 miles down the Mississippi River in 90 hours.
7. The smallest bird is the bee hummingbird, measuring only two and a half inches.
8. In Ohio someone found an eagle's nest weighing two tons.
9. The highest wind velocity recorded in the United States was 231 miles per hour.
10. Oranges and cantaloupes are fruits containing vitamin C.

EXERCISE *Finding Participial Phrases*

Number your paper 1 to 10. Write the participial phrase in each sentence. Then beside each one, write the word it modifies.

1. We watched the chickadees fluttering around the bird feeder.
2. Quacking loudly, the ducks paddled toward the shore.
3. The soybean, first grown in the United States as fodder for livestock, is rich in vitamins.

4. Rearing up on its hind legs, the deer nibbled on the lower branches of the juniper tree.

5. The huge swordfish has a powerful snout shaped just like a sword.

6. The nest of the weaver bird looks like a bottle hanging down from a tree branch.

7. The storm heading toward us could have winds over 50 miles per hour.

8. Costing only a few dollars, the old bookcase was a real bargain.

9. In his lifetime John D. Rockefeller gave away sums totaling $550 million.

10. A piece of pie eaten once each week can add three pounds of body weight in a year.

Punctuation with Participial Phrases

A participial phrase that comes at the beginning of a sentence is always followed by a comma.

Speaking softly, the mother encouraged the child.

However, participial phrases that come in the middle or at the end of a sentence may or may not need commas. If the information in the phrase is essential, no commas are needed. Information is essential if it identifies a person, place, or thing in the sentence. If the information is nonessential, commas are needed to separate it from the rest of the sentence. A participial phrase is nonessential if it can be removed without changing the meaning of the sentence.

ESSENTIAL   The painting **hanging near the door** is Lee's. [Commas are not used because the participial phrase is needed to identify which painting is Lee's.]

NONESSENTIAL   My down vest, **given to me as a present,** keeps me toasty warm. [Commas are used because the participial phrase could be removed from the sentence without changing its meaning: *My down vest keeps me toasty warm.*]

EXERCISE *Writing Sentences*

Write a sentence for each of the following participial phrases. Use commas where needed.

1. lost in the woods
2. walking down the street
3. enjoying the picnic
4. laughing hysterically
5. found in the backyard
6. using a dictionary
7. recently discarded
8. stored in the attic
9. broken into pieces
10. cooking dinner

Gerunds

Another kind of verbal is called a *gerund*. Both the gerund and the present participle end in *-ing*. A gerund, however, is used as a noun, not as an adjective.

Rule 25c A **gerund** is a verb form that is used as a noun.

A gerund is used in all the ways in which a noun is used.

SUBJECT	**Singing** is my best talent.
DIRECT OBJECT	Do you like **skiing?**
INDIRECT OBJECT	His trimmer waistline gave his **dieting** a big boost.
OBJECT OF A PREPOSITION	I can't stop her from **speaking.**
PREDICATE NOMINATIVE	My favorite pastime is **reading.**
APPOSITIVE	I have a new exercise, **jogging.**

EXERCISE *Finding Gerunds*

Number your paper 1 to 10. Write the gerund in each sentence. Then label it *subject, direct object, indirect object, object of a preposition, predicate nominative,* or *appositive*.

1. Swimming is one of the best forms of exercise.
2. She has just finished a course in typing.
3. Please stop that yelling!

4. An early method of food preservation was pickling.
5. The hungry boys gave eating their full attention.
6. That rude couple's whispering bothered everyone in the audience.
7. Lee has a new hobby, painting.
8. A common experience for everyone is dreaming.
9. The hardest part of skating is balance.
10. Kim has always enjoyed cooking.

Gerund or Participle?

It is easy to confuse a gerund and a present participle because they both end in *-ing*. Just remember that a gerund is used as a noun. A participle is used as an adjective.

GERUND   My neighbor earns extra money by **sewing.**
         [*Sewing* is the object of the preposition.]

PARTICIPLE   I think I'll take a **sewing** class. [*Sewing* modifies *class*.]

EXERCISE *Distinguishing between Gerunds and Participles*

Number your paper 1 to 10. Write the underlined word in each sentence. Then label it *gerund* or *participle*.

1. Are you a member of the <u>rowing</u> team?
2. <u>Reading</u> does not weaken the eyes.
3. I'm joining the <u>swimming</u> team this year.
4. Connie's <u>singing</u> has greatly improved.
5. Do you have a copy of the ninth grade <u>reading</u> list?
6. The movie showed the hazards of <u>smoking</u>.
7. <u>Swimming</u> is the best exercise for asthmatics.
8. The local <u>singing</u> group is becoming famous.
9. By noon my muscles were sore from <u>rowing</u>.
10. The <u>smoking</u> oven meant that the meat and potatoes had burned.

Gerund Phrases

Like a participle, a gerund can be combined with modifiers or a complement to form a *gerund phrase*.

Rule 25d A **gerund phrase** is a gerund with its modifiers and complements—all working together as a noun.

Following are four variations of the gerund phrase.

GERUND WITH AN ADJECTIVE	**The loud talking** bothered the people in the library.
GERUND WITH AN ADVERB	**Exercising daily** is important for everyone.
GERUND WITH A PREPOSITIONAL PHRASE	**Jogging in a park** is a pleasant form of exercise.
GERUND WITH A COMPLEMENT	**Watching a football game** is one of my favorite pastimes.

Note: Use the possessive form of a noun or a pronoun before a gerund. A possessive form before a gerund is considered part of the phrase.

We were surprised at **Tom's** winning the award.
Mom encouraged **our** climbing Mount Snow.

EXERCISE 8 *Finding Gerund Phrases*

Number your paper 1 to 10. Write the gerund phrase in each sentence. Then underline the gerund.

1. Galileo made his first telescope by placing a lens at each end of an organ pipe.
2. Sinking 499 free throws in a row is Ellen's present claim to fame.
3. A snail can cross the edge of the sharpest razor without cutting itself.
4. The ancient Egyptians avoided killing any sacred animal.
5. Josh's plan, rushing the passer, seemed sound to us.

6. Kingfishers build nests by tunneling into the sides of riverbanks.

7. I appreciate your helping me with my homework.

8. There are many different ways of growing vegetables and flowers in small containers.

9. Decreasing the Amazon rain forests threatens one of the earth's most important natural resources.

10. Bagdad, California, once went 767 days without receiving a single drop of rain.

EXERCISE *Finding Gerund Phrases*

Write the gerund phrase in each sentence. Then label it *subject, direct object, indirect object, object of a preposition, predicate nominative,* or *appositive.*

1. Next week Missy will try diving from the high board.

2. You can call almost anywhere by dialing directly.

3. My plan for the future is going to college.

4. David enjoys reading science fiction.

5. Part of Una's morning routine is getting up at seven.

6. Rubbing paraffin on the shoe part of your ice skates will prevent cracks.

7. Arriving on time for a job interview creates a good impression.

8. My part-time job, baby-sitting for the Murphys, pays well.

9. Walking the dog is one of my afternoon chores.

10. Gabriel Fahrenheit made the thermometer more accurate by substituting mercury for alcohol.

EXERCISE *Writing Sentences*

Write a sentence for each of the following gerund phrases.

1. cleaning my room

2. meeting with the principal

3. calling long distance

4. falling asleep at night

5. driving a car

6. writing quickly

7. flying to Texas

8. getting a suntan

9. doing my homework

10. swimming ten laps

Infinitives

A third kind of verbal is called an *infinitive*. It looks very different from a participle or a gerund because it usually begins with the word *to*.

Rule 25e An **infinitive** is a verb form that usually begins with *to*. It is used as a noun, an adjective, or an adverb.

An infinitive is used in almost all the ways in which a noun is used. It can also be used as an adjective or an adverb.

NOUN	**To succeed** was his only goal. [subject]
	They wanted **to eat.** [direct object]
ADJECTIVE	That is a big question **to answer.** [*To answer* modifies the noun *question.*]
	The book **to read** is a mystery. [*To read* modifies the noun *book.*]
ADVERB	She was eager **to study.** [*To study* modifies the adjective *eager.*]
	She ran **to catch** the bus. [*To catch* modifies the verb *ran.*]

EXERCISE *Finding Infinitives*

Number your paper 1 to 10. Write the infinitive in each sentence. Then label it *noun, adjective,* or *adverb*.

I. Do you know the name of the person to see?
2. Jeff just learned to ski.
3. The best way to go would be Route 62.
4. Your teacher will give you the topic to research.
5. To relax is difficult for some people.
6. The items to sell are on the table.
7. The crossword puzzle is easy to do.
8. Mia is planning to return.
9. Their words were too muffled to understand.
10. The movie to see is showing at the Plaza.

Infinitive or Prepositional Phrase?

Because an infinitive usually begins with the word *to*, it is sometimes confused with a prepositional phrase. Just remember that an infinitive is *to* plus a verb form. A prepositional phrase is *to* plus a noun or a pronoun.

INFINITIVE	I'm finally learning **to drive.** [ends with the verb form *drive*]
PREPOSITIONAL PHRASE	I'll take this duffel bag **to camp.** [ends with the noun *camp*]

EXERCISE *Distinguishing between Infinitives and Prepositional Phrases*

Number your paper 1 to 10. Write the underlined words. Then label them *infinitive* or *prepositional phrase*.

 1. Now I would like <u>to speak</u>.
 2. Should we take the dog <u>to Tennessee</u> with us?
 3. That stereo is too expensive <u>to buy</u>.
 4. What do you want <u>to say</u>?
 5. The oboe is the hardest woodwind <u>to master</u>.
 6. Of all brass instruments, the French horn is generally considered the most difficult <u>to play</u>.
 7. Let's walk <u>to school</u> today.
 8. I need some time <u>to rest</u>.
 9. Give that message <u>to Larry</u>.
 10. Take this pencil <u>to class</u> with you.

Infinitive Phrases

Like a gerund, an infinitive can be combined with modifiers or a complement to form an *infinitive phrase.*

Rule 25f An **infinitive phrase** is an infinitive with its modifiers and complements—all working together as a noun, an adjective, or an adverb.

The following examples show three variations of the infinitive phrase.

INFINITIVE WITH AN ADVERB	We hope **to finish early.**
INFINITIVE WITH A PREPOSITIONAL PHRASE	Tomorrow my family plans **to leave for Utah.**
INFINITIVE WITH A COMPLEMENT	Does he want **to grill some fish?**

Sometimes *to* is omitted when an infinitive follows such verbs as *dare, feel, hear, help, let, need, see,* and *watch.*

Did you watch me **play** tennis? [to play]
No one dared **go** without permission. [to go]
Chris helped his uncle **paint** the canoe. [to paint]

EXERCISE *Finding Infinitive Phrases*

Write the infinitive phrase in each sentence. Then underline the infinitive. Remember that *to* is sometimes omitted.

Facts and Figures

1. Europeans were the first people to use wallpaper.
2. Joseph Lister was the first doctor to use antiseptic methods during surgery.
3. Benjamin Franklin went to Paris to enlist French aid for the American Revolution.
4. In colonial days children helped make candles and soap with their families.
5. Henry Ford was the first employer in America to guarantee a minimum daily wage of five dollars.
6. Warren G. Harding was the first president to speak over the radio from the White House.
7. Until 1937, a basketball referee had to toss a jump ball after every basket.
8. To prevent snow blindness, Eskimos have been wearing sunglasses for 2,000 years.
9. Helene Madison was the first woman to swim 100 yards in one minute.
10. In Baltimore it is a crime to mistreat an oyster.

EXERCISE *Finding Infinitive Phrases*

Number your paper 1 to 10. Write the infinitive phrase in each sentence. Then label it *noun, adjective,* or *adverb.*

1. My plan is to work every other weekend.
2. We left early to catch the bus.
3. People begin to shrink after the age of thirty.
4. Ralph is eager to know his grade on the test.
5. To be on time won't be easy.
6. Dad promised to take us to the rodeo in Salinas.
7. To become a lawyer is one of my ambitions.
8. Until 1944, women were not allowed to vote in France.
9. The Chinese were the first people to use paper money.
10. An old remedy for too many mice is to get a cat.

EXERCISE *Writing Sentences*

Write a sentence using each of the following infinitive phrases.

1. to complete the report as soon as possible
2. to hear clearly
3. to play in the school band
4. to win the championship
5. to answer the question correctly

EXERCISE *Cumulative Review*

Number your paper 1 to 15. Write each verbal or verbal phrase. Then label it *participial, gerund,* or *infinitive.*

A Very
Strong Man
1. Weighing over 300 pounds, Louis Cyr may have been the strongest man in recorded history.
2. Lifting a full barrel of cement with one arm was an easy task for him.
3. One story, known to everyone in Quebec, tells about his pushing a heavy freight car up an incline.
4. To entertain townspeople, Cyr also would lift 588 pounds off the floor—by using only one finger!

5. Pitting himself against four horses in 1891 was, however, his greatest feat.
6. Standing before a huge crowd, Cyr was fitted with a special harness.
7. The horses, lined up two on each side, were attached to the harness.
8. Cyr stood with his arms on his chest and his feet planted wide.
9. The signal was given, and the horses began to pull.
10. Moving either arm from his chest would disqualify him.
11. The horses strained hard to dislodge him.
12. The grooms urged the slipping horses to pull harder.
13. Not budging an inch, Louis held on.
14. After minutes of tugging, the winner of the contest was announced.
15. Louis Cyr bowed before the cheering crowd.

Application to Writing

If you were in charge of planning a new school, what changes would you make from your present school? Write a paragraph that explains the most important change and the reasons for it. Try to include one participial phrase, one gerund phrase, and one infinitive phrase.

Misplaced and Dangling Modifiers

Participial phrases and infinitive phrases can be used as modifiers. Therefore, they should be placed as close as possible to the word they modify. When they are placed too far from the word they modify, they become *misplaced modifiers*.

MISPLACED   We saw a bear hiking along with our cameras.

CORRECTED   **Hiking along with our cameras,** we saw a bear.

At other times verbal phrases that should be functioning as modifiers have nothing to describe. These phrases are called *dangling modifiers.*

DANGLING   To enter the contest, a form must be signed.

CORRECTED   **To enter the contest,** you must sign a form.

EXERCISE *Correcting Misplaced and Dangling Modifiers*

Number your paper 1 to 15. Then write the following sentences, correcting the error in each one. To do this, follow one of two steps: (1) Place a verbal phrase closer to the word it modifies or (2) add words and change the sentence around so that the phrase has a noun or a pronoun to modify. Remember to use commas where needed.

1. Jack noticed two robins bicycling to school.
2. I came upon an accident turning the corner.
3. Weighed down by our packs, the trail seemed endless.
4. Driving to Miami, our road maps were a big help.
5. Jogging along the street, my ankle twisted.
6. We saw a deer riding along in our car.
7. Turning the pages, my eye noticed the record sale at Rick's Records.
8. That gift was given by Eric wrapped in silver paper.
9. After glancing at the clock, the book was closed by Linda.
10. Growing in the garden, I picked some tomatoes.
11. We admired the autumn leaves gliding along in our canoe.
12. Having waited up for the election results, weariness overcame us.
13. Leaping out of the water, the trainer threw a fish to the porpoise.
14. We noticed a stranger at the front door looking out the upstairs window.
15. To avoid any last-minute problems, reservations should be made in advance.

USING YOUR TEXT

Expository
Paragraphs
(120–163)

Grammar: Revising by Combining Sentences

Two short sentences can be combined by changing the information in one sentence into a verbal phrase.

TWO SENTENCES	Miguel found the hamster. It was hiding in the closet.
ONE SENTENCE	Miguel found the hamster **hiding in the closet.** [participial phrase]
TWO SENTENCES	Donald makes his livelihood in Maine. He repairs wood stoves.
ONE SENTENCE	Donald makes his livelihood in Maine **by repairing wood stoves.** [gerund phrase]
TWO SENTENCES	The director needs Roy. He will construct the scenery.
ONE SENTENCE	The director needs Roy **to construct the scenery.** [infinitive phrase]

Checking Your Understanding Combine each pair of sentences by changing the information in one sentence into a verbal phrase. Remember to use commas where needed.

1. Melanie saw Jake. He was rehearsing for the play.
2. Lucia has written a report. It is based on the life of Dr. Mary Walker.
3. The octopus shoots a cloud of black fluid. In this way it conceals itself from enemies.
4. I sleep eight hours a night. This amount of sleep is necessary for me.
5. The pelican flew close to the water. Suddenly it dived for a fish.
6. We should talk with Mavis. We should find out the dates of the games from her

7. I prepared for the tryouts. I jogged every day for two hours.
8. We tested the water first. Then we jumped in and swam to the boat house.
9. Kate is coming over. She will help me with my science project.
10. The tomatoes tasted delicious. They were canned last August.
11. Mr. Mann makes wooden models of seabirds. This is his hobby.
12. In the salad we used three ripe tomatoes. They were grown in our garden.
13. One creature has 50 joints in each leg. It is known as a daddy longlegs.
14. In the backyard we have huge barrels. That is how we catch rainwater.
15. Bloodhounds are trained by the police. Bloodhounds track people who are lost.
16. The Romans believed that onions made men braver. They fed the vegetable to their soldiers.
17. For a few years Sam Clemens worked as a riverboat pilot. Then he became a reporter and a writer.
18. Throughout history a typical village was small. It consisted of 5 to 30 families.
19. Janice carved three pumpkins. She will take them with her to the Halloween party.
20. The experts had studied the unusually large diamond for six months. Then they were ready to make the first cut.

Explaining a Choice   If you had one chance to travel in space, where would you go? Brainstorm for a list of ideas. Choose the one destination that interests you most and write the reasons for your choice. Then list those reasons in order of importance—from most important to least.

Write a paragraph that explains why you chose the place you did—out of all possible ones in the universe. *Application:* As you reread and revise your work, check for sentences that can be combined by using verbal phrases. To create sentence variety, begin one or two sentences with a verbal phrase. Then edit your paragraph and make a final copy.

Diagraming Verbal Phrases

How a verbal phrase is used in a sentence will determine how it is diagramed.

Participial Phrases Because a participial phrase is always used as an adjective, it is diagramed under the word it modifies. The participle, however, is written in a curve.

Hiking through the mountains, we used the trails marked by the rangers.

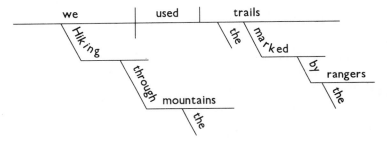

Gerund Phrases Because a gerund phrase is used as a noun, it can be diagramed in any noun position. In the following example, a gerund phrase is used as a direct object. Notice that the complement *plants* and a prepositional phrase are part of the gerund phrase.

José enjoys growing plants in his room.

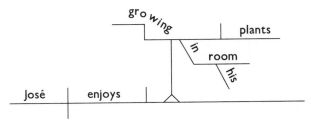

Infinitive Phrases Because an infinitive phrase may be used as an adjective, an adverb, or a noun, it is diagramed in several ways. The following example shows how an infinitive phrase used as an adjective is diagramed.

This is the best place to stop for lunch.

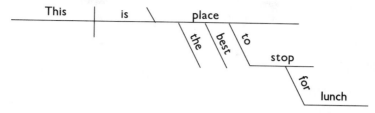

An infinitive phrase used as a noun can be diagramed in any noun position. In the following example, an infinitive phrase is used as the subject of the sentence.

To arrive on time is important.

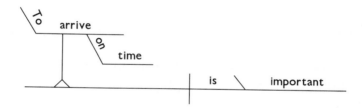

EXERCISE *Diagraming Verbal Phrases*

Diagram the following sentences or copy them. If you copy them, draw one line under each subject and two lines under each verb. Put parentheses around each verbal phrase. Then label each one *participial, gerund,* or *infinitive.*

1. Sitting on the doorstep, the dog waited for its owner.
2. Spilled by accident, the milk dripped from the counter.
3. No one noticed Sally tiptoeing down the stairs.
4. I enjoy speaking before an audience.
5. The team practiced kicking the football between the goalposts.
6. Eating food in the halls is not permitted.
7. This is the best shovel to use for that job.
8. To rush into a decision is a mistake.
9. The uniform to wear to the banquet is the blue one.
10. We want to watch this movie.

25 Review

A **Recognizing Participial Phrases** Number your paper 1 to 10. Then write each participial phrase.

1. Stopping for a moment, Jill untangled the reins.
2. Steam is water expanded 1,600 times.
3. Discovering the entrance, the boys explored the cave.
4. The ship, suffering damage to its hull, finally arrived in New York.
5. We could hear the planes circling overhead, waiting for instructions from the control tower.
6. One out of every four human beings living in the world today is Chinese.
7. Traveling due south from Chicago, you would never reach South America.
8. The location of Chicago, situated west of every point in South America, is often misjudged.
9. Walking to the museum, Isabel met a group of friends.
10. Miguel frowned when he discovered the toast burned to a crisp.

B **Recognizing Gerund Phrases** Number your paper 1 to 10. Then write each gerund phrase.

1. I enjoy riding a bike, but Ed likes using a moped.
2. Cleaning up after the party took Tim three hours.
3. Upon hearing the good news, Marta didn't know what to say to the radio announcer.
4. Performing on the stage is a new experience for me.
5. Forgetting your homework could result in remaining after school.
6. What did you think of José's winning the high jump?
7. Ancient Egyptian boats were constructed by binding together bundles of papyrus stems.

8. Yolanda enjoyed talking with the actors.

9. Rehearsing for the play is the best part of my day.

10. After arriving at the airport, Mom waited two hours for the plane.

C **Recognizing Infinitive Phrases** Number your paper 1 to 10. Then write each infinitive phrase.

1. Our schedule must be changed to accommodate our visitors.

2. It takes about ten seconds to slice six cucumbers in a food processor.

3. Clara hopes to win the golf tournament next weekend.

4. The first apples to reach America arrived from England in 1629.

5. A house cat can be expected to live from 8 to 20 years.

6. To wake up early in the morning is easy for some people.

7. My sister has agreed to paint your portrait.

8. To avoid an accident, Kim drove slowly through the fog.

9. Lee would like to visit Austria someday.

10. To play the piano well requires hours of practice.

Mastery Test

Number your paper 1 to 10. Write the verbal phrase in each sentence. Then label it *participial, gerund,* or *infinitive.*

1. Walking along, Meg saw Gordon and spoke to him.

2. Mom likes playing tennis.

3. The plane is scheduled to arrive at six o'clock.

4. Across the room I could see Greg grinning at me.

5. Finding a four-leaf clover isn't easy.

6. Seeing the date, I suddenly remembered your birthday.

7. To sleep soundly all night is a big blessing.

8. Picking blueberries requires care.

9. The hikers found him resting beside a waterfall.

10. I plan to fly a plane by the age of twenty.

26

Clauses

Diagnostic Test

Number your paper 1 to 10. Write the underlined clause in each sentence. Then label it *independent, adjective, adverb,* or *noun.*

EXAMPLE <u>When Mom returned from work</u>, she took us swimming.

ANSWER When Mom returned from work—adverb

1. <u>You use about 35 gallons of water</u> when you take a bath.
2. <u>Because we left the game early</u>, we missed the winning touchdown.
3. Give that book to Andrea, <u>who will return it to the library</u>.
4. <u>As long as you're here</u>, you should stay for dinner.
5. Stacy didn't hear <u>what you said</u>.
6. <u>Whichever movie you choose</u> is all right with me.
7. The cereal <u>that I like so much</u> has no sugar in it.
8. Since I have taken skiing lessons, <u>I hardly ever fall</u>.
9. The computer <u>that you want</u> is very expensive.
10. I want a job <u>so that I can save money for college</u>.

Independent and Subordinate Clauses

In the preceding chapter, you learned about a group of words, called a *phrase*, that can be used as a noun, an adjective, or an adverb. In this chapter you will learn about another group of words, this one called a *clause*, that can also be used as a noun, an adjective, or an adverb.

Rule 26a A **clause** is a group of words that has a subject and a verb.

From the definition of a clause, you can easily see the difference between a clause and a phrase. A clause has a subject and a verb, but a phrase does not have a subject and a verb.

PHRASE   We arrived home **after dinner.**
CLAUSE   We arrived home **after dinner was finished.**
        [*Dinner* is the subject; *was finished* is the verb.]

There are two kinds of clauses. One kind is called a main clause or an *independent clause*.

Rule 26b An **independent (or main) clause** can stand alone as a sentence because it expresses a complete thought.

An independent clause is called a *sentence* when it stands by itself. However, it is called a *clause* when it appears in a sentence with another clause. In the following example, each subject is underlined once, and each verb is underlined twice.

I will wash the dishes, and you can dry them.

This sentence has two independent clauses. Each clause could be a sentence by itself.

I will wash the dishes. You can dry them.

The second kind of clause is called a dependent clause or a *subordinate clause*.

Rule 26c A **subordinate (or dependent) clause** cannot stand alone as a sentence because it does not express a complete thought.

The subordinate clause in each of the following examples does not express a complete thought—even though it has a subject and a verb.

┌── subordinate clause ──┐   ┌── independent clause ──┐
If they win this game, the championship is theirs.

┌─ independent clause ─┐┌── subordinate clause ──┐
We bought a clock that chimes every hour.

EXERCISE *Identifying Independent and Subordinate Clauses*

Number your paper 1 to 10. Write each underlined clause. Then label each one *independent* or *subordinate*.

Hidden
Traits
1. Graphology, which is the study of handwriting, has existed for many years.
2. Many people think that handwriting can reveal personality traits.
3. Because some businesses accept this theory, an applicant's handwriting is analyzed.
4. If your writing slants to the right, you are probably friendly and open.
5. If your writing slants to the left, you may very well be a nonconformist.
6. Writing uphill indicates an optimist, and writing downhill suggests a reliable person.
7. Capital letters that are inserted in the middle of a word reveal a very creative person.
8. An *i* dotted with a circle shows an artistic nature, and a correctly dotted *i* indicates a careful person.
9. When an *i* is dotted high above the letter, the writer is thought to be a serious thinker.
10. None of this should be taken too seriously, however, since graphology is not a technical science.

Uses of Subordinate Clauses

A subordinate clause can be used in several ways. It can function as an adverb, an adjective, or a noun.

Adverb Clauses

A subordinate clause can be used like a single adverb or like an adverb phrase. When it functions in one of these ways, it is then called an *adverb clause.*

SINGLE ADVERB   Leroy awoke **early.**

ADVERB PHRASE   Leroy awoke **at dawn.**

ADVERB CLAUSE   Leroy awoke **when the sun rose.**

Rule 26d   An **adverb clause** is a subordinate clause that is used like an adverb to modify a verb, an adjective, or an adverb.

An adverb clause answers the adverb question *How? When? Where? How much?* or *To what extent?* An adverb clause also answers the question *Under what condition?* or *Why?*

WHEN?   I will stay on my diet **until I lose 15 pounds.**

UNDER WHAT CONDITION?   **If the train is late,** will you wait for me at the station?

WHY?   I saw the movie **because everyone was talking about it.**

The adverb clauses in the preceding examples all modify verbs. Notice that they modify the whole verb phrase. Adverb clauses also modify adjectives and adverbs.

MODIFYING AN ADJECTIVE   Lynn is happy **whenever she is riding a horse.**

MODIFYING AN ADVERB   The play began later **than it usually does.**

Subordinating Conjunctions All adverb clauses begin with a *subordinating conjunction.* Keep in mind that *after, as, before, since,* and *until* can also be used as prepositions.

Common Subordinating Conjunctions			
after	as soon as	in order that	until
although	as though	since	when
as	because	so that	whenever
as far as	before	than	where
as if	even though	though	wherever
as long as	if	unless	while

Unless you hear from me, I will meet you at six o'clock. The date was not changed **as far as I know.**

EXERCISE **2** *Finding Adverb Clauses*

Number your paper 1 to 10. Write the adverb clause in each sentence. Then underline the subordinating conjunction.

1. United States Marines are called leathernecks because their coats once had big leather collars.

2. A tornado once sheared a whole herd of sheep while they grazed.

3. I will exercise as long as you do.

4. Although Columbus made four voyages to the Americas, he never discovered the coast of the mainland.

5. Unless I set the alarm, I will sleep until nine o'clock and be late for school.

6. The quality of programs on television declines when summer comes.

7. The Battle of New Orleans was fought after the peace treaty had been signed.

8. As Mother drove, Father studied the road map.

9. If all cod eggs produced live fish, there would be no room left in the ocean for water.

10. We can attend the meeting even though we aren't members.

EXERCISE *Supplying Subordinating Conjunctions*

Choose an appropriate subordinating conjunction to fill each blank. (Do not use the same subordinating conjunction more than once.) Then write each complete adverb clause.

1. _____ my brother is accepted by Ohio State, he plans to go there.
2. _____ you find the answer, please call me.
3. _____ you complete your term paper, return your books to the library.
4. Jeb is much stronger _____ I am.
5. _____ we put out the sunflower seeds, the cardinals came to the feeder.
6. Terry studied the piano, _____ she never plays.
7. _____ it was pouring, we enjoyed ourselves in the cabin.
8. We chose a beagle _____ we wanted a small dog.
9. _____ I won't be finished by seven o'clock, you'll have to go in my place.
10. _____ I know, the track meet was canceled.

EXERCISE *Finding Adverb Clauses*

Number your paper 1 to 10. Write the adverb clause in each sentence. Then beside each clause, write the word or words it modifies.

1. Meet me in the library before class starts.
2. As far as I know, Suki fed the dog.
3. When one cup of rice is cooked, it expands to three.
4. I can type faster than anyone else I know.
5. If you could jump like a grasshopper, you could jump over a house!
6. They acted as if nothing had happened.
7. I cannot leave until I do my homework.
8. Whenever you're ready to go, just tell me.
9. Since cowbirds don't build nests, they lay their eggs in the nests of other birds.
10. This week is colder than the last two weeks have been.

Punctuation with Adverb Clauses

Always place a comma after an adverb clause that comes at the beginning of a sentence.

Since you have finished your chores, you may leave for the party.

Sometimes an adverb clause will interrupt an independent clause. If it does, place a comma before and after the adverb clause.

The schedule, **as far as I can tell,** is excellent.

EXERCISE *Writing Sentences*

Write sentences that follow the directions below. Then underline each adverb clause. Include commas where needed in your sentences.

1. Include an adverb clause that begins with *than*.
2. Include an adverb clause that begins with *even though*.
3. At the beginning of a sentence, include an adverb clause that begins with *since*.
4. At the end of a sentence, include an adverb clause that begins with *because*.
5. Include an adverb clause that begins with *unless* and interrupts an independent clause.

Adjective Clauses

A subordinate clause can be used like a single adjective or an adjective phrase. It is then called an *adjective clause.*

SINGLE ADJECTIVE   My uncle has an **antique** chair.

ADJECTIVE PHRASE   My uncle has a chair **with a long history.**

ADJECTIVE CLAUSE   My uncle has a chair **that was built in the 1600's.**

Rule 26e   An **adjective clause** is a subordinate clause that is used like an adjective to modify a noun or a pronoun.

An adjective clause answers the adjective question *Which one?* or *What kind?*

WHICH ONE?   I know the actor **who has the lead role.**

WHAT KIND?   The only store **that sold cordless phones** just went out of business.

Relative Pronouns   Most adjective clauses begin with a *relative pronoun*. A relative pronoun relates an adjective clause to its antecedent—the noun or pronoun it modifies.

Relative Pronouns				
who	whom	whose	which	that

Yvonne is the person **whom I met yesterday.**

The casserole **that I made for dinner** was very tasty.

Note: Sometimes a word such as *where* or *when* can also introduce an adjective clause.

Rhode Island is the place **where I was born.**

Morning is the time **when I most enjoy jogging.**

EXERCISE *Finding Adjective Clauses*

Number your paper 1 to 10. Write the adjective clause in each sentence. Then underline the relative pronoun.

1. The crocus, which usually flowers in early spring, is a native of Europe and Asia.
2. Cleopatra, who is perhaps the most famous Egyptian queen, was actually of Greek ancestry.

3. Did they test the water that comes into your house?

4. Benjamin Franklin, whom we know best for his political activities, was also a scientist and an inventor.

5. Near Los Angeles there is a single wisteria vine that covers an entire acre.

6. Special certificates will be awarded to the freshmen whose scholarship and citizenship are outstanding.

7. Jake handed the net to Ted, whom he mistook for Joe.

8. The impala, which can easily leap 30 feet, is one of the most graceful antelopes.

9. The player who caught the line drive threw the ball to first.

10. Clyde Beatty, whose life was devoted to the circus, was probably the greatest animal tamer of all time.

EXERCISE **7** *Finding Adjective Clauses*

Number your paper 1 to 10. Write the adjective clause in each sentence. Then beside each one, write the word it modifies.

The *Titanic*

1. In 1912, the *Titanic* was crossing the North Atlantic, where icebergs were a constant threat.

2. The passengers, who felt secure on this great ship, were enjoying themselves.

3. Several iceberg warnings, which should have been heeded, were ignored by the crew.

4. An iceberg, whose size was tremendous, suddenly appeared in front of the ship.

5. A slight impact, which scarcely disturbed the passengers, had actually struck a fatal blow.

6. At first the passengers, who were unaware of their danger, chatted casually about the accident.

7. The lifeboats that were on board could carry only a fraction of the passengers.

8. Boats that were launched quickly were not even filled.

9. The panic that overcame the passengers at the end might have been avoided.

10. The disaster, which resulted in the loss of 1,513 lives, will never be forgotten.

The Functions of a Relative Pronoun   In addition to introducing an adjective clause, a relative pronoun has another function. It can serve as a subject, a direct object, or an object of a preposition within the adjective clause itself. It can also show possession.

SUBJECT	The program, **which begins at eight o'clock,** should be interesting. [*Which* is the subject of *begins*.]
DIRECT OBJECT	The job **that I want** pays very well. [*That* is the direct object of *want*, answering the question *Want what?*]
OBJECT OF A PREPOSITION	The stamp club **of which I am a member** is open to anyone. [*Which* is the object of the preposition *of.*]
POSSESSION	Harvey is the person **whose voice sounds like yours.** [*Whose* shows possession of *voice.*]

Sometimes the relative pronoun *that* is omitted from an adjective clause. Nevertheless, it is still part of the clause and has its function within the clause.

This is the book **I need for my report.** [*That I need for my report* is the adjective clause. *That* (understood) is used as the direct object within the adjective clause.]

EXERCISE **8** *Finding Adjective Clauses*

Number your paper 1 to 10. Write the adjective clause in each sentence. Then underline each relative pronoun. Remember, the relative pronoun *that* may be omitted from the clause.

1. The Carters, whose dog I walk, will be away for three weeks.
2. Lions that are raised in captivity are surprisingly tame.
3. Are you wearing the coat you bought last week at the mall?
4. The longest tunnel through which we drove was about a mile long.

5. Daniel Webster, who became famous for his work in law, never went to law school.
6. The records I gave him dated back to the 1950's.
7. The story, whose author was unknown, was comical.
8. A rat can gnaw through concrete that is two feet thick.
9. He is the man to whom you must speak.
10. The ostrich, which is the largest of all birds, can outrun a horse.

EXERCISE *Determining the Function of a Relative Pronoun*

Number your paper 1 to 10. Using the following abbreviations, label the use of each relative pronoun in Exercise 8. If an adjective clause begins with an understood *that*, write *understood* and then write how *that* is used.

subject = *subj.*   object of a preposition = *o.p.*
direct object = *d.o.*   possession = *poss.*

Punctuation with Adjective Clauses

If an adjective clause contains information that is essential to identifying a person, place, or thing in the sentence, do not set it off with commas from the rest of the sentence. However, if a clause is nonessential, do set it off with commas. A clause is nonessential if it can be removed without changing the basic meaning of the sentence.

ESSENTIAL   The radio station **that plays the best music** is WXTR. [No commas are used because the clause is needed to identify which radio station plays the best music.]

NONESSENTIAL   The radio station, **which went on the air in 1947,** broadcasts interviews with recording artists. [Commas are used because the clause could be removed from the sentence without changing its meaning.]

Always use the relative pronoun *that* in an essential clause and *which* in a nonessential clause.

EXERCISE ◆10◆ *Writing Sentences*

Write a sentence for each relative pronoun. Then underline each adjective clause. Use commas where needed.

1. who   **2.** whom   **3.** whose   **4.** which   **5.** that

Misplaced Modifiers

Place an adjective clause as near as possible to the word it modifies. A clause that is too far away from the word it modifies is called a *misplaced modifier.*

MISPLACED   Mark has a computer **who lives across the street.**

CORRECT   Mark, **who lives across the street,** has a computer.

EXERCISE ◆11◆ *Correcting Misplaced Modifiers*

Write the following sentences, correcting each misplaced modifier. Use commas where needed.

1. The birds ignored the dog that chirped in the trees.
2. The present is on the table that I received for my birthday.
3. The ten-speed bicycle is in the garage that my father bought for me.
4. The movie will be shown in the auditorium which has Antarctica as the setting.
5. Glenn repaired my car who's a good friend of mine.
6. We met Mrs. Walker in the park who lives nearby.
7. The note was a reminder to order Pat's birthday cake that was written on the calendar.
8. The record album is in the cabinet that I thought I had lost.
9. The rain flooded our basement which lasted a week.
10. The oak tree provides us with shade that grows in our backyard.

Noun Clauses

A subordinate clause can also be used like a single noun. It is then called a *noun clause.*

SINGLE NOUN   I just learned an interesting **fact.**
NOUN CLAUSE   I just learned **that trees can become sunburned.**

Rule 26f   A **noun clause** is a subordinate clause that is used like a noun.

A noun clause can be used in all the ways in which a single noun can be used.

SUBJECT   **Whatever you order** is fine with me.
DIRECT OBJECT   Do you know **when they arrived?**
INDIRECT OBJECT   Give **whoever comes to the party** a paper hat.
OBJECT OF A PREPOSITION   Terry was confused by **what the clerk said.**
PREDICATE NOMINATIVE   The science of astronomy is **what interests me most.**

Following is a list of words that often begin noun clauses.

Common Introductory Words for Noun Clauses			
how	whatever	which	whomever
if	when	who	whose
that	where	whoever	why
what	whether	whom	

Keep in mind that the words *who, whom, whose, which,* and *that* may also begin an adjective clause. Therefore, do not rely on the introductory words themselves to identify a clause. Instead, decide how a clause is used in a sentence.

NOUN CLAUSE   **Who is running for office** is common knowledge. [used as a subject]

ADJECTIVE   Sam Jones, **who is running for office,** is
CLAUSE   young. [used to modify *Sam Jones*]

EXERCISE *Finding Noun Clauses*

Number your paper 1 to 10. Then write the noun clause in each
sentence.

 1. That Miriam deserved the prize for the best costume was
 not disputed by anyone.
 2. I don't know what you mean.
 3. Are you really concerned with what is best for me?
 4. What you say is true up to a point.
 5. Some botanists believe that the cabbage is the most ancient
 vegetable still grown today.
 6. Does Pilar know where she stored the decorations?
 7. The parrot speaks to whoever comes into the house.
 8. I wondered why the group had gathered at the mall.
 9. Some people believe that snake meat is healthful.
 10. The police always give tickets to whoever parks in front of
 a hydrant.

EXERCISE *Finding Noun Clauses*

Number your paper 1 to 10. Then write the noun clause in each
sentence.

 1. For many years no one knew where tuna spawned.
 2. We will go along with whatever you decide.
 3. Give whoever calls the directions to our house.
 4. I don't know why I said that.
 5. How Jerry lost my bicycle is a big mystery.
 6. I'll vote for whoever is best qualified.
 7. Life is what you make it.
 8. Send whoever answers the ad a brochure.
 9. The problem is whether he should play in the band or sing
 in the chorus.
 10. Rachel Carson wrote that some waves may travel thousands
 of miles before breaking on shore.

EXERCISE *Labeling Noun Clauses*

Using the following abbreviations, label the use of each noun clause in Exercise 13.

subject = *subj.*	object of a preposition = *o.p.*
direct object = *d.o.*	predicate nominative = *p.n.*
indirect object = *i.o.*	

EXERCISE *Supplying Subordinate Clauses*

Complete the following skeleton sentences. Then label each subordinate clause *adverb, adjective,* or *noun.*

EXAMPLE   The runner who _____.
POSSIBLE   The runner <u>who came in first</u> is Joel. (adjective)
ANSWER

I. What _____ amazed the entire audience.
2. Since _____, we were all late for the meeting.
3. Those are the books that _____.
4. Today's newspaper mentioned that _____.
5. The actor who _____.
6. Did you know that _____?
7. Because _____, we left early.
8. That some persons _____ is certainly true.
9. We were not disappointed even though _____.
10. The pup that _____.

EXERCISE *Cumulative Review*

Number your paper 1 to 15. Write each subordinate clause in the following paragraphs and label each *adverb, adjective,* or *noun.*

A Tragic Start   The Panama Canal, which connects two oceans, is the greatest constructed waterway in the world. Because it was completed over 80 years ago, few people can remember the tragic problems that occurred during its construction. In 1881, a French firm that was headed by Ferdinand de Lesseps began to dig the canal. Although the work was hard, it was possible. What wasn't possible was finding a way to overcome the mosquitoes that infested the whole area. Within 8 years, nearly 20,000 men died of malaria as they worked on the canal. The French company that had first built the Suez Canal finally went bankrupt after it had lost $325 million.

After 18 years had passed, some Americans tried their luck. They first found a plan that wiped out the mosquitoes. Their work then proceeded without the hazard that had doomed the French. The construction, which began at both ends, moved inland through the dense jungle. Finally, after 10 billion tons of earth had been removed, the canal was opened in 1914.

Kinds of Sentence Structure

Once you know the difference between independent and subordinate clauses, you can understand the four kinds of sentence structure: *simple, compound, complex,* and *compound-complex.*

Rule 26g A **simple sentence** consists of one independent clause.

The subject and the verb in a simple sentence, however, can be compound. In the following examples, each subject is underlined once, and each verb is underlined twice.

The <u>cat</u> <u>slept</u> in the afternoon sun.
<u>Henry</u> and <u>Frank</u> <u>met</u> and <u>walked</u> to school together.

Rule 26h A **compound sentence** consists of two or more independent clauses.

⌐————— independent clause —————¬   ⌐— independent
<u>Mom</u> just <u>baked</u> an angel food cake, and <u>I</u> <u>can</u> hardly
clause ——————¬
<u>wait</u> to taste it.

⌐——— independent clause ——¬ ⌐————— independent
<u>Pat</u> and <u>I</u> <u>pitched</u> the tent; <u>Barb</u> <u>started</u> the fire
clause ——————¬
and <u>cooked</u> dinner.

Note: A compound sentence should include only closely related clauses. If two ideas are not related, they should be placed in separate sentences.

COMPOUND SENTENCE	Earth has only one moon, but Jupiter has at least fourteen.
SEPARATE SENTENCES	Earth has only one moon. Jupiter is the largest planet of all.

Punctuation with Compound Sentences

There are several ways to connect the independent clauses in a compound sentence. You can join them with a comma and a conjunction.

The club's bicycle trip lasted a whole week, **but** everyone enjoyed it.

You also can join independent clauses with a semicolon and no conjunction.

Noreen likes team sports; her sister prefers swimming and jogging.

Rule 26i A **complex sentence** consists of one independent clause and one or more subordinate clauses.

─────── subordinate clause ───── ─────independent
Since I joined the swim team, I have practiced

clause ─────
every day.

──subordinate clause ─── ────── independent clause ──────
After the game is over, we will go to Toby's house,

────subordinate clause ─────
which is near the stadium.

Rule 26j A **compound-complex sentence** consists of two or more independent clauses and one or more subordinate clauses.

─────────── independent clause ───────────
My science project isn't required until Friday, but

———independent clause——— ———subordinate

I <u>have</u> already <u>turned</u> it in because I <u>finished</u> the

clause——— ——subordinate clause——

work sooner than I <u>had expected</u>.

EXERCISE *Classifying Sentence Structure*

Number your paper 1 to 10. Then label each sentence *simple, compound, complex,* or *compound-complex.*

Burgers

1. The hamburger came from Hamburg, Germany, and the frankfurter came from Frankfurt.
2. The idea of placing meat on a bun, however, came from the United States.
3. When the hamburger first arrived in the United States, it was eaten almost raw.
4. The French still prefer rare meat, but the Germans eat raw hamburger meat.
5. Hamburger first became popular among German immigrants who lived in Cincinnati.
6. Hamburger wasn't placed on a bun until this century.
7. Officially, the first hamburger sandwich appeared in 1904 in St. Louis, Missouri, which was also the birthplace of the ice-cream cone.
8. Today the frankfurter is not so popular, but the hamburger is on the rise.
9. Chopped meat now accounts for about 30 percent of all meat sales.
10. Scientists are working on the hamburger, and it may change drastically in the future because it may be made of soybeans or cotton!

 Application to Writing

Use your imagination to describe what a car of the future will look like. Tell what options or features it will offer. Be prepared to identify the kinds of sentences in your paragraph.

Grammar: Revising by Combining Sentences

Good writing style includes sentence variety. To create sentence variety, you can combine related simple sentences into a compound or a complex sentence.

TWO SIMPLE SENTENCES	I wanted to watch television. The set was broken.
A COMPOUND SENTENCE	I wanted to watch television, **but the set was broken.**
TWO SIMPLE SENTENCES	Bianca gave up her paper route. Steve took over for her.
A COMPLEX SENTENCE	**When Bianca gave up her paper route,** Steve took over for her. [adverb clause]
TWO SIMPLE SENTENCES	Dennis is captain of the hockey team. He is my cousin.
A COMPLEX SENTENCE	Dennis, **who is my cousin,** is captain of the hockey team. [adjective clause]
TWO SIMPLE SENTENCES	Dinner will be ready in ten minutes. Do you know that?
A COMPLEX SENTENCE	Do you know that dinner will be ready in ten minutes? [noun clause]

Checking Your Understanding   Combine each pair of sentences into a compound sentence. Use commas where needed.

1. Wolves may live up to 16 years in captivity. In the wild their lives are much shorter.
2. Insects have six legs. Spiders have eight.
3. Bennett threw the ball to third base. Carlos tagged the runner out.

4. My shoes need new heels. The shoe-repair store is closed today.
5. The Indian rhinoceros has one horn. The African rhinoceros has two.
6. The treasure is buried on the islands. No one can find it.
7. The apple tree has blossoms. The tulips are in full bloom.
8. Take my bicycle. Dad might drive you.
9. I'm going to the game today. I'll have to leave early.
10. I like math very much. This year science is very interesting.

Checking Your Understanding   Combine each pair of sentences into a complex sentence. Use commas where needed.

1. Leo painted our house. He lives next door.
2. Peanuts contain protein. They are a healthful snack.
3. School will end early today. The principal said that.
4. Ann answered the doorbell. Brian answered the phone.
5. The first Ferris wheel was constructed in 1893. It was 250 feet in diameter.
6. Snowflakes are raindrops. These have been carried high into the cold layers of air.
7. In northern Scandinavia the sun doesn't set for nearly three months. Did you know that?
8. I ran to the window. I heard a loud crash.
9. Birds have no teeth. They grind their food in the gizzard.
10. I found a ring. It looks very old.

Writing a Persuasive Paragraph   For about five minutes, write down anything that comes to mind in response to the proverb *Every advantage has its disadvantage*. Choose from your notes the best examples or illustrations that support or disprove this proverb.

Write a paragraph to persuade others to agree with your views about the truth or falsehood of the proverb. Convince them by including examples and illustrations to support your opinion.   *Application:* As you revise your paragraph, look for any opportunities to combine sentences into compound or complex sentences. Then edit your paper and write a final copy.

Diagraming Sentences

The simple sentences that you diagramed earlier in this book had only one baseline. In the diagrams for compound, complex, and compound-complex sentences, each clause has its own baseline.

Compound Sentences These sentences are diagramed like two simple sentences, except that they are joined by a broken line on which the conjunction is placed. The broken line connects the verbs.

Mysteries are interesting, but I prefer biographies.

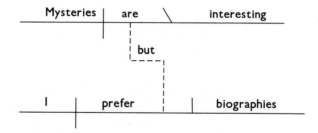

Complex Sentences In a complex sentence, an adverb clause is diagramed beneath the independent clause. The subordinating conjunction goes on a broken line that connects the verb in the adverb clause to the word the clause modifies.

I read my report after I typed it.

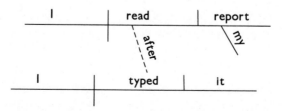

An adjective clause is also diagramed beneath the independent clause. The relative pronoun is connected by a broken line to the noun or pronoun the clause modifies.

This song is one that I will never forget.

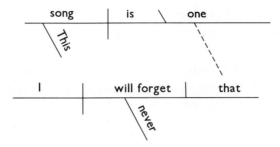

A noun clause is diagramed on a pedestal in the same place a single noun with the same function would be placed. The noun clause in the following diagram is used as the subject.

What the teacher said pleased Jane.

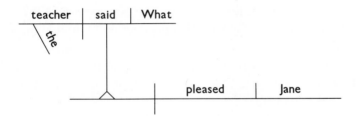

Compound-Complex Sentences   To diagram this kind of sentence, apply what you just learned about diagraming compound and complex sentences.

EXERCISE *Diagraming Sentences*

Diagram the following sentences or copy them. If you copy them, draw one line under each subject and two lines under each verb. Put parentheses around each subordinate clause. Label each clause *adverb, adjective,* or *noun.*

I. My homework is done, but I still must walk the dog.
2. We drove Justin to college when his vacation ended.
3. The bird that you just saw is a cardinal.
4. What Tom said surprised me.
5. I liked the jacket that you gave to me, but it was too small.

26 Review

A **Identifying Subordinate Clauses** Number your paper 1 to 10. Write the subordinate clause in each sentence. Then label each one *adverb, adjective,* or *noun.*

1. Your jacket, which is too small, should be given to your brother.
2. Some of our friends joined us when we were walking to the subway.
3. Most people see what they want to see.
4. Wood is seasoned before it is used in construction.
5. Although I didn't say anything, I agreed with you.
6. Did you know that Mike reads the newspaper daily?
7. The fifth person who calls this number will win five hundred dollars.
8. I can't figure out how these pieces fit together.
9. New York was the first state that required the licensing of motor vehicles.
10. Even though I'm tired, I want to go to the concert.

B **Identifying Subordinate Clauses** Number your paper 1 to 10. Write the subordinate clause in each sentence. Then label each one *adverb, adjective,* or *noun.*

1. Do you know what metal is used to make most cans?
2. If you can crush a can, it probably was made from aluminum.
3. Aluminum, which makes up nearly 8 percent of the earth's crust, is the most common metal in the world.
4. Although aluminum is so abundant, it has been used for only about 100 years.
5. The problem is that aluminum is found only in combination with other substances in the rocks.
6. In 1886, it was Charles Hall who finally discovered a way to separate the aluminum from these substances.
7. He eventually learned that a powerful electrical current worked effectively and efficiently.

8. Today you see aluminum products wherever you look.
9. Aluminum is useful because it is strong and lightweight.
10. Some aluminum products that you have heard of are pots and pans and parts for airplane and automobile engines.

C Recognizing Kinds of Sentences   Number your paper 1 to 10. Then label each sentence *simple, compound, complex,* or *compound-complex.*

1. Many dogs and cats get along very well together.
2. The island of Puerto Rico was originally called San Juan, and the city was called Puerto Rico.
3. Because the books that I need for my report are not available at the library, I will have to find a new topic.
4. Penguins are good swimmers but cannot fly at all.
5. After you left the party, Ken left too, but I stayed for an hour.
6. Children played on swings while parents talked.
7. Plants manufacture food in the light, but they absorb their food during the evening hours.
8. Haven't you heard the news on the radio?
9. Dinner was delicious, but I wasn't hungry because I had eaten a pizza just an hour before.
10. I didn't know what I should say to her.

Mastery Test

Number your paper 1 to 10. Write the underlined clause in each sentence. Then label it *independent, adjective, adverb,* or *noun.*

1. When I joined the club, <u>I paid my dues</u>.
2. <u>Since it's already ten</u>, will you have time to finish?
3. I just bought a bicycle, <u>which I paid for out of my savings</u>.
4. You must explain <u>why you're late</u>.
5. Meg couldn't see the person <u>who was talking</u>.
6. <u>Don't you know</u> which plane you're taking?
7. I played tennis <u>after I had finished the chores</u>.
8. <u>Because I lost the library book</u>, I paid for it.
9. The cat <u>that you found</u> belongs to the Stevensons.
10. Please return this vase to <u>wherever you found it</u>.

27 Sound Sentences

Number your paper 1 to 10. Then label each group of words *sentence, fragment,* or *run-on.*

EXAMPLE   After we ate our dinner.
ANSWER   fragment

1. Fish make up the largest group of animals with backbones.
2. An exciting movie about deep-sea exploration.
3. Waiting for a call from my older brother.
4. I started down the hill smoothly then my skis went out of control.
5. Although I had never seen a barracuda before.
6. On the road leading to Lake Wentworth.
7. I really like tempura, it's a Japanese dish.
8. Frame the picture and hang it in your room.
9. To finish cleaning my room before noon.
10. Jennifer and her brother are on a seafood diet they see food but don't eat it.

Sentence Fragments

Writers sometimes express an incomplete thought as a sentence. These incomplete thoughts are called *sentence fragments*.

Rule 27a A **sentence fragment** is a group of words that does not express a complete thought.

Kinds of Sentence Fragments

There are several kinds of sentence fragments. Each one of them is missing one or more essential elements to make it a sentence.

Phrase Fragments   A phrase does not have a subject and a verb; therefore, it can never stand alone as a sentence. Following are examples of phrase fragments. Notice that they are capitalized and punctuated as if they were sentences.

PREPOSITIONAL PHRASES

The coach gave us a pep talk. **During halftime in the game against Bolton.**

Before my usual breakfast of cereal and toast. I like to read the newspaper.

PARTICIPIAL PHRASES

We found the newspaper. **Lying in a mud puddle.**

Flipping the pancake into the air. Dad caught it with the frying pan.

INFINITIVE PHRASES

The yearbook staff met yesterday. **To elect an editor.**

To appear friendly. The mayor shook hands with everyone and held a baby.

APPOSITIVE PHRASES

Roberta works at Grayson's. **The dress store on Cornell Street.**

Have you seen my library books? **The ones about solar energy.**

EXERCISE *Finding Phrase Fragments*

Label each group of words *sentence* or *fragment*. If a group of words is a fragment, add the words necessary to make it a sentence. Use punctuation where needed.

 1. My bicycle can be repaired for fifteen dollars.
 2. Speaking at the assembly for all ninth graders.
 3. To think of something funny to say.
 4. Mowing the lawn is my responsibility.
 5. Put the groceries away.
 6. The director and also the author of the play.
 7. At ten o'clock on Friday, the meeting will be held.
 8. Slugging the ball with all her might.
 9. The library on the corner of Evergreen Street.
 10. To answer as promptly as possible.

Clause Fragments   All clauses have a subject and a verb. Only an independent clause, however, can stand alone as a sentence. A subordinate clause is a fragment when it stands alone because it does not express a complete thought. Following are examples of clause fragments punctuated and capitalized as if they were sentences.

> ADVERB
> CLAUSES
>
> You could save money. **If you took your lunch to school.**
>
> **Because the game went into extra innings.** We didn't get home until 11 o'clock.

> ADJECTIVE
> CLAUSES
>
> This is the basketball. **That we bought for Harold.**
>
> Is this the road? **That we should take to get to the civic center.**

EXERCISE *Finding Clause Fragments*

Label each group of words *sentence* or *fragment*. If a group of words is a fragment, add words of your own to make it a sentence. Use punctuation where needed.

EXAMPLE Since my brother left.

ANSWER fragment—Since my brother left, I have been very lonesome.

 1. After the painting was framed and hung on the wall.
 2. That the witness told the police after the accident.
 3. Before he left, he spoke with her.
 4. Dry the dishes while you're standing there.
 5. After we know the results of the tests.
 6. Who is the new captain of the football team?
 7. While the weather is still cool.
 8. Until we know, there's nothing to do.
 9. She's the one who told me.
10. Even though we couldn't see well from the second balcony.

Other Kinds of Fragments Other groups of words can also be mistakenly thought of as a sentence.

PART OF A Will you wait for us? **Or come back to**
COMPOUND VERB **get us?**

ITEMS IN We will have to take warm clothes with us.
A SERIES **Coats, wool scarves, and gloves.**

EXERCISE *Finding Sentence Fragments*

Label each group of words *sentence* or *fragment*. If a group of words is a fragment, add the words necessary to make it a sentence. Use punctuation where needed.

 1. Red, purple, and blue are my favorite colors.
 2. And write as clearly as possible.
 3. Before the voting booths close.
 4. A pencil, four sheets of paper, and a ruler.
 5. Flying a kite on a windy day.
 6. I haven't spoken with him yet.
 7. Or take the bus to Haley Street.
 8. Light bulbs, a hammer, and some tape.
 9. We should leave very shortly.
10. Which falls on a Tuesday this year.

Ways to Correct Sentence Fragments

There are two ways to correct a sentence fragment. First, you can add words to make it into a separate sentence as you have done in the previous exercises. Second, you can attach it to the sentence that is next to it.

SENTENCE AND FRAGMENT	We're going to Kansas City in the spring. **To see our cousins.**
SEPARATE SENTENCES	We're going to Kansas City in the spring. **We're planning to see our cousins.**
ATTACHED	We're going to Kansas City in the spring **to see our cousins.**
SENTENCE AND FRAGMENT	This is Mr. Jefferson. **My last year's math teacher.**
SEPARATE SENTENCES	This is Mr. Jefferson. **He was my math teacher last year.**
ATTACHED	This is Mr. Jefferson, **my last year's math teacher.**

EXERCISE *Correcting Sentence Fragments*

Write the following sentences, correcting each sentence fragment. Either make the fragment a complete sentence by adding words or attach it to the other sentence. Add capital letters and punctuation marks where needed.

1. Tennessee was known as Franklin. Before it was granted statehood in 1796.
2. Hernandez can program computers. To do whatever he wants them to do.
3. We could unload the boxes from the truck. Or unpack them in the store.
4. The chow is the only dog. That has a black tongue.
5. History has had some famous marble players. George Washington, Thomas Jefferson, and John Adams.
6. The first house numbers appeared in 1463. On a street in Paris.

7. Tonight I must go to hockey practice. And write a report.
8. Aspirin was first marketed in 1899. And was available only by prescription.
9. Did you hear about Jim's new job? Running errands for his neighbors.
10. Amateur astronomers can tell a star from a planet. Because only stars twinkle.
11. Some jets require tremendous amounts of fuel. Eleven thousand gallons an hour.
12. Fortunately jets can use kerosene. A cheaper fuel than high-octane gasoline.
13. During our trip west, we will stay with my sister. Who lives in Arkansas.
14. Last summer we traveled to Boston. Where we walked the Freedom Trail.
15. Last night I went to the meeting at the school. To learn about the new sports program.

EXERCISE 5 *Correct Sentence Fragments*

Rewrite the following paragraphs, correcting all sentence fragments. Add capital letters and punctuation marks where needed.

Jesse Owens

When Jesse Owens graduated from East Technical High School in Cleveland, Ohio. He had established three national high school records in track. At Ohio State University, Jesse broke a few more world records. Then in the 1936 Olympic Games at Berlin. He acquired world fame by winning four gold medals!

Owens's performance on May 25, 1935, at the Big Ten Conference championships, however, will always be remembered. Getting up from a sickbed. he ran the 100-yard dash in 9.4 seconds. To tie the world record. Ten minutes later in the broad jump. he leaped 26 feet 8¼ inches on his first try. To beat a world record. When the 220-yard dash was over. Owens had smashed another world record. He then negotiated the hurdles in 22.6 seconds. And shattered another record. Within three quarters of an hour. Jesse Owens had established world records in four events.

Run-on Sentences

The second mistake that some writers make is to combine several thoughts and write them as one sentence. This results in a *run-on sentence*. Generally, run-on sentences are written in either of two ways.

WITH A COMMA   John has an extra bat, **mine is lost.**

WITH NO
PUNCTUATION   At camp I will take horseback riding **computer programming sounds like fun.**

Rule 27b A **run-on sentence** is two or more sentences that are written as one sentence and are separated by a comma or no mark of punctuation at all.

EXERCISE *Finding Run-on Sentences*

Number your paper 1 to 10. Then label each group of words *sentence* or *run-on*.

1. Armon has several pets they include two turtles and one hamster.
2. Those earrings are unusual, they are made of genuine jade.
3. The dance will be held at Robinsons' barn, which is just off Old Raven Road.
4. I just took skiing lessons the instructor has been skiing since she was three years old.
5. When you entered the room, did you notice the painting on the wall?
6. I have three favorite subjects they are French, history, and chorus.
7. Just as I was getting comfortable, my mother called me to do the dishes.
8. Have you ever ridden on a roller coaster, my cousin just loves them.
9. I have three brothers two of them are in college.
10. As long as you're going to the kitchen, please get me an apple.

Ways to Correct Run-on Sentences

There are several ways to correct a run-on sentence. You can turn it into separate sentences or turn it into a compound sentence or a complex sentence.

RUN-ON SENTENCE	I was swimming very hard the tide was against me.
SEPARATE SENTENCES	I was swimming very hard. The tide was against me. [separated with a period and a capital letter]
COMPOUND SENTENCE	I was swimming very hard, but the tide was against me. [clauses combined with a comma and a conjunction] I was swimming very hard; the tide was against me. [clauses combined with a semicolon]
COMPLEX SENTENCE	Although I was swimming very hard, the tide was against me. [clauses combined by changing one of them into a subordinate clause]

EXERCISE *Correcting Run-on Sentences*

Correct the following run-on sentences. Write them as separate sentences or as compound or complex sentences. Add capital letters and punctuation marks where needed.

1. The name *Sarah* means "princess," *Linda* means "beautiful."
2. The oldest subway system in the world is in London, it went into service in 1863.
3. I heard the weather report, it is going to rain.
4. Seven men in 100 have some form of color blindness only 1 woman in 1,000 suffers from it.
5. My camera is old I'll be glad to get a new one.
6. Flamingos are usually pink one variety is bright red.
7. A fly has mosaic eyes, it can see in many different directions at the same time.
8. Today is Ellen's birthday we are having a party for her.
9. The crocodile is a cannibal, it will eat another crocodile.
10. A squirrel sees no color it sees only in black and white.

EXERCISE 8 *Correcting Run-on Sentences*

Rewrite the following paragraph, correcting all run-on sentences. Add capital letters and punctuation marks where needed.

The White
White House

The White House wasn't always white, it started out gray. During the War of 1812, British troops invaded Washington they burned the structure on August 24, 1814. Only a shell was left standing. Under the direction of James Hoban, the original architect, the building was finally restored, the work was completed in 1817. "The White House" did not become its official name until 1902. Theodore Roosevelt adopted it.

EXERCISE 9 *Cumulative Review*

Write the following sentences, correcting each fragment or run-on sentence. Add capital letters and punctuation marks.

1. I found a squirrel's nest. Hidden in a box in the attic.
2. Let's study in the library. During our free period.
3. Up to age six or seven months, a child can breathe and swallow at the same time an adult cannot do this.
4. We can eat the bread. After it has cooled awhile.
5. Wyoming was the first state. To allow women to vote.
6. I arrived late, I didn't have a chance to get a seat.
7. Blue eyes are the most sensitive to light, dark brown eyes are the least sensitive.
8. The giraffe is a ruminant it can swallow a meal and chew it later.
9. That is Mrs. Jordan. The wife of the principal.
10. The white rhinoceros is not white, it is gray.

Application to Writing

What modern invention has changed your life most in recent years? Write a paragraph using as many facts and examples as you can to support your choice. Edit your paragraph for any sentence errors.

USING YOUR TEXT

Descriptive Writing (182–195)
Friendly Letters (436–438)

Grammar: Editing for Sentence Errors

When you edit, read your work aloud to find sentence fragments and run-on sentences.

Checking Your Understanding Rewrite the following paragraphs, correcting all sentence fragments and run-on sentences. Add capital letters and punctuation marks where they are needed.

If you owned *Marvel Comics #1*. You would be a rich person. In 1939, it cost a dime today it is worth $15,000! No one knows exactly which comic books to save. There are, however, a few things. To look for when you're buying them. Buy the first issue of any comic book. And hold onto it. Origin issues are also valuable, they are the issues in which a character is born or comes into being. Cross-over issues can be big money-makers too. In a cross-over issue, one famous comic-book character joins up with another famous comic-book character this happened in *Superman #76*. When Batman visits Superman.

Do you have any old comic books? Lying around the house. You can find out how much they are worth by looking in a book it's called *The Comic Book Price Guide* by Robert Overstreet. It can be found in most public libraries.

Writing a Letter How would you describe yourself? Stretch your mind for those features and personality traits that make you a unique individual. When you have lots of exact details, arrange them in a logical order. Then, in a letter to a new pen pal, describe yourself. *Application:* After you revise your paragraph, read it aloud, listening for any sentence errors. Make sure that you correct any errors you find in a variety of ways. Otherwise you will have all short, choppy sentences. Then write a final copy.

27 Review

A **Correcting Sentence Fragments and Run-on Sentences** Number your paper 1 to 15. Then write the following sentences, correcting each sentence fragment or run-on sentence. Use capital letters and punctuation marks where needed.

1. I want Carl on my team he's a terrific pitcher.
2. We have three kinds of trees growing in our yard. Oak, maple, and spruce.
3. "Smith" is a very common name. Appearing in over 40 languages.
4. In 1946, there were 10,000 television sets in the United States, there were 12 million 5 years later.
5. Of all the ore dug in a diamond mine. Only 1 carat in every 3 tons proves to be a diamond.
6. Yesterday I mowed the lawn. And trimmed the bushes and hedges.
7. If the moon were placed on the surface of the United States. It would extend from California to Ohio.
8. The hardiest of all the world's insects is the mosquito, it can even survive at the North Pole.
9. Mom usually flies. Whenever she goes on business trips.
10. We must have loaned the snowblower to Uncle Pete I can't find it.
11. Alaska has a sandy desert. Located in the northwestern part of the state.
12. Many presidents have attended Groton. A prep school in Massachusetts.
13. South American Indians introduced tapioca to the world it comes from the root of a poisonous plant.
14. A large tree had fallen. At the end of the road leading to the lake.
15. About 70 percent of the earth is covered with water only 1 percent of that water is drinkable.

B **Correcting Sentence Fragments and Run-on Sentences** Rewrite the following paragraph, correcting all sentence fragments and run-on sentences. Be sure to correct the errors in a variety of ways. Add capital letters and punctuation where needed.

According to a superstition that has been around for a long time. The groundhog is supposed to come out of its underground home on February 2. National Groundhog Day. If the animal sees its shadow. It hurries back to its snug bed. For another six weeks. This means that there will be six more weeks of winter, people should not put their winter coats away. Of course, if the little critter stays out of its burrow, spring is about to begin. Should you believe this superstition? Pointing to the statistics. The National Geographic Service says that the groundhog has been right only 28 percent of the time that's not a very good record. Still, next February 2, hundreds of reporters will be waiting. To see if the groundhog will see its shadow.

Mastery Test

Number your paper 1 to 10. Then label each group of words *sentence*, *fragment*, or *run-on*.

1. Lucy Hobbs Taylor was the first woman dentist.
2. Stored in a huge box in the cellar.
3. Along the wall on the right side of the driveway.
4. Norman earned some money last week, he deposited it in the bank.
5. Before you storm angrily into the office.
6. An old bicycle with twisted handlebars and a broken seat.
7. Please water the plants and find the newspaper.
8. As a result of John's scream, I stepped back the car missed me by inches.
9. To find just the right shirt to wear with my slacks.
10. My sister tried to make a call the line was dead.

28

Using Verbs

Diagnostic Test

Number your paper 1 to 10. Then write the past or the past participle of each verb in parentheses.

EXAMPLE   Jamie (take) a large bite out of the apple.
ANSWER   took

1. Have you ever (ride) in a helicopter?
2. The second baseman (throw) the ball over the shortstop's head.
3. My watch strap has (break) again.
4. Victor Mandino is the most unselfish person I have ever (know).
5. Yesterday my mother (bring) me breakfast in bed.
6. My baby sister's big yellow balloon hit a sharp twig and (burst).
7. Adam (do) a wonderful imitation of Mr. Martin.
8. I (see) a Broadway play when I visited New York City last month.
9. Have you ever (eat) Hungarian goulash?
10. I've (shrink) my sweater in the dryer.

Principal Parts of Verbs

This chapter begins a unit of usage. In this unit you will learn how to use the various elements of grammar covered in Chapters 18–22. You will learn, for example, about the cases of pronouns. In other words, you will learn which of the following phrases is correct: *between you and I* or *between you and me.* You will also learn which subjects and verbs agree and which form of an adjective to use for comparing two or more things.

First, however, in this chapter you will look more closely at verbs. Because verbs have so many forms, people often make mistakes when they use them in writing and in speech. Even though verbs can be the most informative—and most powerful—words in the language, they can also be the most difficult words to master. This chapter will help you become more familiar with the various forms of the verbs you use every day. The chapter will also show you how the tense of a verb is used to express time when you are writing a story.

The different tenses of a verb are based on its four basic forms, called *principal parts.*

Rule 28a The **principal parts** of a verb are the *present,* the *present participle,* the *past,* and the *past participle.*

The principal parts of the verb *jog* are used in the following examples. Notice that the present participle and the past participle must have a helping verb when they are used as verbs.

PRESENT	I **jog** two miles every day.
PRESENT PARTICIPLE	I was **jogging** early today.
PAST	Today I **jogged** with Bert.
PAST PARTICIPLE	I have **jogged** every day for a year.

Regular Verbs

The past and the past participle of most verbs are formed by adding *-ed* or *-d* to the present. These are called *regular verbs.*

Rule 28b A **regular verb** forms its past and past participle by adding *-ed* or *-d* to the present.

Following are the principal parts of the regular verbs *paint* and *stop*. Notice how the spelling changes when endings are added to the verb *stop*. If you are unsure of the spelling of a verb form, look it up in a dictionary.

PRESENT	PRESENT PARTICIPLE	PAST	PAST PARTICIPLE
paint	painting	painted	(have) painted
stop	stopping	stopped	(have) stopped

EXERCISE *Determining the Principal Parts of Regular Verbs*

Make four columns across your paper. Label them *present, present participle, past,* and *past participle*. Then write the four principal parts of each of the following regular verbs.

1. ask	**5.** share	**9.** taste	**13.** check	**17.** call
2. use	**6.** climb	**10.** weigh	**14.** drop	**18.** talk
3. hop	**7.** wrap	**11.** shout	**15.** cook	**19.** shop
4. row	**8.** jump	**12.** stare	**16.** gaze	**20.** look

Irregular Verbs

Some verbs do not form their past and past participle by adding *-ed* or *-d* to the present. These are *irregular verbs*.

Rule 28c An **irregular verb** does not form its past and past participle by adding *-ed* or *-d* to the present.

The following irregular verbs have been divided into six groups according to the way they form their past and past participle.

Note: *Have* is not part of the past participle. It has been added, though, to help you remember that a past participle must have a helping verb when it is used as a verb.

Group 1

These irregular verbs have the same form for the present, the past, and the past participle.

PRESENT	PRESENT PARTICIPLE	PAST	PAST PARTICIPLE
burst	bursting	burst	(have) burst
cost	costing	cost	(have) cost
hit	hitting	hit	(have) hit
hurt	hurting	hurt	(have) hurt
let	letting	let	(have) let
put	putting	put	(have) put
set	setting	set	(have) set

Group 2

These verbs have the same form for the past and past participle.

PRESENT	PRESENT PARTICIPLE	PAST	PAST PARTICIPLE
bring	bringing	brought	(have) brought
buy	buying	bought	(have) bought
catch	catching	caught	(have) caught
feel	feeling	felt	(have) felt
find	finding	found	(have) found
get	getting	got	(have) got or gotten
hold	holding	held	(have) held
keep	keeping	kept	(have) kept
lay	laying	laid	(have) laid
lead	leading	led	(have) led
leave	leaving	left	(have) left
lose	losing	lost	(have) lost
make	making	made	(have) made
say	saying	said	(have) said
sell	selling	sold	(have) sold
send	sending	sent	(have) sent
sit	sitting	sat	(have) sat
teach	teaching	taught	(have) taught
tell	telling	told	(have) told
win	winning	won	(have) won

EXERCISE ◆ **2** ◆ *Using the Correct Verb Form*

Number your paper 1 to 25. Then write the past or past participle of each verb in parentheses.

EXAMPLE   Have they (build) their new garage yet?
ANSWER   built

1. The left fielder has (hit) his second long, high fly.
2. Deirdre (win) first place in the marathon.
3. After you have (set) the table, call everyone to dinner.
4. The police officer (tell) us about crime prevention.
5. I have never (find) my watch.
6. Amanda has (leave) her cashier's job at the mall.
7. The balloon floated into the sky and (burst).
8. My mother has (sell) her first painting.
9. Our coach (lead) the way to the tennis courts.
10. Ralph (keep) the card you sent him.
11. Lai Kim has already (bring) hot dogs and the potato salad.
12. He (sit) backstage during the entire performance.
13. She had (make) tacos for dinner.
14. My mother has (keep) a lock of my baby hair in her locket for many years.
15. The divers have (hold) their breath for a long time.
16. Four large crows had (sit) on the scarecrow's shoulders for 15 minutes.
17. The contractor (lay) the foundation of the house before the cold weather set in.
18. The students (say) the Pledge of Allegiance.
19. Has anyone ever (catch) the measles more than once in a lifetime?
20. Woodrow Wilson (teach) at Princeton University for 12 years.
21. I haven't (feel) so happy in a long time.
22. You should have (buy) a new pair of sneakers yesterday at Dane's.
23. Thomas (send) a letter to the newspaper and complained about its poor sports coverage.
24. Lucía (get) the majority of the votes.
25. I have (lose) five pounds in the past month.

Group 3

These irregular verbs form their past participle by adding *-n* to the past.

PRESENT	PRESENT PARTICIPLE	PAST	PAST PARTICIPLE
break	breaking	broke	(have) broken
choose	choosing	chose	(have) chosen
freeze	freezing	froze	(have) frozen
speak	speaking	spoke	(have) spoken
steal	stealing	stole	(have) stolen

Group 4

These irregular verbs form their past participle by adding *-n* to the present.

PRESENT	PRESENT PARTICIPLE	PAST	PAST PARTICIPLE
blow	blowing	blew	(have) blown
draw	drawing	drew	(have) drawn
drive	driving	drove	(have) driven
give	giving	gave	(have) given
grow	growing	grew	(have) grown
know	knowing	knew	(have) known
rise	rising	rose	(have) risen
see	seeing	saw	(have) seen
take	taking	took	(have) taken
throw	throwing	threw	(have) thrown

EXERCISE *Determining the Correct Verb Form*

Write the correct verb form for each sentence.

1. The team members just (choose, chose) a mascot.
2. Pat (stole, stolen) three bases in the third inning.
3. My sister has (drove, driven) to Boston many times.
4. Mr. Beck has (grew, grown) corn for years.
5. The quarterback (threw, thrown) a 50-yard pass.
6. Mom (knew, known) the poem by heart.
7. No one has (saw, seen) our new neighbors.

8. Luis may have just (broke, broken) a window.

9. The pond has finally (froze, frozen) over.

10. Two nurses (gave, given) us a demonstration of CPR.

EXERCISE *Using the Correct Verb Form*

Number your paper 1 to 15. Then write the past or past participle of each verb in parentheses.

1. Until last summer I had never (drive) my grandfather's tractor.

2. Mr. Foster has (grow) his own vegetables for five years.

3. I don't think Dad has ever (rise) later than 7:00 A.M.

4. Our clumsy puppy (break) two lamps this morning.

5. The cake (rise) above the sides of the pan.

6. He (draw) me a map of the fairgrounds.

7. The judges of the contest haven't (choose) a winner yet.

8. I don't think the wind has ever (blow) harder than it did last night.

9. Jean has always (give) her dog a birthday present.

10. Alani (see) the comet early this morning.

11. The high winds on Saturday (blow) down the sign.

12. Max (throw) the baseball past the third baseman and allowed two runners to score.

13. I wish I had (take) piano lessons when I was a child.

14. Until Monday I had never (speak) before a large audience.

15. I have (know) him for many years.

Group 5

These irregular verbs form their past and past participles by changing a vowel.

PRESENT	PRESENT PARTICIPLE	PAST	PAST PARTICIPLE
begin	beginning	began	(have) begun
drink	drinking	drank	(have) drunk
ring	ringing	rang	(have) rung
shrink	shrinking	shrank	(have) shrunk
sing	singing	sang	(have) sung
sink	sinking	sank	(have) sunk
swim	swimming	swam	(have) swum

Group 6

These irregular verbs form the past and the past participle in other ways.

PRESENT	PRESENT PARTICIPLE	PAST	PAST PARTICIPLE
come	coming	came	(have) come
do	doing	did	(have) done
eat	eating	ate	(have) eaten
fall	falling	fell	(have) fallen
go	going	went	(have) gone
lie	lying	lay	(have) lain
ride	riding	rode	(have) ridden
run	running	ran	(have) run
tear	tearing	tore	(have) torn
wear	wearing	wore	(have) worn
write	writing	wrote	(have) written

EXERCISE *Determining the Correct Verb Form*

Write the correct verb form for each sentence.

1. My hat has (fell, fallen) into the lake before.
2. Sal has (did, done) many household chores.
3. Polly (drank, drunk) all the orange juice.
4. Has the boat (sank, sunk) to the bottom?
5. My family has (went, gone) to Disneyland twice.
6. Play rehearsals have not (began, begun) yet.
7. I have just (wrote, written) for a free sample.
8. Cal just (rode, ridden) the roller coaster.
9. Juan (swam, swum) to shore from the reef.
10. Has the homeroom bell (rang, rung) yet?

EXERCISE *Using the Correct Verb Form*

Write the past or past participle of each verb in parentheses.

1. After the storm the sailboat (lie) on its side.
2. The birds have (eat) all the suet we put out.
3. The chorus (sing) several songs by Gilbert and Sullivan.

4. Before his campaign for the presidency of the Student Council, Griffin had never (run) for office.
5. I would have (come) by earlier, but I had to work late.
6. Oh, no! I just (tear) a hole in my new coat.
7. What he (wear) to the dance was most inappropriate.
8. I (write) a description of Taylor Pond.
9. Church bells across the country (ring) when the Iran hostages were released.
10. I have never (drink) goat's milk.
11. The images on the screen gradually (shrink).
12. Caesar's Roman troops first (come) to Britain in 55 B.C.
13. Have you ever (swim) to that island?
14. Before the formation of the Republican party, Lincoln (run) for office as a Whig.
15. Sharon has (ride) every horse at the Elmtree Stables.

EXERCISE *Finding Principal Parts in a Dictionary*

Look up each of the following irregular verbs in a dictionary. Then write the principal parts of each one.

1. swing	6. arise	11. bend	16. pay
2. strive	7. become	12. forget	17. mean
3. swear	8. weave	13. lend	18. creep
4. spin	9. build	14. meet	19. hold
5. shake	10. sleep	15. fight	20. sweep

EXERCISE *Cumulative Review*

Number your paper 1 to 10. Then write the past or the past participle of each verb in parentheses.

Ice Cream
1. In first-century Rome, Nero had snow (bring) from the nearby mountains.
2. With the snow he (make) the first frozen dessert.
3. He (experiment) with mixtures of snow, honey, and fruit.
4. Until the thirteenth century, no one in Europe had (see) a frozen milk dessert.

5. Marco Polo (introduce) an early version of ice cream to Europe.
6. Improvements on this dessert (lead) to the creation of ice cream in the sixteenth century.
7. Ice cream, however, (remain) a treat for only the rich.
8. For years the great chefs (keep) the secret of ice cream to themselves.
9. After a French café (begin) serving ice cream, it (become) everyone's favorite.
10. Only a few Americans had (eat) ice cream before 1700.

Verb Tense

All verbs express time, called the *tense* of a verb. The principal parts of a verb are used to form the six tenses: *present, past, future, present perfect, past perfect,* and *future perfect.* In the following examples, the six tenses of *run* are used to express action at different times.

PRESENT	I **run** a mile every day.
PAST	I **ran** a mile yesterday.
FUTURE	I **will run** a mile tomorrow.
PRESENT PERFECT	I **have run** a mile every day since June.
PAST PERFECT	I **had** not **run** much before that.
FUTURE PERFECT	I **will have run** almost 100 miles before the end of the year.

Conjugation of a Verb

One way to see or study all the tenses of a particular verb is to look at a conjugation of that verb. A *conjugation* is a list of all the singular and plural forms of a verb in its various tenses.

Regular verbs are conjugated like irregular verbs. The only variations result from the differences in the principal parts of the verbs themselves. Following is a conjugation of the irregular verb *ride.* The principal parts of *ride* are *ride, riding, rode,* and *ridden.*

Note: The present participle is used to conjugate only the progressive forms of a verb. Those forms are covered on page 717.

CONJUGATION OF *RIDE*

Present

This tense expresses action that is going on now.

SINGULAR	PLURAL
I ride	we ride
you ride	you ride
he, she, it rides	they ride

Past

This tense expresses action that took place in the past.

SINGULAR	PLURAL
I rode	we rode
you rode	you rode
he, she, it rode	they rode

Future

This tense expresses action that will take place in the future. It is formed by adding *shall* or *will* to the present.

SINGULAR	PLURAL
I shall/will ride	we shall/will ride
you will ride	you will ride
he, she, it will ride	they will ride

Present Perfect

This tense expresses action that was completed at some indefinite time in the past or action that started in the past and is still going on. It is formed by adding *has* or *have* to the past participle.

SINGULAR	PLURAL
I have ridden	we have ridden
you have ridden	you have ridden
he, she, it has ridden	they have ridden

Past Perfect

This tense expresses action that took place before some other action. It is formed by adding *had* to the past participle.

SINGULAR	PLURAL
I had ridden	we had ridden
you had ridden	you had ridden
he, she, it had ridden	they had ridden

Future Perfect

This tense expresses action that will be completed by some given time in the future. It is formed by adding *shall have* or *will have* to the past participle.

SINGULAR	PLURAL
I shall/will have ridden	we shall/will have ridden
you will have ridden	you will have ridden
he, she, it will have ridden	they will have ridden

EXERCISE *Conjugating a Verb*

Using the conjugation of *ride* as a model, write the conjugation of the following verbs.

1. play, playing, played, played
2. know, knowing, knew, known

Progressive Forms   Each of the six tenses has a *progressive form*. It consists of a form of *be* plus the present participle of the verb. The progressive form is used to express continuing action. Following are the progressive forms of *ride*.

PRESENT PROGRESSIVE	am, is, are riding
PAST PROGRESSIVE	was, were riding
FUTURE PROGRESSIVE	shall/will be riding
PRESENT PERFECT PROGRESSIVE	has, have been riding
PAST PERFECT PROGRESSIVE	had been riding
FUTURE PERFECT PROGRESSIVE	shall/will have been riding

EXERCISE *Forming the Progressive*

Using the model of *ride* above, write the progressive forms of the verbs *play* and *run*.

Conjugation of the Irregular Verb *Be* Since the principal parts of the verb *be* are highly irregular, the conjugation of that verb is very different from other irregular verbs. The principal parts of *be* are *am, being, was,* and *been.*

CONJUGATION OF *BE*

Present

SINGULAR	PLURAL
I am	we are
you are	you are
he, she, it is	they are

Past

SINGULAR	PLURAL
I was	we were
you were	you were
he, she, it was	they were

Future

SINGULAR	PLURAL
I shall/will be	we shall/will be
you will be	you will be
he, she, it will be	they will be

Present Perfect

SINGULAR	PLURAL
I have been	we have been
you have been	you have been
he, she, it has been	they have been

Past Perfect

SINGULAR	PLURAL
I had been	we had been
you had been	you had been
he, she, it had been	they had been

Future Perfect

SINGULAR	PLURAL
I shall/will have been	we shall/will have been
you will have been	you will have been
he, she, it will have been	they will have been

EXERCISE *Using Tenses of the Verb* **Be**

Number your paper 1 to 10. Then for each blank, write the tense of the verb *be* that is indicated in parentheses.

1. The bat _____ *(present)* the only mammal that can fly.
2. Some cats who lived 40 million years ago _____ *(past)* 14 feet long.
3. April _____ *(present perfect)* a very rainy month.
4. Kent and Barbara _____ *(future)* our representatives at the conference.
5. No two snowflakes _____ *(present)* exactly alike.
6. Jeff _____ *(past perfect)* my friend before I met Brian.
7. Lady Jane Grey _____ *(past)* queen of England for only nine days.
8. We _____ *(future perfect)* the only ones to see the election returns before Friday.
9. Lynn _____ *(future)* the captain of the field hockey team for another year.
10. Today _____ *(present perfect)* an unpredictable day!

EXERCISE *Cumulative Review*

Number your paper 1 to 15. Then write the tense of each underlined verb.

1. My brother <u>borrowed</u> Dad's car last night to go to the library.
2. We <u>were eating</u> an early dinner when the phone <u>rang</u>.
3. Earl and I <u>have collected</u> baseball cards for more than five years now.
4. Leon <u>was</u> here earlier and <u>will be</u> back momentarily.
5. Your birthday <u>will have passed</u> by the time you <u>receive</u> your present.
6. The pilot <u>told</u> us why the plane <u>had landed</u> in Buffalo.
7. You <u>will understand</u> my reasons for resigning if you <u>think</u> about them.
8. I <u>had been</u> sick with a head cold for two weeks before I <u>felt</u> better.
9. Harvey <u>had been working</u> at the garage.

10. I <u>will miss</u> dinner because the team <u>will be staying</u> late.

11. By the time the ambulance <u>came</u>, the lifeguard <u>had revived</u> the swimmer.

12. Matt <u>was</u> my tennis partner in the last match.

13. We <u>have known</u> each other for three years.

14. Mom <u>saw</u> that John <u>had decorated</u> the living room.

15. I <u>took</u> your advice and <u>opened</u> a savings account.

Shifts in Tense

When you write, it is important to keep your tenses consistent. For example, if you are telling a story that took place in the past, use the past tenses of verbs. If you suddenly shift to the present, your reader might be confused.

Rule 28d Avoid shifting tenses when relating events that occur at the same time.

A shift in tense can occur incorrectly within a sentence or within related sentences.

INCORRECT We **opened** the closet door, and suddenly
┌past┐

┌present┐
something **flies** past us.

CORRECT We **opened** the closet door, and suddenly
┌past┐

┌past┐
something **flew** past us.

INCORRECT When everyone **had finished,** our teacher
┌past perfect┐

┌past┐   ┌present┐
collected the tests. Then she **dismisses** us.

CORRECT When everyone **had finished,** our teacher
┌past perfect┐

┌past┐   ┌past┐
collected the tests. Then she **dismissed** us.

EXERCISE *Correcting Shifts in Tense*

Number your paper 1 to 10. If the sentence contains a shift in tense, write the second verb in the correct tense. If a sentence is correct, write *C* after the number.

EXAMPLE   After Doreen spent the day at the beach, she suffers from a terrible sunburn.

ANSWER   suffers—suffered

1. That large motorboat always slows down before it stopped at the dock.
2. Chris walked bravely to the front of the room and faces his classmates.
3. The kitten stalked into the room and pounces on the rubber mouse.
4. After I had begun to mow the lawn, the rain starts.
5. The sight-seeing boat leaves at noon and returned at three o'clock.
6. The halfback lost his balance but hung onto the ball.
7. Huge jets always pass directly over our house and headed west.
8. When Cider ran away, Ken searches for him everywhere.
9. I had played the video game before I order it.
10. After I had seen the movie, I told everyone about it.

EXERCISE *Correcting Shifts in Tense*

Rewrite the following paragraph, correcting any shifts in tense. Then underline each verb you changed. There are ten mistakes.

The Early Days   Modern baseball was once named town ball. It first become popular in the United States in the 1830's. Wooden stakes are the bases, and the playing field is square. A pitcher is called a feeder, and a batter was called a striker. After a batter hits the ball, he runs clockwise. After a fielder catches the ball, he gets a runner out by hitting him with the ball. In the early days of baseball, balls are soft and are made by winding yarn around a piece of rubber.

Active and Passive Voice

In addition to tense, a verb has voice. A verb is used in either the *active voice* or the *passive voice*.

Rule 28e   The **active voice** indicates that the subject is performing the action.

Rule 28f   The **passive voice** indicates that the action of the verb is being performed upon the subject.

In the following examples, the same verb is in the active voice in one sentence and in the passive voice in the other. The verb in the active voice has a direct object. The verb in the passive voice does not have a direct object. *(For information about direct objects, see pages 617–618.)*

ACTIVE VOICE   Everyone **enjoyed** the concert. [*Concert* is the direct object.]

PASSIVE VOICE   The concert **was enjoyed** by everyone. [There is no direct object.]

EXERCISE *Recognizing Active and Passive Voice*

Number your paper 1 to 20. Write the verb in each sentence. Then label it *active* or *passive.*

1. Ancient ruins have been discovered in our backyard.
2. The White House has 132 rooms.
3. Some businesses are guarded at night by watchdogs.
4. Jupiter's moons can be seen with good binoculars.
5. Dry the dishes with that towel.
6. The Gulf Stream warms the west coast of Europe.
7. The dog left a trail of muddy footprints.
8. Jade can be shattered by a sharp blow.
9. Tonight I must write a report for science.
10. Computers are used to predict the monthly rainfall over the next five years.

11. Jim is always called J.J. by his family.
12. Did you plant those tulips yourself?
13. The lead part was played by Jayne.
14. My report on solar energy will be finished soon.
15. A terrible thunderstorm followed the rain.
16. Bart found two dimes under the cushions of the sofa.
17. The wedding vows were written by the couple.
18. Many deer chew the bark on our trees.
19. Joshua made a lamp for his mother.
20. The kitchen window was broken this afternoon.

Forming the Passive Voice

Only transitive verbs—verbs that take direct objects—can be used in the passive voice. When an active verb is changed to the passive, the direct object of the active verb becomes the subject of the passive verb. The subject of the active verb can be used in a prepositional phrase.

ACTIVE VOICE Ned gave a wonderful **speech.** [d.o.]

PASSIVE VOICE A wonderful **speech** was given by Ned. [subject]

A verb in the passive voice consists of a form of the verb *be* plus a past participle.

Old newspapers **were collected** by the club members.
Awards **will be presented** at dinner.

Use the active voice as much as possible. It adds more directness and forcefulness to your writing. However, you should use the passive voice when the doer of the action is unknown or unimportant. Use it also when you want to emphasize the receiver of the action.

Collies are still used as sheep dogs in Scotland. [The doer is unknown.]
The leaking faucet was repaired today by the plumber. [Emphasis is on the receiver.]

EXERCISE *Using the Active Voice*

Number your paper 1 to 5. Then write each sentence, changing the passive voice to the active voice if appropriate. If any sentence is better in the passive voice, write *C* after the number.

1. Orchids are grown as a hobby by my science teacher.
2. More than 100 different types of dogs are bred in the United States.
3. A diary was kept by Admiral Byrd during his expedition to the South Pole.
4. Great interest in conservation has been shown lately by Americans.
5. Religious freedom was promised to the settlers by William Penn.

EXERCISE *Editing for the Active Voice*

In the following paragraph, find any sentences that are written in the passive voice. Then write them in the active voice if appropriate.

Animals to the Rescue!

   In 1814, the small South American country of Chile was ruled by Spain. However, the freedom of Chile was being fought for by Bernardo O'Higgins and a small band of Chilean patriots. For a while all seemed lost for them. Then an unusual idea came to O'Higgins. A large herd of sheep, mules, goats, and dogs were rounded up by O'Higgins's men. When the Chileans startled the animals, they charged off toward the Spaniards. The Spaniards, of course, got out of their way, and right behind the animals were the patriots. After the battle the Chileans reorganized in the hills. Eventually the Spaniards were defeated by them.

Application to Writing

Write a paragraph that describes your first plane, train, trolley, boat, bus, or subway ride. Write it in the active voice.

USING YOUR TEXT

*Clustering
(22)
Expository Essays
(244–283)*

Usage: Editing for Verb Errors

Looking for errors in the use of verbs should always be a part of the editing you do when you finish writing. If you find any errors, always correct them before you write your final copy.

Checking Your Understanding Edit the following paragraph. Check for (1) incorrect verb forms, (2) shifts in tense, and (3) the inappropriate use of the passive voice. Then rewrite the paragraph to include your changes.

Mozart   Mozart's father play in a string quartet. One day the quartet had planned to practice at his home. When the second violinist didn't appear, Mozart takes his place. Even though he had never saw the music before, Mozart plays it perfectly. He was only five years old at the time! Three years later Mozart's first complete symphony was wrote by him. No one has ever doubted that Mozart is the greatest musical genius of his time.

Writing an Expository Essay Make a list of five historic events—anything from Magellan's voyage around the world to the first modern Olympic Games. Then choose one event as a subject and write the name of it in the center of a piece of paper. In clusters write everything you know about the event. If you do not have enough information, you may want to read about your subject in a library reference book. Then write a short expository essay about one aspect of the event you chose.

As you revise your work, make sure that you have included specific facts or examples. Check to see that you have arranged your information in chronological order. *Application:* Edit for any errors in the use of verbs. Look specifically for shifts in tense and for the correct use of active or passive voice. When you have finished, write a final copy.

28 Review

A **Using the Correct Verb Form** Number your paper 1 to 25. Then write the past or the past participle of each verb in parentheses.

1. Ten minutes after the downpour, the sun (come) out.
2. How long have you (know) about the party?
3. The sun (rise) at 5:36 yesterday.
4. Lake Erie has never (freeze) over completely.
5. My sister has (sing) twice on television.
6. Have you (write) your history report yet?
7. Who (write) the screenplay for that movie?
8. The telephone hasn't (ring) all day.
9. You should have (go) to the dance last night.
10. Dana has already (take) those books back to the library.
11. Before World War II, the United States had (give) the Philippines a guarantee of independence.
12. I should have (do) my homework earlier.
13. Until 1875, no one had ever successfully (swam) the English Channel.
14. My wallet hadn't been (steal) after all.
15. Who (choose) brown as the color for this room?
16. Tom (fall) off his skateboard yesterday, but fortunately he was wearing a helmet.
17. Have you ever (wear) those hiking boots on a hike of more than two miles?
18. Who (draw) that picture of Mr. Turner's barn?
19. Lately I have (grow) more confident using the computer.
20. Waiting on the windy corner, we nearly (freeze).
21. Chris Denn has (steal) more bases than any other player.
22. Martin (ride) his bicycle to school today in the rain.
23. My sweater has (shrank) two sizes!
24. Who (eat) all the strawberries?
25. Otis has already (break) two school records in track.

B **Understanding Tenses** Number your paper 1 to 10. Then write the tense of each underlined verb.

1. I <u>am going</u> to the library.
2. Lenny <u>has seen</u> Sarah somewhere before.
3. On Monday Mrs. Saunders <u>will announce</u> the names of the new class officers.
4. Tim <u>was</u> enthusiastic about the project.
5. I <u>have been practicing</u> for my recital every night for a month.
6. Next year will be the third year he <u>will have played</u> for the soccer team.
7. Laura <u>discovered</u> that she <u>had left</u> the theater tickets at home.
8. Pilar <u>knows</u> that we <u>will be working</u> together on the dance committee.
9. Marie <u>has been</u> happy ever since she <u>won</u> the stereo in the contest.
10. Susan and Greg <u>were riding</u> the bus when they first <u>met</u> each other.

Mastery Test

Number your paper 1 to 10. Then write the past or the past participle of each verb in parentheses.

1. I (see) the figure-skating championships last year.
2. Our puppy has (grow) eight inches in two months.
3. Mandy (begin) her research paper for history.
4. We (go) to Mobile, Alabama, last August.
5. Dad (drive) our new car to San Francisco.
6. The police officer (give) us directions to the new stadium.
7. Cocker spaniels have (fall) from first place as the favorite breed in the United States.
8. Juan (write) invitations to his party last night.
9. Steve (run) the bases for a home run.
10. The mail carrier (ring) the bell impatiently.

29 Using Pronouns

Diagnostic Test

Number your paper 1 to 10. Then write the correct form of the pronoun in parentheses.

EXAMPLE   Anna and (I, me) decided to have a tag sale.
ANSWER   I

1. Jonah asked Andy and (she, her) to bring suntan lotion and beach towels.
2. (We, Us) science lovers also like science fiction.
3. To (who, whom) did you give the award?
4. The coach gave Nels and (they, them) some help.
5. Do you know if (them, their) skiing has improved since last winter?
6. Sally and (he, him) will be our debaters.
7. Carl divided the duties between Aaron and (he, him).
8. The finalists in the diving competition were Alani and (she, her).
9. I think Bert is a better batter than (he, him).
10. Peter is the only person (who, whom) was absent from choir practice.

The Cases of Personal Pronouns

In German words change their form depending upon how they are used in a sentence. You say *kinder* if *children* is the subject, but *kindern* if *children* is the indirect object. This is because all nouns and pronouns have *case*.

Rule 29a **Case** is the form of a noun or a pronoun that indicates its use in a sentence.

There are three cases in English: the *nominative case,* the *objective case,* and the *possessive case.* Unlike nouns in German, nouns in English change form only in the possessive case. For example, *Mary* is the nominative form and is used as a subject. *Mary* is also the objective form and is used as an object. *Mary's,* though, is the possessive form and is used to show that Mary has or owns something. Unlike nouns, pronouns usually change form for each of the three cases.

Nominative Case

(Used for subjects and predicate nominatives)

SINGULAR   I, you, he, she, it
PLURAL   we, you, they

Objective Case

(Used for direct objects, indirect objects, and the objects of a preposition)

SINGULAR   me, you, him, her, it
PLURAL   us, you, them

Possessive Case

(Used to show ownership or possession)

SINGULAR   my, mine, your, yours, his, her, hers, its
PLURAL   our, ours, your, yours, their, theirs

EXERCISE *Determining Case*

Write the pronouns in each sentence. Then write the case of each one: *nominative, objective,* or *possessive.*

1. Why wasn't he invited to your party?
2. I hope Sally left me some paper.
3. Mother will pick us up at the airport.
4. Did my brother go with them to the game?
5. We don't know whether the record is his or hers.
6. They often speak of their love of horses.
7. Our dog likes to be at your house rather than ours.
8. You should speak to him about a job.
9. She knew that the lost watch was mine.
10. Are the cassettes yours or theirs?

The Nominative Case

The personal pronouns in the nominative case are *I, you, he, she, it, we,* and *they.*

Rule 29b The **nominative case** is used for subjects and predicate nominatives.

Remember that a predicate nominative is a word that follows a linking verb and identifies or renames the subject. *(See pages 579–580 for lists of linking verbs.)*

SUBJECTS **She** and **I** are applying for the job.
If **they** are late, **he** will go alone.

PREDICATE   The highest scorer on the team was **he.**
NOMINATIVES   That was **she** with Tony last night.

In everyday conversation, people do not always use the nominative case for predicate nominatives. It is common to hear someone say, "It's *me*" instead of "It is *I*," or "That's *him*" instead of "That is *he*." As common as this usage is in conversation, it should be avoided when you write.

A pronoun that is used as a subject or a predicate nominative can have a noun appositive. An *appositive* is a word that comes right after the pronoun and identifies or renames it. The appositive in the following sentence is underlined.

We members must work very hard on the drive.

An appositive, however, will never affect the case of a pronoun. In fact, you can check whether you have used the correct pronoun by dropping the appositive.

We must work very hard on the drive.

EXERCISE **2** *Supplying Pronouns in the Nominative Case*

Number your paper 1 to 10. Complete each sentence by writing an appropriate pronoun in the nominative case. (Do not use *you* or *it*.) Then write how the pronoun is used—*subject* or *predicate nominative*.

EXAMPLE   Did _____ do well on the test?
POSSIBLE ANSWER   I — subject

1. Don't make a decision until _____ give their side of the story.
2. The only ones voting will be _____ students.
3. The person who answered the ad was _____.
4. _____ had to wait at the airport for an hour.
5. The two most popular performers are _____.
6. Neither my mother nor _____ can attend the next meeting.
7. No one remembers what _____ did next.
8. If _____ are patient, a solution will be found.
9. The project leader will be _____.
10. _____ reporters must remain objective.

Compound Subjects and Predicate Nominatives

Choosing the right case for a single subject or a predicate nominative does not usually present any problem. Errors occur more often, however, when the subject or predicate nominative is compound. For compound subjects there is a test that will help you check your answer.

Brenda and (I, me) are cooking dinner tonight.

To find the correct answer, say each choice separately.

I am cooking dinner tonight.
Me is cooking dinner tonight.

The nominative case *I* is the correct form to use.

Brenda and **I** are cooking dinner tonight.

Also use this test if both parts of a compound subject are pronouns.

EXERCISE *Using Pronouns in the Nominative Case*

Write the correct form of the pronoun in parentheses.

1. (She, Her) and Naomi will be the hostesses at the open house.
2. The leads in the play were Pepe and (he, him).
3. (They, Them) and the Wallaces have gone to the rodeo.
4. (She, Her) and (I, me) were born on a farm.
5. Is that (he, him) or Tony on the pitcher's mound?
6. Neither the Andersons nor (we, us) can attend the meeting.
7. Was that (she, her) or Janice with Alison?
8. The announcer will be either (he, him) or (I, me).
9. The audience and (we, us) reviewers enjoyed the play.
10. (They, Them) and their old friends met for a reunion.

 Application to Writing

Write a paragraph that tells about a humorous experience you have shared with a friend. It can be something that happened either recently or some time ago. Your incident will be more humorous to your reader if you add specific details and examples. Begin one sentence with *he and I* or *she and I*.

The Objective Case

The personal pronouns in the objective case are *me, you, him, her, it, us,* and *them.*

Rule 29c The **objective case** is used for direct objects, indirect objects, and objects of a preposition.

A direct object answers the question *What?* or *Whom?* after a verb. An indirect object answers the questions *To* or *for whom?* or *To* or *for what?* A sentence cannot have an indirect object unless it has a direct object. The object of a preposition is always part of a prepositional phrase.

DIRECT OBJECTS	Lana will join **us** after the game.
	Mom took **him** to the dentist.
INDIRECT OBJECTS	Mr. Kent showed **me** the new lab equipment.
	Please give **her** some sweet potatoes.
OBJECTS OF PREPOSITIONS	This agreement is between Pat and **me.**
	People like **him** are handy to have around.

Pronouns in the objective case can also have appositives.

Today's practice really helped **us** <u>violinists</u>.

EXERCISE **4** *Supplying Pronouns in the Objective Case*

Number your paper 1 to 20. Complete each sentence by writing an appropriate pronoun in the objective case. (Do not use *you* or *it.*) Then write how the pronoun is used—*direct object, indirect object,* or *object of a preposition.*

1. Mrs. Martinson gave _____ good advice.
2. The award for best actor came as a big surprise to _____.
3. Uncle Fred drove _____ to the movies.
4. Please take _____ with you.
5. Did you send _____ a birthday card?
6. Mr. White gave _____ our marks.
7. The class elected _____ unanimously.

8. I want to talk to _____ after school.

9. Dad gave _____ a lesson on changing a tire.

10. Have you called _____ yet?

11. There is disagreement among _____ students about the date of the dance.

12. For getting things done, there's no one like _____.

13. The waitress brought _____ a big piece of honeydew.

14. Meet _____ in the library after school.

15. Tell _____ curious friends about your trip.

16. To their surprise Julia invited _____ to the party.

17. Jaime will spend a week with _____ at the lake.

18. My parents bought _____ a watch for my birthday.

19. Will you send _____ a postcard during your vacation in Germany?

20. Do you expect a telephone call from _____ today?

Compound Objects If an object is compound, use the same test you used for compound subjects. Say each pronoun separately.

Isn't Marta going with Greg and (I, me)?
Isn't Marta going with **I?**
Isn't Marta going with **me?**

The objective form *me* is the correct form to use.

EXERCISE **5** *Using Pronouns in the Objective Case*

Number your paper 1 to 20. Then write the correct form of the pronoun in parentheses.

1. A very large package just arrived for my brother and (I, me).

2. The mayor praised the police and (we, us) scouts for rescuing the young child.

3. Who is sitting between Derek and (he, him)?

4. Bring Sam and (she, her) a glass of milk.

5. The lifeguard warned (I, me) and (he, him) of the strong undertow.

6. Greta sent Peg and (she, her) pictures from Texas.

7. The principal assigned (he, him) and (she, her) the same homeroom.

8. Mrs. Gray took the twins and (they, them) to the circus parade in Boston.

9. Athletes like you and (I, me) need to exercise regularly.

10. Gloria's parents invited the coaches and (we, us) team members to their house after the game.

11. Mr. Ames sent Paula and (he, him) to talk with the vocational counselor.

12. My parents planned a barbecue for (I, me) and my friends.

13. Arnie shouted at Wayne and (we, us) from the other side of the pool.

14. Nearsighted people like you and (I, me) usually need glasses.

15. This weekend I'll send Otis and (she, her) a letter about my graduation.

16. Seat Mike and (he, him) beside their parents at the banquet.

17. For help when you really need it, there is no one like Gwen or (he, him).

18. The bill should be divided between (they, them) and (we, us).

19. Give Lian and (I, me) the tickets to the play at the Wilbur Theater.

20. Follow (she, her) and (I, me) to Pat's house.

Application to Writing

Imagine that Sherlock Holmes has asked you to go with him on one of his cases. Write a scene that might take place as you and the great detective capture a notorious jewel thief. First include a brief description of the locale of the capture. Then create suspense by telling what happens just before you nab the most wanted criminal in London. When referring to Sherlock Holmes and yourself, include both *he and I* and *him and me* at least once in your scene.

The Possessive Case

The personal pronouns in the possessive case are *my, mine, your, yours, his, her, hers, its, our, ours, their,* and *theirs.*

Rule 29d   The **possessive case** is used to show ownership or possession.

Some possessive pronouns can be used to show possession before a noun or before a gerund. Others can be used by themselves.

BEFORE A NOUN	Pat shared **her** dessert with Laura.
BEFORE A GERUND	Jerry takes **his** writing seriously.
BY THEMSELVES	This pencil could be **mine.**

Personal possessive pronouns are not written with an apostrophe. Sometimes an apostrophe is incorrectly included because possessive nouns are written with an apostrophe.

POSSESSIVE NOUN	**Rob's** bike is in the garage.
POSSESSIVE PRONOUN	The bike is **hers.** [not *her's*]

Also, do not confuse a contraction with a possessive pronoun. *Its, your,* and *their* are possessive pronouns. *It's, you're,* and *they're* are contractions.

POSSESSIVE PRONOUN	The cat drank all **its** milk.
CONTRACTION	**It's** [it is] time to go.

EXERCISE *Using Pronouns in the Possessive Case*

Number your paper 1 to 10. Then write the correct word in parentheses.

  1. Are (their, they're) shoes dry yet?
  2. (Your, You're) report is due tomorrow.
  3. The box of old baseball cards is (hers, her's).
  4. (Me, My) exercising has slimmed my waist.
  5. Has Lisa borrowed (your, you're) notebook?
  6. I think the radio is (hers, her's).
  7. Was the cat interested in (it's, its) new toy?

8. We thought that car was (ours, our's).
9. Do you know whether these are (their, they're) coats?
10. Dad spoke about (me, my) watching too much TV.

EXERCISE **7** *Supplying Pronouns in All Cases*

Number your paper 1 to 10. Then complete each sentence by writing appropriate pronouns. (Do not use *you* or *it*.)

1. Tell _____ and _____ the story.
2. _____ sat with _____ and Joe.
3. _____ watched the bird build _____ nest.
4. _____ sent for Meg and _____.
5. Pat showed _____ and _____ the poster.
6. _____ was skating with Carl and _____.
7. _____ went camping with _____.
8. _____ invited Rose and _____ to go with _____.
9. The Taylors took _____ dog with _____.
10. Did _____ take _____ to the movies?

EXERCISE **8** *Cumulative Review*

Number your paper 1 to 15. Find and write each pronoun that is in the wrong case. Then write each one correctly. If a sentence is correct, write *C* after the number.

EXAMPLE   Mr. Dale blamed we boys for the broken window.
ANSWER   we—us

1. Without you and he, the party would have been boring.
2. My grandfather told Judy and I amusing stories about his childhood in Rome.
3. Last week we campers went on a backpacking trip.
4. You and me are invited to the surprise party for Christine.
5. Divide the rest of the melon between you and him.
6. Maureen invited we three to dinner.
7. Last year the cleanup committee was headed by Ryan and her.

8. Ellen and me are planning a trip to Wyoming.

9. Mr. Trapani took Joe and I to a soccer game.

10. Are those tennis shoes yours?

11. Divide the jobs among Kate, you, and her.

12. The instructor gave we divers some good tips.

13. With Jed and he as guides, we set out at dawn.

14. Between you and I, we can't fail.

15. Aunt Fran always sends them and us taffy from Atlantic City.

EXERCISE *Writing Sentences*

Write ten sentences that use the following expressions correctly. Then write the case of the pronouns you use.

1. Corey and I   **6.** you and me

2. us students   **7.** we players

3. him and me   **8.** Mom, Dad, and I

4. she and Jan   **9.** she and I

5. Don and he   **10.** Alex or her

Pronoun Problems

Pronoun choice can be a problem. Should you say, "Who is calling?" or "Whom is calling?" Should you say, "Is Jim taller than I?" or "Is Jim taller than me?"

Who or *Whom*

Who is a pronoun that changes its form depending on how it is used in a sentence.

NOMINATIVE CASE   who, whoever

OBJECTIVE CASE   whom, whomever

POSSESSIVE CASE   whose

Who and its related pronouns are used in questions and in subordinate clauses.

Rule 29e The correct case of *who* is determined by how the pronoun is used in a question or a clause.

In Questions Forms of *who* are often used in questions. The form you choose depends upon how the pronoun is used.

NOMINATIVE CASE **Who** is coming to the party? [subject]
OBJECTIVE CASE **Whom** did you call? [direct object]
To **whom** is the letter addressed? [object of the preposition *to*]

When deciding which form to use, turn a question around to its natural order.

QUESTION **Whom** did you ask?
NATURAL ORDER You did ask **whom.**

EXERCISE *Using Forms of* Who *in Questions*

Write the correct form of the pronoun in parentheses. Then, using the following abbreviations, write how each pronoun is used in the question.

subject = *subj.*   object of the preposition = *o.p.*
direct object = *d.o.*

1. (Who, Whom) is on the phone?
2. (Who, Whom) did you meet on the way to school this morning?
3. With (who, whom) did Lee eat lunch?
4. (Who, Whom) will address the students at the computer workshop?
5. From (who, whom) did you get my name?
6. (Who, Whom) sent that package to you?
7. (Who, Whom) will you choose for your partner for the mountain hike?
8. (Who, Whom) is your best friend?
9. (Who, Whom) has the lead in the play?
10. With (who, whom) did you go to the dance at school last night?

In Clauses Forms of *who* can be used in both adjective clauses and noun clauses. The form you use depends on how the pronoun is used within the clause—not on any word outside the clause. The following examples show how *who* and *whom* are used in adjective clauses.

NOMINATIVE CASE — She is the doctor **who spoke at the opening assembly.** [*Who* is the subject of *spoke.*]

OBJECTIVE CASE — Mr. Rowland is the man **whom I met yesterday.** [I met whom yesterday. *Whom* is the direct object of *met.*]

Have you met Mr. Keats, **from whom I take piano lessons?** [I take piano lessons from whom. *Whom* is the object of the preposition *from.*]

The following examples show how forms of *who* are used in noun clauses.

NOMINATIVE CASE — Our dog will obey **whoever will feed it.** [*Whoever* is the subject of *will feed.*]

Do you know **who the winners are?** [The winners are who. *Who* is a predicate nominative.]

OBJECTIVE CASE — Invite **whomever Betsy wants.** [Betsy wants whomever. *Whomever* is the direct object of *wants.*]

I don't know **to whom I should address the envelope.** [*Whom* is the object of the preposition *to.*]

EXERCISE *Using Forms of* Who *in Clauses*

Number your paper 1 to 15. Write the correct form of the pronoun in parentheses. Then, using the following abbreviations, write how each pronoun is used in the clause.

subject = *subj.*   object of a preposition = *o.p.*
predicate nominative = *p.n.*   direct object = *d.o.*

1. Melba didn't know (who, whom) sent the flowers.
2. The club accepts (whoever, whomever) wants to join.
3. Sam couldn't tell to (who, whom) she was referring.
4. (Whoever, Whomever) answers the phone should take messages.
5. Did Gene know (who, whom) the judge was?
6. The person (who, whom) they select will get a screen test.
7. (Whoever, Whomever) is the sixth caller wins ten dollars.
8. No one questioned (who, whom) made that decision.
9. Everyone admires the person (who, whom) you are.
10. This is Willie, to (who, whom) all the credit must be given.
11. The parade was led by two drum majors (who, whom) were dressed in white and gold.
12. Glenn Carlson, (who, whom) is the team's best runner, sprained his ankle.
13. Two men, one of (who, whom) dived into the icy water, are responsible for saving the boy's life.
14. Take (whoever, whomever) you need to get the job done.
15. I spoke with the people from (who, whom) I had received the invitation.

EXERCISE *Cumulative Review*

Number your paper 1 to 10. Write the correct form of the pronoun in parentheses. Then, using the following abbreviations, write how each pronoun is used in the question or the clause.

subject = *subj.*   object of a preposition = *o.p.*
predicate nominative = *p.n.*   direct object = *d.o.*

1. (Whoever, Whomever) is best qualified will get the cashier's job.
2. Did the police find out (who, whom) the burglars are?
3. Those (who, whom) need advice most like it least.
4. The person from (who, whom) you'll get all the answers is Mrs. Chin.

5. (Who, Whom) called me last night?
6. Isn't Ray the one (who, whom) you recommend?
7. Send (whoever, whomever) answers the ad a brochure and a price list.
8. (Who, whom) did you meet at the conference?
9. I'd like to know for (who, whom) you're substituting.
10. Is he the child (who, whom) you found?

Elliptical Clauses

Over the years writers have introduced shortcuts into the language. One such shortcut is an *elliptical clause*. This is a subordinate clause in which words are omitted but are understood to be there. Elliptical clauses begin with *than* or *as*.

Peter takes more courses **than I.**
Wade weighs as much **as I.**

Rule 29f In an elliptical clause, use the form of the pronoun you would use if the clause was completed.

In the following examples, both of the expressions in heavy type are elliptical clauses. Both are also correct because they have two different meanings.

Nancy is with us more **than he.**
Nancy is with us more **than him.**

He is correct in the first example because it is used as the subject of the elliptical clause.

Nancy is with us more **than *he* is with us.**

Him is correct in the second example because it is used as an object of a preposition.

Nancy is with us more **than she is with *him*.**

Because the meaning of a sentence with an elliptical clause sometimes depends upon the case of a pronoun, you must be careful to choose the correct case. One way to do this is to complete the elliptical clause mentally. Then choose the form of the pronoun that expresses the meaning you want.

Ted cares for her as much as (I, me).
Ted cares for her as much **as I care for her.**
Ted cares for her as much **as he cares for me.**

In the example above, decide which meaning you want. Then choose either *I* or *me*.

EXERCISE *Using Pronouns in Elliptical Clauses*

Number your paper 1 to 15. Write each sentence, completing the elliptical clause. Be sure to choose the pronoun that correctly completes each clause. Then underline the pronoun you chose.

EXAMPLE Ronald is a better storyteller than (he, him).
ANSWER Ronald is a better storyteller than he is.

 1. Greg spends more time with them than (I, me).
 2. Do you think I'm as tall as (he, him)?
 3. Our teacher didn't review the test with us as much as (they, them)?
 4. Is Toby as old as (she, her)?
 5. I studied longer than (he, him).
 6. The tennis tournament seemed more exciting to them than (we, us).
 7. Helmut lifts as many weights as (he, him).
 8. I think Marvin is a better singer than (she, her).
 9. Our cat means more to Shelby than (I, me).
10. Hayes likes hot weather as much as (they, them).
11. Everyone should be as cheerful as (he, him).
12. Did you collect as many old newspapers as (they, them)?
13. I think Robin will run faster than (I, me) will run at the county track meet.
14. The people from the television station talked longer to us than (they, them).
15. At the school crafts fair last week, no one worked harder than (we, us).

Pronouns and Their Antecedents

In Chapter 19 you learned that a pronoun takes the place of a noun. That noun is called the pronoun's *antecedent.* In the first example, *Ralph* is the antecedent of *his.* In the second example, *students* is the antecedent of *their.*

Ralph left **his** notebook in the band room.

The **students** wrote down **their** assignments.

There must be agreement between a pronoun and its antecedent in both number and gender.

Rule 29g A pronoun must agree in number and gender with its antecedent.

Number is the term used to indicate whether a noun or a pronoun is *singular* or *plural.* Singular indicates one, and plural indicates more than one. *Gender* is the term used to indicate whether a noun or a pronoun is *masculine, feminine,* or *neuter.*

MASCULINE	FEMININE	NEUTER
he, him, his	she, her, hers	it, its

Note: The pronouns *I, you,* and *they* do not show gender because they can be either masculine or feminine.

If the antecedent of a pronoun is one word, there usually is no problem with agreement.

Our **dog** likes **its** new house.

Kate just sang in **her** first concert.

If the antecedent of a pronoun is more than one word, there are two rules you should remember.

Rule 29h If two or more singular antecedents are joined by *or, nor, either/ or,* or *neither/nor,* use a singular pronoun to refer to them.

These conjunctions indicate a choice. In the following example, only *one* person should read a story. Maud should read her story, or Rosa should read her story.

> Either **Maud** or **Rosa** should read **her** story in front of the class.

Rule 29i If two or more singular antecedents are joined by *and* or *both/ and,* use a plural pronoun to refer to them.

These conjunctions always indicate more than one. In the following example, Anthony and Martin—together—volunteered *their* help.

> Both **Anthony** and **Martin** volunteered **their** help on the project.

Sometimes you will not know whether an antecedent is masculine or feminine. Standard written English solves this agreement problem by using *his* or *his or her* to refer to such vague antecedents.

> Each **worker** will donate two hours of **his** time.

> Each **worker** will donate two hours of **his** or **her** time.

You can avoid this problem completely if you rewrite such sentences, using the plural form.

> All **workers** will donate two hours of **their** time.

EXERCISE *Making Pronouns and Antecedents Agree*

Number your paper 1 to 10. Then write the pronoun that correctly completes each sentence. Make sure that the pronoun agrees in both number and gender with its antecedent.

1. Either Bart or Joe left _____ lunch in the library.
2. All camera-club members should choose five of _____ best pictures for the exhibit.
3. Otis and Roy will give _____ speeches tomorrow.
4. Neither Ruth nor Virginia remembered _____ key.
5. Nathan took five suitcases with _____ to Florida.
6. All players were responsible for _____ own uniforms.
7. After the Cases bought the house, _____ painted it.
8. Dad carried the groceries and put _____ in the car.
9. A robin built _____ nest near the back porch.
10. Either Kate or Sue will play _____ own sonata.

Indefinite Pronouns as Antecedents

Sometimes an indefinite pronoun is the antecedent of a personal pronoun. Making the personal pronoun and the indefinite pronoun agree can be confusing because some singular indefinite pronouns suggest a plural meaning. Other indefinite pronouns can be either singular or plural.

The following lists break the common indefinite pronouns into three groups.

Singular Indefinite Pronouns			
anybody	either	neither	one
anyone	everybody	nobody	somebody
each	everyone	no one	someone

One of the girls left **her** book bag on the table.

Sometimes the gender of a singular indefinite pronoun is not indicated in a sentence. Standard written English solves this problem by using *his* or *his or her.*

Everyone must bring **his** own tennis racket.

Everyone must bring **his** or **her** own tennis racket.

Plural Indefinite Pronouns			
both	few	many	several

Few of my neighbors have **their** own garage.

Singular or Plural Indefinite Pronouns				
all	any	most	none	some

Agreement with one of these indefinite pronouns depends upon the number and the gender of the object of the preposition that follows it.

Some of the **crystal** has lost **its** shine.

Most of the **performers** played **their** own musical compositions.

EXERCISE *Making Personal Pronouns Agree with Indefinite Pronouns*

Number your paper 1 to 10. Then write the pronoun that correctly completes each sentence.

1. Each of the girls won _____ school letter.
2. All of the trees in our yard have lost _____ leaves.
3. No one on the girls' team likes _____ uniform.
4. Many of the citizens cast _____ votes early.
5. Some of the cheese has lost _____ flavor.
6. Neither of the girls received _____ driver's license.
7. Several of the employees bring _____ lunches.
8. Someone in the boys' choir had forgotten _____ part.
9. One of the bridesmaids lost _____ bouquet.
10. Both of the Schlaffman twins jog on the path near _____ home.

USING YOUR TEXT

*Expository Paragraphs
(120–163)
Business Letters
(439–446)*

Usage: Editing for Pronoun Errors

When you edit your writing, make sure each pronoun you have used is in the proper case and has the correct number and gender. Also check for pronoun shifts and missing antecedents. For example, did you shift to the pronoun *you* when you should have used another pronoun—*he* or *she* or *they*—to agree with its antecedent? Is the antecedent of a pronoun you have used missing or unclear?

PRONOUN SHIFT Tim applied for the job but was told that **you** should wait a week.

CORRECT Tim applied for the job but was told that **he** should wait a week.

MISSING ANTECEDENT We tried to call Joanne, but **it** was busy.

CORRECT We tried to call Joanne, but **the line** was busy.

VAGUE ANTECEDENT Ellen filed the letter in the briefcase, but she can't find **it.**

CORRECT Ellen can't find **the letter** that she filed in the briefcase.

CORRECT Ellen can't find **the briefcase** in which she put the letter.

Checking Your Understanding Number your paper 1 to 20. Then rewrite each sentence that has a vague antecedent or a pronoun shift to make the meaning clear.

1. When the teacher gives you the reading assignment, open it at once to the right page.
2. Almost all people can learn to swim reasonably well if you try hard enough.

3. Please try to remove the bandage from your arm and throw it away.
4. Almost everyone likes to read if it is interesting.
5. Ants attacked the chips and sandwiches before we could eat them.
6. I like sailing because you get plenty of sun.
7. Although I never make a goal, I like it anyway.
8. The next time the children come home with wet sweaters, don't hang them up by their necks.
9. Alexander and his brother Phil like to jog, but you get really tired.
10. Henry and Michael took the rugs off the floors and cleaned them.
11. The boy stared at the actor, but he said nothing.
12. I watch the TV news because you learn a lot.
13. After the doctor had seen Sue's foot, she went home.
14. We went fishing but caught only one of them.
15. Lynn's mother ran for political office when she was ten years old.
16. Though I have never surfed before, I really enjoy that.
17. I like dog walking because you don't work too hard.
18. At the firehouse, the children saw where they eat.
19. Marcia asked her mother where her umbrella was.
20. As the outfielder caught the ball, he hit his head on the wall and then dropped it.

Writing a Letter Brainstorm for a list of services you could perform to earn spending money. The services should be practical and realistic, but they should be as imaginative as possible—for example, pet sitting or bicycle repairing. Choose one service and make a list of ways in which it could benefit other people. Arrange the benefits in order of importance.

Write a letter to a prospective customer, explaining your service and its benefits. Follow the form for a business letter on page 441. *Application:* After you have revised your letter, edit it for correct form. Make sure you have used all pronouns correctly. Then write a final copy.

29 Review

A Using Pronouns Correctly   Number your paper 1 to 25. Then write the correct form of the pronoun in parentheses.

1. Neither Dina nor Candy has had (her, their) turn at bat.
2. Will someone lend me (his, their) pen?
3. Please explain to (we, us) students how the computer works.
4. To (who, whom) should I send the invitations?
5. Do other students study as hard as (we, us)?
6. (They, Them) made a delicious dinner for us.
7. Sandra went to the movies with David and (I, me).
8. Both Raoul and Ted forgot (his, their) skates.
9. Our debaters will be Hans and (he, him).
10. It was (she, her) who won the local marathon.
11. Jessica and (he, him) went to the game with us.
12. (Whoever, Whomever) picks the most apples will win a prize.
13. That was quick thinking for an inexperienced quarterback like (he, him).
14. There is no one who is as fast as (she, her) on a word processor.
15. Between you and (I, me), we're never going to get there on time.
16. She is the only person (who, whom) arrived early.
17. (We, us) joggers need to pay special attention to the traffic lights.
18. I think that's (she, her) in the blue coat.
19. Yes, I think she dives as well as (I, me).
20. I think Mr. Pentose is someone (who, whom) we met in Florida last year.
21. Someone shouted at Wayne and (we, us) from the car.
22. The club accepts (whoever, whomever) wants to join.
23. Is this (their, they're) house?
24. The best actors were Tim and (she, her).
25. With (who, whom) were you just dancing?

B **Making Personal Pronouns Agree with Their Antecedents** Number your paper 1 to 15. Then write the personal pronoun that correctly completes each sentence.

1. Either Tim or Morris will bring _____ guitar.
2. One of my brothers just received _____ diploma.
3. Both Heidi and Irene turned in _____ reports early.
4. The tire has lost most of _____ air.
5. All students will be assigned to _____ homerooms.
6. Several of my friends want to add mechanics to _____ schedules.
7. Both of the girls think that _____ will compete.
8. Anton or Elroy should drive _____ car to the fair.
9. After we painted the posters, we hung _____.
10. Either Claire or Erica will have _____ camera.
11. Either of the boys will share _____ lunch.
12. Several of the tourists lost _____ way.
13. That tree is beginning to lose _____ leaves.
14. Neither Mindy nor Sue can finish _____ picture.
15. None of the silver pieces had lost _____ shine.

Mastery Test

Number your paper 1 to 10. Then write the correct form of the pronoun in parentheses.

1. Please loan (we, us) would-be campers a tent.
2. Send an application to (whoever, whomever) calls.
3. Neither my mother nor (I, me) can ski.
4. It's between Marco and (she, her).
5. Travel is more important to Shirley than (I, me).
6. Mr. Hanson is the only teacher (who, whom) I ever consult after school.
7. The man in the tuxedo is (he, him).
8. Hard workers like you and (I, me) need to relax!
9. (Who, Whom) is the best candidate?
10. Rick and (I, me) mow lawns for extra money.

30 Subject and Verb Agreement

Diagnostic Test

Number your paper 1 to 10. Write the subject in each sentence. Then next to each one, write the form of the verb in parentheses that agrees with the subject.

EXAMPLE   Where (is, are) the bananas for breakfast?
ANSWER   bananas—are

1. (Was, Were) you at the class picnic on Saturday?
2. Carl (doesn't, don't) remember the combination.
3. Either the battery or the bulb in my flashlight (has, have) just failed.
4. There (is, are) only a few swimmers entered in the 100-meter race.
5. Two students from our school (was, were) sent to a press conference in Washington.
6. Brad, as well as Dee, (is, are) running for office.
7. (Does, Do) a warm day and a cool evening cause fog?
8. In Vermont there (is, are) several big ski resorts.
9. Not one of the climbers (was, were) able to reach the summit.
10. A compass and a pocketknife (is, are) standard equipment for every hiker.

Agreement of Subjects and Verbs

Language is very much like a jigsaw puzzle. You must put all the pieces of a jigsaw puzzle together correctly to end up with a completed picture. You must also fit all the parts of a sentence together correctly in order to communicate clearly. For example, some subjects and verbs fit together, while others may seem to fit together but actually don't. In the English language, when a subject and a verb fit together, they are said to have *agreement*.

This chapter will show you how to make subjects and verbs agree so that your writing will communicate a complete, clear picture to your reader. One basic rule applies to this entire chapter.

Rule 30a A verb must agree with its subject in number.

Number

In the last chapter, you learned that *number* refers to whether a noun or a pronoun is singular or plural. You learned that *singular* indicates one and that *plural* indicates more than one. In this chapter you will learn that verbs also have number and that the number of a verb must agree with the number of its subject.

Number of Nouns and Pronouns In English the plural of most nouns is formed by adding *-s* or *-es* to the singular form. However, some nouns form their plural in other ways. You should always check a dictionary to see whether a noun has an irregular plural.

SINGULAR	floor	tax	child
PLURAL	floors	taxes	children

In the last chapter, you also learned that pronouns have singular and plural forms. For example, *I, he, she,* and *it* are singular, and *we* and *they* are plural. *(See page 567 for a list of these forms.)*

EXERCISE ◆ **I** ◆ *Determining Number of Nouns and Pronouns*

Write each word and label it *singular* or *plural*.

I. Jessica	**6.** hats	**II.** they	**16.** bike
2. everyone	**7.** mice	**12.** both	**17.** he
3. children	**8.** rakes	**13.** women	**18.** Dennis
4. several	**9.** anyone	**14.** cap	**19.** it
5. schools	**10.** lights	**15.** we	**20.** radio

Number of Verbs   The singular and plural forms of nouns and pronouns are fairly easy to recognize. You can easily see, for example, that *eagle* and *it* refer to only one, while *eagles* and *they* refer to more than one.

The number of verbs, however, is not so easy to recognize. Only the form of the verb indicates its number. Most verbs form their singular and plural in exactly the opposite way that nouns form their singular and plural. Most verbs in the present tense add *-s* or *-es* to form the singular. Plural forms of verbs in the present tense drop the *-s* or *-es*.

	SINGULAR		**PLURAL**
The eagle	{ soars. swoops. flies	The eagles	{ soar. swoop. fly.

Note: Most verbs have the same form for both the singular and the plural when they are used in the past tense.

SINGULAR   The eagle **soared.**

PLURAL   The eagles **soared.**

The irregular verb *be* shows number differently from most verbs. The singular is not formed by adding *-s* or *-es*.

Forms of Be			
SINGULAR FORMS	am	is	was	has been
PLURAL FORMS	are	were	have been

SINGULAR   The eagle **is** a majestic bird.
PLURAL   Eagles **are** majestic birds.

EXERCISE *Determining the Number of Verbs*

Write each verb and label it *singular* or *plural*.

1. breaks	**6.** works	**11.** is	**16.** swim
2. freezes	**7.** was	**12.** tear	**17.** see
3. are	**8.** reads	**13.** look	**18.** speak
4. have been	**9.** am	**14.** sings	**19.** were
5. keep	**10.** has	**15.** walk	**20.** barks

Singular and Plural Subjects

Because a verb must agree in number with its subject, you must remember two rules.

Rule 30b A singular subject takes a singular verb.

Rule 30c A plural subject takes a plural verb.

To make a verb agree with its subject, ask yourself two questions: *What is the subject?* and *Is the subject singular or plural?* Then choose the correct verb form.

SINGULAR   A large shrub **grows** in the front yard.
PLURAL   Large shrubs **grow** in the front yard.
SINGULAR   She **types** rapidly.
PLURAL   They **type** rapidly.
SINGULAR   That light **is** (or **was**) very bright.
PLURAL   Those lights **are** (or **were**) very bright.

The pronouns *you* and *I* are the only exceptions to these agreement rules. The pronoun *you*, whether singular or plural, always takes a plural verb.

SINGULAR   You **sing** the solo.   You **are** the captain.
PLURAL   You two **sing** the duet.   You **are** teammates.

The pronoun *I* also takes a plural verb—except when it is used with a form of *be*.

SINGULAR   I **am** the owner.   I **was** his assistant.

PLURAL   I **like** that one.   I **have** the key.

EXERCISE *Making Subjects and Verbs Agree*

Number your paper 1 to 20. Write the subject in each sentence. Then next to each one, write the form of the verb in parentheses that agrees with the subject.

EXAMPLE   My history report (was, were) in my notebook.

ANSWER   report—was

 1. Butterflies (tastes, taste) with their hind feet.
 2. My brother (knows, know) her address.
 3. Sight (accounts, account) for 90 to 95 percent of all sensory perceptions.
 4. I (takes, take) my lunch to school every day.
 5. The bananas (seems, seem) ripe.
 6. You (is, are) now the club's new president.
 7. The hippopotamus (is, are) a close relative of the pig.
 8. One 75-watt bulb (gives, give) more light than three 25-watt bulbs.
 9. These chairs (needs, need) repairing.
 10. I (was, were) busy at the time.
 11. Normally a whale's heart (beats, beat) only nine times per minute.
 12. The right lung (takes, take) in more air than the left one.
 13. The human body (has, have) 45 miles of nerves.
 14. Carrots (contains, contain) vitamin A.
 15. Flamingos (is, are) not naturally pink.
 16. You (walks, walk) too slowly for me.
 17. A cat's eyes (shines, shine) in the dark.
 18. They (freezes, freeze) many of their own vegetables.
 19. I (likes, like) spring more than autumn.
 20. The Empire State Building (exceeds, exceed) the height of the Eiffel Tower by only 265.5 feet.

Agreement with Verb Phrases If a sentence contains a verb phrase, make the first helping verb agree with the subject.

Rule 30d The helping verb must agree in number with the subject.

> Ralph <u>was working</u>. [*Ralph* is singular, and *was* is singular.]
> They <u>have been working</u> on the committee. [*They* is plural, and *have* is plural.]

The following chart shows the singular and plural forms of common helping verbs.

Common Helping Verbs	
SINGULAR	**PLURAL**
am, is, was, has, does	are, were, have, do

SINGULAR	Lynn **is** making the dessert.
	The actor **does** answer his mail.
PLURAL	The biscuits **are** burned on the bottom.
	Our library books **have** been returned.

EXERCISE *Making Subjects and Verb Phrases Agree*

Write the subject in each sentence. Then next to each one, write the form of the verb in parentheses that agrees with the subject.

1. They (has, have) finished their science projects.
2. Italian (is, are) spoken at Donato's Restaurant.
3. You (was, were) really missed at the dance.
4. The milk (does, do) taste sour to me.
5. A hippopotamus (is, are) born underwater.
6. Oak trees (is, are) often struck by lightning.
7. Kevin (has, have) applied for a job at the bank.
8. The invitations (was, were) mailed on Monday.
9. I (was, were) just leaving when you called.
10. Those daisies (does, do) make a beautiful centerpiece.

Agreement and Interrupting Words If the subject is separated from the verb by a phrase or a clause, a mistake in agreement may occur. The reason is that either the object of a preposition or some other word is closer to the verb than the subject is. Agreement of the verb may then be incorrectly made with that word—rather than with the subject.

Rule 30e The agreement of a verb with its subject is not changed by any interrupting words.

In the following examples, notice how the subjects and the verbs agree in number—in spite of the words that come between them. Each subject is underlined once, and each verb is underlined twice.

> A <u>bouquet</u> of roses <u>was</u> given to the prom queen. [*Was* agrees with the singular subject *bouquet*. The verb does not agree with *roses*, the object of the preposition—even though *roses* is closer to the verb.]

> The <u>engine</u> together with the first three cars <u>was</u> derailed. [*Was* agrees with the subject *engine*—not with *cars*, the object of the preposition.]

> The <u>paintings</u> that hang in the museum <u>are</u> insured for millions of dollars. [*Are* agrees with the subject *paintings*—not with *museum*, the object of the preposition.]

EXERCISE **5** *Making Interrupted Subjects and Verbs Agree*

Number your paper 1 to 15. Write the subject in each sentence. Then next to each one, write the form of the verb in parentheses that agrees with the subject.

1. The hands of the mole (is, are) very much like human hands.
2. Every Sunday many people who live on Pine Street (organizes, organize) a baseball game.

3. Flags of France, Spain, and England (has, have) flown over areas of Mississippi.
4. The craters of the moon (is, are) visible through a low-powered telescope.
5. One of Sumi's sisters (goes, go) to Wheaton College in Illinois.
6. The election of the Student Council officers (was, were) held last week.
7. A town in the Dutch West Indies (is, are) located in an extinct volcano.
8. Shape, as well as size, (helps, help) determine the value of a pearl.
9. Three people in our group (was, were) swimming in the ocean.
10. Ammonia, which is used in household cleaners, (is, are) poisonous.
11. One of the New England states (was, were) admitted to the Union in 1820.
12. That tree, including branches and leaves, (weighs, weigh) 100 tons.
13. The front tires of the abandoned car (was, were) worn smooth.
14. Until the nineteenth century, solid blocks of tea (was, were) used as money in Siberia.
15. A representative of several colleges (is, are) visiting our school.

EXERCISE 6 *Cumulative Review*

Number your paper 1 to 20. Find and write the verbs that do not agree with their subjects. Then write them correctly. If a sentence is correct, write *C* after the number.

EXAMPLE   Two sheets of that color is enough.
ANSWER   is—are

1. My dog, Muscles, chase toads in the backyard.
2. You needs a new alarm clock.
3. The location of the volcanic islands are not marked on that map.

4. The roses in our garden smells very fragrant.
5. Each year many people, mostly fans of country music, go to Opryland in Nashville.
6. I were the only person there on time.
7. A new display of sports photographs have been hung on the gym bulletin board.
8. At one time helicopters was considered impossible.
9. The apples that are on the table is for a pie.
10. The runways at the airport is covered with ice.
11. You is perfect for the job.
12. Summer nights in Denver are usually cool.
13. A person who is dressed in bright colors look larger than a person in dark colors.
14. A group of lions is known as a *pride*.
15. Four rows of plants in the front is enough.
16. A good milking cow gives nearly 6,000 quarts of milk every year.
17. Four people on our team was late for practice.
18. Two methods of preserving food is canning and freezing.
19. Earthworms in Australia reach a length of as much as ten feet.
20. The steps on the old porch are hazardous.

Compound Subjects

Agreement between a verb and a compound subject can sometimes be confusing. The following two rules will help you avoid errors of agreement.

Rule 30f **When subjects are joined by *or*, *nor*, *either/or*, or *neither/nor*, the verb agrees with the closer subject.**

This rule applies even when one subject is singular and the other subject is plural.

Either <u>brown</u> or <u>orange</u> <u>is</u> a good color for the poster.
[The verb is singular because the subject closer to it is singular.]

<u>Winds</u> or rising <u>temperatures</u> <u>dispel</u> fog. [The verb is plural because the subject closer to it is plural.]

Neither my <u>brother</u> nor my <u>parents</u> <u>are eating</u> at home tonight. [The helping verb is plural because the subject closer to it is plural—even though the other subject, *brother,* is singular.]

The conjunctions *and* or *both/and* may also be used to form a compound subject. Because these conjunctions always indicate more than one, a plural verb is used.

Rule 30g When subjects are joined by *and* or *both/and*, the verb is plural.

With *and* or *both/and,* the verb should be plural—whether the subjects are singular, plural, or a combination of singular and plural.

Both the <u>desk</u> and the <u>chair</u> in Carol's room <u>are painted</u> yellow. [Two things—the *desk* and the *chair*—*are painted* yellow. The verb must be plural to agree.]

<u>Clara</u> and the other <u>cheerleaders</u> at school <u>have learned</u> a new cheer. [Even though one subject is singular, the verb is still plural because *Clara* and the *cheerleaders*—together—are more than one.]

There are two exceptions to the second rule. Sometimes two subjects that are joined by *and* refer to only one person or thing. Then a singular verb must be used.

The cocaptain and quarterback **is** Bert Roberts. [one person]

Bread and butter **is** served with every meal. [one dish]

The other exception occurs when the word *every* or *each* comes before a compound subject whose parts are joined by *and.* Since each subject is being considered separately in these sentences, a singular verb is called for.

Every pot and pan **has** been packed already.

Each girl and boy **is** allowed to bring one guest.

EXERCISE 7 *Making Verbs Agree with Compound Subjects*

Number your paper 1 to 20. Then write the correct form of the verb in parentheses.

1. The plans and arrangements for the picnic (has, have) not been finalized yet.
2. Either Jennie or her brothers (delivers, deliver) the Sunday newspaper.
3. Ham and cheese (is, are) my favorite sandwich.
4. Every student and teacher (was, were) present at the special assembly.
5. Neither Mars nor Jupiter (is, are) as bright as Venus.
6. Each pencil and pen (was, were) marked with Karen's name.
7. Moisture and warm air (is, are) needed to raise orchids.
8. Mums or carnations (was, were) requested for the centerpiece on the table.
9. My softball coach and Spanish teacher (is, are) Mrs. Gomez.
10. Strawberries and cream still (remains, remain) my favorite dessert.
11. Red, white, and blue (is, are) the colors in many flags.
12. After more than 30 years, rock and roll (is, are) still a popular kind of music.
13. Either Pat or Cathy (has, have) the key to the costume room.
14. Earthquakes and volcanoes (has, have) caused cities to sink beneath the sea.
15. Some tape or nails (is, are) needed to hang this poster.
16. The passenger and driver of the truck (was, were) not hurt in the accident.
17. Today, great ice caps and glaciers (covers, cover) one tenth of the earth's surface.
18. Both Paul Bunyan and Pecos Bill (is, are) legendary heroes in American folklore.
19. Every bicycle and car in the parade (was, were) decorated with streamers and balloons.
20. Neither the President nor his aides (was, were) prepared for such a warm welcome.

EXERCISE 8 *Cumulative Review*

Write the verbs that do not agree with their subjects. Then write them correctly. If a sentence is correct, write *C*.

1. *Animal Farm* and *1984* were written by George Orwell.
2. The collie, as well as many other dogs, were originally raised as a work animal.
3. Neither the king snake nor the water snake is harmful.
4. Spaghetti and meatballs are my favorite dinner.
5. The leaves of the ginkgo tree looks like tiny fans.
6. Limestone and sandstone is easily split into sheets.
7. The king penguins of the Antarctic is over three feet tall.
8. Snow or showers is predicted for tomorrow.
9. Every box and trash can by the school were filled.
10. The number of atoms in a pound of iron is nearly five trillion trillion.
11. The votes for the position of secretary is being counted.
12. Ham and eggs are my favorite Sunday breakfast.
13. Each performer and guest were given an entrance pass.
14. Neither the canoe nor the rowboats was damaged.
15. Both intensive training and a thorough knowledge of anatomy is required in judo.
16. The captain and first baseman this year are Ike Saunders.
17. The fastest elevators in the world is located in Chicago.
18. An island or a reef is barely visible near the horizon.
19. In 1610, the population of all the English colonies in America were 350.
20. My uncle, aunt, and cousin are staying with us.

Application to Writing

Over the years movies and TV have pictured weird creatures from outer space. Write a paragraph describing what you think a creature from outer space would look like. Write as if you are describing a creature you have seen. Then edit your paragraph for correct subject and verb agreement.

Special Agreement Problems

Some subjects, unfortunately, create special agreement problems. They will be discussed in this chapter.

Indefinite Pronouns as Subjects   In the last chapter, you learned that not all indefinite pronouns have the same number.

Common Indefinite Pronouns	
SINGULAR	anybody, anyone, each, either, everybody, everyone, neither, nobody, no one, one, somebody, someone
PLURAL	both, few, many, several
SINGULAR/PLURAL	all, any, most, none, some

A verb must agree in number with an indefinite pronoun that is used as a subject. The number of an indefinite pronoun in the last group in the box is determined by the object of the preposition that follows the pronoun.

Rule 30h   A verb must agree in number with an indefinite pronoun used as a subject.

SINGULAR	<u>Everyone</u> in the room <u>is</u> a member of the debating team.
PLURAL	<u>Many</u> of the students <u>want</u> shorter homeroom periods.
SINGULAR OR PLURAL	<u>Most</u> of the money <u>has</u> been collected. [Since *money,* the object of the preposition, is singular, *has* is also singular.]
	<u>Most</u> of the tomatoes <u>are</u> ripe now. [Since *tomatoes,* the object of the preposition, is plural, *are* is also plural.]

EXERCISE **9**   *Making Indefinite Pronoun Subjects and Verbs Agree*

Number your paper 1 to 10. Write the subject in each sentence. Then next to each one, write the correct form of the verb in parentheses that agrees with the subject.

1. Several of her dogs (is, are) collies.
2. Each of you (is, are) needed to help.
3. Some of the broken glass (is, are) still on the floor.
4. One of the eggs in the carton (was, were) cracked.
5. Many of the bags (contains, contain) old clothes.
6. None of the lights (was, were) on in the house.
7. Nobody (remembers, remember) the secret code.
8. Both of the twins usually (eats, eat) together.
9. Most of the snow (has, have) melted.
10. Either of the books (is, are) interesting to read.

Subjects in Inverted Order   A verb must agree in number with the subject, regardless of whether the subject comes before or after the verb.

Rule 30i   **The subject and the verb of an inverted sentence must agree in number.**

There are several types of inverted sentences. *(See pages 552–553.)* To find the subject in an inverted sentence, turn the sentence around to its natural order, placing the subject first.

INVERTED ORDER	At the bottom of the trunk <u>were</u> my father's <u>medals</u>. [My father's <u>medals</u> <u>were</u> at the bottom of the trunk.]
QUESTIONS	<u>Have</u> the <u>birds</u> been fed yet? [The <u>birds</u> <u>have been fed</u>.]
SENTENCES BEGINNING WITH *HERE* OR *THERE*	There <u>are</u> three <u>men</u> waiting to see you. [Three <u>men</u> <u>are waiting</u> to see you.]

EXERCISE *Making Subjects and Verbs in Inverted Order Agree*

Number your paper 1 to 10. Write the subject in each sentence. Then next to each one, write the form of the verb in parentheses that agrees with the subject.

 1. There (is, are) 2,500,000 rivets in the Eiffel Tower.
 2. In the newspaper (was, were) two ads for collies.
 3. (Does, Do) rings really tell the age of a tree?
 4. At the head of the parade (was, were) two bands.
 5. There (is, are) the photos of the class party.
 6. In the basket (was, were) apples, pears, and grapes.
 7. Here (is, are) the photos of the class party.
 8. (Was, Were) you able to find the book in the library?
 9. At the foot of the dock (was, were) two old rowboats.
 10. (Is, Are) there any good remedies for poison ivy?

Doesn't and **Don't** These contractions and other contractions often present agreement problems. When you write a contraction, always say the two words that make up the contraction. Then check for agreement with the subject.

Rule 30j The verb part of a contraction must agree in number with the subject.

Doesn't, isn't, wasn't, and *hasn't* are singular and agree with singular subjects. *Don't, aren't, weren't,* and *haven't* are plural and agree with plural subjects.

> He <u>doesn't</u> <u>know</u> the address. [He *does* (not).]
> <u>Don't</u> <u>they</u> <u>know</u> the address either? [They *do* (not).]

EXERCISE *Making Subjects and Contractions Agree*

Number your paper 1 to 10. Write the subject in each sentence. Then next to each one, write the contraction in parentheses that agrees with the subject.

 1. (Doesn't, Don't) you want to join the softball team?
 2. (Isn't, Aren't) they joining us for dinner?
 3. That (doesn't, don't) sound like a normal jet engine.
 4. Chihuahuas usually (doesn't, don't) like other Chihuahuas.
 5. (Wasn't, Weren't) they told about the meeting?
 6. (Doesn't, Don't) plants give off oxygen?
 7. The glass animals on the mantle (hasn't, haven't) been dusted.
 8. (Doesn't, Don't) your neighbors own a Siamese cat?
 9. These (isn't, aren't) the books I wanted.
10. I (doesn't, don't) have the information you need.

EXERCISE **12** *Cumulative Review*

Write the verbs that do not agree with their subjects. Then write
them correctly. If a sentence is correct, write *C*.

 1. Here comes three buses all at once.
 2. In this container is the refreshments for tonight's party.
 3. Everyone in the burning buildings were rescued.
 4. Many of my friends has part-time jobs.
 5. Are there more telephones in the United States than in any
     other country?
 6. Some of the blueberries was kept for you.
 7. Was you going for a swim with Darrell and me?
 8. None of the tomatoes is ripe.
 9. There was once no difference between right and left shoes.
10. Someone in the bleachers was waving a flag.
11. He don't understand the question.
12. On a football team there are 11 players.
13. Most of the candidates is advertising on TV.
14. In 1921, there were a 76-inch snowfall in 24 hours at Silver
     Lake, Colorado.
15. Was you afraid of the huge waves?
16. In the center of the table was red and yellow tulips.
17. The penguin don't use its flipperlike wings for flight.
18. No one in the pictures were smiling.
19. Don't he know his lines for the second act yet?
20. There is several snowy mountain peaks right on the equator.

Collective Nouns In Chapter 19 you learned that a *collective noun* names a group of people or things. Words such as *group, flock, audience,* and *family* are collective nouns.

Rule 30k Use a singular verb with a collective-noun subject that is thought of as a unit. Use a plural verb with a collective-noun subject that is thought of as individuals.

> The <u>committee</u> <u>is</u> planning to hire a band. [The committee is working as a single unit. Therefore, the verb is singular.]
>
> The <u>committee</u> <u>are</u> unable to agree on a band. [The individuals on the committee are acting separately. Therefore, the verb is plural.]

Words Expressing an Amount Words that express an amount of time or money or that express a measurement or weight are usually considered singular.

Rule 30l A subject that expresses an amount, a measurement, or a weight is usually singular and takes a singular verb.

Words expressing an amount can be confusing because they are sometimes plural in form.

> <u>Twelve dollars</u> <u>was</u> all Jody could spend. [one sum of money]
> <u>Nine tenths</u> of Pat's spare time <u>is spent</u> reading. [one part of her time]

Once in a while, an amount is thought of in individual parts. When this happens, a plural verb must be used.

> <u>Three quarters</u> <u>were found</u> in the pockets of the pants.

Singular Nouns That Have a Plural Form Words such as *measles, mathematics, economics,* and *news* all end in *-s;* but they name single things, such as one disease or one area of knowledge.

Rule 30m Use a singular verb with certain subjects that are plural in form but singular in meaning.

Mathematics <u>is</u> Gail's favorite subject.
The <u>news</u> of her award <u>delights</u> all of us.

Subjects with Linking Verbs Sometimes a sentence will have a subject and a predicate nominative that do not agree in number.

Rule 30n A verb agrees with the subject of a sentence, not with the predicate nominative.

In the following examples, the number of the predicate nominative does not affect the number of the verb.

One <u>problem</u> in our town <u>is</u> huge potholes.

<u>Problems</u> in the cafeteria <u>are</u> one issue that will be discussed at the school-board meeting.

Titles Titles may have many words, and some of those words may be plural. Nevertheless, a title is the name of only one book or one work of art.

Rule 30o A title is singular and takes a singular verb.

Wuthering Heights by Emily Brontë <u>was dramatized</u> on public television last fall.
Three Musicians by Picasso <u>is hanging</u> in the museum.

EXERCISE *Making Subjects and Verbs Agree*

Number your paper 1 to 15. Then write the correct form of the verb in parentheses.

1. Those singers (is, are) a big hit now.
2. My pottery class (is, are) learning about glazes.
3. *Thirteen Days* (is, are) a book by Robert Kennedy.

4. Computers (is, are) a great learning tool.
5. Eight miles of the River Seine (is, are) inside the city of Paris.
6. Economics (is, are) the subject I enjoy most this year.
7. Nearly three fourths of the earth's surface (is, are) covered by salt water.
8. One result of inflation (is, are) higher interest rates.
9. *The Cardsharps* (was, were) painted about 1590.
10. Thirty dollars (was, were) donated by our class.
11. Three days (was, were) spent studying for final exams.
12. The athletic club (is, are) holding a fund-raising drive.
13. (Is, Are) mathematics one of your favorite subjects?
14. (Has, Have) the family agreed on a name for the puppy?
15. *Gulliver's Travels* first (tells, tell) about Gulliver's voyage to Lilliput.

EXERCISE *Cumulative Review*

Number your paper 1 to 10. Find and write the verbs that do not agree with their subjects. Then write them correctly. If a sentence is correct, write *C* after the number.

They Can Tell

1. The groundhog for years have been used to predict the arrival of spring.
2. The fuzz on woolly caterpillars are used to determine how hard a winter will be.
3. Neither a groundhog nor caterpillars is really dependable for forecasting, though.
4. Many of the predictions are wrong.
5. There are reports that animals can sense earthquakes.
6. Ten catfish in a laboratory was observed for two years.
7. During that time 20 earthquakes was experienced.
8. Most of the earthquakes was inaccurately forecast by humans.
9. Seventeen of the quakes, nevertheless, were sensed early by the fish.
10. Catfish doesn't talk, of course, but they wiggled their whiskers just before the quakes struck.

USING YOUR TEXT

*Reference Skills
(494–513)
Expository Writing
(120–163)*

Usage: Editing for Subject and Verb Agreement

One of the most important steps in editing your writing is to check for correct subject and verb agreement. Lack of agreement will make your writing hard to understand.

Checking Your Understanding   Find each verb that does not agree with its subject. Then write the correct form of the verb and its subject.

Everyone have read folktales about cunning wolves. Movies have shown wolves attacking people. Is all these stories about wolves really true? According to Boye Rensberger, they aren't. He says that a wolf don't like to fight. In fact, wolves often go out of their way to avoid harming humans. Rensberger goes on to say that a wolf pack are a tightly knit family. Both males and females raise the young. When both of the parents goes out to hunt, another wolf baby-sits for the pups.

Writing an Interview   If you could interview any person living today, whom would you choose? Select someone interesting and write a list of questions you would ask. Next write the answers to the questions—as the person you chose might answer them. Use specific information from the media and from your reading. Refer to such sources as the *Readers' Guide* and *Current Biography* to help you find up-to-date information about your subject. The answers should give an idea of your subject's personality.

As you revise the answers, make sure that they sound as if the person you chose to interview—not you—has given them. ***Application:*** Edit the interview, looking especially for any errors in subject and verb agreement. Then write a final copy and read it to a friend.

30 Review

A **Making Subjects and Verbs Agree** Number your paper 1 to 20. Write the subject in each sentence. Then next to each one, write the form of the verb in parentheses that agrees with the subject.

1. (Isn't, Aren't) these four loaves of bread enough?
2. There (is, are) still horse ranches within the city limits of San Diego.
3. Neither of the loudspeakers (was, were) working.
4. Two members of the golf team (was, were) able to finish the course at five under par.
5. Off the coast of Maine (is, are) many rocky islands.
6. Ten dollars (was, were) a fair price for the used tennis racket.
7. My height and weight (is, are) average for my age.
8. (Doesn't, Don't) you think we can win?
9. The team (was, were) fighting among themselves over the choice of a new captain.
10. *Incredible Athletic Feats* (is, are) an interesting book by Jim Benagh.
11. Every student and teacher (was, were) at the dedication ceremony.
12. Both Ellen's sister and my sister (is, are) at the University of Wisconsin.
13. One fourth of the world's population (lives, live) on less than two thousand dollars a year.
14. (Wasn't, Weren't) you able to solve the math problem?
15. One of our best pitchers (was, were) unable to play in the county championships.
16. Either Amanda or Mary (is, are) sure to win the race.
17. My friends from school (doesn't, don't) ride the bus.
18. Some of the pages in this book (is, are) missing.
19. The two longest rivers in the world (is, are) the Nile and the Amazon.
20. Many of the participants (has, have) already arrived.

B **Subject and Verb Agreement** Number your paper 1 to 10. Find and write the verbs that do not agree with their subjects. Then write them correctly. If a sentence is correct, write *C* after the number.

1. Was you with Les in the crowd after the game?
2. In the picnic basket were sandwiches for everyone.
3. Fifty dollars were contributed by my friends and me.
4. Crackers and cheese are my favorite snack.
5. Either red or green looks good on you.
6. Every actor and dancer were dressed in a colorful costume.
7. Don't that dripping faucet bother you?
8. There are few poisonous snakes in northern regions.
9. Each of the members are assigned to a committee.
10. Is your father and mother at home this evening?

Mastery Test

Number your paper 1 to 10. Write the subject in each sentence. Then next to each one, write the form of the verb in parentheses that agrees with the subject.

1. (Doesn't, Don't) you have your driver's license yet?
2. The food, tents, and supplies (is, are) on the truck.
3. My family (is, are) planning to drive to Florida.
4. On Dale's workbench (was, were) several unfinished boat models.
5. Some of the old photos (has, have) lost their color.
6. A big breakfast including home fried potatoes and biscuits (was, were) eaten by everyone.
7. Neither Madison nor the nearby towns (was, were) touched by the tornado.
8. Every glass and cup in the house (was, were) sitting in the sink.
9. Three fourths of the crop (was, were) damaged.
10. One of the algebra problems (is, are) too hard.

Chapter 31

Chapter

Using Adjectives and Adverbs

Diagnostic Test

Number your paper 1 to 10. Then write the correct form of the modifier in parentheses.

EXAMPLE   Paula is the (friendlier, friendliest) club member.
ANSWER   friendliest

1. Which of the three routes to Manchester is the (shorter, shortest)?
2. Of the three, Sal can whistle (louder, loudest).
3. Which is (heavier, heaviest), a ton of bricks or a ton of feathers?
4. Of the three trails up Mount Keating, which is the (more, most) scenic?
5. I don't know which is (worse, worst), having a tooth filled or thinking about having it filled.
6. Of all the runners, Phyllis wins (more, most) consistently.
7. Wilbur was the (older, oldest) of the two Wright brothers.
8. Which twin made the (better, best) grades?
9. Of the ten problems, this one was (easier, easiest).
10. Which one do you think has the (less, least) chance of getting the job: Martha, Jane, or Zelda?

Comparison of Adjectives and Adverbs

Before you buy a bicycle, you should do some comparison shopping. You might find out, for example, that one make of bicycle is a *good* buy. A second make, however, is a *better* buy, but a third make is the *best* buy of all. This example shows that different forms of a modifier are used to show comparison.

Most adjectives and adverbs have three forms. These forms are used to show differences in degree or extent.

Rule 31a   Most modifiers show degrees of comparison by changing form.

The three degrees of comparison are the *positive,* the *comparative,* and the *superlative.* The *positive* degree is the basic form of an adjective or an adverb. It is used when no comparison is being made.

Eric is a **tall** basketball player.

The *comparative* degree is used when two people, things, or actions are being compared.

Eric is **taller** than Bruce.

The *superlative* degree is used when more than two people, things, or actions are being compared.

Eric is the **tallest** player on the team.

Following are additional examples of the three degrees of comparison.

POSITIVE	Today is a **hot** day. [adjective] Holly exercises **often.** [adverb]
COMPARATIVE	Today is **hotter** than yesterday. Holly exercises **more often** than Pat.
SUPERLATIVE	Today is the **hottest day** of the year. Holly exercises the **most often** of all the team members.

Note: Some adverbs, such as *too, somewhere, very,* and *never,* cannot be compared.

EXERCISE *Determining Degrees of Comparison*

Number your paper 1 to 10. Write each underlined modifier in the following sentences. Then label its degree of comparison *positive, comparative,* or *superlative.*

EXAMPLE   Pepper is <u>friendlier</u> than Muffin.

ANSWER   friendlier—comparative

1. Which is <u>longer</u>, a yard or a meter?
2. Of all the states east of the Mississippi, Georgia is the <u>largest</u>.
3. Quartz is <u>harder</u> than feldspar.
4. Mario made his bed <u>hurriedly</u>.
5. Who can run <u>faster</u>, Carla or Ellen?
6. That was the <u>funniest</u> movie I have ever seen.
7. It is <u>easier</u> to make biscuits than it is to make bread.
8. Who is the <u>most</u> <u>considerate</u>, Larry, Meg, or Glen?
9. Today was a <u>wonderful</u> day!
10. Hematite is the <u>most</u> <u>important</u> of all iron ores.

Regular and Irregular Comparison

Most modifiers form the comparative and superlative degrees regularly, but a few modifiers form them irregularly.

Regular Comparison   The number of syllables in a modifier determines how it forms its comparative and superlative degrees.

Rule 31b   Add -er to form the comparative degree and -est to form the superlative degree of one-syllable modifiers.

POSITIVE	COMPARATIVE	SUPERLATIVE
brave	braver	bravest
kind	kinder	kindest
soon	sooner	soonest

The comparative and superlative degrees of many two-syllable modifiers are formed the same way. However, some two-syllable modifiers sound awkward when *-er* or *-est* is added. For these modifiers, *more* or *most* should be used to form the comparative and superlative degrees. (*More* and *most* are always used with adverbs that end in *-ly.*)

Rule 31c Use *-er* or *more* to form the comparative degree and *-est* or *most* to form the superlative degree of two-syllable modifiers.

POSITIVE	COMPARATIVE	SUPERLATIVE
happy	happier	happiest
helpful	more helpful	most helpful
quickly	more quickly	most quickly

When deciding whether to add *er/est* or to use *more/most* with a two-syllable modifier, let your ear be your guide. If adding *-er* or *-est* makes a word awkward or difficult to pronounce, use *more* or *most* instead. Your ear tells you to avoid awkward comparisons such as "helpfuler" and "faithfuler" or "helpfulest" and "faithfulest."

The comparative and superlative degrees of modifiers with three or more syllables are always formed by using *more* and *most*.

Rule 31d Use *more* to form the comparative degree and *most* to form the superlative degree of modifiers with three or more syllables.

POSITIVE	COMPARATIVE	SUPERLATIVE
trivial	more trivial	most trivial
serious	more serious	most serious
vigorously	more vigorously	most vigorously

Since *less* and *least* mean the opposite of *more* and *most,* use these words to form negative comparisons.

trivial	less trivial	least trivial
serious	less serious	least serious
vigorously	less vigorously	least vigorously

EXERCISE ◆2◆ *Forming the Comparison of Regular Modifiers*

Number your paper 1 to 20. Write each modifier. Then write its comparative and superlative forms.

1. difficult	**6.** quick	**11.** safe	**16.** slow
2. colorful	**7.** sure	**12.** high	**17.** seasick
3. eagerly	**8.** muddy	**13.** lively	**18.** dark
4. swiftly	**9.** hastily	**14.** loudly	**19.** easily
5. abrupt	**10.** heavy	**15.** fast	**20.** frisky

EXERCISE ◆3◆ *Forming the Negative Comparison of Modifiers*

Number your paper 1 to 5. Write the first five modifiers in Exercise 2. Then write the negative comparison of each one by using *less* and *least*.

Irregular Comparison The following adjectives and adverbs are compared irregularly. The comparative and superlative forms of these modifiers should be memorized.

POSITIVE	COMPARATIVE	SUPERLATIVE
bad	worse	worst
badly	worse	worst
ill	worse	worst
good	better	best
well	better	best
little	less	least
many	more	most
much	more	most

Do not add the regular comparison endings to the comparative and superlative degrees of these irregular modifiers. For example, *worse* is the comparative form of *bad*. You should never use "worser."

EXERCISE ◆**4**▶ *Forming the Comparison of Irregular Modifiers*

Number your paper 1 to 5. Write the comparative and super-lative forms of the underlined modifier.

1. That movie was really <u>bad</u>.
   It was _____ than the movie I saw last week.
   In fact, it was the _____ movie I have ever seen.
2. Frank shows <u>little</u> concern about the pollution in our neighborhood.
   Betty shows even _____ concern than Frank.
   Amazingly, Paula shows the _____ concern of all.
3. <u>Many</u> households have a dog.
   _____ households have a cat.
   However, _____ households have more than one pet.
4. Your corn muffins are <u>good</u>.
   They certainly are _____ than your first ones.
   In fact, they are the _____ you have ever made.
5. My brother is <u>ill</u>.
   He was _____ yesterday.
   Three days ago he was the _____.

EXERCISE ◆**5**▶ *Cumulative Review*

Number your paper 1 to 10. Find each incorrect modifier and write it correctly. If a sentence is correct, write *C*.

1. The thinnest twin is Roberta.
2. Norman Rockwell was one of America's best-known illustrators.
3. Colleen is the youngest of the two Compton sisters.
4. Of the three finalists, Greg has the least chance to win.
5. Rita thinks spring is the more beautiful season of all.
6. Of all the mountains in the Andes, which is the higher?
7. Tony can mow the lawn faster than his brother.
8. Which way is quickest, bus or subway?
9. Yesterday was the happiest day of my life!
10. Of the two movies, I enjoyed this one most.

Application to Writing

Tall tales are fun to read because of their exaggerations. Paul Bunyan, for example, could even reposition a river. Make up a Paul Bunyan-like character and write a tall tale about him or her. Check for the correct form of each modifier.

Problems with Modifiers

A few special problems can arise when you use modifiers.

Double Comparisons Use only one method of forming the comparative or superlative degree of a modifier.

Rule 31e Do not use both *-er* and *more* to form the comparative degree, or both *-est* and *most* to form the superlative degree.

DOUBLE COMPARISON	Joan is **more kinder** than Greta.
CORRECT	Joan is **kinder** than Greta.
DOUBLE COMPARISON	This is the **most violentest** storm I have ever seen.
CORRECT	This is the **most violent** storm I have ever seen.

***Other* and *Else* in Comparisons** Be sure that you do not make the mistake of comparing one thing with itself when it is part of a group. You can avoid this by adding *other* or *else* to your comparison.

Rule 31f Add *other* or *else* when comparing a member of a group with the rest of the group.

In the first example on page 781, the television tower is supposedly being compared with the *other* structures in the city. However, without the word *other,* the tower is also being compared with itself. It is a structure in the city.

INCORRECT   The television tower is taller than any structure in the city.

CORRECT   The television tower is taller than any **other** structure in the city.

INCORRECT   Edgar runs faster than anyone on the track team.

CORRECT   Edgar runs faster than anyone **else** on the track team.

EXERCISE *Correcting Mistakes in Comparisons*

Number your paper 1 to 10. Then write the following sentences, correcting each mistake.

EXAMPLE   Leo is paid more than anyone in the store.

ANSWER   Leo is paid more than anyone else in the store.

1. Diagrams help make directions and explanations more clearer to a reader.

2. The sperm whale has a heavier brain than any animal.

3. More turkeys are raised in California than in any state in the United States.

4. Frank is the most strongest student in our class.

5. You are the most happiest person I have ever known.

6. Wanda, the captain of the team, can swim faster than anyone on the team.

7. We need to walk more faster to get there on time.

8. Swift, graceful greyhounds have better eyesight than any breed of dog.

9. I think this was the most hardest test I have ever taken in my life.

10. Florida is more farther south than any state except Hawaii.

Double Negatives   Words such as *but* (when it means "only"), *hardly, never, no, nobody, not* (and its contraction *n't*), *nothing, only,* and *scarcely* are all negatives. Two negatives should not be used to express one negative meaning.

Rule 31g   Avoid using a double negative.

A double negative often cancels itself out, leaving a positive statement. For example, if you say, "There isn't no more time," you are really saying, "There is more time."

DOUBLE NEGATIVE   **Don't never** scare me like that again!

CORRECT   **Don't ever** scare me like that again!

CORRECT   **Never** scare me like that again!

EXERCISE   **7**   *Correcting Double Negatives*

Write the following sentences, correcting each mistake.

1. I didn't go nowhere near the beach today.
2. She was so sleepy she couldn't hardly stay awake.
3. Uncle Al can't hardly wait to see the Colts play again.
4. Pam hasn't done nothing about getting us tickets.
5. Because of fog, we couldn't scarcely see the road.
6. Don't tell nobody what I just told you.
7. Cheryl didn't say nothing about the invitation.
8. I can't hardly wait for summer vacation.
9. I'm never going to walk in no more poison ivy again.
10. The fire fighters couldn't do nothing to save the house.

EXERCISE   **8**   *Cumulative Review*

Number your paper 1 to 10. Write the following sentences, correcting each mistake. If a sentence is correct, write *C.*

1. The Dead Sea forms part of the most deepest chasm on the earth's surface.
2. Which is more fiercer, the leopard or the lion?
3. Sometimes my grandfather is livelier than I am.
4. Notre Dame is more famous than any French cathedral.
5. Don't feed Bruno nothing before his dinner.
6. Is there an animal more smarter than the beaver?
7. Pam draws better than anyone I know.
8. Don't never answer in that tone of voice.
9. We couldn't scarcely see the eclipse.
10. Of these three shirts, which do you like more?

USING YOUR TEXT

Persuasive Writing
(196–205)
Speeches
(450–456)

Usage: Editing for Correct Use of Modifiers

Factual writing often contains comparisons. This means that you will use comparisons in your reports. When you edit a report, always check to see if you have used the correct form of comparison.

Checking Your Understanding Rewrite the following paragraph, correcting each mistake.

The Olympic decathlon is held in greater esteem than any event in sports. The champion of this event is generally considered the most greatest athlete in the world. The performances in the decathlon are watched more than those in any Olympic event. A decathlon performer must be able to jump the highest, run the fastest, and throw the javelin the most farthest. The winner must be the bestest.

Writing a Persuasive Speech Imagine that your local school board proposes ending all physical education courses in the public schools. At the board's next meeting, you will have five minutes to explain why you agree or disagree with the proposal. Think about your position on the matter. List reasons and examples that support your position, being as specific as possible. Then arrange your notes in a logical order and write the first draft of your speech.

As you revise your speech, make sure that the topic sentence states your opinion clearly. Check whether you have used enough facts and examples to persuade others to agree with your view. Decide whether your concluding sentence summarizes your position forcefully. *Application:* Now edit your work, paying special attention to comparative and superlative forms of any modifiers. Then write a final draft and practice reading your speech aloud.

31 Review

A **Using Modifiers Correctly**   Number your paper 1 to 25. Then write the following sentences, correcting each mistake. If a sentence is correct, write *C* after the number.

1. For its size, the honeybee is much more stronger than a person.
2. Paul hasn't done nothing yet about the garden.
3. Rainbow Bridge in Utah is larger than any other natural arch.
4. Woodworking is the bestest class I have this year.
5. Sean hasn't never seen *Star Wars*.
6. English contains more words than any language.
7. There isn't no more hamburger for the picnic.
8. The Great Dane is among the most largest of all dogs.
9. I think Molly is smarter than anyone in her class.
10. The copies seem brightest than the originals.
11. Which is hardest, ice-skating or roller-skating?
12. Do people in the United States have a higher standard of living than anyone in the world?
13. Nobody knew nothing about the defective fuse.
14. The flood last week was the worst yet.
15. That was the less expensive gift I could find.
16. Even an expert could hardly tell the difference between the real and the counterfeit bill.
17. Lee plays the drums better than anyone in his band.
18. Of Sarah's parents, her dad is the most easygoing.
19. Tulips haven't never done well on that side of the house.
20. Of the two finalists, Carl has the best chance of winning.
21. I think our phone is the most busiest in town.
22. Friday's storm was the worst of the year.
23. I've never seen a more larger dog.
24. We didn't have no time to make other plans.
25. Which of these three ropes is stronger?

B **Writing with Modifiers** Number your paper 1 to 15. Write the correct form of each modifier indicated below. Then use each word in a sentence.

1. the comparative of *quickly*
2. the comparative of *wide*
3. the superlative of *good*
4. the superlative of *generous*
5. the comparative of *little*
6. the superlative of *bright*
7. the comparative of *carefully*
8. the superlative of *bad*
9. the comparative of *brave*
10. the comparative of *many*
11. the superlative of *angry*
12. the superlative of *evenly*
13. the comparative of *zany*
14. the superlative of *courageous*
15. the comparative of *nervous*

Mastery Test

Number your paper 1 to 10. Then write the correct form of the modifier in parentheses.

1. Who is (taller, tallest), Vincent or Tom?
2. Of all the routes, this way to school is the (longer, longest).
3. Which do you consider (sweeter, sweetest), honey or maple syrup?
4. The (younger, youngest) of the two girls is very tall.
5. Of the three pups, I like this one (more, most).
6. Kent is the (stronger, strongest) in our family.
7. I felt (worse, worst) yesterday than today.
8. Which of the two cars is (more, most) economical?
9. Of the three brothers, Bart gave the (less, least) support.
10. Lightning is the (shyer, shyest) of the two colts.

A Writer's Glossary of Usage

In the last four chapters, you covered all the fundamental elements of usage. A Writer's Glossary of Usage will present some specific areas of usage that were not covered in those chapters. Because this section is intended to be a reference tool, the items in the glossary are listed alphabetically.

References in this section will be made to standard English and nonstandard English. The term *standard English* refers to the rules and the conventions of usage that are accepted and used most widely by English-speaking people throughout the world. *Nonstandard English* has many variations because it is influenced by regional differences and dialects, as well as by current slang. Since nonstandard English lacks uniformity, you should always use standard English when you write.

a, an   Use *a* before words beginning with consonant sounds and *an* before words beginning with vowel sounds.

Did you buy **a** new record?
No, it was given to me as **an** early birthday gift.

accept, except   *Accept* is a verb that means "to receive with consent." *Except* is usually a preposition that means "but" or "other than."

Everyone **except** Bernie **accepted** the news calmly.

advice, advise *Advice* is a noun that means "a recommendation." *Advise* is a verb that means "to recommend."

I usually follow Marvin's **advice.**
My doctor **advised** me to exercise more often.

affect, effect *Affect* is a verb that means "to influence" or "to act upon." *Effect* is usually a noun that means "a result" or "an influence." As a verb, *effect* means "to accomplish" or "to produce."

Does the weather **affect** your mood?
No, it has no **effect** on me.
The medicine **effected** a change in his condition.

ain't This contraction is nonstandard English. Avoid it in your writing.

NONSTANDARD   Ken **ain't** here yet.
   STANDARD   Ken **isn't** here yet.

all ready, already *All ready* means "completely ready." *Already* means "previously."

We were **all ready** to go by seven o'clock.
By the time he called, I had **already** left.

all together, altogether *All together* means "in a group." *Altogether* means "wholly" or "thoroughly."

Let's try to sing **all together** for a change.
This cereal is **altogether** too sweet.

a lot People very often write these two words incorrectly as one. There is no such word as "alot." *A lot,* however, should be avoided in formal writing.

INFORMAL   Famous movie stars receive **a lot** of fan mail.
   FORMAL   Famous movie stars usually receive **a large quantity** of fan mail.

among, between These words are both prepositions. *Among* is used when referring to three or more people or things. *Between* is used when referring to two people or things.

> Put your present **among** the others.
> Then come and sit **between** Judith and me.

amount, number *Amount* refers to a singular word. *Number* refers to a plural word.

> Although there were a **number** of rainy days this month, the total **amount** of rain was less than usual.

EXERCISE *Determining the Correct Word*

Number your paper 1 to 10. Then write the word in parentheses that correctly completes each sentence.

1. Have you finished your homework for tomorrow (all ready, already)?
2. The choice is (between, among) these two ties.
3. There will be (a, an) evening meeting on Tuesday.
4. Did you (accept, except) the job?
5. How did the hurricane (affect, effect) your town?
6. I don't think I'm in a position to (advice, advise) him.
7. The (amount, number) of rainfall has decreased in the past five years.
8. We met (all together, altogether) before the meeting.
9. I can't tell you (a lot, much) about the accident.
10. This (ain't, isn't) the right road.

anywhere, everywhere, nowhere, somewhere Do not add -*s* to any of these words.

> I looked **everywhere** but could not find my keys.

at Do not use *at* after *where*.

NONSTANDARD Do you know **where** we're **at?**
STANDARD Do you know **where** we are?

a while, awhile *A while* is made up of an article and a noun that are used mainly after a preposition. *Awhile* is an adverb that stands alone and means "for a short period of time."

We can stay for **a while.**
After we work **awhile,** we can take a break.

beside, besides *Beside* is always a preposition that means "by the side of." As a preposition *besides* means "in addition to." As an adverb *besides* means "also" or "moreover."

I want Grandfather to sit **beside** me. [by the side of]
Besides Mom Aunt Peg was there. [in addition to]
Some other relatives are coming **besides.** [also]

bring, take *Bring* indicates motion toward the speaker. *Take* indicates motion away from the speaker.

Bring me the stamps.
Now please **take** this letter to the post office.

can, may *Can* expresses ability. *May* expresses possibility or permission.

I **can** baby-sit for you tonight.
May I watch TV after Kenny is asleep?

doesn't, don't *Doesn't* is singular and must agree with a singular subject. *Don't* is plural and must agree with a plural subject.

This article **doesn't** make sense to me.
These articles **don't** make sense to me.

double negative Words such as *but* (when it means "only"), *hardly, never, no, none, no one, nobody, not* (and its contraction *n't*), *nothing, nowhere, only, barely,* and *scarcely* are all negatives. Do not use two negatives to express one negative meaning.

NONSTANDARD I **hardly never** see you anymore.
STANDARD I **hardly** see you anymore.
STANDARD I **never** see you anymore.

etc. *Etc.* is an abbreviation for a Latin phrase, *et cetera,* that means "and other things." Never use the word *and* with *etc.* If you do, what you are really saying is "and and other things." You should not use this abbreviation at all in formal writing.

INFORMAL	We had to pack our clothes, books, records, **etc.**
FORMAL	We had to pack our clothes, books, records, **and other belongings.**

fewer, less *Fewer* is plural and refers to things that can be counted. *Less* is singular and refers to quantities and qualities that cannot be counted.

There seem to be **fewer** hours in the day.
I seem to have **less** time to get everything done.

EXERCISE 2 *Determining the Correct Word*

Number your paper 1 to 10. Then write the word in parentheses that correctly completes each sentence.

1. That shade of red (doesn't, don't) look good on you.
2. During the year there are (fewer, less) lunar eclipses than solar eclipses.
3. Let's stop for (a while, awhile) and rest.
4. Don't put the bag of ice (beside, besides) the hot stove.
5. He never gives money to (anyone, nobody) except friends.
6. I haven't been able to find the directions to their house (anywhere, anywheres).
7. (Can, May) I help you with those packages?
8. (Beside, Besides) the sunscreen lotion, take a beach umbrella.
9. We didn't have (anything, nothing) to keep us dry in the rain.
10. Please (bring, take) this note to your teacher.

good, well *Good* is an adjective and often follows a linking verb. *Well* is an adverb and often follows an action verb. However, when *well* means "in good health" or "satisfactory," it is used as an adjective.

The biscuits smell **good.** [adjective]
Janice cooks **well.** [adverb]
I feel quite **well** now. [adjective—"in good health"]

have, of   Never substitute *of* for the verb *have.* When speaking, many people make a contraction of *have.* For example, they might say, "We should've gone." Because *'ve* sounds like *of, of* is often mistakenly substituted for *have* in writing.

NONSTANDARD   We should **of** started earlier.
  STANDARD   We should **have** started earlier.

hear, here   *Hear* is a verb that means "to perceive by listening." *Here* is an adverb that means "in this place."

I can't **hear** the music from **here.**

hole, whole   A *hole* is an opening. *Whole* means "complete" or "entire."

Have you noticed the **hole** in your coat?
Did you see the **whole** movie twice?

in, into   Use *into* when you want to express motion from one place to another.

Is the money **in** your coat pocket?
Be careful that you don't walk **into** those glass doors.

knew, new   *Knew,* the past tense of the verb *know,* means "was acquainted with." *New* is an adjective that means "recently made" or "just found."

Michael's sneakers looked so clean and white that I **knew** they were **new.**

learn, teach   *Learn* means "to gain knowledge." *Teach* means "to instruct" or "to show how."

I just **learned** how to use the word processor.
I can **teach** you how to use the word processor.

leave, let *Leave* means "to depart" or "to go away from." *Let* means "to allow" or "to permit."

NONSTANDARD **Leave** me help you with those packages.
STANDARD **Let** me help you with those packages.
STANDARD Don't **leave** before you help me.

lie, lay *Lie* means "to rest or recline." *Lie* is never followed by a direct object. Its principal parts are *lie, lying, lay,* and *lain. Lay* means "to put or set (something) down." *Lay* is usually followed by a direct object. Its principal parts are *lay, laying, laid,* and *laid.*

LIE Our dogs always **lie** near the fireplace.
They are **lying** there now.
They **lay** there all last evening.
They have **lain** there now for an hour.
LAY **Lay** the mat on the floor. [*Mat* is the direct object.]
George is **laying** the mat on the floor.
Melvin **laid** the mat on the floor the last time.
Usually Gina has **laid** the mat on the floor.

like, as *Like* is a preposition that introduces a prepositional phrase. *As* is usually a subordinating conjunction that introduces an adverb clause.

STANDARD Betty talks exactly **like** her mother. [prepositional phrase]
NONSTANDARD Betty usually does **like** she is told. [clause]
STANDARD Betty usually does **as** she is told.

EXERCISE ▶3▶ *Determining the Correct Word*

Write the word that correctly completes each sentence.

1. The seal slipped through the (hole, whole) in the ice.
2. Chico is (learning, teaching) me Spanish.
3. No one could (have, of) known about the secret key.
4. That hot chocolate tastes unusually (good, well).
5. Put the packages down (hear, here).

EXERCISE *Using* Lie *and* Lay *Correctly*

Number your paper 1 to 5. Then complete each sentence by writing the correct form of *lie* or *lay*.

1. The blame for the broken bicycle should not be _____ entirely on Pete.
2. For 50 years this guitar _____ in the attic.
3. _____ the new blanket at the bottom of the bed.
4. The huskies turned around three times and _____ down in the snow to sleep.
5. Trash was _____ all over the sidewalk.

passed, past   *Passed* is the past tense of the verb *pass*. As a noun *past* means "a time gone by." As an adjective *past* means "just gone" or "elapsed." As a preposition *past* means "beyond."

In the **past** I have **passed** all math tests. [*past* as a noun]
I have walked **past** that store for the **past** few days without noticing its new name. [*past* as a preposition and then as an adjective]

rise, raise   *Rise* means "to move upward" or "to get up." *Rise* is never followed by a direct object. Its principal parts are *rise, rising, rose,* and *risen. Raise* means "to lift (something) up," "to increase," or "to grow something." *Raise* is usually followed by a direct object. Its principal parts are *raise, raising, raised,* and *raised*.

The sun will **rise** at 6:23 A.M.
Raise the blinds. [*Blinds* is the direct object.]

shall, will   Formal English uses *shall* with first person pronouns and *will* with second and third person pronouns. Today *shall* and *will* are used interchangeably with *I* and *we*, except that *shall* is used with *I* and *we* for questions.

Shall I invite her to join the club?
I **will** ask her tonight.

sit, set   *Sit* means "to rest in an upright position." *Sit* is never followed by a direct object. Its principal parts are *sit, sitting, sat,* and *sat. Set* means "to put or place (something)." *Set* is usually followed by a direct object. Its principal parts are *set, setting, set,* and *set.*

> After you have **set** the table, everyone should **sit** down.
> [*Table* is the direct object.]

than, then   *Than* is a subordinating conjunction and is used for comparisons. *Then* is an adverb and means "at that time" or "next."

NONSTANDARD	Jupiter is much larger **then** Saturn.
STANDARD	After learning that Jupiter is much larger **than** Saturn, we **then** learned some other interesting facts about our solar system.

that, which, who   As relative pronouns, *that* refers to people, animals, or things; *which* refers to animals or things; and *who* refers to people.

> The books **that** I found in the attic were very old.
> We watched the baby goats, **which** were in the field.
> The flight attendant **who** was on our plane seemed tired.

their, there, they're   *Their* is a possessive pronoun. *There* is usually an adverb, but sometimes it begins an inverted sentence. *They're* is a contraction for *they are.*

> Tell them to take **their** time.
> **There** were many reporters **there.**
> **They're** meeting at seven o'clock.

theirs, there's   *Theirs* is a possessive pronoun. *There's* is a contraction for *there is.*

> These are ours; those are **theirs.**
> **There's** a message for you in the office.

them, those   Never use *them* as a subject or a modifier.

NONSTANDARD   **Them** are freshly picked tomatoes. [subject]
STANDARD   **Those** are freshly picked tomatoes.
NONSTANDARD   Did you like **them** tomatoes? [adjective]
STANDARD   Did you like **those** tomatoes?

EXERCISE *Determining the Correct Word*

Number your paper 1 to 5. Then write the word in parentheses that correctly completes each sentence.

  I. Did you see the car that just (passed, past)?
  2. These gloves are warmer (than, then) those gloves.
  3. I didn't see them (their, there, they're).
  4. (Shall, Will) we ask him to join us?
  5. The people (which, who) attended the meeting were interested in solar energy.

EXERCISE *Using* Rise/Raise *and* Sit/Set *Correctly*

Number your paper 1 to 5. Then complete each sentence by writing the correct form of *rise/raise* or *sit/set*.

  I. During the performance we _____ in the balcony.
  2. By ten o'clock the tide had come in, and the water had _____ ten feet.
  3. After dinner everyone _____ around the campfire.
  4. Who _____ the toolbox on the table?
  5. People _____ and applauded.

this here, that there   Avoid using *here* or *there* in addition to *this* or *that*.

NONSTANDARD   **That there** chair is very comfortable.
STANDARD   **That** chair is very comfortable.

threw, through   *Threw* is the past tense of the verb *throw.* *Through* is a preposition that means "in one side and out the other."

Denny **threw** the ball to first base.
Have you ever looked **through** a high-powered
telescope before?

to, too, two *To* is a preposition. *To* also begins an infinitive.
Too is an adverb that modifies a verb, an adjective, or another
adverb. *Two* is a number.

Keith went **to** the gym **to** practice.
Two of the members were **too** late to vote.
Jim was invited, but Greg came **too.**

way, ways Do not substitute *ways* for *way* when referring to
a distance.

NONSTANDARD We have gone a long **ways** since noon.
STANDARD We have gone a long **way** since noon.

weak, week *Weak* is an adjective that means "not strong" or
"likely to break." *Week* is a noun that means "seven days."

That chair is too **weak** to hold you.
School will be closed all next **week.**

when, where Do not use *when* or *where* directly after a linking verb in a definition.

NONSTANDARD A *presbyope* is **when** a person is farsighted.
STANDARD A *presbyope* is a farsighted person.
NONSTANDARD A *domicile* is **where** people live.
STANDARD A *domicile* is a place where people live.

where Do not substitute *where* for *that.*

NONSTANDARD I heard **where** crime rates are going down.
STANDARD I heard **that** crime rates are going down.

who, whom *Who,* a pronoun in the nominative case, is used
as either a subject or a predicate nominative. *Whom,* a pronoun
in the objective case, is used as a direct object, an indirect object,
or an object of a preposition. *(See pages 738–739.)*

Who is coming to your party? [subject]
Whom did you choose? [direct object]

whose, who's *Whose* is a possessive pronoun. *Who's* is a contraction for *who is.*

Whose bicycle did you borrow?
Who's living next door to you?

your, you're *Your* is a possessive pronoun. *You're* is a contraction for *you are.*

Are these **your** gloves?
You're the one we want for president of the class.

EXERCISE *Determining the Correct Word*

Number your paper 1 to 5. Then write the word in parentheses that correctly completes each sentence.

I. The action in that movie was much (to, too, two) slow.
2. *Pioneer 10* has passed (threw, through) the solar system.
3. The signals from Channel 4 are very (weak, week).
4. Why aren't you taking (your, you're) tent with you?
5. You have a long (way, ways) to go before you finish.

EXERCISE *Cumulative Review*

Write the word that correctly completes each sentence.

I. Please (bring, take) the hammer to your brother.
2. My uncle (learned, taught) me how to bait a hook.
3. Tell the operator we will (accept, except) the charges.
4. Will Mr. Ames (leave, let) you use his computer?
5. William went (in, into) the restaurant to use the phone.
6. She has looked just about (everywhere, everywheres).
7. The full moon has already (raised, risen).
8. There are (fewer, less) mosquitoes this year.
9. Bud dances better (than, then) Mickey.
10. Mom divided the coins (among, between) her and me.

32 Capital Letters

Diagnostic Test

Number your paper 1 to 10. Then write each word that should begin with a capital letter.

EXAMPLE   i would like to spend the winter in florida.
ANSWER   I, Florida

1. i baby-sit for mrs. martha anderson every tuesday night.
2. my brother bill just moved to houston, texas.
3. does labor day fall on september 3 this year?
4. the senator from ohio is running for reelection.
5. has washington, d.c., always been the capital of the united states?
6. everyone in my science class enjoyed the american museum of natural history.
7. henderson high school is the largest school in butler county.
8. have you ever read the book *the call of the wild* by jack london?
9. next year i plan to take english, french, art, biology, european history, and advanced math II.
10. on our trip to the south, we flew into atlanta, georgia, on delta airlines.

Rules for Capital Letters

Written English is a bit like a detective story. It is filled with many clues that help readers understand a writer's message. Capital letters and punctuation are two such clues. If some of the clues are missing, the message can easily become confused and misleading.

By now you probably know most of the rules for capital letters. This chapter, however, can serve as a review—especially since capital letters are such important clues to the meaning of your writing.

First Words

A capital letter signals the beginning of a new idea or a new line in a poem.

Rule 32a Capitalize the first word of a sentence or a line of poetry.

SENTENCE	**A** lone rose stood in the vase.
LINES OF POETRY	**W**ater, water, everywhere,
	Nor any drop to drink.

SAMUEL TAYLOR COLERIDGE

Note: A few modern poets deliberately misuse or eliminate capital letters. If you are quoting one of their poems, copy it exactly as the poet has written it.

I and *O*

Some words are always capitalized.

Rule 32b Capitalize the pronoun *I*, both alone and in contractions. Also capitalize the interjection *O*.

I   **I** hope **I**'ve heard the last of that story.
O   "Build thee more stately mansions, **O** my soul."
O   "They be of foolish fashion, **O** Sir King . . ."

Note: The interjection *oh* is not capitalized unless it comes at the beginning of a sentence.

Proper Nouns

A proper noun is the name of a particular person, place, or thing.

Rule 32c Capitalize proper nouns and their abbreviations.

Names of Persons and Animals Capitalize the names of particular persons and animals.

PERSONS   **G**rant, **L**isa **A**nn **T**hompson, **S**usan **B**. **A**nthony, **J**ames **F**oster, **T. H. M**urphy, **J**r., **T**immy
ANIMALS   **S**pot, **M**uffin, **M**orris, **L**ightning, **P**eppy

EXERCISE *Using Capital Letters*

Number your paper 1 to 10. Then write each word that should begin with a capital letter.

1. why did you name your dog roger?
2. with one blow of his ax, paul bunyan toppled an oak.
3. what did carol t. haver say at the conference?
4. exult o shores, and ring o bells!
　　 but i with mournful tread,
　　　 walk the deck my Captain lies,
　　　　 fallen cold and dead.   WALT WHITMAN
5. i went to the play, but oh, how bored i was!
6. sean connery starred in six movies about james bond.
7. if i find the book, i'll call you.
8. between 1890 and 1895, george w. vanderbilt II had a 280-room house built for himself.
9. with only $28,000 henry ford began his motor company in 1903.
10. my mother named her cats charlie and esther.

Geographical Names Capitalize particular places and bodies of water.

STREETS, HIGHWAYS	Maple Avenue, the Pennsylvania Turnpike, Marcy Boulevard, Route 30, Forty-second Street [The second part of a hyphenated numbered street is not capitalized.]
TOWNS, CITIES	Canton, San Francisco, Memphis
COUNTIES, TOWNSHIPS	Pike County, Franklin Township
STATES	Ohio, North Carolina, Arizona
COUNTRIES	Canada, the United States, France
SECTION OF A COUNTRY	the Midwest, the Southwest, the East [Compass directions do not begin with a capital letter. *Go east on Route 4.*]
CONTINENTS	Europe, Asia, North America
ISLANDS	the Hawaiian Islands, Long Island
MOUNTAINS	the Rocky Mountains, the Appalachian Mountains, Mount McKinley
PARKS	Yosemite National Park, the Grand Canyon, Elizabeth Park
BODIES OF WATER	the Missouri River, the Great Lakes, the Pacific Ocean, Niagara Falls

Note: Words such as *street, lake, ocean,* and *mountain* are capitalized only when they are part of a proper noun.

Which is the smallest lake of the Great Lakes?

EXERCISE 2 *Capitalizing Geographical Names*

Number your paper 1 to 20. Then write the following geographical names, adding capital letters only where needed.

1. new delhi, india
2. munroe falls
3. thirty-third street
4. great smoky mountains
5. lake michigan
6. south america
7. central park
8. north on route 20
9. el paso, texas
10. dawson county

11. a river in georgia
12. fort lauderdale
13. north dakota
14. the south
15. antarctica

16. the indian ocean
17. saudi arabia
18. catalina island
19. mount rushmore
20. the memorial highway

EXERCISE *Using Capital Letters*

Number your paper 1 to 10. Then write each word that should begin with a capital letter.

1. did both of you know that the capital of manitoba, canada, is winnipeg?
2. lake titicaca in south america is the highest large lake above sea level.
3. the first pay phone was installed in hartford, connecticut, in 1889.
4. located in california, mount whitney towers 14,494 feet above sea level.
5. on one of his voyages for spain, christopher columbus discovered the virgin islands.
6. leather money was used in the soviet union until the seventeenth century.
7. the first straw hat was produced in america in 1798 by a 12-year-old girl from rhode island.
8. the city of paris, france, is over 2,000 years old.
9. louis blériot became the first person to fly across the english channel.
10. brazil, the largest country in south america, is also the most populous latin american country.

Application to Writing

Write a paragraph that describes a place you have visited, read about, or seen on television. Mention its location and points of interest. Be sure to capitalize all geographical names.

Nouns of Historical Importance   Capitalize the names of historical events, periods, and documents.

EVENTS	World War II, the Battle of Bull Run
PERIODS	the Renaissance, the Middle Ages, the Industrial Revolution, the Ice Age
DOCUMENTS	the Declaration of Independence, the Constitution, the Treaty of Versailles

Note: Prepositions are not capitalized.

Names of Groups and Businesses   Capitalize the names of organizations, businesses, institutions, government bodies, and political parties.

ORGANIZATIONS	the American Red Cross, the United Nations, the Boston Red Sox
BUSINESSES	the Ford Motor Company, the Xerox Corporation, Lexington Lumber
INSTITUTIONS	the University of Chicago, Emerson High School, Memorial Hospital [Words such as *high school* and *hospital* are not capitalized unless they are a part of a proper noun. *Where is the nearest hospital?*]
GOVERNMENT BODIES	Congress, the State Department, the Bureau of Labor Statistics
POLITICAL PARTIES	Democratic Party, Republican Party, a Democrat, a Republican

Specific Time Periods and Events   Capitalize the days of the week, the months of the year, civil and religious holidays, and special events.

DAYS, MONTHS	Tuesday, Sunday, February, June
HOLIDAYS	Valentine's Day, New Year's Day, Labor Day, the Fourth of July
SPECIAL EVENTS	the Orange Bowl Parade, the New York Marathon, the Junior Prom

Note: Do not capitalize the seasons of the year unless they are part of a proper noun.

I like **w**inter best.   Did you go to the **W**inter Fair?

EXERCISE *Capitalizing Proper Nouns*

Write the following, adding capital letters only where needed.

1. world war I
2. thanksgiving
3. summer
4. olympic games
5. the senate
6. december
7. the stone age
8. veterans day
9. monday
10. the united way

11. a hospital in new jersey
12. a fourth of july parade
13. acme company
14. the rock island railroad
15. a high school in detroit
16. the monroe doctrine
17. the defense department
18. the library of congress
19. the treaty of paris
20. the republican party

EXERCISE *Using Capital Letters*

Write each word that should begin with a capital letter.

1. many students in school memorize the preamble to the constitution of the united states.
2. next year memorial day falls on the last monday in may.
3. william c. potts of the detroit police department is credited with the invention of traffic lights.
4. the treaty of paris ended the american revolution.
5. two religious holidays are christmas and hanukkah.
6. my report about the united nations focused on the general assembly and the security council.
7. many years ago the george b. carpenter company sold tents for $6.85 each.
8. the symbol of the democratic party is a donkey.
9. the truman doctrine marked a turning point in the foreign policy of the united states.
10. last winter i took a tour of the senate and the house of representatives.

Application to Writing

Write a paragraph about a historical event. Be sure to capitalize each proper noun.

Nationalities, Races, and Languages   Capitalize the names of nationalities, races, and languages.

NATIONALITIES   an **A**merican, a **C**anadian, a **M**exican
RACES   **C**aucasian, **O**riental, **A**frican-**A**merican
LANGUAGES   **S**panish, **G**erman, **I**talian, **R**ussian

Religions and Religious References   Capitalize the names of religions and names referring to the Deity, the Bible, and divisions of the Bible. Capitalize pronouns that refer to the Deity.

RELIGIONS   **C**hristianity, **J**udaism, **B**uddhism
RELIGIOUS   **J**ehovah, the **L**ord, **G**od and **H**is children, the
REFERENCES   **B**ible, **E**xodus, the **S**criptures

Note: The word *god* is not capitalized when it refers to mythological gods.

Neptune was the **g**od of the sea.

Names of Stars, Planets, and Constellations   Capitalize the names of the stars, planets, and constellations.

STARS   the **D**og **S**tar, **C**anopus, the **N**orth **S**tar
PLANETS   **M**ars, **S**aturn, **V**enus, **P**luto, **J**upiter
CONSTELLATIONS   the **M**ilky **W**ay, the **B**ig **D**ipper

Note: The words *sun* and *moon* are not capitalized. *Earth* is not capitalized if it is preceded by the word *the.*

Other Proper Nouns   Other proper nouns should also begin with a capital letter.

AIRCRAFT, SPACECRAFT   the *Concorde, Titan II*

AWARDS   the **N**obel **P**rize, an **O**scar, an **E**mmy, the **H**eisman **T**rophy

BRAND NAMES	**P**rell shampoo, **C**amay soap [The product itself is *not* capitalized.]
MONUMENTS, MEMORIALS	the **W**ashington **M**onument, the **L**incoln **M**emorial
BUILDINGS	the **E**mpire **S**tate **B**uilding, the **E**iffel **T**ower, the **F**irst **N**ational **B**ank
SHIPS, TRAINS	the *Mayflower*, the *Chesapeake*
NAMES OF COURSES	**H**istory 1A, **A**rt II, **L**atin, **E**nglish

Note: Do not capitalize the name of an unnumbered course such as *history, math,* or *biology*—unless it is the name of a language.

Last year I studied **h**istory, **a**rt, and **J**apanese.

Also do not capitalize class names such as *freshman* and *senior* unless they are part of a proper noun.

Eighty percent of the **s**eniors are going to the **S**enior Prom.

Note: For capitalization within letters, see Chapter 12, pages 436–446.

EXERCISE *Capitalizing Proper Nouns*

Number your paper 1 to 20. Write the following items, adding capital letters only where needed.

1. typing and spanish
2. kraft cheese
3. the new testament
4. nine lives cat food
5. god and his kingdom
6. the vietnam memorial
7. advanced geometry II
8. the pulitzer prize
9. judaism
10. *spirit of st. louis*

11. the sun and mars
12. polish and russian
13. a presbyterian
14. the *hindenberg*
15. a canadian
16. the statue of liberty
17. a methodist
18. the war of 1812
19. the world trade center
20. sirius and other stars

EXERCISE *Using Capital Letters*

Number your paper 1 to 10. Then write each word that should begin with a capital letter.

1. like venus, jupiter has a thick cloud cover.

2. twenty-one million americans now play the piano.

3. the greatest concentration of catholics in the united states is in rhode island.

4. is exodus the second book in the old testament?

5. in 1976, *viking 1* landed on mars.

6. after the thirty years' war, the french, not the germans, became the leading watchmakers.

7. at night, north can be determined almost exactly by locating the position of polaris, the north star.

8. three out of four people living in utah are mormon.

9. the diameter, density, and gravity of venus are similar to those of earth.

10. the lincoln memorial in washington, d.c., is the work of daniel chester french.

EXERCISE *Cumulative Review*

Write each word that should begin with a capital letter.

Who's Who

1. was william sherman a general in the american revolution or the civil war?

2. who wrote the declaration of independence?

3. who carried the message that the british were coming through massachusetts?

4. is andrew wyeth a painter or a member of the united states senate?

5. who were the two explorers who led an expedition from st. louis, missouri, to the pacific ocean in 1804?

6. is george c. scott a composer or the winner of an oscar?

7. who was the couple that tried to rule the roman empire from the nile river?

8. what famous person's address is 1600 pennsylvania avenue, washington, d.c.?

9. is sara lee a winner in the olympics or a brand name?

10. did captain james kirk or captain bligh command the *star-ship enterprise?*

11. who joined the boston bruins at age eighteen and led the team to win the stanley cup?

12. who was the first american to set foot on the moon?

13. who flew across the atlantic ocean in the *spirit of st. louis?*

14. who paid for the statue of liberty in new york by giving donations, the french or the americans?

15. did thomas edison or george eastman invent the first kodak camera?

16. who delivered the gettysburg address during the civil war?

17. who painted the ceiling of the sistine chapel in the vatican in rome?

18. washington, jefferson, lincoln, and who else are shown on the mount rushmore memorial?

19. who was the fictitious character who lived on baker street in london, england?

20. who led his troops across the delaware river to attack the british during the american revolution?

Proper Adjectives

Proper adjectives are formed from proper nouns. Like proper nouns, proper adjectives begin with a capital letter.

Rule 32d Capitalize most proper adjectives.

PROPER NOUNS	PROPER ADJECTIVES
France	French doors
Rome	Roman numerals
Alaska	Alaskan oil
Boston	Boston baked beans

Note: Some adjectives that originated from proper nouns are so common that they are no longer capitalized.

Be careful not to drop the china plate.

EXERCISE 9 *Capitalizing Proper Adjectives*

Number your paper 1 to 10. Then write the following items, adding capital letters only where needed.

1. a chinese restaurant
2. a british naval officer
3. a former french colony
4. an ancient egyptian tomb
5. irish stew

6. new england weather
7. a german clock
8. a turkish towel
9. maine lobster
10. a swedish ship

Titles

Capital letters indicate the importance of titles of people, written works, and other works of art.

Rule 32e Capitalize certain titles.

Titles Used with Names of People Capitalize a title showing office, rank, or profession when it comes directly before a person's name.

BEFORE A NAME Have you met **D**r. Anna Richman?
AFTER A NAME Jennifer Kemp is also a **d**octor.

BEFORE A NAME Did you vote for **G**overnor Harper?
AFTER A NAME Did you think George Harper would be elected **g**overnor?

Titles Used Alone Capitalize a title that is used alone when the title is being substituted for a person's name in direct address.

USED AS A NAME Please, **D**octor, may I speak with you?
I didn't see the sign, **O**fficer.

Titles of high government officials, such as *President, Vice President, Chief Justice,* and *Queen of England,* are almost always capitalized when they stand alone.

The **P**resident made a trip to China.

Note: *President* and *vice president* are capitalized when they stand alone only if they refer to the current president or vice president.

Titles Showing Family Relationships Capitalize a title showing family relationship when it comes directly before a person's name, when the title is used as a name, or when the title is being substituted for a person's name in direct address.

BEFORE A NAME   Did you call **Aunt Harriet?**

USED AS A NAME   May we watch the late movie, **M**om?

Do not capitalize titles showing family relationship when they are preceded by a possessive noun or pronoun—unless the titles are considered part of a person's name.

Have you met Ted's **a**unt?

Have you met Ted's **A**unt Katherine?

EXERCISE *Capitalizing Titles of People*

Number your paper 1 to 10. Then write each word that should begin with a capital letter. If a sentence is correct, write *C* after the number.

 1. My uncle is coming for a visit.
 2. The president of the united states and the queen of england met for the first time recently.
 3. My aunt ruth is going to marry senator tobin on Valentine's Day.
 4. Thanks, sis, for helping me with the dishes.
 5. My brother jeff is running for president of the Foreign Language Club.
 6. The senators from our state will visit our school next Wednesday.
 7. Could I make a suggestion, coach?
 8. When did you decide to become a dentist?
 9. Do you know who is the superintendent of your school district?
 10. The pastor of our church knows ambassador lang.

Titles of Written Works and Other Works of Art Capitalize the first word, the last word, and all important words in the titles of books, newspapers, periodicals, stories, poems, movies, plays, musical compositions, and other works of art. Do *not* capitalize a preposition, a conjunction, or an article (*a*, *an*, and *the*) unless it is the first word of a title.

BOOKS AND CHAPTER TITLES	I just finished reading a chapter called "**T**he **M**an on the **T**or" in the book *The Hound of the Baskervilles*.
NEWSPAPERS, MAGAZINES	My family subscribes to the *Chicago Tribune* and to *Field and Stream*. [Generally, do not capitalize *the* as the first word of a newspaper or a magazine title.]
MOVIES	I saw *Star Wars* in a theater and on TV.
MUSICAL WORKS	"**W**hen **Y**ou **W**ish upon a **S**tar" became the theme song for a Disney TV program.
WORKS OF ART	When I was at the museum, I especially enjoyed the paintings *The Sleeping Gypsy* and *Fur Traders on the Missouri*.

EXERCISE *Capitalizing Titles of Things*

Number your paper 1 to 10. Then write each word that should begin with a capital letter.

 1. My sister is a reporter for the *washington post*.
 2. The best song in the musical *cats* is "memory."
 3. Do you know who wrote the book *sawdust in his shoes*?
 4. Yesterday I memorized the poem "casey at the bat."
 5. Here is a picture of the famous statue *the thinker*.
 6. My favorite short story is "to build a fire."
 7. Many paintings, such as *the ceiling of saint matthew*, have religious themes.
 8. I read an article called "solar energy."
 9. I just saw a local production of *the pirates of penzance*.
 10. Isn't the song "somewhere over the rainbow" from *the wizard of oz*?

EXERCISE ◆12◆ *Cumulative Review*

Number your paper 1 to 20. Then write each word that should begin with a capital letter.

1. what are the names of the stars in the movies *duck soup* and *a night at the opera*?

2. what are the seven roman numerals?

3. what god in greek mythology held the world on his shoulders?

4. an old form of what sport takes place in the story "rip van winkle"?

5. what is the name of the fictional reporter who worked on the *daily planet* in the city of metropolis?

6. what is the name of the movie in which fay wray, the empire state building, and a giant ape were featured?

7. what is the name of the captain of the *nautilus* in the film *20,000 leagues under the sea*?

8. what is the motto of the boy scouts of america?

9. what does the initial stand for in president john f. kennedy's name?

10. what is the name of the football team in dallas, texas, the cowboys or the broncos?

11. what was the name of the president of the confederacy during the civil war?

12. what are the chief ingredients of english muffins?

13. what group recorded "i want to hold your hand"?

14. what television series has run longer, *meet the press* or *general hospital*?

15. who is the author of *the red badge of courage*?

16. in the united states, what is the first monday after the first tuesday in september called?

17. what property is lower priced in monopoly, baltic avenue or mediterranean avenue?

18. in what art museum does the *mona lisa* hang?

19. what is the name of the first american writer to win the nobel prize?

20. in what book is captain ahab a character, *two years before the mast* or *moby dick*?

USING YOUR TEXT

*Descriptive Paragraphs
(182–195)
Specific Words
(59–60)*

Mechanics: Editing for Capital Letters

When you are finished writing, always edit your work for proper capitalization. Writing that is not capitalized properly looks immature and unfinished.

Checking Your Understanding Write all the words in the following two paragraphs that should begin with a capital letter. You do not need to include any words that are already capitalized.

A Mighty River

High in the lofty, snow-covered andes mountains, the amazon river begins. It runs eastward across the continent of south america, flowing through the jungles of brazil. Finally it empties into the atlantic ocean.

The mighty amazon river has more water flowing through it than north america's mississippi, egypt's nile, and china's yangtze river—all put together! The reason for this amazing fact is that the drainage basin of the giant south american river lies in one of the rainiest regions of the world.

Writing an Advertisement Brainstorm for a list of interesting cities, towns, or other areas you have been to. List places you would be able to write about for a travel brochure. For example, name such places of interest as historic sites or unusual stores, restaurants, parks, or buildings in the cities, towns, or other areas.

As an employee of the Rambling Rose travel agency, write a newspaper advertisement for the place you chose. As you revise your ad, substitute clear, specific words for any dull, general ones. *Application:* As a part of your editing, check the capitalization of all proper nouns and proper adjectives. After you make a final copy, draw an illustration to go with your ad.

32 Review

A **Using Capital Letters Correctly** Number your paper 1 to 25. Then write each word that should begin with a capital letter.

1. the world's largest church is st. peter's in rome.
2. the *voyager* missions studied jupiter and saturn.
3. the soviet union is the largest country in the world.
4. during thanksgiving vacation i read about the *titanic*.
5. required courses for juniors are english, math II, biology, and american history.
6. in his novel *the grapes of wrath*, john steinbeck tells about the problems of the poor in oklahoma.
7. the houston oaks hotel is in the southwest.
8. last fall my aunt pat flew to athens on world airways.
9. did michigan ever beat nebraska in the cotton bowl?
10. yes, senator parks will speak at logan high school.
11. have you read the book *dr. jekyll and mr. hyde*?
12. the west indies form an island arc in the atlantic ocean.
13. the irish potato originated in south america.
14. the *orient express* train ran from france to turkey.
15. the snake river flows from wyoming to washington.
16. the university of utah was founded in 1850.
17. pasta appeared in italy after the renaissance.
18. the nickname for utah is the beehive state.
19. the treaty of versailles ended world war I.
20. the *apollo 16* carried a special camera to take pictures of the moon.
21. the statue of liberty's nose is over four feet long.
22. who is coming to the barbecue on the fourth of july?
23. animals of the ringling brothers barnum and bailey circus eat 37,600 pounds of carrots every year.
24. last summer we drove through new england.
25. was president reagan in the white house for two terms?

B **Editing for the Correct Use of Capital Letters**   Write all the words in the following paragraph that should have a capital letter. Do not include words that are already capitalized.

Every few years a city in a country such as canada, japan, france, or the united states hosts a world's fair. One of the earliest fairs was held in london, england, in 1851. That was during the early reign of queen victoria. The queen hired joseph paxton, an english architect, to design the exhibition hall in london's hyde park. He created the largest glass building ever made. It contained 300,000 panes of glass and 3,300 columns to support its three stories. After the exhibition, it was taken down and moved to a different part of london. There it became known as the crystal palace. Unfortunately it was destroyed by a fire in 1936.

Mastery Test

Number your paper 1 to 10. Then write each word that should begin with a capital letter.

1. last monday we ate in an italian restaurant.
2. do you mind, mom, if i invite mrs. reese to dinner?
3. the mississippi river flows from minnesota to the gulf of mexico.
4. a museum in maine is closed on mondays during november and december.
5. the elizabethan era was named after queen elizabeth I of england.
6. during the american revolution, the battle of bunker hill was actually fought on breed's hill.
7. our new ambassador to turkey was formerly a senator from new mexico.
8. an english army defeated a much larger french army at the battle of agincourt in 1415.
9. *christina's world* is a painting by andrew wyeth.
10. from earth the andromeda galaxy is faintly visible to the eye.

33

End Marks and Commas

Diagnostic Test

Number your paper 1 to 10. Write each sentence, adding commas where needed. Then write an appropriate end mark.

EXAMPLE   Yes Paul was born in Des Moines Iowa

ANSWER   Yes, Paul was born in Des Moines, Iowa.

1. Mrs Burns my sixth grade teacher just got married
2. Jeffrey does not play baseball tennis or hockey
3. Sandy did Sue move to Phoenix Arizona
4. Write to Harold Fox 950 Ridley Avenue Folsom PA 19033 for more information
5. When Arlene first entered the contest did she have any hope of winning
6. Roberta has such a playful friendly puppy
7. Well I never saw two people do the dishes so quickly
8. The peas not the lima beans should have been picked
9. Ida and Lee however are the two best science students
10. I was born on September 3 1974 in a small town

Kinds of Sentences and End Marks

Imagine New York City without any traffic lights or stop signs. There would be utter confusion. The result of writing without end marks or commas would be very much the same.

In this chapter you will review the three different end marks as well as the four different types of sentences to which those end marks are added. In addition, you will review the use of the period with abbreviations and the uses of the comma.

A sentence may have one of four different purposes or functions. The purpose of a sentence determines the punctuation mark that goes at the end. A sentence may be *declarative, imperative, interrogative,* or *exclamatory.*

One purpose of a sentence is to make a statement or to express an opinion.

Rule 33a   **A declarative sentence** makes a statement or expresses an opinion and ends with a period.

Following are two examples of declarative sentences. Notice that the second sentence makes a statement, even though it contains an indirect question.

Modern highways go around cities, not through them.

I asked them what time they were leaving. [A direct question would be *What time are they leaving?*]

A second purpose of a sentence is to give directions, make requests, or give commands. The subject of these kinds of sentences is usually an understood *you.*

Rule 33b   An **imperative sentence** gives a direction, makes a request, or gives a command. It ends with either a period or an exclamation point.

Although all of the following examples are imperative, two are followed by a period, and one is followed by an exclamation point.

Turn left.

Please answer the phone.

Call the fire department! [This command would be stated with great excitement or emphasis.]

Sometimes an imperative sentence is expressed in the form of a question, but no reply is actually expected. Because the purpose of the sentence still is to request or command, the sentence is followed by a period or an exclamation point—not by a question mark.

May I please have your attention.

A third purpose of a sentence is to ask a question.

Rule 33c An **interrogative sentence** asks a question and ends with a question mark.

Following are two examples of interrogative sentences. Notice that the second example is phrased as a statement but is intended as a question.

What is the capital of Illinois?
You've been here for 20 minutes?

Note: Some questions are not expressed completely; nevertheless, they are followed by a question mark.

You didn't return my call. Why not?

A fourth purpose of a sentence is to express a feeling—such as excitement, joy, anger, fear, or surprise.

Rule 33d An **exclamatory sentence** expresses strong feeling or emotion and ends with an exclamation point.

Following are two examples of exclamatory sentences. Notice they express strong feeling.

I should have thought of that myself!
It's too late now!

Use exclamatory sentences sparingly when you write. They lose their impact when they are used too often.

Note: Remember that an exclamation point also follows an interjection. *(See page 611.)*

Wow**!** That was a wonderful surprise.

EXERCISE *Classifying Sentences*

Number your paper 1 to 15. Write an appropriate end mark for each sentence. Then label each sentence *declarative, imperative, interrogative,* or *exclamatory.*

1. How far north do palm trees grow
2. I just won ten thousand dollars
3. Would everyone please follow me
4. After you mow the lawn, rake up the clippings
5. Reno, Nevada, is farther west than Los Angeles
6. Which planet is closest to Earth
7. Only rarely do whooping cranes breed in captivity
8. Mother asked why you didn't empty the rubbish can
9. Go to bed right this minute
10. Two professional sports many people watch regularly are baseball and basketball
11. How much does a ten-gallon hat really hold
12. You should do warm-up exercises before jogging
13. Answer the doorbell for me
14. The flood water in the basement is getting higher and higher
15. Don't go near that burning building

Application to Writing

Write a paragraph about space travel in the future. At least one sentence in the paragraph should be declarative, one should be imperative, one should be interrogative, and one should be exclamatory. Be prepared to identify each sentence according to its purpose.

Periods with Abbreviations

Abbreviations save time when you take notes or messages. However, most abbreviations should be avoided in formal writing. Following are a few abbreviations that are acceptable in formal writing.

TITLES WITH NAMES	Mr.	Ms.	Rev.	Sgt.	Jr.
	Mrs.	Dr.	Gen.	Lt.	Sr.
TIMES WITH NUMBERS	A.M. (*ante meridiem*—before noon)				
	P.M. (*post meridiem*—after noon)				
	B.C. (before Christ)				
	A.D. (*anno Domini*—in the year of the Lord)				

Rule 33e Use a period after most abbreviations.

If an abbreviation is the last word of a statement, only one period is used. Two marks are needed when a sentence ends with an abbreviation and a question mark or exclamation point.

I'd like to introduce you to Ronald Franklin, Jr.
Should I meet you at 10:00 P.M.?

Note: If you are unsure of the spelling or punctuation of an abbreviation, look it up in the dictionary. Some abbreviations are used without periods. Following are a few examples.

UN   CIA   FM   TV   IBM   TWA   TX   NY

EXERCISE 2 *Writing Abbreviations*

Number your paper 1 to 15. Then write the abbreviations that stand for the following items. Include periods where needed.

1. dozen
2. major
3. ounce
4. latitude
5. mountain
6. Fahrenheit
7. Rhode Island
8. television
9. association
10. boulevard
11. incorporated
12. before Christ
13. Bachelor of Arts
14. miles per hour
15. *post meridiem*

Commas

Although there may seem to be many uses for the comma, there are basically only two. Commas are used to separate items and to enclose items.

Commas That Separate

Commas are used to prevent confusion and to keep items from running into one another. Following are some specific rules for commas that are used to separate items.

Items in a Series   Three or more similar items—words, phrases, or clauses—coming together form a series.

Rule 33f   Use commas to separate items in a series.

WORDS   Blackberries, raspberries, and strawberries are all members of the rose family. [nouns]
Anita will sing, dance, or tell jokes. [verbs]
We were tired, dirty, and wet. [adjectives]

PHRASES   The cat could be in the closet, under the bed, or behind the couch.

CLAUSES   We don't know when we are leaving, where we are going, or what we should take.

When a conjunction connects the last two items in a series, some writers omit the last comma. Although this is acceptable, it can be confusing. Therefore, it is always better to include the comma before the conjunction.

CONFUSING   I had juice, bacon and corn pancakes.
CLEAR   I had juice, bacon, and corn pancakes.

When conjunctions connect all the items in a series, no commas are needed.

We pushed **and** shoved **and** fought our way out of the toy department. [no commas]

Note: Some pairs of words, such as *bacon and eggs,* are thought of as a single item. If one of these pairs of words appears in a series, consider it one item.

For dinner you could have franks and beans, fish and chips, or pork and sauerkraut.

EXERCISE **3** *Using Commas in a Series*

Write each sentence, adding commas where needed. If a sentence does not need any commas, write *C* after the number.

1. The longest known sentence ever written contains 823 words 93 commas 51 semicolons and 4 dashes.
2. Among the strangest names of towns in the United States are Accident Soso Helper and Battiest.
3. Could you tell me when the library opens where it is and how I can get there?
4. The *H* in *4-H Club* stands for "head heart hands and health."
5. Tadpoles develop hind legs first grow front legs next and finally lose their tails.
6. Two Adamses and two Harrisons and two Roosevelts have been president.
7. A minuet is slow stately and dignified.
8. Interstate 95 goes from New England around Washington and into Florida.
9. How did you get your jacket shoes socks and slacks so muddy?
10. Harvesting machines reap grain thresh it and clean it.
11. My cousin Shawn practices the tuba in the morning during the late afternoon and at night.
12. Down coats are light very warm and rather bulky.
13. The graphite and clay in pencil lead are ground together pressed into thin sticks and baked.
14. Do you like raisin and nut apple and cinnamon or peanut butter and oatmeal granola bars?
15. Did Thomas Edison invent the phonograph in 1833 or in 1877 or in 1903?

EXERCISE ◆4◆ *Writing Sentences*

Number your paper 1 to 10, skipping a line after each item. Then, write each sentence, filling the blank with a series of three or more appropriate items. Finally, add commas where needed.

1. On his hamburger Jerry put _____.
2. This year in school I am studying _____.
3. My favorite foods are _____.
4. The birds _____ outside our kitchen window every morning.
5. Before leaving for school in the morning, I usually like to _____.
6. The weather yesterday was _____.
7. Look for the suitcase _____.
8. The old car _____ up the hill.
9. _____ are my favorite sports.
10. A _____ tree stood on the edge of the cliff.

Adjectives before a Noun If a conjunction is missing between two adjectives that come before a noun, a comma is sometimes used to take its place.

> The rabbits disappeared into the tall, thick grass.
> That is the oldest, most beautiful tree in the park.
> Several tall, thin boys passed the ball.

Rule 33g Use a comma sometimes to separate two adjectives that precede a noun and are not joined by a conjunction.

There is a useful test that can help you decide whether or not a comma is needed between two adjectives. If the sentence reads sensibly with the word *and* between the adjectives, a comma is needed.

COMMA NEEDED	Today was a damp, dismal day. [*A damp and dismal day* reads well.]
COMMA NOT NEEDED	Today was a damp spring day. [*A damp and spring day* does not read well.]

EXERCISE *Using Commas with Adjectives*

Number your paper 1 to 10. Then write each sentence, adding commas where needed. If a sentence does not need any commas, write *C* after the number.

1. Zip is the biggest strongest dog on the block.
2. Some cacti produce beautiful delicate flowers.
3. My mother just bought a musical Swiss clock.
4. My uncle's house is surrounded by small green shrubs.
5. My father couldn't read the torn wet newspaper.
6. We store tools in a sturdy wooden box.
7. The loud piercing alarm awakened us.
8. The bright clear colors of the old photographs were amazing.
9. The large white house on Baker Street has been sold.
10. Mr. Roberts is the tall dignified man in the blue suit.

Compound Sentences A comma is usually used to separate the independent clauses in a compound sentence.

Rule 33h Use a comma to separate the independent clauses of a compound sentence if the clauses are joined by a conjunction.

A coordinating conjunction most often combines a compound sentence.

Coordinating Conjunctions						
and	but	for	nor	or	so	yet

Notice in the following examples that the comma comes before the conjunction.

Don't tease the dog, or it may bite you.
I play the flute, and my sister plays the cello.

A comma is not needed in a very short compound sentence.

Otis left but I stayed.

Note: Do not confuse a compound sentence with a sentence that has a compound verb. No comma comes between the parts of a compound verb unless there are three or more verbs.

COMPOUND SENTENCE We waited for ten minutes, but Ben never came. [A comma is needed.]

COMPOUND VERB We waited for ten minutes and then left. [No comma is needed.]

Note: A compound sentence can also be joined by a semicolon. *(See page 866.)*

EXERCISE **6** *Using Commas with Compound Sentences*

Write each sentence, adding commas where needed. If a sentence does not need any commas, write *C* after the number.

1. Most animals remain on land but a few are equipped for gliding.
2. Terry caught the fish and Bryan cooked them.
3. The squirrel ran up and darted across the roof.
4. Palm trees are desert trees but people have transplanted them to other areas.
5. The gorilla looks fierce but it is a rather gentle animal.
6. Gourds are hard-shelled and may be used as cups.
7. You wash and I'll dry.
8. A schooner has at least two masts but a sloop has only one.
9. The skink looks like a snake but has very tiny legs.
10. Either the rain soaked the mats or someone spilled water on them.

EXERCISE **7** *Writing Sentences*

Write one compound sentence for each of the following topics. Make sure that the clauses in each compound sentence are related. Add commas where needed.

1. food **2.** hobbies **3.** friends **4.** jobs **5.** sports

Introductory Elements Some words, phrases, and clauses at the beginning of a sentence need to be separated from the rest of the sentence by a comma.

Rule 33i Use a comma after certain introductory elements.

Following are examples of introductory elements that should be followed by a comma.

WORDS	**No,** I cannot attend the meeting. [Other words include *now, oh, well, why,* and *yes*— except when they are part of the sentence. *Why did you do that?*]
PREPOSITIONAL PHRASE	**After the earthquake in town,** we all helped one another. [A comma comes after two or more prepositional phrases or a single phrase of four or more words. (Punctuation of shorter phrases varies. See the last set of examples below.) Also, never place a comma after a phrase or phrases followed by a verb: *At the bottom of the sea lay the Spanish treasure ship.*]
PARTICIPIAL PHRASE	**Hearing the noise outside,** I rushed to the window.
ADVERB CLAUSE	**As Toby walked closer,** the cat hissed at him.
OTHERS	**In Room 47,** 35 students were studying. **In the road,** blocks of wood were a traffic hazard. [The commas prevent confusion.]

EXERCISE ◆ 8 ◆ *Using Commas with Introductory Elements*

Write each sentence, adding commas where needed. If a sentence does not need a comma, write *C* after the number.

1. Above a glider soared gracefully.

2. Yes that is a wonderful idea.

3. Before the final exam I studied all my old tests.

4. Deciding the trail was too steep the hikers turned back after two hours.

5. After practice in the gym we will meet in room 3B.

6. No announcement was made prior to the meeting.

7. In 1776 54 delegates signed the Declaration of Independence in Philadelphia.

8. After dinner I will meet you at the library.

9. Down the chimney of our house dropped a bird's nest.

10. While cooking vegetables lose some of their vitamins.

11. After he was deaf Beethoven still wrote music.

12. Well water often tastes better than tap water.

13. Waving to Mary Sue entered the bus.

14. Insulated by thick layers of blubber whales can dive deep into the icy depths of the ocean.

15. Into the pool jumped Randy and his friends.

EXERCISE ◆9◆ *Cumulative Review*

Write the following paragraphs, adding commas where needed.

At Home in the Water

Pinnipeds are fin-footed mammals with limbs that are used as paddles or flippers. The three main kinds of pinnipeds are the walrus the sea lion and the seal. All pinnipeds are meat eaters and they all live in the water. Most pinnipeds live in the cold waters of the Arctic and the Antarctic oceans but several forms live in freshwater lakes. Since pinnipeds spend most of their lives in the water they have become well adapted to this kind of existence. Their tapered streamlined bodies make them excellent swimmers. Their thick layer of blubber gives them added buoyancy and helps keep them warm.

Searching for food pinnipeds can dive two or three hundred feet below the water's surface. When they are underwater their nostrils close. Most pinnipeds have sharp backward-pointing teeth. This feature makes it possible for a pinniped to seize prey and direct it down its throat. Since pinnipeds are sociable animals they live together much of the time in large herds.

Commas That Enclose

Some expressions interrupt the flow of a sentence. These expressions generally add information that is not needed to understand the main idea of the sentence. If one of these interrupters comes in the middle of a sentence, a comma is placed before and after the expression to set it off.

The movie**, to tell the truth,** was rather boring.

Sometimes an interrupting expression comes at the beginning or the end of a sentence. When an interrupter appears in one of these places, only one comma is needed to separate it from the rest of the sentence.

To tell the truth, the movie was rather boring.
The movie was rather boring**, to tell the truth.**

Direct Address   Names, titles, or words that are used to address someone are set off by commas. These expressions are called nouns of *direct address*.

Rule 33j   Use commas to enclose nouns of direct address.

Norm, may I borrow your camera?
Your essay**, Marc,** was excellent.
Have you had dinner**, Marian?**

EXERCISE **10**   *Using Commas with Direct Address*

Write each sentence, adding commas where needed.

1. What's for dinner tonight Mom?
2. Ladies and gentlemen please be seated.
3. Yes Thomas you may work with Toni.
4. I had a wonderful time my friend.
5. Could you tell me Ms. Rann if Dr. Saltus is in?
6. Of course Margaret you can join us.
7. I'll give you the list Tim at Saturday's meeting.
8. Perhaps the next bus will be less crowded Mary.

9. Joan did I leave my books at your house?

10. In ten minutes class you should finish your tests.

Parenthetical Expressions   A parenthetical expression provides additional information or related ideas. It is related only loosely to the rest of the sentence. The parenthetical expression could be removed without changing the meaning of the sentence.

Rule 33k   Use commas to enclose parenthetical expressions.

Common Parenthetical Expressions		
after all	for instance	of course
at any rate	generally speaking	on the contrary
by the way	I believe (guess,	on the other hand
consequently	hope, know)	moreover
however	in fact	nevertheless
for example	in my opinion	to tell the truth

By the way, did you buy a newspaper?
The movie, **in my opinion,** was very realistic.
We'll attend the meeting, **I guess.**
José, **on the other hand,** can come with us.

Other expressions, as well, can be used as parenthetical expressions.

The temperature, **although it is colder than usual,** is still within the normal range.
According to this article, only 3 percent of Norway is under cultivation.
Dolphins, **it is known,** communicate with each other.

Contrasting expressions, which usually begin with *not*, are also considered parenthetical expressions.

Nashville, **not Knoxville,** is the capital of Tennessee.
East St. Louis is in Illinois, **not in Missouri.**
Marie, **not Saul,** is president of our class.

EXERCISE **11**   *Using Commas with Parenthetical Expressions*

Number your paper 1 to 10. Then write each sentence, adding commas where needed.

1. A fly's taste buds surprisingly enough are in its feet.
2. Ostriches for instance have wings but cannot fly.
3. Eighty degrees I suppose is too hot for you.
4. My weight because I have been exercising is down a bit.
5. The movie after all won an Academy Award.
6. Jefferson was the third president not the second.
7. The witch-hazel plant blooms only in winter I think.
8. Nina like her two brothers is good in math.
9. The book in my opinion was the best I ever read.
10. On the other hand palm trees live up to 100 years.

Appositives   An appositive with its modifiers identifies or explains a noun or pronoun in the sentence. *(See pages 640–642.)*

> The old firehouse, **a town landmark,** is being restored.

Rule 331   Use commas to enclose most appositives and their modifiers.

Notice in the following examples that an appositive can come in the middle of a sentence or at the end of a sentence. If an appositive comes in the middle of a sentence, two commas are needed to enclose it.

> Aerobics**, a type of exercise,** is fun to do.
> Hanna received a wonderful present**, a down vest.**

Commas are *not* used if an appositive identifies a person or thing by telling which one or ones. Usually these appositives are names and have no modifiers.

> My sister **Barbara** will travel to Ohio with me.
> The book *Oliver Twist* was written by Charles Dickens.
> We **students** want more time on the computers.

EXERCISE *Using Commas with Appositives*

Number your paper 1 to 10, skipping a line after each item. Then write each sentence, adding commas where needed. If a sentence does not need any commas, write *C* after the number.

1. Antarctica a large mass of land wasn't really explored until the twentieth century.
2. The name *Caroline* means "strong."
3. Carmel one of the oldest towns in California was founded as a Spanish mission.
4. Have you and Joanie ever visited Columbia the capital of South Carolina?
5. Zachary Taylor the 12th president never voted in his life.
6. Francisco Coronado a Spanish explorer brought the first horse to America in 1540.
7. The novelist Rudyard Kipling wrote *Kim*.
8. Hindi the official language of India is spoken by only 35 percent of the population.
9. Alvin Parker once flew a glider a plane without a motor 644 miles.
10. I just bought a new pocket-size thesaurus a most useful reference book.

EXERCISE *Writing Sentences*

Number your paper 1 to 5. Then write sentences that follow each set of directions below. Be sure to use commas where needed.

1. Include the word *Dad* as an expression of direct address at the beginning of a sentence.
2. Include the parenthetical expression *I know* in the middle of a sentence.
3. Include the words *a good friend of mine* as an appositive at the end of a sentence.
4. Include a noun of direct address in the middle of a sentence.
5. Include a parenthetical expression and an appositive within the same sentence.

EXERCISE *Cumulative Review*

Write each sentence, adding commas where needed. If a sentence does not need any commas, write *C* after the number.

1. Women not men are a majority in the United States.
2. No the peak month for colds is not July.
3. The vanilla plant a member of the orchid family is cultivated in various tropical countries.
4. Everyone is fond of my dog Bruno.
5. Please wait Loretta while I make a telephone call.
6. No one knows the origin of the story of Paul Bunyan the legendary lumberjack.
7. Many people you will find do not enjoy television.
8. Book reports like essays should be well organized.
9. Let's have hamburgers for dinner tonight Mom.
10. Why that's a wonderful idea!

Nonessential Elements   Sometimes a participial phrase or a clause is not essential to the meaning of a sentence.

Rule 33m   Use commas to set off nonessential participial phrases and nonessential clauses.

A participial phrase or a clause is nonessential if it provides extra, unnecessary information.

NONESSENTIAL   Homing pigeons**, used as messengers,** fly at a speed of 30 miles an hour. [participial phrase]

NONESSENTIAL   Three inches is the annual rainfall in Yuma, Arizona**, which is in the southwestern part of the state.** [clause]

If the nonessential phrase and clause in the preceding examples were dropped, the main idea of the sentences would not be changed in any way.

Homing pigeons fly at a speed of 30 miles an hour.
Three inches is the annual rainfall in Yuma, Arizona.

If a participial phrase or a clause is essential to the meaning of a sentence, no commas are used. Essential phrases and clauses usually identify a person or thing and answer the question *Which one?* Adjective clauses that begin with *that* are always essential.

ESSENTIAL We enjoyed the film **playing at the Plaza.** [participial phrase]

ESSENTIAL The runner **who crossed the finish line second** is my sister. [clause]

ESSENTIAL The house **that has stood for years on the corner of Elm and Park** will be torn down. [clause]

If the essential phrase and clauses in the preceding examples were dropped, necessary information would be missing. The main idea of the sentences would be incomplete.

We enjoyed the film. [Which film?]
The runner is my sister. [Which runner?]
The house will be torn down. [Which house?]

Note: Nonessential and essential elements are also called *nonrestrictive* and *restrictive* elements.

EXERCISE *Using Commas with Nonessential Elements*

Number your paper 1 to 25. Then write each sentence, adding commas where needed. If a sentence does not need any commas, write *C* after the number.

1. Home-grown vegetables that are not properly canned can cause botulism.
2. We saw two bear cubs hiding in a hollow tree.
3. The pronghorn antelope living only in North America has no close relatives.
4. A sport that many Scots enjoy is curling.
5. Curling which resembles bowling is played on ice.
6. Huskies warmed by their thick coats are able to sleep in the snow.

7. Ogunquit which is on the ocean is a resort town in south-eastern Maine.

8. Where is the quartz watch that Dad gave you for your birthday?

9. Mount McKinley located near the Arctic Circle may well be the world's coldest mountain.

10. An English novel that I really enjoyed reading is *David Copperfield.*

11. Samuel Houston for whom the city of Houston was named was a frontier hero.

12. Mozart gave a concert at an age when most children are just starting school.

13. The stag alarmed by the loud and sudden noise raised its magnificent head.

14. People who work on high bridges and buildings must have nerves of steel.

15. A flock of wild geese flying in a V-shaped formation passed high above us.

16. The man who is pictured on the $10,000 bill is Salmon P. Chase.

17. Arthur's uncle wants to buy the fishing pole that is made of fiberglass.

18. The Sandwich Islands which are now called the Hawaiian Islands were discovered by Captain Cook.

19. An inch of rain covering one city block weighs about 160 tons.

20. This is the tulip that won first prize at the flower show yesterday.

21. The poisonous Portuguese man-of-war has tentacles that may trail as long as 40 feet.

22. This cuckoo clock made in Germany is a present for our grandparents' anniversary.

23. The other morning we saw Patty who was waiting for a bus at the corner of Munsey Street.

24. Playing cards were issued as money to French soldiers stationed in Canada in the seventeenth century.

25. The heaviest organ in the human body is the liver which weighs an average of three and a half pounds.

EXERCISE ⟨16⟩ *Cumulative Review*

Write the following paragraph, adding commas where they are needed.

    A man who lives in California constructed a musical robot. The amazing thing about this achievement however is that the man made it in 1940! The robot named Isis looked like a woman. Sitting on a couch Isis would play the zither. The zither a musical instrument has 30 to 40 strings. Anyone who was within a 12-foot radius could ask Isis to play any of about 3,000 tunes. A person's voice explained one computer expert touched off her controls. The machinery that was inside Isis included 1,187 wheels and 370 electromagnets. No one knows in spite of extensive research whatever happened to Isis the world's first robot musician.

Commonly Used Commas

When you tie your shoelaces, you no longer have to think how to do it, as you did when you were a toddler. You do it automatically. There are some comma rules that you have been using for so many years now that they probably have also become automatic. Following is a brief review of those rules for using commas.

Dates and Addresses For clarity, commas are used to separate the various elements in a date or an address from each other.

Use commas to separate the elements in dates and addresses.

Notice in the following examples that a comma is also used to separate a date or an address from the rest of the sentence.

DATE   On Tuesday, March 3, 1985, my sister Jennifer was born.

ADDRESS   I have lived at 29 Bank Street, Long Beach, California, for ten years.

A comma is not used to separate the state and the ᴢɪᴘ code.

> Send your letter to Art Supplies, 500 West 52nd Street, New York, NY 10019.

Titles and Degrees Titles or degrees that follow a person's name should be set off by commas.

Rule 33o Use commas to enclose titles or degrees after a name.

ᴛɪᴛʟᴇ Did Harry Chen, Jr., attend the meeting?
ᴅᴇɢʀᴇᴇ Elizabeth Marshall, D.D.S., is my sister.

Note: For commas used within letters, see Chapter 12, pages 436–446.

EXERCISE *Using Commas*

Number your paper 1 to 10. Then write each sentence, adding commas where needed.

1. On July 4 1826 John Adams and Thomas Jefferson died.
2. Send the check to Rob Matthews Jr. 365 Jade Street Springfield IL 62702.
3. On May 30 1896 the first automobile accident in the United States occurred in New York New York.
4. On July 4 1956 1.23 inches of rain fell in one minute at Unionville Maryland.
5. *Ebony* is published by Johnson Publishing Company 820 South Michigan Avenue Chicago IL 60695.
6. Mail your requests to Ms. Lois Burbank 59 Chatham Street Greenville SC 29609.
7. On December 16 1773 the American colonists staged the famous Boston Tea Party.
8. Address the envelope to Patricia Hartman Ph.D. and include extra postage.
9. On April 30 1812 Louisiana was admitted to the Union.
10. Write to Curtis Circulation Company 645 Madison Avenue New York NY 10014 for information.

USING YOUR TEXT

*Persuasive Writing
(196–205)*

Mechanics: Editing for Commas

After you write, edit your work to be sure you have used commas correctly. Check for missing commas and for unnecessary ones.

Checking Your Understanding Write the following three paragraphs, adding commas wherever they are needed to make the sentences correct.

The bald eagle of course is not bald. It was named at a time when *bald* meant "white." Because it has white feathers on its head the adult eagle has its present name. In contrast to its white head and tail the bald eagle's body and wings are brown. Its eyes beak and feet are yellow. An eagle can be over three feet long and its wingspan may be over seven feet. Its toes end in talons which are strong claws.

An eagle is a hunter. It feeds mainly on dead or dying fish but sometimes will eat small animals. It swoops down picks up its prey in its talons and flies off. An eagle which weighs 8 to 12 pounds is able to carry an animal weighing as much as 17 pounds!

Even though the bald eagle is the national emblem it has become an endangered species. Steps have been taken in recent years however to protect this magnificent bird.

Expressing an Opinion Make a list of all the birds that you would prefer to the bald eagle as a national symbol, keeping in mind what each one represents. Choose one bird and write a paragraph explaining the reasons for your choice. Include enough facts and examples to support your view. *Application:* After you have revised your paragraph, read over your first draft and check for any missing or incorrectly used commas. Then write a final copy.

A **Understanding Kinds of Sentences and End Marks** Number your paper 1 to 10. Write an appropriate end mark for each sentence. Then label each sentence *declarative, imperative, interrogative,* or *exclamatory.*

1. The longest worm ever measured was 180 feet long
2. Have you ever tasted homemade peanut butter
3. Will you please erase the board
4. Store the snow tires in the basement
5. The most common blood type is type 0
6. Look out for that live wire
7. How tall is the Washington Monument
8. No birds have teeth
9. Mom asked if you want dessert
10. Is the tomato a fruit or a vegetable

B **Using Commas Correctly** Number your paper 1 to 20. Write each sentence, adding commas where needed. If a sentence does not need any commas, write *C* after the number.

1. Pablo is your birthday on Tuesday March 6?
2. Gazelles and prairie dogs seldom drink water.
3. The Mariana Trench in the Pacific the lowest point on Earth is 36,198 feet below sea level.
4. Jennifer is only one day older than her cousin.
5. An old farmhouse owned by Ito stands near a meadow.
6. On Monday January 16 my brother will enter the Army at Fort Dix New Jersey.
7. After our long hike up Mount Washington we were very tired but we had big appetites.
8. In Switzerland official notices are printed in French German Italian and Romansch.
9. Generally speaking a worker bee may live for six months but a queen bee may live for six years.

10. No Leslie doesn't live in Louisville Kentucky anymore.
11. The pumpkin like other squashes was unknown in Europe before the discovery of America.
12. Why I hardly know how to answer your question.
13. Where in the world Alice did you find that old book?
14. The Mayo Clinic one of the world's largest medical centers treats patients from all over the world.
15. The first woman's rights convention met at Seneca Falls New York on July 19 1848.
16. A brilliant crescent moon shone above us.
17. During our trip to New Hampshire we saw the Presidential Range.
18. My cousin Cathy will be visiting us next summer.
19. Before locking up the custodian turned off the lights.
20. Using the computer for the first time Jill learned fast.

Mastery Test

Number your paper 1 to 10. Write each sentence, adding commas where needed. Then write an appropriate end mark.

1. The impala which can leap 30 feet is one of the most agile graceful antelopes
2. Yes the divers raised the submarine *Squalus*
3. William Henry Harrison died on April 4 1841 after being president for only one month
4. Anne don't forget to bring your bathing suit a towel and your sneakers
5. Mules according to my uncle are not stupid at all
6. Before you could enter the stadium how long did you have to stand in line
7. The pecan not the peanut is a true nut
8. Will you make a dress out of this soft silky material
9. After nearly sinking the boat was towed to shore
10. Order the tools from Ace Company 1790 State Street Chicago IL 60629 before Friday

34 Underlining and Quotation Marks

Diagnostic Test

Number your paper 1 to 10. Then write each sentence, adding underlining, quotation marks, and other punctuation marks needed with direct quotations. Only a sentence with a speaker tag *(he said, she asked)* should be considered a direct quotation.

EXAMPLE   Sail the boat with care Sue cautioned.
ANSWER   "Sail the boat with care," Sue cautioned.

1. Which trail do you want to take the guide asked.
2. Jud requested Please don't disturb me.
3. Your assignment is to read the chapter Floods of Gold in Tom Sawyer.
4. There are two i's in my name.
5. Since we won't finish today replied Agnes let's quit early.
6. Please lend me your bicycle Nat pleaded.
7. I felt so good today Kathleen said The sun was out for the first time in three days.
8. The pep rally was very exciting Doreen exclaimed.
9. The phrase draggin' wagons referred to racing cars in the Fifties.
10. Have you seen the most recent edition of TV Guide?

Underlining

Try to imagine what it would be like if no one spoke for one whole hour during the school day. That probably would never happen. Most people are involved in conversations from the moment they get up in the morning to the moment they go to sleep.

As a result, you should easily see why learning the rules for quotation marks is indispensable. Quoting someone's exact words, for example, adds realism to stories and letters. Direct quotations also add support and interest to reports and compositions.

This chapter will cover the uses of quotation marks with direct quotations, as well as with titles. First, however, the uses of underlining for italics will be reviewed.

Italics are printed letters that slant to the right. Since you cannot write or type—except on some word processors—in italics, you must use underlining instead.

ITALICS   George has just finished reading *Robinson Crusoe*.

UNDERLINING   George has just finished reading <u>Robinson Crusoe</u>.

Certain letters, numbers, words, and titles should be underlined.

Rule 34a   Underline letters, numbers, and words when they are used to represent themselves. Also underline foreign words that are not generally used in English.

LETTERS, NUMBERS   My <u>2</u>'s look like <u>Q</u>'s.
WORDS, PHRASES   The word <u>bud</u> has several meanings.
The expression <u>chill out</u> means "calm down" or "relax."
FOREIGN WORDS   <u>E pluribus unum</u> is printed on several United States coins.

Notice in the first example above that only the *2* and the *Q* are underlined—not the apostrophe and the *s*.

Underlining is also used to set off certain titles.

Rule 34b / Underline the titles of long written or musical works that are published as a single unit. Also underline titles of paintings and sculptures and the names of vehicles.

BOOKS	<u>Jane Eyre</u>, <u>White Fang</u>
NEWSPAPERS	<u>Washington Post</u>, <u>Chicago Tribune</u>
PERIODICALS	<u>Newsweek</u>, <u>Reader's Digest</u> [In general, do not underline *the* before newspaper or periodical titles.]
PLAYS, MOVIES	<u>Our Town</u>, <u>The Wizard of Oz</u>
BOOK-LENGTH POEMS	<u>Evangeline</u>, <u>Gareth and Lynette</u>
RADIO AND TV SERIES	<u>Mystery Theater</u>, <u>Nova</u>
LONG MUSICAL WORKS	<u>Faust</u>, <u>La Traviata</u>
WORKS OF ART	<u>Totem Head</u> [a sculpture]
SHIPS, PLANES, OTHER CRAFT	<u>Titanic</u>, <u>Spirit of St. Louis</u>, <u>Voyager 2</u>, <u>Columbia</u>

EXERCISE *Using Underlining*

Number your paper 1 to 15. Write each sentence. Then underline each letter, number, word, or group of words that should be italicized.

1. The expression going full blast began in the steel mills.
2. Before preparing his speech, Peter bought a copy of the book 10,000 Jokes, Toasts, and Stories.
3. The word committee has two m's, two t's, and two e's.
4. Who sang the tenor's part in The Marriage of Figaro?
5. The Boston Globe recently ran an article on nutrition.
6. What does the expression vincit omnia veritas mean?
7. I hope to fly on the Concorde some day.
8. About 1500, Bosch painted The Ship of Fools.
9. Who is the hero in The Last of the Mohicans?
10. In the Sixties the expression flake out meant "to sleep."
11. The Pirates of Penzance is a famous light opera.
12. Is the Daily Mirror London's largest newspaper?
13. Facetious contains the vowels a, e, i, o, and u.
14. The launching of Sputnik I began the Space Age.
15. The Mona Lisa hangs in the Louvre in Paris.

Quotation Marks

When you use quotation marks, always remember that they come in pairs. They are placed at the beginning and at the end of uninterrupted quotations and certain titles.

Quotation Marks with Titles

You have learned that titles of long works are underlined. Most long works are made up of smaller parts. The titles of these smaller parts should be enclosed in quotation marks.

Rule 34c Use quotation marks to enclose the titles of chapters, articles, stories, one-act plays, short poems, and songs.

CHAPTERS   Read "I Am Born," the first chapter in <u>David Copperfield</u>.

ARTICLES   Have you seen the article "Frozen Foods Get Hot Again" in <u>Newsweek</u>?

SHORT POEMS   My favorite poem in the book <u>Famous Twentieth Century Poetry</u> is "Sea Lullaby."

EXERCISE   2   *Using Quotation Marks with Titles*

Number your paper 1 to 10. Then write each sentence, adding quotation marks and underlining where needed.

1. Tourism Is Up is the lead story in the Miami Herald.
2. The familiar lullaby Rock-a-Bye Baby dates back to the Elizabethan Age.
3. Edgar Allan Poe wrote the short stories The Pit and the Pendulum and The Gold Bug.
4. I read Mending Wall in the book Selected Poems of Robert Frost.
5. Did you read the chapter Health and Nutrition in your science book?
6. The Old Lady Shows Her Medals is a one-act play, but The Diary of Anne Frank has two acts.

7. Who sang the song Bridge over Troubled Waters?
8. Glorious Jones or the Catnip Hangover is a very humorous chapter in the book The Fur Person.
9. The Sea and Sinbad's Ship is the first part of Rimsky-Korsakov's symphonic suite Scheherazade.
10. Two of Robert Frost's most famous poems are Birches and Stopping by Woods on a Snowy Evening.

Quotation Marks with Direct Quotations

The most important thing to remember when writing direct quotations is that quotation marks enclose only the *exact words* of a speaker. In other words, quotation marks are used only with a *direct quotation*.

Rule 34d   **Use quotation marks to enclose a person's exact words.**

"I just finished my homework," Tammy said.
Roberta said, "I can't stay after school today."

Sometimes, when you write, you may paraphrase what someone has said—without using his or her exact words. When you paraphrase, you are indirectly quoting a person. Do not use quotation marks with *indirect quotations*.

Tammy said that she had just finished her homework.
Roberta said she couldn't stay after school today.

In the first example above, the word *that* signals the indirect quotation. In the second example, *that* is understood.

A one-sentence direct quotation can be written in several ways. It can be placed before or after a speaker tag such as *she said* or *Bill asked*. In both cases quotation marks enclose the person's exact words—from beginning to end.

"Yesterday we went skating," Beth added.
Beth added, "Yesterday we went skating."

For variety or emphasis, a quotation can also be interrupted by a speaker tag. When this interruption occurs, you need two pairs of quotation marks because quotation marks enclose *only* a person's exact words—not the speaker tag.

"Yesterday," Beth added, "we went skating."

To quote more than one sentence, put quotation marks at the beginning and at the end of the entire quotation. Do not put quotation marks around each sentence within a quotation—unless a speaker tag interrupts.

Beth added, "Yesterday we went skating. We got to the lake early and left when the sun began to set. What a great day we had!"

EXERCISE *Using Quotation Marks with Direct Quotations*

Number your paper 1 to 10. Then write each sentence, adding quotation marks where needed. Place a comma or an end mark that follows a quotation *inside* the closing quotation marks.

1. Report to the field now, ordered the coach.
2. Elbert Hubbard once said, Don't make excuses—make good.
3. It is easy, said Aesop, to be brave from a safe distance.
4. I always forget my locker combination when I'm in a rush, announced Leslie.
5. Rain is forecast for tomorrow. Maybe we should cancel the picnic, Betty suggested.
6. Don't be nervous, the drama coach told everyone.
7. Of course, said Mom, I'm going to the open house.
8. The park attendant cautioned, Don't feed the bears.
9. I'm sorry, Ann apologized, that I forgot the tapes.
10. Margo stated, We all need to help. Our goal is to raise one hundred dollars. A car wash could be our answer.

Commas with Direct Quotations   When you are reading quoted material aloud, your voice naturally pauses between the speaker tag and the direct quotation. In written material these pauses are indicated by commas.

Rule 34e   Use a comma to separate a direct quotation from a speaker tag.
Place the comma inside the closing quotation marks.

"The apples aren't ripe yet**,**" Jordan cautioned.
Jordan cautioned**,** "The apples aren't ripe yet."
"The apples**,**" Jordan cautioned**,** "aren't ripe yet."

Notice in the last example that two commas are needed.

EXERCISE *Using Commas with Direct Quotations*

Number your paper 1 to 20. Then write each sentence, adding
quotation marks and commas where needed. Place commas
and end marks that follow a quotation *inside* the quotation marks.

1. Come with us to the baseball game Eugene and Betsy urged.
2. Hale said My Chihuahuas each weigh only a pound.
3. There are two sides to every argument he said until you
take a side.
4. The traffic was terrible Dad complained.
5. Moy reported Terns migrate halfway around the world twice
a year.
6. Roy boasted I passed my driver's test today.
7. You're taking my coat Alice warned.
8. I just learned Kara stated that lightning often strikes the
same spot more than once.
9. Ken announced The answer to the bonus question on the
test is quite simple.
10. Ocean waves Bryan said are sometimes 80 feet high.
11. Mrs. Lewis asked us Have you ever eaten oysters?
12. Did you know Roy asked that George Washington left no
direct descendants?
13. Mercury can be seen by the naked eye a few times a year
the lecturer explained.
14. Basketball the coach told us is a matter of good sense and
teamwork.
15. An angry man opens his mouth and shuts his eyes said
Cato.
16. The mango explained Robert is a tropical fruit.

17. One should eat to live wrote Benjamin Franklin not live to eat.
18. The young of the opossum said the speaker are smaller at birth than a honeybee.
19. Jerry shouted Watch out for that car!
20. From one of the rooms in the deserted house, a voice cried out Who's there?

End Marks with Direct Quotations   End marks come at the end of a quoted sentence—just as they do in a sentence that is not a quotation.

Rule 34f   Place a period inside the closing quotation marks when the end of the quotation comes at the end of the sentence.

Carlos said, "Tonight I'll dry the dishes**.**"
"Tonight," Carlos said, "I'll dry the dishes**.**"

If a quotation comes at the beginning of a sentence, the period follows the speaker tag.

"Tonight I'll dry the dishes," Carlos said**.**

A period comes at the end of each sentence within a quotation that has more than one sentence.

"Tonight I'll dry the dishes," Carlos said. "I washed them last night**.** I also washed them the night before that**.**"

Sometimes you may want to quote a question someone has asked or a sentence someone has said with strong feeling.

Rule 34g   Place a question mark or an exclamation point inside the closing quotation marks when it is part of the quotation.

Martin asked, "Is that the telephone or the doorbell**?**"
"Is that the telephone," Martin asked, "or the doorbell**?**"
"Is that the telephone or the doorbell**?**" Martin asked.

Kim screamed, "Watch out for that hole**!**"
"Watch out for that hole**!**" Kim screamed.

A question mark or an exclamation point is placed *inside* the closing quotation marks when it is part of the quotation. When either of these punctuation marks is part of the whole sentence, however, it is placed *outside* the closing quotation marks.

Did I hear Roger say, "I found your tennis shoes"**?** [The whole sentence—not the quotation—is the question.]

It was the happiest moment of my life when Dan said, "We're home"**!** [The whole sentence is exclamatory, not the quotation.]

Notice that in these cases, the end marks for the quotations are omitted.

EXERCISE **5** *Using End Marks with Direct Quotations*

Number your paper 1 to 20. Then write each sentence, adding commas and end marks where needed.

1. "The ancient Egyptians first began to make glass in 3500 B.C." Karen explained
2. Quentin asked "Did you know that the Navahos are the largest Indian tribe in America"
3. "I just learned" Mary said "that a year on Jupiter is 12 times longer than a year on Earth"
4. Tim suggested "You can cook the hot dogs at the picnic I have other things to do"
5. Marvin exclaimed "That greyhound was clocked at 14.17 miles an hour"
6. I almost fell out of my chair when Mr. Banner announced "We'll skip the quiz today"
7. "You're picking poison ivy" Mavis screamed
8. "Did you know" Clyde asked "that blood is six times thicker than water"
9. Did you hear Betty say "I second the motion"
10. "When is the test in English" Cindy asked
11. From the rock they shouted "Have you found the trail yet"
12. "Look out for that rattlesnake" cried Muriel

13. "Why did you throw away the map" Lee asked "I thought you were saving it as a souvenir"
14. The guide shouted "Don't go so close to the edge"
15. "We have nothing to fear" said Franklin Roosevelt "but fear itself"
16. Hurry and tell everyone that the health inspector said "Don't drink the tap water"
17. "Watch this" Allison cried "I've learned to do a figure eight"
18. Dan boasted "I made ten baskets tonight"
19. "Who owns this diving suit" Mark asked his brother
20. Who wrote "All the world's a stage"

Capital Letters with Direct Quotations   Each sentence of a quotation begins with a capital letter—just as a regular sentence does.

Rule 34h   Begin each sentence of a direct quotation with a capital letter.

"**C**all Jean at six o'clock," my sister said.
My sister said, "**C**all Jean at six o'clock."

If a single-sentence quotation is interrupted by a speaker tag, use only one capital letter—at the beginning of the sentence.

"**C**all Jean," my sister said, "at six o'clock."

EXERCISE   **6**   *Using Capital Letters with Direct Quotations*

Number your paper 1 to 20. Then write each sentence, adding capital letters and end marks where needed.

1. "is Finland or California larger" we asked
2. someone answered, "the state of California is larger"
3. "the end of reading is not more books," Holbrook Jackson said, "but more life"
4. my science teacher joked, "if it weren't for Edison, we'd be watching TV by candlelight"
5. "it doesn't matter where a man comes from," Henry Ford once said "we hire a man, not his history"

6. "there are at least 1,500 varieties of mosquitoes," reported Karen

7. "a baby is born every 8½ seconds in the United States," Alice stated "that's amazing"

8. "did you know," Lai asked, "that President Tyler was the father of 15 children"

9. my brother announced, "practice starts in ten minutes"

10. "the toast was burned," he complained, "and the eggs were hard what's more, the orange juice had seeds in it"

11. "have you seen Mary this afternoon" Kevin asked

12. "come to the light," said Mother "do you expect me to see your splinter in the dark"

13. the teacher asked, "can anyone describe an atom"

14. "look out" shouted Jonathan

15. did Mr. Dean say, "come here"

16. "that's outrageous" Jim exclaimed "a birdhouse costing ten thousand dollars was built in Quebec in 1975"

17. "did you know," Carol asked, "that Eskimos have more than 20 words to describe snow"

18. "we should meet after school we need to discuss the freshman dance," Kenneth said

19. it was the most exciting moment of my life when Mrs. Altman said, "you got the job"

20. "this is an interesting fact," Joe said "milk is heavier than cream"

EXERCISE ◄7► *Cumulative Review*

Number your paper 1 to 20. Write each sentence, adding capital letters, quotation marks, and other punctuation marks where needed. Then check your answers carefully.

About Beasts

1. a cat has absolute honesty Ernest Hemingway noted

2. someone once said it's nice for children to have pets— until the pets start having children

3. if things went by merit Mark Twain announced you would stay out and your dog would go in

4. young gorillas are friendly Will Cuppy said

5. Samuel Butler said the hen is an egg's way of producing another egg

6. if insects ever take over the world he mused I hope they remember that I invited them to all my picnics

7. all animals are equal George Orwell said but some are more equal than others

8. money will buy a pretty good dog commented Josh Billings but it won't buy the wag of its tail

9. what modest claim do kittens make David Irvine asked they claim the ownership of humans

10. animals are such agreeable friends George Eliot stated they ask no questions and pass no criticisms

11. it amuses me to talk to animals George Bernard Shaw said

12. He added the intellectual content of our conversation, however, may to some extent escape them

13. can one love animals or children too much Jean-Paul Sartre once asked

14. a cat can be trusted to purr when she is pleased said William Inge which is more than can be said for humans

15. it is odd Frederick Goodyear once said that few animals are more unsteady on their feet than centipedes

16. William Lyon Phelps asked what is a dog's ideal in a life that's easy; it is a life of active uselessness

17. Of this I am sure: someone once said that nothing is sure

18. Emily Dickinson said my ideal cat always has a huge rat in its mouth

19. the caribou seem to have no idea whatever of personal comfort William Parker Greenough noted

20. to me someone once said the noblest of dogs is the hot dog it feeds the hand that bites it

Application to Writing

From a book of quotations—or from a relative—find an old proverb. Then write it correctly as a direct quotation.

USING YOUR TEXT

*Freewriting
(11–12)
Creative Writing
(400–433)*

Mechanics: Punctuating Dialogue Correctly

Dialogue means "a conversation between two or more persons." In writing, dialogue is treated in a special way so that a reader always knows who is speaking, even if there are no speaker tags such as "he said" or "she asked."

Rule 34i When writing dialogue, begin a new paragraph each time the speaker changes.

In the following excerpt from *Dr. Jekyll and Mr. Hyde,* each sentence follows the rules that you have just studied for direct quotations. Notice, however, that a new paragraph begins each time Mr. Utterson or Poole speaks.

> "I saw Mr. Hyde go in by the old dissecting door, Poole," he said. "Is that right, when Dr. Jekyll is from home?"
>
> "Quite right, Mr. Utterson, sir," replied the servant. "Mr. Hyde has a key."
>
> "Your master seems to repose a great deal of trust in that young man, Poole," resumed the other.

Quoting Long Passages When you write a report and want to support a point, you may want to quote more than one paragraph from a book.

Rule 34j When quoting a passage of more than one paragraph, place quotation marks at the beginning of each paragraph—but at the end of only the last paragraph.

Closing quotation marks are omitted at the end of each paragraph, except the last one, to indicate to a reader that the quotation is continuing.

"Chicagoans were out in force on Thanksgiving Day, 1895. They came to see a new-fangled contraption called the automobile. A few of the gasoline-powered horseless carriages were going to race. [no quotation marks]

"The route lay from the heart of Chicago to a nearby suburb and back. The road measured exactly 54.36 miles. The winner would have to cover that terrific distance without breaking down. [no quotation marks]

"J. Frank Duryea busted the tape 7 hours and 17 minutes after the start of the race. He had covered the distance at an average speed of 7.5 miles an hour!" [closing quotation marks]

Checking Your Understanding Correctly rewrite the following dialogue between Sherlock Holmes and Sir Henry. Add any needed punctuation and indent each time there is a change of speaker.

The practical point which we now have to decide Sir Henry said Holmes is whether it is or is not advisable for you to go to Baskerville Hall. Why should I not go? There seems to be danger. Do you mean danger from this family fiend Sir Henry asked or do you mean danger from human beings? Well, that is what we have to find out.

Arthur Conan Doyle
"The Hound of the Baskervilles"

Writing a Short Story Think about the word *trunk*. Then write freely for several minutes, jotting down anything your mind associates with that word. When you are finished, choose one of the ideas as the basis for a short story. (Plan to limit the number of characters to two or three.) Write the first draft of your short story in which a trunk has some part. Be sure to include dialogue between the two main characters in your story. *Application:* As you edit, correct any punctuation errors in the dialogue. Make a final copy and read your story to a friend.

C
h
a
p
t
e
r

34 **Review**

A **Punctuating Quotations Correctly** Number your paper 1 to 30. Then write each sentence, adding underlining, capital letters, quotation marks, and other punctuation marks where needed.

1. where asked Ina did you find those earrings
2. a hairstylist's sign read we curl up and dye for you
3. I just read Oliver Twist Jan said it was better than any movie version I have ever seen
4. news Ben Bradlee once said is the first rough draft of history
5. have you ever read the Christian Science Monitor Dan asked
6. Cathleen asked is the ocean rough today
7. Ken declared I'm going to be the new class president
8. please don't break us apart the sign over the bananas read we grew up together
9. that was an incredible pass exclaimed Dave
10. work is the best escape from boredom Eleanor Dean once said
11. who said little things affect little minds
12. defeat is not the worst of failures said G. E. Woodberry not to have tried is the true failure
13. we saw a production of the Shakespearean play As You Like It at the Lyric Stage Cheryl announced
14. life shrinks or expands in proportion to one's courage Anaïs Nin commented
15. Voltaire once said common sense is not so common
16. it was an extremely exciting moment when he said we will win in spite of the odds
17. it is easier to fight for one's principles said Alfred Adler than to live up to them
18. he's here Jill shouted Dad's home
19. what is happiness Albert Schweitzer asked it is nothing more than health and a poor memory

20. Jamie exclaimed what a surprise this is
21. the only way to have a friend said Ralph Waldo Emerson is to be one
22. if you're too busy Pat stated please call me
23. why are you sitting there Julia asked
24. Thomas H. Bayly is famous for saying absence makes the heart grow fonder
25. have you seen the movie Casablanca Ari asked
26. don't eat now Mom said dinner is in ten minutes
27. your assignment for tonight Mr. Franklin said is to read the feature article in Newsweek
28. are we supposed to read the book Grapes of Wrath or the poem by Robert Frost Cynthia asked
29. I was amazed to hear the coach say no practice today
30. The concert Greg said is tomorrow night

Mastery Test

Number your paper 1 to 10. Then write each sentence, adding underlining, quotation marks, and other punctuation marks needed with direct quotations. Only a sentence with a speaker tag should be considered a direct quotation.

1. The article in Time was titled Computers in Class.
2. That Jeff proudly proclaimed is a soft sculpture of a tomato.
3. Does that word have one or two l's?
4. Stop that car the woman yelled.
5. Did anyone take the dog out Mom asked.
6. In the Forties moolah was a slang word for "money."
7. The special exhibit at the museum was great Pat said I learned so much.
8. This is my history textbook, We the People.
9. Mr. Henry explained This chair is an antique.
10. I want to hear the weather forecast Meg said.

35

Other Punctuation

Diagnostic Test

Number your paper 1 to 10. Then write each sentence, adding apostrophes, semicolons, colons, and hyphens where needed.

EXAMPLE   Sixty two passengers arrived at 9 15 A.M.
ANSWER   Sixty-two passengers arrived at 9:15 A.M.

1. Senator Allens speech received a standing ovation.
2. A two thirds majority was all that Jason needed to win.
3. Tree bark once served many purposes clothes, homes, canoes, and weapons.
4. Lets meet with the new officers at 7 30 P.M. in Room 212.
5. Rain is predicted for tomorrow nevertheless, we still plan to hold Robertas party outdoors.
6. Im taking the Romeros youngsters to the new childrens museum tomorrow.
7. The dragonfly has large compound eyes each eye is made up of thousands of tiny eyes.
8. The ex governor of Alabama will be interviewed on the *Today* show.
9. Evas coat and someones keys were found in the office.
10. Her handwritten *n*s look like *m*s.

Apostrophes

The most costly punctuation error of all time occurred in 1962. A hyphen was omitted from a set of directions that was being sent to the *Venus* space-probe rocket. As a result of the omission, the rocket self-destructed. Most errors that you make in punctuation will not have such disastrous results. Nevertheless, correct punctuation is necessary for clear communication—right here on Earth.

Omitting a tiny apostrophe, for example, can make a big difference in a sentence. In fact, including apostrophes in certain words is as important as spelling those words correctly. Without an apostrophe, the first sentence in the following examples does not make any sense. With an apostrophe, however, the meaning of the sentence instantly becomes clear.

Well go with you to the game tonight.
We'll go with you to the game tonight.

In addition to being used in contractions, apostrophes are commonly used with nouns and some pronouns to show ownership or relationship.

Possessive Forms of Nouns and Pronouns

The possessive form of a noun shows ownership, possession, or relationship. The possessive form is used when an *of* phrase could be substituted for the noun.

Lani's guitar = the guitar of Lani
the Spensers' garage = the garage of the Spensers

As you can see from these examples, nouns have a special form to show possession. An apostrophe or an apostrophe and an *s* are added.

Possessive Forms of Singular Nouns To form the possessive of a noun, first decide whether the noun is singular or plural.

Rule 35a   Add 's to form the possessive of a singular noun.

Do not add or omit a letter. Just write the word and put 's at the end.

baby + 's = baby's	Give me the baby's blanket.
Gary + 's = Gary's	That is Gary's baseball glove.
week + 's = week's	What were your week's wages?
boss + 's = boss's	Where is your boss's office?

The 's goes on the last word of compound words and the names of most businesses and organizations.

The passerby's report of the accident was accurate.
The jack-in-the box's spring was broken.
The Mahoney Oil Company's service is dependable.
Lord & Taylor's advertisements are very artistic.

Note: Occasionally a singular noun, such as the name *Prentiss*, will end in *s*. If the noun—especially a name—is two or three syllables long, it might be awkward to pronounce with 's. In that case add only an apostrophe.

EXERCISE *Forming the Possessive of Singular Nouns*

Number your paper 1 to 15. Write the possessive form of each noun. Then use five of the forms in sentences of your own.

1. apple	**6.** mother-in-law	**11.** morning
2. Pep Club	**7.** brother	**12.** Bess
3. starfish	**8.** Mike	**13.** Hope College
4. Georgia	**9.** sailor	**14.** maid-of-honor
5. month	**10.** Reese Company	**15.** Mr. Rogers

Possessive Forms of Plural Nouns   There are two rules to follow to form the possessive of plural nouns.

Rule 35b   Add only an apostrophe to form the possessive of a plural noun that ends in *s*.

Rule 35c Add 's to form the possessive of a plural noun that does not end in *s*.

Deciding which rule to follow is simple if you take two steps. First, write the plural of the noun, as is. Second, look at the ending of the word. If the word ends in *s,* add only an apostrophe. If it does not end in *s,* add an apostrophe and an *s.*

PLURAL	ENDING	ADD		POSSESSIVE
babies	s	'	=	babies'
foxes	s	'	=	foxes'
mice	no *s*	's	=	mice's
children	no *s*	's	=	children's

EXERCISE *Forming the Possessive of Plural Nouns*

Number your paper 1 to 20. Write the possessive form of each noun. Then use five of the forms in sentences of your own.

1. friends   **6.** wolves   **11.** books   **16.** men
2. boxes   **7.** tomatoes   **12.** geese   **17.** Smiths
3. weeks   **8.** girls   **13.** stores   **18.** women
4. deer   **9.** Lutzes   **14.** clouds   **19.** papers
5. boys   **10.** cities   **15.** albums   **20.** Ryans

EXERCISE *Forming the Possessive of Nouns*

Number your paper 1 to 10. Then write the possessive form—singular or plural—of each underlined word.

1. Are <u>men</u> shoe sizes different from <u>women</u>?
2. The <u>Drama Club</u> presentation this year was superb.
3. My <u>uncle</u> store is a few <u>minutes</u> walk from here.
4. My <u>brother</u> picture appeared in <u>Madison</u> newspaper.
5. The <u>girls</u> and <u>boys</u> uniforms have been handed out.
6. <u>Sarah</u> sisters got jobs at a <u>children</u> day camp.
7. Jill won the <u>National</u> <u>Film</u> <u>Association</u> annual award.
8. A <u>secretary</u> job involves more duties than a <u>typist</u>.
9. After the <u>day</u> ride, the horses were put in <u>Carlos</u> barn.
10. My <u>sister-in-law</u> car is pale blue.

Possessive Forms of Pronouns Unlike nouns, personal pronouns do not use an apostrophe to show possession. Instead, they change form: *my, mine, your, yours, his, her, hers, its, our, ours, their,* and *theirs.*

Rule 35d Do not add an apostrophe to form the possessive of a personal pronoun.

The bicycle is **hers.** A spider spun **its** web.

Indefinite pronouns, however, form the possessive the same way singular nouns do—by adding *'s.* *(See page 568 for a list of common indefinite pronouns.)*

Rule 35e Add **'s** to form the possessive of an indefinite pronoun.

This seems to be everyone**'s** favorite song.
Someone**'s** purse was left under the seat.

EXERCISE **4** *Using the Possessive of Pronouns*

Number your paper 1 to 10. Then write the correct form of the pronoun in parentheses.

1. Are these gloves (yours, your's)?
2. (Anyone's, Anyones') solution is better than none.
3. The mountain is beautiful with (its, it's) top covered with snow.
4. I gave my speech, but Jan hasn't given (hers, her's) yet.
5. (No one's, No ones') predictions came true.
6. I hope (everybody's, everybodys') time was well spent.
7. Those sandwiches are (ours, our's).
8. Has (everyones, everyone's) test been graded?
9. It was (nobody's, nobodys') fault but my own.
10. The blue towels are (their's, theirs).

Apostrophes to Show Joint and Separate Ownership
Sometimes it is necessary to show that something belongs to more than one person.

Rule 35f   To show joint ownership, make only the last word possessive in form.

These are Nan and Joanne**'s** records. [The records belong to both Nan and Joanne.]

The only exception to this rule applies when one word showing joint ownership is a possessive pronoun. In such cases the noun must also show possession.

This is Karen**'s** and **my** computer.

Separate ownership is shown in a different way from joint ownership.

Rule 35g   To show separate ownership, make each word possessive in form.

These are Nan**'s** and Joanne**'s** records. [Each girl has her own records.]

EXERCISE *Using Joint and Separate Ownership*

Number your paper 1 to 10. Then correctly write each word that needs an apostrophe or an apostrophe and an *s*.

EXAMPLE   Don and Jan father is a Little League umpire.
ANSWER   Jan's

1. I picked up Dad and Mike shirts from the cleaners.
2. Mrs. Hayden is Joyce and my history teacher.
3. Martha and Nick car was just painted red.
4. Donna and Ray poems were published in the paper.
5. My father hobbies include golfing and fishing.
6. Someone hat was found under the bleachers.
7. Eli Whitney inventions changed the course of history.
8. In Ambrose Bierce story, a snake eyes seemed to have a hypnotic effect.
9. Dad and Uncle Fred farm has 1,000 acres of corn.
10. Dan spent three weeks vacation on Mr. Murray farm.

EXERCISE *Using the Possessive of Nouns and Pronouns*

Write each incorrect word in the following sentences correctly.

1. My uncles ranch is a days ride from Rock Springs.
2. In almost all cities', buses have replaced trolleys.
3. The winter coats in the mens' department are on sale.
4. Everyone's is coming to you're party.
5. Frank and Judy's suggestions' were accepted.
6. Have you seen Mrs. Ryans bulletin board?
7. Teds efforts were well rewarded, but her's were not.
8. The girls' auditioned for the plays director.
9. Eds cats' have a separate entrance to the house.
10. These tapes are our's, not their's.

Other Uses of an Apostrophe

Apostrophes have other uses besides showing the possessive of nouns and some pronouns.

Apostrophes with Contractions   A contraction is a shortcut. It usually combines two words into one. An apostrophe is added to take the place of one or more missing letters.

Rule 35h   Use an apostrophe in a contraction to show where one or more letters have been omitted.

These examples show how some contractions are formed.

do + not = don't	there + is = there's
we + are = we're	who + is = who's
let + us = let's	of + the + clock = o'clock

In most contractions, no letters are added or changed around. There is one common exception: *will* + *not* = *won't*.

Note: Do not confuse the contractions *it's, you're, they're, there's,* and *who's* with the possessive pronouns *its, your, their, theirs,* and *whose.*

EXERCISE *Using Apostrophes with Contractions*

Number your paper 1 to 20. Write the contraction for each pair of words. Then write a short conversation in which you use at least five of the contractions.

1. are not	**6.** do not	**11.** we will	**16.** were not
2. will not	**7.** is not	**12.** that is	**17.** they are
3. did not	**8.** let us	**13.** I would	**18.** there is
4. has not	**9.** I have	**14.** does not	**19.** I am
5. you are	**10.** we have	**15.** have not	**20.** who is

EXERCISE *Distinguishing between Contractions and Possessive Pronouns*

Number your paper 1 to 10. Then write the correct word in parentheses to complete each sentence.

1. (Its, It's) now or never.
2. Please tell me how you would like (your, you're) breakfast eggs cooked.
3. I don't know if (their, they're) home or not.
4. If (theirs, there's) anything you and your family need, let me know.
5. (Whose, Who's) taking care of your cats?
6. Do you know if (your, you're) invited?
7. These suitcases must be (theirs, there's).
8. (Whose, Who's) bicycle did you borrow?
9. (Its, It's) wingspread is seven feet.
10. Did you speak to (their, they're) teachers?

Apostrophes to Form Some Plurals Certain items form their plurals by adding 's.

Rule 35i Add 's to form the plural of numbers, letters, symbols, and words that are used to represent themselves.

You often write *g*'s for *q*'s. You use too many *and*'s. Why did you put two *!*'s after that sentence?

EXERCISE ❾ *Using Apostrophes*

Number your paper 1 to 10. Then correctly write each word that needs an apostrophe or an apostrophe and an *s*. If a sentence is correct, write *C* after the number.

EXAMPLE   Isnt this blue notebook yours?
ANSWER   Isn't

1. If you take our spare tire, leave theirs.
2. Is that everyone decision?
3. Ina writes all her capital *P* with style.
4. That red plaid suitcase is hers.
5. My locker combination had two *3* and two *5* in it.
6. Someone jacket was left in the gym.
7. This green windbreaker doesnt come in both boys and men sizes.
8. Couldnt that boat be theirs?
9. My brother bookkeeper is planning to take a month vacation in Puerto Rico.
10. Theres a surprise waiting for you at the bottom of the kitchen drawer.

EXERCISE ❿ *Cumulative Review*

Number your paper 1 to 10. Then correctly write the words that need an apostrophe.

Is It a Moth?   Has a moth ever turned one of your favorite sweaters into a tasty meal for itself? If so, you might be able to prevent future feasts by knowing the difference between a moth and a butterfly. Listen carefully. Recognizing the difference wont be easy. First, look at the insects feelers. If theyre thin, they belong to a butterfly. A moths feelers are usually broad and feathery. Next, observe the insect in question when its resting. Butterflies wings are folded in an upright position, with the wings undersides facing toward you. A moth sits holding its wings horizontally, with only the upper sides of the wings showing. If this information doesnt help, youd better buy a summers supply of mothballs.

Semicolons and Colons

A *semicolon* (;) is used to indicate a pause greater that that of a comma, but not a full pause like that of a period. Semicolons are used mainly between the clauses of a compound sentence. A *colon* (:) is used mainly to introduce a list of items.

Semicolons

Independent clauses in a compound sentence can be joined by a conjunction and a comma. *(See page 824.)*

Ken's favorite sport is tennis, **but** mine is hockey.

The clauses in a compound sentence can also be joined by a semicolon.

Ken's favorite sport is tennis; mine is hockey.

Rule 35j   Use a semicolon between the clauses of a compound sentence that are not joined by a conjunction.

Use a semicolon only if the clauses are closely related.

INCORRECT   A mosquito bite is not a bite; mosquito bites can be painful.

CORRECT   A mosquito bite is not a bite; it is a puncture.

Semicolons with Transitional Words   The following list contains transitional words that, with a semicolon, can be used to combine the clauses of a compound sentence.

Common Transitional Words		
accordingly	furthermore	moreover
consequently	hence	nevertheless
for example	however	otherwise
for instance	instead	therefore

Rule 35k Use a semicolon between clauses in a compound sentence that are joined by certain transitional words.

Notice in the following examples that the transitional words are preceded by a semicolon and followed by a comma.

> The weather was perfect**; nevertheless,** I stayed indoors and studied.
>
> The camping trip was fun**; for instance,** we swam each day in the lake.

Note: Some of the transitional words listed on page 865 can also be used as parenthetical expressions within a single clause. *(See page 829.)*

JOINING CLAUSES   The meeting started at eight o'clock**; however,** we were late.

WITHIN A CLAUSE   The meeting**, however,** won't start until eight o'clock.

EXERCISE *Using Semicolons with Compound Sentences*

Number your paper 1 to 10. Then write each sentence, adding a semicolon where needed. If a sentence does not need a semicolon, write *C* after the number.

1. Panama hats are not made in Panama most are made in Ecuador.
2. Over 60,000 deaths a year result from high blood pressure nevertheless, most are avoidable.
3. The American jay is bright blue however, its Canadian cousin is gray.
4. Lee was elected president furthermore, she was elected by a unanimous vote.
5. Irrigation is used on many farms in fertile areas moreover, it is an absolute necessity in desert areas.
6. The first baseball catcher's mask was worn in 1875 the first chest protector was used in 1885.
7. The Kennedys, nevertheless, were able to join us for dessert.

8. The *knot* is not a measure of length it is a measure of speed.

9. Almost everyone is born farsighted nevertheless, most people develop 20/20 vision at about five years of age.

10. Babe Ruth was elected to baseball's Hall of Fame in 1936 Lou Gehrig became a member in 1939.

EXERCISE **12** *Using Semicolons with Compound Sentences*

Number your paper 1 to 10. Then write each sentence, adding a semicolon and a comma where needed.

Facts and Figures

1. An ailurophile loves cats an ailurophobe dislikes cats.

2. George Washington chose the site of the White House however he never lived there.

3. The sweet potato and the yam are not the same moreover the yam is almost never seen in this country.

4. A male kangaroo is called a boomer a female kangaroo is called a flyer.

5. The emu is an unusual species of bird for example it is the male that cares for the young.

6. Type O is the most common blood type in the world type AB is the rarest.

7. A polecat is not a cat at all the term actually designates a skunk.

8. Saying just one word uses 72 muscles therefore talking on the phone for an hour can be exhausting.

9. A crocodile cannot move its tongue it is rooted to the base of its mouth.

10. The giant panda of western China resembles a bear however it is more closely related to the raccoon.

Semicolons to Avoid Confusion   Sometimes a semicolon is used to take the place of a comma between the clauses of a compound sentence.

Rule 35l   Use a semicolon instead of a comma between the clauses of a compound sentence if there are commas within a clause.

> To get to Maine from New York, we travel through Connecticut, Massachusetts, and New Hampshire; but the trip takes us only four hours.

A semicolon takes the place of a comma in another situation as well.

Rule 35m Use a semicolon instead of a comma between the items in a series if the items contain commas.

> I have relatives in Rochester, New York; in Boulder, Colorado; and in Tallahassee, Florida.

Note: See Chapter 33 for the rules for commas.

EXERCISE 13 *Using Semicolons to Avoid Confusion*

Number your paper 1 to 10. Then write each sentence, adding a semicolon and commas where needed.

1. In 1976, there were over 100 million TV sets in the United States over 375 million radios and over 125 million telephones and today there are even more.
2. The awards were presented at a special ceremony on Friday February 2 1985 and a press conference with the winners was held afterward.
3. This year I am taking math history English and Spanish but my favorite subject is science.
4. Popular tourist attractions around the world include Parliament in London England the Eiffel Tower in Paris France and the Colosseum in Rome Italy.
5. Receiving awards were the pitcher the catcher and the second baseman but the third baseman won a college scholarship.
6. The bloodmobile will be at the school on Wednesday October 12 Friday October 14 and Friday October 21.
7. We had a choice of going bowling seeing a movie or visiting friends but we decided to stay home.
8. They visited Jacksonville Miami and Tampa but they chose to live in Daytona Beach.

9. The students elected to the school board's special committee are Jenny Young a freshman Wayne Gray a sophomore and Kevin Seymour a senior.
10. Jennifer's address is 32 Beverly Drive Springfield Illinois but she will be moving soon to Indiana.

EXERCISE **14** *Cumulative Review*

Number your paper 1 to 15. Then write each sentence, adding a semicolon and commas where needed.

1. We have Mother's Day in the United States but the English have Mothering Sunday.
2. I have packed the books the records and the tapes but I don't know what to do next.
3. Computer chips were unknown a generation ago however they now play an important role in industry.
4. I spoke with our advisor the principal and the committee members and they are all in agreement.
5. The Arabian camel has one hump the Bactrian camel has two humps.
6. Viking ships had oars as well as sails consequently the vessels were not completely dependent upon the wind.
7. The tourist trap looked expensive but its wares were reasonable.
8. The movie however was much too long.
9. The porpoise is not a fish it is a mammal.
10. I didn't win the marathon nevertheless running in it was a good experience.
11. Yesterday the temperature was 32 degrees in Lima Ohio 58 degrees in Waycross Georgia and 80 degrees in Hollywood Florida.
12. The world is not round it is an oblate spheroid.
13. Please get my homework assignments for I'll be out of town on Friday.
14. Some things are not what they seem for example "magic" is only a series of illusions.
15. Termites are not related to ants they are part of the cockroach family.

Colons

A colon is used most often to introduce a list of items.

Rule 35n Use a colon before most lists of items, especially when the list comes after an expression like *the following*.

All volunteers will need the following: a notebook, a pen, and a comfortable pair of walking shoes.

There are four methods of catching fish: hooking, netting, spearing, and trapping.

Note: Commas should separate the items in the series.

Never use a colon directly after a verb or a preposition.

INCORRECT   My three favorite subjects are: math, science, and woodworking.

CORRECT   My three favorite subjects are math, science, and woodworking.

CORRECT   These are my favorite subjects: math, science, and woodworking.

Colons are also used in a few other situations.

Rule 35o Use a colon in certain special situations.

HOURS AND MINUTES   5:30 A.M.
BIBLICAL CHAPTERS AND VERSES   John 3:16
SALUTATIONS IN BUSINESS LETTERS   Dear Sir or Madam:

EXERCISE *Using Colons*

Number your paper 1 to 10. Then write each sentence, adding a colon where needed. If a sentence does not need a colon, write *C* after the number.

1. Kathleen left the Boston airport at 10 40 A.M. and arrived in Bermuda at 1 10 P.M.

2. I have relatives in Kentucky, Utah, and Arizona.

3. While you're at the drugstore, please buy aspirin, toothpaste, and cotton balls.
4. Mariella made note of her favorite Biblical verse, I Corinthians 13 13.
5. For the hike you should bring the following a snack, a canteen of water, and sunscreen.
6. The ocean floor is divided into three main regions continental shelf, slope, and abyss.
7. At 11 15 A.M. the minister read Psalms 62 5, the text for his sermon.
8. I've been very busy taking care of two rabbits, one cat, three dogs, and a turtle.
9. In colonial times medicines included the following powdered frogs, crabs' eyes, and pine bark.
10. Cargo planes carry almost anything white mice, toupees, and even small private planes.

Hyphens

Although a hyphen is used mainly to divide a word at the end of a line, it has other uses as well.

Hyphens with Numbers and Words

Hyphens are used with certain numbers and fractions.

Rule 35p   Use a hyphen when writing out the numbers *twenty-one* through *ninety-nine.* Also use a hyphen when writing out a fraction that is used as an adjective.

Thirty-two people entered the writing contest.
Jane owned a two-thirds share of the property.

When a fraction is used as a noun, no hyphen is needed.

The recipe calls for **two thirds** of a cup of flour.

Hyphens with Compound Nouns The parts of some compound nouns should be separated by hyphens.

Rule 35q Use a hyphen to separate the parts of some compound nouns.

Mrs. Knight is my great-grandmother.
Ray was elected secretary-treasurer.

Hyphens with Certain Prefixes Hyphens are used to separate certain prefixes and the suffix *-elect* from their root words.

Rule 35r Use a hyphen after certain prefixes and before the suffix *-elect.*

Hyphens Used with Prefixes and Suffixes

Use hyphens in the following situations.

1. Between a prefix and a proper noun or proper adjective (all-American, mid-Atlantic, pre-Columbian) [Notice that only the proper noun or the proper adjective begins with a capital letter—not the prefix.]
2. After the prefix *self-* (self-righteous, self-satisfied)
3. After the prefix *ex-* when it means "former" or "formerly" (ex-mayor, ex-governor, ex-senator)
4. After a person's title when it is followed by the suffix *-elect* (president-elect)

EXERCISE *Using Hyphens*

Number your paper 1 to 10. Then correctly write each word that should be hyphenated. If no word in the sentence needs a hyphen, write *C* after the number.

1. I will enjoy having a new sister in law.
2. Did the convention follow the two thirds rule?
3. Sixty eight freshmen attended the assembly.
4. Instead of depending upon her parents so much, Lynn should become more self reliant.
5. The ex mayor of Philadelphia ran again.

6. I have typed one half of my report.

7. The president elect will hold a news conference.

8. I'm giving Jamie a jack in the box as a gift for his second birthday.

9. Send a stamped, self addressed envelope with your inquiry to the agency.

10. My brother Ian is the ex president of the Swampscott High School Student Council.

Hyphens with Divided Words

Whenever possible, avoid dividing words in your writing. Sometimes, however, it is necessary to divide words in order to keep the right-hand margin of a composition, story, or report fairly even.

Rule 35s   Use a hyphen to divide a word at the end of a line.

Using the following six guidelines will help you divide words correctly.

Dividing Words

1. Divide words only between syllables.
  gym nas tics: gym-nastics or gymnas-tics

2. Never divide a one-syllable word.
  myth   rhyme   strength

3. Never separate a one-letter syllable from the rest of the word. For example, the following words should never be divided.
  DO NOT BREAK   e-vent   sleep-y   o-boe   i-tem

4. A two-letter word ending should not be carried over to the next line.
  DO NOT BREAK   cred-it   hang-er   part-ly

5. Divide hyphenated words only after the hyphens.
  mother-in-law   maid-of-honor   attorney-at-law

6. Do not divide a proper noun or a proper adjective.
  Beckerman   Memphis   Atlantic   Indian

EXERCISE *Using Hyphens to Divide Words*

Number your paper 1 to 15. Add a hyphen or hyphens to show where each word can be correctly divided. If a word should not be divided, write *no* after the number.

1. event	**6.** amazement	**11.** gathering
2. hamster	**7.** action	**12.** Timothy
3. growth	**8.** jury	**13.** forgery
4. invoice	**9.** syllable	**14.** flip-flop
5. son in law	**10.** Cairo	**15.** avoid

EXERCISE *Cumulative Review*

Number your paper 1 to 5. Then write each sentence, adding semicolons, colons, and hyphens where needed. If a sentence is correct, write *C* after the number.

1. There are four commonwealths in the United States Kentucky, Massachusetts, Pennsylvania, and Virginia.

2. The life span of a trout is four years a goldfish can live to be twenty five.

3. Kevin White, an ex mayor of Boston, held that office for four terms.

4. A cheetah can run about 70 miles per hour, an ostrich 30, and a jackrabbit 35 but the top speed for a human is only 27 miles per hour.

5. More than three fourths of all flowers have an unpleasant odor or no odor at all.

Application to Writing

Imagine that you had to be away from your home for two months. What—besides essential clothing and toiletries—would you decide to take with you? Write a paragraph that explains what you would pack. Explain why you chose those items. Use at least one semicolon and one colon in your paragraph.

USING YOUR TEXT

*Brainstorming
(20–21)
Expository Paragraphs
(120–163)*

Mechanics: Editing for Correct Punctuation

When you revise your work, remember that capital letters and punctuation marks are like road signs. If the signs are incorrect, your readers may get lost before they reach the end.

Checking Your Understanding   Write the following paragraphs, adding apostrophes, semicolons, colons, and hyphens where needed.

Whos the worlds champion jumper? If youre thinking of a person, youre wrong. The kangaroo lays claim to this title. This curious-looking Australian mammal cannot walk however, it surely can jump. It can easily hop over a parked car. It can also travel over thirty nine miles an hour.

The kangaroo has some quite unusual physical characteristics a small head, large pointed ears, very short front limbs, and hindquarters the size of a mules. Its feet sometimes measure ten inches from the heel to the longest toe. The kangaroos thick tail is so strong that it can use the tail as a stool. The kangaroo is strictly a vegetarian it will not eat another animal.

Writing to Inform   Across the top of a piece of paper, write the first five common, everyday objects that come to mind. You could, for example, write *pencil, book, shoe, window,* and *school.* Choose just one and brainstorm for a list of unusual uses for it. Rather than using a pencil to write, for instance, you could use one to conduct an orchestra. Think of as many different uses as you can. Then write a paragraph that states what your object is and describes new ways of using it that have occurred to you. *Application:* As you edit your paragraph, check for correct punctuation. Then write a final draft.

35 Review

A **Using Punctuation Correctly** Number your paper 1 to 20. Then write each sentence, adding all needed punctuation.

1. Rattlesnakes don't lay eggs they bear live young.
2. The worlds largest gem is a 596-pound topaz.
3. The soybean is a versatile vegetable for example 400 different products can be made from it.
4. Greg wont be satisfied until hes totally self sufficient.
5. The following famous people had red hair George Washington, Thomas Jefferson, and Mark Twain.
6. Lenny Burns received a two thirds majority vote.
7. When Snuffys leash broke, he jumped the Becks fence.
8. The official name of India is not *India* it is *Bharat*.
9. My brother in law is president elect of the club.
10. Salt is found on Earth in three basic forms salt water, brine deposits, and rock salt crystal.
11. A snake has no ears however its tongue is extremely sensitive to sound vibrations.
12. The poet H. D.s real name is Hilda Doolittle.
13. The people on the panel included Terry Hayden, an editorial writer Thelma Casey, a fashion consultant and Judith Howe, a high school teacher.
14. Today there are more than 7,000 varieties of apples nevertheless only 20 varieties are widely grown.
15. Twenty two people will arrive for dinner at 6 30 P.M.
16. The hot dog is not an American invention it was first produced in Germany.
17. No ones script was left in the auditorium.
18. Sources for his report included books, magazines, and filmstrips but he forgot to document them.
19. Dont leave the dog outside if its going to rain.
20. Shuffleboard has had many names over the years shoveboard, shovel-penny, and shovelboard.

B **Editing for Correct Punctuation**   Write the following paragraph, adding any needed apostrophes, semicolons, colons, and hyphens.

Everyone has heard of the Nobel Prizes, but most people havent heard about Alfred Nobel, the man who established the prizes. He was born in Sweden in 1833. Thirty three years later he invented dynamite. This invention made him very rich it also made him feel very guilty later on. As a result his will set up a trust fund that annually awards prizes to people throughout the world who excel in the following categories literature, physics, chemistry, medicine, and peace. Now, every December 10, the anniversary of Nobels death, each winner receives up to $125,000.

Mastery Test

Number your paper 1 to 10. Then write each sentence, adding apostrophes, semicolons, colons, and hyphens where needed.

1. A chameleons tongue is as long as its body.
2. Sometimes a camel doesnt drink water for days, weeks, or even months yet it can drink 25 gallons of water in half an hour.
3. The ex mayors speech will be televised tonight.
4. To almost everyones surprise, elephants can swim.
5. Shouldnt we be at the theater by 8 15 P.M.?
6. In the laboratory all the mices and rats cages must be kept spotlessly clean.
7. In his later years, George Frideric Handel was blind nevertheless, he continued to compose music.
8. Henrys story contains too many *and*s and *so*s.
9. The smallest antelope is the size of a rabbit the largest antelope can weigh up to 1,500 pounds.
10. Two beautiful countries will be visited on the tour Switzerland and Sweden.

Appendix

Using a Word Processor

Word processors have features that will help you in all stages of the writing process. Using a word processor, you can open and name documents, create and store files, and input first drafts. After drafting compositions, you can then revise, edit, and even publish them. If you take the time to master word-processing skills, you will be able to accomplish writing assignments more easily and quickly than by writing longhand or using a typewriter.

Prewriting

Almost any prewriting activity that you complete with paper and pencil can be done on a word processor. For example, you can input journal entries, freewrite, brainstorm, and use computer conferencing to explore subjects. You can create files listing ideas for possible writing subjects and then add to those lists any time you have a new idea. You can even create a file called "Subjects" and then create subfiles for ideas for each of the writing purposes. Consequently, a subfile entitled "Explain" would contain expository writing ideas, "Describe" would contain descriptive writing ideas, "Persuade" would contain persuasive writing ideas, "Express" would contain thoughts and feelings you would like to express, and "Creative" would contain ideas for short stories, poems, and plays. All of these subfiles would go into the file entitled "Subjects."

When you are writing expository essays or reports, you can use the word processor to help you gather and organize information. If your computer is linked to an information network, for instance, you can use electronic bulletin boards to access computerized reference materials. You may even be able to communicate by electronic mail with experts on your subject. Then, as you gather information, you can maintain a computer file listing all your sources. Some programs will automatically generate citations or entries for a works cited page in the correct form. *(See pages 389–390.)* Other ideas for using the word processor when prewriting are listed on the next page.

Prewriting on a Word Processor

- Create a subject file by inputting your answers to questions for exploring your own interests and knowledge. *(See pages 10–11.)*
- Create a reader's response file in which you record your responses to literature. *(See page 13.)*
- Store your learning log in the computer or on a disk and update it by logging interesting information you learn in other subject areas. *(See page 13.)*
- Explore a subject by listing elements or aspects of it, possible focuses or main ideas for a composition about it, possible working thesis statements for it, and supporting details. *(See pages 14–15, 259–260, and 18–22.)*
- Freewrite about your observations, experimenting with descriptive and sensory details. *(See pages 18–19.)*
- List questions for developing a subject through inquiring. *(See pages 23–24.)*
- Input audience profiles or freewrite letters to real or imaginary members of your audience to help you clarify your ideas. *(See pages 17–18.)*
- If you are working on a computer network—in which computers are interconnected—use computer conferencing to explore a subject through dialogue with a partner. For group brainstorming, you and your classmates can move from terminal to terminal and keyboard questions and responses directly onto one another's monitors.

Whatever your writing purpose is, take advantage of any software available to you that lets you create clusters, diagrams, outlines, and charts for classifying or for comparing and contrasting. Even without special software, grouping and ordering ideas and information are easy on a word processor because keyboard commands let you copy and move, or cut and paste, blocks of text.

Drafting

On a word processor, drafting is a simple procedure. You can keyboard freely—type and enter commands—without worrying about the ends of lines, the beginnings of paragraphs, or any mechanical errors. Keyboard functions let you move back and forth between drafting and revising as you rearrange, delete, or insert words, sentences, or paragraphs. Because you can delete any unwanted writing at the touch of a key, you are free to include alternative ways of expressing an idea or alternative versions of an introduction or a conclusion.

Drafting on a Word Processor

- Start by setting the format so that all your writing will automatically be in standard manuscript form. Double or triple space for easy marking on hard copies, or printouts.
- With your outline on the monitor, expand your outline into a composition by inserting writing after each heading.
- Save your work often—about every 20 minutes—and print hard copies often to work on when you are not at the computer.

Revising

The box below suggests ways to use the word processor when you revise.

Revising on a Word Processor

- Use the **insert** command to add ideas, details, transitions between sentences and paragraphs, and parenthetical citations.
- Use the **move** or **cut and paste** command to rearrange the order of words, sentences, and paragraphs.
- Use the **delete** command to eliminate unneeded words and details and any sentences or paragraphs that detract from the unity of your composition.
- Use the **find** or **search and replace** feature to substitute words and phrases.

When you are ready to revise, you can use a word processor for networking, or electronic conferencing, to help you evaluate your work. After reading your composition on their monitors, for example, your classmates or other readers can directly input their reactions, questions, and suggestions for improving your draft. Another timesaving strategy is to store revision checklists in the computer or on a disk for easy reference. You can also use software that includes a dictionary and a thesaurus.

Editing and Publishing

The same keyboarding functions that help in revising also help in editing. For instance, you can use the search and replace commands to correct automatically a particular kind of error simultaneously in all the places where it occurs. In addition, most word-processing programs have a spell feature that automatically checks your spelling.

Before you edit your revised draft, mark final corrections on a hard copy, or printout, using proofreading marks. To guide you in marking your copy, you could store your Personalized Editing Checklist and other editing checklists in the computer or on a disk for quick reference.

Word processors make publishing your work a creative challenge. You can experiment with the design features of the computer program to enhance the layout and appearance of your composition before the final printout. Design features include different sizes, styles, and decorative treatments of type, called fonts. Many programs also let you use files of ready-made graphics or even let you create graphics of your own.

Printing out a manuscript that you have designed yourself and giving it to your readers to enjoy can give you great satisfaction. Remember, however, that you can publish electronically too. In electronic publishing, you share your work with readers through electronic mail or on a network bulletin board.

From prewriting to publishing, word processing simplifies many aspects of the writing process and saves time. Although using a word processor cannot automatically make you a good writer, it can help you to work at your best.

Useful Conventions of Writing

Writing Numbers In general, spell out the numbers one through ten. Use numerals for numbers above ten.

> three   ten   11   105   3,487   425,297

To avoid six or more zeros, a combination of numerals and words may be used.

> one million   11 million   55 billion   2.5 billion

Note: An alternate style for writing numbers is to spell out numbers under 101 and most round numbers. Whichever style you choose, it is important to be consistent.

> ten   ninety-nine   105   3,487   eleven million

Always spell out a number at the beginning of a sentence or revise the sentence.

> One hundred fifty-six scientists attended last year.
> Last year 156 scientists attended.

Use numerals for dates, street and room numbers, page numbers, percents, decimals, and times with A.M. or P.M.

> July 4, 1776   room 5   page 3   9 percent   8:30 A.M.

Using Abbreviations Most abbreviations should be avoided in formal writing. Do not, for example, abbreviate the names of states, countries, days of the week, months, weights, or measurements. *(See page 820 for examples of abbreviations that may be used in formal writing.)*

Quoting Long Passages When you write a report, you might want to support a point by quoting a long passage from a book. When quoting a passage of more than one paragraph, place quotation marks at the beginning of each paragraph—but at the end of only the last paragraph. *(See pages 852–853.)* Remember to give credit to the author for the quoted material. *(See pages 387–391.)*

Glossary of Terms

A

Abbreviation An abbreviation is a shortened form of a word. A period is used after most abbreviations. *(See page 820.)*

Action verb An action verb tells what action a subject is performing. *(See page 575.)*

Active voice Active voice indicates that the subject is performing the action. *(See page 722.)*

Adjective An adjective is a word that modifies a noun or a pronoun. *(See page 587.)*

Adjective clause An adjective clause is a subordinate clause that is used like an adjective to modify a noun or a pronoun. *(See page 677.)*

Adjective phrase An adjective phrase is a prepositional phrase that is used to modify a noun or a pronoun. *(See page 634.)*

Adverb An adverb is a word that modifies a verb, an adjective, or another adverb. *(See page 595.)*

Adverb clause An adverb clause is a subordinate clause that is used like an adverb to modify a verb, an adjective, or an adverb. *(See page 673.)*

Adverb phrase An adverb phrase is a prepositional phrase that is used like an adverb to modify a verb, an adjective, or an adverb. *(See pages 635–636.)*

Alliteration Alliteration is the repetition of a consonant sound at the beginning of a series of words. *(See page 333.)*

Analogies Analogies show the logical relationships between pairs of words. *(See page 480.)*

Antecedent An antecedent is the word or group of words that a pronoun replaces or refers to. *(See pages 566 and 744.)*

Antonym An antonym is a word that means the opposite of another word. *(See page 478.)*

Appositive An appositive is a noun or a pronoun that identifies or explains another noun or pronoun in a sentence. *(See page 640.)*

Audience Audience is the person or persons who will read your work or hear your speech. *(See pages 17 and 254.)*

B

Brainstorming Brainstorming means writing down everything that comes to mind about a subject. *(See pages 20–21.)*

Business letter A business letter has six parts: the heading, inside address, salutation, body, closing, and signature. *(See pages 439–441.)*

C

Card catalog The card catalog is a cabinet of drawers containing author, title, and subject cards for all materials in a library. *(See pages 497–500.)*

Case Case is the form of a noun or a pronoun that indicates its use in a sentence. In English there are three cases: the *nominative case,* the *objective case,* and the *possessive case.* *(See page 729.)*

Characterization Characterization is a variety of techniques used by writers to show the personality of a character. *(See pages 162 and 335.)*

Chronological order Chronological order arranges events in the order in which they happened. *(See pages 143, 175, and 176.)*

Clarity A paragraph or essay has clarity if the meaning of each paragraph, sentence, and word is clear. *(See page 232.)*

Clause A clause is a group of words that has a subject and a predicate. *(See page 671.)*

Cliché A cliché is a worn out, overused expression that has lost its power to call any clear images to a reader's mind. *(See page 63.)*

Clustering Clustering is a brainstorming technique in which the writer writes a subject at the center of a page, writes supporting details, and connects those details to the subject with lines. *(See page 22.)*

Coherence A paragraph or an essay has coherence if the ideas in it are presented in logical order with clear transitions. *(See pages 111, 153, and 231.)*

Colloquialism A colloquialism is an informal phrase or expression appropriate for conversation but not for formal writing. *(See page 470.)*

Comparison and contrast Comparison and contrast is a method of development in which the writer examines similarities and differences between two subjects. *(See pages 186, 264, 265–267.)*

Complement A complement is a word that completes the meaning of an action verb. *(See page 617.)*

Complete predicate A complete predicate includes all the words that tell what the subject is doing or that tell something about the subject. *(See page 543.)*

Complete subject A complete subject includes all the words used to identify the person, place, thing, or idea that the sentence is about. *(See page 540.)*

Complex sentence A complex sentence consists of one independent clause and one or more subordinate clauses. *(See page 686.)*

Compound-complex sentence A compound-complex sentence consists of two or more independent clauses and one or more subordinate clauses. *(See page 686.)*

Compound noun A compound noun is a common noun with more than one word. *(See page 562.)*

Compound sentence A compound sentence consists of two or more independent clauses. *(See page 685.)*

Compound subject A compound subject is two or more subjects in one sentence that have the same verb and are joined by a conjunction. *(See page 549.)*

Compound verb A compound verb is two or more verbs that have the same subject and are joined by a conjunction. *(See page 550.)*

Concluding paragraph A concluding paragraph completes an essay and reinforces its main idea. *(See pages 233–234.)*

Concluding sentence A concluding sentence adds a strong ending to a paragraph by summarizing the major points, referring to the main idea, or adding an insight. *(See page 102.)*

Conflict Conflict is the struggle between opposing forces around which the action of a work of literature revolves. *(See pages 118 and 333.)*

Conjugation of a verb A conjugation of a verb lists all the singular and plural forms of a verb in its six tenses. *(See pages 715–717)*

Conjunction A conjunction connects words or groups of words. *(See page 610.)*

Connotation The connotation of a word is the feeling that a word creates. *(See pages 60–61.)*

Context clue A context clue is the clue to a word's meaning provided by the sentence or passage in which the word is used. *(See page 472.)*

Contraction A contraction is a word that combines two words into one. It uses an apostrophe to replace one or more missing letters. *(See page 862.)*

Cooperative learning Cooperative learning occurs when a group works together to achieve a goal or accomplish a task. *(See page 463.)*

Coordinating conjunction A coordinating conjunction is a single connecting word used to connect compound subjects, compound verbs, and compound sentences. *(See page 610.)*

Correlative conjunction Correlative conjunctions are pairs of conjunctions used to connect compound subjects, compound verbs, and compound sentences. *(See page 610.)*

D

Dangling modifier A dangling modifier is a phrase that has nothing to describe in a sentence. *(See page 663.)*

Declarative sentence A declarative sentence makes a statement or expresses an opinion and ends with a period. *(See page 817.)*

Demonstrative pronoun A demonstrative pronoun points out a person or a thing. *(See page 569.)*

Denotation The denotation of a word is the dictionary definition of a word. *(See pages 60–61.)*

Descriptive paragraph A descriptive paragraph creates in words a vivid picture of a person, an object, or a scene. *(See page 182.)*

Dewey decimal system The Dewey decimal system is used by libraries to arrange nonfiction books on shelves in numerical order according to ten general subject categories. *(See pages 495–496.)*

Dialect A dialect is a regional variation of a language distinguished by distinctive pronunciation and some differences in word meanings. *(See page 469.)*

Dialogue A dialogue is a conversation between two or more persons. In writing, a new paragraph begins each time the speaker changes. *(See page 852.)*

Direct object A direct object is a noun or a pronoun that receives the action of a verb. *(See page 617.)*

Direct quotation A person's exact words are quoted in a direct quotation. Quotation marks are used before and after a direct quotation. *(See pages 844–845.)*

Double negative A double negative is the use of two negative words to express an idea when only one is needed. *(See pages 781–782.)*

E

Editing Editing is the stage of the writing process that follows revising. In this stage, writers polish their work by correcting errors and making a neat copy. *(See page 37.)*

Elliptical clause An elliptical clause is a subordinate clause in which words are omitted but understood to be there. *(See page 742.)*

Encyclopedia An encyclopedia contains general information about a variety of subjects. The information is arranged alphabetically by subject. A specialized encyclopedia focuses on one subject. *(See pages 500–501.)*

Essay An essay is a composition that presents and develops one main idea in three or more paragraphs. *(See page 216.)*

Essential phrase or clause An essential phrase or clause is essential to the meaning of a sentence and is therefore not set off with commas. *(See page 833.)*

Etymology An etymology of a word is its history from its earliest recorded use to its present use. *(See page 468.)*

Exclamatory sentence An exclamatory sentence expresses strong feeling and ends with an exclamation point. *(See page 818.)*

Expository paragraph An expository paragraph explains or informs with facts and examples or gives directions. *(See page 128.)*

F

Fact A fact is a statement that can be proved. *(See pages 198 and 459.)*

Fiction Fiction refers to prose works of literature, such as short stories and novels, that are partly or totally imaginary. *(See page 333.)*

Figurative language Figurative language is the imaginative, nonliteral use of language. *(See pages 62 and 282.)*

First draft Writing the first draft is the second stage of the writing process. At this stage, writers use their prewriting notes to get their ideas on paper as quickly as possible. *(See page 29.)*

Freewriting Freewriting is a prewriting technique of nonstop writing that encourages the flow of ideas. *(See page 11.)*

Friendly letter The parts of a friendly letter are the heading, salutation, body, closing, and signature. *(See pages 436–438.)*

G

Gerund A gerund is a verb form ending in *-ing* that is used as a noun. *(See page 654.)*

H

Helping verb A helping, or auxiliary, verb and the main verb make up a verb phrase. *(See page 546.)*

I

Idiom An idiom is a phrase or expression that has a meaning different from what the words suggest in their usual meanings. *(See page 470.)*

Imperative sentence An imperative sentence makes a request or gives a command and ends with either a period or an exclamation point. *(See page 817.)*

Indefinite pronoun An indefinite pronoun refers to an unnamed person or thing. *(See page 568.)*

Independent clause An independent (or main) clause can stand alone as a sentence because it expresses a complete thought. *(See page 671.)*

Indirect object An indirect object is a noun or a pronoun that answers the question *to or for whom?* or *to or for what?* after an action verb. *(See page 619.)*

Infinitive An infinitive is a verb form that usually begins with *to* and is used as a noun, an adjective, or an adverb. *(See page 658.)*

Inquiring Inquiring is a prewriting technique in which the writer asks questions such as *Who? What? Where? Why?* and *When? (See page 23.)*

Interjection An interjection is a word that expresses strong feeling. *(See page 611.)*

Interrogative pronoun An interrogative pronoun is used to ask a question. *(See page 569.)*

Interrogative sentence An interrogative sentence asks a question and ends with a question mark. *(See page 818.)*

Intransitive verb An intransitive verb is an action verb that does not have an object. *(See page 577.)*

Introduction An introduction to an essay introduces a subject, states or implies a purpose, and presents a main idea. *(See page 219.)*

Irregular verb An irregular verb does not form its past and past participle by adding *-ed* or *-d* to the present. *(See page 708.)*

J

Jargon Jargon is the specialized vocabulary used in particular professions. *(See page 471.)*

Journal A journal is a daily notebook in which a writer records thoughts and feelings. *(See page 13.)*

L

Linking verb A linking verb links the subject with another word in the sentence. This other word either renames or describes the subject. *(See page 579.)*

Listening Listening occurs when a person comprehends, evaluates, organizes, and remembers information presented orally. *(See page 457.)*

M

Metaphor A metaphor implies a comparison by saying that one thing *is* another. *(See page 62.)*

Meter Meter is the rhythm of stressed and unstressed syllables in each line of a poem. *(See page 333.)*

Misplaced modifier A misplaced modifier is a phrase or a clause that is placed too far away from the word it modifies, thus creating an unclear sentence. *(See pages 639 and 662.)*

Mood Mood is the atmosphere or feeling created by a work of literature. *(See pages 84 and 335.)*

N

Narrative paragraph A narrative paragraph tells a real or an imaginary story. *(See page 173.)*

Nominative case The nominative case of a pronoun is used for subjects and predicate nominatives. *(See pages 730–731.)*

Nonessential phrase or clause A nonessential phrase or clause is not essential to the meaning of a sentence and is therefore set off with commas. *(See page 832.)*

Nonfiction Nonfiction is prose writing that contains facts about real people and real events.

Noun A noun is a word that names a person, a place, a thing, or an idea. A common noun gives a general name. A proper noun names a specific person, place, or thing and always begins with a capital letter. A collective noun names a group of people or things. *(See pages 561–563.)*

Noun clause A noun clause is a subordinate clause that is used like a noun. *(See page 682.)*

Novel A novel is a long work of narrative fiction. *(See page 328.)*

O

Objective case The objective case of a pronoun is used for direct objects, indirect objects, and objects of a preposition. *(See page 733.)*

Onomatopoeia Onomatopoeia is the use of words whose sounds suggest their meaning. *(See page 333.)*

Opinion An opinion is a judgment that varies from person to person. *(See pages 198 and 459.)*

Order of importance, interest, size, or degree Order of importance, interest, size, or degree is a way of organizing information by arranging details in the order of *least to most* or *most to least*. *(See pages 142 and 199.)*

Outline An outline organizes information about a subject into main topics and subtopics. *(See pages 268–269.)*

P

Paragraph A paragraph is a group of related sentences that present and develop one main idea. *(See page 96.)*

Parenthetical citation A parenthetical citation is a brief reference in the body of a research paper to the source of borrowed information. *(See page 387.)*

Participial phrase A participial phrase is a participle with its modifiers and complements—all working together as an adjective. *(See page 651.)*

Participle A participle is a verb form that is used as an adjective. *(See page 649.)*

Passive voice The passive voice indicates that the action of a verb is being performed upon its subject. *(See page 722.)*

Peer conference A peer conference is a meeting with one's peers, such as other students, to share ideas. Peer conferences are commonly used as a prewriting and revising strategy. *(See pages 21 and 36.)*

Personal pronoun A personal pronoun refers to a particular person, place, thing, or idea. *(See page 567.)*

Personification Personification is a comparison in which human qualities are given to an animal, an object, or an idea. *(See page 186.)*

Persuasive paragraph A persuasive paragraph states an opinion and uses facts, examples, and reasons to convince readers. *(See page 196.)*

Phrase A phrase is a group of related words that functions as a single part of speech and does not have a subject and a verb. *(See page 633.)*

Play A play is a composition written for dramatic performance on the stage. *(See page 329.)*

Plot Plot consists of the events in a story or a play. *(See page 333.)*

Poem A poem is a highly structured composition with condensed, vivid language, figures of speech, and often the use of meter and rhyme. *(See pages 329 and 333.)*

Point of view In first person point of view, the narrator takes part in the story. In third person point of view, the narrator tells what happens to others and is not a character in the story. *(See pages 177–178 and 333.)*

Possessive pronoun A possessive pronoun is used to show ownership or possession. *(See page 736.)*

Predicate adjective A predicate adjective is an adjective that follows a linking verb and modifies the subject. *(See page 623.)*

Predicate nominative A predicate nominative is a noun or a pronoun that follows a linking verb and identifies, renames, or explains the subject. *(See page 621.)*

Prefix A prefix is a word part that is added to the beginning of a word and changes its basic, or root, meaning. *(See page 475.)*

Preposition A preposition is a word that shows the relationship between a noun or a pronoun and another word in the sentence. *(See page 605.)*

Prepositional phrase A prepositional phrase is a group of words that begins with a preposition, ends with a noun or a pronoun, and is used as an adjective or an adverb. *(See pages 278, 606–607.)*

Prewriting Prewriting is the first stage of the writing process. It includes all the planning steps that come before writing the first draft. *(See page 10.)*

Principal parts of a verb The principal parts of a verb are the *present*, the *past*, and the *past participle*. The principal parts help form the tenses of verbs. *(See page 707.)*

Pronoun A pronoun is a word that takes the place of one or more nouns. *(See page 566.)*

Proofreading symbols Proofreading symbols are a kind of shorthand that writers use to correct their mistakes while editing. *(See pages 37–38.)*

Propaganda Propaganda is the effort to persuade by distorting and misrepresenting information or by disguising opinions as facts. *(See page 459.)*

Protagonist A protagonist is the principal character in a story. *(See page 356.)*

Publishing Publishing is the final stage of the writing process. At this stage, writers present their work to an audience in final, correct form. *(See page 37.)*

Purpose In writing, purpose is the reason for writing. *(See page 16.)* The purpose of a speech is the reason for speaking. *(See page 451.)*

R

Readers' Guide to Periodical Literature The *Readers' Guide* is an index of magazine and journal articles. *(See page 503.)*

Regular verb A regular verb forms its past and past participle by adding *-ed* or *-d* to the present. *(See page 708.)*

Relative pronoun A relative pronoun relates an adjective clause to the modified noun or pronoun. *(See page 677.)*

Research report A research report is a composition of three or more paragraphs that uses information from books, magazines, and other sources. *(See page 364.)*

Revising Revising is the third stage of the writing process. At this stage, a writer changes a draft as often as needed to improve it. *(See page 32.)*

Rhyme scheme Rhyme scheme is a pattern of rhymed sounds at the end of lines in a poem. *(See page 333.)*

Root A root is the part of a word that carries the basic meaning. *(See pages 474–475.)*

Run-on sentence A run-on sentence is two or more sentences that are written as one sentence. They are separated by a comma or have no mark of punctuation at all. *(See pages 115 and 700.)*

S

Sensory detail A sensory detail appeals to one of the five senses: seeing, hearing, touching, tasting, and smelling. *(See pages 184–185.)*

Sentence A sentence is a group of words that expresses a complete thought. *(See page 539.)*

Sentence combining Sentence combining is the method of combining short sentences into longer, more fluent sentences by using phrases and clauses. *(See pages 66–70.)*

Sentence fragment A sentence fragment is a group of words that does not express a complete thought. *(See pages 39, 114, and 695.)*

Sequential order In a paragraph of directions or steps in a process, sequential order presents the details in the proper sequence. *(See page 143.)*

Setting The setting is the location and time of a story. *(See page 333.)*

Short story A short story is a short work of narrative fiction. *(See page 328.)*

Simile A simile states a comparison by using the word *like* or *as*. *(See pages 62 and 282.)*

Simple predicate A simple predicate, or verb, is the main word or phrase in the complete predicate. *(See page 544.)*

Simple sentence A simple sentence consists of one independent clause. *(See page 685.)*

Simple subject A simple subject is the main word in a complete subject. *(See page 541.)*

Slang Slang expressions are non-standard expressions developed and used by particular groups. *(See page 470.)*

Sound devices Sound devices are ways to use sounds in poetry to achieve certain effects. *(See page 333.)*

Spatial order Spatial order arranges details according to their location. *(See pages 143, 144, and 188–189.)*

Speech A speech is an oral composition presented by a speaker to an audience. *(See page 450.)*

Subordinate clause A subordinate (or dependent) clause cannot stand alone because it does not express a complete thought. *(See page 672.)*

Subordinating conjunction A subordinating conjunction is used in a complex sentence to introduce an adverb clause. *(See page 674.)*

Suffix A suffix is a word part that is added to the end of a word and changes its basic, or root, meaning. *(See page 475.)*

Supporting sentences Supporting sentences explain or prove a topic sentence with specific details, facts, examples, or reasons. *(See page 101.)*

Synonym A synonym is a word that has nearly the same meaning as another word. *(See page 478.)*

T

Tense Tense is the form a verb takes to show time. The six tenses are the *present, past, future, present perfect, past perfect,* and *future perfect. (See page 715.)*

Theme Theme is the underlying idea, message, or meaning of a work of literature. *(See page 333.)*

Thesaurus A thesaurus is a special dictionary that gives several synonyms for one word. *(See page 478.)*

Thesis statement A thesis statement states the main idea and makes the purpose of an essay clear. *(See pages 220 and 271.)*

Timed writing Timed writing is an essay test that must be written in a prescribed amount of time. *(See page 522.)*

Tone Tone is the attitude of a writer toward the subject of a composition. *(See page 226.)*

Topic sentence A topic sentence states the main idea of the paragraph. *(See page 98.)*

Transitions Transitions are words and phrases that show how ideas are related. *(See pages 153–154, 175, and 188.)*

Transitive verb A transitive verb is an action verb that has an object. *(See page 577.)*

U

Understood subject An understood subject of a sentence is a subject that is understood rather than stated. *(See page 553.)*

Unity A paragraph or an essay has unity if all the supporting sentences relate to the main idea expressed in the topic sentence. *(See pages 109–110, and 231.)*

V

Verbal A verbal is a verb form used as some other part of speech. *(See page 649.)*

Verb phrase A verb phrase is a main verb plus one or more helping verbs. *(See pages 546 and 575.)*

W

Works cited page A works cited page comes at the end of a research paper and lists all the sources cited in the paper. *(See page 389.)*

Index

A

a, an, 786

abbreviation: in dictionary entry, 505, 510, 511; in formal writing, 820; with or without period, 820

accent mark in dictionary, 509

accept, except, 786

action verb, defined, 575

active voice, 722

address, comma with, 442, 835–836

address, direct, 828

adjective, 586–603, 774–785; articles (*a, an, the*), 588; comparative and superlative form in dictionary entry, 507; comparison of, 193, 775–782; compound, 590; defined, 587; distinguished from noun, 591; noun used as, 591; position of, 589; predicate, 623–624; pronominal, 592; pronoun used as, 592; proper, 590, 808–809; punctuation with, 194

adjective clause, 676–680; defined, 394, 677; distinguished from noun clause, 682–683; as misplaced modifier, 681; punctuation with, 395, 680; relative pronoun in, 677, 679; in sentence combining, 395, 688

adjective phrase, 634–635; defined, 634; as misplaced modifier, 639

adverb, 586–603, 774–785; common, list of, 595; comparison of, 775–782; defined, 595; distinguished from *-ly* adjective, 598; distinguished from preposition, 607; introductory, for sentence variety, 600; that modifies adjective and other adverb, 597–598; that modifies verb, 595–597; uses of, 595

adverb clause, 673–676; defined, 394, 673; punctuation with, 394–395, 676, 826; in sentence combining, 395, 688

adverb phrase, 635–637; defined, 635; as misplaced modifier, 639; punctuation with, 637

advice, advise, 787

affect, effect, 787

agreement of pronoun and antecedent, 744–747

agreement of subject and verb, 39–40, 752–773; collective noun, 768; compound subject, 760–762; contraction, 766; indefinite pronoun, 764–765; interrupting word, 547, 758; inverted order, 765–766; linking verb, 769; number, 753–755; singular noun with plural form, 768; title, 769; verb phrase, 757; words expressing amount, 768

ain't, 787

all ready, already, 787

"All Summer in a Day," 49–56, 57, 84

all together, altogether, 787

almanac, 502

a lot, 787

among, between, 236, 788

amount, number, 788

an, a, 786

anachronism, 240

analogy, 480–482, 528–530

analyzing, 7, 95, 137, 405

Angelou, Maya, 3–6, 46

antecedent, 566; agreement of pronoun with, 744–747; defined, 744; vague or missing, 748

antonym, 478–480, 526–528

anywhere, 788

apostrophe, 80, 857–864; contraction with, 862–863; forming plural with, 863; possessive noun or pronoun with, 736, 857–862; to show joint or separate ownership, 860–861

application, job, 436–449; completing, 447–448

appositive: comma with, 642, 830–831; defined, 640, 731; after pronoun, 731

appositive phrase, 312–313, 640–642; punctuation with, 642, 830–831; in sentence combining, 643

Writing Is Thinking

analyzing, *137;* classifying, *26;* comparisons, *65;* conclusions, *223;* evaluating, *202, 261;* generalizing, *100;* imaging, *419;* inferring, *338;* interpreting, *296;* synthesizing, *376*

Acknowledgments

The authors and editors have made every effort to trace the ownership of all copyrighted selections found in this book and to make full acknowledgment of their use. Grateful acknowledgment is made to the following authors, publishers, agents, and individuals for their permission to reprint copyrighted material.

Page 3: From *I Know Why the Caged Bird Sings*, by Maya Angelou. Copyright © 1969 by Maya Angelou. Reprinted by permission of Random House, Inc.   **49:** "All Summer in a Day," by Ray Bradbury. Copyright 1954; renewed © 1982 by Ray Bradbury. Reprinted by permission of Don Congdon Associates, Inc.   **87:** "The Confidence Game," by Pat Carr, from *Young Miss*. Copyright © 1977 by Parent's Magazine Enterprises, Inc. Reprinted by permission of Gruner and Jahr U.S.A. Publishers, Inc.   **121:** From "The Life and Death of a Western Gladiator," copyright by Charles G. Finney, from *Harpers* magazine. By permission of Barthold Fles.   **162:** "To a Brown Spider: en el cielo," by Angela de Hoyos. From *Arise Chicano! and Other Poems*, Bilingual Edition, Spanish translations by Mierya Rebles, Backstage Books, copyright © 1975. Reprinted with permission of the author.   **165:** From *A Flag at the Pole*, by Paxton Davis, copyright © 1976 by Paxton Davis. Reprinted by permission of Curtis Brown, Ltd.   **174:** "Rescue!" Adapted from *Rescue! True Stories from Heroism*, by L.B. Taylor, Jr. Copyright © 1978 by L.B. Taylor, Jr. Used by permission of Franklin Watts, Inc.   **211:** "The Trouble with Television," by Robert MacNeil. Reprinted with permission from the March 1985 *Reader's Digest,* by Reader's Digest and Robert MacNeil.   **245:** "Single Room, Earth View," by Sally Ride, published in the April/May 1986 issue of *Air & Space/Smithsonian* Magazine. Published by The Smithsonian Institution. Reprinted by permission of the author.   **250:** "Space," by Evangelina Vigil-Piñón, from *The Computer Is Down*, copyright © 1987 Evangelina Vigil-Piñón. Reprinted by permission of Arte Publico Press, University of Houston.   **285:** From *Barrio Boy*, by Ernesto Galarza. Copyright © 1971 by University of Notre Dame Press. By permission of the University of Notre Dame Press. **290:** "Lineage," from *For My People*, by Margaret Walker Alexander, Yale University Press. Copyright 1942. By permission of the author.   **319:** "Say It with Flowers," from *Yokohoma, California*, by Toshio Mori, is reprinted by permission of Steven Mori for the Estate of Toshio Mori.   **359:** From "Rancho Buena Vista," by Fermina Guerra, from *Texan Stomping Ground*, by J. Frank Dobie. Published by the Texas Folklore Society, 1931. Reprinted by permission of the publisher.   **401:** "The Open Window," by Saki, from *The Complete Short Stories of Saki*, by H.H. Munro, Penguin Books, USA, Inc.   **410:** "A Day's Wait," from *Winner Take Nothing*. Copyright 1933 by Charles Scribner's Sons; copyright renewed 1961 by Mary Hemingway. Reprinted with permission of Charles Scribner's Sons.

Cover   Design: Studio Goodwin-Sturges. Illustration: Mahler Ryder. Calligraphy: Colleen

Unit Openers   Design: Studio Goodwin-Sturges. Photography by Ken O'Donoghue © D.C. Heath. Calligraphy: Colleen

Interior Calligraphy   Lisa Tarca

Illustrations   **2–8:** Dale Gottlieb.   **28:** Amy L. Wasserman.   **48–57:** Bruce Hogarth.   **74:** collage, Joan E. Paley.   **86, 96:** Patrice M. Rossi.   **113:** Cynthia Carrozza.   **116:** collage, Amy L. Wasserman.   **120–128:** Ka Botsis.   **139:** Pedro Gonzales.   **152:** Amy L. Wasserman.   **164–172:** Joan Hall.   **211–216:** Peter Kuper.   **252:** Patrice M. Rossi.   **256, 258:** Alan Witshonke.   **284–290:** Connie Connally.   **330, 336:** Judith DuFour Love.   **354:** Bruce Hogarth.   **400–405:** Elizabeth S. Lada.   **406:** *t*, Bruce Hogarth; *b*, Elizabeth S. Lada.   **413:** Caroline Alterio.   **421:** Judith DuFour Love.   **425:** Robert de Michiell.   **430:** collage, Patty de Grandpre. Writing Process logo: Paul Metcalf.

Picture Research   Carole Frohlich and Po-yee McKenna.

Photography   **9:** Ralph Mercer © D.C. Heath.   **14:** Rick Falco/Sipa.   **19:** Hugh Rogers/Monkmeyer Press.   **25:** *l*, Richard Frances/TSW Worldwide; *r*, Dave Cannon/TSW Worldwide.   **35:** Culver Pictures.   **44:** Mario Ruiz/Picture Group.   **58:** NASA, Goddard Space

Center.   **61:** Ted Russell/The Image Bank.   **62:** Georgia O'Keeffe, *Road Past the View I*, 1964. Photo by Malcolm Varon, N.Y.C. © 1990. Courtesy, The Estate of Georgia O'Keeffe. **72:** NASA.   **79:** Jim Sulley/The Image Works.   **82:** SUPERMAN™ & © DC Comics Inc. All rights reserved. Used by permission.   **86:** G. Glod/Superstock.   **87, 89, 90*l*, 91–93*r*, 94*l*, r:** Lorraine Rorke/The Image Works.   **90:** *m*, G. Glod/Superstock.   **93:** Dorothy Littell. **94:** *m*, G. Glod/Superstock.   **95:** William L. Hamilton/Superstock.   **96, 99:** Bob Daemmrich/ Stock, Boston.   **105:** *l*, Hans Neleman/The Image Bank; *r*, Steve Niedorf/The Image Bank. **107:** Wide World Photos.   **109:** Doug Mindell © D.C. Heath.   **128:** Tarsila do Amaral, *Setting Sun* (Sol Poente), 1929. Collection Jean Boghici, Rio de Janeiro, Brazil.   **132:** Bob Daemmrich/ The Image Works.   **145:** Superstock.   **156:** D. Wiley, International Wildlife Coalition. **160:** Stephen Dalton/Animals Animals.   **167:** Central Independent Television, Birmingham, England.   **172:** W.C. Burn Murdock, *Whalers Active, Balaena and Diana in the Antarctic*. Dundee Art Galleries and Museums.   **180:** Pablita Velarde, *Old Father the Story Teller*. Photograph by Cradoc Bagshaw.   **183:** Wiley/Wales/Profiles West.   **185:** Bonnie McGrath.   **192:** *tr*, Stan Aggie/The Picture Group; *b*, Bill Anderson/Monkmeyer Press; *tl*, Bob Daemmrich/Stock, Boston.   **197:** Fortean Picture Library.   **200:** "Vince & Larry" © 1985 U.S. DOT Poster art used by permission.   **203:** Matt Lambert/TSW Worldwide; *inset*, Mark Antman/The Image Works.   **206:** Illustration by J.R.R. Tolkien, from J.R.R. Tolkien, *THE HOBBIT or There and Back Again* (Houghton Mifflin Company). Reprinted with permission.   **208:** Scott Kuckler © D.C. Heath.   **219:** Michael Holford.   **222:** *The City of St. Louis*, 1874, color lithography by Parsons & Atwater; published by Currier & Ives, NY. Missouri Historical Society #RIVER 624.   **224:** Karl Kummels/Superstock.   **233:** © 1990 David Muench.   **238:** Margaret Miller © D.C. Heath; *inset*, Bob Daemmrich/Stock, Boston.   **244–252, 280:** NASA, Johnson Space Center.   **270:** The Bettmann Archive.   **290:** Photography by Dorothea Lange, 1936. Library of Congress. **292:** Milton Avery, *Two Figures at Desk*, 1944; oil on canvas, 48″ × 32″. Collection of Neuberger Museum, State University of New York at Purchase; gift of Roy R. Neuberger. Photograph by Jim Frank.   **293:** Anthony Barboza/Ken Barboza Associates.   **299:** Don Williams, *Night Intersection*, 1989. Courtesy, J. Noblett Gallery.   **307:** Scott Kuckler © D.C. Heath.   **311:** Paul Merideth/TSW Worldwide.   **314:** Mary Cassatt, *The Boating Party*, 1893/1894; oil on canvas, 35½″ × 46⅛″. National Gallery of Art, Washington, D.C.; Chester Dale Collection. **318–327:** Ralph Mercer © D.C. Heath.   **328:** Copyright © 1987 by The New York Times Company. Reprinted by permission. Courtesy, International Creative Management; *inset*, Charlie Erickson.   **345–350:** Ralph Mercer © D.C. Heath.   **358:** *t*, Jim Richardson/West Light; *b*, Allen Russell/Profiles West.   **359*l*, 360*l*, 362*l*:** Jim Brandenburg/West Light.   **359*r*, 361*r*, 362*r*:** Jim Richardson/West Light.   **359:** Lois Ellen Frank/West Light.   **362*m*:** Craig Aurness/West Light.   **363:** Kent Vinyard/Profiles West.   **364:** Doug Mindell © D.C. Heath.   **366:** Memory Shop West/MGM.   **380:** Louis Glanzman, *Signing the Constitution*. Commissioned by the DAR, Delaware, NJ, State Societies, Daughters of the American Revolution. Independence Historic Park Collection. Copyright Louis Glanzman.   **390:** NASA/JPL.   **393:** *l*, Joe Viesti/Viesti Associates, Inc.; *r*, Michael Melford/The Image Bank.   **396:** Joe Viesti/Viesti Associates, Inc.   **408:** Robert Farber/The Image Bank.   **453:** Photofest.   **458, 464:** Museum of Modern Art, Film Stills Archives.   **468:** Russ Kinne/Comstock.   **486:** Don Smetzer/TSW Worldwide.   **492:** Steven Kaufman/Peter Arnold, Inc.   **496–513:** Doug Mindell © D.C. Heath. Handcolored by Margery Mintz.

Cartoons   **68:** The Far Side cartoon, by Gary Larson, is reprinted by permission of Chronicle Features, San Francisco, CA.   **475, 481:** Elivia Savadier.   **520:** The Far Side, © 1990 Universal Press Syndicate. Reprinted with permission.   **526:** Drawing by M. Stevens, © 1985 The New Yorker Magazine, Inc.   **531:** Rothco.